# *Transcendence*

"*Transcendence* is an incredible work. With rich, layered narrative populated with very strong, approachable characters . . . An astonishing tale."
—*St. John's Telegram* (Newfoundland)

"The sequel to *Ascendance* illustrates Salvatore's gift for combining swiftly paced, action-filled adventure with mature storytelling and engaging characters. A strong addition to the author's growing body of work."
—*Library Journal*

"The author displays a deeper understanding of motivation and emotional development than most commercial fantasists."
—*Publishers Weekly*

Also by R. A. Salvatore

# TRANSCENDENCE

## BOOK II OF THE SECOND DEMONWARS SAGA

# R. A. SALVATORE

**BALLANTINE BOOKS • NEW YORK**

*Transcendence* is a work of fiction. Names, places, and incidents either are products of the author's imagination or are used fictitiously.

A Del Rey® Book
Published by The Random House Ballantine Publishing Group

Copyright © 2002 by R. A. Salvatore
Excerpt from *Immortalis* by R. A. Salvatore copyright © 2003 by R. A. Salvatore

All rights reserved under International and Pan-American Copyright Conventions. Published in the United States by The Random House Ballantine Publishing Group, a division of Random House, Inc., New York, and simultaneously in Canada by Random House of Canada Limited, Toronto.

Del Rey is a registered trademark and the Del Rey colophon is a trademark of Random House, Inc.

www.delreydigital.com

Map by Laura Maestro

ISBN 0-345-43044-1

Manufactured in the United States of America

First Hardcover Edition: May 2002
First Mass Market Edition: May 2003

10 9 8 7 6 5 4 3 2 1

# TRANSCENDENCE

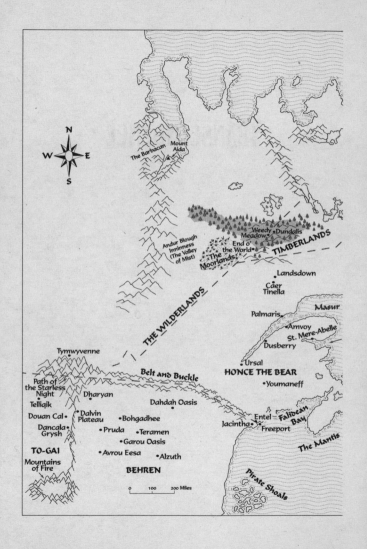

ALPINADOR

THE JULIANTHES

(The Weathered Isles)

Pireth
Vanguard

Delaval

Gulf of Corona

MIRIANIC
OCEAN

All Saints
Bay

Pireth
Dancard

Pireth Tulme

Tinson

Macomber

St. Gwendolyn
by the Sea

The Broken Coast

Arm

**THE LANDS OF
CORONA**

# CONTENTS

# CONTENTS

## PART THREE
## ENLIGHTENMENT

## PART FOUR
## THE DRAGON OF TO-GAI

# Prelude

Brynn Dharielle looked back over her shoulder repeatedly as she slowly paced her pinto mount, Diredusk, along the descending mountain trail. Though she had only been on the road for a half hour beyond the edge of Andur'Blough Inninness, the enchanted elven valley, the ridges that marked the place were already lost from sight. The mountainous landscape was a natural maze that had been enhanced by the magic of Lady Dasslerond of the Touel'alfar to be unsolvable. Brynn had marked the trail well along her route, but she understood that she would have a hard time finding her way back—even if she were to turn about right then.

This was the first time Brynn had been out of that misty valley in a decade, and she truly felt as if she was leaving her home. The Touel'alfar, the diminutive, translucent-winged elves of Corona, had come to her when she was a child of ten, orphaned and alone on the rugged and unforgiving steppes of To-gai, far to the south. They had taken her in and given her food and shelter. And even more importantly to Brynn, they had given her life purpose. They had trained her and made her a ranger.

And now they were sending her home to find her destiny.

The young brown-skinned woman crinkled her face at that thought, as she continued to stare back along the trail behind her, to the place that she knew to be her real home, the place she would likely never see again. Tears misted in her almond-shaped brown eyes, the sparkling eyes of a child, still, though so much had they seen. Already she missed Aydrian, the fourteen-year-old who had shared some of her training. Many times,

Brynn had found the boy to be exasperating, often infuriating. But the truth was, he was the only other human she had seen in these last ten years, and she loved him like a brother.

A brother she would likely never see again.

Brynn shook her head forcefully, her raven hair flying wildly, and pointedly turned back to the trail heading south. Certainly leaving the valley was a sacrifice for Brynn, a dismissal of the trappings and the companionship that had made the place her home. But there was a reason for her departure, she reminded herself, and if the pain of this loss was the greatest sacrifice she would be expected to make, then her road would be easier by far than anyone, herself included, had ever imagined possible.

Her future was not her own to decide. No, that road had been laid out before her a decade before, when the Behrenese Yatol priests and their armies had tightened their grip on To-gai, had abolished almost completely the last remnants of a culture that had existed for thousands of years. Brynn's road had been set from the moment Tohen Bardoh, an orange-robed Yatol priest, had lifted his heavy falchion and lopped off her father's head; from the moment Tohen and his lackeys had dragged off her mother, eventually killing her, as well.

Brynn's jaw tightened. She hoped that Tohen Bardoh was still alive. That confrontation alone would be worth any sacrifice.

Of course, Brynn understood keenly that this journey, this duty, was about much more than personal gain. She had been trained for a specific reason, a destiny that was bigger than herself. She was to return to the cold and windy steppes of harsh To-gai, the land she loved so much, and find those flickers of what had once been. She, little Brynn Dharielle, just over five feet tall and barely weighing a hundred pounds, was to fan that flicker into a flame, then feed the flame with the passion that had burned within her since that fateful day a decade ago. She was to find the To-gai spirit, to remind her fierce and proud people of who they truly were, to unite the many divided tribes in the cause against a deserving enemy: the Yatol-led Behrenese, the Chezru.

If the plan went as Brynn and the elves hoped, then Brynn would be the harbinger of war and all the land south of the great Belt-and-Buckle Mountains would be profoundly changed.

That was the hope of Lady Dasslerond, who rarely involved herself in the affairs of humans, and that was the burning hope of Brynn Dharielle. Liberation, freedom, for the To-gai-ru would avenge her parents, would allow them to sleep more comfortably in their graves.

"We will move down to the east, along that open stone to the tree line," came a melodic voice from the side and above. Brynn looked up to the top of a boulder lining the rocky trail to see a figure far more diminutive than she. Belli'mar Jura-viel of the Touel'alfar, her mentor and companion, looked back at her with his golden eyes. His hair, too, was the color of sun-light, and his features, though angular, with the high cheek-bones and pointy ears characteristic of all of the Touel'alfar, somehow exuded gentleness.

Brynn glanced back once again toward the land that had been her home.

"Keep your eyes ahead," Juraviel remarked. "Andur'Blough Inninness is no more to you than a dream now."

"A pleasant dream," Brynn replied, and Juraviel grinned.

"They say that memories often leave out the more terrible scenes."

Brynn looked at him hard for a moment, but when he started laughing, she understood his meaning well. Indeed, there had been many hard times for Brynn in Andur'Blough Inninness, under the tutelage of the often-stern elves, including Belli'mar Juraviel—though he was considered by his kin to be among the most kindhearted of the people. Particularly Brynn's early years in the valley had been filled with seemingly impossible trials. The elves had pushed her to the very limits of her physi-cal and emotional being, and often beyond those limits—not to break her, but to make her stronger.

And they had succeeded. Indeed they had! Brynn could fight with sword and bow, could ride as well as any of the people of To-gai, who were put on the back of the sturdy ponies before they could even walk. And more importantly, the Touel'alfar had given her the mental toughness she would need to hold true to her course and see it through. Yes, she

wanted revenge on Tohen Bardoh—indeed she did!—but she
understood that such personal desires could not supersede
the greater reason for this journey. She would hold fast to the
course and the cause.

Juraviel left that part of the discussion right there, and so
did Brynn, following the elf's gaze to the sloping stone facing
he had indicated. Brynn frowned, not thrilled with the angle.

"Diredusk will have trouble navigating that," she stated.
She looked back to her pinto pony, who stood calmly munching grass and seemed not to mind the saddlebags he carried,
full of foodstuffs and bedrolls for the pair.

Juraviel nodded. "We will get him through. And once we
cross under the canopy of the trees, the ground will be softer
under his hooves and the trail will slope more gently."

Brynn looked down to those trees, rows of evergreens neatly
defined by elevation, and frowned again. The ground down there
didn't look very level to her.

"We will be out of the mountains soon enough," Juraviel said,
seeing her thoughts clearly reflected on her pretty face.

"Sooner if we had gone straight to the east, then turned south,"
the irascible Brynn had to say, for she and Juraviel had spent
the better part of the previous week arguing about this very
topic. Considering what Brynn had been told about this mountain range, which ran more north–south than east–west, they
certainly could have gotten to flatter ground more quickly by
heading to the east.

"Yes, and then poor Diredusk would be running swiftly until he dropped from exhaustion, or until the goblin hordes
caught up to us. Or until he mired down in the mud," Juraviel
said, again with a chuckle. That had been his argument from
the beginning, for the lands immediately east of the mountains were far from hospitable, with goblins and swamps and
great areas of muddy clay.

"A Touel'alfar and a ranger, afraid of goblins," came Brynn's
huffing reply.

"A Touel'alfar wise enough to know that danger is best defeated by avoiding it altogether," Juraviel corrected. "And
a ranger too proud and too stubborn to recognize that her
body, though hardened by our training, is not impervious to a

goblin spear! You have heard of Mather, uncle of Elbryan, great-uncle of Aydrian. 'Twere goblins that struck him down."

Juraviel started to turn away, and so Brynn took the opportunity to stick her tongue out at him. He looked back immediately, catching her in the act, and just sighed and shook his head, hardly surprised. For surely Belli'mar Juraviel was used to such playful behavior from this one, named by many of the Touel'alfar as the most irreverent—and irresistible—of any of the humans they had ever taken in for training. Brynn saw the world differently from most humans, and had done so even before falling under the demanding influences of the Touel'alfar. Despite the darkness that had found her at a young age, she remained the one with the brightest and most sincere smile, the one willing to solve any problem thrown her way through cunning and wit as much as through disciplined training.

That was the charm of Brynn Dharielle, and also, to Juraviel's thinking, it was the strength that would carry her through this, her ultimate trial, where sadness and guilt loomed large in places unexpected.

If anything could.

# PART ONE

# TO THE EDGE
# OF DARKNESS

*I cannot begin to explain the tremendous shift that has come
to Caer'alfar since the demon Bestesbulzibar left its stain, its
growing rot, upon our fair valley. For centuries, we of the People
have lived in relative seclusion, peaceful and content. Only the
rangers knew of us, truly, and a select few of Honce-the-Bear's
ruling families. Our concern with the ways of the wider world
ended with the potential impact any happenings might have upon
us. Thus the rangers, while protectors of the human settlements
on the outskirts of human civilization, were also our link to that
world, our eyes in the field.*

*That was enough.*

*Bestesbulzibar has apparently changed all of that. During the
time of the DemonWar, I was assaulted by that demon, while
transporting some poor human refugees away from the goblin and
powrie hordes. I would have perished in that battle—perhaps I
should have!—except that Lady Dasslerond arrived and took up
my battle. She, too, would have perished, but she used her magical
emerald to take us back to the place of her greatest power, back to
Andur'Blough Inninness, just outside of Caer'alfar. There,
Dasslerond drove the demon away, but not before Bestesbulzibar
had left its indelible stain upon our fair land, a mark enduring,
and growing.*

*I believe that if Dasslerond had understood the cost, she never
would have brought us all back to the valley, that she and I would
have died on the field that day.*

*For then we would be gone, but Andur'Blough Inninness would
live on.*

*That rotting stain has done more than change the complexion of* our fair valley, it has changed the perspective of Lady Dasslerond. The Touel'alfar have existed by remaining on the outskirts, passive observers in a world too frenzied for our tastes. We do not involve ourselves in the affairs of humans—how many times have I been chided by Lady Dasslerond and my peers for my friendship with Elbryan and Jilseponie?

Now, though, Lady Dasslerond has assumed a more active role outside of Andur'Blough Inninness. She sends Brynn south to free To-gai from the Behrenese, mostly because the nomads of To-gai will prove much more accommodating and friendly toward our people should the demon stain force us out of our home. In that event, we would go south, through the Belt-and-Buckle and across To-gai, to another of our ancient homelands, Caer'Towellan, where perhaps our brethren still reside.

Still, despite the potential gains should that event occur, I am surprised that Dasslerond has sent Brynn Dharielle to begin a war, human against human. If we were forced to journey southward, we could do so, I am certain, whether the To-gai-ru or the Yatol Chezru Chieftain ruled the steppes. But Lady Dasslerond insisted upon this, as much so as on anything I have ever witnessed. She is truly fearful of the demon stain.

And so she undertakes her second unusual stance, and this one frightens me even more than the journey she has determined for Brynn. She took Jilseponie's child, unbeknownst to the mother. She took the child of Elbryan and Jilseponie, right from its mother's womb! True, her action saved the lives of both Jilseponie and Aydrian that dark night on the field outside of Palmaris, for had not Dasslerond intervened to drive away the demon-possessed Markwart, both humans would surely have perished.

Still, to raise the child as her, as our, own . . .

And the manner of that upbringing scares me even more— perhaps as much as the reason for the upbringing. Lady Dasslerond has plans for Brynn, but they pale compared to her goals for young Aydrian. He will be the one to deliver Andur'Blough Inninness from the demon stain, at the sacrifice of his own blood and his own life. He will become the epitome of what it is to be a ranger, and then, when that is achieved, he will become Dasslerond's sacrifice to the earth, that the demon stain be lifted.

She has foreseen this, my Lady has told me, in no uncertain terms. She knows the potential of her plan. All that she must do is bring Aydrian to the required level of power and understanding.

*But there's the rub, I fear. For Aydrian Wyndon, raised without the gentle touch of his mother or the love of his father, raised in near seclusion with harsh treatment and high standards from the moment he was old enough to understand them, will not be complete as a man, let alone as a ranger. There was a side to Elbryan, the Nightbird, beyond his abilities with the sword and his understanding of nature. The greatest gift of Nightbird, the greatest strength of the man Elbryan, was compassion, was a willingness to sacrifice everything for the greater good. Nightbird's gift to the world was his death, when he threw his wounded form fully into Jilseponie's final battle with the demon-possessed Markwart, knowing full well that he could not survive that conflict, that, in aiding Jilseponie, he would be giving his very life.*

*He did that. He didn't hesitate, because Nightbird was possessed of so much more than we of the Touel'alfar ever gave to him—because Elbryan the Nightbird was a man of true character and true community.*

*Will the child raised alone and unloved be as much?*

*This is my fear.*

—BELLI'MAR JURAVIEL

# CHAPTER 1

## *First Blood*

They were out of the mountains now, and the going was smooth and easy. Diredusk most of all seemed to revel in the softer and flatter ground, the powerful pinto pony striding long and eagerly under Brynn's expert handling. True to his noble To-gai heritage, the pony could trot for many miles before needing a break, and even then, he was quickly ready to be back on the trail, straining against Brynn's hold to travel faster and faster.

For Brynn, riding along quiet forest trails on a late-spring or early-summer day was about as wonderful as things could get, and would have been perfect—except that with every passing mile the young ranger's eyes turned back less and looked forward ever more eagerly. She couldn't enjoy the ride as much when the destination was all-important.

Belli'mar Juraviel rode with the woman at times, Diredusk hardly feeling the extra weight of the diminutive creature. The elf typically sat in front of Brynn, turned to face the woman and lying back along the pony's powerful neck. He didn't speak to Brynn much along the trails, though, for he could see that the woman was falling deeper and deeper into thought about the destination awaiting them. That's what Juraviel wanted from the young woman; that's what the Touel'alfar demanded of the ranger. The goal was all-important, because Lady Dasslerond had said it was, and nothing else should clutter Brynn Dharielle's mind—not the fragrance of the summer forest awakening fully, not the sounds of the songbirds, not even the sparkle of the morning sun on the dewy grasses and leaves.

And so they rode quietly, and sometimes Juraviel leaped from Diredusk's back and fluttered up to the branches of the trees, moving to higher vantage points to scout the road ahead.

Their evenings, too, were for the most part quiet, sitting about a fire, enjoying their evening meal. In this setting, with little stimulation about them, Brynn would sometimes tell Juraviel stories of her homeland, of her parents and their small nomadic tribe, Kayleen Kek. On one such night, with Andur'Blough Inninness a hundred miles behind them, the woman became especially nostalgic.

"We always went to the higher ground in the summer," she told her companion. "Up the sides of the great mountains in the range you call the Belt-and-Buckle, but that we called *Uleshon Twak*, the Dragon Spines. We'd camp so high sometimes that it was hard simply to draw in sufficient air. You'd always feel as if you couldn't catch your breath. Every step seemed to take minutes to execute, and a tent in sight might take you an hour to walk to. I remember that at times blood would run from my nose, for no reason. My mother would fret over me, but my father would just say that the high-sickness could do that and it was nothing to bother about."

Juraviel watched her as she continued her tale, her head tilted back so that her eyes were staring up at the night canopy. It wasn't starry that night, with thickening clouds drifting in from the west. The full moon, Sheila, shone behind those clouds, sometimes seeming a pale full light, other times disappearing completely behind a dark and thick blanket.

Brynn wasn't seeing it, any of it, Juraviel knew. She was looking across the years as much as across the distance. She was seeing the crisp night sky from a camp of deerskin tents nestled among great boulders on the high slopes of the Belt-and-Buckle. She was hearing her mother's laugh, perhaps, and her father's stern but loving commands. She was hearing the nickers of the nearby To-gai ponies, so loyal that they didn't need to be tethered, as they protested the sparse grasses at the great elevation.

That was good, Juraviel knew. Let her recall the feeling of the old days, of her life before Andur'Blough Inninness. Let her remember clearly how much she had lost, how much To-gai had lost, so that her calls to her people to reclaim their heritage would be even more full of passion and conviction.

"Do they still go to the high passes?" Juraviel prompted.

Brynn's expression changed as she lowered her gaze to regard the elf, as if one of the clouds from the sky had dropped down to cross over her fair features. "I know not," she admitted somberly. "When I was taken by your people, the Chezru were trying to establish permanent villages."

"The To-gai-ru must walk the land with the creatures," said Juraviel. "That is their way."

"More than our way. It is our spirit, our path to . . ." She paused—unsure, it seemed.

"Your path to what?" the elf asked. "To heaven?"

Brynn looked at him curiously, and then nodded. "To our heaven," she explained. "There on the high plateaus. There in the autumn valleys, full of the golden flowers that bloom to herald the cold winds. There by the summer streams, swollen with melt. There, following the deer."

"The Chezru do not see the value of such a life," Juraviel noted. "They are not a wandering people."

"Because their deserts are not suited to such a lifestyle," said Brynn. "They have their many oases, and their great cities, but to wander through the seasons would not show them much beauty beyond those defined enclaves. Behren is not like To-gai, not a land of differing beauties in differing seasons. Thus they do not understand us and thus they try to change us."

"Perhaps they believe that in giving villages to the To-gai-ru, they will be showing the To-gai-ru the path to a better life."

"No," Brynn was answering before the elf even finished the statement, and Juraviel knew that he would elicit strong disagreement here—indeed, that was his goal. "They want us in villages, even cities, that they might better control us. In villages, they can watch the clans, but out on the plains, we would be free to practice the old ways and to speak ill of our conquerors."

"But the gains," the elf said dramatically. "The stability of existence."

"The trap of possession!" Brynn was quick to argue. "Cities are prisons and nothing more. When they run correctly, they trap you, they make you dependent on the comforts they provide. But they take from you—oh, they take so much!"

"What do they take?" There was an unintended urgency to Juraviel's tone. He could tell that he was getting to Brynn, driving her on, which was precisely his duty.

"They take away the summer plateaus, the mountain wind, and the smell. . . . oh, the scents of the high fields in the summer! They take away the swollen rivers, full of leaping fish. They take away the rides, the ponies charging across the open steppe. Oh, you should hear that sound, Belli'mar! The thunder of the To-gai-ru charge!"

She was breathing hard as she finished, her brown eyes sparkling with energy, as if she were witnessing that charge—as if she was leading that charge. She finally came out of her trance a bit and looked to the elf.

"I will witness it," came Belli'mar Juraviel's soft and assuring answer. "I will."

Their road remained fairly straight south over the next few days, and Brynn was under the impression that they had but a single goal here: to get to To-gai and begin the process of liberation.

That's what Juraviel and the others had told her, but the elf knew that he and Brynn had other things to attend to before beginning the long process of placing Brynn at the front of a revolution. Brynn Dharielle had been trained in the rigorous manner that had produced rangers from Andur'Blough Inninness for centuries, but, as fine as that training might be, Juraviel knew that it had its limitations. Even the most difficult trials—for Brynn, one had involved shooting targets from the saddle and at a gallop—were without the greatest of consequences, and hence, without the true understanding of the disaster that could be failure. For failing a test in Andur'Blough

Inninness could mean humiliation and weeks of intense corrective training, but failing a test out here would likely mean death. Brynn had to learn that, had truly to appreciate all that she had to lose.

And so, on that morning when Belli'mar Juraviel took note of some curious tracks crossing the soft ground in front of them—tracks so subtle that Brynn didn't even notice them from horseback—he allowed the woman to move obliviously past the spot, then studied the trail more closely. Juraviel knew the tracks, had seen them many, many times during the days of the DemonWar, when he had traveled beside Nightbird and Jilseponie battling Bestesbulzibar's minions. The tracks were like those of a human, a young human, perhaps. But those made by shod feet revealed a poorly crafted boot, and those made by bare feet showed a telltale flatness in the arch and a wide expanse at the toes narrowing almost to a point at the heels.

Goblins. Moving east and in no apparent hurry.

Juraviel looked up and studied the area, even going so far as to sniff the breeze, but then he smiled at himself and shook his head. The tracks were probably a day old, he knew. These goblins were likely long gone.

But he knew the direction.

To Brynn's surprise, Juraviel announced that they had to turn to the east for a bit. She didn't argue, of course, for he was her guide, and so with a shrug, she brought Diredusk in line behind the moving elf. When that day ended, the pair had put twenty miles behind them, but in truth, they were no closer to the steppes of To-gai than they had been the previous day, something that Brynn surely took note of.

"Are we to travel around the world, then?" she asked sarcastically after they had eaten their dinner of vegetable stew. "Perhaps that way, we can sneak up on the Chezru from behind."

"The straight line is always the shortest distance, 'tis true," the elf replied. "But it is not always the swiftest."

"What does that mean? What have you seen up ahead?" Brynn got up and looked to the south. "Monsters?"

"There is no barrier looming to the south, but this road is better, I believe."

Brynn stared hard at the cryptic elf for some time, but Juraviel went back to his eating and didn't return the look. He wanted to keep the mystery, wanted to have Brynn off-balance and wondering. He didn't want her to know what was coming, and likely coming the very next day.

Later on, when Brynn was asleep, Juraviel hopped, flew, and climbed up the tallest tree he could find and peered through the dark night to the east.

There was the campfire, as he had expected. It was a long way off, to be sure.

But the goblins, he believed, weren't in any hurry.

Brynn stared through the tangle of trees, sorting out the distinct and confusing lines until she was fully focused on the ugly little creatures beyond. They were diminutive—not as much so as the Touel'alfar, but smaller than Brynn. Their skin color ranged from gray to sickly yellow to putrid green, and hair grew in splotches about their heads, backs, and shoulders. Elongated teeth, misshapen noses, and sloping foreheads only added to the generally wretched mix. Brynn wasn't close enough to smell the creatures, but she could well imagine that such an experience wouldn't be pleasant.

She turned and looked up to Juraviel, who was sitting comfortably on a branch. "Goblins?" she asked, for though she had heard of the creatures during her stay with the elves, she had never actually seen one.

"The vermin are thick about these stretches," Juraviel answered, "outside the borders of the human kingdoms."

Brynn thought things over carefully, particularly their unexpected change in course of the previous day. "You knew they were here," she reasoned. "You brought me here to see them. But why?"

Juraviel spent a long moment looking through the trees to the goblin group. Several of them were visible, and he suspected that more were about, probably out destroying something, a tree or an animal, just for the fun of it. "You do not know that I brought you here to see them," he said.

Brynn chuckled at him. "But why?" she asked again.

Juraviel shrugged. "Perhaps it is merely a fortunate coincidence."

"Fortunate?"

"It is good that you should view these creatures," the elf explained. "A new experience to broaden your understanding of a world much larger than you can imagine."

Brynn's expression showed that she could accept that, but Juraviel added, "Or perhaps I feel it is my—our—duty to better the world wherever we may."

Brynn looked at him curiously.

"They are goblins, after all."

The woman's expression didn't change. "Goblins who seem not to be bothering anybody or anything."

"Perhaps that is because there is no one or nothing about for them to bother at this moment," Juraviel replied.

"Am I understanding your intent correctly?" the young ranger asked, turning back to survey the distant, undeniably peaceful scene of the small goblin camp. "Do you want us to attack this group?"

"Straight out? No," Juraviel answered. "Of course not—there are too many goblins about for that to be wise. No, we must be more stealthy and cunning in our methods."

When Brynn looked back to him, she wore an expression that combined curiosity, confusion, and outrage. "We could go around them and leave them in peace."

"And fear forever after for the mischief they would cause."

Brynn was shaking her head before Juraviel ever finished, but the elf pressed on dramatically. "For the families who would soon enough grieve for loved ones slain by the evil creatures. For the forests destroyed and desecrated, the animals senselessly slaughtered—not for food or clothing, but just for entertainment."

"And if we murder this band, then we are no better than the goblins, by any measure," Brynn declared, and she tilted her head back, her expression proud and idealistic. "Is it not our compassion that elevates us? Is it not our willingness to find peace and not battle, that makes us better than creatures such as this?"

"Would you be so generous if those were Yatol priests about that distant encampment?" the elf slyly asked.

"That is different."

"Indeed," came the obviously sarcastic reply.

"The Yatol priests chose their course—one that invites revenge from To-gai," Brynn reasoned. "The goblins did not choose their heritage."

"Thus you reason that every single Yatol priest took part in the atrocities perpetrated upon your people? Or are they all guilty for the sins of the few?"

"Every Yatol priest, every Chezru, follows a creed that leads to such conquest," Brynn argued. "Thus every Yatol priest is an accomplice to the atrocities committed by those following their common creed!"

"The goblins have visited more grief upon the world than ever did the Yatol priests."

"Being a part of that group, goblins, is not a conscious choice, but merely a consequence of parentage. Surely you of the Touel'alfar, who are so wise, can see the difference."

Belli'mar Juraviel smiled widely at the compassionate young ranger's reasoning, though he knew, from his perspective garnered through centuries of existence, that she was simply wrong. "Goblins are not akin to the other thinking and reasoning races," he explained. "Perhaps their heritage is not their choice, but their actions are universally predictable and deplorable. Never have I seen, never have I heard of a single goblin who goes against the creed that is their culture and heritage. Not once in the annals of history has a goblin been known to step forward and deny the atrocities of its wretched kin. No, my innocent young charge, I'll not suffer a goblin to live, and neither will you."

Brynn winced at the direct edict, one that obviously did not sit well on her slender shoulders.

"I brought you here because there before us is a stain upon the land, a blight and a danger, and there before us is our duty, clear and obvious."

Brynn glanced back as she heard the commanding, undebatable tone.

"We will search the forest about the encampment first," Juraviel went on. "Thinning the herd as much as possible before going to an open battle."

"Striking with stealth and from behind?" Brynn asked with clear sarcasm.

But her accusation, for that is what was obviously intended, was lost on Juraviel, who replied simply and with ultimate coldness, "Whatever works."

Less than an hour later, Brynn found herself crawling through the brush south of the goblin camp, for she and Juraviel had worked themselves around the location. The ranger moved with all the stealth the Touel'alfar had taught her, easing each part of her—elbow, knee, foot, and hand—down slowly, gradually shifting her weight and feeling keenly the turf below, taking care to crunch no old leaves and snap no dried twigs.

A dozen feet before her, a pair of goblins labored noisily, one of them breaking little limbs from the trees and tossing them back to its ugly companion, who was hard at work with a small stick and bow, trying to start a fire. Brynn and Juraviel had overheard a pair of the creatures a short way back, and Juraviel understood enough of the guttural language to relay to Brynn that the goblins were planning to set great fires to flush out easy kills.

Brynn paused as she considered that conversation, for she had argued against Juraviel's clear implication that the goblin plans proved his point about the creatures' temperament. Humans hunted, after all—the To-gai were particularly adept at it. Perhaps this was only a difference in method. Lying there, Brynn understood how weak her argument had been. The amount of kindling that was being piled and the sheer joy on the face of the goblin who intended to set the blaze told her that this was about much more than a simple hunt for food.

Still . . .

Juraviel had given Brynn his sword for this unpleasant business, though in her hands it was no more than a large and slender dagger. That would work better than her staff or bow for now, though, for this had to be done quickly and quietly. Especially quietly.

She continued forward another couple of feet, then a bit more. She could hear the creatures clearly, could smell them. With mud streaked about her face, and leaves and twigs strapped to her clothing, Brynn understood logically that she was somewhat camouflaged, but still she could hardly believe that the goblins hadn't taken note of her yet!

The one bent over trying to start the fire yelped suddenly and started to stand. Its companion, closer to Brynn, looked to regard it, smiling stupidly, apparently thinking that the fire was starting to catch.

But there were only wisps of smoke, then the goblin, halfway upright, yelped again, and then again, and its companion's expression shifted to curiosity.

And then Brynn was behind it, her hand coming around to clamp over its mouth, her dagger, Juraviel's silverel sword, driving deep into the creature's back, just to the side of the backbone, sinking deep to reach for the goblin's heart. Brynn felt that keenly—so very keenly! She felt the flesh tearing, the varying pressures as the dagger slid through, and then felt an almost electrical shock, as if she had touched the very essence of the creature's life force, the point of the weapon acting as a channel to let that life force flow freely from the goblin's body.

The other goblin yelped again and fell over. Then it yelped—or tried to—yet again, and clutched at its throat.

The goblin in her arms went limp and she eased it to the ground, thinking that she should go and finish the other. It was a forced thought, though, for all that Brynn wanted to do at that horrible moment was fall to her knees and scream out in protest. She growled those feelings away and steadied herself for the necessary task at hand, pulling free the bloodied sword and considering her next kill. Belli'mar Juraviel was at the other goblin before her, though, standing over the creature, his small bow drawn back fully.

He put another arrow into the squirming goblin, then another. And then a third, and the creature seemed as if it would not die!

The next arrow drove through the side of its head. It gave a sudden, vicious spasm, and the light went out of the goblin's eyes.

It was all Brynn could manage to keep tears flowing from her eyes, to keep from crying out in horror and revulsion, and pain.

So much pain.

Was this why she had trained as a ranger? Or was "ranger" even the proper word? Was it, perhaps, merely a cover for the true intention of her training, the true title she should drape across her shoulders: assassin?

"Come, and quickly," Juraviel said to her, drawing her back from her inner conflict. Hardly thinking, she followed the elf along the circuitous route, until they happened upon another goblin, out collecting kindling.

It was dead before it even knew they were there.

The perimeter was secured then, and so the pair focused their attention on the encampment itself, where a band of more than a half dozen of the creatures milled about and sat around the smoldering embers of the previous night's fire. They had a large, rusty pot sitting atop it, and every once in a while, one went over to it and ladled out some foul-looking stew.

"We could wait to see if others wander out alone," Juraviel said to her. "Take them down one or two at a time."

Brynn winced visibly at the thought, wanting all of this to be over as quickly as possible.

"The time for stealth is ended," she said determinedly, and started to rise, intending to charge straight into the band.

Juraviel caught her by the arm and held her fast. "What is a To-gai-ru warrior's greatest weapon?" he asked. "Even beyond courage and the bow?"

Brynn nodded and handed him his small sword, then turned about, understanding.

A few minutes later, the goblins in the encampment stood and looked curiously to the north, to the crashing and thumping echoing out of the forest.

Brynn Dharielle, astride Diredusk, came through the last line of brush with bow drawn. She took the goblin farthest to the right first, dropping it with hardly a squeak, then got her second arrow away, knocking a goblin away from the cooking pot, a bowlful of stew flying over it as it toppled backward.

A quick and fluid movement had the bow unstrung, and Brynn tucked it under her right arm like a lance as she guided Diredusk to a course right past a third, stunned creature. The goblin's face exploded in a shower of blood, the sturdy dark-fern bow smashing through. Brynn cut Diredusk hard to the left, the pony trampling the next goblin in line, then running down yet another as it tried to flee. Now Brynn swung the staff like a club, whistling it past another goblin's face, a near miss that had the creature diving back to the ground.

By then, though, her momentum had played out. She reached the far end of the encampment, leaving three goblins standing, no longer surprised, and collecting their weapons. Where was Juraviel? Why hadn't she heard the high-pitched twang of his small bow or the yelps of stuck goblins?

Brynn tugged hard on the reins, bringing her pony to a skidding stop and quick turn. She flanked around to the left, going to a half seat and bending low over Diredusk's neck as the horse easily leaped a pair of logs set out as benches.

Brynn yanked him hard to the left as he landed, lining up a second run at the center of the camp. The three goblins, though, had wisely retreated to the fringes of the forest, using brush and trees for cover, and the only target she found was the goblin she had narrowly missed on her first pass, the creature stumbling as it tried to rise. Her aim was better this time, the swinging bow smacking it across the back of the head as she thundered past, launching the creature facefirst. It crashed against the cooking pot, knocking it over, then it tumbled down right onto the hot embers. How that goblin howled and thrashed! Its scraggly hair ignited, its skin burned and curled!

With movements so fast and so fluid that they defied the goblins' comprehension, Brynn bent and strung her bow as she lifted her leg over the horse's back, then set an arrow as she dropped from Diredusk into a charge.

She pegged the closest goblin right between the eyes, dropped into a roll to avoid a thrown spear from a second, set an arrow as she rolled, and came up firing.

Then there was one.

A flick of Brynn's wrist had the bow unstrung as she charged.

The goblin, obviously unsure, obviously terrified, started to run. Then it changed its mind and turned, crude spear presented before it. It thrust out as Brynn came in, but the skilled ranger slapped the awkward attack aside and started forward for what looked like a quick victory.

Started forward, but stopped abruptly as the brush to the side parted and a second goblin burst through, charging at the ranger with a small and rusty dagger.

Brynn turned sidelong and started to bring her bow-staff to bear, but the first goblin came back in hard. The ranger adeptly changed the momentum of her weapon, grabbing it up high with her left hand, reversing the grip, then thrusting the staff right back to the side in an underhand movement, guiding it with her right hand, holding on with her left. The charging spear-wielder had its weapon back, trying to gain momentum for its thrust at that moment, and so there was nothing in place to block Brynn's stab before the staff connected with the goblin's face.

Brynn let her weapon drop then, confident that the goblin was out of the fight for a while at least. She wove her hands furiously before her to set a defense against the goblin with the knife. Her balanced and precise movements slowed the goblin just a bit, as it tried to find some hole in the sudden defense, and that was all Brynn needed. She sent her left hand out wide to the left and lifted her right hand up above her head, giving an apparent opening.

And the goblin dove into that hole, thinking to sink its knife into her chest.

Up snapped Brynn's right foot, smacking the goblin's lead arm out wide. She caught the back of the goblin's wrist in her left hand and yanked it down, twisting to lock the creature's elbow, its palm and Brynn's facing upward. The ranger turned right inside the hold, then bringing her left arm over and around, then down under the caught arm, turned her back right before the goblin's torso as she went. Brynn ignored the expected punch from the goblin's free hand, keeping her momentum, locking her forearm under that trapped elbow, and yanking up, while throwing her weight farther out over that trapped hand and tugging down hard.

The goblin yelped in pain, though it still managed to throw a second punch into Brynn's back.

It couldn't maintain its hold on the dagger, though, as Brynn's fingers worked the hand of the pained arm to force it free. As it fell, Brynn pulled straight out with her left hand, keeping the goblin off-balance, and released the arm from her right arm's hold, stepping forward and snapping out her right hand to catch the dagger before it ever hit the ground. She flipped it over in a sudden reversal and, even as the goblin slugged her again, thrust out straight and hard behind her, planting the dagger deep into the goblin's chest.

The goblin punched her yet again, but there was no strength in the blow. Brynn pumped her arm once and again, tearing up the goblin's chest and guts, then turned hard and shoved the dying creature to the ground.

The goblin she had smacked in the face was up by then, but not charging. The creature had seen enough of this fighter, apparently, and started to run off into the forest.

Hardly even thinking of the movement, Brynn launched the dagger, hitting it in the back of the leg. The goblin howled and went down hard, then kicked and thrashed, trying to tug the dagger out, but in too much pain even to grasp it.

Now Brynn was thinking again, and watching every terrible movement. As much in horror as in pragmatism, she picked up her staff, rushed over, and smashed the goblin in the head.

It just yelled and thrashed even more.

Brynn hit it again and again, just wanting this nightmare to be over, just wanting the wretched thing to lie still.

A long while later, after what seemed like many, many minutes to Brynn, the goblin finally stopped its thrashing and its whining.

Brynn slumped to her knees. There were still goblins about, some hurt, others perhaps not so, but she couldn't think of that right at that moment, couldn't think of anything except for the dead creatures about her, the goblins she had killed, and brutally so. She fought against the tears and against the urge to throw up, trying hard to steady her breathing and her sensibilities. She reminded herself that danger was all about her, told herself that a goblin might be creeping up even then, ready to drive a spear into her back.

Brynn glanced over her shoulder at the unsettling thought, but all was quiet behind her. Even in the encampment, nothing seemed to be stirring, though she knew she had not killed all of the creatures back there in her initial charge. She noted Diredusk off to the side, standing calmly, tugging at some low brush, then lifting his head with a great haul of small branches and leaves in his munching mouth.

Brynn took up her bow and strung it, then pulled the dagger out of the dead goblin's leg and set it into her belt. Fitting an arrow, she crept along a circuitous route, gradually working her way back in sight of the camp.

None of the goblins was moving. Belli'mar Juraviel walked about them, kicking at them, and when any showed signs of life, the elf bent down and slashed open its throat.

Brynn hated him at that moment. Profoundly. Why had he done this to her? Why had he taken her off the straight trail to the south and toward To-gai, only to slaughter these creatures?

It took the young ranger a few moments to realize how tightly she was gripping her bowstring about the set arrow, or the fact that she had inadvertently begun to pull back, just a bit, on the bow. She eased it to rest, then grabbed it up in one hand, clenching the bow at midshaft and wrapping one finger about the arrow to hold it steady. Then she determinedly, angrily, strode back into the encampment.

Juraviel looked up at her. "A bit sloppy," he said. "Your first charge through was beautifully executed, efficient and to the point. But you spent far too long with the pair in the brush. Three of these were not dead, and two could have soon enough gathered their wits and strength enough to come in at you. What would you have done if I had not been here to clean up?"

His voice trailed away at the end, his expression showing

Brynn that she was correctly conveying her outrage with her steely look.

"Is there a problem?" the elf asked, his condescending tone alone telling Brynn that he knew well enough what was bothering her.

"Was there a purpose?"

"Need I give you another lecture about the wretchedness of goblins? How many examples should I provide you to settle your guilt, young ranger? Should I tell you about the forests they have burned to the ground, about the human settlements they have raided, slaughtering even the children, and eating more than a few? Should I recount for you again the great DemonWar and point out the hundreds of instances of misery the goblins perpetrated upon the land and upon the humans in that dark time?"

"Raided human settlements," Brynn echoed, looking about sarcastically.

"Yes, and took pleasure in every kill."

"As did you!" Brynn knew that she was moving over the line even as the words left her mouth.

"Not so," Juraviel answered quietly and calmly, seeming to take no offense. "I—we—did as we had to do. With expediency and efficiency. Without true malice, and with actions spawned from pragmatism. Did I enjoy the killing? Not really. But I take heart in knowing that our actions here just made the entire world a bit brighter and a bit safer."

"And seasoned your ranger a bit more." There was no mistaking the heavy sarcasm and anger in her tone.

"And that, yes," the elf answered, unperturbed.

Brynn quivered on the verge of an explosion. "And do rangers often gain their first battle experience against goblins?" she asked. "Is that where they draw first blood, where they first can enjoy the sweet smell of death?"

"Goblins or rabid animals, likely," the elf was quick to respond, and still he seemed completely unshaken. "Though it could be argued that they are much one and the same."

His tone as much as his words only brought even more tension into poor Brynn, and she wanted to scream out in protest at that moment more than she ever had since the murder of her parents.

"As worthy an enemy as can be found, if not so worthy as an opponent," Juraviel went on.

Brynn turned away and squeezed her eyes shut tightly, then opened them and stared off into the forest. She felt Juraviel's gentle hand upon the small of her back.

"How steep are the mountains you must climb if you cannot scale this tiny hillock?"

"I did not leave Andur'Blough Inninness to become a murderess," Brynn answered through her gritted teeth.

"You left Andur'Blough Inninness to begin a war," Juraviel reminded, with even more intensity. "Do you think that your revolution will be bloodless?"

"That is different."

"Because the Chezru are deserving?"

Brynn, her eyes narrowed, turned to face him directly, and said with an air of confidence, "Yes."

"And only the deserving Chezru will die?"

"Many of my people will die, but they will do so willingly, if their sacrifice helps to free To-gai!"

"And many innocents will die," the elf pointed out. "Children too young to understand what is happening. The infirm. Women on both sides will be raped and slaughtered."

Brynn worked hard to hold firm her gaze, but she did wince.

"War is not fought along clear lines, Brynn. The Yatols at war will call upon the fierce Chezhou-Lei warriors, and they, by reputation, will not suffer any of the enemy race to live. And will your own people be more generous? How many of the To-gai-ru have suffered horrible tragedies under the press of the Yatols? When you press into Behren, as surely you must if you are to force the people of the sand kingdom truly to allow you your freedom, you will overtake Behrenese villages, full of people who know nothing of To-gai and the plight of the To-gai-ru. But will not some of your own warriors take revenge on those innocents for the wrongs of the Yatol occupation?"

Brynn didn't relent in her stoic gaze. She could not, at that moment of dark epiphany. But she heard well Belli'mar Juraviel's every word, and knew in her heart, if her head would not yet admit it, that he was correct.

# CHAPTER 2

## *The Blood of Centuries*

Yakim Douan, Chezru Chieftain of all Behren, opened his eyes on this, the 308,797th day of his life.

The sun looked the same, peeking into his bedroom window. The springtime air, laced with the scents of flowers and spices and pungent camels, felt the same as it always had.

Yakim Douan smiled at that thought, for he liked it this way, too much ever to let it go. He groaned a bit as he rolled off his bed—a hammock, as was customary in the city of Jacintha, where the aggressive and deadly brown-ringed scorpions often crawled into the padded bedding of mattresses or straw. Slowly the old man straightened, cursing the sharp pain in both his knees and the way his back always seemed to lock up after a long night's sleep.

His room was beautifully adorned, with all the trappings one would expect for the most powerful and the richest man south of the Belt-and-Buckle—and arguably north of it, as well. Wondrous tapestries lined the walls, their rich colors capturing the morning light, their intricate designs drawing in Yakim Douan's gaze and holding it there. How long had he been studying those same images? Depictions of war and of the human form, of beauty and of tragedy? And still, they seemed as fresh and inspiring to him as they had when first he had gazed upon them.

Thick woven rugs felt good on his bare feet. He stretched and widened his toes, taking it in fully, then made his creaking way across the large room to the decorated washbasin, all of shining white-and-pink marble, with a golden-framed mirror hanging above it. The Chezru Chieftain splashed cold water onto his old and wrinkled face and stared hard into the mirror, lamenting the way age had ravaged him. He saw his gray eyes and hated them most of all, and wished he had known their color before he had chosen this corporeal coil as his own.

Blue eyes next time, he hoped. But, of course, some things were quite beyond his control.

His current set of orbs was quite telling to him. Never did they seem white about the pupils anymore, just a dull yellowish hue. His body was sixty-two years old, and he had hated every minute of the last decade. Oh, of course he could have any luxuries he wanted. He kept a harem of beautiful young women at his beck and call, and should he desire a plaything, he could bring in any other woman he chose, even if she was already married. He was the Chezru Chieftain, the God-Voice of Behren. With a word he could have a person burned at the stake, or order one of his subjects to take his own life, and the idiot would unquestioningly comply.

All the world was Yakim Douan's to take, and so he did, over and over again.

A soft, polite knock on his door turned the old Chezru from the mirror. "Enter," he said, knowing full well that it was Merwan Ma, his personal attendant.

"Your pardon, Great One," Merwan Ma said, peeking his head around the door. He was a handsome young man in his early twenties, with short, black, tightly curled hair, and large black eyes that seemed all the darker because they were set in pools of white, pure white, with no veins and no yellow discoloration at all. The eyes of a child, Yakim thought, every time he looked upon them. Merwan Ma's face was boyish as well, with hardly a shadow of hair, and his nose and lips were somewhat thin, which only made his eyes seem all the larger. "Shall I have your breakfast brought to you up here, or do you prefer a litter to take you to the Room of Morning Sun?"

Yakim Douan suppressed his chuckle. He heard these same words every morning—every single morning! Without fail, without the slightest deviation. Exactly as he had ordered them spoken fifty-two years and seven personal attendants ago.

"God-Voice?" Merwan Ma asked.

A telling question, Yakim Douan realized, for the younger man had spoken out of turn, without prompting and without permission. The Chezru Chieftain glared at the attendant, and Merwan Ma shrank back, nearly disappearing behind the door.

Yes, Yakim could still keep the overly curious young man in line, and with just a look. That, and the fact that he honestly liked Merwan Ma, was the only reason Yakim kept this one around. While one would normally expect intelligence to be a prized attribute for a personal attendant, Yakim Douan usually went out of his way to avoid that particular strength. The Chezru Chieftain was safer by far if those closest to him were somewhat dim-witted. Unfortunately for Yakim, though, by the time he had realized Merwan Ma's brightness, he was already enamored of the young man, who had been only sixteen when he had begun to serve. Even after he had come to understand Merwan Ma's intellect and curiosity, Yakim had kept him on, and now, with the day of his death approaching, he was glad that he had. Merwan Ma was bright and inquisitive, but he was also fiercely loyal and pious, dedicated enough to Yatol to rise into the priesthood. When Merwan Ma called Yakim "God-Voice," he honestly believed the title to be literal.

"Come in," the Chezru Chieftain bade the attendant.

Merwan Ma came around the door, standing straight. He was tall, well over six feet, and lean, as were most of the people of Behren, where it was hot all the time and extra pounds and layers of fat did not sit well. He'd seem even taller if he ascended to the priesthood, Yakim realized, for then he'd grow his hair up high, as was the custom for Yatols.

Yakim nearly chuckled again as he considered the fact that his attendant was not a Yatol priest. For centuries, the Chezru Chieftain had been attended *only* by Yatol priests; for centuries, none but Yatol priests were even allowed to speak to the God-Voice. But Yakim Douan had changed that nearly four hundred years before, after one almost disastrous transformation when several of his attending Yatols had decided to make a try for the principal Chezru title themselves, claiming that the new God-Voice could not be found, despite the fact that they had a two-year-old in hand who could fully recite the Codex of the Prophet.

Luck alone had allowed Yakim Douan to continue his reign in that instance, and so when he had risen to Consciousness at the tender age of ten, one of his first edicts was to change the strata at Chom Deiru, the Chezru Palace, putting those whose power was closest to the Chezru Chieftain out of the loop, removing personal ambition from the formula in times of Transcendence.

"The Room of the Morning Sun is prepared for break-fast?" Yakim asked.

"Yes, God-Voice." Merwan Ma was careful to avert his eyes as he spoke. "But you have risen late this day and I fear that the room is already heated beyond comfort."

"Yes . . . well, then have my food delivered here."

"Yes, God-Voice." Merwan Ma bowed quickly and turned to leave, but Yakim called out after him.

"Have a second meal delivered, as well. You will dine with me this morning, I think. We have things that we should discuss."

"Yes, God-Voice."

Merwan Ma hustled out, and Yakim Douan nodded know-ingly at the tremor in his last answer. Merwan Ma had always enjoyed sitting with Yakim—the two had become friends of a sort, a mentor-student relationship—but Merwan Ma knew now the reason for the invitation. Yakim wanted to speak with him about Transcendence again, about the Chezru Chieftain's impending death and the duties that Merwan Ma must carry out perfectly during the time that would follow, the Behead-ing, it was called, a period when the Yatol Church would be without an official leader, when the Yatol priests would rule by consensus and were bound to make only little changes in standing policy.

Yakim Douan was glad that his talks about the time of Transcendence so unsettled Merwan Ma. That revealed the young attendant's love for his Chezru master, and that love, Yakim believed, would help to carry them both through the vulnerable few years they must face between Yakim's death and his subsequent ascension.

Merwan Ma returned a short while later, along with several younger attendants, all bearing trays of fruits and seasoned cakes, plates and fabulous utensils, and pitchers filled with many different types of juice. They quickly set the table at the northern window in the circular chamber, the one affording a spectacular view of the Belt-and-Buckle Mountains, towering black stone and white snowy peaks. The Belt-and-Buckle was the most imposing range in the known world, with few passes, and even those full of danger, rockslides and avalanches, great bears and cats and other monsters more dangerous by far. The view of the range from Yakim Douan's palace displayed that awesome power in all its glory. That view, with the sun splayed on the eastern slopes and shining on the white caps, and with the dark shadows looming behind every jag, was considered quite spiritual by most who looked upon it. For the Yatols in particular, it held a reminder that there was a greater power than any they might witness in the domain of humankind. It was a spiritual and humbling view—humbling even to immortal Yakim Douan.

When the pair sat down, the attendants hustled all about, pouring juice and serving the food, but Yakim Douan waved them away and ordered them out of the room. A couple of them hesitated, staring at the Chezru Chieftain with confusion, even disbelief, for they customarily served throughout the meal.

"We are capable of pouring our own drinks," Yakim Douan assured them. "And of cutting our own fruit. Now be gone." He ended by waving his hands at them, and they skittered away.

He looked back to Merwan Ma, smiling, and noted that the young man seemed to want to say something.

"You will speak openly at this meal," he instructed, and Merwan Ma shifted uncomfortably.

Yakim went quiet then, but didn't begin eating. He just sat there staring at his attendant, his expression prompting the young man to speak out.

"You wish to discuss your death again, God-Voice. I am not fond of this topic."

"Everyone must die, my young friend," said Yakim, and he smiled inwardly at the irony of the statement.

"But you are still a young man," Merwan Ma blurted, and he lowered his eyes immediately upon saying the words, as if he believed that, despite Yakim's claim, he had overstepped the bounds of propriety.

"In my bones, I feel the weight, the wrath, of every year and every morning," Yakim replied with a warm smile, and he put his hand on Merwan Ma's forearm, comforting the younger man.

"But God-Voice, you seem as if you are surrendering to age without a fight."

"Do you believe in the Revelation of Yatol?" the Chezru Chieftain said suddenly, sternly, reminding the student of who he was, of his—of their—supposed purpose in life. The Revelation of Yatol was the binding force of the Yatol religion, a promise of eternal life on the Cloud of Chez, a place of Paradise. All of the rituals and practices, all of the codes of behavior that governed the Yatol religion were based upon that promise.

"Of course, God-Voice!" Merwan Ma retorted, blurting the response with surprise and horror.

"I am not accusing you, my son," said the Chezru Chieftain. "I am merely reminding you. If we are to believe in the Revelation of Yatol, then we should accept the onset of death with open arms, confident that we have lived a life worthy of the Cloud of Chez. Am I to be sad, then, to think that Paradise is soon to be my home?"

"But we do not ask for death, God-Voice—"

"I know, however, when death begins to ask for me," Yakim Douan interrupted. "This is part of my station, to understand when death approaches so that those around me—so that you, Merwan Ma—can begin their preparations for the search for the new God-Voice. Do you understand?"

Merwan Ma lowered his eyes. "I am afraid, God-Voice," he said.

"You will not fail."

"But how will I know?" asked the young attendant, looking up suddenly at the Chezru Chieftain. "How can I be sure that I will select the correct replacement? It is a terrible burden, God-Voice. I fear that I am not worthy to bear it."

"You are," Yakim Douan said, laughing. "The child will be obvious to you, I assure you. When I was selected, I was reciting the entire Fourth Book of Prophecy."

"But could not a mother so teach her young child, if she wished him to ascend?"

"I had not yet seen my second birthday!" said a laughing Yakim. "And I could answer any question put to me by the Yatol Council. Do you doubt that they chose correctly?"

Merwan Ma blanched.

"It is not an accusation, my young friend," said Yakim. "It is merely a reassurance to you that you will know. Your predecessor voiced similar concerns . . . so I have heard," the Chezru Chieftain quickly added, for how could he have firsthand knowledge of what Merwan Ma's predecessor might or might not have said?

"Even so, God-Voice," the obviously nervous Merwan Ma continued. "Once the child is found—"

"Then your duties are clear and with many recorded precedents," Yakim Douan interrupted. "And those duties are minimal, do not doubt. You will watch over the child and see that he is well cared for through the early years of his life. Not so difficult a job, I would say."

"But what of his training? Who will tutor the new God-Voice in the ways of Yatol?"

Yakim Douan was laughing before Merwan ever finished. "He will tutor you, if you so desire! Do you not understand? The child will be born with full consciousness, and full understanding of all that is Yatol.

"Do you doubt?" the Chezru Chieftain asked into Merwan Ma's scrunched-up face. "Of course you do!" Yakim added to alleviate the tension before it could ever really begin. "Because you have not witnessed the miracle of Transcendence. I have, firsthand! I remember those early days well, and I needed no tutoring. I needed nothing, just the climb to Consciousness, and by that time, I understood everything about our beloved Chezru, both good and bad, better than any of those around me. Fear not, my young friend. Your time of indenture in the house of the Chezru Chieftain is to end in scarcely more than a decade, it would seem."

If those words were of any comfort at all to Merwan Ma, he didn't show it; in fact, his expression revealed just the opposite.

"You know this to be true," Yakim prompted.

"As with your anticipated death, it is not a subject I am comfortable discussing, God-Voice."

"Ah," Yakim answered with a great laugh, and again he patted the young attendant's arm. "You are to serve me, and then to see the next God-Voice to Consciousness, and then you are freed of all responsibility to the Chezru. That is the way it has always been, and the way it must continue to be."

"All that I love—"

"That does not preclude you from joining Chezru more formally," Yakim went on. "In truth, I would be sorely disappointed if you do not pursue your calling to piety. You will make a fine Yatol, my friend, and as such, will prove a valuable asset to the next Chezru Chieftain. Why, I have already penned a long letter to my successor and to the Yatol Council expressing my beliefs in your potential."

That seemed to calm Merwan Ma considerably, and he blushed with embarrassment and lowered his eyes.

Just the effect Yakim Douan had hoped for. He truly liked the young man, and would indeed miss him when he came to Consciousness in the next incarnation. But on this point of ritual, Yakim had to hold fast. He couldn't take the chance of keeping one as bright as Merwan Ma around for too long.

Familiarity might bring danger.

Merwan Ma made his way through the great columned hallways of the airy palace. The whole of the place was made of stone, mostly marble, pink and white and the subtle pale yellow of Cosinnida marble from the south. The many columns, ridged and decorated, were of the type that came from the northwest, from the foothills of the Belt-and-Buckle near the borderland of Behren and To-gai. This stone was the brightest white of all, but streaked with red veins throughout, so much so that it appeared to Merwan Ma as if red vines grew all along the columns. He could almost envision large grapes hanging from the vine, ready to be plucked and savored.

Merwan Ma's sandals were leather, and not hard-soled, but his footfalls echoed along the vast chambers of the palace, where every ceiling was delicately arched to catch the sound and roll it about. The young attendant often lost himself on walks such as this, wandering the great ways past the inspiring tapestries and the amazing mosaics tiled on the great floors. On such jaunts, he felt alone in the vast universe, and yet at one with it, as well.

He needed that now, that comfort that he was part of something larger than himself, larger than human flesh. His master had done it again, another conversation about the God-Voice's impending death. How could the Chezru Chieftain be so calm about that? How could he speak in such commonsensical terms about the end of his life?

Merwan Ma gave a great exhale, thoroughly jealous of his master, of any man who could be so at ease with mortality. Merwan Ma was a dedicated and pious Shepherd, a rank above the common Chezru folk but a rank below the Yatols. He prayed every day, and followed every ritual and precept of the religion. He believed in an afterlife, in a reward for his good behavior. Truly he did. And yet, how pale his convictions seemed next to the supreme calm held by Yakim Douan!

Perhaps he would come to such a place of tranquillity as he aged, Merwan Ma hoped. Perhaps he would find a day when he could so easily accept the inevitability of his own death, when he could be so confident that one journey was ending only so that another journey could begin.

"No," he said aloud, and he fell to his knees briefly and pressed his palms against his eyes, prostrating himself on the floor, an expression of submission, obedience, and repentance for his last thought. He could never find a place as content as that of the God-Voice! He could never come to understand the mysteries of life and death as the Chezru Chieftain, and he alone, obviously understood! Not in this life, at least. Perhaps enlightenment awaited him on the other side of that darkest of doors.

With another deep breath, Merwan Ma pulled himself up from the floor and resumed his journey. He was late, he knew, and the others were likely already gathered about the sacred chalice, the Chezru Goblet, in the Room of Forever. Mado Wadon, the overseeing Yatol, had probably already prepared the sacrificial knife, filling its hollowed hilt with the oils of preservation. But certainly, without Merwan Ma there, the others had not begun the bleeding.

Yakim Douan continued to enjoy his meal at the northern window, staring out at the towering majestic peaks. He knew what was going on in the Room of Forever, and he knew well the ultimate danger to him and to his secrets whenever the seven gathered for the ritual. But the centuries had taken the edge from the Chezru Chieftain concerning this anxiety. He had watched the bleeding closely all those early years, centuries before when he had instituted the ritual.

No, not instituted it, but merely altered it to cover his secret. Since the beginning of Yatol, the selected group had kept the sacred Chezru Goblet filled with their blood, standing in a circle about it and taking turns slicing their wrists until the deep and wide chalice was full to the appointed line. That ritual of blood-brotherhood and the resultant pool of blood had proven to be a wonderful binding force for Yakim Douan, for embedded in the base of that sacred chalice was a single gemstone, a powerful hematite. When Yakim added his own blood to the pool, every week immediately following the bleeding ritual, he somehow created a bond to that embedded hematite that he had learned to exploit from a great distance, from the other side of the palace, even. That was important to Yakim, not because he often utilized the hematite, but because he understood that if a sudden tragedy should befall him—the dagger of a rival, perhaps—he would be able to establish enough of a connection to the hematite to free his spirit from his dying corporeal form.

The only real danger to Yakim, then, came during the process of changing the blood pool, for though all of the attending bleeders would be blindfolded and instructed, strictly so, never to glance into the chalice, one look with the blood level low might be enough to arouse great suspicions. For the Yatols were not fond of gemstones, magical or not, and to see one embedded in their most-prized religious symbol, the Chezru Goblet itself, would strike a sour note in the heart of any true Yatol. Gemstones were the province of the hated Abellicans to the north, the source of Abellican magical powers, and for centuries, since before Yakim Douan's first ascension even, the Yatol priests had denounced the enchanted stones as instruments for channeling demon magic.

Seeing a gemstone—and a hematite, a soul stone, at that!—embedded in the base of that deep chalice would bring about questions that Yakim Douan did not want to answer.

But the Chezru Chieftain held all confidence that it would not come to that. In all the nearly eight hundred years he had been secretly using the magical hematite, the blood level in the chalice had only dropped to a revealing level once, when a young Yatol priest had inadvertently tripped and spilled the contents.

That unfortunate Yatol, so flustered, so horrified by what he had done, hadn't even paused long enough to consider the ramifications of what he had seen. He had only stammered apology after apology when Yakim Douan had come upon him, to find him kneeling on the bloody floor and crying, his head in his hands. He had begged forgiveness from the God-Voice, even as Yakim's knife had reached for his unprotected, undefended throat.

That one had died confused.

Yakim Douan shuddered at the memory of that awful day. He had never wanted to kill the man, but so much had been at stake. How could he jeopardize his own theoretical immortality, centuries of life, against the few decades the poor fool might have remaining?

To Yakim all these years later, it had been pragmatism, and not hatred and not any evil lust for power, that had guided his dagger hand that fateful day.

Yakim Douan couldn't even remember the clumsy Yatol's name. Nor could anyone else.

Merwan Ma stood perfectly still, chanting softly the intonation of sacrifice, his voice blending beautifully with the others standing in a circle about the small table that held the

Chezru Goblet. The young attendant held his left hand out across his chest and to the right side, ready to take the knife, while his right arm was out before him, his forearm resting on a padded shelf, his wrist dangling above the sacred vessel.

He was blindfolded, as were the others. In fact, Merwan Ma, as principal attendant to the Chezru Chieftain, had been the only one to enter this holy room with his eyes open, guiding the others to their respective positions. Then, with a prayer, Merwan Ma had taken his place and reached below the table and turned the lever. He had watched the red fluid level slowly dropping as he had applied his own blindfold.

That lever and release under the table was counterweighted, designed to slow the flow and then close altogether as the blood in the bowl drained. This group would not replace all of the liquid, but only about three-quarters. A bell sounded as the lever closed, the signal for the sacrifice to begin. And so it had, with the chanting. The man immediately to Merwan Ma's left took up the treated knife, reached forward, and cut his right wrist, then counted out the appropriate time, in cadence with the verse of the common chant, as his lifeblood dribbled down into the chalice. When the verse ended, the man passed the blade to the man on his left and the process was repeated.

And so on, until the knife came full circle, back to Merwan Ma. The attendant, his right wrist crisscrossed with lines and lines of scarring, finished his duty stoically and efficiently, then reverently placed the blade back on the table.

As the song finished, Merwan Ma lifted the blindfold off of his head and looked down at their work. Some blood had spattered outside of the great goblet, as usual, and the level wasn't as high as it should have been, though it was well within the marks of tolerance inside the chalice. Had it not been, then the sacrifice would have been declared void and one of the men gathered about the table would have been killed and replaced, with only the attending Yatol and Merwan Ma exempt from that fate.

But the sacrifice was acceptable, the level of red fluid more than sufficient to hold the sacred goblet until the month had passed and the next sacrifice ensued.

Merwan Ma nodded at the handiwork—he'd have to come back in later and clean up the sacred vessel, of course, but other than that, the duty was done. With perfect precision wrought of months and months of practice, he took up the hand of the man on his left and led the group, joined as one line, out of the room.

In the anteroom, as soon as the door was closed, the others pulled off their blindfolds and tightened the bandages on their wrists, congratulating each other on a job well-done.

The exception, as usual, was the one Yatol in attendance. The older man looked to his wrist first, securing the bandage, but then, as he did after every sacrifice, he glanced at Merwan Ma.

The attendant saw little fondness in that look. Many of the Yatols were not fond of him, allowing their own jealousies to overcome their dedication to their religion and their god. He was not a Yatol, after all, not a priest, and yet, when the Chezru Chieftain went to his reward, Merwan Ma would, in all practicality, become the most powerful man in all of the Chezru domain. He would be the initial selector of the new God-Voice, and would have full voice at the ensuing council of confirmation. He would then oversee the early years of the chosen child's life, and while he would then have no voice in Yatol formal policy, it would be his voice most often heard in the next chosen God-Voice's ear.

Some of the Yatols were not pleased at this arrangement. Merwan Ma had even overheard a pair of particularly obnoxious priests mumbling that in times long past, a Yatol, the highest ranking of the order below the Chezru Chieftain, had served as attendant, and not a mere Shepherd.

Merwan Ma took it all in stride. He had been selected, for whatever reason, and his duty was clear and straightforward. He could not allow petty human frailties and emotions to deter him from his duty. His calling was to God, through the words and edicts of the God-Voice, his beloved Chezru Chieftain. It was not his place to question, nor—he reminded himself then and there—was it his place to accept or internalize the expression the attending Yatol was now sending his way. That look reflected that man's weakness, and it was not a weakness that Merwan Ma meant to share.

He ushered the group out of the anteroom, then went back into the sacred room, consecrated cloth in hand, and reverently wiped clean the sides of the Chezru Goblet, satisfied that the sacrifice of blood that day would secure the goblet and the health of the church for the next month.

# CHAPTER 3

# Walking with Purpose

Brynn and Juraviel rode in virtual silence for many days after their fight with the goblin band. Despite Juraviel's cutting words and sound reasoning, Brynn could not let go of her anger toward the elf for what he had done to her, for what he had forced from her. For he had made her kill, had taken her out of their way so that she could feel her blade sinking deep into the heart of an enemy, so that she could smell spilled blood and see the stains, so that she could witness death at her own hands, horrible in a way that she had never known. Brynn Dharielle had witnessed much death in her early years in To-gai, after the coming of the Behrenese. She had witnessed the murder of her parents—from afar, but close enough to hear the screams. Nothing could be more terrible than that!

But this last experience was troubling and horrible in a different way. This time she had been forced into the role of assassin, and the smell of blood and the screams had come to her of her own doing, and with a sizable amount of guilt attached.

Belli'mar Juraviel had done that to her, and his justifications rang hollow in Brynn's ears as the pair made their way along the southern trails. For more than a week, they went about their duties with hardly a word exchanged. They each knew what was expected of them, in setting the camp and preparing the meals, and in keeping watch throughout the night. Every now and then, Juraviel would offer a friendly comment, but Brynn usually just deflected it with a grunt or a halfhearted chuckle.

Things began to warm again between them the second week.

When Juraviel offered a sarcastic or teasing comment Bryn started to give him back one of her own, and by the end of the second week, the pair had even traded exchanges longer than single sentences.

"The Belt-and-Buckle," Juraviel said to her near the end of the third week after the goblin fight, when Brynn walked Diredusk up beside him. They stood atop a ridge that had sloped up gradually from the forest, but dropped off dramatically before them. Below, the forest spread wide and thick, and, far to the south, they could see the jagged outline of distant mountains.

Far distant, and Juraviel was quick to dampen the brightened look that came over the woman. "Do not be deceived. The mountains of that range are more huge than anything you can imagine."

"I came through them once," Brynn reminded. "And I walked their southern slopes."

"When you were a child, so many years ago that you hardly remember the truth of their scope."

"I saw them every day when I was a child, and from much closer than this vantage point!"

"Indeed," Juraviel replied. "Much, much closer. We can see them, and each day they will seem a little taller. But just a little, and by the time we actually reach them, they will tower so high above us that they will block out the sun itself. Our road is far from finished."

Brynn looked down at the elf, who stood staring to the south. To her surprise, her irritation at Juraviel's words could not take hold. No, Brynn appreciated Juraviel at that moment, more so perhaps than she had since their departure from Andur'Blough Inninness. Only then and there, standing with their goal somewhat in sight and yet still so far away, did Brynn truly understand the sacrifice that her mentor, her friend, was making for her. He was giving up months and months, years even, away from his home and kin, and for what? For no personal gain that Brynn could see, however much Lady Dasslerond preferred the To-gai-ru over the Behrenese. When Juraviel returned home to Andur'Blough Inninness, if he managed to stay alive throughout the war and return home, the daily routines, the daily joys and sorrows of his existence would not be dependent upon whether or not Brynn had prevailed in To-gai. What did it truly matter to Juraviel and the Touel'alfar whether the To-gai-ru or the Behrenese ruled the windy steppes of that far-distant land?

And yet, here he was, uncomplaining, traveling beside her, leading her to her destiny.

Brynn stooped a bit and draped her arm across Juraviel's small shoulders. He turned a curious expression toward her, and she smiled in response and kissed him on the cheek, and then, when he returned her smile, she nodded, silently conveying her appreciation, silently explaining to him—and she knew that he understood—that she at last understood and appreciated that she could not possibly make this journey without him.

That was the truth that Brynn Dharielle realized, standing there on that warm afternoon, the southern breezes blowing through her dark, silken hair. And as she had grown on that day of her dark epiphany, when she had learned what it was to kill, so she believed that she had grown even more this day, the day of her second epiphany, the next stage of her maturation along the road to her destiny.

A good leader understood her enemies.

A better leader understood, and appreciated, her allies.

The days blended together, but with each dawn Brynn noted that the mountains did indeed seem taller, if only just a bit. She tried to put it out of her mind, for she was becoming as anxious as if those mountains were not just the landmark that would lead into her land, but marked the very steppes of To-gai itself.

One day on the road, with Brynn leaning forward eagerly, her body language speaking clearly to the fact that she believed her final goal was already in sight, and almost in hand, Belli'mar Juraviel threw a bit of cold water over her.

"It is good that we make the foothills of the Belt-and-Buckle before midsummer," he said casually. "For then we have a chance, at least, of finding our way through the divide before the winter snows begin."

Brynn's expression as she turned to regard him was one of curiosity and confusion.

"For winter will come early up in those high passes," Juraviel explained. "Oh, down here, amidst the trees and this far south, I doubt the snows ever pile very deep, or indeed, if it ever snows at all. But note that the caps of the mountains are still encased in snow, though summer nears its midpoint. I suspect that we will not have to climb very high, and not very late into the winter season, before we find the passes fully blocked.

"Of course, that is assuming that we even find a pass," he finished grimly.

That last sentence had Brynn's eyes widening tellingly. "You do not know the way through?" she asked, almost with a gasp. "But you were there—or your people were—barely a decade ago! When you rescued me from the Chezru! Surely the Touel'alfar have not forgotten the way already!"

"Lady Dasslerond was the one who rescued you," Juraviel explained. "She has ways, with her gemstones, to travel great distances quickly. When she had you in tow, though you remember it not, she and her attendants lulled you to sleep, then used the power of the emerald stone to turn a hundred miles into a short walk."

"Then why didn't Dasslerond do the same thing now?" Brynn demanded. "We could have saved weeks of travel! And the mountains would be no barrier, while you sit there telling me that we might not even be able to get through them!"

"The road is preparation for the trials at its end."

Brynn snorted, obviously not impressed with that argument. "And what do we do if we cannot find a way through the mountains? Do we sit in their shadows and share dreams that we know cannot come true? Do we turn back for Caer'alfar and beg Lady Dasslerond to do that which she should have done before?"

That last statement brought a glare of disapproval that reminded the young ranger that there were boundaries concerning the Touel'alfar she should not cross.

She pressed on anyway, but in more reserved tones, trying to justify her outrage. "My people are enslaved. Every day that we tarry is another day of misery for the To-gai-ru. The revolution could be taking place by now."

Belli'mar Juraviel chuckled and shook his head, and Brynn, thinking that she was being mocked, narrowed her brown eyes.

"If Lady Dasslerond had summoned the power of the emerald and placed you within a To-gai-ru village enclave, do you believe that you would have stepped forward and simply taken control?" the elf asked. "By what declaration would you have been named as hero and leader?"

"By the same declaration I must use, I suppose, when at last we arrive in To-gai," came the sarcastic response, and Brynn added under her breath, "If we ever arrive in To-gai."

"If we find no way over the mountains, then we shall turn east along the foothills, all the way to the coast, to the city of Entel, where we will secure passage to Jacintha easily enough."

Brynn knew the name of the second city, Jacintha, and understood the extent of the hike.

"Jacintha," Juraviel said again. "The seat of Behrenese power. The home of the Chezru Chieftain who rules the Yatols."

Predictably, Brynn's expression became one of intense anger.

"You are worldly in many ways," Juraviel said to her. "And yet, in many others, you know so little of the wide world. Perhaps that is our fault, but we are, by need, a reclusive people. So, instead of begrudging the delays in returning to To-gai, consider this journey, and the one far to the east that we might well have to make, as a continuation of your training, as preparation for the trials you will soon enough face."

Brynn stared at Juraviel long and hard, but she had heard the words clearly, and could accept that explanation to some degree. She reminded herself that the Touel'alfar had rescued her from a life of certain slavery, an existence that would never have led to the possibilities spread wide before her. She reminded herself that the Touel'alfar had trained her in the arts she would need to make an attempt to lead her people. In light of all that history and training and friendship, Brynn suddenly felt very foolish indeed for so severely questioning Belli'mar Juraviel!

She looked down and gave a self-deprecating chuckle,

then said, "Perhaps I have spent too much time in the company of Aydrian."

She glanced back up as she finished and saw that her words had indeed brought a smile to the elf's fair face.

"Aydrian will find his own way in the world, I doubt not," Juraviel replied. "But his temperament would never have proven suitable to the task you have at hand. You are a warrior, but foremost you are a diplomat, a leader with words above the sword, an inspiration through courage and . . ." The elf paused, raising a finger into the air to signify the importance of his point. "An inspiration through wisdom. Without the second quality, you will lead your people into nothing but disaster. It will take more than force to pry To-gai from the grasp of Behren, my young friend. It will take unparalleled courage and cunning, and will take a leader so elevated that her people will die for her willingly, gratefully. Do you fully appreciate the gravity of that position?"

Brynn suddenly found it hard to draw breath.

"Do you truly understand that you will one day order your warriors into battle, knowing that many of them will die on the field?"

Breathing didn't get any easier.

"Do you truly understand that you may have to turn your army aside, knowing full well that in doing so you will leave a To-gai-ru village unprotected, and that the Behrenese will likely take out their anger against your insurrection on that unprotected village? Perhaps your actions will lead to more children watching their parents die—or even more horrifying, will lead to some parents watching their children die. Are you ready to take that responsibility, Brynn Dharielle?"

She stood there, trembling, unblinking.

"Is the potential cost worth the gain?"

That last question grounded her again, tossed aside the images of potential horror and clarified the potential victory. Victory for To-gai meant only one thing, in truth, but to Brynn Dharielle, that one thing outweighed all the pain and all the deaths.

"Freedom," she whispered, her teeth clenched tightly.

Belli'mar Juraviel stared at her for a few moments, then nodded his approval.

She was learning.

Lozan Duk watched the curious couple sitting at the camp-fire that warm summer night in the rolling foothills of the Belt-and-Buckle, a mountain range that Lozan Duk's people considered the very end of the world. Lozan Duk was not too concerned with the female, for though her skin was darker and her eyes a bit unusual in shape, she did not seem so much different from the other bumbling humans who every so often wandered into these lands.

But the other one, with his angular features and diminutive form . . .

At first Lozan Duk and his companion, Cazzira, had thought the second creature a human child, but closer inspection had nullified that viewpoint. He was no child, and indeed spoke in the tones of a leader. And more than that, this one had a set of features that neither of the onlookers could have expected: a pair of nearly translucent wings.

A branch to the side shuddered slightly as Lozan Duk's companion returned, leaping through the boughs as nimbly as any squirrel might. "Debankan," she said with a nod, confirming their suspicions that the wings were akin to those of a debankan, a butterfly.

The two hesitated, staring at each other, at a loss. Their histories told of only one race of creatures who sported such ornaments, the Tylwyn Tou, the elves of the day.

But those creatures, the Tylwyn Tou, had receded into the oldest memories of the Tylwyn Doc. To many of the younger people, they had become no more than legends.

Was this, then, a legend come to life? For the diminutive creature down by the campfire surely resembled the Tylwyn Doc, with his deceivingly delicate stature and his angular features, except that his hair was light, where the Tylwyn Doc had hair almost universally black. And his skin, though creamy, seemed somewhat colored by the sun, where the skin of all the Tylwyn Doc, creatures who rarely if ever ventured out from under the nearly solid canopy of their forest home of Tymwyvenne, was milky white.

"Tylwyn Tou?" Cazzira asked, echoing Lozan Duk's thoughts exactly.

"And what does that mean?" Lozan asked with a shrug.

Normally, the procedure for dealing with intruders was fairly straightforward, and certainly of uniform intent. No reasoning being who wandered into the realm of the Tylwyn Doc, the Doc'alfar, would wander back out.

Intruders were given to the peat bog.

Lozan Duk looked back down at the duo, particularly at the curious creature who seemed in many ways a mirror image of himself, and wondered.

# CHAPTER 4

## *Details, Details*

Their bickering was becoming more than an annoyance to Yakim Douan.

"The pirates must be handled more delicately!" yelled Yatol Peridan, the highest-ranking priest of southeastern Behren, the land known as Cosinnida—and a man well known to be in league with many of the notorious coast runners. The argument that he was now making in Jacintha—that the crackdown Yatol De Hamman had imposed along his section of the coast, the area north of Peridan's territory and just south of Jacintha, was unreasonable and dangerous for security—almost had the Chezru Chieftain laughing aloud. How transparent this one was! Yakim always got a good chuckle out of Peridan's antics; he had only appointed the man as a Yatol because Peridan had done a fine job in getting valuable marble up to the palace in Jacintha for recent improvements.

"The pirates must be handled!" Yatol De Hamman countered angrily. "Leave it at that. You call for delicate handling because you fear for your own purse!"

Yatol Peridan's eyes widened at the blunt accusation, but Yakim Douan was paying more attention to the other seven priests, who were sitting back and watching the rising conflict with obvious amusement. The only analogy the Chezru Chieftain could draw upon at that moment was that of a group of youngsters, encircling a pair that had squared off, calling for them to fight.

Yes, this was more than an annoyance. Yakim Douan wanted to begin the time of Transcendence, wanted a new and younger body. But how could he leave the Chezru flock so vulnerable when it was in such disarray, when even the Yatols, the supposed leaders of the Chezru, were bickering amongst themselves? The verbal sparring between Peridan and De Hamman continued to escalate dangerously, until finally the Chezru Chieftain slammed his fists down on the round whitewood table and rose so forcefully that his chair skidded out behind him.

"Do you use the pirates, Yatol Peridan?" he asked, the bluntness of his question drawing gasps from all in attendance. It was one thing for a pair of priests to spar and accuse, but something altogether different for the Chezru Chieftain, the God-Voice of Yatol, to ask a question with such implications.

"God-Voice, how can you ask me . . ." Yatol Peridan stammered clumsily.

"Exactly as I have asked you," Yakim Douan replied with all calm and confidence. "Do you use the pirates, for your own gain or for the gain of the church?"

Peridan continued to squirm, obviously seeking an escape, but Yakim Douan fixed him with a withering glare—a look perfected over the centuries, a look that allowed no possibilities of dodge here.

"The pirates have tithed to my church, yes, God-Voice," Peridan finally admitted, lowering his eyes. The other priests all looked to each other with concern. Peridan's admission was not news to them, of course, for everyone there knew the truth of Yatol Peridan's relationship with some of the most notorious thugs sailing the coastline. But to hear the admission openly, in front of the Chezru Chieftain, was no small thing!

Yatol De Hamman sat back and crossed his arms over his chest, seeming quite pleased with himself.

"And you have used this . . . tithing, for the betterment of your church and flock?" the Chezru Chieftain asked, and all eyes looked at him then with continued surprise.

"I have," Yatol Peridan answered enthusiastically after the shock of the question had worn off. "And I have spoken with many of the pirates about their activities, God-Voice. I try to alter their behavior. I seek to channel their strengths into the betterment of all."

"They are killers!" Yatol De Hamman cried out. "Killers all!"

He started to spout on, but Yakim Douan held up his hand, halting the man. "You speak truly, Yatol De Hamman," the Chezru offered. "And I hold little sympathy for those pirates your warships have sent into the depths of the dark waters. But as they are killers, they are also an inevitability. The pirates have run their catamarans across the coral reefs and away from Behrenese warships for centuries. They have always been there and will always be there. Accept that truth, and you will come to understand that Yatol Peridan's profiting from the pirate activities is beneficial to the Chezru."

"Bless you, God-Voice," Yatol Peridan started to say.

"But," Yakim Douan said sternly, lifting his pointing, accusatory finger Peridan's way, "do not confuse the issue. You complain that Yatol De Hamman is sinking pirate ships, and thus sinking your profits, but to do so shows a disregard for the needs of Yatol De Hamman. How is he to rule his flock effectively if they do not believe that he can be trusted to protect them? So come not to Jacintha with complaints that your fellow Yatols are upholding the laws, Yatol Peridan. Come not to Jacintha with complaints that your temple will not be layered in gold."

Yatol Peridan again lowered his eyes. "Yes, God-Voice."

"And for the rest of you, find some insight!" Yakim Douan went on. "There are unpleasant inevitabilities to society, much as we see with the pirates off our coastline. We try to diminish these unpleasantries, indeed, but we are not wrong to find gain from them. As for you, Yatol Grysh," he said, referring to, and looking to, the Yatol of the northwesternmost reaches of Behren, who presided under the shadows of the great mountains and the plateau along the borderlands of To-gai, in the great Behrenese city of Dharyan. Grysh, a bald, heavyset man with sleepy eyes who noticeably lacked any chin, was, in effect, Yakim Douan's principal sheriff over the conquered To-gai-ru. The Yatol who had done the conquering, Tohen Bardoh, had been so brutal in his tactics that Douan had been forced to pull him back from the steppes. There were other Yatol priests in To-gai, of course, but they were either quick-promoted and expendable, eager young men, lifted from the ranks of the Shepherds and sent to the wilderness of the steppes, or they were of To-gai-ru descent, traitors to their own people, who obviously, therefore, could not be trusted by the Chezru Chieftain. That left Grysh, a cunning and often callous man, the perfect liaison to handle the savages of To-gai.

"There are many, many bandits running just west of your domain, are there not?" Yakim Douan asked the large man.

Yatol Grysh blinked sleepily, smiled, and nodded.

"Do you not find a way to tap into their growing resources?" Yakim Douan asked slyly.

Yatol Grysh, who was easily the most confident and self-assured of all those gathered, excepting of course Yakim Douan himself, merely smiled and nodded again, his demeanor drawing a chuckle or two from the others seated about the table.

"Inevitabilities," Yakim Douan said to them all. "We cannot achieve perfection of our world. This is the teaching of Yatol. Perfection is to be found in an existence beyond this mortal realm. We know of this, and so, while we cannot be publicly tolerant of such behaviors or risk losing our hold, I applaud a Yatol wise enough to turn unpleasantness into gain."

He finished with a pleading look toward Yatol De Hamman.

"Yes, God-Voice," the humbled priest said, and though he offered one disapproving, even angry, look toward Yatol Peridan, he lowered his eyes obediently, giving Yakim Douan at least the hope that this troublesome business had been settled.

And how Douan needed it settled! If the rivalry between De Hamman and Peridan continued to escalate, it would likely come to a head during the time when the Yatol Council, and not Yakim Douan—for he would be in a woman's womb, or in the body of small child—would be holding power in all the church. De Hamman and Peridan would no doubt be strong voices in that council, as strong as any, and if they went to war with each other, the church Yakim Douan inherited at the age of ten would be in complete disarray.

If he even was able to inherit the church, for such infighting could destroy the customs that now allowed for such a transition.

A weary Yakim Douan walked away from the contentious meeting sometime later, feeling satisfied that he had put the beast back into its cage, at least for the time being. He would have to reinforce the lessons he had given to the two troublesome Yatols many times over, he knew. And if he could not find a compromise that seemed binding, he would have to hold on to his earthly coil—would have to suffer the aches in the morning, would have to suffer the uninterested looks the harem girls gave to him when they didn't think he was looking—for a long time to come.

The tired Chezru Chieftain knew that his day was only going to get busier when he saw Merwan Ma rushing down the long hall toward him, the young man's face bright with excitement.

"God-Voice," Merwan Ma breathed, sliding to a stop before Yakim.

The Chezru managed to straighten his shoulders and eye the young man squarely.

"Master Mackaront of Entel has come to speak with you."

Mackaront, the personal assistant of Abbot Olin of St. Bondabruce, was an Abellican monk of great power and Yakim Douan's principal liaison to the northern kingdom. The Chezru Chieftain did well to offer a slight smile and nod in response, did well to hide his trepidation upon hearing the name of the unexpected visitor. If Mackaront had come south with more bad news—that Abbot Olin had died, perhaps—it could put yet another tear in the carefully drawn plans for Transcendence.

"I will meet with him in the Study of Sunset," Yakim explained to his assistant, and he walked past, turning down the next corridor.

He heard Merwan Ma's eager footfalls, sandals clapping on mosaic floors, and hoped again that the news from the north would not bode ill.

Master Filladoro Mackaront was surely one of the ugliest men Yakim Douan had ever met. His face was cratered and blotchy, his nose bulbous and seeming almost to glow with painful rawness. His brown eyes drooped and his teeth were all broken and twisted. As if all that wasn't enough, several huge warts adorned Mackaront's head and neck, including one cracked black-and-brown blemish in the center of his high forehead.

"It is good to see you again, God-Voice of the Yatols," Mackaront said with a bow. The man spoke perfect Mohdan, the predominant language of eastern Behren.

Yakim Douan motioned for him to sit in a chair to his left, with both seats facing the window, which afforded a wonderful view of sunset over the western-stretching Belt-and-Buckle. Yakim Douan had placed them this way purposely before Merwan Ma and Mackaront had caught up to him, partly because he enjoyed watching the glorious sunsets, but mostly so that he would not have to sit facing his ugly guest. He liked Mackaront quite a bit, actually, but he didn't want to look at the man!

"Pray tell me that my friend Abbot Olin fares well."

"Indeed, God-Voice," Mackaront happily replied. "Abbot Olin remains strong and well, his eyes clear."

"And his mind sharp."

"Yes, God-Voice!"

Yakim Douan did turn then to regard the ugly master from St. Bondabruce, noting how the man's lips could not sit straight on his face because of the jagged teeth beneath. He wondered, and not for the first time, if that physical ugliness had been the catalyst for Filladoro Mackaront to join the Abellican Church. The Abellicans, after all, frowned upon any relationships between brothers and women—mostly because the powers of the Abellican Church wanted to make certain that no widows or children were left behind to claim any inheritance over Abellican property or wealth!—so it seemed plausible that entering the Church offered Mackaront the excuse for the obvious truth that no woman would ever want to share his bed.

"Why do you call me that?" Yakim Douan asked the Abellican, quite off the cuff. Behind him, he heard the sharp intake of Merwan Ma's breath.

Mackaront looked at him curiously.

"In your religion, I am not such a God-Voice, am I?" the Chezru Chieftain asked. "We worship different gods, do we not? We assign different meanings to greatness, and yet you address me by the title normally reserved for my personal attendants and visiting Yatol priests. Are you prepared to convert to the true religion of Yatol, Abellican Master Mackaront?"

Mackaront's droopy eyes widened considerably at that remark, and he started shaking his head, his crooked lips moving as if he were trying to find appropriate words with which to respond.

"Or are you merely being polite?" the Chezru Chieftain asked with a grin that allowed both poor Mackaront and Merwan Ma to sigh with relief.

"God-Voice," Mackaront began tentatively, and he quickly corrected it to, "Chezru Douan, I am sent with all humility from my master, Abbot Olin of St. Bondabruce."

Yakim Douan didn't even hide his smile. He liked the way lackeys like Mackaront always reverted to the formalities of station when they were backed into a corner.

"I intend no offense to you," Mackaront went on. "Never that. I offer you the respect afforded your position, using titles you have earned among your people."

"Earned?" Yakim Douan said with a chuckle. "I was born to this position. There was nothing to 'earn,' because this was all decreed by Yatol, by God himself. Do you not understand?"

Master Mackaront's expression could not have been more stupefied. He understood the reasoning, of course, for he was well versed in the customs of the Yatols. What had him stunned beyond words here, Yakim Douan knew, was the Chezru's tone and insistence, this whole line of questioning—a conversation that Yakim Douan knew to be out of bounds.

"I am not qualified to debate the relative beliefs and strengths of our religions, Chezru Douan," Master Mackaront said after a few uncomfortable moments.

Yakim Douan's laughter had the man leaning back defensively in his seat.

"Nor should you wish to enter such a debate," he said lightheartedly. "Nor do I ever desire such a course. Our worlds are very different, Master Mackaront. Abbot Olin and I have understood that for years, and that understanding has been the cornerstone of my friendship with your abbot for decades. We accept each other's beliefs, with humility and respect, though I know that he, and you, are wrong."

Mackaront frowned; Yakim Douan watched his every flinch and movement, taking a measure for every step along this tricky road. He wasn't sure why he had decided to pursue this course this day. It was almost a replay of the conversation he had shared with young Abbot Olin soon after the man had ascended to the leadership of St. Bondabruce, a necessary understanding before the two men could pursue an honest friendship.

Yakim Douan came to recognize his own instincts then. When he had heard of Mackaront's visit, he had at once assumed that Olin might have died. Thus, his instincts had sent him into this unexpected conversation, one that might lead him down a road of friendship with Master Mackaront, Abbot Olin's possible successor. Better for Yakim Douan, for the end of this corporeal incarnation and for the early years of the next, if Master Mackaront of St. Bondabruce came to a higher understanding and appreciation of the Yatol religion.

"I know you are wrong because I am the God-Voice of Yatol," the Chezru Chieftain explained. "As your Father Abbot Agronguerre knows that I . . . that we," he added, sweeping his hand out toward Merwan Ma, "are wrong in our beliefs." Yakim Douan gave a shrug, as if it didn't really matter. "Your Abbot Olin understands this. What we, together, have come to know is that, though our beliefs are very different, our goals are not so much so. Pious Abellicans are closer to Yatol than the highwaymen of your lands, as pious Yatols should be far more welcomed into the gates of your heaven than the unlawful pirates running the Behrenese coastline."

Yakim Douan glanced back at Merwan Ma as he spoke, noting how the man's eyes widened! Of course they did, and if Yakim Douan had not trusted Merwan Ma implicitly to keep this conversation private, he never would have spoken in such a manner with the man present. For the formal and public declarations of the Yatol religion were quite clear concerning the Abellicans. Their gemstone use alone damned them! To the Yatols, the gemstones were the instruments of the demon dactyls, and by that reasoning, "pious" Abellicans should have been placed at the end of the line for those seeking to enter the Paradise promised by Yatol.

While Merwan Ma was obviously confused and stunned, Master Mackaront seemed to ease back into his seat, a bit more relaxed. Yes, Yakim Douan saw, and was glad: the seeds were being planted well.

"Enough of philosophy," the Chezru Chieftain announced. "You did not come here for such a discussion as this, I am sure, and my time is pressing. What news from Abbot Olin?"

Master Mackaront spent a moment collecting himself, clearing his throat and snorting a few very unpleasant sounds. Yakim Douan tried to ignore the man, looking back out to the west and the long line of mountains.

"Abbot Olin bade me come to Jacintha to tell you that Father Abbot Agronguerre's health has turned for the worse," the man from Entel explained. "He is very old and very frail, and a College of Abbots is expected within a year or two."

"And does Abbot Olin expect to ascend to your highest post at that College of Abbots?"

"He does. He has rivals, of course . . ."

"That is why our ascension is placed in the hands of God, and not mortal man," Yakim Douan couldn't resist interjecting.

Mackaront bristled and coughed, but worked past the remark. "There is one master at St.-Mere Abelle who will strive hard against him. And another, perhaps, a younger man, but one who was fortunate enough to find himself beside the disciples of Brother Avelyn, whose miracle rescued the kingdom from the rosy plague. That man is not ready, of course, but the emotions are high and favorable toward deceased Brother Avelyn."

"Ah yes, the wandering heretic who blew up a mountain and defeated the demon," Yakim Douan said with just a hint of sarcasm. "Who raised his dead arm toward the heavens and invoked the miracle you speak of, bringing down the power of God to create a mystical cure for the plague that ravaged your land." The Chezru Chieftain resisted the temptation to point out that this supposedly God-cured plague should logically be considered a God-sent plague. And if that was the case, then why hadn't God visited this horror upon Behren and the heathen Yatols?

For mortal men, such questions could bring great distress, but for Yakim Douan, who had lived through the centuries and who planned on living forever more, such questions were the stuff of pure amusement.

*Not now,* the Chezru Chieftain silently told himself. *Not here and with this man.*

"How much of a threat does Abbot Olin perceive from this young follower of Brother Avelyn?" he asked.

Master Mackaront shrugged and seemed content with the change of subject. "Young Abbot Braumin should not pose too great a threat. He is not a dynamic man, of himself, and it is only his ties to Avelyn's disciples—one martyred, the other held in the highest regard of all the land, Church and State alike—that even allows his name to be seriously mentioned. It is more the other rival, a powerful Master of St.-Mere-Abelle, and thus, sitting at Father Abbot Agronguerre's right hand, who concerns Abbot Olin, and he will have to wage a strong campaign if he is to defeat the man."

*Wage a strong campaign,* Yakim Douan echoed in his mind. The words were telling indeed, and explained much about Master Mackaront's visit.

Abbot Olin had come begging.

"Abbot Olin is prepared to wage such a battle," Mackaront went on with great enthusiasm. "He understands the great gain to both our peoples if he can ascend to the position of Father Abbot while Yakim Douan is hailed as Behren's Chezru Chieftain. Perhaps then our respective flocks can mend old wounds in a way that kings and ambassadors have never envisioned! Perhaps the bonding, then, of Jacintha to Entel will strengthen the ties to a point where few would ever consider war between our peoples ever again!"

"Entel?" Yakim Douan asked skeptically. "Why, Master Mackaront, if your Abbot Olin ascends, will he not be forced by custom to move to the north, far from his beloved Entel, to the dark halls of St.-Mere-Abelle?"

"Perhaps," Mackaront responded, his momentum a bit deflected. "Abbot Olin has spoken of moving the Abellican seat of power to Entel."

"Old traditions die hard."

"Or, even if he is forced to move to St.-Mere-Abelle, he will ensure that St. Bondabruce and St. Rontlemore of Entel are headed by men who understand the growing relationship between our peoples. Abbot Olin wishes me to assure you that his loyalties to you as his friend will not end—"

"Of course not," interrupted Yakim Douan, who had heard more than enough. "And please, when you return to Entel, assure your master that I am no less loyal than he. Though I suspect you will not even have to speak the words when Abbot Olin views your cargo." As he finished, he stood up and turned for the door, and an elated Master Mackaront was quick to take the cue.

As Mackaront bowed and turned to leave, Merwan Ma rushed ahead of him to open the door.

"Return to me at once," Yakim Douan instructed his assistant, and then he turned to Mackaront. "I will instruct good Shepherd Ma on how properly to prepare your wagons."

"You are most generous, God-Voice," the overwhelmed Mackaront said with another clumsy bow.

Yakim Douan just smiled and showed him out of the room, nodding to Merwan Ma, a signal for the man to hurry. Then, comfortably alone, the Chezru Chieftain returned to his seat and his wonderful view, awaiting Merwan Ma's return and taking this quiet moment to reflect on all of the events happening about him, all of those circumstances that would determine when he could at last shed his aching mortal coil.

"I do not understand, God-Voice," came Merwan Ma's voice behind him sometime later, startling Yakim from a pleasant nap. He jumped a bit and turned, and Merwan Ma blanched at the realization that he had just wakened the Chezru Chieftain.

"My pardon . . ." he stammered, and bowed repeatedly, heading for the door.

"I prefer that my attendants are not blabbering fools,"

Yakim said to him, stopping him cold. "Do not act the part of one, Merwan Ma. It is not becoming."

"Yes, God-Voice."

"What did you say when you entered?"

"I said that I do not understand," Merwan Ma repeated. "Master Mackaront left here in fine spirits."

"As I intended."

"Of course."

"Then what is not to understand?"

"All of . . . " Merwan Ma started, but he stopped and just shook his head, seeming quite flabbergasted.

"You are surprised that I would help to finance Abbot Olin's ascension?"

"That is the business of the Abellicans, and something whose effect should end at the mountain range, God-Voice. I do not understand why we would choose to get involved. I know that Abbot Olin is your friend—"

"My friend?" Yakim gave a heartfelt laugh. "No, he is not my friend. Or at least, I would not call him my friend—except, of course, to those who need to hear such assurance, such as Master Mackaront. Abbot Olin and I have an understanding."

"And a mutual respect?"

"He respects me, as he should. We recognize the gains that may be made from our contact. He has things that benefit Behren, and I have things that benefit Honce-the-Bear. Such as my wealth, you see?"

"Yes, God-Voice," Merwan Ma said unconvincingly.

Yakim Douan gave yet another laugh. "Surely you can recognize the benefit to us in having a man such as Abbot Olin seated in power over the Abellican Church. Entel is an important sister city to Jacintha, a way of trading for goods that are hard to secure south of the mountains. Most of the wood within Jacintha, including the great masts for our fleet, was brought here by Entel ships, as were many of the delicacies that we enjoy regularly at our table."

"I do understand." Again, Merwan Ma was not very convincing and seemed to be quite upset.

"But you know, as well, that it is not our place to help the Abellican heathens, and that is what troubles you," the Chezru

Chieftain reasoned. Merwan Ma didn't respond verbally, but his expression showed Yakim Douan that his guess had been on the mark.

"In friendship and in trade will we infiltrate the kingdom to the north with the word of Yatol," Yakim Douan explained. "We know that we are right. We know that our faith is strong and that the Abellicans err in their devotion to gemstones. And we are secure that they, too, will come to see the light that is Yatol. The more they see of us, the more our true faith will mock their pitiful religion in the eyes of the Abellican flock."

Merwan Ma was standing straighter by that point and nodding eagerly, and Yakim Douan understood that he had settled this matter for good. Of course, he didn't really believe much of what he was preaching. He knew that any who watched the transition from Chezru Chieftain to the next chosen child would be stunned, would likely fall on their knees at the sight of the "miracle." But he knew, too, that the crafty Abellicans were pretty good at manufacturing miracles of their own, and given all the stir concerning the upraised hand of the dead Avelyn and the way that it "miraculously" cured the deadly plague, Yakim Douan knew that it would be a long, long time before many Abellicans even thought to change their spiritual course!

But still, he did want Olin to ascend, did want allies within the northern kingdom, men who would not put any pressure on Behren during the time of Transcendence, and men who, through trade and gifts, would make his life a little bit more pleasurable in the next incarnation.

"Our relationship with the Abellicans will prove of utmost importance in the crucial time that will soon be before us," Yakim Douan went on, and as Merwan Ma's eyes widened, just a bit, the Chezru Chieftain recognized that an urgency had crept into his voice.

A burst of laughter from Yakim mocked the attendant's fearful expression. "All is in place, and you know your duties."

"Are you not afraid?"

Yakim Douan waved the question away with such confidence that Merwan Ma's shoulders slumped. "We will not travel this circular path again, my young companion, nor will I tolerate your continued lack of faith."

Merwan Ma stepped back and lowered his eyes, and Yakim Douan was touched by the moisture rimming those brown orbs, touched that the very pious young Shepherd was so concerned about him.

He walked over and draped an arm across Merwan Ma's shoulders, giving a slight tug to jostle the man from his slumping posture.

"I will be reborn, and you will be there to watch over me, until we are again united," the older priest said. "The word of Yatol is, in this case, literal. I know this because I have been reborn time and time again, and so, no, my young friend, I am not afraid. And after you witness the great Transcendence, after you hear the words of consciousness spoken from the mouth of the babe, you will rest easier at night, in full confidence that Yatol is with us, every step of the way."

He coaxed a smile from Merwan Ma, then hustled the man out of the room. The sun was almost down behind the western-stretching line of the Belt-and-Buckle and Yakim Douan wanted to enjoy the sunset alone.

He was asleep again before darkness engulfed the city.

# CHAPTER 5

# *Conflicting Responsibilities*

"What is it?" Brynn asked Juraviel, for the elf was up again from his seat before their small fire, pacing the small clearing they had selected for that evening's camp.

Juraviel stared out into the dark forest for a moment, then just shook his head. "There is something . . ." he tried to explain.

"I feel it, too," said Brynn. "A scent in the air . . . like death."

Belli'mar Juraviel turned to regard her, considering her words. He could sense something, some feeling about the forest, a bit of a hush, perhaps. Perceptive Brynn had put a proper label to it, though she wasn't exactly right.

"Not death," he corrected. "Decay. There is the smell of decay in the air, like old logs rotting on the ground."

"There are many dead logs about us."

Juraviel shook his head again. "No, this is different," he explained, but he couldn't quite find the words. It was as if there was a wetness in the air, heightening the scent of decay, though the week had been dry and there were no streams or swamps or ponds about that could account for the odor.

What might it be?

"It is getting stronger," Brynn remarked a few moments later, and she rose and moved near to Juraviel, who still stood on the perimeter of the encampment, at the edge of the firelight, staring out into the dark woods.

It was indeed getting stronger, Belli'mar Juraviel understood, and since there was no wind, that had to mean that the source of the smell was growing or moving closer. Soon

Juraviel had to twitch his nose, so full was it of the scent, and only then did he recognize it for what is was.

"Peat," he explained, and even as the word got out of his mouth, he choked it off and turned suddenly, his attention caught by a flicker of movement out in the forest.

"Peat?" Brynn echoed curiously, scratching her head, and Juraviel realized that she didn't even know the word. No time to explain it to her now, though, for something—or perhaps several somethings—was moving out in the dark.

The elf bent lower and crept out a bit farther from the light, his keen eyes scanning the forest. Another movement caught his attention to the side, then another back the other way. He actually caught a silhouette of this last mover. Too big to be an elf, powrie, or goblin, he realized with a bit of relief. It had appeared much the same size as a human man, but stood up very straight and walked stiffly, barely bending torso or legs.

"Go back by the fire," he instructed Brynn. The elf's first instinct was to tell her to put out the fire, but he realized it was far too late for that, that the light of the flames had already shown whoever or whatever was out there the location of the camp. "Stoke it up, and keep your bow ready by your side."

"What do you see?"

"Go," the elf repeated, and as Brynn started away, Juraviel slipped into the cover of the brush. Likely these were humans, frontier huntsmen and trappers. Or perhaps they were outlaws, chased out of civilized lands. Either way, Brynn and Juraviel would be better off if the elf was out of sight.

Sitting back by the fire, Brynn Dharielle seemed the picture of calm, and indeed, there was little nervousness about the confident young woman. She was a ranger, elven-trained, and whatever Juraviel had seen out there in the darkness, she was confident that she and he could handle it. Her hand closed about the smooth, burnished darkfern wood of her elven-crafted bow, its rich and dark hue crossed by thin lines of the silverel metal that the towering darkferns leached out of the ground.

Yes, Brynn believed, she and Juraviel could handle anything they might expect out there.

But what walked into the light of the encampment a moment later was certainly nothing that either Brynn or Juraviel could have ever expected!

It looked like a man, a Bearman of Honce-the-Bear, but it was covered in a muddy substance that made Brynn think of the rich and rotting mud she had seen under the edge of mossy carpets after a heavy spring rain. Straight and stiff, the intruder was more than a foot taller than Brynn. His clothing, too, was filthy, soaked with the mud, and was torn in several places, and his eyes . . .

Yes, those eyes! When Brynn looked into them—or rather, at them—a shudder coursed down her spine. She saw the firelight reflected there, but not in any sparkling gleam. No, the eyes of this one showed no life, no inner spark at all.

They were dead eyes.

"What do you want?" Brynn managed to ask, and she rose fast, bringing her bow across in front of her, an arrow ready in her other hand. "Who are you?"

The man, the zombie, didn't respond in any way, just kept moving toward her, and now Brynn was backing to keep pace, to keep the distance between them. She heard movement behind her, though, out in the forest, and knew she didn't have far to retreat.

"Stay back!" she warned, fitting the arrow and lifting the bow before her.

The intruder continued its calm approach.

"Last warning!" shouted Brynn, drawing back and taking deadly aim.

"It is inhuman," came Juraviel's quiet assurance from above. "Shoot it!"

And as the creature came another step forward, Brynn did exactly that, letting fly, her arrow smacking into the intruder, right between the eyes.

The creature flinched and missed a step, wavering off to the side. But that was just a matter of the weight and momentum of the missile, a horrified Brynn realized, for the creature, seemingly uninjured, soon righted its course and calmly came on.

Brynn had another arrow up and away in the blink of an eye, this time aiming lower and putting her shot right through the creature's heart. Right through it went, and out the other side, drilling a hole through which came a greenish, milky substance.

The intruder passed the fire then, and Brynn scrambled to the side, fitting yet another arrow.

"What is it?" she cried out, but no voice came back in response.

"Who are you?" she demanded, but the creature just continued to pursue her, walking slowly and deliberately.

She let fly again, and again after that, scoring hits that would have dropped any living man, but again, to no apparent effect.

Brynn turned toward Diredusk, thinking to flee.

She gasped in horror and froze at the sight, for the pony was surrounded by more of these foul-smelling intruders, these undead creatures of her nightmares.

But they couldn't have her horse! Never that! With a snarl and a flick of her wrist, Brynn unstrung her bow, the solid wood straightening into a deadly club. Seeing Diredusk in trouble, whinnying and stomping its hooves, even kicking one of the creatures to launch it back into the brush, washed away Brynn's fears for herself. Staff spinning and twirling, she charged in, coming up short before one turning zombie. She fell to one knee as the staff came around, transferring all of her running energy into that perfectly aimed swing.

With a sickening thud, the staff smashed against the side of the zombie's head, leaving a huge and grotesque dent. The creature rocked to the side, skipping on one foot several times. But it did not fall over, showed no sign that it was feeling any pain, and came on again.

Brynn let out a cry and smashed it again, the squishy head flattening a bit more, and then, when that didn't work, the ranger retracted the weapon, repositioned her hands, and stabbed its end straight out, smashing the creature, which was offering absolutely no defense at all, square in the face.

The head snapped back. The zombie moved forward.

Again, Brynn hit it in the face, then lower in the exposed throat. Then she brought the staff back in and turned it over in her hands, spinning and spinning. Around it went, behind her back, coming out into her other hand for another strike, then going back around the other way and coming in hard from the other side, again scoring a square and brutal hit.

The zombie's head lolled as if without any support. As Brynn leaped aside, the creature continued forward, arms reaching and outstretched, as if it couldn't see her. She took up her staff in both hands as it passed and, just because she wanted to, took a mighty swing and smashed the passing zombie on the back of the skull, sending the head into a bobbing motion.

The zombie started to turn toward her, but just toppled over to the ground.

Brynn didn't even watch the descent, leaping into the pair of creatures grabbing at Diredusk's flank. She landed between them, both hands set firmly on her staff, and jabbed it out left and right, and then again, scoring two wicked hits on the zombies' heads.

Diredusk whinnied and bucked, kicking out with both hind legs, splattering the chest of another zombie and launching it into a short flight through the trees. The pony landed and bucked again, throwing its head, spinning and leaping.

Brynn went with that movement, made her way past the pony's shoulders and head, to the tether, which she quickly undid.

"Go! Go!" she cried to Diredusk, and the pony, bucking and leaping, dragging two zombies with it, charged off into the forest night.

Tears streaked Brynn's face, and she was glad, at least, that Diredusk had a chance to get away. For herself, though, there seemed no such escape, walls of zombies were coming at her from every direction. She growled away her fears and charged the nearest group, staff stabbing and swinging mightily, scoring splattering hit after splattering hit. Twisting and dodging, Brynn somehow got through that line and seemed for a moment to be running free.

But more zombies moved before her, and one of those behind, toppled by her burst of speed, grabbed on to her ankle with a grip inhumanly strong.

Brynn wailed and stumbled, stopped in her tracks, but managing, at least, not to fall over. She spun back on the grabbing zombie and punished it with a series of smacks all about its head, frantically bashing and bashing.

Others closed all about her.

The zombie on the ground lay very still, seemingly back in the realm of death where it belonged, but still it held on stubbornly, its fingers locked about Brynn's slender ankle. She kicked and twisted, stomping the wrist with her free foot.

But then she had to alter her attacks, as the other zombies descended over her.

High in the boughs before the zombies ever entered the encampment, Belli'mar Juraviel put his bow to work, the string humming as the elf launched arrow after arrow into the circling mob of intruders. Unlike Brynn, Juraviel had understood the nature of this perversion, the undead state of the intruders, right away, and so he did not hesitate at all, just set his small, but normally effective, bow to its work.

He had half emptied his quiver before he even realized that the arrows were having absolutely no effect.

With a groan of frustration, Juraviel leaped and fluttered down to a lower branch, just above the heads of the zombies. Intent on Brynn and on Diredusk, the horrid creatures seemed not to notice him, and so the elf waited and quietly moved from limb to limb until he came to one creature relatively isolated from its undead companions.

Down slashed the small sword, cutting a deep gash in the zombie's head.

The zombie stopped and looked around stupidly.

Juraviel slashed it again, and then a third time, in the face, as it at last looked up.

Showing no pain, the zombie reached stiff arms up for the nimble elf. Juraviel wasted no time in slashing one hand, then the other, taking off a couple of fingers. Greenish pus flowed from the stumps, and Juraviel could smell the disease. He backed off a few skittering steps and, apparently realizing that it could not reach him, the zombie clamped both arms about the branch and began pulling itself into the tree.

Juraviel saw his opening and didn't hesitate, leaping right to the spot on the branch between the zombie's arms, taking up his sword in both hands and slashing it down with all his might, cleaving the zombie's head right down the middle. He retracted the blade immediately, brought it back around to his left, then in a circular motion up over his head and back down to the right, driving it in hard against the side of the zombie's head, creasing all the way to the gash of the great downward cut.

A huge piece of head fell away, but the zombie kept pulling itself up.

Eyes wide with disbelief, Juraviel transferred his horror into power and slashed away with abandon.

The zombie slowly turned and looped one leg over the branch, and Juraviel promptly slashed and slashed at that limb until it, too, fell free of the body. Down tumbled the undead monster, holding on with just one hand.

Juraviel cut that hand away.

The creature fell to the ground and tried to rise, but just fell over again and again.

Watching it struggling, but not lying still, Juraviel knew that this fight could not be won. The creatures were not difficult enemies, one at a time. But the sheer amount of punishment they could take ensured that no fight against the mob would be one against one for any amount of time.

"We must flee!" Juraviel called out to Brynn, as he ran along the branches, trying to find his companion. Diredusk's frenzy cued him in, and he ran toward it until horse and woman were in sight.

Brynn's work was nothing short of magnificent, a tribute to the woman and the training of the Touel'alfar. Juraviel watched her bow-staff swinging this way and that, coming in for a sudden clutch and stab, then working back out for a devastating smash. Or at least, it should have been devastating, for it would have felled a living opponent.

He watched Brynn shift her tactics to more effect, watched her drop a zombie with a brilliant combination, watched her free up Diredusk and send him galloping off into the forest night.

That was all-important to her, Juraviel knew, and he managed a slight smile despite the terrible situation. For the To-gai-ru, the bond with their mounts could not be underestimated. A To-gai-ru would risk her life gladly in an effort to save her horse.

Again Brynn worked brilliantly against the closing horde.

Juraviel realized then that he should not simply be standing there in the safety of the boughs, watching her, that he should rush down to her side!

But, despite that realization, the elf did not explode into motion, did not move at all toward his young ranger friend.

Because Belli'mar Juraviel understood the truth of it, understood that he and Brynn could not win out and could not escape. Or at least, that the woman could not get away.

His heart torn, Belli'mar Juraviel chewed his bottom lip, his hand grasping his sword so tightly that his knuckles whitened. He wanted to go to Brynn, wanted to fight beside her and die beside her, if that was the ultimate ending. And he would have done that, he knew in his heart, would have willingly given his life for her.

But he could not.

For this horror, this atrocity, held implications beyond the lives of Belli'mar Juraviel and Brynn Dharielle, beyond even the failure of returning Brynn to To-gai to try to lead her people in revolt against the Behrenese. This horror, a perversion of life itself, held implications that went right to Caer'alfar and Juraviel's people. His duty was clear to him, though it was a duty that burned his heart. His duty was to his people above Brynn, was to return with all speed to Caer'alfar to report to Lady Dasslerond, to warn the Touel'alfar of the grotesque army that walked the southern night.

The elf watched as Brynn was borne down to the ground by a mob of zombies, the stubborn woman fighting all the way.

Juraviel turned his back and started away, picking a course

along the higher boughs that would take him far from the scene of horror and send him running on his way back to the north.

The elf stopped before he had gone three strides.

No, he could not do this. Despite his heritage, despite the Touel'alfar code that elevated his people to the highest regard and placed all of the other races, including humans, including human rangers, far below, Belli'mar Juraviel could not leave Brynn to her fate.

As the woman had done for Diredusk, so Juraviel did for her, turning back and half-flying, half-leaping from limb to limb and then from limb to the back of one zombie, his small sword thrashing violently.

He managed to get that one creature off the woman, then rushed into two of the others, slashing wildly and forcing them back, creating enough of an opening for Brynn, who was still fighting fiercely, somehow to climb back to her feet.

She held her staff out horizontally before her, hands widespread on its solid shaft. She punched out, left and right repeatedly, forcing two zombies back, then went out with a stab hard to the right, crushing the face of a third.

"There is no escape!" she cried out, as Belli'mar Juraviel came up behind her, so that they were back-to-back.

"Then die well," the elf calmly replied.

And so they tried to do just that, as the walls of zombies closed upon them, sword and staff flailing wildly, tirelessly, brutally.

They had several of the creatures down soon after and had forced their way back toward the encampment, back toward the fire.

Juraviel found the new weapon first, grabbing up a flaming stick and thrusting it into the nearest zombie's face. A puff of smoke carried with it a sickening smell, but the torch had much more effect than either sword or staff, igniting the creature. Juraviel worked frantically to keep its burning arms away.

The zombie beside it began to burn as well.

"A torch! A torch!" Juraviel yelled, hope creeping back into his voice.

Brynn reacted quickly, throwing her staff into the nearest creatures to make them hesitate, then spinning back to the fire and trying desperately to find a torch. She burned her hand as she grabbed up one long stick, but ignored the pain and spun about, thrusting the flaming end right into the eye of a zombie.

And so the tide of battle turned, briefly, as zombies fell back from the flames. One toppled, fully ablaze, and then another.

But even so, Juraviel and Brynn knew that they could not win out against so many, for their supply of firebrands was limited indeed, and would fast exhaust itself.

"Cut through one line and run away!" Juraviel instructed.

Brynn nodded and turned to move beside the elf, but then stopped suddenly, feeling a burning sting in the side of her neck. She reached up, her expression curious.

"Brynn?" Juraviel cried.

The woman exploded into motion, coming forward again, thrusting her brand into the face of one zombie and driving it back.

But then Juraviel watched as her movements unexpectedly and inexplicably slowed, as her arms drooped.

"Brynn!" he cried again, slapping his torch to the side, then leaping out the other way as the zombie went up in a blaze of fire.

Juraviel turned just in time to see Brynn tumbling down, zombies falling over her, thrashing and punching.

He could not get to her, could do nothing to help her!

Now Juraviel knew that he had to escape, to flee to Caer'alfar with this horrible news. He turned a complete circuit, his outstretched torch forcing the mob back. He ended the turn by throwing the torch into the face of one creature, then leaped straight up, his wings fluttering to carry him to the boughs.

He almost made it, but one zombie caught him by the ankle.

Juraviel fought against it, his little wings flapping frantically. But elven wings were not meant for flight. They were meant for enhancing leaps and breaking falls, and the zombie's grip was too strong and unrelenting.

Juraviel felt himself spinning down to the side, then swinging about fast.

He saw the tree right before the zombie smacked him into it.

Dazed and on the ground, Juraviel's thoughts were for Brynn, and for his own failure in coming back to her. He should have flown off immediately for the north. His duty to the Touel'alfar demanded it.

But what of his duty as a friend?

He saw Brynn, then, briefly, lifted from the ground by a zombie and thrown back down hard, while others fell over her limp form, kicking and punching, though she was offering no resistance at all. She appeared to Belli'mar to be dead already.

He kicked and thrashed, trying to break free. He scrambled away as soon as he felt the grip relent, climbing to his feet and taking two quick strides.

But he was tackled, then he was punched, and, finally, half-conscious and helpless against the rain of blows, he saw another creature, this one fully engulfed in flames, coming toward him.

In his last flicker of consciousness, Juraviel felt fortunate that one of the other zombies smashed him into blackness before he felt the burning flames.

Belli'mar Juraviel knew no more.

# CHAPTER 6

## *The Iron Hand of Yatol*

The long caravan snaked its way across the broken brown clay. It appeared like a giant centipede, its torso a long line of camels and covered coaches, its legs the flanking soldiers riding tall horses. In the middle of that center line, in the largest and most lavish coach, Yatol Grysh sat back in his cushy seat, complaining about the heat constantly, though he had several attendants, all beautiful young women, fanning him and patting his brow with moistened towels.

"I do so hate this," the Yatol said repeatedly. "With the To-gai dogs, there is never any rest from my duties."

The two of his four attendants who were of obvious To-gai-ru descent, with their softer and straighter hair and almond-shaped eyes, didn't flinch at the remark, having long ago gotten used to Grysh's demeaning manner.

"It will calm the outposters," said Carwan Pestle, Grysh's advisor Shepherd, and the sixth and final person in the wide coach. "They fear that the thieves grow bolder by the day."

The caravan had been barely out of Jacintha, making its way along the southern shadows of the Belt-and-Buckle toward Dharyan, the town controlled by Yatol Grysh, the seat of his power in northwestern Behren, when couriers from Temple Yaminos of Dharyan had caught up to them, informing the ruling Yatol that the thieves of the Corcorca region of To-gai, just west and south of Yaminos, always a thorn, had become even more active. That, of course, had unsettled the outposters, the Behrenese emigrants who had begun to settle outside the old Behren-To-gai border.

Yatol Grysh had campaigned for those settlements, to the Behrenese people and to Chezru Douan, figuring that his job would become all the easier as the Behrenese settlers gradually began to civilize the wild To-gai-ru. But the early transition was proving to be something of a trial for the lazy man.

Thus, Grysh had diverted his caravan to the south and ridden right past Dharyan, determined to enter Corcorca with his two hundred escorting soldiers, a contingent that included a score of fierce Chezhou-Lei warriors. He'd teach the dogs. Though there weren't all that many miles separating Dharyan from the To-gai region, it was a difficult trek, with the wagons bouncing along a narrow, rocky, steeply ascending trail, up to the higher elevations of the To-gai plateau. Yatol Grysh did not enjoy the several days of discomfort.

Grysh leaned back and looked out his window at the wide and barren landscape. In the distance to the north, he could see the towering peaks of the mountain range that had been a backdrop to his home for his entire life. He wanted to be back under their cooling shadow, in the temple that was his palace, full of luxuries and sweet foods, of clean baths and beautiful and dutiful women.

But Yatol Grysh understood that the only way to ensure the continuation and safety of his precious palace was to rule these eastern stretches of To-gai with an iron hand. He hated the To-gai-ru, with their barbaric, nomadic ways. He hardly considered them human.

Grysh looked at his To-gai-ru attendants and smiled lewdly. He did like their women, though.

"The people of Douan Cal near completion of their wall?" he asked Carwan. Douan Cal, named after the Chezru Chieftain, was the largest and most important of the Behrenese settlements, and also the one most plagued by the rogue To-gai-ru bandits.

"They work tirelessly, Yatol," Carwan replied. "But their life is difficult. Water must be carried far and crops constantly tended. Their hunters have not learned the way of the local game yet, and thus often return without food. They are not many, but still, they work as they can, whenever they can, at cutting the blocks for their encircling wall."

"Have they not enough To-gai-ru servants to complete the work?"

"Many have left, Yatol. The To-gai-ru traditionally wander to the foothills in the summer season."

"And many, it seems, have wandered to the nearby desert, to come forth whenever it is convenient to steal from our people."

Carwan nodded. "Life is difficult," he said somberly.

Grysh sat back and stared out the window, considering the new responsibilities that had befallen him since Chezru Chieftain Yakim Douan had decided that the time had come for Behren to "reclaim" its ancient province of To-gai. True, the subjugation of the To-gai-ru had provided many slaves for Behren, and a seemingly endless supply of the wonderful and valuable ponies so prized by the men of Honce-the-Bear. But Grysh, who witnessed the hardships of controlling the wild folk of the steppes on a nearly daily basis, still wondered about the wisdom of the conquest, still wondered if the bother was worth the gain.

For Yatol Grysh was wise enough to recognize that his people, the Behrenese, were not well suited for the trials of the cold wind and grassy steppes of brutal To-gai. How many years would it take the outposters to adapt? How many seasons would it take for them to come to understand the ways of the desert animals, the huge hares and spry deer, the giant and powerful chochunga buffalo?

But that was his charge from Jacintha, to continue to build new settlements, stretching farther and farther to the west, a supply line of small towns across the windblown stretch of grassland that separated the heart of To-gai from Behren, so that the assimilation of the wild To-gai-ru could begin in earnest. Yatol Grysh was more a pragmatic man than a religious one, but both sides of that conflict saw prudence in following the Chezru Chieftain's edicts to the letter.

And so he had turned south and continued west, to the call of his people. Late that afternoon, as the summer sun began its descent behind the line of mountains, the call came back that the eastern wall of Douan Cal had been spotted by the point scouts.

"Continue on through the darkness, then," Yatol Grysh instructed. "Have a rider go ahead fast to instruct the outposters to light guiding signal fires atop the highest point of their eastern wall."

"It may be dangerous to travel after dark," Carwan pointed out, but Grysh silenced him with a stern look.

"Then tighten the line and move the wagons into three side-by-side columns," he instructed. He turned to his military commander, Chezhou-Lei Wan Atenn, who had personally delivered the news of the sighting. "You will protect us from the fierce To-gai-ru bandits, will you not?"

The Chezhou-Lei, proud and loyal, sat up very straight on his tall horse, staring at his Yatol with a frozen and determined expression.

"I thought so," Yatol Grysh said, and he closed the window's shutter, for the sun was descending, and on the steppes, even in summertime, it was amazing to Grysh how fast the air cooled, the scorching daytime heat dissipating to an uncomfortable chill.

Grysh slapped away the fanning ladies then, and motioned for them to huddle about his large form, using them as living blankets.

He wanted to be home, true, but Yatol Grysh was a man who knew how to take his comforts as he found them. Surely the ride that night was not so unpleasant.

The stories Yatol Grysh heard within the compound of Douan Cal were predictable. Bands of To-gai raiders had struck at the town repeatedly, taking their livestock, hurling curses and hurling missiles. None of the Behrenese settlers had been killed as yet, but several had been injured, including one old woman who had been hit in the head with a rock.

"What is your assessment of our enemy?" Yatol Grysh asked Carwan later on when they were alone—alone concerning anyone who mattered, for Yatol Grysh did not think enough of his serving wenches to bother watching his words around them.

"Young men," Carwan answered after giving the question a bit of thought. "Teenagers, perhaps. The older To-gai-ru would have been more straightforward and more brutal in their attacks."

"Because the older To-gai-ru would be fighting for more than livestock," Yatol Grysh said, and Carwan nodded eagerly.

"The older ones once caused trouble throughout To-gai, fighting fanatically," Carwan said. "They slaughtered entire villages without regard for the women or children."

"Because the older outlaws—and praise Yatol that few remain alive—fought with the names of their gods on their lips," Yatol Grysh explained, "they believed that their fighting and murdering was paving their road to whatever they envision as their heaven. Men who do battle in such a manner are always the worst enemies, my young student."

"Like our own Chezhou-Lei?" Carwan dared to remark.

"And always the best allies," Yatol Grysh finished with a sly smile. "And tell me, what are we to do about these raiders? Do you believe that we will find them in the open desert?"

Carwan leaned back and considered the problem. The outposters had become fairly competent at navigating this area of desert, by their own boasts, but none knew the region as did the To-gai-ru. There in Corcorca's rugged landscape, valleys opened up unexpectedly at one's feet and huge and towering mesas formed dizzying arrays of interlocking channels. Chasing the raiders about in that, their home ground, seemed a fool's errand indeed.

"We'll not catch up to them if we spend the rest of the season in pursuit," Yatol Grysh went on, for Carwan's expression made his feelings on the matter quite clear. "And likely, they'll strike behind us at every opportunity, to embarrass us more than to cause any serious mischief. But in that inevitable embarrassment lies a danger, my student. Do you see it?

"We will turn a band of young thieves into a band of legends," Yatol Grysh answered after only a brief pause. "And that legend will give the To-gai-ru of the region great hope that the veil of Behren will be lifted from their land."

"Then what are we to do, Yatol?"

"The nomads' latest encampment is not far from here," Yatol Grysh explained. "We will pay them a visit on the morrow, I think, and see what we may learn."

Something about the manner in which he said the words had the hairs on the back of Carwan's neck standing up. Something about the set of his expression at that moment, a bit of a grin, perhaps, but more a smug and determined look, told Carwan that his master meant to see to this thorny problem with all efficiency.

Whatever the cost.

Most of the caravan remained behind at Douan Cal the next day, with Grysh's coach the only wagon riding out. Surrounding the Yatol, though, was the whole of his military escort, along with a few men from Douan Cal who knew some of the nearby To-gai-ru.

Carwan Pestle rode with Grysh. He tried to start a few conversations at first, but it became obvious to him that his master was agitated and wanted to be left to his own thoughts. Carwan could guess what that foretold, for he had seen Grysh in similar moods, always before issuing a most unpleasant order. As Yatol of Dharyan, Grysh also served as principal magistrate, and so he was the one who ordered the executions of convicted criminals. It was not a duty that he seemed to enjoy, but neither was it one from which he ever shied.

Soon after midday, Carwan was leaning out of the coach window, peering ahead intently, for the call had come back that the To-gai-ru encampment was in sight. Carwan Pestle had never seen a To-gai-ru settlement, and he held a healthy curiosity toward these strange nomadic savages.

The wagon came over a ridge, the ground falling away gradually beyond, down to a wide and shallow river that meandered across the clay, the ever-eager flora of the desert springing to life about its inevitably temporary banks. A cluster of tents was set near one bend, the thin gray smoke of cooking fires lazily snaking into the pale blue sky. No horses were tethered within the camp that Carwan could see, but there was a fair-sized herd milling about. Above all else, the To-gai-ru were famous for their ways with horses, and Carwan could well imagine that this seemingly wild herd was far from untamed.

At least to the commands of a To-gai-ru rider.

The lead riders fanned out left and right, forming a semi-circle about the camp, the only open route leading right into the river. With perfect discipline, the second line of twenty warriors, led by Wan Atenn, kicked their mounts into a thundering run, galloping right to the edge of the camp and forming a tighter, threatening perimeter.

Many cries of alarm came out to Carwan Pestle's ears, and he noted that all of them were in the voices of women or young children.

A moment later, Wan Atenn signaled that the village was secure, and the driver cracked the whip on the draft horses and Yatol Grysh's coach rambled down to the encampment.

Carwan Pestle peered intently all the way, as the small forms took on more definitive shapes, and he knew that his reasoning upon hearing the cries was correct. There seemed to be no adult men in the encampment.

Wan Atenn rode up beside the window. "It is safe, Yatol," he reported.

"No weapons shown?"

"Only the young and the old and the women," Wan Atenn explained.

Carwan Pestle turned a curious expression on Grysh. "Perhaps the men are out on a hunt."

"Indeed," the Yatol replied slyly. "But it is well-known that the To-gai-ru hunt early in the morning. Only early in the morning."

"But—"

"So if they are indeed out on the hunt, then what, my young friend, might they be hunting?"

Carwan sat back and stared at the Yatol. He was beginning to get a very bad feeling about all of this, his stomach turning over and over. The coach came to an abrupt stop and Carwan was quick to the door, throwing it open and leaping out, then turning about and rolling out the retracting stairs for his Yatol.

Grysh came out slowly, allowing Wan Atenn to set his warriors in defensive posture about the small stairway. The Yatol paused on each step, his heavy head swiveling to take in all the sights: the many tents, the many small children peeking out from under the shadows of the folds.

"These people breed like hares," he snickered, and he sighed. "Find out who is in charge of this wretched camp."

Wan Atenn snapped to attention, then spun off, motioning for one of the Douan Cal men to come with him. Together, they went tent to tent, Wan Atenn saying something to the outposter, and the man translating it to the To-gai-ru.

Always, a shake of the head came back in response, followed by a more insistent bark from Wan Atenn and a more insistent reiteration from the outposter.

When that, too, brought no apparent acceptable response, Wan Atenn stepped forward and, with a simple and balanced twist and push movement, shoved the To-gai-ru to the ground, and the pair moved along.

"They are afraid," Yatol Grysh explained to Carwan. "They do not answer because they know not what to say."

"Your man, Atenn, inspires fear."

"No," Yatol Grysh replied. "They know not what to answer because the truth would damn them. The fools have not properly rehearsed their lies because they did not expect that such a force would come against them. Their hesitance is telling, do you see?"

"Yes, Yatol."

"Do you?" Grysh asked again, more emphatically, turning to face Carwan. "Why are they afraid?" he asked when Carwan gave him his full attention.

Carwan knew the answer, but he chewed on it for a few seconds, not even wanting to speak it aloud, fearing the consequences. "Because they are guilty," he said at last, and Yatol Grysh nodded slowly and deliberately, turning his head as he did, his eyes narrowing, to face the gathered To-gai-ru.

Carwan could not deny the logic of his claim, for it seemed obvious to him that this village was at least aware of, if not in league with, the bandits. But as he looked around at the gathering, frightened women and children, and a few old men staring out from the shadows, the word "guilty" just did not seem appropriate.

A commotion to the side caught his attention, and he turned

that way to see a Behrenese warrior emerging from a tent, a young To-gai-ru man held before him, arm wrapped painfully and effectively behind his back.

"They say that their men are all out hunting, Yatol," Wan Atenn said at that same moment, for the Chezhou-Lei warrior and the translator had continued the conversation to the side.

"All but one, it would seem."

The soldier with the prisoner moved before Wan Atenn and threw the man at his leader's feet. "A tunnel concealed within the tent," he explained.

Wan Atenn nodded to a pair of soldiers and they ran off to the tent, disappearing within its folds without hesitation.

"Who is this?" Yatol Grysh said to Wan Atenn and the interpreter, and the outposter immediately turned to the To-gai-ru woman with whom he had been speaking and barked out a series of questions. The woman was slow to answer at first, but the outposter began screaming at her, the same question over and over.

She started screaming back, answering with such enthusiasm that her lie was easy for all to see, even for those who didn't understand the To-gai-ru language.

Then it stopped, suddenly, the outposter and the defiant woman staring hard at each other.

"Where are the others?" Yatol Grysh calmly asked, and his translator echoed the question in the same tone.

"No others," the woman answered, and both Carwan and Grysh understood the simple phrase before their man turned to explain.

"Where are the others?" Grysh asked again, in the same calm tones, and again, it was properly translated.

The woman responded exactly the same way, and as the outposter turned to Grysh, the Yatol held up his hand and turned to Wan Atenn.

"No trees to hang the prisoner properly," he said. "Stake him."

Carwan's eyes widened with shock. "Yatol . . ." he started to say, but the look Grysh shot him clearly said that he was out of bounds.

Wan Atenn began barking orders, and in short order, the

prisoner had been dragged to the side of the encampment and laid out, spread-eagled, staked down by his wrists and ankles. Every time he tried to struggle, a Behrenese soldier kicked him in the ribs.

The gathering of To-gai-ru screamed and jostled, but Grysh's escorting contingent was more than able to hold them at bay.

At the next moment of calm, Grysh again nodded to Wan Atenn, and the fierce warrior, no novice to these techniques, fetched a torch from the fire his companions were preparing. Another soldier dutifully ran to intercept Wan Atenn, handing him a bulging waterskin.

A waterskin of lamp oil, Carwan knew. Carwan was at a loss, hardly able to draw breath, let alone speak a word of protest. A word that his unquestionable master did not want to hear, in any case.

He watched, fighting hard to hide his revulsion, as Wan Atenn stuck the torch into the ground between the man's knees.

"Ask her again where the others might be," Grysh instructed his outposter interpreter.

The woman, her eyes wide and unblinking, hesitated for a long, long time, then answered with the same words, though in a much more subdued tone.

Grysh nodded to his fierce Chezhou-Lei warrior, who immediately began splashing the lamp oil all over the staked man.

Then the Yatol turned to the woman, a wide smile on his face. "One last time," he said, somewhat flippantly.

The woman looked away, and Carwan wanted to as well, but found that he could not, mesmerized by the sight of his master calmly nodding to Wan Atenn, by the sight of Wan Atenn, showing no emotion at all, as he grabbed up the torch and touched it to the oiled prisoner.

Carwan knew that the man was screaming, knew that the gathered To-gai-ru were screaming, but he didn't really hear any of it. He was trapped by the vision before him, locked by horror and sheer amazement.

"Now," he at last heard from the side, and realized that Yatol Grysh, who was motioning for him to follow to the coach, had likely called to him several times.

Carwan spun away and sprinted to the stairs, guiding his master up, then retracting the stairs and leaping into the coach, eager to close the door on the gruesome scene.

"Do as you will," Yatol Grysh said to Wan Atenn, then ordered his driver to be off.

They all left then, except for the twenty warriors and their fierce Chezhou-Lei leader. For a long, long time, Carwan Pestle sat in the quiet coach, determined not to look back. Eventually, though, he did peek out.

The encampment was not in view, lost behind the sloping ridgeline, but several lines of smoke rose into the pale air. Not thin gray smoke, as from the campfires, but evil black snaking lines.

Carwan shuddered and fell back into his seat, trying hard not to throw up.

# CHAPTER 7

# *Tymwyvenne*

Belli'mar Juraviel was surprised indeed when he opened his eyes to look upon a strange, almost preternatural scene. A thick fog blanketed the ground, with dark patches of moss and muddy mounds showing sporadically. He was in a copse of trees, but they were all dead, black-armed, empty things, their crooked limbs snaking out like the last desperate limb-waving pleas of a doomed man. At first the elf saw no signs of life, but then he heard a groan, and managed with great effort to roll over.

Brynn stood there, or at least, hung there, her arms up high above her head, tied at the wrists to a thick, dead branch. Her head lolled about her shoulders and she kept trying to stand up straight—to take the painful pressure off of her arms, Belli'mar reasoned. Her legs would not support her, though, and she kept sagging, often uttering a groan as her arms straightened.

"Brynn," Juraviel whispered. "Waken, ranger."

She didn't answer, so Juraviel repeated his words, more loudly and insistently.

Still no answer.

Not from Brynn. However, at the second call, forms rose up out of the fog. Hulking, stiff-limbed forms, rising silently and moving deliberately toward the pair.

Shaken by the gruesome image, Juraviel tried to stand, only to find that he was strapped down tightly to his make-shift cot, another dead limb, by a series of looped cords.

"Brynn!" he cried out. "Wake up, girl!"

The zombies moved methodically about the woman. One

grabbed her about the ribs, and with seemingly no effort at all, lifted her into the air. A second zombie grabbed the woman's arms and hoisted them back up straight, lifting the loop of the rope over the peg that was holding it.

Brynn started, suddenly awake, and her initial thrash broke her free of the zombies. But again, her legs would not support her, and she tumbled down into the mist, and as she tried to scramble away, the zombies fell over her, grabbing her, punching her.

Belli'mar Juraviel cried out to her repeatedly and thrashed about, to no avail. A few moments later, one of the zombies lifted the limp form of the young ranger into its arms, cradling her under the knees and shoulders, and started away on its stiff legs.

Juraviel continued to thrash, thinking that the undead creatures would come for him next. But to his surprise, they all continued away, a solemn and gruesome procession.

Juraviel fought hard to suppress his revulsion and collect his wits. What was going on here? As he settled, he realized that there had to be a higher intelligence about other than the zombies; they seemed unthinking creatures. But why, then, had both Juraviel and Brynn been tied up? Why hadn't the creatures simply battered them both into the realm of death?

It made no sense to Juraviel, but how could it, after all? He had never seen an animated corpse before, had never even heard of such a thing!

The zombies and their captive disappeared into the fog, and Juraviel heard Brynn utter a plaintive cry, helpless and hopeless.

The elf sagged back, staring up into the dark sky. He noted only then, and curiously, that his perch had been made somewhat comfortable. A thick blanket was under him, between him and the gnarly branch. He craned his neck, trying to find some clues, but he could only see the edge of a wayward flap, nothing that offered him any information. Why had he been treated with some consideration, while Brynn had been mercilessly hung up by her wrists? And why was he still lying there, while his friend had been dragged away to some unknown horror?

Juraviel figured that he was about to get some answers—
and likely none that he wanted to hear!—when a hulking
form came up beside him, down by his legs, stiff arms reaching out to him!

Panic welled in Juraviel, but was soon overwhelmed by
anger—anger at himself, mostly, for the elf knew then that he
had done wrong in standing beside Brynn. He should have
run off to report this atrocity to Lady Dasslerond; all of his
people might be threatened now because of his miserable
failure.

*"Hefle!"* came a shout, a word that sounded vaguely familiar to Juraviel. When the zombie halted and lowered its arms,
the elf understood the word more clearly, for it sounded like
an offshoot of the elven word *"hefele,"* which meant, "desist."

Juraviel craned his neck again, straining to get a look at the
speaker, and when he did, his eyes went wide indeed! For
there, standing beside him, were a pair of creatures, a male
and female, of similar stature to his own. Their hair was dark,
black like a raven's wing, and the eyes of the male seemed
like an inky black pool, while the other's were the lightest
shade of blue, a stark and startling contrast to her black hair.
They had no wings, as did the Touel'alfar, but their features
were similarly angular and pronounced. Juraviel's own skin
had been tanned under the sun, but these two looked as if they
had never seen the sunlight, their skin chalky white, almost
luminescent in the gray fog.

The female started hurling words Juraviel's way. Questions, he supposed, or threats, but the creature was speaking
too fast for him to catch up to the meaning or the intent.

But then he did catch a word, "intruder," and another,
"thief," and he was surprised indeed when he paused long
enough to recognize that the creature was speaking to him in
his own tongue! Or in a tongue that resembled that of the
Touel'alfar, both in specific wording and in the various inflections that could be placed on any word.

The female continued to ramble, with Juraviel's ears keeping pace with the flow of the words now, and the elf truly
understood that the danger was far from past, that these two,
and their kinfolk, apparently, were not pleased that he and

Brynn had stumbled onto their land. The creature spoke of "the severest of penalties" for the human woman and mentioned that they might kill Juraviel instead of that worst of fates if he cooperated appropriately.

Finally, Juraviel had recovered his wits enough for him to look the rambling and outraged creature in the eye, and say, "We meant no harm."

Both creatures fell back, their eyes going wide. The female stammered over a few syllables, while she trembled, with nerves, with rage, with . . . something.

"Who are you who know my language?" Juraviel said, trying to use inflections similar to those the creatures had used, though his tone was obviously far less confrontational.

The pair looked at each other curiously, as if trying to sort through the question. They each repeated the last word, "language," several times, shaking their heads and wearing confused expressions.

Juraviel rattled off several synonyms and tried to explain what he meant, and the thought came clear to the pair.

"Who are you who know our . . . language?" the one with the dark eyes asked.

"Who are you?"

"Who are you?" the two demanded in unison.

Belli'mar Juraviel lay back on his branch and closed his eyes, trying to sort out the web of confusion and surprise. Could it be? the elf wondered. Was it possible? He took a deep breath, and answered, knowing full well that he was taking a great chance here, "Touel'alfar. I am Touel'alfar."

"Tylwyn Tou!" the female cried, her bright eyes going wide, and her tone made it sound like an accusation.

Belli'mar Juraviel looked at her directly. If this was what he now suspected, then he certainly understood that tone. In times long past, the Touel'alfar and these creatures, the Doc'alfar, had lived together as one race. But the primary difference in the elves, the fact that some were adorned with wings while others were not, had caused strife among the people. Add to that a devastating disease that had afflicted the elves without wings for some reason, but not their cousins, and the elven peoples of Corona had been split apart, Touel and Doc.

Juraviel didn't blink, but neither did he frown or show any intentions of intimidation. He was walking a fine line, he knew, balancing on a perch where a fall would cost him his life—and cost him any chance at all to save Brynn, if she was even still alive.

"Doc'alfar," Juraviel said quietly, and as the elf mouthed the word, he became even more certain that he should have abandoned Brynn in the initial fight.

"Tylwyn Doc," the male corrected, calmly, though his companion seemed as if she was about to leap forward and throttle Juraviel.

"Tylwyn Doc," Juraviel conceded.

"And you are Tylwyn Tou," said the elf with the bright eyes.

"We name ourselves Touel'alfar, but I accept Tylwyn Tou."

"You accept?" the female said with a snort. "Have you a choice?"

Juraviel merely shrugged, or tried to, for his bindings were too tight for such movement.

"What is your name?" the male demanded.

"Belli'mar Juraviel," he answered without hesitation.

"Where have you come from?" the female snapped.

Juraviel tightened his lips. "I am Belli'mar Juraviel," he said again, aiming the words at the male, who seemed the more reasonable of the two.

The male Tylwyn Doc stared at him hard for a short while, then said, "I am Lozan Duk." He paused and looked to his companion, as did Juraviel.

The Tylwyn Doc with the remarkable light eyes didn't look at her companion, but continued to stare ominously at Juraviel. "Cazzira," she said at length. "Know that your doom is named Cazzira, Belli'mar Juraviel."

The elf's question came out simply, "Why?"

Cazzira narrowed her bright eyes, her face tightening with anger.

"You have intruded where you do not belong," Lozan Duk explained. "The Tylwyn Doc make no exceptions."

Juraviel pondered that for a bit. "You routinely execute any who wander onto your land, though you have no warning markers to ward intruders away?"

"Warning markers would tell the world where we are, would they not?" Cazzira asked with biting sarcasm. "Perhaps we do not want the world to know."

Juraviel lay back again, considering the words, trying to figure out what was going on, and what steps he might take, what words he might say to try to calm the situation.

"Where is my companion?" he asked. "Brynn Dharielle is her name. A ranger, trained by the Touel'alfar and returning to her home beyond the mountains. She poses no threat to the Tylwyn Doc."

"She is being prepared for the bog," Lozan Duk answered matter-of-factly.

"All humans are given to the bog," Cazzira eagerly added. "We throw them in, and then our priests return them to us as slaves."

A shudder coursed Juraviel's spine. He pictured Brynn as one of those "slaves," an undead monstrosity under the complete control of these creatures.

"We have not taken much of the land as our own," Lozan Duk explained. "But that which is ours, we guard with all diligence."

Those words rang true to Belli'mar Juraviel, for his own people held beliefs not so different. The Touel'alfar guarded Andur'Blough Inninness fanatically. They didn't often kill intruders, because their elven magic, along with Lady Dasslerond's emerald gemstone, could make those who wandered onto their lands forget the way. But if there was any doubt—if the intruder learned too much about the Touel'alfar, if a ranger, perhaps, failed in his training—then Juraviel knew that Dasslerond would not hesitate to kill the human.

Juraviel thought of Aydrian at that moment, for the young ranger had been walking a fine line for some time. Another shudder coursed through him.

"You cannot do this," Juraviel said suddenly, hardly thinking before he blurted the words. He craned his head up again, staring at the two intently. He read Lozan Duk's expression as one of sympathy, though Cazzira's tightened features showed little understanding.

"There is a possibility here," Juraviel went on. "How many centuries have passed since our peoples were torn asunder?"

"Since the Tylwyn Tou expelled the Tylwyn Doc from their lands, you mean," Cazzira remarked.

"Who can know the truth of that distant past?" Juraviel replied. "Perhaps you are right—there was a plague, by all accounts. But whatever the truth, are we two peoples to be held prisoner by it?"

Cazzira started to respond, but Lozan Duk held his hand up before her. "This is not our decision to make," he said. "King Eltiraaz will have much to say concerning your fate, Belli'mar Juraviel."

"And what of Brynn?"

"She is for the bog," Cazzira was quick to answer.

Juraviel shook his head defiantly. "Then that will be your error. And one the Touel'alfar will not soon forgive."

"You threaten us?" asked the angry female.

"I speak honestly, and in the hope that this meeting need not be a tragedy. Brynn Dharielle—"

"Is a human, and we do not suffer humans who wander onto our lands to live!"

"Brynn Dharielle is a ranger," Juraviel calmly went on. "She is not like others of her race. She has been trained for many years within the home of the Touel'alfar. She has been given an understanding of my—of our—people that elevates her above her sorry kin. My people have placed much faith and responsibility in her. I tell you this now so that there will be no mistaking the implications if you proceed. I want you to hold no misconceptions on this point. Brynn Dharielle is Touel'alfar in all but heritage, and we protect our own as fiercely as do the Doc'alfar."

Cazzira was tightening her angular features throughout his speech, and she winced visibly when Juraviel referred to her people using the title of his people and not hers.

"Are we to learn from each other, or are you to sever all possibilities of friendship and alliance before they are ever explored?"

Lozan Duk looked at his companion, holding the stare until Cazzira tore her glare away from Juraviel and returned the look. Then, with a glance at Juraviel, Lozan Duk motioned for Cazzira to follow him a short distance away, that they could speak in private.

Belli'mar Juraviel lay back and tried to sort through the amazing turn of events that night, trying to discern his responsibilities. Had he erred in so forcefully protecting Brynn? Perhaps his duty to his people demanded that he try to save himself, whatever the cost to Brynn, that he could flee back to the north and inform Lady Dasslerond that the Doc'alfar were very much real and alive.

No, Juraviel decided. He would not sacrifice Brynn. Not for himself, not for anyone. He intended to get out of this, and intended to have Brynn right beside him when he did.

Lying there, cocooned by an unyielding rope on a tree branch and with a powerful zombie hovering over him, Juraviel had to admit that intentions were a far cry from reality.

"Tell the priests to await the judgment of King Eltiraaz," Lozan Duk instructed Cazzira when they had moved away from their prisoner.

"His judgment concerning humans was rendered centuries ago," Cazzira protested.

Lozan Duk looked to Juraviel, then back to Cazzira. "He must speak with this one before rendering his judgment over the ranger."

Cazzira stared at him hard.

"You know that I am correct in this," Lozan Duk replied. "King Eltiraaz would not be pleased if we proceeded after what this one has told us."

Cazzira looked back at their prisoner, her hard look softening, and finally gave a helpless chuckle. "This is amazing," she admitted. "A legend walks into our midst. Who can tell what that will portend for the Tylwyn Doc?"

"Or the Tylwyn Tou?" Lozan Duk added, nodding, and when he turned to Cazzira, he saw that she was nodding, too.

So many possibilities.

\*     \*     \*

It hurt to move at all, but Brynn turned her head to the side and opened her eyes.

She was lying on her stomach, on soft and smelly ground. It was a cave, she realized, as she turned her head more to regard the light hanging on the earthen wall. Her gaze lingered there, for this was like no lantern the woman had ever seen. It had a short wooden handle and was capped by a glowing, blue-white globe, with no flames anywhere that Brynn could see.

She continued her scan as far as her aching neck and back would allow. Many, many small roots hung out of the walls and the ceiling, and it seemed to Brynn as if this whole place, however large it might be, had simply been torn out of the ground.

Brynn coughed, and her ribs felt as if they would break apart under the pressure!

Too weary and battered even to cry, the young ranger turned her face back toward the earth and slowly lowered her head back in place. She closed her eyes, wishing it was all just a nightmare, but knowing better. Knowing that she had failed, that she would not be the savior of her enslaved people.

Fitful dreams awaited her.

When the woman next opened her eyes, she was lying on her back, still bathed in the same bluish white light, and still in the small earthen cave.

"I thought that you would be more comfortable this way," came a sudden voice, and Brynn started, then groaned from the pain. Her panic was gone by the time she winced through the agony, for she surely recognized the voice of Belli'mar Juraviel. Slowly and with great effort, the young ranger managed to turn enough to glimpse her mentor, who sat at the side of the room, not bound, apparently.

"They can animate the dead, but they have little in the way of healing magic," Juraviel mused, and it seemed to Brynn that he was talking more to himself than to her.

"They?" she managed to say, and her lips were so dry and parched that they hurt to move.

"Doc'alfar," Juraviel explained, coming over to her and putting a small waterskin to her lips. He poured, and Brynn

tried to gulp the fresh water, but Juraviel quickly pulled
it back.

"Not too fast," he warned, bringing it forward and giving
her another sip. "You have been asleep for a long time. If you
drink too quickly, you will shock your body, to no good end."

"How long?"

Juraviel looked around and shrugged. "Three days at least,
I would guess, though time is not easy to measure in here."

*Three days,* Brynn thought. But how had she and Juraviel
escaped? And where was the pursuit, for how far might the
diminutive elf have traveled with an unconscious woman to
drag along?

Those questions swirled about in her thoughts for a short
while, gradually blending in with the more general gray that
seemed to permeate her thoughts, guiding her back to the
realm of slumber.

She knew before Juraviel even told her that another day
had slipped past. Brynn turned to the side, to where Juraviel
had been—and still was—sitting.

"Ah, Brynn, you have returned to me." As he spoke, Juraviel lifted the waterskin and came back to her, putting it to
her parched lips.

"Help me to sit up," the young ranger said after taking a
few sips and then a few deep breaths—breaths that showed
her that her ribs were far from healed.

Juraviel was beside her in a moment, easing her into a sitting position, then helping her to turn so that she could put
her back against the wall.

"I remember getting hit," she said after a lengthy pause. "I
tried to fight back, but they were all about me. I tried . . ."

"You fought well, but the numbers were too great, and the
creatures seemed nearly immune to our weapons."

"How did we get out?"

Juraviel's expression corrected her even before she had
finished speaking the words. They had not gotten out of anything, and were obviously prisoners.

"What do they want of us? And what are they?"

"They—the ones who attacked us—were unthinking animations," the elf explained. "Zombies raised as an army by the Doc'alfar."

"Doc'alfar," Brynn echoed, thinking that there was a familiar ring to the word, though she couldn't place it.

"We have been through this all before," Juraviel said to her. "Though I would not expect you to remember it."

"Doc'alfar?" Brynn said yet again, for she understood the word to mean "the dark people," as Touel'alfar meant "the fair people," or simply, "the People."

"In a time long past the longest memories of the eldest elves, there was but one race," Juraviel explained somberly, his eyes staring to the side, as if looking across the miles and the centuries. "Touel'alfar, or Tylwyn Tou. Some had wings, some not, and most of those who had wings had hair of gold and light eyes, while most of those who did not had dark hair and dark eyes."

"These are your cousins, then," Brynn reasoned. She glanced all around. "And this is the home of . . . ?"

"This is a prison, and nothing more."

"But they are of *the People*. You are kin and kind. Why would they treat you—"

"Did I mention the banishment?" Juraviel remarked, somewhat flippantly.

"They're going to kill us, aren't they?"

Juraviel looked at her directly. "You, likely," he confirmed. "They are not overly fond of humans, it seems."

Brynn considered the undead force that had come against them, human zombies all.

"Though they may keep me alive," Juraviel went on, "for information or for barter, if ever they should venture to find Lady Dasslerond and Andur'Blough Inninness."

"Then we have to find a way to fight our way out of here."

Juraviel shrugged and motioned to the side, to a dark hole in the floor, seeming barely wide enough to crawl into. "One tunnel, through which we'll have to crawl, blocked at the one exit by a boulder and a host of zombies, to say nothing of any Doc'alfar who might be about. And I trust that my kin have not lost their proficiency in battle."

Brynn's shoulders slumped and her gaze fell to the floor. "I

cannot die here," she said. "Not now. My people are in need
and I will not forsake them!" She finished with a snarl, but
it was one, she knew, more of frustration than determination. For what could she and Belli'mar Juraviel do? They were
overmatched, plain and simple, and so much so that there were
no apparent options.

She wanted to punch the wall, and turned, meaning to do
just that. But a thought came to her suddenly and her face
brightened, and her hand unclenched and tore at the soft wall
instead, pulling away a sizable chunk of root-filled earth.
Brynn spun right about, ignoring the pain in her shoulder and
ribs, determined to tear a tunnel out of the soft soil.

"Do not!" came Juraviel's emphatic cry, and the woman
stopped and turned back to regard him.

"The cave is not solid enough," Juraviel explained. "Our
captors understood how to build a prison properly here, and if
we weaken the integrity of the walls, it will all fall in on us."

Brynn closed her eyes, her ribs aching as she gasped in
deep breaths, reconsidering her exertion.

"We are very deep," Juraviel grimly added.

Brynn fell back over to a sitting position, her back against
the cool, smelly mud. "What are we to do? To sit and wait,
and pray for the beneficence of our captors?"

"How I wish I had an answer."

And so they did just that, sitting and waiting, Juraviel's
mind whirling as he tried to come up with some manner of
negotiation that he might use, should he get the chance, to get
both of them out of there. Brynn sat thinking of her failure, of
the loss to To-gai and the enslaved To-gai-ru. She would not
be their savior, apparently.

Inevitably, the woman's thoughts turned to her own mortality. What did it mean to die? Would her murdered parents
be there at the end of the dark tunnel, as the shamans of To-
gai claimed, ready to welcome her to the Great Hunt? Or
would there be nothing at all, just an empty blackness, a ces-
sation of existence?

Many times, the woman tried to bring her thoughts back to
the situation at hand, tried to fathom some solution to the ter-

rible dilemma. But she was dragged back over and over to the unavoidable contemplations of that greatest of mysteries.

Time slipped past; Brynn knew not if it was minutes or hours or days. She wasn't hungry, and figured that trying to eat would pain her greatly, anyway. She just sat there and waited, and every so often, she glanced across the way to Juraviel, who sat cross-legged, his elbows propped on his legs, his chin in his cupped hands.

Time slipped past.

The sound of movement in the tunnel shook Brynn from a trancelike slumber some long hours later. The young ranger instinctively started to move, and quickly, to a defensive position, but a sudden stabbing pain in her side forced her back to her sitting posture, gasping for breath.

Juraviel didn't move very much at all, just turned his head to regard the approaching sound. It wasn't from weakness or pain, though, Brynn understood, but from simple resignation. They were beaten, and Juraviel had fully accepted that. If their captors walked Juraviel to the edge of a cliff, clipped his wings, and told him to jump, Brynn believed that he just might do it, and without complaint!

A covered pot was the first thing that came through the dark hole at the base of the wall across from Brynn, ushered forward by a pair of peat-covered, stiff-fingered hands. The zombie continued to crawl its way into the room, moving more like a worm than a bipedal creature. It set the pot down, then began to recede into the hole, moving slowly backward down the tunnel.

The perfect delivery system, Brynn realized, for the zombie would not panic in the tight tunnel and could take its time in leaving, inch by inch.

"What is it?" Brynn asked after the gruesome zombie was finally gone from sight.

"Food and water," Juraviel explained. "You go first and take as much as you require. It has been far too long since your last meal."

Brynn stared at the pot for a long moment, considering the

pain in her ribs and the nausea it had created in her stomach. She didn't want food, but she needed it, she knew.

Or did she? What was the point, if she was just to be executed anyway?

Brynn dismissed those dark thoughts before they could ever gain a hold, and crept forward and pushed the cover from the pot. In the dim light, she couldn't make out much within the shadows beneath the lip, but her nose told her that it was merely bread—stale bread, she determined as she lifted it out—and a small flask of water. It was her first meal in four days, and it hurt too much for her to enjoy a single bite or sip of it. But Brynn forced fully half of the bread and water down, treating each bite as a small victory in her resistance against her captors, her determination to win out and get out.

Juraviel finished the food and drink with the same resigned manner as he had welcomed the zombie waiter.

Brynn just stared at him, trying to impart some fighting spirit. It occurred to her, only briefly, that Juraviel was taking such a passive attitude so that his chances of getting out alive would be heightened, even if his apparent determination not to fight back doomed his companion.

No, Brynn told herself forcefully. Juraviel was resigned because he believed that they had no chance of any substantive resistance.

She would have to show him differently!

The zombie returned after what Brynn estimated to be the turn of a full day. It put the new pot down and grabbed the old one, now serving as a commode, and started backing down the hole.

Brynn started to move, thinking to kill the undead creature while it was vulnerable in the tight passageway, but her expression betrayed her to her companion.

"Do not!" Juraviel commanded, and Brynn stopped and stared at him, then looked back to the zombie, which continued to back away mindlessly, oblivious to the threat.

"If you kill it, then it will lie stinking in the hole," the elf explained, his tone flat and even. "Then we will have to tolerate the added smell of rot, and that I do not desire."

Brynn sank back against the wall and gave a great sigh. "Are we to do nothing?"

"We are to eat," replied Juraviel. "And more slowly this day, for they do not always replace the pot they take away on their rounds."

The cycle continued day after day, and while Brynn's ribs began to hurt less, she was weakening, not getting stronger, she knew. Their captors were apparently not novices at this business, for they kept the food and drink to an absolute minimum, gradually breaking down the strength and will of the prisoners.

Brynn knew not how many days had passed, and hardly took note when movement sounded in the tunnel. Even after the Doc'alfar emerged from the tunnel, it took the woman a few seconds to realize that this was not their usual zombie waiter!

"Belli'mar Juraviel," the Doc'alfar greeted.

"Hail, Lozan Duk," Juraviel replied, and Brynn's eyes went wide with surprise.

"King Eltiraaz awaits you."

Juraviel nodded and rolled up to his knees, and it took him a long while to steady himself. Brynn, too, started to move, but Juraviel fixed her with a stare and motioned for her to sit back, and Lozan Duk turned a threatening glare at her.

"You will have your chance to explain yourself to my king," the Doc'alfar said to Juraviel. "This is your trial."

"And am I to have my say to your King Eltiraaz?" Brynn boldly asked.

Lozan Duk slowly turned to regard her. "You have nothing to say, *n'Tylwyn Doc*."

*N'Tylwyn Doc*. The word played over and over in Brynn's mind, for she had heard a similar word many times during her tenure with the Touel'alfar, particularly in the beginning, when her training in the ways of the ranger, in the ways of the elves, was in its infancy. Many times, the Touel'alfar had called her *n'Touel'alfar*, a derisive term that meant, simply, that she was not of *the People*, of the important people, of the only ones who truly counted. There was some hope to be garnered here, in the fact that the Doc'alfar had not similarly referred to Juraviel. By pointedly using the phrase in regard to Brynn as the reason she would not be allowed to go along, he had, in effect, somewhat included Juraviel in his clan.

That hope was lost on Brynn as she slumped back against the wall, though, for the derisive title, *n'Tylwyn Doc,* sounded to her like the call of the executioner.

The two elves moved out of the room with far more ease and grace than had the zombie waiter. Brynn again considered moving, not to follow, but to attack their jailor, though she realized that she would likely have no chance against an elf in her weakened state. The only thing that held her back were the implications for Belli'mar Juraviel. Brynn was likely doomed, as Juraviel had admitted, but perhaps her friend would find some way to get out of this.

So she sat back against the cool wall and let the minutes slip into uneventful hours.

Juraviel followed Lozan Duk into a smaller chamber down near the exit of the earthen tunnel—which was still blocked, as far as he could tell—where Cazzira was waiting. Without a word from the female, and without a word of protest from Juraviel, the Doc'alfar moved and slipped a thick belt about Juraviel's waist, tightening it down and pinning his wings, then buckling the front with some locking mechanism.

"You will not fly away, little bird," Cazzira remarked as she fastened the lock, and Juraviel noted that the Doc'alfar word for "bird" was exactly the same as the word in his own tongue: *marrawee.*

"Do you believe that I wish to fly away?" he answered. "Perhaps this is a long-overdue meeting between the alfar, and fate has guided me to you for a reason."

"Perhaps," Lozan Duk said.

"Or perhaps it was simply bad fortune on your part," Cazzira was quick to add. Juraviel maintained a nonchalant visage until the female added, "And even worse fortune for your *n'Tylwyn Doc* companion."

"Come," Lozan Duk instructed, seeming as eager to be done with this particular line of conversation as was Juraviel.

The Doc'alfar crawled into the ascending tunnel then, Juraviel right behind, and Cazzira following a short distance back.

Soon after, Juraviel crawled out of the tunnel, but not into the light, though he was outside and the sun was up.

But not there. The fog was even thicker than it had been in the graveyard of trees by the peat bog, casting the place in a moist and perpetual gloom.

"King Eltiraaz has accepted your request to speak with him," Lozan Duk explained. "You should be honored."

"Indeed I am," Juraviel replied with all sincerity. A twinge of guilt struck him as he responded, as he thought of Brynn and her likely fate. Still, Juraviel had to admit his excitement in seeing his white-skinned and wingless cousins. For the Touel'alfar, this was monumental news, at least as important as anything Brynn might accomplish in To gai, and though Juraviel was surely torn and upset about the possibilities of Brynn's lack of future, he couldn't deny his excitement, his thrill, at the opportunity to represent his people to the king of the Doc'alfar!

"Though I fear that I am hardly properly attired for an audience with your king," Juraviel added.

"Your clothing will do," Cazzira remarked. "The road-worn, weathered outfit of a traveler, of a thief, perhaps."

Juraviel took the comment in stride and thought he detected a bit of softening in Cazzira's tone, if not her actual words.

Lozan Duk motioned for Juraviel to follow, leading him down a winding trail to a large, hollowed tree stump. Juraviel found two depressions within, one with soapy oil and the other with clear rainwater.

The washing felt good indeed!

He turned when he was done, just in time to catch a towel Cazzira threw his way, then they were off again, walking the winding, fog-enshrouded trails, through skeletal black trees that all looked the same. Juraviel doubted he would be able to retrace his steps on his own, and he suspected that his two guards were tracking all about on purpose, to obscure the true path even more. They seemed a lot like the Touel'alfar, he mused.

Almost without warning, Juraviel found himself on a narrow trail amidst towering mountain walls, a narrow gorge trail that led to a huge cave. The two Doc'alfar each picked up one of those strange-glowing lanterns right inside the cave and paused, turning to their prisoner.

Juraviel looked all about, though the other walls of the cavern were far beyond the limit of the light. When his gaze at last settled on Lozan Duk and Cazzira, he found Lozan Duk coming toward him, a black hood in hand.

Juraviel didn't protest at all as they popped it over his head, pulling a drawstring set about its opening to somewhat close it. Lozan Duk took him by the arm and led him off, and they walked for a long and winding way, down corridors that closed in on Juraviel and through chambers that he sensed were very vast indeed.

A long while later, they stopped again, and Juraviel was surprised when Cazzira pulled off his hood, staring at him intently with her icy blue eyes. They were in a large chamber, and it seemed to Juraviel that he was actually out of doors again, in some secret mountain hole.

His eyes scanned up, up, eagerly, but as he turned, he quickly forgot all about the chamber itself, for there before him towered the magnificent gates of the Doc'alfar city.

"Tymwyvenne," Lozan Duk explained. "You are the first who is not Doc'alfar to look upon the gates of Tymwyvenne in many centuries."

"I am honored," Juraviel said, again with all sincerity and more than a bit of awe, for the entrance to Tymwyvenne was what he would expect of any cousins of the Touel'alfar—and more! The doors, huge doors, as thick as ten elves side by side, were of some golden-hued wood. They hung open, flanked by two huge round pillars of the same material, which were set against a wall of gray-and-black stone. Across the top of the pillars was a third, lying horizontally above the doorway, and made of the same wood, with thousands of designs carved into it, many of them shining of various colors. Juraviel looked more closely and noted that many, many gemstones were set in that beam, a king's treasure, and he was glad to see that there was an appreciation of beauty there, as in Caer'alfar—though his own people's ideal of beauty was evidenced in the perfection of nature itself. Juraviel understood that such appreciation often signaled an understanding of the higher orders and stations of life, including mercy.

Through the doors, the trio came into an immense cavern, a place of quiet, but steady, light, where the fog was not so thick. Structures loomed all about them, made of burnished wood of varying hues and textures. There was no one singular dominant design, but each house, for that is what they obviously were, was its own free-flowing work of art.

Many other Doc'alfar milled about, making Juraviel's path a veritable parade route. All wanted to catch a glimpse of the captured Tylwyn Tou, obviously, and he noted many expressions there, from curiosity to some almost giddy faces, to many, many profound scowls.

The place had a somber tone about it, to Juraviel's thinking, gloomy but not dark. It wasn't hard for him to figure out his escorts' intended destination as they crossed a large central open area. Ahead of them, a crisscross of balconies lined the back wall, climbing up above the city. There, on a higher level, sat the grandest house of all, which he knew without doubt was the palace of King Eltiraaz.

Belli'mar Juraviel fixed his gaze on that house and the many surrounding landings and ornate railings and balusters, trying to get a feeling for the occupants through their choice of design. The alfar could do this more easily than could humans because elven houses were rarely handed down—were, ultimately, a product of centuries of choices and intuitions and creativity from a single driving heart and mind.

This house looked inviting enough, very much like a place expecting many guests and revelers.

Of course, a pair of Doc'alfar guards darkened that notion. They were dressed in strange skin and wooden armor and held thin and nasty-looking hooked clubs, their full-faced helms showing only their dark eyes, and those eyes revealing nothing of their feelings toward this strange newcomer to their land.

The trio entered a wide foyer, then turned down a side passage and around a series of bends, at last coming into another wide room, set with two rows of decorated columns, with a thick green carpet running the length of the room between them. The only piece of furniture in the room was a large golden-wood throne near the far wall, behind which a fire blazed in a great hearth, and upon which sat a Doc'alfar with long black hair and large dark eyes. Like that of the rest of his kin, his skin was creamy white. His clothing, though, was far more remarkable. Thus far, most of the Doc'alfar Juraviel had seen were either in that curious armor or in rather plain garb. Lozan Duk and Cazzira both wore dark brown outfits—suitable for hunting the foggy bogs, Juraviel figured.

This one—King Eltiraaz, Juraviel knew before the formal introduction—wore light-colored breeches, embroidered with many gemstones, and a rich purple shirt. A cape that seemed a combination of the two hung back off his shoulders, bunching on the chair behind him. His vest was full of sewn images, in a thread that seemed almost metallic to Juraviel. He wore a crown of leafy vines wrapped about a silvery band, metal that the Touel'alfar recognized as silverel. That was very telling to Juraviel, for no race other than the Touel'alfar knew how to farm the exotic metal from the ground, as far as he knew; that crown proved to him that either the Doc'alfar had held that secret during the centuries of separation, or that this particular crown was a relic left over from the days when the races were one. Likely the second, he surmised, for he had seen no darkferns about, and no other silverel. If the Doc'alfar had the knowledge and the means to farm the wondrous silverel, they surely would not have their soldiers carrying wooden clubs!

Unless, of course, the wood of those clubs, a variety that Juraviel did not know, carried a few special properties of its own.

Flanked by Lozan Duk and Cazzira, Juraviel walked along the carpet to stand before Eltiraaz.

The King of Tymwyvenne sat very straight on his throne, staring hard at Juraviel, his expression stern and regal, his shoulders perfectly squared. He had his hands on his lap, holding a gem-capped scepter fashioned out of that same strange wood.

"You will tell King Eltiraaz your tale, Belli'mar Juraviel of the Touel'alfar, from the very beginning of the road that brought you to our lands," Lozan Duk explained. "And of why you walk the trails with a living human beside you."

Juraviel winced a bit at that last statement, further confirmation that the Doc'alfar's contempt for humans was nearly absolute. He pushed past his emotions, though, and did as instructed, relating his tale from the battle with the goblins south and east of Andur'Blough Inninness—whose whereabouts he had no intention of disclosing—to the night of his and Brynn's capture.

King Eltiraaz listened intently to his every word, sometimes tilting his head to the side, as if he wanted to ask a question. But he remained silent and patient throughout the tale.

"Long have we known that our kin, the Tylwyn Tou, remained in the northland," Eltiraaz said after Juraviel had finished. His voice was both regal and melodic, a great baritone that seemed strange to Juraviel, coming out of so diminutive a creature. "Yet no less is our surprise in seeing one, in seeing you, walk into our lands. Know that you are the very first of our lost brethren to look upon Tymwyvenne."

"I am truly honored, King Eltiraaz." Juraviel thought it appropriate to bow at that solemn moment.

The King of the Doc'alfar nodded, then looked to Lozan Duk.

"King Eltiraaz wishes to know why you were in the company of a human," Lozan Duk asked.

Juraviel looked from the king to the other male, curious as to why Eltiraaz had not simply asked him himself. "Brynn Dharielle is a ranger," he explained. "Trained by the Touel'alfar. It is a practice that we have employed for centuries—taking in human orphans who show promise and training them in the ways of the Touel'alfar, that they might serve as eyes and ears for my Lady Dasslerond in the wider human world."

"Why not just kill every human who wanders into your domain?" Cazzira asked, and Juraviel noted, in all seriousness. "They are lesser creatures, and if a threat, should be eliminated."

"We view them more highly than do you, perhaps," the

Touel'alfar replied, trying to remain civil, knowing that Brynn's life might be on the line here. "We have come to see the humans as valuable allies at times, if often a bit troublesome."

"More than troublesome," said Cazzira.

"Rangers are not like other humans," Juraviel stated clearly, aiming the words at King Eltiraaz. "They understand much more about the world than their clumsy kin. They are expert warriors, and with the temperament and instilled discipline to use their fighting prowess wisely. They are friends to the natural world, friends to the Touel'alfar, and surely no ranger would be a threat or enemy to the Doc'alfar."

"How do you know?" asked Eltiraaz.

Juraviel started to echo the question, but caught himself, understanding it, and replied, "Rangers who do not show the proper temperament and judgment are not allowed back out into the wide world."

"And your companion has passed these tests?" Eltiraaz asked.

"Brynn is as fine a ranger as has ever walked out of Andur'Blough Inninness and Caer'alfar."

"Then why does she need the company of Belli'mar Juraviel?"

The Touel'alfar took a deep breath and considered the question, and considered how much he should reveal to Eltiraaz and the others. He had already spoken the name of his valley, his Lady, and his city, and sensed that he should trust these kin somewhat, but how might they feel about a human heading through their lands on her way to begin a war?

"Brynn Dharielle was selected among the To-gai-ru of the wild steppes south of the great mountains," he explained.

"We know of the To-gai-ru," Eltiraaz replied.

"Then you know that they are not like their kinfolk," Juraviel said. "They are more attuned to the land and to—"

"A few of our soldiers are of To-gai-ru descent," Cazzira said, and her grim tone reminded Juraviel of the type of "soldier" to which she was referring. He looked at her, wondering how deep her enmity truly ran, and was taken in again by those exotic eyes of hers, shining icy orbs layered in emotion and thought.

He shook off his revulsion and focused on an interesting question: how had any To-gai-ru come to the land of the Doc'alfar? And how did the Doc'alfar know of Brynn's people? True, the To-gai-ru settled the land only a hundred miles or so south of this region, but on the other side of supposedly impassable mountains. Or perhaps, not so impassable?

But how to bring the conversation to that point, to where he could even begin to hope that these captors would allow him and Brynn to go free at all, let alone tell them of a possible way through the mountains?

"Have you found no redeeming qualities in the To-gai-ru?" he dared to ask. "Are they no more than the other humans to you?"

"Should we look, Belli'mar Juraviel?" King Eltiraaz asked. "Is it your word to us that the To-gai-ru can be better trusted by our people? Do you believe, perhaps, that we have erred in judging them so harshly?"

Juraviel saw the potential trap, particularly in that last question, but he knew that he had to hold fast to his principles, both for his own heart and for any chance that he might find in getting past those fierce people. "I believe that you should look, if that is what you desire," he said. "It is my word to you that the To-gai-ru are more attuned to the ways of both the Tylwyn Tou and Tylwyn Doc, if the Tylwyn Doc hold at all to the old ways of our people."

"More, perhaps, than the Tylwyn Tou, Belli'mar Juraviel," King Eltiraaz replied, "if the Tylwyn Tou have come to befriend the humans."

Juraviel conceded the point without any countering statement at all, for indeed, during the old times when the races of elves were united, they had no contact with anyone who was not of *the People*.

"I would not say that you have erred, King Eltiraaz. That is not a judgment for me to make. In my own land, we preserve our secrecy with equal ferocity; a human who cannot be trusted is treated in the same manner in which we would deal with a goblin who wandered onto our land. Well, perhaps not as harshly as that—we would kill the human more quickly and mercifully.

"But not a To-gai-ru," he quickly added, though he had no idea if he was speaking the truth or not, since no To-gai-ru had ever wandered anywhere near to Andur'Blough Inninness, except for those taken in as rangers-in-training, of course. He felt that his reasoning was sound, though, and so he continued. "My Lady Dasslerond would hold back on the killing blow against a To-gai-ru until the intruder's intent could be discerned."

"By then, it is often too late," Cazzira remarked.

"Too late for what? We fear no threat from anything short of an invading army."

That set all three of the Doc'alfar back on their heels a bit, Juraviel noted.

"Perhaps your clan is more numerous than our own," King Eltiraaz said after a short pause and a glance at his two kinfolk. "We are not numerous, and thus we take threats against our land more seriously."

"Or you are more quick to judge intrusion as threat," Juraviel dared to say, and Cazzira at his side sucked in her breath sharply. Juraviel started to modify the statement, to make it seem less an accusation, but he stopped himself short, letting King Eltiraaz weigh the words.

"Perhaps we must be," the king said a short while later. "And I doubt not that we will hold on to our ways, Belli'mar Juraviel. They have served us well through these centuries, have kept Tymwyvenne alive. I care not enough for the clumsy and bumbling humans to risk a single Tylwyn Doc life, and if I had to destroy the entire human race to safeguard my people, then I would do so, without hesitation."

"And what of a Tylwyn Tou who inadvertently wandered onto your land, good King Eltiraaz? Would such an unfortunate—or perhaps fortunate—distant cousin be similarly executed, or would the King of the Doc'alfar think that preserving the life of a relative was worth the risk to his people?"

King Eltiraaz stood up out of his throne, his gaze set grimly and sternly upon Juraviel. "Is there a threat to my people, Belli'mar Juraviel?"

Juraviel squared his shoulders and matched the king's unblinking gaze in intensity. "No."

A long, long silence ensued, the two standing there, Eltiraaz a step higher than Juraviel, and thus, looking down at him. But in truth, that height difference did nothing to diminish Juraviel in this contest of wills.

Finally, after several minutes of the locked stares, Eltiraaz turned to each of the others, left and right, then declared, "There is no threat."

Juraviel held firm his gaze and determined posture, though in truth, he wanted to blow a long and deep sigh. So he was not to die there, it seemed.

But that wasn't enough.

"And what of Brynn Dharielle?" he asked. "She is To-gai-ru, and even more than that, much more than that, she is a ranger, trained by my people in the ways of the Tylwyn Tou. She sees the world as a Tylwyn Tou sees the world, and is more kin and friend to my people than to her own."

"So you say," Lozan Duk put in.

Juraviel looked at him, and he only shrugged in reply, as if his words were spoken in all simplicity and honesty.

"I do say," Juraviel answered, and he turned again to face Eltiraaz directly. "Brynn Dharielle is no threat to you or your people. Indeed, she is, or would be, a friend to Tymwyvenne, if you choose to allow it."

"I need no humans for friends, Belli'mar Juraviel."

Juraviel nodded and conceded the point. "She is my friend," he said then, and somberly. "I ask of you, King Eltiraaz, to allow my friend to leave with me. On my word, she is no threat."

"I have not yet said that you could leave," the King of the Tylwyn Doc reminded.

Juraviel did blow that sigh, and he nodded.

Soon after, he was back in the small room of peat with Brynn, sitting there silently in the soft light of the glowing torch. Brynn had immediately started to ask him about his visit with the king when he had first returned, but Juraviel had waved the question away, not wanting to discuss any of that. For the first time in his long life, Belli'mar Juraviel felt perfectly helpless in determining his fate, and he did not like the feeling at all.

The rest of that day passed, and the next, and the only contact came from the zombie waiter delivering their food.

On the second day after his visit with Eltiraaz, though, Juraviel was summoned again from the peat cave, escorted again by Lozan Duk and Cazzira to the same throne room, where King Eltiraaz sat waiting.

"I have considered your words, Belli'mar Juraviel," the king greeted. "And I find that I believe you."

Juraviel did not reply or make any sign at all, not sure exactly what that meant.

"I will have your word that, once you have left here, you will not disclose the location of Tymwyvenne."

"I will not."

"And I will have, from you, the location of Caer'alfar," King Eltiraaz went on.

Juraviel rocked back on his heels, chewing his lip as he considered the request. "King Eltiraaz, I am similarly sworn to secrecy by Lady Dasslerond," he answered.

Beside him, Cazzira and Lozan Duk bristled.

"But this is not equal footing," King Eltiraaz replied. "Now you, a member of Tylwyn Tou, know of Tymwyvenne, but none of us know of Caer'alfar."

"King Eltiraaz, if one of your people wandered to our lands and was captured, you would not expect, nor accept, that your subject would betray the location of Tymwyvenne, even at the cost of his or her own life."

"And do you accept similar consequences for yourself and for Brynn?" the king came back without hesitation, his voice rising more than Juraviel had previously heard.

"I do, if that is your judgment," Juraviel answered just as quickly. "If that is your decision, then I damn the fates, and not King Eltiraaz and his people, in bringing me here. But I do argue against such a course. Perhaps there will come of this a rejoining of our peoples, or at least a growing understanding of each other. A distant alliance, long overdue."

King Eltiraaz stared at him sternly for some time, then

broke into a sudden, tension-breaking burst of laughter. "You would willingly die, and without judgment, I believe."

"I would!"

"And that sincerity makes me believe you even more, Belli'mar Juraviel, friend of Tymwyvenne. Nay, we will not kill you, or hold you any longer as our prisoner. Though I would be pleased if you would remain for some time as my guest."

"And I would be pleased to do so, King Eltiraaz of Tymwyvenne," Juraviel answered formally, and with a bow. "But not alone, and not while my companion, my friend, sits in a prison of peat. You say that you believe me, and well you should. But I'll not accept anything from you—not my own freedom, not your invitation—without a free Brynn Dharielle at my side."

"And if we kill her? Are we then enemies?"

Juraviel took a deep breath. "We are," he declared, and he couldn't believe the words as they came out of his own mouth! How could he take such a chance when so much might be at stake for the Touel'alfar? Surely, this offered friendship could blossom into something wonderful for his people. Given that, was he acting in the best interest of Caer'alfar—and did he have the right to act in any other way?—by so protecting Brynn?

He didn't honestly know, and he found that he didn't honestly care.

"Go and bring the human woman," King Eltiraaz instructed Cazzira and Lozan Duk. "Allow her to bathe and feed her well. It seems that perhaps we have made two new friends this day."

It took all the willpower Belli'mar Juraviel could muster to remain upright at that wonderful moment.

"You are not the first human permitted to walk through our lands," King Eltiraaz said to Brynn when she—fresh from her bath and with her clothes wonderfully cleaned—and Juraviel met with the King of Tymwyvenne later on that day.

"Before you continue, I demand to know what happened to Diredusk!" the young ranger demanded.

King Eltiraaz sat back, his expression turning stern, his

eyes narrowing and focusing on Brynn. Juraviel put his hand on her arm, squeezing tightly in an attempt to silence her.

"Her horse, good King Eltiraaz," he explained. "When we were taken, Brynn had her horse with her, a beautiful creature."

Eltiraaz relaxed visibly, and so did Juraviel.

"What happened to him?" the stubborn Brynn demanded, and Juraviel squeezed even more tightly, thinking that his companion might be throwing it all away, pushing too hard when they were obviously in no position to demand anything.

But again, King Eltiraaz's expression only softened. "You have enough concern for that creature—Diredusk, you name him—to speak in this manner to me?"

"I do." There wasn't a hint of anything other than grim determination in Brynn's voice.

"And if your insolence costs you my patience?"

"If you have harmed Diredusk, then I want not your patience, King Eltiraaz. If you have harmed Diredusk, then—"

Eltiraaz held up his hand, but it was his smile that stopped her more than any hand gesture. "We of the Tylwyn Doc do no harm to our fellow creatures of Ga'na'Tyl. Your horse, Diredusk, is running free in the fields to the east, among his own kind. Free, I say, and where he belongs."

Brynn breathed a huge sigh of relief, and so did Juraviel.

"You do not wish him recaptured?" Eltiraaz asked.

Brynn looked up at him, and it was obvious that the king was testing her here. "My concern was for Diredusk, not for myself," she answered. "If he is running free and safe, then I am satisfied."

King Eltiraaz smiled, warmly. "Once, many years ago, a man crossed through our lands, coming from the north, and it was the decision of King Tez'nezin that he not be hindered," he went on with the tale he had been relating when Brynn had interrupted. "King Tez'nezin, my predecessor to the throne, was rumored to have gone out to the man for a secret meeting, though what he discerned that allowed him to change his policies—long-standing policies of the Tylwyn Doc against humans—I cannot say.

"That human was To-gai-ru, like Brynn Dharielle, seeking

a way home, over the mountains or under them. Whether or not he succeeded in returning to the land south of the mountains, I cannot say."

"What was his name?" a very curious Belli'mar Juraviel asked. "And when was this? A century ago?"

"His name I do not know, and it was much longer in the past. Three centuries, at least, perhaps four. The years, the decades, do all seem the same."

Juraviel sat back and considered the words. A To-gai-ru coming through this region from the north would be a rare thing indeed, especially centuries before, when Honce-the-Bear and Behren were avowed enemies, and To-gai was not even known to the humans north of the mountains. But there had been other To-gai-ru rangers, several over the centuries, and none before Brynn had left Andur'Blough Inninness with an elvish escort, though all of them had been assigned back in their ancient homeland. Was it possible that the human Eltiraaz now spoke of had been one of the To-gai-ru rangers? Emhem Dal, perhaps? Or Salman Anick Zo?

Intrigued, Juraviel rubbed a hand over his chin.

"Did he find a way over the mountains, at least?" Brynn asked. "Or did he start on a path that he hoped would take him home?"

"No," King Eltiraaz replied, and Brynn's hopeful smile disappeared, though it brightened again as the King of Tymwyvenne continued. "Not over the mountains. That human was guided to a way known to the Tylwyn Doc as the Path of Starless Night."

"Under the mountains," Juraviel reasoned, and King Eltiraaz nodded.

"And will you take me and Juraviel to the entrance to this Path of Starless Night?" Brynn asked eagerly, seeming oblivious to the frown worn by the Doc'alfar King.

Juraviel caught that look, though, and he understood that this ominously named underground passageway likely lived up to some grim reputation!

"What say you, Belli'mar Juraviel?" King Eltiraaz asked. "Do you wish to head to this path, a dark road indeed?"

Juraviel looked to Brynn, and her eagerness prodded him

into agreeing to a choice that he feared he would later regret.
"We do. If this Path of Starless Night can save us a journey all
the way to the sea to the east, then perhaps it is worth the try."

King Eltiraaz sat back and nodded, his expression grave.
"Perhaps, then, my people will have to worry less that you
will betray us to the Tylwyn Tou."

Juraviel looked to Brynn again, but she held her determined expression.

"And what will Belli'mar Juraviel tell his Lady Dasslerond
about us?" King Eltiraaz went on. "When finally you walk the
ways of your homeland again, what will you say?"

"I will say that I have found a legend come to life," Juraviel
answered. "Or I will say nothing at all. The choice is yours,
King of Tymwyvenne, earned by your mercy and gracious-
ness. I owe you this, at least, for my own life and for Brynn's.
If you wish this entire episode to retreat into the realm of
Belli'mar Juraviel's hopeful dreams, then so it shall."

Eltiraaz spent a long while mulling that over. He looked to
his Doc'alfar companions, Lozan Duk, Cazzira, and several
others he had invited to the meeting that day, gauging their
silent answers.

"No," he said at length. "You will tell your Lady Dasslerond that you have looked upon Tymwyvenne and met your
long-lost kin. You will tell her that she, upon the invitation of
King Eltiraaz, is most welcome to visit us, that we might both
learn if our peoples, Doc and Tou, should find their way together again."

Juraviel could hardly believe what he was hearing, and in
truth, he was terribly torn at that moment. His immediate
duty was to Brynn and their journey to To-gai-ru. Or was it?
Was this potential reunification more important? Should he
abandon Brynn here and now and head back to the north with
all speed? Or perhaps he could take Brynn back with him and
delay her mission to her homeland. There was no pressing issue there, after all, nothing more than had been going on
since before Brynn had been taken in by the Touel'alfar.

But then Eltiraaz settled it for him. "But that is in the future," the king said. "For now, your road is, and must be, to
the south. We will show you the Path of Starless Night and

tell you more of what we know of the dangers that lie within the deep mountains. You may choose to enter, or choose to turn to the east. But not to the north, not now. My people are not ready for this meeting, and I'll not force it upon them."

Juraviel nodded his agreement.

"And what if Belli'mar Juraviel does not return from the southland?" Lozan Duk interjected. "What if Belli'mar Juraviel does not emerge again into the sunlight from the Path of Starless Night? Is this hope that we have just shared of reunion to die with him, then?"

As he finished, Lozan Duk looked to King Eltiraaz, and Juraviel recognized then that the question was not likely spontaneous.

"I would speak with you privately," Juraviel bade the king, and with a wave of his hand, Eltiraaz cleared the room of all but himself and Juraviel.

"If you desire the meeting, and I cannot return, then send a trusted courier or two to the north, staying west of the human lands, to the mountain region three weeks' journey from here. Once there, call out the name of Lady Dasslerond to the night wind, every hour every night. She will find your couriers, do not doubt, and the Touel'alfar will speak with them before passing swift judgment. Have them relay the tale of Belli'mar Juraviel and Brynn Dharielle, and tell of how they came to the lands of the Touel'alfar."

"And they will not be harmed?"

Juraviel took a deep breath. "I cannot commit to anything," he admitted. "My people are no less reclusive than are your own—it is part of our shared heritage, it would seem. The Lady of Caer'alfar is stern and strong, but she is blessed with the wisdom of the centuries. I trust she will choose correctly."

"Though you have less to lose."

"There is that," Juraviel admitted. "It is the best I can offer, King Eltiraaz of Tymwyvenne, and more, I fear, than I should have said."

"And nothing more than we could have discerned, in any case," Eltiraaz answered with a chuckle, and he offered his hand to Juraviel, and the Touel'alfar took it in a firm shake.

"Stay with us a few weeks more," Eltiraaz offered. "Enjoy the customs of my people, walking freely about Tymwyvenne."

"And Brynn?"

"Likewise! Let her be the most blessed of humankind, to have looked upon both Caer'alfar and Tymwyvenne! When you are ready, we will take you to the Path of Starless Night, and you may choose your course. We will provide you with ever-burning light and with all the supplies you can carry." He paused and assumed a pensive posture, his look quizzical. "And perhaps with more."

Juraviel understood that he should not press for more than that cryptic statement at that time. Already he had been offered far more than he could ever have hoped for, far more than he ever would have dared to ask for!

"The season means little in the Path of Starless Night," Eltiraaz went on. "In truth, the closer you wait toward winter, the more passable will be the dark tunnels, for the spring melt will have flowed from them by then, and the new snows atop the mountains will be locked frozen in the days it will take you to cross under."

It was an invitation that Belli'mar Juraviel could not refuse, and—given that last bit of logic, one that he knew would calm Brynn's eagerness—he believed that his companion would readily agree. Perhaps if they stayed in Tymwyvenne, their trip to the south would prove no less time-consuming than the long journey around the mountains, but in truth, it was more than the loss of time that had Juraviel trying to avoid that circuitous route. He had little desire to cross the human lands of Honce-the-Bear, and even less to try to find his way through hostile Behren. There Brynn would be considered no more than a pig looking for a slave owner and he, if his true identity as a Touel'alfar was ever discovered, would likely be put to a swift death, a sacrifice to Yatol.

Yes, this would be a most-welcomed rest, not for weeks, perhaps, but for a short while.

"Do you believe him?" Brynn asked Juraviel that same night, the two spending some quiet time trying to sort through the momentous events of the day. How swiftly their fate had changed! And how unexpectedly!

"If King Eltiraaz meant us harm, then why would he go to all this trouble?" the elf replied. "He had garnered all of the information he will get from me, from us, concerning Andur'Blough Inninness, and he knows that. No, he is sincere." As he finished, smiling, he noted that Brynn's sour expression had not changed. He looked at her curiously, silently prompting her to elaborate.

"I meant about Diredusk."

"They said he was running free with other horses."

"But did they say that merely to calm me?" the young woman asked. "Are they merely telling us what we need to hear?"

Belli'mar Juraviel settled back. "No," he answered with the calm of complete confidence. "Have you noticed the tables they set? The meals they have brought to us?"

Brynn tilted her head, staring at him intently, needing to find the same conclusions as he obviously already had.

"They eat the produce of the earth, the gifts of Ga'na'Tynne. They eat the fruits and vegetables, the fungi of the tunnels. But not the animals. King Eltiraaz spoke truly of his people when he said that they hold the creatures of Ga'na'Tyl in the highest reverence and would not harm them. Diredusk is running free and unharmed, I am sure."

"They harm no creatures of Ga'na'Tyl," Brynn echoed with a sarcastic chuckle. "Except for humans."

"Whom they believe deserving of their wrath," Juraviel was quick to point out. "Consider those of your race with whom they have had contact. Trappers and hunters, loggers and rogues who have been chased from their own lands. Humans who clear-cut the trees and slaughter the animals, often merely for a pelt to sell in the east. Humans who set traps that cause excruciating pain to their prey, without regard for the animal. If the Doc'alfar feel a kinship to the living animals, then how could they not feel anger at some of the tactics that trappers and hunters of your race employ?"

Brynn merely shrugged and shook her head, hardly seeming convinced of the argument that the Doc'alfar were, in some way, justified in the horrible executions they routinely practiced on humans inadvertently walking onto their lands.

Juraviel didn't try to convince her otherwise, didn't believe that she would ever truly understand. For she was human, if Touel'alfar trained and To-gai-ru, and she understood there to be a redeeming side to her race. Juraviel recognized that as well, but, seeing the world as a Touel'alfar, he was much more sympathetic to the Doc'alfar view of things. In many ways, he saw these distant cousins as even more honorable than his own people, who hunted the deer, pigs, fowl, and rabbits of Andur'Blough Inninness. The Doc'alfar only did harm to living creatures they believed deserving of their wrath. It wouldn't occur to Eltiraaz to have a great deer slaughtered to fill his own table with venison steaks. It wouldn't occur to any of the Doc'alfar to kill foraging creatures that happened onto their gardens. No, but humans were not like the animals, for they were possessed of reason.

To the Doc'alfar way of thinking, then, that reason condemned them for actions against the precepts of Doc'alfar life.

When he thought of the horrid zombies, Juraviel shuddered and could not totally agree with the Doc'alfar ways. But neither could he deny that there was a consistent simplicity to that philosophy, and one that had more than a little justification.

He looked over at Brynn, who had settled back and seemed ready to sleep, and he did not press the point any further.

The pair felt the looks, most merely curious, but some truly suspicious, on them at all times as they walked the ways of Tymwyvenne over the next week. They were allowed practically free rein, except that they could not leave the city—King Eltiraaz didn't want to give away too much of the exact location, after all—and could not enter anything other than public structures unless invited, which they were not.

It was pleasant enough, though, and surely interesting. For Brynn, this was yet another new world, widening her already wide horizons; and for Belli'mar Juraviel, this was a glimpse into a different branch of his own history. Many of the Doc'alfar customs were familiar to him, the notes of their communal songs so similar to those of Caer'alfar that at times he was able to join in. But so much else was different, and strangely fascinating! His own people worked with the living, with great trees and flowers, blending into the harmony of the flora and fauna of Andur'Blough Inninness. The Doc'alfar, though, worked with the dead, with cut logs and zombie slaves. Their artisans carved masterwork pieces on the walls of every structure. Their armorers turned slabs of wood into fantastic shields and body pieces, backing them with thick mosslike blankets the gatherers brought in. Their culture seemed somewhat coarser to Juraviel, as much a matter of destruction as creation, but in truth, it seemed strangely beautiful to him, and equally harmonious with the ways of nature, if in a more severe manner.

Their guides through all of those days were again Lozan Duk and, surprisingly, Cazzira. The female Doc'alfar seemed much different to Juraviel and Brynn after the proclamation of King Eltiraaz, almost as if she now wanted to learn all that she could of the strangers, though whether that was out of any desire for friendship, or for the information to give her the edge over an enemy, neither Juraviel nor Brynn could tell. While Cazzira constantly peppered the pair with questions, Lozan Duk took the lead in pointing out landmarks and particularly interesting artworks. But it was Cazzira, and not Lozan Duk, who called Brynn aside into a building where the females of Tymwyvenne used paints and oils to highlight their beauty, to style their hair.

By the end of the week, Cazzira and Brynn were spending much time together, with Cazzira listening to Brynn's tale over and over again, leaning forward eagerly as the young ranger recounted it each time. Juraviel watched the pair curiously and closely, fearing that Cazzira was trying to pry valuable information from Brynn, but he did nothing to warn Brynn away from speaking too openly. The Doc'alfar were in complete command, and Juraviel and Brynn had no choice but to trust them and simply go along.

Still, Belli'mar Juraviel had a feeling, or perhaps it was just a desperate hope, that something good would come of the unexpected encounter.

"Belli'mar Juraviel was correct in telling us that this ranger is not akin to humans," Cazzira reported to King Eltiraaz one evening after hearing Brynn's tale yet again, from beginning to end. "If humans have such potential, then perhaps we should not be so quick—"

Eltiraaz held up his hand, stopping the uncomfortable thought short. "Our ways were created for prudence and survival," he explained. "They will not change quickly, whatever exception we might make for this unusual pair."

Cazzira sat back and considered the grim reality of Eltiraaz's words. She could be among the most hardened and callous of the Tylwyn Doc, but only through putting up an emotional wall, a barricade against guilt. Cazzira, however tough she might talk, did not enjoy the killings, even of inferior beings such as humans, though she surely held no love for the big and bumbling creatures.

"It may be time for some of our ways and tenets to change," King Eltiraaz admitted, catching his subject by surprise.

Cazzira looked at him curiously, blinking her blue eyes repeatedly.

"It may be time for us to explore beyond the boundaries of Tymwyvenne," the king went on after Cazzira had recovered.

"To the north or south?" Cazzira asked, her blue eyes narrowing as she scrutinized Eltiraaz, trying to discern his meaning. Did he want someone to head out to the north in search of Caer'alfar? Or was he suggesting that one of the Tylwyn Doc accompany the two strangers to the south, through the Path of Starless Night and onto the southern steppes?

"I think we would be ill-advised to approach this land, Andur'Blough Inninness, that Belli'mar Juraviel has told us about, without Belli'mar Juraviel to serve as our guide," Eltiraaz clarified. "Or to offer a formal introduction to his Lady Dasslerond, that she will take the time and effort to better learn of us before making any rash judgments."

"Are you asking me to walk the Path of Starless Night?"

"I am suggesting that perhaps one of the Tylwyn Doc should accompany Belli'mar Juraviel and Brynn Dharielle," Eltiraaz replied, somewhat defensively, sitting back in his throne and holding his hands up as if to fend off the legendary explosive wrath of Cazzira. "Am I asking you? No, not asking, Cazzira, not if you mean that I am somehow imploring you or commanding you to go. I am asking only in the sense that I am offering it to you first, as the first to make contact with these intriguing strangers."

Cazzira sat back, trying to hide the surprise from her fair features. It wasn't often that King Eltiraaz asked, truly asked, instead of commanded, for that was his place in Tylwyn Doc society. He was the king, bound to make those decisions that he thought most beneficial to the Tylwyn Doc people as a whole, whatever sacrifices any individual might have to make. Yet, here he was, *offering* the duty of accompanying Juraviel and Brynn to Cazzira. That told Cazzira exactly how important, and dangerous, that duty might prove to be. They were going to walk the Path of Starless Night, after all, and while Tylwyn Doc individuals and parties had sometimes ventured through the lightless tunnels, and To-gai-ru humans had exited them on the northern side of the mountains, most who entered those dark ways had never been heard from again.

"Do you think it wise that one of us accompany them?" King Eltiraaz asked, again surprising Cazzira.

"I do," she blurted before she could even sort through a more thorough and informative response.

Eltiraaz settled back, allowing her to collect her thoughts.

"This is an opportunity that we must explore," Cazzira went on after a while. "I did not wish to believe Belli'mar Juraviel when first I encountered and spoke with him. I thought him even worse, even more dangerous, than the human intruders who sometimes cross our lands. Here was a creature above those humans, a kin of ours, who perhaps held the power to destroy us utterly. We cannot let him walk away unobserved."

"And yet, I have come to understand that there is no such malice in Belli'mar Juraviel's heart, and if the rest of his people are of similar feelings toward the *Doc'alfar*"—King Eltiraaz stumbled over that Touel'alfar word, mimicking Juraviel's voice inflections as closely as possible—"then I believe we would be wise to make contact with our lost kin."

"It may be no more than wishful thinking."

King Eltiraaz gave a great sigh. "Perhaps. I feel that there is sincerity in Belli'mar Juraviel's words of friendship, but I am afraid," King Eltiraaz admitted. "In making such a choice to let him and Brynn Dharielle go, I am putting all of Tymwyvenne in danger."

"In allowing Belli'mar Juraviel and Brynn Dharielle to live, you are doing that," Cazzira replied. "Yet I do not, nor does anyone else, suggest that you kill them now. Indeed, if you chose to give Brynn to the bog and execute or imprison Juraviel, you would find opposition to that course, silent if not overt."

"From you?"

"No."

King Eltiraaz laughed at the honesty of those words. Cazzira was speaking plainly, and it seemed to Eltiraaz that she, too, preferred their present course toward the strangers. But fierce Cazzira never let compassion get in the way of prudence. "Yet I am not ready boldly to approach Lady Dasslerond," he admitted. "I am not ready to confront the past of Tylwyn Doc and Tylwyn Tou. I know my intuition toward Belli'mar Juraviel and his ranger companion, but it is just that, intuition. I will need more than that to attempt to bring the alfar together again."

Cazzira nodded with every word, understanding completely. "Then you need not ask me," she said. "It is right that one of us accompany Belli'mar Juraviel, to the south and then back again, if this way he comes. And it is right that I am the one. I first saw the pair."

"But it was Lozan Duk who suggested that Belli'mar Juraviel and Brynn Dharielle be captured and not killed," Eltiraaz reasoned.

"Qui'mielle Duk is with child," Cazzira replied without the slightest hesitation, referring to Lozan Duk's wife, who was indeed pregnant—the first pregnancy in Tymwyvenne in nearly forty years. "Lozan Duk should not leave."

King Eltiraaz stared long and hard into Cazzira's icy blue eyes, measuring her resolve.

*     *     *

Juraviel and Brynn removed their hoods on Cazzira's command, blinking their eyes against the brilliant late-summer sunlight. Despite Juraviel's original decision against a long delay, they had spent several weeks in Tymwyvenne, where the sun did not shine, and now the brilliant warmth felt good indeed!

So good that it took Juraviel a long while to realize that he and Cazzira and Brynn were apparently alone, with no sign of the contingent of more than a dozen other Doc'alfar who had accompanied them out of the city.

They were in the foothills of the giant mountains, so close that Juraviel understood that this area just north of the divide would be bathed in shadow at this time of day in a few weeks, when the sun lowered in the sky farther to the south.

"Where are we?" Brynn asked. "And where are your kinfolk?"

"We are where you said you wanted to be," Cazzira answered. "Close to it, at least. And why would the Tylwyn Doc wish to accompany you to the Path of Starless Night, a place where we do not often choose to go?"

"Then why are you here?"

Juraviel was sharing a stare with Cazzira as Brynn asked the question, reading her thoughts. "You intend to come with us," he reasoned, and when there came no immediate argument, he went on, "This is our road, one chosen by fate and by need. There is no reason—"

"My king believes that there is a reason," Cazzira interrupted. "You have wandered onto our lands, Belli'mar Juraviel. Do not pretend that your presence in Tymwyvenne means nothing to Tylwyn Doc, or to Tylwyn Tou. Perhaps it means nothing immediately significant, but now the races know of each other once more, and that is a door that, once opened, cannot be closed, for good or for ill."

"Unless I die in the southland, or on my way to the southland."

"Yet we still know of you, of Caer'alfar and Andur'Blough Inninness. And so King Eltiraaz would learn more. Slowly and in proper time. He would like to keep you in Tymwyvenne for many months, years perhaps, that he might truly learn your heart and your thoughts. But he cannot in good conscience, of course—and despite my counsel—because of your need to be away to the south."

"We are grateful for King Eltiraaz's understanding of our situation."

"And he wishes your response to be the gratitude of a friend," Cazzira said. "He hopes that more will come of our chance meeting—much more. Thus, he must continue his exploration of Belli'mar Juraviel's heart, through Cazzira, who serves as his eyes and ears."

"And what of me?" Brynn asked, her tone showing that she felt a bit left out.

"You are still alive, and on your way," Cazzira replied, never taking her stare from Juraviel. "Be pleased, Brynn Dharielle, for that is more than most humans who wander onto the land of Tylwyn Doc can ever say!"

Brynn sighed and did not press the point.

"And so you will serve as King Eltiraaz's eyes and ears all the way to the entrance to the Path of Starless Night?" Juraviel asked.

Cazzira gave a little laugh and swept around, waving her arm out toward a dark shadow at the base of a nearby jag of stone. "We are at the entrance," she explained, pulling off her pack as she spoke. She untied and opened the pack, producing three of the blue-white glowing torches, tossing one to each of her companions while keeping the third for herself. "The continuation of your road, the beginning of my own."

Cazzira started toward the shadowy opening, but Juraviel grabbed her arm to stop her. She turned about and the two locked stares again.

"This is not your business," Juraviel said.

"Is it yours?"

"It is because Lady Dasslerond decided that it was."

"As it is mine because King Eltiraaz decided that it was," Cazzira answered. "Perhaps the Tylwyn Doc have no place in the affairs of the Tylwyn Tou, or in the affairs of the To-gai-ru or any humans at all. Or perhaps we simply do not trust you enough to let you walk out freely. That is what we intend to discover. Consider my company the price of your freedom, if you must: a return favor from Belli'mar Juraviel and Brynn Dharielle."

Juraviel continued to stare at Cazzira for a long, long while, and then he blinked and gave a helpless, defeated laugh. How could he refuse her companionship after the amazing trust the Doc'alfar had placed in him and in Brynn?

Another part of Belli'mar Juraviel wondered why he would *want* to refuse her, as well. Would it not be more pleasant for him to have another along who understood his perspective of the world, the elven viewpoint? Brynn was a fine companion, but she was a human, and would soon be among her own kind, heavily involved in their politics and ways, and during that transition, Juraviel knew that he would be little more than a distant observer. Perhaps those days would be brighter indeed with the companionship of one more akin to him.

Besides, there was something about Cazzira that Juraviel found quite appealing, despite her stern face—or possibly, because of it. Her often fiery and volatile remarks reminded him of another he had once known, a Touel'alfar named Tuntun who had been his dearest friend. Cazzira even looked a bit like Tuntun.

"Lead on," he said, and so she did, and so Cazzira and Juraviel and Brynn entered a narrow tunnel that widened into a large and airy cave. Two exits ran off the back of the cave, deeper into the mountains, and Cazzira considered each for a few moments, then nodded and went into the one to the left.

Soon all daylight was left behind, the trio entering a darkness so profound that, without the strange torches, they would not have been able to see a hand flapping an inch from their faces.

# CHAPTER 8

# *Trial of Faith*

"The child will be of full consciousness," Yakim Douan said to his newest gathering of Yatols, most of them from the region just interior to Jacintha. The Chezru Chieftain had chosen the invitation lists to his meetings very carefully, pulling together disparate, often feuding, priests. He didn't want any secret alliances building, to fester during the time when he would be most vulnerable. Thus, in the small gatherings during which he would give the traditional Transcendence speech, Yakim drew together opposing Yatols, such as Peridan and De Hamman, who would never trust each other enough to form any destructive alliances.

"What does that truly mean, God-Voice?" asked Yatol Bohl, who led a flock at the great Dahdah Oasis, nine days' journey west of Jacintha. "Will the child be able to speak? Words or sentences?"

Yakim studied Bohl carefully. At thirty, he was among the youngest of the Yatol priests, and he was certainly among the most fit. He ruled Dahdah with an iron hand, Yakim knew, collecting outrageous fees for shelter and supplies from any caravan coming in from the west toward Jacintha, or heading out to the west from the main city. No doubt, Yatol Grysh had been forced to reach deep into his pockets for a needed stop at Dahdah on his way back to Dharyan.

"Full consciousness," Yakim replied. "The child, of no more than a year, will be able to speak as fluently as you or I. The child will know of our ways, will know of me, his predecessor, and will know of his destiny."

"Surely a peasant mother seeking to elevate her family could teach—"

"The child will know more of Yatol and the Chezru religion than any peasant could possibly guess," Yakim interrupted the ever-petulant Bohl. "You will see, you will understand, and you will believe."

"God-Voice, please do not believe that I am a doubter," Yatol Bohl said, holding his hands out wide, assuming a posture of perfect innocence.

Yakim Douan just smiled at the pose. He knew exactly that, of course, that Bohl and all the others, except for those most pious, like the poor fool Merwan Ma, held grave doubts about the Transcendence, the mystical hand-off of power to the next Chezru Chieftain. Of course they did—how could they not? For someone to believe that a baby, an infant, would arise speaking fluently and knowing all the secrets of their culture's wisest priests was a stretch, certainly, a test of faith against logic, of belief against experience.

How well Yakim Douan could sympathize with those doubts! He remembered that time, so many hundreds of years before, when he had first learned of the Transcendence. Things were done very differently back then, for it was not the Chezru Chieftain delivering a speech such as this one. No, the Chezru Chieftain would die, often unexpectedly, and then the leaders of the Chezru religion would initiate the search.

Yakim Douan, a young Yatol, had been just a bit older than Bohl was now when he had participated in that search those centuries ago. He remembered how full of eagerness, full of great joy he had been at the thought that he was about to witness a miracle, a confirmation of his faith that every man so desires, whether he admits it or not. They had discovered the blessed infant soon after, and full of anticipation and the expectation of extreme joy, Yakim Douan had gone in to witness the miracle child.

And he had found a baby. Not a blessed baby, not a miracle child speaking the words of Yatol, but a normal baby.

The leaders of Chezru, their names lost to him now, had

told him and the other Yatols of the "miracles" they had witnessed the child perform, of the words they had heard this
goo-gooing infant speaking. Many of the other Yatols had
taken those proclamations as proof enough that this was indeed the miracle child, the new God-Voice of Yatol.

But Yakim Douan had known better. He had understood instinctively that this baby was nothing more than a pawn,
through which the leaders of the Yatol priests could spend the
rest of their days in control of the religion, and thus, of all
Behren.

He knew.

And so he understood the doubts and the fears that Yatols
such as Bohl must now be feeling in this time of approaching
crisis. If Yakim could only hand them enough teasing to hold
them in check until after the birth, until they saw proof positive that their faith was not misplaced, that the selected child
was indeed the God-Voice, then men like Bohl could become
very valuable allies to the next incarnation.

"When I was chosen, I knew as much about the truth of
Yatol as I do now," he told them all. "I could recite the Verses
of Propriety as well as I can now . . ." He gave a little laugh.
"No, better, for then my physical body had not begun to fail
me, my memory did not lapse as it sometimes does now."

The gathering of ten Yatols all chuckled at the Chezru
Chieftain's uncharacteristic comedy—all except for Yatol Bohl,
who sat staring hard at Douan, obviously taking a careful
measure of the man.

Yakim resisted the temptation to call him on that look, and
merely smiled disarmingly in response.

"You are human, reasoning beings, and so you hold your
doubts," he said, and there came a chorus of denials, to which
Yakim merely looked away and held up his hands. "It is the
expected response, my children, for you cannot make logical
sense of faith. Who here has seen the paradise of the afterlife?" He paused and let the gathered Yatols all look to each
other questioningly. "Nay, you cannot see the spirit or hear
the spirit. For you in your current state of existence, only the
empty and lifeless corpse remains, and logic would tell you,
then, that death is the end of consciousness.

"I know better, and I tell you that this Transcendence will show you, too, that there is more to this existence than what our physical senses can show us. When you look upon the reincarnated God-Voice, when you hear him speak the words of Truth, you will know and you will be content.

"Fear not for those doubts you now harbor," Yakim went on, trying to hold that fierce edge of passion in his voice, trying not to lapse into the simple recitation of this, a speech he had spoken many times over the centuries. "Fear not that you will be disappointed, and fear not that your doubts somehow mark you as less than true to Yatol. You are supposed to question and supposed to doubt! Else, how will you be certain that you have selected the correct child? Question and doubt everything! When you find the new God-Voice, your questions will catch in your throats and your doubts will vanish so completely that you will be befuddled as to how you ever held them. And then you will know true peace, my children, for then you will understand the truth of your faith. To witness a miracle is to ease the fear of dying itself. Look upon those few living Yatols who remember the last Transcendence! See the contentment in their old eyes, my children, and take heart that you, too, will know that supreme comfort."

It was true enough. Only three Yatols remained alive who remembered the last Transcendence, when Yakim Douan had been identified as the next God-Voice of Yatol, and those three were considered among the happiest of all the Yatol priests. Happy because they had seen a miracle and knew that heaven awaited them. Happy because they understood the value of their lives in service to Yatol.

Happy because Yakim Douan had ultimately deceived them.

When the gathering dispersed a short while later, most of the Yatols left the audience chamber grinning and speaking excitedly about the coming Transcendence. Two notable exceptions caught Yakim Douan's eye and attention as he watched the departing flock. Merwan Ma sat at the side of the stage, in the shadows, staring at him with a long look upon his face. The man was deeply troubled by Yakim's expected and hoped-for death, the Chezru Chieftain knew, and was deeply troubled by his own inability to accept that reality, to brush aside his logical fears of mortality and logical sadness at losing a man he considered as mentor and friend.

His posture and his fears did not bother Yakim Douan, though, for he knew that Merwan Ma would rejoice when the God-Voice was discovered. The Chezru Chieftain decided then and there that when they found him, one of his first spoken revelations would be to tell poor Merwan Ma that Yakim Douan was still with him, looking over him and taking pride that his student was performing his ultimately important duties so very well.

The second exception to the common joy troubled Yakim Douan much more, though, for Yatol Bohl left the chamber neither smiling nor chatting excitedly. His face was stern and locked into an expression of deepest reflection.

That one could prove to be dangerous, Yakim Douan knew. He was young and strong and eager and impatient. And he was ambitious—too much so, perhaps, to sublimate himself to a mere child. The one true concern that had followed Yakim Douan through his centuries of power was the weakness of true spirituality in the face of human emotions. A Yatol priest, for all of his piousness, even heroics, in the eyes of the church, could only ascend so far, could never be greater than the second rank of the hierarchy. Certainly if Bohl witnessed the selected child, the God-Voice who could tell him of the Yatol tenets and codes as well as any scholar priest, then he would be convinced and would put aside his earthly ambitions and human weaknesses.

But would Yatol Bohl show enough patience? Would he wait the nearly two years it would take after Yakim Douan's death to even find the new Chezru? Or was he plotting a more direct route to install a new leader of Yatol?

Yakim Douan smiled knowingly. The same magic that allowed the deception of Transcendence would soon provide him with practical information.

"We are to wait years to be disappointed?" Yatol Bohl asked his guest, Yatol Thei'a'hu, incredulously. "Surely you cannot believe this chatter of a speaking infant!"

"Chezru Chieftain Douan has asked us to trust in our faith,

and what is faith without trust?" replied the other Yatol, older than Bohl by more than a decade and seeming worn and thin, with sleepy eyes and a badly balding head, and a jaw that constantly trembled from a disease he had contracted many years before. "Are we to believe in the miracle of Paradise if we cannot hold faith in this relatively minor miracle?"

"Minor?" Bohl echoed with the same unyielding skepticism. "An infant is to recite the tenets of Yatol? An infant? Have you even known an infant to speak in a complete sentence, Yatol, let alone in any manner that makes sense?"

"Minor," Yatol Thei'a'hu insisted. "If Yatol can fashion Paradise, if Yatol can transcend death, then how can you doubt this?"

Bohl settled back on his comfortable seat, a relatively shapeless stuffed bag, and took a deep draw on the hose extending from a watery tube beside him. "And yet, you doubt it, too, for all of your reasoning now. Else, friend, why are you here?"

Yatol Thei'a'hu similarly sat back on his shapeless chair, staring at his counterpart. Bohl's words were true enough, he had to admit to himself. His feelings toward this impending Transcendence were not positive at all, and his expression and posture showed that clearly. In truth, Thei'a'hu had never been overly fond of Yakim Douan, and had often privately disagreed with the man. While he accepted the Chezru Chieftain's unchallenged leadership and obeyed Douan's commands to the letter, Douan had made several very damaging decisions concerning Yatol Thei'a'hu's province of Eh'thu, located two weeks to the south and west of Jacintha. Ten years before, Douan had clipped off the northernmost stretch of Thei'a'hu's province and given it to Yatol Presh, who rode with the nomads of Tossionas Desert, in an effort to settle the often-troublesome nomadic warriors. That ploy had hardly worked, for the Tossionas nomads were causing as much grief as ever, and yet, that redrawing of province lines had cost Thei'a'hu an important oasis. For all of his faith, Yatol Thei'a'hu could hardly believe that Douan's decision had been god-inspired—how could Yatol have made such an obvious mistake? That was the most grievous example, but there were others, always gnawing at the reasonable Thei'a'hu's logic.

"For centuries, we have followed the Transcendence of Yatol," Thei'a'hu said. "When the Chezru dies, the search begins for the next God-Voice, and that God-Voice will be identified through the miracle of premature knowledge and voice. That is our way, and so Chezru Douan prepares us now for the next Transcendence. What would you have us do, Yatol Bohl? Are we to seize the title for ourselves? Do you believe that the other two hundred Yatols of Behren will accept a religious coup?"

"I have suggested no such thing!" Bohl sputtered in reply.

"Then what?"

"We must be aware and alert," the fiery young Yatol insisted. "We must insinuate ourselves into the process of the search, to find a child who will be sympathetic to our needs."

"You believe that you can know such a thing about an infant? You believe that you can find a child who will be acceptable to the other Yatols, if this child is not speaking as Chezru Douan has told us?"

"Do you believe that there will be such a child, a clear-cut God-Voice speaking the tenets as fluently as our present Chezru Chieftain?"

Thei'a'hu settled back even farther at the continuing blunt, bordering on heretical, declarations of Yatol Bohl. That was it, was it not? Either they believed that such a creature would be born into their midst, literally as Chezru Douan had said, or they did not. And if they did not, then perhaps they would do well to find a child whose mother would favor Bohl and Thei'a'hu.

"My friend, if such a child is found, then perhaps we should abandon our selection and fall in line with the others," Bohl went on. "And if not, then what have we lost?"

"If we find a bright child to elevate, there remains the problem of Chezru Douan's choice of Shepherd Merwan Ma as tutor and mentor for the child," Yatol Thei'a'hu reminded. "Merwan Ma above all others will help to shape the next Chezru, and he is likely of similar mind and heart as Douan, else he would not have been chosen. That heart is not sympathetic for Eh'thu, I am sure."

"Merwan Ma is insignificant," Yatol Bohl insisted. "He will be a minor player in the future of Yatol."

"Not according to Chezru Douan."

"Who will be dead and buried," the other reminded.

Yatol Thei'a'hu narrowed his sleepy eyes at the obvious threat, for Bohl's tone made it quite clear that he believed he could have Merwan Ma eliminated, if the need arose, and that he would not hesitate to do so.

Yakim Douan watched it all with a considerable amount of amusement—for he, too, was in that quiet room in the luxurious northern quarter of Jacintha. Not physically. Physically, Yakim Douan was in Chom Deiru, the Chezru palace in Jacintha, in his meditation room, where none would dare disturb his private communion with Yatol. Little did they know that his true communion on that day, as on many, was with a certain hematite, a magical soul stone. Using that magic, Yakim walked out of his body, his spirit silently making its way along the streets, following troublesome Yatol Bohl to his temporary quarters in the city.

How convenient that Bohl had chosen that very day, the same day as the speech of Transcendence, to further his nefarious plotting with Yatol Thei'a'hu.

It saddened Yakim Douan to learn that Thei'a'hu was in on Bohl's growing conspiracy. He had always been rather fond of the man, and though he knew that Thei'a'hu harbored some resentment about the loss of his northern reaches, Yakim hadn't imagined that his decision had put the man so far into Bohl's dangerous court.

Bohl's last statement, though, hinting at eliminating Merwan Ma, had not surprised Yakim Douan in the least. He understood Bohl well, had over the centuries seen many men of similar impatience and weakened faith. Indeed, Yakim Douan was one of them!

How could he not sympathize with Bohl? The man, who obviously wasn't sold on the specific concept of Yatol Paradise, was merely being pragmatic, much as the disillusioned

Yakim Douan had acted pragmatically those centuries before when he had discovered his own secret to immortality, one that made logical sense to him.

If he had a body about him at that moment, Yakim Douan would have issued a revealing sigh. In looking at Bohl, so much a younger version of his own first incarnation, Yakim Douan considered, and not for the first time, not even for the hundredth time, that he had the power to offer true immortality to others, a select few, perhaps, friends and lovers who could coast through the centuries beside him. His was not necessarily a lonely existence, for in each incarnation as God-Voice, he was able to surround himself with friends, and certainly the Chezru Chieftain had little trouble in finding the carnal companionship of many, many women.

But what might it be like to walk the centuries with another? With Bohl, perhaps, or Merwan Ma?

It was a passing thought, as always. For taking such a course would surely invite great risk. A companion who knew the truth of the hematite and Transcendence might speak out to a friend, or might allow himself to fall in love and wish to take yet another on the century-walking journey. Or even worse, a companion might harbor ambitions to become the God-Voice, threatening a position that Yakim Douan did not wish to relinquish.

For who but a pragmatic, not overly spiritual man might Yakim Douan convince to follow him on his eternal journey. Only a man like young Yakim, or like Bohl, a man who harbored innermost doubts about Yatol, would desire this journey, and a man such as that, Yakim Douan knew firsthand, could not truly be trusted. A man without the true belief in Paradise, and thus, without the true fear of Yatol, was a man who desired to make Paradise his own in this life.

Whatever the cost.

His body would have sighed again had it been there, as Yakim Douan realized what he now had to do to eliminate this latest threat, to eliminate Yatol Bohl.

And yes, he realized, Yatol Thei'a'hu, as well.

How might he do that without causing a major disruption in all the church, a ripple that would shake the groundwork he had struggled so hard to put in place? If it was but one man, one caravan, he could order his Chezhou-Lei warriors out, disguised as bandits. Even if the great warriors were recognized by any survivors of that caravan for who they were, no one would believe mere escorts. But two Yatol priests and two caravans?

It would have to be orchestrated carefully and over time.

*Over time.* Yakim Douan was biting his lip in frustration even as he reentered his corporeal form back in the palace. He did not want to delay the resolution to this newest problem, did not want to spend the next weeks—even months, perhaps in executing the deserving Yatols, then waiting for the results to shake out.

"But how might . . ." he started to say, but he stopped short, his lips curling into a wicked grin.

He went right back out in spiritual form, leaping through the hematite portal, then soaring across the city to the house occupied by Yatol Thei'a'hu. He found the man lying in a bath, surrounded by pretty, scantily clad young attendants, both male and female. Yakim considered the scene with both pity and amusement. It was common knowledge that Thei'a'hu had lost his ability to perform sexually, and so it had been rumored that the man took his pleasures vicariously.

Pitiful wretch.

Ignoring those standing about the Yatol, Yakim Douan's spirit soared right to the reclining man, and right into the reclining man.

Yatol Thei'a'hu's eyes popped open wide and he let out a shriek that turned all heads in the room his way. Some of those onlookers started to approach him, but then they all backed off, eyes wide with shock, as Thei'a'hu thrashed about in his tub, splashing soapy water all about the room.

His mouth opened and twisted as if he was trying to spout out some words, some cry for help, and indeed he was.

But he had no control. For Yakim Douan was in there with him, two spirits, two wills, fighting for control over one body. Muscles knotted and twisted from contrasting signals. Eyes bulged and Thei'a'hu's mouth continued to twist and snap, biting into his lip and tongue.

*Do you know me, Yatol Thei'a'hu?* Yakim Douan's spirit telepathically demanded.

The body stopped thrashing, lying very still in what remained of the bathwater.

*Look upon me!* Yakim Douan went on. *Let your heart tell you who has come to visit!*

*Chezru Chieftain Douan?* Thei'a'hu's mind silently asked.

*That is one incarnation,* came the teasing, cryptic response.

The onlookers in the room, some of them just gathering the nerve to approach the man once again, leaped back as Thei'a'hu's body jerked in surprise.

*Yatol! Yatol! Yatol!* Thei'a'hu's spirit screamed.

*You are a nonbeliever!* Yakim Douan accused. *You disappoint me, Yatol Thei'a'hu.*

*No!*

*You consort with heretics who deny the truth of Yatol!*

Thei'a'hu's call, both telepathic and physical, held the inflections of a whimper then, as he repeated over and over, "Mercy."

*Correct your sacrilege, Yatol Thei'a'hu! This night! Now! You have but one chance to again walk the path to Paradise!* Yakim Douan ended by imparting more specific visual instructions, and then he departed Thei'a'hu's physical body, his spirit drifting up to the ceiling to observe, and though he was invisible and silent, those others in the room sensed that spirit, or something. Yakim Douan was amused again to watch the looks of confusion and fear upon their faces, to see the hairs standing up on the back of their necks, to see the women hugging themselves as if suddenly chilled. The Chezru Chieftain even went back down among them, a cold ghost brushing close, heightening the fear. More than one of those attendants ran out of the room, screaming.

But the show hadn't even yet begun, Yakim Douan knew, and so he continued to watch, taking great pleasure as Yatol Thei'a'hu climbed out of the tub, pushing past any attendants who moved to help him, or to try to put a robe about his naked shoulders.

Thei'a'hu did have a blanket wrapped about him as he exited the house, more to ward the chill than out of any modesty, for it was obvious to all looking upon him, Yakim Douan's spirit included, that the man was suddenly obsessed and single-minded.

That blanket also conveniently hid the tool Thei'a'hu would need to find his way back to Paradise.

The visiting Yatols had all been quartered in the same area, and so Thei'a'hu did not have far to walk to get to the house of Yatol Bohl, pushing right through the two soldiers standing guard at the door and banging on it loudly. When it was opened, by yet another soldier, Yatol Thei'a'hu did not wait to offer an explanation, but just forced his way through, screaming for Yatol Bohl.

The man came down the sweeping staircase at the back of the foyer a moment later, dressed exactly as he had been when Yatol Thei'a'hu had left him three hours earlier.

"Thei'a'hu," he said, obviously stunned at the man's appearance. "What is wrong?"

Thei'a'hu stormed up to him, Bohl holding his arms wide, his expression incredulous.

That look grew even more incredulous when Thei'a'hu's knife jabbed into his belly.

"Heretic! Unbeliever!" Thei'a'hu cried, pumping his arm repeatedly, and with the strength of a man possessed and with the determination of a man who truly believed that his own salvation was at stake.

By the time Bohl's stunned soldiers could restrain the intruding Yatol, Yatol Bohl lay curled on the floor, his lifeblood pouring out into a widening puddle that already took in more than half of the foyer.

Hovering above the entryway, the spirit of Yakim Douan watched it all, with a bit of regret, but in truth, thoroughly enjoying the spectacle. He considered his voyeurism there and felt a twang of guilt, wondering if he was no better than Thei'a'hu, taking his pleasure vicariously.

It mattered not, he decided, and he retreated back to his waiting corporeal form, preparing himself, for he knew that Yatol Thei'a'hu would soon be paraded before him to answer for the crime of murder.

Yakim Douan decided to play this delicately, and with ultimate contempt for those around him. He would hear Thei'a'hu's story, then would retreat to consult with Yatol, then would return and proclaim Thei'a'hu a hero of Yatol.

The old Chezru Chieftain was still chuckling at the beautiful irony of it all when Merwan Ma rushed into his meditation room to tell him that he was needed in the audience chamber immediately.

# CHAPTER 9

## *Dark Solitude*

The Path of Starless Night offered a darkness beyond anything that Brynn had ever known, deeper even than the blackness of the peat cave. Walking the tunnels, descending under the mountains beside Juraviel and Cazzira, Brynn began to understand a second element to the darkness, a profound sense of brooding, a quiet so intense that it numbed the ears and made her retreat within herself. She tried to consider the goal ahead, tried to find strength and determination in the realization that this dark path marked the end of her journey home. When they exited the Path of Starless Night, they would look upon To-gai, the grassy steppes of her homeland.

Brynn couldn't hold the thought against the pounding silence, stifling and seeming almost hungry.

They had lamps, those curious glass-and-wood creations of the Doc'alfar, all glowing bluish white. But even the light seemed uncomfortable there, diminished and out of place. Given the limited range of the glow, it occurred to Brynn that their lamps served to highlight them to predators more than they revealed any predators to them.

The air was warm and still—so still that it settled about them like a heavy blanket, weighing down their steps. The tunnel was broken and uneven, so that even they, two elves and an elven-trained ranger, had to take care with every step not to stub their toes or trip and fall. Similarly, the walls were broken, with jags of stone all about, casting ominous shadows in the dim light.

"How much worse are these shadows in the flickering light of a flaming torch," Cazzira said suddenly, her voice breaking the stillness so starkly that both Juraviel and Brynn jumped. "With each flicker, the shadows come to life," Cazzira went on. "Many died in here in times long past, before we learned the secrets of the fazl pods. Those who traveled these paths became so numbed to any danger from the repeated dancing of the shadows that when real danger presented itself, they were caught unawares."

Brynn regarded her glowing scepter, its carved wood handle and the frosted glass ball set at its top. The light was fairly constant, but in looking closely, the ranger did note that there were some things moving about within the frosted sphere.

"Fazl pods?" Juraviel asked, as if reading Brynn's mind.

"Small centipedes of the deep peat," Cazzira explained. "They make the light, though it normally dissipates into the air like a glowing mist. Encased in an airless globe, they glow for many weeks. Without them, we would have little chance of crossing under the mountains, for we could not carry enough wood and I doubt we'll find any down here!"

The conversation died at that, and the trio went on. They came to many forks in the trail, and intersections, and crossed a few wider chambers, some that had many exits. But Cazzira went on in seeming confidence that she knew the way, and it took Brynn a long while to catch on to the secret: all choices in the path had been marked, subtly, in flowing elven script delicately carved upon the walls.

"Your people come down here often," she said, and she winced, for her words sounded as an accusation.

Cazzira looked at her hard, as did Juraviel, the Touel'alfar silently signaling for Brynn to tread cautiously.

"You know the way, because the passages have been marked by Tylwyn Doc, I mean," Brynn stuttered, trying hard to keep her tone nonconfrontational. "Your people are not strangers to the Path of Starless Night, I would assume."

"We used to come in here quite often," Cazzira answered after a long pause. "Once, many centuries ago, Tymwyvenne was comprised of two settlements, the one you have walked and one in here."

"Why was the second abandoned?" Juraviel asked before

Brynn could, the elf apparently past his trepidation at broaching the subject.

"The reasons are many, but in truth, this is not our place. Dark things crawl along these corridors, and after a few more days in here, you will understand why we prefer the open air."

"I understand it already," Brynn remarked, and Juraviel laughed in agreement.

They walked through the rest of the day—to the best of their estimation—and set a camp in a small side chamber, placing their glowing lamps strategically in the corridor outside, so that whoever was on watch would see the approach of a threat before it saw them.

The next day went the same way, with brief conversations punctuating the silent blackness. The second day, Cazzira showed them some moss and fungi that they could eat, and some other mushrooms that they would be wise to avoid. On and on they walked, and oftentimes crawled in corridors too low for even the two elves, and then set a similar camp.

The next day was much the same, and the next after that, and the next after that, where the only highlight was the discovery of a small stream where they could refill their waterskins, and even bathe a bit. Brynn was glad of that, very glad, but despite the clear water, every day they got a bit dirtier and a bit smellier.

On and on they walked, and the paths were so winding, left and right, that they had to wonder how much progress they were really making to the south. At times, the trail before them ascended at such an angle that they had to climb hand over hand, struggling for finger- and toeholds. At other times, the path dropped so dramatically that they had to take out the fine silken ropes Cazzira's kin had provided, and slide down.

None of them complained; they just kept putting one foot in front of the other.

So many wondrous things did Brynn, Juraviel, and Cazzira see in the days to come: a wide underground lake, its water gently lapping at the shore, disturbed somewhere out in the darkness by something unseen and unknown; an underground waterfall, tumbling noisily, echoing like tumultuous music in all of the caverns and corridors about; strange and beautiful formations of crystals squeezed from the rocks, twisting and turning into exotic, shining shapes as they became pushed out over the eons.

The trio were walking through another wondrous place, a three-tiered plateau of gigantic mushrooms, thicker of trunk than a large oak and thrice Brynn's height, when they came to know, for the first time, that they were not alone.

It came as a flicker of movement, a subtle brushing of darker shadows at the edge of Brynn's consciousness. The woman couldn't react defensively, couldn't get her staff up to intercept the rushing creature as it ran past her, but she did let out an alarmed yelp.

His muscles toned to their finest warrior edge, Belli'mar Juraviel dove immediately to the side, launching himself into a somersault. As he came around, easily finding his feet again, he noted the shiny line of a thick blade, slashing through the air where he had just been. He started to call out to Cazzira, but saw that the Doc'alfar was already exploding into motion.

She came around on her tiptoes, her arms out wide, her small, golden-wood club flying at the end of one extended limb. She whipped it past the dark attacker, too far away for a strike, but with enough of a whipping sound to freeze the creature in place for an instant.

That was all Brynn needed. As the creature jerked upright, the woman dashed forward, slipping her bow between its widespread legs. She caught the leading edge of her bow with her now free hand and continued on, lowering her shoulder as she lifted with both hands, slamming into the creature, which was somewhat smaller than she, while her lifting bow took away its balance.

Down it went, crashing to the floor.

Before Brynn could pursue, she noted other movement, all about, and she came up just in time to set herself in a defensive posture against a second attacker.

"Goblins!" Juraviel yelled, as a pair of the creatures rushed through a well-lit area, their ugly features showing clearly. The elf leaped toward Brynn, then fell into another roll to avoid the thrust of a pair of spears.

Brynn shifted her bow out toward him, and Juraviel grabbed on, welcoming the momentum assist as Brynn pulled him right past her, to dive into yet another roll that brought him up between Brynn and Cazzira, and closer to the Doc'alfar. He started toward her, alarmed, but realized almost at once that Cazzira needed no help at that time.

Her movements were every bit as fluid, graceful, and beautiful as *bi'nelle dasada*, the elven sword dance. She twirled about, spinning on a pointed toe, leaping and kicking, and all the while shifting her small club from hand to hand, letting it flow out from her, an extension of her perfectly controlled body.

She seemed to leave an opening, and a goblin rushed in at her back, spear leading.

But Cazzira spun and the spear went past her turning back, and the goblin got too close, inside the reach of her club.

The crack was so pronounced that Juraviel and Brynn figured the Doc'alfar's club must have split apart, but when the strike was finished, Cazzira continued her dance, intact weapon in hand, and the goblin skidded down and lay very still, the side of its head caved in.

Cazzira's club swiped past another goblin, which hunched back out of range, then came on, for it seemed clear that the diminutive Cazzira had overbalanced.

Nothing could have been further from the truth. The club went sliding harmlessly past, but the Doc'alfar flipped it over to her other hand, her left hand, weaving against the flow of her body as she turned right to left. Her left turned under and handed the club back to her right, reversing the weapon so that Cazzira took its thick end.

Out snapped that right hand, stabbing the thinner, handle end of the club into the face of the attacker, whose own momentum worked against it.

Two goblins down and the dance went on.

Belli'mar Juraviel's fascination with the tantalizing dance of Cazzira nearly cost him dearly, for the goblins coming at him paid no heed to anything other than their intended prey.

The elf got his sword out in front to parry one spear and force the wielder of the second to hold back its thrust.

And then Brynn was there, right behind the attacking pair, her bow-staff held horizontally before her with widespread hands. She punched out, left and right, smacking both goblins hard, one on the back of the head, one on the shoulder, and both stumbled forward.

Where Juraviel's fine-tipped sword stabbed them, one-two, one-two.

The elf spun about, and Brynn leaped up beside him, but the remaining goblins on the flank ran off screaming and shouting, shadowy forms blending into the darkness.

Both Brynn and Juraviel spun about to regard Cazzira, who seemed stuck in place, like a statue fashioned after a dancer caught in a pose, one arm extended above her head, her weapon held perpendicularly to it, back over and across her head, and her other arm out before her like some targeting instrument. She was up on one foot—on one toe, actually—with her other leg looped about the supporting limb, lending to her perfect balance.

No goblins approached; no goblins, save those on the ground about her, were to be seen.

"We must move from this place," Juraviel said. "To tighter tunnels where goblins cannot throw spears at us from the shadows!"

"Some are wounded," Brynn remarked, but if that meant anything to the two elves, they did not reveal it.

"Away! Away!" Juraviel demanded, and on the trio ran, past the towering mushrooms and out of the wide chamber, rushing down one narrow corridor.

Around the first bend, Juraviel, in the lead, came face-to-face with yet another goblin, its sickly eyes wide with surprise.

A fine sword slid into its belly; a club came past Juraviel's shoulder to smash it in the face.

The three ran over it as it fell back, stomping it flat to the stone.

They heard the loud flapping of wide goblin feet in pursuit sometime later.

Brynn handed her lamp to Juraviel, then strung her bow as they ran, and when the sound closed in at their backs, she turned suddenly and let fly, her arrow disappearing into the darkness. She knew not if she hit anything, or if her arrow skipped harmlessly across the stones, but the sound of pursuit stopped for a bit, and the three ran on.

They crossed a large chamber, keeping near to the wall, then turned into the first opening, only to hear goblins, many goblins!

They passed that, and the second opening and the third, as well. Then, using nothing more than a simple guess, they charged down the next. In the dim light of her glowing lamp, Cazzira in the lead nearly stumbled over the edge of a precipice. She fell to her knees, watching in horror as a few loose stones fell before her, dropping out of sight.

Seconds later, the three heard the echoes of the stones bouncing along the deeper rocks.

"Back!" Juraviel yelled. "Quickly, before the goblins cut us off!"

"They already have!" cried Brynn.

"There is a way!" said Cazzira, pointing to the right, past the precipice.

Peering into the gloom, just at the edge of the lights, Brynn noted a rocky descending trail that seemed full of loose stones. She was about to point out the obvious danger there, but Juraviel and Cazzira weren't waiting, with the Doc'alfar leaping out and beginning her controlled slide, and Juraviel hopping out behind her, his wings flapping furiously so that he put as little weight on the unstable slope as possible.

Brynn turned and let fly another couple of arrows, wanting the other two to be far below before she tried the slope with her greater mass. Then she went out, gingerly, and lay out on her side, using her bow like a guiding oar as she slid down, down, into the deeper blackness.

She caught up to Juraviel and Cazzira at an apparent dead end: a lip overlooking a deep, deep drop.

The two were working furiously—to set up some defense, Brynn figured at first, but she looked on curiously as they unpacked the fine silken rope, Cazzira taking one end and handing the bulk of it to Juraviel.

With a shared nod, the Touel'alfar leaped out into the blackness, wings beating furiously. He disappeared from sight, but the fact that the rope didn't seem to be tugging at all gave Brynn hope that his descent was controlled, at least.

"He has found footing," Cazzira told Brynn a few seconds later.

Brynn glanced back to see Cazzira tying off the rope around the stub of a stalagmite with one of her patented slip-knots. Holding the rope in both hands, the Doc'alfar set her feet against the mound and pulled with all her strength, tightening the slack as much as possible.

"Use your belt," she said to Brynn, then she looped her own belt over the rope and swung out, sliding away into the darkness.

Leaving Brynn, who had given her lamp to Juraviel, in absolute darkness, and with the sounds of goblins approaching.

The woman worked furiously, pulling off her belt and falling down to her knees, groping her way to the stalagmite mound and the taut rope. She had no time to pause and consider what she was about to do, no time to yell out and make sure that Cazzira was clear and she could come on, no time even to shout and ask how far she would have to slide. She just looped her belt over the rope, grabbed up her precious bow, and slipped out, tucking her feet defensively as she blindly slid over the rim of a deep chasm.

Juraviel and Cazzira put up lamps to guide her in on the other end, the pair standing on a landing, with a dark tunnel behind them. As soon as Brynn touched down, Cazzira grabbed up the rope and gave a deft twist and tug that detached it across the way.

They pulled it in and ran on, and this time, with a gorge blocking the way behind them, they did not hear the flapping feet of goblin pursuit. Still, they went on for a long, long time, until sheer exhaustion stopped them. They made their camp in as defensible a position as they could find, set their order of watch, and, despite their nervousness, each of them slept soundly.

\*          \*          \*

They moved off with all speed the next day, along the only tunnel available to them, though Cazzira admitted that she had little idea of where they were.

"In Tymwyvenne, we have a saying that most who perish in the Path of Starless Night do so of old age," she told them with a half-hearted chuckle. If she was trying to be humorous, neither of the other two caught it.

They seemed to be going generally in the right direction, south, as far as their instincts could tell, but more troubling, they were going down more than up. And the air grew warmer and more stifling with each passing hour.

The next change came so gradually that it took them all many, many steps to even notice.

Juraviel stopped, and the other two glanced at him and were held by the curious expression on his face. "The tunnels are not natural," he explained. "They have been worked."

Both Cazzira and Brynn moved to the side of the tunnel, holding aloft their respective lights to study both wall and flooring. Sure enough, they found crafted supports along walls and ceiling, and worked blocks flooring the somewhat even slope beneath their feet.

Brynn and Juraviel inevitably turned to Cazzira for some explanation, but the Doc'alfar had none to offer. "There are no cities down here, no settlements at all, that the Tylwyn Doc know of," she explained. "Unless these are goblin tunnels."

Juraviel was shaking his head before she ever finished that last, ominous thought. "No goblins made these," he said with some confidence. "Goblins tear down, they do not create."

"The world is a wide place, Belli'mar Juraviel," Cazzira reminded. "By your own words, not all humans are alike—the men of the kingdom north of the mountains are not so closely akin to the To-gai-ru. Perhaps the same can be said of goblins."

Juraviel considered the words briefly, but shook his head again. Not goblins.

"We should know soon enough," Brynn put in, and she started away, the other two falling into step beside her.

The worked tunnel went on for more than a hour of walking, opening finally into a wide chamber sectioned by walls of mortared stone, each running out from a wall, left and right, and with a narrow doorway set in the middle. Gingerly, ready for fight or flight, the trio moved up to the door, to find that it was not fully closed, and was swinging unevenly on its old and rusty hinges.

Juraviel took the lead, gently pushing it open, studying the stonework immediately beyond, then rushing ahead, glancing left and then spinning around to the right, looking past the door.

Then he looked back to his companions and shrugged.

The trio went left, moving along a corridor of stonework walls, six to seven feet high, all the way to the wall, and finding only a dead end, with no other doors or openings apparent.

Juraviel looked at his companions, shrugged again, then hopped, beating his wings to lift him to the top of the wall. Then he leaped higher, a short flight that gave him an overview of the wide chamber for as far as his light source would illuminate. Knowing that he would make quite a fine target up there, the elf came down almost immediately.

"A maze of walls," he explained. "There seem to be openings, but at opposite ends of each successive corridor."

"A defensive design," Cazzira noted. "To force enemies to battle along hundreds of feet of narrow corridors merely to cross this one chamber."

"Then let us hope it is not now defended," said Juraviel, and he started along the corridor the other way, all the way to the far wall, where they found an opening that turned back into the second corridor. All the way back to the other end, they found the entrance to the third.

Entering that third corridor, Brynn jumped up, caught the top of the wall, and pulled herself into a sitting position atop it. "My feet ache from the walking," she explained, reaching back toward Cazzira. The Doc'alfar took her hand, and Brynn easily pulled her over the wall, while Juraviel fluttered up and over to join them.

And so they crossed, wall by wall, gradually working their way back toward the center of the room, and finally they came over the last of the thirty barriers, to find a series of carved steps leading between four fabulously decorated columns, and with a great iron door set in the chamber's back wall.

The carvings on those columns told them much.

"Powries," Juraviel said breathlessly as he inspected the worn reliefs. He looked to Cazzira, who seemed not to understand. "Bloody caps. Dwarves."

The Doc'alfar shrugged and shook her head, even after moving beside Juraviel to see the fairly accurate depiction of one of the fierce powries sculpted into the column. Fittingly, that relief showed the powrie in threatening pose, hooked sword at the ready and in full battle gear.

"If we go through that door to find a city of powries awaiting us, then we are surely doomed," Juraviel remarked.

Cazzira looked up at him, a knowing grin on her face. "Yet you wish to open it as much as I do."

A strange feeling washed over Brynn as she watched the two elves exchange smiles, a sudden intuition that some deeper connection was forming between them. She didn't say anything about it, just followed, her bow in hand and ready, as Juraviel and Cazzira walked up to the large iron door, studied it for a few moments, then pushed it open, its rusted hinges creaking.

A thin, glowing fog awaited them.

"Fazl pods," Cazzira noted, moving forward. Just inside the doors was a landing, a balcony overlooking a wide chamber with a series of plateaus stepping down into the bowels of the mountains. Hundreds of structures, houses and larger communal buildings, sat on those various plateaus, connected level to level by stone-worked stairways, all of it illuminated in dull white. They saw the pockets of fazl pod colonies, dozens and dozens of great living lamps and each containing pods numbering in the millions, by Cazzira's guess. So many were there, that few corners of the various plateaus were hidden in shadows, and this city spreading beneath them was surely huge, level upon level upon level.

But, they learned as they descended the stairway from the balcony to the nearest plateau, it was a city long in decay. Upon closer inspection, the trio noted that the stones of the various buildings were crumbling, their mortar gone. What few items they found in the many houses, pots and clay vessels, utensils and stone furniture, were broken and dusty, with no sign of any continuing society.

They moved along, down another stairway, then across a narrow stone bridge to a small section of what seemed to be more lavish houses.

"Back!" Cazzira warned as soon as they had stepped off the bridge, and the other two froze in place.

Following her gaze, they saw the threat, first one gigantic subterranean lizard and then another, slithering across an area of tumbled stones. The creatures went on their way, bodies swaying in a fluid, mesmerizing manner, forked tongues flicking out before them.

"The new inhabitants," Cazzira whispered.

"But what happened to the old ones?" Brynn asked; and intending to find out exactly that, the three went down again to another level, then down from there, and down again.

On what seemed to be the bottommost section of the city, in a chamber similar to the first they had crossed, full of defensible walls, and even with the rotted wooden remains of what seemed to be a ballista, they found their answers.

The room was full of skeletons, piled at every portal.

"Short and thick," Juraviel remarked, holding up one broken femur. "Powrie bones." He shook his head in disbelief as he searched on, for the bones were devastated, smashed and clawed. "What could have done this to a colony of hardy powries?" he asked, and the other two, having no experience with the powerful dwarves, didn't truly understand the weight of that statement.

They made their way from pile to pile, coming to a wide-open anteroom, where they found many more bones, but with wounds very different.

Brynn bent low and picked one up, holding it for the other two to see. It was charred on one side, as if some intense heat had blasted across it with tremendous force. Likewise, one wall of the room was blackened and blasted.

"What war engine could have done this?" Juraviel asked.

"A dread wurm," came a quiet answer from Cazzira a few

moments later, and when both Juraviel and Brynn looked at her directly, she added, "Dragon."

"Dragon?" Brynn echoed, and she looked to Juraviel, her expression full of doubt.

But Juraviel's look dispelled those doubts, for he was nodding in agreement.

"Perhaps they dug too deep," Cazzira remarked. "Perhaps they uncovered that which should have been left undisturbed."

"Do you notice that something is missing?" Juraviel asked, and the other two looked at him curiously.

"Their weapons," he explained. "Their armor. All of their treasures. The entire city, as far as we have seen, has been picked clean."

"By centuries of pillagers," Cazzira reasoned, and they left it at that and went back to their searching.

By the tunnel opening of the anteroom, Brynn found the next surprise. "This was no powrie," she said, holding up a longer and narrower femur, charred on one side. Several other larger bones, human bones, they seemed, were about it, some crushed, others just burned.

"Humans and powries did battle in here?" Cazzira asked.

"Why would they leave only one set of human bones, then?" Brynn asked. "A traitor, perhaps, who betrayed his clan to the dwarves?"

"You assume too much," said Cazzira, but her scolding was cut short by a cry of surprise from Juraviel, who had exited the anteroom to inspect the beginning of the tunnel beyond. He emerged from that shadowy place holding a piece of wood as long as his arm.

"What is it?" asked Cazzira.

"Darkfern," Brynn answered as she inspected the piece, to see the silverel lines encircling it. "That was part of a bow, a Touel'alfar bow!"

Juraviel turned it over to reveal a tiny signature near the tapered end. "With the mark of Joycenevial, my father," he explained. "This was the bow of a ranger—of that ranger," he said, pointing to the human remains. He considered the piece of the bow and the mark and searched his distant memories.

"Emhem Dal," he decided a few moments later. "Bow your

head, Brynn Dharielle, for here before you is the final resting place of Emhem Dal, trained by the Touel'alfar to return to his home of To-gai more than three hundred years ago."

"What does it mean?"

"It means that he never made it home," said Cazzira.

"And that his sword, Flamedancer, was lost here," Juraviel added. He looked at Brynn, his golden eyes narrowing with determination. "Are you ready to find and earn your ranger sword, Brynn Dharielle?"

The woman stared back at him hard, then nodded grimly.

"If the dread wurm has it, then you'll not likely get it back," Cazzira was quick to put in. "Behold the devastation of the beast." She swung her arm about at the piles of charred and crushed bones as she spoke. "Behold the fate of the last ranger who stood before the dragon!"

"That was hundreds of years ago," Brynn put in. "Can the dragon still be alive?"

"We shall see," was all that Belli'mar Juraviel replied, his tone more grave and angrier than Brynn had ever heard it before. Clearly, the sight of the remains of Emhem Dal had unsettled him.

Cazzira suggested that they should return to the city to search for more clues, but Juraviel pushed on down the tunnel, his pace strong.

They followed their instincts, they followed the heat they could feel pulsing beneath their feet, then they followed the smoke, wafting through cracks in the floor on hot updrafts.

After three long marches, with only short rests in between, they came to a huge and broken chamber, with a shattered stone bridge that had once crossed a deep gorge. Far below, they saw the orange glow of fire, the heat radiating up to flush their faces.

"If the dragon remains, it is down there," Juraviel said. "If Flamedancer remains, it is down there."

"You cannot know that," said Cazzira.

"I feel it," was all the answer she was going to get.

Juraviel stood up straight, peering across the way. "We can work our way to the entrance of the tunnel."

"Or we can go down there," said Brynn. She spent a long

time staring down into the gorge, then looked up at Juraviel, whose gaze led her to Cazzira.

The Doc'alfar chuckled under the intensity of those two looks. "What is life without adventure?" she asked at length.

And so they descended even farther, so far that they had to set their hundred foot rope several times. Sweat stung Brynn's brown eyes as she hand-walked down rope and stone, finally coming out on what seemed to be the floor of the place.

On they went, the air smoky about them. Soon the reflected light of flames was enough so that they did not need their torches, and rounding a bend in the corridor, they happened upon the source of the light and the heat, a wide and winding chamber full of what seemed to be water—except that the water was burning at various points.

"There is oil leeching onto the water," Juraviel reasoned.

"But what ignited it?" came Cazzira's response.

"Let us learn," said Brynn, and she stepped out from the bank onto a stone, then hopped to another. She paused there and bent low, and gradually lowered her hand to the water, dipping it below the surface. "Warm, but it does not burn."

"Take that as comfort if you fall in," said Cazzira. "A pleasant thought before the dread wurm eats you."

For many minutes, they made their way along the only trail open to them, a broken walk of small ledges and stepping-stones that wound through the fires and across the waters.

"Do we even believe that the dragon is still alive?" Brynn asked. "Three hundred years is a long time."

"Only in the measurement of humans," said Juraviel. "Not in the memory of the Tylwyn Tou or Tylwyn Doc, and certainly not in the memory of the great wurms, the longest living creatures of Corona."

"What do you know of dragons?" Cazzira asked.

"Only what you do, I presume," Juraviel answered. "Since our legends on the matter should be similar."

Brynn started to join in, but she stopped abruptly—so abruptly that the other two turned to regard her.

She stood there on a stepping-stone, looking down at the orange-glowing water, and when her companions similarly looked to the base of her stone, they recognized the potential problem—for the water was lapping at the rock, as if something had disturbed its stillness.

"Move along, and be quick," Cazzira instructed. "I have little desire to meet a dread wurm out here."

"I have little desire to meet a dread wurm anywhere," Juraviel added.

Brynn pushed on with all speed, hopping from stone to stone, running along ledges, ducking stalactites when they dipped low to block her way, and choosing left or right without bothering to ask whenever they came to a fork in the way. They had to double back more than once, and saw more ripples spreading out toward them on several occasions, though they never discerned the source.

Finally, they found an opening in the sidewall, another dark tunnel beyond, and though they had to leap and even swim a bit to get to it, they went on without question, just glad to be away from the fiery lake.

The tunnel only went on for a short distance, opening up into a wide chamber, a pit, and with a larger chamber up above, one that glowed from some unseen light source. The climb was easy enough for Juraviel with his wings, and he went up without question, then sat there on the ledge above his two companions, staring into the larger chamber, his mouth dropping open.

"What is it?" Cazzira called up to him softly.

"Juraviel?" Brynn chirped in when the elf didn't make any move to answer.

"It was worth the trouble," he finally said, motioning for them to climb up and join him.

The wall was nearly fifty feet high, but it was of broken stone. Cazzira verily ran up it, and agile Brynn wasn't far behind, and as each crested the larger room's floor, each assumed an expression as dumbfounded as that worn by Belli'mar Juraviel.

There, spread before them, were mounds of treasure, gold and silver coins and glittering gemstones, pieces of armor and furniture, sculptures and dozens of metallic weapons.

"So we know what happened to the powries," Brynn remarked dryly.

"But more importantly, what happened to the one who assembled this hoard?" asked Cazzira.

Juraviel motioned to the side of the largest mound of gold and silver, to a single curving white rib bone. A gigantic bone, that even a tall human could walk under without ducking.

"And so the wurm is dead," Cazzira said as they approached. "And its treasure lies unguarded."

"And so one of the wurms is dead," came a correction, in a voice that was neither human nor elf.

The pile of gold and silver shifted and broke apart, and from within came the dread wurm, the great dragon, its scales all red and gold, its horns taller than a tall man, its blazing eyes slitted, like those of a cat, and with wisps of smoke coming forth from its great nostrils. Three sets of eyes went wide with surprise and horror, three mouths dropped open in simple awe at the most magnificent beast.

"Welcome, thieves!"

"Not so . . ." Juraviel started to say, gasping and stuttering through each word. But he stopped his sentence and started his legs, leaping aside as a great foreleg came swatting down at him, smashing into the gems and coins where he had been standing, rending the very stone of the floor!

Cazzira leaped in near to that foreleg and whipped her wooden club about hard, smacking it against the scaly limb.

She might as well have smashed it against the side of a rocky mountain.

"Run away!" Belli'mar Juraviel cried, and all three scattered, diving about the treasure mounds, using them for cover from the beast. The dragon thrashed its tail, sending a fountain of coins, gems, and trinkets flying about the room, showering poor Brynn, who went tumbling down over a smaller pile of spears and other weapons. She hit hard and turned about, fearing that the wurm was upon her.

But the dragon had gone the other way, in pursuit of Cazzira. The Doc'alfar cut around one pile of coins; the dragon lowered its head and plowed right through.

Apparently anticipating the move, Cazzira came right back out the way she had gone in, scaling another nearby pile and rolling right over the top, to slide down the other side.

"Good!" bellowed the dragon, and its voice boomed off the rock and seemed as if it would sunder the very stones that supported the chamber. "Make me work for my meal, that I might enjoy it all the more!"

In her worst nightmares, Brynn Dharielle had never imagined anything as powerful and monstrous as the dragon. It seemed as if it could kill her with its voice alone, and every time it spouted a word, a bit of flame came out with it! All that Brynn could think of was running away, diving back down the pit and rushing back across the fiery lake. Despite the plight of her two companions, the young ranger actually started on that very course—until something else caught her eye.

A specter hovered by the pile of weapons over which she had just tripped, the ghost of a man, a To-gai-ru.

"Emhem Dal," she whispered, though she had no idea of how she knew the ghost's identity.

The specter lifted a translucent arm, pointing to the side, and Brynn felt a command, one that she could not ignore. Pushing away the continuing thunder of the dread wurm, the shouts of Juraviel and Cazzira, the screeching of dragon claws on stone, Brynn rushed out to the side, toward a mound of assorted treasures, following the specter's command. She reached the pile and began digging, having no idea of what she might be looking to find, for she had not taken the moment to consider any of this.

She just dug and dug, tossing aside goblets and jewelry, strangely shaped coins stamped with a dwarven face, and even a helm and short sword. And then another sword . . .

Brynn almost threw that second one, until she felt a wave of comprehension as her hand closed about its fashioned golden hilt, beautiful in design. It was formed into a sculpture of an elf dancing, her arms outstretched as she twirled, forming the crosspiece, and her head, fashioned of a light red ruby, serving as the joint between the slender blade and the pommel.

The blade was no less magnificent, razor thin and with delicate carvings running the length of the flat sides. It wobbled as Brynn flicked her wrist, but despite that, the woman could sense its immense strength.

Understanding the truth of the sword, a ranger sword, Brynn looked back to the ghost . . . but the specter was gone.

She came out of her trance then, and abruptly, seeing Juraviel flying over one mound, his bow in hand, launching a series of arrows back at the pursuing dragon.

Brynn sucked in her breath as Juraviel approached another treasure mound, thinking that it would stop him and that serpentine neck would catch up to him!

But the clever elf dropped right before he got there, and the lunging dragon snapped over him as he fell, colliding with the mound and sending a shower of coins and gems flying about the chamber.

"Run away!" Juraviel cried again. "To each your own, and find a way out!"

"No escape!" the dragon promised.

"Not for me, perhaps," Brynn said under her breath, and with a howl, she charged forward, rushing past the surprised Juraviel as he continued his flight, rushing right toward the dread wurm, her sword held high.

"Feel the sting of Flamedancer!" the furious ranger cried, rolling past the snaking head, coming up between the gigantic forelegs. She chose her mark carefully, the hollow of the breast, and threw all of her momentum into the powerful strike, stabbing the mighty ranger sword for the dragon's heart with all of her strength and passion.

To the sword's credit, it did not break.

And to Brynn's credit, she did manage to scratch the targeted scale a little bit.

"Brynn!" Juraviel cried.

The young ranger considered the mark on the scale, realizing that if she had the time to strike a hundred times more, she might manage to get through that outer armor. With a sigh, she looked up, to see the wurm's retracted head, those awful catlike eyes beaming down at her.

Up went a foreleg.

Brynn dove aside.

The dragon hit the floor with enough force to split the

stone, the shudder knocking Brynn from her feet. The foreleg bore right through the floor, and the overbalanced wurm fell to the side, against yet another pile of treasure, disturbing it so that it began to flow out of the chamber and into the opened crack. It wasn't nearly enough of a flow to topple the dragon, but the momentum of it did catch poor Brynn, carrying her along on a river of gems and gold, to spill out of the chamber, to tumble and bounce and fall along a rocky decline, smashing her body and head, tearing her clothing.

She didn't know how far she had fallen, for she lost consciousness long before she settled far, far below the chamber of the dragon.

Cazzira never even tried to go in against the great dragon. As soon as the beast made its presence known, the elf turned and fled, and she almost made it into a side passage. Almost, but a great tail stamped down in front of the opening, blocking the way even as she reached it.

She stumbled into the tail, regained her balance immediately, and started off to the side, but a sudden swish of the great tail caught her and sent her flying away.

She hit the side of a treasure mound, and the unstable nature of that pile alone saved her from serious injury. For the mound gave beneath her, then tumbled about her, and she went down in a heap, coins and gems and jewels spilling over her, burying her as she lay there unconscious.

The dragon wasn't even paying attention to her. The human woman had fallen down the hole, and so the beast had started into the hole in pursuit, its head snaking down after the tumbling human and dropping treasure. But the descent narrowed too quickly for the dragon to continue the pursuit to catch up, and the great head came back out, the beast roaring in anger!

That rage focused almost immediately upon a second figure, Belli'mar Juraviel, skittering for the open hole.

A huge claw slammed down in front of the running elf, barring the way—or seemed to, for the elf leaped, his wings flapping furiously, getting him up and around the blocking leg. And then he dropped, like a stone, into the opening.

But this time the dragon was not caught by surprise, and with frightening speed, the quickness of a striking serpent, the great head snapped down.

And when it came back up, the elf's flailing legs stuck out between the beast's huge fangs.

Brynn Dharielle opened her eyes, or rather, one eye, for the other was caked closed by dried blood. She was not in darkness, for her glow torch had fallen beside her, but she knew at once that the globe had been cracked, for unlike the sharp edge of light it had previously shown, it was now dulled, surrounded by a glowing white mist.

She remembered Cazzira's explanation of the torches and feared that she would soon be in total blackness.

Spurred by that, Brynn rolled to her side and forced herself into a sitting position. At first, her thoughts went right back to the cavern above, to the huge beast and her fall, to her friends and the grim fate they had likely found before the dragon. But soon enough, Brynn noted all the glittering items about her: gems and jewels, and her newfound sword, a ranger sword.

Brynn picked it up reverently, then nearly threw it aside in anger, feeling that it had betrayed her with its inability even to pierce the great monster's scaly hide.

She didn't throw it, though, but held it up before her eyes. "Flamedancer," she said, reciting the name Juraviel had spoken. She studied the fabulous detailing of the long and very slender blade, her eyes and her free hand roaming down to feel the cool metal and the sculpted hilt, the female elven form with the ruby head.

Brynn stood up and with a nod, slid the sword into her belt. She considered the tunnel far above her and realized that she could hardly retrace her steps back to the dragon's lair.

Nor did she want to. The woman closed her eyes in a silent salute to Belli'mar Juraviel, and to Cazzira, who had become somewhat of a friend over the days of traveling the Path of Starless Night. But they were dead, she told herself—or else they, too, had escaped, and would likely do better than she in these dark tunnels. Either way, Brynn understood that she had to be strong, had to put Juraviel and Cazzira behind her, had

to find her way out of those black tunnels and to her homeland, where she could lead the To-gai-ru to freedom and do
honor to Belli'mar Juraviel and to all the elves who had
trained her for the task.

She searched all about the fallen treasure then, ignoring
the gems and the coins, seeking a light source, or anything
else that might help her on her way.

The first thing of note that she happened upon was a beret,
shining red even in the dimming light. She picked it up and
put it on, more to keep her bloody and sticky hair out of her
face than out of any fashion sense.

Almost immediately, Brynn began feeling a little better,
but it was a subtle thing and she didn't make the connection.

A gem-studded bracer lay nearby. Looking at her left wrist,
which had been cut and bruised in the fall, she took the bracer
and tightly strapped it in place. She completed the outfit by
replacing her torn shirt with a fine-looking surcoat, lined with
sown metal rings and tied with a red sash that held her sword
perfectly.

And then she picked up her broken glow torch and started
off along the hot and dark tunnels, determinedly putting one
foot in front of the other. She shrugged off the pain as the
hours passed, and searched out some food as Cazzira had
taught her.

She made her camp in a side alcove and spent some time,
futilely, in trying to repair her broken lamp.

Then she fell into a fitful sleep, remembering her lost
friends in terrible dreams and awakening in a cold sweat.

But she dragged herself up and moved on, step after step,
day after day.

The fourth day out, with miles of snaking tunnels behind
her, her light source grew dimmer and dimmer, then winked
out altogether, leaving her in total darkness. Overwhelmed by
the sudden blackness, more profound than anything she had
ever known, the ranger fell into a crouch and drew out her
sword, praying for light, some light, any light.

And then her magical blade erupted in flames, and Brynn
shrieked in surprise and dropped it to the stone. It lay there,
burning, for just a moment, then the fire went away.

After she had recovered from the shock, Brynn fell to her knees, searching all about and finally gathering up the fallen blade. Then she stood again and presented the sword before her, and willed it to ignite once again.

It did so, as bright as any torch. Since she had no idea of how long the fire might last, Brynn started away immediately, and with renewed hope.

Days slipped past. Brynn walked among the shadows, climbed hand over hand up black chutes, and crossed an underground river, the waters freezing cold. She went on at times with the sounds of other creatures, predators likely, off in the shadows about her, and at other times in complete silence. She kept her focus on her goal, wherever it might lie and tried not to think of Cazzira's remark that most who died in the Paths of Starless Night did so of old age.

On and on she went, through the hours and the days, and though her torch did not seem to be based upon any finite fuel, for it did not dim, the battered woman nearly surrendered on many, many occasions.

Nearly. For Brynn was a ranger, elven-trained, and Brynn was To-gai-ru. Her people needed her; she could not fail. It was as simple as that.

One morning, or perhaps it was evening, Brynn squeezed through a narrow opening into a wider, ascending chamber. It was a tight crawl, and an exhausting one, and so she paused in the larger area to catch her breath.

And felt a current of air.

Not the rising hot air of lava, but a true breeze.

Invigorated by the thought that her ordeal might at last be at its end, Brynn rushed along the tunnel. But as the minutes became an hour, she slowed; and when another hour passed, and then another, the woman had to stop and take her rest.

She walked on again after a short nap, and the feeling of the air became lighter about her, and the breeze seemed to intensify, just a bit.

And then she saw it, far ahead: a dot of light, real light, daylight!

Brynn extinguished her fiery sword and stood there staring numbly at the pale light.

And then she ran, as fast as her legs would carry her.

She exited the tunnel on the side of a mountain, but not too high up. Down below her, spread wide, were the blowing, brown-green grasses of her homeland, of To-gai.

At long last, Brynn Dharielle had come home.

# PART TWO

# GRASSES IN
# THE WIND

*I have a strong belief that where we live greatly influences who we are and how we view the wider world. The people of Behren are quite different than To-gai-ru, and both are different from those people I met, Aydrian Wyndon included, from the kingdom north of the mountains, Honce-the-Bear. And by all accounts, the fierce barbarians of Alpinador are far removed from any of the other three human races.*

*Many people confuse the implications of these differences, though, for in truth, we all share a similar hope for our lives, that of improvement for self and community, for a better world for our children, for the continuation of our ways. Many people use the differences of the four cultures, exemplified by variations in appearance, to demean another race, and thus to elevate themselves. Even with my profound hatred of the Behrenese Yatols who conquered my homeland, I must try not to do that. I must try to recognize that their beliefs are the result of different experiences in a different land. Societies, like individuals, develop in response to the world about them, to the realities of the climate and the environment, the dangers and the joys they can find.*

*For the To-gai-ru, I prefer the old ways, the culture that evolved in response to the realities of the steppes. I believe with all of my heart that the old ways are the better ways—for us.*

*For we are a product of our culture, and our culture is, in great part, a product of the land around us. The people of To-gai are nomadic, because our survival is dependent upon the animal herds; whereas the people of Behren are settled, for the most part, in city enclaves. Their cities, all on fertile grounds, are often separated by miles of barren, blowing sand, and thus, their travels*

*are limited by the harsh environment. Many of the characteristics
that define the two races, To-gai-ru and Behrenese, are results of
those different lifestyles. The To-gai-ru are riders, the finest in all
the world, hunting on strong and swift ponies; we love our ponies
as brothers sharing a journey. The To-gai-ru are archers, the finest
in all the world, using great bows from horseback to bring down
the beasts that bring us shelter and food. Because our lifestyle is
so intertwined with the fruits of the steppes, we revere those
beasts. We thank them for that which they give to us. We
understand the delicacy of the land about us, the balance that
must not be disturbed if our culture and our people are to survive.*

*The Behrenese, in contrast, more often ride the plodding camels
that carry them across the great expanses of desert dunes. They
farm more than hunt, for their land provides little game. They
fashion and practice with weapons meant for war, not for hunting.
There is a different mind-set necessary for a culture based on
farming, I think. The Behrenese harvest and hoard; they do not
live day to day, as do my people. They look to that which will
increase their yield and their wealth, rather than merely reveling
in the simple joys of existence. As they huddle deeper within the
cities and farms, as they fashion the land more and more to their
specific needs, they lose sight of the greater world about them, one
that thrives on diversity.*

*And as they hoard, they covet, and greed feeds upon itself. They
remove themselves from the natural pleasures and beauties, and
replace these honest joys with created necessities: wealth and
dominance. Only in assembling hoards of useless wealth do the
Behrenese leaders, Yatols mostly, justify their existence to
themselves. Only by building great burial mounds, filled with
glittering jewels and sculpted artifacts, and built on the broken
bones and backs of slaves, do the Behrenese leaders seek to assure
their stature in the netherworld.*

*How they have lost their way! A presiding Yatol might have a
treasury of golden goblets, too many to inspect or to hold, while
his people live in squalor outside the crafted walls of his home—
walls that he must construct for his own defense because his
people live in poverty.*

*A To-gai-ru chieftain who so hoarded the wealth would be put
out by his tribe—if he was fortunate. A nomad cannot build such
defensive walls.*

*The hierarchy of Behrenese society established itself, Yatol to
peasant, and the wealth of Behren was long ago divided among*

*the leaders, though they are in constant strife attempting to redistribute the specifics. But as a whole, that wealth total is settled, and so to elevate the whole, wealth and class, the Behrenese needed to look beyond their own borders. With To-gai-ru serving as slaves, even the peasants of Behren are uplifted; and with To-gai ponies to sell to Honce-the-Bear, the kingdom increases its overall wealth.*

*So their useless treasuries will grow.*

*So their tombs will become larger and more elaborate, filled with more wasted jewels, and built upon more broken bodies.*

*It is a simple fact of my life that I hate the Behrenese. But I must not err, as I spoke of earlier, in confusing the society with the individual. I hate the culture that has grown in the desert kingdom, the culture that has felt a need to invade my own land and enslave my own people. I hate the Yatols who did not turn away from this murderous and heinous course, who instead claimed this conquest as their religious right, the true path of their god. Greed and arrogance go hand in hand, it seems.*

*I hate them, and I will free my people, or will die in the attempt.*

*But I must not err. I do not hate the Behrenese subject, the poor peasant caught up in the whirlwind of Yatol furor.*

*I must remind myself of that through every step of my journey if I am to remain true to the goal. I must remind myself of that through every battle and conquest, or I am surely to have my heart shattered and my purpose perverted to that which I most despise.*

—BRYNN DHARIELLE

# CHAPTER 10

# *Kin and Kind*

Brynn wandered the hills and valleys of the southern slopes of the Belt-and-Buckle Mountains for nearly two weeks before finding a pass that would take her down to the grassy steppes. The going was easy, though, with plenty of food and cold, fresh water to be found, and no monsters or animals threatened her step.

The only battle she knew during those days and especially those nights was the one that continued to rage in her heart and mind. She had lost Belli'mar Juraviel, who had been her truest friend for the last decade of her life. She had escaped where he had not; she had run away while the dragon had burned him, or eaten him, or just crushed him flat to the stone.

Still, the young ranger knew that she had been given no options, that by the time she had awakened far below the dragon's lair, Juraviel was already long dead. And she knew, in her heart and in her mind, that her present road was the correct one, the one that would be expected of her by Lady Dasslerond, and by Juraviel himself. Her life's goal was not to avenge her dead friend, or even to return to his people to report his death.

No, Brynn Dharielle's life's goal lay before her, spread wide on the grassy fields of To-gai.

And so it was with a heart both heavy with sorrow and light with anticipation that Brynn made her way, day by day, step by step, with the sights and smells of her beloved To-gai thickening about her.

On one splendid morning, the young ranger awoke to the

sound of thunder, and it came not from the sky, but from the ground below. Eagerly, Brynn crawled to the lip of the plateau where she had camped, looking down upon a grassy lea set among the mountain stones. A herd of pinto ponies, brown and white and black and white, charged about the field below her, agitated.

Brynn looked around, but saw no sign of any predators in the area, and no sign of any men. She studied the herd more closely and realized that the mares and the foals were running about mostly to stay out of the way of several agitated stallions.

Brynn nodded her understanding. One of the younger stallions was likely challenging the dominant male. The woman propped herself on her elbows and watched the spectacle unfold before her.

She soon discerned that there were three stallions involved in the ruckus. A large old male, scarred by many bites and kicks, was chasing two others in turn, warding them away. He was the leader, obviously, and the largest of the three—Brynn put him at fifteen hands and near to eight hundred pounds. He was more brown than white, showing only a few splotches about his thick torso, as was the second of the stallions, who seemed to be the primary challenger.

But it was the third of the group that truly caught Brynn's eye. She figured him to be the youngest of the three, and he seemed to be spending more time keeping out of the way than in mounting any real challenge to the dominant male. His legs were white, his splotches rich brown and outlined with a lighter shade of brown. His mane was white, with a black tuft, and his tail black, and showing a white tuft; unlike most of the others in the herd, he had not the single blue eye, but a pair.

He seemed to Brynn to be a smaller version of Diredusk!

The young ranger bit her lip, hoping that the small pony wouldn't be too badly injured in the ruckus.

The dominant male rushed at him, and he lowered his ears and head, ducking away in submission.

Or at least, he seemed to be, for as soon as the dominant male swung back to deal with the more aggressive challenger, the small pinto spun about and bit him hard on the rear flank, and when he turned to respond, the smaller horse bolted past, running in between the dominant male and the other challenger, leaving both startled and rearing, their forelegs clapping together hard.

The little pony cut a sharp turn and barreled back in, and it seemed to Brynn as if he hesitated, as if he was studying the ongoing battle to determine which of the others was gaining an upper hand! Then he went in hard and fast, kicking and butting the dominant male, who was clearly getting the best of the challenger, and by the time the smallest of the three ran out the other way, the two opponents were back on equal footing.

Soon after, the small pinto came in hard again, this time making a run at the challenger, who had gained the upper hand, and then a third pass, where he clipped both horses, who were fighting evenly at that point.

"Clever runt," Brynn whispered with a chuckle, for she knew that this was more than coincidence. This pony was doing all it could to drag the fight between the larger horses out for as long as possible, and she understood that the clever pony meant to wear them both down and win the day!

And soon after, it happened just like that, with the small pony running off first the dominant male, then the exhausted and battered challenger.

"And so enjoy the spoils," Brynn whispered, as the pony turned its attention to the mare that had started it all.

The young ranger was still chuckling as she packed up her gear and began her day's march. She kept looking back, though, at the clever little pony. Something about him—and it was more than the resemblance to Diredusk—made her feel a connection to this one.

She was still thinking of the pony the next day, while walking through a wide canyon along the lower trails, when she heard the thunder of the running herd. Brynn quickly moved to the rocky wall and crouched behind a boulder.

The horses entered the canyon behind her, running hard, running scared, and an ensuing roar, low and rumbling, explained it all to the woman.

A mountain cougar, and not far away.

The horses thundered past; they weren't in much danger, Brynn knew, as long as the trail was open before them, and unless the great cat was already up above them, ready for the spring. The young ranger ducked lower and instinctively clutched the hilt of her fine sword. If the cat couldn't catch the horses, it might settle for a bit of human flesh . . .

She saw it, then, running along the rocky wall behind the herd, moving so smoothly across the uneven rocks that it seemed as if it was cruising across an open field. It was losing ground but stubbornly continuing the chase, ears flat and great legs pumping, adjusting perfectly to the uneven ground.

Until it saw Brynn.

The cat froze so quickly, so quietly and completely, that it seemed to melt into the brownish gray stone behind it. Brynn held very still, locking her stare on the spot until she was again able again to mark the large and powerful cat. And it was a big one—Brynn estimated its shoulders at over four feet, which meant that one of its paws would more than cover her entire face. While it didn't seem so formidable compared to the young ranger's last foe, that horrid dragon, Brynn knew well the dangers of the brown mountain cats, for her people had often encountered them in the summer months, when their travels took them north to the foothills, and often with disastrous results. Many To-gai-ru had been buried in these foothills.

But Brynn was no normal To-gai-ru and had been trained in ways superior even to the best of her people's proud warriors. She resisted the urge to rush back around the boulder, knowing that any sudden movement on her part would surely bring the cat flying in—and it was not too far away for a single great leap at her.

No, she had to let the cat move first, to trust in her abilities to react properly.

The passing moments seemed all the longer because the woman didn't dare even draw breath.

The patient cat stared down at her, measuring her, and Brynn noted only a very slight, but very telling, movement: the cat subtly shifting its weight from hind leg to hind leg, tamping them down for better footing.

"Do not do it," Brynn whispered under her breath.

Even as she spoke the words, the great cat sprang, flying down from the mountainside at her. With reflexes honed to near perfection, Brynn fell into a sidelong roll, angling her dive around the boulder so that the cat could not easily adjust its course toward her after landing. She came up in a defensive stance a few feet away, the mountain cat standing atop the boulder, eyeing her with slitted eyes. Head low, back legs settling for another charge, it gave an angry roar that shook Brynn to her bones.

She pushed her thoughts into her sword, then, and fire erupted along the blade.

The cat roared again, and shrank back, but only for a moment. This one was hungry, Brynn knew, and angry.

It came on with a suddenness that would have had almost any other warrior caught flat-footed, too fast for most to bring the fiery sword across in any semblance of defense. But Brynn was a ranger, and was so attuned to animals that she instinctively knew the spring was coming before it had even begun.

She spun back and to her left, sword coming all the way around as she completed the circuit to swat at the passing cat's rump.

The cat cut quick, turning right around and leaping, this time high, for Brynn's head.

She fell forward and to the ground, and while she didn't have the time to turn her sword about to stab the cat as it flew above her, she did manage to punch out hard with the pommel, thumping the cat in the belly, and to push out with her newfound gem-studded bracer, forcing those deadly rear paws aside.

And as she did, the woman's eyes widened with surprise, for a pulsing white light, bent and rounded like a shield, came forth from that bracer! As she regained her footing, she tapped her sword against it, and sure enough, it was a tangible thing, a shield of some kind of glowing energy. She wanted to inspect it more, but she had other matters to attend.

"Go away!" she yelled at the beast, as it turned again, and as she fell to her standard defensive stance.

This time, the clever cat stalked in.

Brynn stabbed at it, but it ducked back, then came forward, up on its hind legs, forelegs swatting.

Brynn worked her sword back and forth, batting the claws, stinging the cat with fire. But then it leaped, suddenly, and Brynn had to dive aside, and she felt a burn in her shoulder as one claw raked past. Her roll interrupted, she lay on her back and clutched at the wound reflexively, but had to let go and punch out, and try to bring her sword to bear as the great cat fell over her, all muscle and tearing claws and biting teeth.

She fended frantically, got in a hit or two, then just rested the flat of her fiery blade against the neck and head of the cat, holding it back, pushing it out to arm's length so that those powerful claws could not get a firm hold, and she worked her pulsing shield all about, fending them further.

With a growl of protest, the cat retreated, and Brynn threw herself right over backward, moving lightly back to her feet.

The great cat circled to her right, seeming unsure, and stung, though not badly wounded.

Brynn went on the offensive, seizing the moment to rush forward, working her sword in an overhand slash rather than her customary straightforward stab to accentuate the flames and perhaps chase the cat off.

It did skitter back, dropping low on its front legs, ears flat, mouth open in a winding screech of protest and outrage.

Then the cat came forward and Brynn leaped back, and then she charged again, and the cat, after a moment, reversed its charge, retreating one stride, then turning back toward her.

Neither dared follow through, each respecting the other's formidable weapons.

Brynn had no idea of how this might end. She couldn't try to run away, obviously, for the cat was far too swift. And apparently she couldn't scare the beast off.

The cat came on again, this time more forcefully, and Brynn had to continue her retreat, step after step, her sword slashing back and forth before her to keep the determined beast at bay. It roared all the while, and in the tumult, Brynn was caught completely by surprise as another form, the largest of all, entered the fray.

The small pinto pony cut between the combatants, head

lowered and forelegs kicking at the surprised mountain cat. The cat leaped away and the pony reared and whinnied mightily.

As it came down to all fours, Brynn, hardly thinking, wasted not a second, grabbing its mane and leaping astride its strong back, and the pony jumped away.

On came the mountain cat, springing and roaring.

Brynn didn't have her seat well enough to control her mount, but the pony needed no guidance. Ducking its head low in a full gallop, it went left and then right, then left again, putting a bit of ground between it and the pursuing cat, and then it ran full out and straight on, angling for an area of fallen logs and boulders. Instinctively, Brynn started to tug the horse to the side, to avoid the rough ground, but the pony would not be deterred. In it charged, and Brynn found her balance just in time before the pony leaped the first boulder, gave two quick strides, and soared over a log that was propped up by stones on one end. There weren't two strides before the next hurdle, though, and the footing was bad, and so the pony came down and went right back up on its hind legs, not quite releasing into the jump, but rather, giving a short hop and then a second to clear the way.

*Like a rabbit,* Brynn thought. Looking back, she saw that the pony's choice had proven correct, for the mountain cat had gone around the first boulder and had then lost ground ducking under the log. Now, coming past the last obstacle, the cat bolted, but the pony had already gained its momentum and was in full stride. The mountain cat kept up with it for a few more strides, even managing a swipe at the pony's hind leg, but it could not hold the pace.

Brynn and the pony came out the other side of the canyon at a full gallop, and when the woman finally managed to look back, she saw the mountain cat standing there, staring back in obvious frustration.

The pair rode on for some time, and Brynn did little to guide the pony. She sat comfortably, her legs hardly pressing its strong sides and her hands gentle on its snowy mane, for she knew instinctively that the pony would not throw her. As a child, Brynn had seen many horses taken in and broken for riding, and so she understood just how extraordinary this entire encounter had been. For the pony to come back anywhere near the mountain cat was amazing, and for it to stop and then allow Brynn to climb atop its back was even more so.

Still, there were many stories about such encounters, such immediate bonding between rider and mount, scattered among the legends of the To-gai-ru, a people intimately tied to the marvelous horses of the steppes.

Finally, convinced that the mountain cat was long gone, Brynn shifted her weight back a bit and gave a gentle tug on the pony's mane, whispering into its ear, "Ho."

The pony eased down to a stop and Brynn slid off. She came around the front, scratching the side of the pony's face, looking into its smooth blue eyes, and seeing intelligence there. "Thank you," she said, and she kissed the pony on the nose. When she backed up a bit, the young stallion tossed his head a few times, up and down.

Brynn smiled and scratched its ears again. "Where are your friends?" she asked quietly. "Did they send you back to defend the rear?"

The pony nickered and lowered its head to the grass, munching contentedly. Truly, it seemed in no hurry to be off to rejoin the others.

Brynn knew that she couldn't push this budding relationship, though she dearly hoped that the pony would remain with her. She didn't have a rope, and even if she did, she wouldn't use it on the pony after it had just saved her from that difficult battle!

No, she wanted the pony to become her mount, her friend and ally—even more so, she understood, because she now felt so alone, with Belli'mar Juraviel and Cazzira gone. But it would have to be a friendship of mutual agreement, and on that note, it was all up to the pony.

Brynn petted the pony again for a few moments, then sighed and turned about and began deliberately—if not too swiftly—walking away.

Her smile could not be contained when she realized that the little pony was walking behind her.

An hour later, Brynn came upon a small lea, sheltered by

rocks and by trees, and decided to make camp under the boughs of some thick pines, with plenty of grass about for the pony.

"Well, what am I to name you?" she asked, and the pinto looked at her as if it understood her every word. "So clever and such a hero, and here I thought that you were the runt of the herd!"

She smiled as she finished and looked into the pinto's blue eyes knowingly. When she was a young girl, she and her mother used to play many word games, nonsensical and simple fun, and one song in particular stood out to her as she looked upon the beautiful pony, a rhyme that she and her mother had made up about another smallish horse, the runt of the clan's herd. Brynn could not completely remember the rhyme, but she did remember the word, "runtly," that her mother had used to both describe the horse and fit lyrically into the song.

"Runtly, then," Brynn announced to the pony. "I will call you Runtly!"

The pony threw its head up and down, several times.

Brynn knew that it had understood, and she couldn't have been more delighted.

The young ranger and her pony spent the next several days together, sometimes riding the lower trails, but more often just walking, with Brynn leading the way and Runtly plodding along, seemingly contentedly, behind. The weather remained mostly clear and chilly, for though they were moving lower in the foothills, the season was pushing on.

All the while, Brynn tried to get her bearings, looking for some landmark—the jagged, peculiar face of a mountain, perhaps, or a winding stream—that would jog her childhood memories and give her some idea of where a tribe of To-gairu might be encamped. She knew that the season was somewhat late for any of the tribes to be so close to the mountains, and so she was relieved indeed when she saw a line of thin smoke, marking a camp.

She climbed onto Runtly's strong back and urged the willing pony along at a swift pace. Goose bumps showed on her bare arms, and her mouth went dry, her hands damp, at the thought of seeing her people again for the first time in more than a decade, for the first time since becoming an adult. She grew more nervous with each passing stride and had to remind herself over and over again that she was well prepared for the meeting. The Touel'alfar had trained her in many of the arts that her people held dear, and had gone out of their way to tutor her, often using her own language and not their singsong tongue.

It occurred to her, then, that the elves had not similarly treated Aydrian concerning language. Brynn never recalled Lady Dasslerond, nor any of the others, speaking to Aydrian in the tongue common to the folk of Honce-the-Bear, but only in the elven tongue. That struck her as odd indeed and, for some reason she did not understand, set the hairs at the back of her neck on edge, but she couldn't pause and ponder it just then. Aydrian's road out of Andur'Blough Inninness was years away, she believed—not knowing that the young man, barely more than a boy, was even then in fast retreat from Dasslerond's captivity—while hers lay right before her, right under that line of gray smoke, perhaps.

She bent lower and urged Runtly along, soon cresting a ridge and pulling the pony up to a stop, her smile wide.

And fast disappearing. For there below her was not a To-gai-ru encampment as Brynn remembered them, with deer-skin tents set about in a rough circle around a large cooking pit, with horses running free in the fields all about and watchers guarding those fields from high vantage points, protecting the herd that was so vital to the To-gai-ru survival. Brynn had even suspected that she might encounter a watcher up there on the northern ridge.

There was no watcher. There were no horses running in the fields, as far as Brynn could tell. And no tents! The settlement below her was not the temporary encampment of To-gai-ru, but a true settlement, with permanent structures, and even a trench-and-wall barrier surrounding the whole of it. There were houses fashioned of wood and clay, with sod roofs. They were connected by cleared pathways, roads, all centered around a wide town square. Directly across that square from Brynn stood the largest structure in the town, a long and tall building with a sloping roof constructed of interlocking beams that formed a row of X's, front to back, and with small towers, minarets, at each of the four corners.

It was a distinctive design, and one that Brynn would come to mark well and despise in the days ahead.

Her eyes scanned the structure for a bit, but were drawn away, to the side, to the second-largest structure in the settlement, long and wide and low, and with several fenced-in areas about it. A stable, she knew, for more than a dozen horses milled about those corrals, and even from that distance, she could hear more whinnying from within.

Her mouth open now, with shock and with anger, Brynn just shook her head helplessly.

It took her a long, long while to muster up the strength to prod Runtly down the slope to the settlement. As she neared the gate, Brynn noted that there were many Behrenese about, wearing their typical light-colored robes and turbans, and more than a few suspicious expressions turned her way. The To-gai-ru who saw her looked on with equal curiosity, but with expressions that showed less sinister undertones.

Brynn feared that wearing her surcoat and her armor, and particularly the beret and that fabulous sword hanging at Runtly's side, might have been a mistake. Perhaps she should have stripped off the pilfered items and bagged them, coming in as a simple To-gai-ru wanderer.

"Too late now," the young woman said with a shrug of her shoulders, and she pushed Runtly forward at an easy, unthreatening pace.

"Halt!" came the expected cry from one of the four guards standing about the gate area.

Brynn shifted back and gave a slight tug on the pony's mane.

The four guards, Behrenese all and with one of them, a woman, wearing the distinctive overlapping scale armor of the Chezhou-Lei, came forward. The three common Behrenese soldiers looked a bit nervous at first, but quickly settled beside their mighty Chezhou-Lei companion.

The female warrior regarded Brynn gravely, then grunted at one of her companions.

"Who are you?" the man said immediately, and obediently, Brynn thought.

"I am Brynn Dharielle," she answered honestly, for she could think of no reason to hide the name she was best known by, though it was not her true name.

"From where have you come?"

Brynn shrugged and looked back over her shoulder at the mountains. "From there, the foothills."

The To-gai-ru quickly translated to the Chezhou-Lei, and the mighty warrior regarded Brynn even more closely, her dark eyes narrowing. She said something in the Behrenese tongue, which Brynn did not understand.

"What village do you call home?" the translator asked. "And what tribe?"

"I was of Kayleen Kek," Brynn answered, again honestly. "But that was many years ago."

"And now?"

"Now, a wanderer."

The man tilted his head, as if not understanding.

"A wanderer," Brynn said again. "Surely you have encountered To-gai-ru wanderers, in this season, in this region near to the mountains." The man still didn't seem to catch on, and Brynn worked hard to suppress her smile. In Behren, there were nomads, mostly desert bandits riding from oasis to oasis, and in To-gai, wanderers—as they were called, for they were even more nomadic than the tribes—were even more common, and much respected among the tribes. Wanderers were the information bearers, informing the tribes of news from other encampments and often guiding the hunters to areas with better game signs. Brynn remembered well the excitement among her friends whenever a wanderer approached Kayleen Kek.

"You are young."

"Not so young," she answered. "But I am tired and desire a warm bed this night, and a fine, cooked meal."

The Behrenese translated to the Chezhou-Lei woman, and she paused for a long moment, then nodded at the man.

"Dee'dahk would not turn you away, Brynn Dharielle," the man explained. "If the Ru will have you, then enter. But be warned," he added grimly, staring hard at Brynn, "Champion Dee'dahk will tolerate no insolence from any under her watchful eye."

Keeping her face devoid of expression, revealing nothing that could be viewed as threatening or mocking, Brynn slipped down from Runtly and straightened her clothing, then pointedly untied the sword and strapped it about her slender waist. Dee'dahk was watching her every movement, she knew, and so she tried to appear a bit clumsy, at least.

"You can stable your horse inside," the Behrenese soldier continued. "Bargain the price as you desire. For your lodging, you will have to seek out among the other Ru, but expect that my master, Yatol Daek Gin Gin Yan, will wish to speak with you."

Brynn held her ground for a long moment, digesting the names and the tone, trying to make some sense out of the obviously huge changes that had come over her homeland. So, there was a Yatol here, and a Chezhou-Lei? Was every "village" like this, under close scrutiny?

She started forward, Runtly stepping easily behind her, but she stopped suddenly and turned to her pony. She scratched his face and neck and pulled his ears and whispered to him comfortingly, then she turned him about and gave him a smack on the rump, and the pinto trotted off for greener grasses.

Dee'dahk immediately exploded with a stream of agitated words.

"That is not allowed!" the Behrenese translator shouted at her. "The horse will be brought in!"

"This is their land as much as ours," Brynn explained.

"This is the land of Yatol Daek Gin Gin Yan!" the man screamed at her. "The horse will be brought in!"

Brynn considered it for a moment, telling herself repeatedly that this was not the time to start a fight. She understood that the Behrenese would in no way harm Runtly—a To-gai pony as fine as he would be far too valuable for that! She gave a short whistle and the pony stopped and looked back to regard her. A second whistle turned Runtly around, walking back at his own leisurely pace.

"Then I expect that I shall not be staying here for long," Brynn explained when the pony reached her, and she started toward the open gates, Runtly right behind. She didn't bother to return the glare that Dee'dahk was casting her way.

She reminded herself again, many times, that her duty to her people now was to gain information, to learn all that she could about the present state of affairs in To-gai.

The time for fighting would come soon enough, she knew.

"You are a bit young to be a true wanderer, are you not?" an old woman, Tsolona, said to Brynn that same night, when she joined most of the village adults in a common room set off the village square, in full view of the distinctive and huge Yatol Temple.

"Not so young. And older than I appear in experience, if not in years."

"Ah," said Balachuk, the woman's companion, a wrinkled and leathery old man whose eyes remained as bright and sharp as those of any twenty-year-old. "And where is it that you've been wandering?"

Brynn smiled as she considered the depth of her forthcoming answer. She wanted this discussion to go completely the other way around, with her asking the questions about To-gai, and not the To-gai-ru interrogating her. She had found no trouble in getting lodgings; several To-gai-ru families had offered to take her in at the cost of a few tales, and she had accepted the invitation of this very couple. One Behrenese man had offered, as well, and Brynn had almost accepted, thinking that she might garner much information about her enemies by becoming a confidant of one of them. But then she had looked into the man's eyes and had seen the truth of his intent, though his wife would be in the same house.

"Along the mountains, mostly," Brynn answered slowly, very conscious of the fact that a pair of Behrenese men were sitting at a table not too far away and were listening somewhat more than casually. She knew that she was being watched wherever she went, as the leaders of the town tried to learn as much as they could about this strange woman and her unusual equipment. Brynn looked at the two men out of the corner of her eye, and added, loudly enough for them to hear, "And under the mountains."

The old couple looked to each other in surprise, and others about the immediate area of the large room shared that expression. The whispers began almost immediately, and within a few moments, Brynn found herself surrounded by folk, To-gai-ru mostly, but even with a few Behrenese, all waiting to hear her tales.

And so she told them—the part under the mountains, at least, though she kept out any mention of Juraviel and Cazzira. Every face screwed up with confusion as she told of the dwarf city, for the To-gai-ru and Behrenese alike had little knowledge of powries, and every eye went wide indeed when Brynn told her tale of the great dragon and its hoard of treasure.

She played it to maximum effect, dramatizing her words by standing and even mimicking some of the battle actions as she described the fight. At one point, she cried out, "So I thrust my new sword against the great beast's leg!" and spun to the side as she did, stabbing out with her bare hand, and taking delight, along with all of the others, in the way several of the audience leaped back, one even giving a shriek.

All the while, though, Brynn subtly glanced at the two Behrenese, who were still sitting at their table, still pretending, unsuccessfully, to be ambivalent about the newcomer or her tale. They were hearing her words, she knew, and marking them well, and likely, they'd be speaking with Yatol Daek Gin Gin Yan before Brynn's scheduled meeting with him the next morning.

"They say you are of Kayleen Kek," one man to the side remarked.

"Long ago," Brynn replied, and simply hearing the tribal name evoked memories of her carefree childhood days.

"A fine tribe!" another man offered, and many about nodded and sounded their accord, and at that moment, Brynn knew that she had come home. The tribes of To-gai were not often friendly with each other, and were oftentimes at war.

But there was a mutual respect among them, and an understanding, in the greater scheme of the world, that they were all one people, the proud To-gai-ru.

The one disconcerting expression that Brynn saw came to her from Barachuk, who seemed a bit confused, even suspicious.

She wasn't overly surprised, then, when, after many more tales, including many that Brynn at last coaxed out of the others, old Barachuk turned to her on the way back to the house, and said, "I knew Kayleen Kek. I once traded with them and hunted beside them. I know of no family Dharielle."

Brynn noticed the gentle, but firm, way Tsolona put her hand on Barachuk's forearm, as if reminding him that Brynn was one of them.

Still, Brynn certainly understood Barachuk's concern. Kayleen Kek had not been a large tribe, numbering no more than three hundred, and with only twenty distinctive families. And in this day, under the harsh rule of Behren, there was reason for suspicion.

Brynn stopped walking, as did her two companions. She stared into Barachuk's sharp eyes. "Do you know the family Tsochuk?"

The man assumed a pensive pose for a moment, then his eyes widened. "Keregu and Dhalana," he started to say, hesitantly.

"And their daughter, Dharielle, who was spared on that evil morning when they were murdered, left to carry the image," Brynn finished.

"Brynn Dharielle," Tsolona breathed.

"You are that little girl?" Barachuk asked, then he nodded, scrutinizing her. "The age is appropriate."

"Poor girl," said Tsolona, in a voice that was both sympathetic and strong, resigned to the harsh realities of life. She moved closer and put her hand on Brynn's arm in the same manner she had done to Barachuk a bit earlier.

Brynn shrugged and let it all go, holding her strong expression and posture and refusing to allow herself to bring back that terrible image. There was no room for any show of weakness here, no time to allow her pain to transfer into anything other than that simmering and determined anger that drove her on in her mission.

"I left Kayleen Kek, alone, the next day," Brynn explained. "I know nothing of the tribe—are they still traveling the steppes?"

"In a village, much akin to our own, I would guess," said Tsolona.

"Few follow the old paths," said Barachuk. "To-gai has changed."

"Become civilized," added Tsolona, an obvious frustration in her snappy voice.

They walked on quietly, arriving at the small and unremarkable house a few minutes later. Barachuk waited until after they had settled before pressing on. "How did you survive? Which tribe took you in as their own? And are they still up there, in the foothills?"

The tone of that last question and the glimmer in his dark eyes tipped Brynn off to Barachuk's feelings on that particular subject, and she knew then that she was among allies, among To-gai-ru who longed for the old ways, the customs from before the coming of the hated Behrenese. Relief accompanied that realization, for though Brynn could hardly imagine many of her people surrendering their identity to the conquerors in but a decade, she had indeed feared that very possibility.

"I was with no tribe," Brynn admitted. "I was not even in To-gai. I traveled north of the mountains."

That widened her companions' eyes! The To-gai-ru were a nomadic people, but their travels had distinct borders, the mountains being one of them. Few To-gai-ru had ever traveled through them; fewer still, and none in memory, had ever returned.

"Your words are . . ." Barachuk started to say, but he stopped and just shook his head.

"Hard to believe?" Brynn finished for him. "Trust me, both of you, if you knew all of my tale, your eyes would widen even more." As she finished, she reached into her pouch and pulled forth the powrie beret, placing it on her black hair. The two looked at her curiously, obviously not understanding.

For a moment, Brynn entertained the thought of drawing forth her sword and setting its blade ablaze, but she held back, thinking it wise not to reveal too much, even to this couple, whom she already trusted implicitly. For they would likely talk, to friends at least, and Brynn knew that the Behrenese might well start evesdropping on Barachuk and Tsolona now, as they had already been observing her.

"It is the headpiece treasured by a race of mighty and wicked dwarves, called the powries," Brynn explained. "Much of this armor that I wear is of powrie make, I believe."

"You befriended dwarves?" asked Tsolona.

"No."

"You warred with them, then. The spoils of battle?"

"No, I have never seen a powrie. This was taken from the lair of a much greater foe, in a cavern deep under the mountains. A creature so mighty that it could raze the land!"

The old couple looked to each other, a flash of amazement on their faces, but one fast replaced by a grin of doubt.

"And you killed this creature?" Barachuk asked.

"No, the dragon was quite beyond me," Brynn answered honestly.

"Ah, yes, the dragon," said Barachuk, seeming far from convinced.

Brynn nodded, holding her calm in the face of their obvious doubt. "But I escaped the great beast, and with some treasures."

"Girl, you grow more curious by the moment," the old man remarked.

Brynn smiled, and let it go at that. She was tired, and had an important meeting the next day.

# CHAPTER 11

# *The Sash of All Colors*

Pagonel stared at the red sash hanging on the hook by the door of his small and unremarkable room, at its rich hues, bloodlike, the symbol of life among his order, the ancient and secretive Jhesta Tu mystics. Pagonel was one of only four among the 150 brothers and sisters to have earned the Sash of Life, but when he took it down from the hook and belted it about his waist, securing his tan tunic, he did not wear it with pride.

If he did, he would not have been worthy of the sash.

No, Pagonel wore the sash in simple optimism, for himself and for all the people of all the world. He was Jhesta Tu, dedicated to a life above the common, a life spent in reflection, in the quiet attempts of understanding, and in the hopes that such understanding of life and death and purpose would lead him to a place of absolute enlightenment.

The Jhesta Tu were not a large order; this place, the Walk of Clouds, nestled high among the volcanic mountains along the southern border where both the deserts of Behren and the steppes of To-gai came to an end, was their only temple, and few brothers were out on the roads of the wider world.

Very few, since the Yatols of Behren would not tolerate the Jhesta Tu, and the To-gai-ru had little use for them.

Most of the Jhesta Tu were of Behrenese descent, and most of those who were not, like Pagonel, traced their ancestry to To-gai. But all within the Walk of Clouds had entered at a very young age, and few had any memories other than those at the temple. They got their glimpses of the world outside from the books and oral presentations given within their mountain home, which was built into the side of a towering cliff facing, a walk of five thousands steps from the broken floor of the torn region.

A crackle and then a thunderous boom resounded outside of the one small window in Pagonel's south-facing room, but it only amused, and did not startle, the forty-year-old mystic. Some of the younger Jhesta Tu were practicing with the magical gemstones, he knew, in preparation for the celebration of the autumnal equinox that evening. Lightning bolts and fireballs would light the ever-misty gorge beyond the Bridge of Winds that night, Pagonel knew, and he smiled at the thought, for he truly enjoyed the revelry, and knew that his contributions to the show would bring pleasure to many of the younger mystics. Few at the Walk of Clouds could utilize the gemstones as well as Pagonel, though even he was no master with them, certainly not compared to the mighty Abellican monks of the northern kingdom of Honce-the-Bear. For in the eyes of the Jhesta Tu, the gemstones were not sacred, no more than were the grass and the wind and every natural thing in all the world. Their order was based on inner peace and contentment, a joining of mind and body and external environment that blended into pure harmony and equilibrium. While the Jhesta Tu appreciated the power of the gemstones, and particularly the inner searching required of one attempting to use the gemstones, they did not hold them as sacred and did not consider them a gift from god.

Another crackle and boom combination took Pagonel from his private reflections, and he made his way to his window and peered out, to see a group of younger mystics gathered on the Bridge of Winds, the clouds of mist rising from the gorge before them. Most wore the white belt of air, the first of the sashes, one that signified, more than any attainment of knowledge, the willingness to open one's mind to gain insight. Some wore the second, yellow belt, which signified growth from air toward the brown belt of earth.

One that Pagonel saw, though, wore the blue belt of water, a high rank indeed, and it was this mystic, a woman of about thirty years, who was putting on the lightning display.

Another bolt shot out from her hand, slicing into the mist

and crackling into a thunderous report, and the others on the bridge cheered and clapped their hands with joy.

Pagonel felt that joy, but it was dampened by a sudden insight, a realization that he would not attend the celebration that night.

The mystic moved back from the window, hardly believing the realization.

He would not attend.

He could not, would not, leave his room this day, or this night.

He saw the lightning bolt again and again, following its curious tracing through the misty air before it. A line of pure energy.

His breath coming in shallow gasps—ones that could be corrected by those wearing the white belts of air, who were learning the properties of drawing various breaths—Pagonel fell back farther into his room, fell back further into his thoughts. He pictured that bolt of lightning again, but this time it was inside of him, a line of energy running from his head to his groin, a balance, a line of power.

Pagonel cleared aside some clutter and pulled forth his meditative carpet, an intricately designed weave of sheep's wool, one that he had crafted himself over the course of two years. He sat down upon it, crossing his legs and bringing his hands together in front of his lean and strong chest, then very slowly dropping his hands to his thighs, palms facing upward. Then Pagonel went into his conscious relaxation, visualizing each part of his body and forcing it to sink more deeply into a quiet and relaxed mode. He felt hollow and empty, letting all the clutter leave his body and mind.

Then, when his body and mind were quiet, Pagonel allowed the image of the lightning bolt to grow again in his thoughts. But rather than just picturing the bolt cutting through the mist again, he let it grow beside a sensation of power within him, the line of his own life force, the energy that defined him more than his mortal trappings ever could.

He lost all sensation of time and space, fell into himself more completely than he had ever known possible, touched his life force with his consciousness for the first time.

And he stayed there, finding, for the first time, the most perfect harmony.

Pagonel blinked open his eyes, staring at the dark room. Slowly, very slowly, the mystic lifted his hands out to the side, then brought them in together before his chest. His breath came slow and deep as he used the techniques he had mastered in the many years he had worn his white sash, then he consciously forced that breath into his muscles, his arms, and his legs.

Moving in perfect balance, in the smooth harmony of his muscles, Pagonel unfolded into a standing position, his hands never moving from in front of his chest.

The mystic blinked again and looked around, trying to find some hint of how much time had passed. He went out into the hall, to find it empty, all the doors closed. He went down to the hall of lights, a circular room lined with rows of burning candles, and with several angled mirrors and small rock fountains strategically placed to catch and distort the light.

Pagonel caught sight of himself in one of those mirrors, and he was pleased by the contentment he recognized in his rich brown eyes. Something profound had happened to him in his chamber, he knew, and he understood what it was.

"Three days," came a voice behind him.

Pagonel turned and bowed. "Master Cheyes." In the Walk of Clouds, there were three other mystics of Pagonel's level, the Red Sash of Life, and there were only two who had achieved the level beyond that, the Belt of All Colors, the symbol of enlightenment—Master Cheyes and his wife, Mistress Dasa. In all the centuries of the monastic order, the number who had so achieved this belt was minuscule, under a hundred, and to have two such masters in the Walk of Clouds at one time was almost unprecedented.

And now Pagonel meant to announce that a third would be joining them.

"I have seen the Chi," he said quietly.

Master Cheyes nodded solemnly. "It is as I assumed when you did not emerge from your room for the celebration of the equinox, three days ago."

*Three days?* Pagonel laughed, somehow not surprised.

"I had hoped that you would see it, Pagonel," Master Cheyes continued. "It is good that you have, for now there is a road before you."

"I have touched Chi," Pagonel explained. "I have grasped it. I know it."

His stream of pronouncements had the old and wrinkled master rocking back on his heels. Few dared make such a claim, and for one of Pagonel's tender age to touch and fully grasp Chi, as Pagonel was claiming, was practically unheard of. Master Cheyes' wife, Dasa, had only found Chi two years before, in her seventy-eighth year, her seventy-fifth of formal study.

"I would walk the Path of All Colors, Master Cheyes," the younger man said confidently.

Master Cheyes nodded, for though it seemed obvious to Pagonel that he doubted the claim, he was powerless to say so. The discovery of the Chi, the highest level of enlightenment, was a personal undertaking and claim, one that went beyond the supervision of Cheyes, or of any master.

"You understand the danger?" Master Cheyes did ask, as was required. "And you understand that there is no need to walk the Path of All Colors at this, or at any, set time?"

"To wait is folly, as I am prepared," Pagonel assured him.

"I am bound to say no more, Pagonel." Master Cheyes bowed his head in respect, in acknowledgment that Pagonel was no longer his student or his inferior. If the man succeeded in the walk, then he would instantly become Cheyes' peer. If he did not succeed, then he would be dead. There was no middle ground; at the moment Pagonel announced his intent, his days as the student of Master Cheyes and Mistress Dasa ended. "The chamber is ready, as it is always ready."

Head bowed, Cheyes walked away.

Pagonel nodded confidently. He had seen the Chi, the inner life, the joining of body and soul, and in that recognition, he held no doubts about the outcome of his walk. He went straightaway to a little-used stairway in the far northern reaches of the temple. He moved down three levels, to the bottommost common area, and to an ironbound doorway that had not been opened since Mistress Dasa had made the journey. He grabbed the ring at the center of the door and felt the heat emanating from beyond the portal. A sudden jerk clicked the locking mechanism and the door cracked open, a blast of hot wind hitting Pagonel in the face.

He stepped through, onto a landing, and closed the door behind him, then turned and waited a few moments, allowing his eyes to adjust to the dim, orange light, a glow from far, far below.

He had gone beyond the worked tunnels of the Walk of Clouds, into a natural cavern sloping down to the depths of the mountain. It took him almost half an hour to reach the end of that corridor, a rocky, natural chamber with a single door set in the far wall. Beside that door hung many red sashes, identical to the one Pagonel now wore.

The mystic walked to the wall and nodded as he took note of how well most of the sashes had held up over the years. Most were well over a century old, and the air in that place, with its nasty sulphuric smell, was very acidic, and took a devastating toll on most cloth.

Pagonel removed his own belt and hung it on an open peg. His hand lingered upon it for a long while, for though he had only worn it for a few years, it had become more than just a symbol, but a constant reminder of the road of his life.

The man let go and quickly pushed open the door, stepped through, and closed the door behind him, well aware that he would never see that sash, or the room in which it hung, again.

Now he was in a wide and dimly lit chamber, crowded with life-size statues in various battle poses, a room similar to the one in which he had earned his Sash of Life.

This was not the test of his new enlightenment, though, but rather, a precaution against any who would come in there prematurely. For these statues were set on a "living" floor, a series of pressure plates that incited the manikins to action, and only one skilled enough to have earned his Red Sash could walk through there, avoiding the traps.

With complete confidence, only pausing long enough to remind himself that he had to hold his focus on the present, rather than on that which awaited him, Pagonel removed his soft slippers and started across the room.

His feet felt the subtle vibrations beneath him as he padded across. His mind and body moved in perfect harmony, turning sidelong to avoid a sliding statue, spear outstretched, then, in the same movement, ducking low to avoid a spinning statue, glaive cutting the air above him.

He came up in a leap, anticipating rather than sensing, the spikes stabbing out of the floor beneath him. He landed to the side, balanced perfectly on one foot, then stepped confidently ahead.

A spear shot at him from the shadows.

Pagonel's torso was ducking even as his arm was sweeping up, his forearm catching the spear just under the head and turning it harmlessly high and to the side. He fell into a forward roll that brought him under two slashing swords, came up in a leap that brought him over a thrusting spear, then moved, turning side to side, even spinning about once or twice, to avoid a series of other thrusts and slashes.

And then he stood before the far door, beside a huge lever set into the floor. Grasping it tightly, he pulled it back, settling it into place. Then he waited as the minutes passed, becoming an hour, as the counterweights all refilled with sand, resetting the dangerous room. When all the sliding and scraping ended, Pagonel returned the lever to its resting position, and, with a deep breath, walked through the door, entering onto a tiny landing in a wide but low natural cavern, full of orange light and intense heat. For the chamber was split before Pagonel by the life flow of the mountain, a river of running lava.

The mystic reached quickly into himself, gathering his Chi, willing a defense against the killing heat. Human skin and blood could not suffer the intensity, but the Chi certainly could. Pagonel reached within and brought forth a shield of energy, a determination that blocked out the pain.

Settled again, Pagonel looked at the walkway before him: a narrow metal beam, stretching out across the cavern to a waterfall of orange lava. The walkway, too, glowed with heat.

Pagonel focused his inner strength into a cluster of energy, then brought it down to his feet. Slowly, without fear, the mystic stepped out onto the metal walkway, which was no more than a few inches wide. He placed one bare foot in front of the other, denying the heat and the pain so completely that it did not burn his skin.

Out he went, to the very end of the walkway, standing just a few feet from the lava fall, almost close enough to reach out and touch it. Pagonel regarded all the area around him, for there seemed no other path, and yet he knew that he could not go back.

He nodded as he came to understand, and he backed up several steps, then fell even deeper within himself, to the power of life, and he brought it forth as a shield.

Pagonel exploded into a short run, then leaped, head back, arms outstretched, fists clenched.

He burst through the wall of falling lava, and somehow held his balance as he landed on a narrow walkway on the other side. Suppressing his elation, for this walkway too was glowing hot and any distraction that released Pagonel's grasp of his inner force would almost instantly take the skin from his feet, the mystic walked along, finally entering a second tunnel, again sloping down.

He walked for several hours, soon in almost absolute darkness, before he saw the tiniest glow of daylight up ahead. Pagonel held his determined stride and did not break into a run, reminding himself that this day was a blessing upon him, good fortune, and should not be tainted by foolish pride.

He came out of the tunnel, into the daylight, in a deep, deep pit, a circular area barely ten feet across. There, hanging on a jag in the stone, the mystic saw the symbol of his achievement, the Sash of All Colors. Reverently, he took it in his hands. It was made of fine strands of treated silk, so narrow and finely woven that in all but direct light, the sash appeared black. When the sun hit it, though, the sash shone of every color in the rainbow, and Pagonel tilted it up then to catch the dim rays, to see some hint of its true splendor.

He would spend the next few months weaving the sash for the next one to pass the test of Chi, he understood, and when finished, he would walk to the spot far above him, the lip of this deep, deep pit, and toss it in, to wait here for years and years, decades, even centuries, perhaps.

That was the way of Jhesta Tu.

Pagonel belted on his sash, a reminder of who he was, then looked about him for a way up. The hole was several hundred feet deep, at least, and the walls were sheer.

No obstacle to a Master of Chi.

Pagonel found again the line of energy, head to groin, and brought it forth about him like a shroud, using it to counter his own body weight.

He began to float, near to the wall, and hand-walked his way up, up, until he stood among the boulders.

A short walk through a narrow pass brought him below the Bridge of Winds, at the base of the long, ascending stairway. He resisted the urge to float up to the bridge, to amaze those students who witnessed it, and walked instead, humbly, one foot in front of the other.

Masters Cheyes was waiting for him.

"I am pleased, Pagonel," he said.

"I held no doubts."

"If you had, you would not have survived. There is success or failure, and nothing in between."

Pagonel nodded, understanding perfectly well. Those mystics who had attempted the Path of All Colors out of determined pride, those who had not truly seen and come to understand their Chi, had failed, to their doom. For those mystics who had reached the point of enlightenment, the test could not be failed.

"You must begin the replacement of the sash, of course," Master Cheyes remarked. "Have you determined your road beyond that?"

"To-gai," Pagonel replied. "I have seen the steppes and the grasses in my dreams and I know that I must return there."

"I am old, my friend, as is Mistress Dasa. You may one day return to the Walk of Clouds to find that you alone wear the Sash of All Colors. That is a heavy responsibility, my friend, but one that you will carry well."

Pagonel nodded and smiled warmly. He understood the truth of Cheyes' words, of course, and the realization that his road beyond the temple might take him forever away from this dear man and his dear wife brought a moment of regret.

Only a moment, though, for Pagonel had seen his Chi. He understood now the eternity; he feared neither his own death nor that of any friends, because he knew that there was no true death, only transcendence.

# CHAPTER 12

# *Pragmatism and Patience*

Merwan Ma looked on with surprise and even fear as Chezru Douan grilled Master Mackaront. Merwan Ma had rarely seen his master this agitated, and this particular instance seemed very out of place for the normally controlled Chezru Chieftain.

"How many gifts must I shower upon Olin?" Yakim Douan shouted. "Shall you leave with wagons of gold and jewels, only to return for more wagons of gold and jewels?"

"The monies are not for Abbot Olin," Master Mackaront calmly replied, even patting his hand in the air in a futile effort to calm the uncharacteristically explosive Douan. "They are to convince his followers that their voices at the College of Abbots should be heard loudly."

"The College of Abbots," Douan echoed, spitting the words. "By the time your College is convened, Abbot Olin will be long dead!" He came forward out of his cushioned chair as he spoke, and Mackaront shrank back beneath his withering glare and fiery tones.

"Father Abbot Agronguerre has shown remarkable strength," the Master from St. Bondabruce admitted. "We did not think that he would live through the summer."

"But he has, and now you come here telling me that the process of preparing the vote will take longer, that Agronguerre's health has unexpectedly improved. He will survive the winter, so you now believe, and if that is so, then perhaps the spring and summer, as well. When will you convene your College of Abbots, Master Mackaront?"

"We cannot know."

"Can you not schedule it for next fall in anticipation of the inevitable?"

Mackaront blanched at the suggestion. "We cannot presume to know when God will take Father Abbot Agronguerre to his side."

"God," Yakim Douan spat. "This is not the work of God, fool, but rather the stubbornness of an old man too afraid to lie down and peacefully die. And what does it say of your Church if your leader fears death?"

Mackaront fell back even more, but then reversed his course and stood up forcefully, glaring at the seated Chezru Chieftain.

Merwan Ma narrowed his eyes, ready to spring upon the man should he lift a hand against the God-Voice. And truly, Master Mackaront seemed on the verge of an explosion, trembling visibly, jaw clenched so tightly that his teeth were grinding.

If Yakim Douan was the least bit fearful, he did not show a hint of it. He settled back in his chair, crossing his legs and tapping his fingers together before him.

"You presume . . ." Mackaront started to say, and it was obvious that he had to force every syllable out of his tightened jaw.

"Enough, my friend, enough," Yakim Douan said quietly, holding his hand up before him. "We are all anxious here, all frustrated that old Agronguerre will not quietly pass on and allow Abbot Olin his rightful ascent."

"You cannot insult . . ." Mackaront pressed, apparently bolstered by the Chezru's shift in tone.

But Yakim Douan's fire returned instantly and he lowered his hands, freezing the man with a stern glare. "I say nothing that you do not already fear," he replied, his voice flat and even, which gave it all the more power. "And I do not fear to speak the truth, however painful that truth might be to hear."

"I will not—"

"You will sit down and hear whatever it is I have to say!" Yakim Douan shouted suddenly. "You come here as a beggar, seeking riches and bearing no news that rings sweetly in my old ears. So take your gold and your gems and continue the campaign for Abbot Olin. And pray, Master Mackaront, to whatever god you discover honestly within your heart, that old Agronguerre accepts the inevitable and goes to his reward.

"Because I am running out of patience. Tell that to your Abbot Olin."

Master Mackaront started to reply, but Douan waved him away, and told him to be gone.

As the door closed behind the departing master, Merwan Ma sat looking at Chezru Douan, seeking some signal from the man. When they were told that Master Mackaront was back in Jacintha, they had assumed he had come bearing the news that Agronguerre was finally gone and that the College would be scheduled for the spring. The Chezru Chieftain's surprise at hearing that not only was Agronguerre still alive, but apparently in better health, had not sat well upon him, obviously.

Still, the depth of his angry turn had caught Merwan Ma off his guard. Chezru Douan had voiced his wishes that Abbot Olin ascend in the Abellican Church, but still, Honce-the-Bear seemed a kingdom far, far away, separated by nearly impassable mountains. And though Entel was a short boat ride from Jacintha, neither Behren nor Honce-the-Bear could mount enough of a fleet to threaten the other. Why, then, was the continuing reign of Father Abbot Agronguerre of such great concern?

Yakim Douan sat in his comfortable chair for a long while, staring out the window at the shadowed mountains. Finally, he rose and moved to a small table at the back end of the room and shuffled some parchments about, including a message that had been delivered from the To-gai front, from Yatol Grysh, that very morning.

Yakim Douan lifted the parchment and began to read through it again.

"Do you know what they are calling one of their leaders?" he asked a moment later.

"Who, God-Voice?"

"The To-gai-ru rebels," Douan explained. "One band of raiders has named their leader Ashwarawu." He turned to

Merwan Ma, an amused grin on his face. "Do you know what that means?"

Merwan Ma muddled over the foreign word for a few moments. He recognized the pattern of the name's ending, and thought that the To-gai-ru word, "awu," had something to do with compassion, but finally, he just shook his head.

"Ashwarawu," Yakim Douan said again. "He who kills without mercy." The Chezru Chieftain snorted and chuckled. "The pride of the conquered. They have so little left that they grasp at every fleeting hope."

"Yatol Grysh asks for help?" Merwan Ma asked, though he knew the answer, of course, for he had perused the note before handing it to the Chezru Chieftain, as was expected of him.

"It is not unexpected," Douan said, trying to sound resigned but coming off as more than a little bit perturbed by it all. "He asks for an eight-square of soldiers."

Merwan Ma nodded. An eight-square was one of the basic formations of the Behrenese military, sixty-four men squared up in eight rows of eight, with all flanking soldiers carrying towering protective shields, and those in the middle holding spears to poke through the defensive walls.

"Send him his soldiers," Yakim Douan instructed, and Merwan Ma nodded.

"No," the Chezru Chieftain said a second later, holding up one pointing finger, as if he had just found a revelation. "Send him a twenty-square . . . no, two twenty-squares."

Merwan Ma's eyes popped open wide. It was not his place to question the decisions of the Chezru Chieftain, but two twenty-squares? Eight hundred warriors?

"Yes, God-Voice," he stammered.

"These minor uprisings in To-gai are expected, of course," Yakim Douan explained. "A conquered people is not truly conquered until a full generation has passed, at least. We show them a better life, but it will take the death of the old and stubborn barbarians before the younger To-gai-ru will come to accept the simple truth. These bandits roaming the steppes are not old men, but younger ones trying to please their misguided elders. Better that we eradicate the problem without question, here and now. Two twenty-squares to Yatol Grysh, then, with instructions to Chezhou-Lei Wan Atenn to take these soldiers and scour the countryside."

Yakim Douan's lips curled up into a perfectly wicked smile. "Let Wan Atenn earn the title Ashwarawu."

Despite his confidence in the decision to take powerful action against To-gai, Yakim Douan went through the rest of that day with little joy, for he understood the truth that his time of Transcendence was slipping back. He had hoped that he would not have to suffer another winter, even a mild Jacintha winter, encased in his aging bones. But that would not be, not even if Yatol Grysh took his new army and killed every rebellion-minded person in To-gai.

The Abellican Church in the north did not move quickly, Douan understood. If Father Abbot Agronguerre's health was indeed rallying, then it would be many, many months before they could ever organize and convene a College of Abbots.

For some reason he did not understand, Yakim Douan felt that he should not attempt Transcendence until after the situation in Honce-the-Bear was resolved. The mighty neighboring kingdom seemed at peace, but it had recently been ravaged by plague, and the Abellican Church, in particular, had been turned upside down by a supposed miracle.

All that the Chezru Chieftain had seen as a bedrock base of stability seemed to be shifting under his feet.

But old Yakim Douan could accept that. The centuries had taught him, most of all, pragmatism and patience. This was not the time for him to become vulnerable. So be it.

He glanced back once over his shoulder before he entered the circular room that held the sacred chalice, though entering was certainly no breach of any rules. He was the God-Voice and could do as he pleased.

Still, when dealing with this chalice, Douan always reminded himself that he was harboring a dark secret that must never be revealed.

He approached the central podium nervously, rubbing his fingers together. Then he stopped and chuckled, considering his posture and expression. To any onlooker, he would look perfectly appropriate, for all the followers of Yatol approached this chalice in this uncertain and reverent manner. The irony was not lost on Yakim Douan, for though he was wearing the appropriate mask, he was doing so for very different reasons than his underlings might know. The chalice held nothing of the sacred, or even of the spiritual—in terms of any god-figure—for Yakim Douan. But he held it in no lower esteem. For within this item, within the blood, was the gemstone that he had learned to master, the secret to his immortality.

What were the gods of the others, if not the hope of that very thing?

As soon as he put his hands about the decorated chalice, Yakim Douan felt the connection to his precious gemstone. Though he had known that it was in there, of course, and though he had known that he could access it, it still came as a relief to him when the connection was realized.

He fell deep within the gemstone and deep within himself, exploring all the corners of his aging physical form.

He found those areas of pain, the clenched muscles and weakened bones, and he used the magic of the hematite to bring relief and healing and energy. For a very long while, Yakim Douan stood there, purging his body of impurities and infirmities. He knew that it would be a temporary and imperfect fix for the one ailment that could never be cured: aging. But this would get him through the next months in relative comfort, until the time came for him to cheat the end result of aging once again.

Merwan Ma came upon Chezru Chieftain Yakim Douan quite by accident that day. He went to the chalice chamber merely to clean the place—for the care of such a sacred area could not be entrusted to mere servants.

He was quite surprised to find Douan in there, so much so, in fact, that he gave a little cry when he noticed the Chezru.

But Yakim Douan, deep into the magic by that point, didn't even hear him.

That lack of response piqued Merwan Ma's curiosity. He scolded himself for intruding upon the God-Voice, and started out of the room, but his natural curiosity held him, for just a bit.

Merwan Ma could not understand what was going on in there, for it was no ritual that the God-Voice had ever related to him. And while he understood that Yakim Douan could not be questioned, nor could he err in matters spiritual, something about all of this settled uncomfortably on Merwan Ma's shoulders.

The realization of his discomfort only prompted the loyal servant of Yatol to scold himself again and remind himself that he was ignorant.

Ignorant.

He scurried out of the room, taking care to close the door gently so that he did not disturb the great Chezru Chieftain.

He consciously denied his feelings of discomfort.

His subconscious was not so easily controlled.

# CHAPTER 13

## *Never the Horse*

He was To-gai-ru, and not Behrenese. Brynn had no doubt of that at all from the moment she had entered the tapestried room in the Yatol Temple to stand before Yatol Daek Gin Gin Yan. His hair was straight and raven black, and his skin was not the delicate, chocolate brown most common among the Behrenese, but held a ruddier hue, a touch of yellow within the rich tones so unique to the To-gai-ru. While at first glance, his physique seemed more like that of a Behrenese man, the softer and rounder lines more common among people living in the luxury of cities, Brynn noted the strong underlying musculature along his bare forearms. And when he shifted in his seat so that his flowing robes tightened about one leg, she noted, too, the muscular set of his thighs, both indicative of the hard riding of a To-gai-ru.

He stared hard at Brynn as she stood there calmly before him, with Dee'dakh, who was half a foot taller than she, at her side. The Yatol narrowed his eyes several times, and stubbornly did not blink, obviously trying to intimidate the woman.

Brynn worked hard not to match that stare. Knowing that this man was To-gai-ru made her hate him all the more. He was a traitor to his people, abandoning the old ways and embracing the conquerors'. He was everything that Brynn was not, holding fast to everything she despised—she knew that from his title and his heritage. There was little more, if anything, that needed to be said between them, as far as she was concerned. But Yatol Daek wouldn't see things that way, she knew, and so she let him play his game for the time being.

"Kayleen Kek," he said, a hint of derision in his somewhat

shrill voice speaking perfect To-gai-ru. "I did not know that any of Kayleen Kek remained anywhere to be found. Certainly they do not proudly announce their presence."

The insult rolled from Brynn's shoulders; she gave it hardly a thought. She knew that she was being tested.

"I see that you chose to wear your sword," Yatol Daek observed.

"It would bring dishonor to you if I had not," Brynn replied. "This is a meeting of station, and my station is that of warrior. To come in here adorned differently, for our initial meeting, would be deceptive, would it not?"

She had spoken truthfully concerning To-gai-ru tradition. A sheathed sword was a sign of honesty, not of threat.

At her side, Dee'dahk bristled, giving Brynn the distinct impression that the warrior woman was not nearly as deaf to the To-gai-ru language as she had pretended at their first meeting.

"You fancy yourself a warrior, then," said Yatol Daek.

"I am. There is no pride. There is no ambition. There is only truth."

"A fine warrior, I suppose."

"It is not a measure that I seek," Brynn answered. "My skills have kept me alive through my trials, and thus, they have been sufficient." She couldn't help but twinge a bit as she considered that her skills had not been enough to keep Belli'mar Juraviel and Cazzira alive. Her answer was perfectly in line, again, with To-gai-ru tradition, where such things as battle skill were not measured for vanity, but more for pragmatism. Rather, skill levels were viewed as more akin to one's legs—long enough to reach the ground.

"There is a true warrior standing beside you, you know," Yatol Daek remarked.

"I am well aware of the reputation of the Chezhou-Lei," Brynn calmly answered. She subtly glanced to the side as she spoke, noting that Dee'dahk had stiffened a bit with pride.

"Perhaps I should arrange a contest between you two," Yatol Daek said, speaking more to himself, it seemed, than to Brynn or Dee'dahk. "Yes, that might be a fine idea."

"To what end?"

Brynn's blunt question elicited a glare her way from the traitor To-gai-ru. "Is it your place to question?"

Brynn gave a hint of a shrug, but otherwise did not answer.

"Perhaps I will arrange such a contest for my amusement," Yatol Daek went on. "Yes, watching two women do battle for my enjoyment . . ."

Brynn let it all roll away from her, thinking the man a perfect fool. She entertained a fantasy of allowing Daek Gin Gin Yan his game, of slaughtering Dee'dahk then turning her wondrous blade upon the Yatol, cutting him down in front of the whole, grateful village.

*Patience,* she reminded herself. *Patience.*

"Let me see your sword," the Yatol said suddenly, motioning to her with one outstretched hand.

Brynn drew out the fabulous weapon and presented it vertically before her, but not close enough for the Yatol to grasp it.

"Hand it over," he instructed.

Brynn slowly turned the blade around, allowing him to view the masterwork crafting and design, but did not move it out toward his hand at all. Her expression was not defiant, nor was it confrontational.

"The code of the To-gai-ru warrior prevents me from handing my sword to any but one who has defeated me at *irysh kad'du,*" she said quietly, referring to the greatest challenge in To-gai-ru society, a test of horsemanship and courage.

"*Irysh kad'du* has been outlawed," Yatol Daek said. "You know that, of course."

Brynn most certainly did not know of that. For a moment, she allowed her flash of stunned amazement to show upon her face. Had it gone that far already? Had the To-gai-ru been so completely conquered that they had abandoned the most sacred of their rituals, *irysh kad'du*? How had her proud people allowed this to happen without going back to war with the Behrenese?

Brynn fought hard to put all of that out of her thoughts, reminding herself that this was not the time for violence. She needed to use this place, and this traitorous Yatol, to gain better insights into her enemies.

Yatol Daek reached out a bit farther, motioning for the

sword, and despite her desire to maintain a controlled environment there, she made a quick movement that slid her precious sword back into its scabbard.

Fires burned in Yatol Daek's dark eyes.

"If the challenge is outlawed, then none shall touch my sword until I am dead," Brynn stated, and Dee'dahk at her side bristled again, like a horse straining at the bit.

Yatol Daek sat back and continued to stare at Brynn, an amused expression on his plump face.

For a moment, Brynn thought that she had stepped over the line, that the man would agree to her terms and instruct Dee'dahk to kill her. Still, on this point there could be no other open path; Brynn would certainly not turn over her amazing elven sword to any potential enemy!

Yatol Daek relaxed, though, and the moment of danger seemed to pass. "You may remain in the village," he decided suddenly, and he waved his hand and looked away.

It took Brynn a moment to catch on, but she realized that she had been dismissed, and so, with a shrug, turned and started toward the door.

"Without a proper pronouncement of departure?" came Yatol Daek's question behind her.

Brynn turned, looking at him with confusion. Apparently, she had broken yet another rule.

"I will forgive yet another of your transgressions," Yatol Daek remarked haughtily. "But if you intend to stay here—indeed, Brynn Dharielle, if you intend to survive—then you would do well to learn what is expected of you."

Brynn resisted the urge to show him her sword again, this time horizontally and point out.

She made no gestures at all, though, no sign of confirmation or denial of his last statement, and walked out of the room and out of the building. She knew that Daek Gin Gin Yan was inside conversing with Dee'dahk at that very moment, likely trying to discern the best method for discrediting Brynn in front of the other To-gai-ru, or for simply eliminating her altogether. She knew that she would be watched every step during her stay in Yatol Daek's domain, and she suspected that her refusal to bend to his will would force a confrontation with him, and with Dee'dahk, fairly soon.

She knew, too, the dangers of that course, for this was a fine opportunity for her to come to better understand the truth of the present state of To-gai.

But so be it, she decided.

Layered in skins, from the shaggy and heavy coat of the brown ox to the silver accents of the wolf, and with a tall and strong physique of corded, rolling muscle, Ashwarawu looked every bit as fierce as the reputation that preceded him. His long legs hung far below the belly of his pinto pony, seeming as if he could guide the creature easily through any maneuver.

Which he could.

His jaw was square and firm, his brow furrowed, a line of thick black hair accenting it from one side of his face to the other. That pronounced brow only added to the mystery and intensity of his dark eyes below it.

It was said that many of Ashwarawu's enemies simply surrendered to him on the battlefield, begging for a quick and merciful death. Anyone who looked upon the angry To-gai-ru warrior did not doubt those rumors.

"They have not finished the wall," one of the great leader's scouts reported to him.

Ashwarawu nodded grimly, then turned to regard the single stone marker set in the grass, up from the banks of a dry riverbed: the spot where a young To-gai-ru man, Jocyn Tho by name, had been staked out and murdered.

Ashwarawu had brought his gang there purposely. He wanted them to see this marker—yet another example of the brutality of Yatol Grysh and his murdering soldiers. Many of Ashwarawu's warriors were of that assaulted clan. Many had known Jocyn Tho.

It was just one more insult to the To-gai-ru, one more reminder that they and the Behrenese were not alike and not allies, and that they, whatever the cost, had to expel the conquerors from their sacred lands.

Ashwarawu walked his mount right past the stone marker.

He tapped the tip of his great spear once, twice, thrice on the stone marker, a traditional signal from living To-gai-ru warrior to deceased that his death would soon be avenged. One by one, Ashwarawu's warriors walked past the grave marker, tapping their weapons similarly.

The leader looked at his clansmen, his warriors, his friends, and he knew that they were ready this day.

"The builders understand?" Ashwarawu asked his scout.

"They believe that they can sneak in a score, and hide them," the man answered.

A sly smile crossed the leader's face. The folly of the conquerors to use the conquered in projects as vital as the building of fortifications! It hadn't taken much effort on Ashwarawu's part to make contact with the To-gai-ru wall-building slaves, and had taken even less to convince them to render aid in the attack.

He barked out a command to one of his undercommanders to organize the score of infiltrators, and with precision honed over the months of fighting, the undercommander was soon away, trotting across the steppes with nineteen eager warriors in tow. They would hide in the grass outside the town Douan Cal until dusk, and then, as the slaves arranged for distractions, crawl into the town one by one to their appointed hiding places. It was all too easy.

Ashwarawu led the attack just before the next dawn. With a hundred warriors riding behind him, the great outlaw charged the still-sleeping settlement of Douan Cal.

Cries went up along the wall, from the sentries, calls to all the Behrenese settlers to take up arms and defend their homes. Dozens of men and women went up to those walls, twenty skilled To-gai-ru soldiers filtering up beside them.

Ashwarawu came in straight and strong, his spear held high above his head, the song of the warrior god, Joek, on his lips. The settlers rained arrows down on the attackers, but the thundering horde did not slow and did not turn.

And unlike the frightened Behrenese, the fierce To-gai-ru did not loose their missiles from a distance. They waited until they were in close, drawing back powerful bows—and no race in all the world could handle a bow from horseback better than the warriors of the steppes.

The thunder of the charge held, then, with Ashwarawu and his warriors milling about the base of the wall, which was barely higher than a tall man, firing arrow after arrow.

A Behrenese occasionally rose up to return the fire, but the barrage had him ducking, or had him dead, almost immediately.

Another group within the To-gai-ru archers went to work then, tossing grapnels up over the wall top, then turning their powerful ponies about and starting the pull immediately. As pony after pony hooked up, the wall began to groan and sway.

The Behrenese responded by charging to the spot, ready to loose a fierce barrage, ready to slice through the tugging lines.

But then the score of To-gai-ru infiltrators sprang up among the defenders, disrupting their shots and shattering any coordinated defense. Outposter after outposter was heaved over the wall, to fall to the dust at the feet of the merciless Ashwarawu.

Then the wall came crashing down, and battle was joined, and the mounted To-gai-ru sliced the lines of standing Behrenese apart with devastating precision.

For all of its construction, Douan Cal was not prepared for so large an attack, and had no chance of beginning to repel even the first assault. Many were dead or on the ground screaming in agony within a few minutes. Outmaneuvered, outflanked, and outfought, those who remained soon enough threw down their weapons, pleading for mercy.

Their answer came in one chilling word, "Ashwarawu."

The captive men were bound and taken away, out to the dry riverbed, where a select few were untied and forced to dig holes in the sand, so that their bound kin could be buried up to their waists. In turn, Ashwarawu's own warriors dug the holes for the remaining captive men.

Then, with forty-three Behrenese men squirming in the sand, buried to their waists and helplessly bound and blindfolded, Ashwarawu led in the To-gai-ru nomads of Jocyn Tho's tribe, showing to them the many stones left by the dried-up river.

The stoning went on for hours, until the last Behrenese outposter leaned over limply, dead.

Most of Ashwarawu's men left before it was finished, returning to Douan Cal to have their way with the Behrenese women before killing them outright.

The few children of the outposters were killed mercifully, at least, a single blow to the head before being thrown atop a large bonfire.

Jocyn Tho had been avenged.

Her last transgression when leaving Yatol Daek, she learned, was one that offended her profoundly. In leaving the presence of Yatol Daek, To-gai-ru were expected to drop to one knee and bow their heads.

Brynn took great care over the next few weeks to avoid the Yatol, for she doubted that she could bring herself to do that, whatever the result.

The young ranger also took great care to learn well the rituals of life in the settlement. She tried to fit in as well as she could, though, since she would not go anywhere without her sword and the bracer, at least, she always seemed to stand out.

She also made time every day to go and see Runtly. The pony, who had run free all of his life, was not pleased to be indoors in a stall.

"Not much longer," Brynn promised him every time she went to him. "We will be away to the wide fields again."

The pony seemed to understand, and always calmed down when Brynn came in to see him. The last few days, though, Runtly had continued his cribbing, biting the wood at the front of the stall and tugging it back, even when Brynn was there, a clear sign that he was not happy.

Outwardly, Brynn remained calm, not wanting to distress the pony any more. Inside, though, the woman bit it all in and swirled it about, adding the situation to the list of crimes of the Behrenese, using it to build her hatred even more.

But she refused to allow her simmering anger to boil over. She was learning much there about the Behrenese and about the present state of the proud To-gai-ru. Many were assimilating; to Brynn's distress she heard more than one of her fellow

villagers claiming that the new way of life introduced by the
Behrenese conquerors was preferable to the old ways.

Not all of them felt that way, though. Certainly not old
Barachuk and Tsolona, who peppered Brynn for tales of
Kayleen Kek every night after they had retired to the old couple's home. Though she didn't have many tales to tell of that
long-past time, Brynn always tried to accommodate—and
she always tried to draw out recollections of the past from the
old couple. And so it happened that these two, Barachuk and
Tsolona, became Brynn's informal tutors, schooling her in
the way things had been, and in the way she intended for
things to be again.

All remained relatively stable during those weeks, with the
village preparing for the onslaught of winter. Just north of
the Belt-and-Buckle, winter did not hit hard, but the To-gai
steppes were of high enough elevation for the winter wind
to bite.

One day, the clouds gathering overhead with a threat of the
first snow of the season, Brynn was going about her regular
duties, bringing water from a nearby river, when she noted a
commotion within the village, over by the stables. Sensing
immediately that Runtly might be involved, Brynn dropped
her two buckets and sprinted over, to find many Behrenese,
including a fair number of soldiers and including Yatol Daek
and Chezhou-Lei Dee'dahk, bringing out several of the pinto
ponies.

Brynn winced when she saw Runtly come out of the barn
at the end of a lead, handled by a cursed Behrenese.

She pushed through the gathered folk, to the front of the
To-gai-ru line. "What are they doing?" she asked a young To-
gai-ru woman, Chiniruk, who was standing beside her.

"Yatol Daek thins the herd," the woman explained. "The
chosen horses will be taken to Behren for sale."

Before Chiniruk had even finished, Brynn started across
the short expanse of open ground, toward Yatol Daek, who
was directing the handling. He saw her coming, obviously,
but pretended not to, continuing his stream of commands, including one to Chezhou-Lei Dee'dahk to return to his side—a
clear sign to Brynn that he meant to incite her.

"My horse is among the group on the left," she said, not waiting for an introduction.

"The group on the left is leaving for the market in Dharyan," Yatol Daek replied, turning to regard her.

"My horse is among—"

"You have no horse!" the Yatol snapped suddenly, the volume and intensity of his voice bringing Dee'dahk's hand to the hilt of her sheathed sword and bringing many of the nearby Behrenese soldiers to attention. "By the terms of surrender, all horses are the property of Chezru Chieftain Yakim Douan. Learn the rules and your place, wandering Ru."

Brynn glanced over at Runtly, but only for a second, turning back on the Yatol, her rich brown eyes going narrow. "Runtly is my horse," she said.

Yakim Douan glanced back at her, seeming rather amused by it all. "Truly?"

"Truly." Not a hint of submission sounded in Brynn's cold tone.

"Learn your place, wandering Ru."

"If this is not my place, then I will take my horse and be gone from here," Brynn replied.

Yatol Daek gave a snort and a chuckle. "You have no horse."

"You are To-gai-ru," Brynn declared. "You understand the meaning. There can be no mistake here!"

"Do not allow the mistake that I was born of To-gai-ru parents to bring any misunderstanding, fool. You have no horse. Now go back to the other peasants and be silent, before I lose patience with your ignorance."

Brynn turned to Runtly and gave a shrill whistle, and the horse reared and threw his head, tossing the Behrenese handler to the ground.

"Desist, or I will have the horse killed!" Yatol Daek cried, and when he looked again at Brynn, he looked, too, at her unsheathed sword.

"Release my horse, Yatol," Brynn replied, but Daek was in full retreat already, issuing a shrill cry.

"Kill the girl! Kill the horse!"

As she started to pursue, Brynn saw Dee'dahk coming in

hard, her curving blade out, spinning a vertical circle on her right, then working its way impressively over to the left, then behind her back and back out to the right again. Her charge came in perfect balance, that sword spinning effortlessly, and Brynn knew that in a fair fight, this warrior would be a worthy opponent indeed.

But this was not a fair fight, Brynn knew, for Dee'dahk thought little of Brynn's fighting prowess. To the mighty Chezhou-Lei, Brynn was just another Ru, and unmounted. That did not amount to much in the Behrenese warrior's estimation.

So she came in hard and fast, sword spinning to the right, sword spinning to the left, sword always out too wide to deflect.

Brynn kept her apparent focus on Yatol Daek, pursuing the man, but not really closing ground. She waited until the last possible second, until Dee'dahk was upon her. Then, with muscles honed and balance perfected from all her years of *bi'nelle dasada*, the elven-trained ranger pivoted on her back foot and thrust out, one, two, three, her magnificent sword slicing through the layered armor and driving hard into Dee'-dahk's chest.

The Chezhou-Lei stopped in her tracks. All about gasped in astonishment at the sheer speed of the strike, for none in To-gai had ever before witnessed the precision and straight-forward attack that was *bi'nelle dasada*. Dee'dahk's wide-eyed look was as much in surprise as in pain, Brynn knew. In truth, Brynn wasn't sure that the warrior woman had even registered the fact that she was already mortally wounded.

Mortally wounded, but probably still dangerous, Brynn realized.

Brynn's fourth strike was perfectly aimed, taking her in the heart.

She stood there at the end of Brynn's bloody blade for a long while, staring into the rich brown eyes of her killer.

Then she slid back off the blade, falling to the ground.

The reality of the moment, of the kill, hit Brynn hard indeed, but she pushed it away, having no time, and charged hard at Yatol Daek.

The man put his hands up, begging her for mercy. "Take your horse, wanderer!" he said, and he quickly called out to his soldiers trying to corner Runtly, telling them to desist. "Be gone from here—I have no quarrel with you!"

Brynn stared at him curiously, contemptuously. He was an appointed leader, but he was obviously a coward. So great a coward! Not lowering her sword, and not letting him slip away from her at all, Brynn glanced to the side and called to the pony, who came trotting over.

"There, you see?" said Yatol Daek. "I am not your enemy, wanderer. I am To-gai-ru."

"No!" Brynn screamed at him before he had ever finished the claim.

Yatol Daek put his trembling hands before him. "You cannot kill me and hope to survive," he said. "Please, get on your horse and be gone."

"No, fool," Brynn said, in more controlled tones, and she lowered her blade somewhat, and Yatol Daek's hands similarly drooped. "You are no To-gai-ru."

"The religion of Yatol—"

"This is not about the robes you wear!" Brynn shouted. "No, this goes deeper." Runtly reached her then, and she pulled the brown-and-white head in close and rubbed her cheek against the soft hair.

"No," she said to Daek. "No To-gai-ru would steal a horse."

"The horses are the property—" he started to protest, but Brynn wasn't listening.

"No To-gai-ru would ever order a horse slaughtered." When she finished, she was still nuzzling Runtly, still seeming quite at ease.

But then came that explosive thrust of *bi'nelle dasada*, so suddenly that Yatol Daek never registered the movement. His expression was of genuine astonishment when he looked down to see Brynn's magnificent sword buried deep in his belly.

"Damn you, and damn your new ways," Brynn said, and her thoughts went into the sword, then, calling forth the fire!

Yatol Daek screamed in agony, and Brynn jerked the blade

once and then again, the fine metal slicing him open, the flames consuming him.

She tore it free then, and turned to see the many Behrenese and the many To-gai-ru, staring at her with disbelief.

It didn't hold, and the Behrenese soldiers howled and started to charge.

Brynn went up to Runtly's back, guiding him with her strong legs. She clenched her left fist, bringing forth the pulsing white shield of her enchanted powrie bracer.

She didn't run off, though, but turned and galloped into the heart of the charging Behrenese line. Behrenese soldiers scattered before her; she ran one down, finishing him with a devastating chop, and let Runtly trample another to the dirt.

Brynn charged back the other way, toward the home of Barachuk and Tsolona. To her relief, the couple was waiting for her, throwing her the bow and quiver.

The pursuit was halfhearted at that point, and Brynn could have taken Runtly out of the village easily enough. But the young ranger was far from satisfied. She slid her sword under one leg and took up her bow, charging back toward the Behrenese pursuit.

A couple of enemy soldiers were up on horseback by then.

Brynn smiled wickedly as she thought of the first major challenge Lady Dasslerond had thrown at her. She saw her enemies as she had seen the targets that dark night in Andur'Blough Inninness on the torchlit field, and her aim was no less true.

By the time Brynn Dharielle and Runtly charged out of the small village, her quiver was emptied of its twelve arrows and ten Behrenese, including Yatol Daek and Chezhou-Lei Dee'dahk, lay mortally wounded.

A few arrows arched out of the town in her general direction, none coming close to striking the mark.

Brynn pulled up a short distance away, turning to measure the danger.

But no pursuit was forthcoming.

# CHAPTER 14

# *As Graciously as Possible*

The tribesmen of the southern steppes of To-gai, near to the Mountains of Fire, had never been true nomads, and so the intrusion of Behrenese conquerors had not changed the ways of these To-gai-ru as profoundly as it had their brethren farther to the north. The northern slopes of the volcanic mountain range were so very fertile year-round that there was no need to wander or follow any herd. And there, far removed from Jacintha and the edicts of the Chezru Chieftain, and where the borderland between the two kingdoms was not so clearly defined as the barren sand to plateau steppe change farther to the north, many Behrenese and To-gai-ru had lived and worked in relative proximity for centuries. There were even children of mixed heritage, though they were not common, and the practice had never been openly accepted.

The only real difference since the conquest of To-gai was the presence of Behrenese soldiers, a single eight-square, traveling from settlement to settlement to tribe encampment, fostering many ill feelings among the To-gai-ru, and trying, obviously, to rouse the sentiments of the Behrenese in the region against their Ru neighbors. Typically, though, as soon as the eight-square moved on, those Behrenese and To-gai-ru commoners who were left behind resumed their typical daily routines.

Another thing that the Behrenese and To-gai-ru of the southern stretches had in common was a mistrust, even fear, of the mysterious order of mystics rumored to be wandering the Mountains of Fire, the Jhesta Tu. These reservations were amplified among the Behrenese, for the Yatol religion had long ago condemned the Jhesta Tu as heretics. Even among the To-gai-ru, though, traditionally more tolerant of other beliefs—since their own tribes often varied in their respective deities—the Jhesta Tu had never been looked upon fondly.

Into this environment, following the vision that had been shown to him in the days before he had earned the Sash of All Colors, walked Pagonel, carrying a backpack of various colored threads and sewing supplies so that he could continue work on producing the Sash of All Colors for the next master to walk the path. Pagonel knew that he would be in somewhat hostile territory no matter what direction he took out of the Mountains of Fire, but he had seen the truth, had experienced his Chi life force in a conscious and intimate way, and so he feared nothing.

In the common room of the first village he entered, he felt the many stares focused his way, and since he spoke both Behrenese and To-gai-ru fluently, he understood the many whispered insults surrounding him. But he let them slide right past him. They didn't understand. How could they understand?

The To-gai-ru proprietor of the common room served him as requested—certainly not promptly!—though he charged more pieces of silver than normal, Pagonel knew.

"You offer rooms for the night?" Pagonel asked him.

The proprietor, a To-gai-ru, glanced around at the many patrons whose eyes were upon him.

"Fear not, friend, for I'll not even ask about acquiring shelter," the mystic said, letting the obviously nervous man off the hook. "The night will not be cold, and the stars are the finest roof a man might know." Pagonel drained his glass of water, smiled and bowed at the flustered proprietor, then turned and similarly saluted the rest of the gathering.

He heard many whispered conversations, almost all derogatory, aimed at his back as he exited the building.

At least they had not been openly hostile, and none, not even the few Behrenese in the room, had made any movements to challenge him. Still, Pagonel thought it unwise to remain in the settlement that night, so he went out to the surrounding forest and found a comfortable niche in a tree, settled back, and watched the lazy glide of the moon across the starry sky.

He was gone long before the next dawn, walking north at a leisurely pace. He still was not quite sure why his vision had beckoned him out into the wide world, but he was curious about the continuing assimilation of To-gai-ru into the conquerors' culture. Perhaps that was the experience to which he had been called, to learn more of this clash of cultures that was reshaping the civilizations south of the larger mountain range. Perhaps there, where old traditions were being challenged daily, Pagonel might learn more about the truth of the world and about this life.

That was what the mystic told himself as he wandered north. He never imagined that other, deeper emotions would soon be stirring within him.

The mystic wandered for many days, enjoying the sights about him as the season changed to winter. He wasn't overly concerned for his safety; he was Jhesta Tu and had learned well how to survive in the harshest of climates.

He recognized the signs of an approaching storm—one that would likely be snow and not rain—one afternoon, at about the same time he saw the wispy gray lines of smoke rising from a nearby village.

He crested a ridge, looking down upon the collections of mud and wood houses, the sun setting behind them. He noted a line of tethered horses—not the pinto ponies of the To-gai-ru, but taller mounts, chestnut and roan. Noting movement about the mounts, Pagonel recognized the white robes of a Behrenese man, then looked closer to see the crossed black straps over the man's chest, showing him to be a Behrenese soldier.

"This could be of interest," Pagonel remarked, and he strode down to the village. The stares that greeted the mystic, with his identifying Jhesta Tu tan tunic and sash, were identical to the ones he had felt upon him in the previous village. Except for the Behrenese soldier; when that man took note of Pagonel, his dark eyes widened in obvious horror, and he ran headlong, even tripping to his knees once as he tried to scramble inside the town's common room.

Pagonel went in soon after, to find a dozen soldiers, all adorned in the white robes with the black leather chest straps, staring at him hard. The mystic nodded to them, then moved to the long table that served as a bar.

The scuffling of feet behind him told him that one of the soldiers had scrambled out of the room, no doubt to warn his superiors.

"Long way from your home," said the innkeeper, a broad-shouldered Ru with black stubble on his face that seemed to reach all the way up to his dark eyes.

"Not so long," Pagonel replied. "A week's march and no more, if my pace is brisk."

"Them Behrenese dog-soldiers are going to think that you're far from home," said the innkeeper.

As he finished, Pagonel heard another scuffling, and he turned to see the soldier returning, glancing at him from over the shoulder of an older, stern-faced man who was dressed in Behrenese soldier robes, but with golden straps and not black, crossing his broad, muscled chest.

He stared hard at Pagonel, who took care not to match that look, but rather nodded deferentially and tipped his glass of water. Then the mystic turned back around, facing the bar, and placed his cup down on the table.

"What is your name?" came the question behind him, spoken in To-gai-ru, if a bit strained in dialect.

Pagonel sipped his water, making no move to answer.

"You, Jhesta Tu!" came a snarl. "What is your name?"

Pagonel slowly turned to face the man, and the line of a dozen warriors standing behind him, most of them glancing about nervously. The reputation of the Jhesta Tu preceded him, apparently.

"What is your name?" the leader asked yet again.

"I am called Pagonel. And what is yours?"

"I will ask, you will answer."

"I already have."

"Silence!" The man narrowed his eyes, his stare boring into the mystic. "You mock me?"

"Hardly."

"I am Commander of the Square," the soldier said in haughty tones.

"And that is a source of pride?"

"Should it not be?"

"Should it be?" Pagonel understood that he might be pushing a bit too hard, though all of his remarks had been offered in neutral, matter-of-fact tones, and all had been merely observations and not judgments. Or had they been? the mystic had to honestly ask himself. He reviewed his last few comments—while pointedly not locking stares with the infuriated Commander of the Square—and he had to admit that, while everything he said had been simple truth, it was also bait.

"I am Pagonel, Commander of the Square," he said calmly. "I have journeyed from my home in search of wisdom and enlightenment, and with no desire for any trouble, I assure you." He lowered his eyes as he finished, which he believed that the prideful commander would surely view as a sign of peace and submission.

Like a shark smelling blood, the man moved to grab Pagonel's chin, to lift his head up that he could stare the sheepish mystic down. The commander's hand never got close to connecting, though. Reacting purely on instinct, Pagonel's own hand snapped across, slapping the commander's hand back to back, and with a lightning fast twist and pull, Pagonel rolled his hand back, caught the commander's thumb, and bent it back hard, throwing the commander off-balance, locking him low in pain.

Now the mystic did look up, into a face twisted with pain and outrage.

"I could have you killed for this!" the commander growled through teeth tightly clenched.

"I seek wisdom and enlightenment, not trouble," Pagonel calmly replied. "But I am of the body, Jhesta Tu, and am sworn to protect that body." He released the hand as he explained, and the commander retreated a step and stood straight, rubbing his sore thumb and glaring at the mystic.

"I am the voice of the Chezru Chieftain in this province,"

the commander growled, and Pagonel noted that many of the soldiers were collecting their weapons at that point. He wasn't afraid of them—not for his personal safety, at least—but he was very concerned at the implications of a confrontation here, before he had even really begun to explore To-gai and his vision.

"I question your authority not at all, Commander of the Square," Pagonel said humbly.

The commander held up his hand, motioning for his soldiers to hold calm. "Yet you have committed a crime against the God-Voice," he said.

Pagonel bit back the obvious response. He just sat calmly and listened.

"You are not to touch me, and I will treat you as I deem appropriate. Do you understand?"

Pagonel's expression remained impassive. He suppressed his instincts then, as the commander reached out toward his face again. The man took Pagonel's chin in his hand, a tight and strong grip, and forced the mystic to look at him directly.

Pagonel considered the thirty or so ways he could cripple the fool, but he only entertained those thoughts to distract him from his current revulsion.

"I will have all of your coins as a fine for your insolence," the commander declared, and he pushed Pagonel's face aside.

"I am Jhesta Tu, and without many funds," the mystic replied.

The commander reached over and pulled the small purse from Pagonel's belt, then dumped the silver coins into his open palm. "It is not enough to pay for your crimes," he said. "But I will forgive your transgressions, this one time."

As he finished, he turned and started back toward his soldiers, who were all chuckling and nodding approvingly.

Pagonel let him go. For the price of a few easily replaced coins, he had defused the situation. That was his duty as a brother of Jhesta Tu. They were not a warlike order.

But, if pressed . . .

Pagonel took a long look at the Commander of the Square, imprinting the man's image in his mind.

The soldiers, predictably, began to taunt the mystic then, with a couple tossing small items Pagonel's way, and one even spitting at him.

"He's a bully, that one," the To-gai-ru innkeeper said quietly, bending low so that only Pagonel could hear. "Don't pay him no heed." As he finished, the innkeeper put a second glass of water before the mystic.

"I have no money," Pagonel started to explain, but the innkeeper shook his head and held out his hand, showing that he wouldn't have accepted any money even if it had been offered.

"Perhaps someday you'll tell me tales of your order in payment."

"That I cannot do," said Pagonel.

The innkeeper shrugged and smiled, as if it did not matter.

Pagonel left the common room a short while later, to the jeers and spit of the Behrenese soldiers.

He accepted it.

He filed it away in a place in his mind where he would not forget.

Outside, the mystic brushed himself off and spent a moment in quiet meditation, finding his center.

"You gave him free drink!" he heard the commander shout, back within the common room.

The mystic turned a bit, craning his ear toward the door.

"And so free drinks will be the way of the night," the commander declared.

"It was only water," the innkeeper protested.

"And he was only a Jhesta Tu dog," the commander shouted back. "If he is worth water, then my soldiers are worth all of the drink that you have, and all of the money as well!"

The innkeeper's protest was cut short by a sharp slap.

The cries of the soldiers, calling for drink, and of the commander, demanding an apology and all the money within the common room were cut short, abruptly, as the door banged open.

All eyes turned to see the Jhesta Tu mystic standing in the

open portal, expression calm and arms down by his side, seeming vulnerable.

Deceptively so, the first soldier to attack him realized. The Behrenese charged straight in, spear leading. He hardly saw Pagonel move, and so he was completely off-balance as he somehow missed with the thrust, sliding past, leaning forward.

A hand came up fast in front of his face, barely hitting, but perfectly aimed to snap the man's nose straight up. Pagonel's other hand grabbed at the back of his belt as he stumbled past, heaving him along to tumble out into the street.

Two more soldiers charged in, side by side, the one on Pagonel's right coming with another straight spear thrust, the other slashing a sword horizontally before him. A twitch of his toned muscles and a tight tuck had the mystic somersaulting over the swinging sword. He reversed his momentum immediately as he landed, half-turning and snapping a kick to the side of the soldier's knee, caving in the leg.

Pagonel leaped and shoulder-rolled right over the soldier's shoulders as the man slumped. He landed lightly on his feet next to the dropping man's companion, within reach of the cumbersome spear.

His open-palmed thrust only moved about four inches, but with enough force into the center of the soldier's chest to take his breath and his strength away. The soldier gave a great gasp, gulping air, and collapsed to his knees.

Pagonel reached with his right leg across the kneeling man, hooking him under the arm, then swung back out to the right, launching the man headlong at the feet of another charging soldier, tripping him up. The mystic ran along the back of the sprawling soldier, lifting off lightly into the air, right in the middle of three more startled soldiers.

He kicked left with his left foot, right with his right, then straight ahead with the left, before ever touching the ground, and three more Behrenese went flying away.

As he touched down, the mystic skittered out to the left, toward the bar. As he approached another table, he made a move as if to leap it, then ducked fast and skittered under instead.

A soldier, falling for the ruse, swept his spear across above the tabletop, then tried to recover fast and stoop down to stab at the mystic.

Pagonel's hand exploded through the wooden table, snapping a clean hole. He grabbed the bending soldier by the hair and snapped his arm back down, moving out as he did, so that when the soldier's face smashed into the table with enough force to shatter the piece of furniture, Pagonel was already coming out the far side.

He looked more like a dancer than a warrior as he crossed the room, his feet touching the floor, the chairs, the tables or, impossibly, nothing at all. However the mystic did it, he was standing right before the stunned commander in a matter of moments.

The commander shoved the innkeeper back and turned fast, stabbing at Pagonel with a small serrated knife.

Pagonel's right hand came across, lightning fast, to catch the inside of the commander's wrist. The mystic's left hand came across with equal speed, catching the back of the knife hand and bending it in forcefully and painfully, taking the knife away while hardly slowing.

Up went the knife, into the air, and Pagonel let go with his right and backhanded the commander with a stinging slap across the face, followed by a forehand, followed by a backhand from the returning left, and finishing with a fourth slap, an open forehand with the left.

Pagonel caught the knife as it dropped and snapped his hand across again, replacing the blade in the dazed commander's hand.

"If you strike again, then do so with more precision," Pagonel warned. "That was the one lesson I offer you for free."

The commander's face twisted in rage and he retracted his arm a bit, as if lining up a strike. He held there, though, and looked about at his soldiers, several on the ground and the others staring back with confusion and obvious fear. The leader collected himself and looked back to Pagonel. "I forgave you once," he started, but he was interrupted almost immediately, the mystic whispering so that only he could hear.

"Be gone from this place and this village, and now," Pagonel warned. "Do so immediately and save your pride and save your life."

The commander looked around again, at the fallen and the stunned, then he looked down to his own hand, to the knife replaced, to the knife that had somehow been cleanly taken from his grasp.

"Gather your fellows!" he roared at his command, and he stormed past Pagonel, stomping right out of the common room.

The first man the mystic had felled had the misfortune of heading back into the tavern at that precise moment, and the commander smacked him aside and continued away. Appearing grudging, though all who had witnessed understood their profound relief, the other soldiers followed.

"Commander Aklai will not forgive you for this," the innkeeper warned quietly. "He will see you dead."

"Indeed," Pagonel replied, and he accepted another glass of water and drained it quickly.

Then, after he heard the pounding hooves of Aklai's departing forces, the mystic walked out of the common room for the second time, this time not stopping until he had put the village far behind him.

He continued to head north over the next few days, though the weather became colder and less hospitable. One day, with fine snow flying sidelong in the frigid wind, Pagonel found a comfortably sheltered perch beneath a rocky overhang. He sat cross-legged, hands on thighs, palms upward. He sent his consciousness through his body, one step at a time, inviting deep relaxation and also slowing the rhythms of his body, insulating it from the cold.

In that trancelike state, Pagonel's mind replayed the events of the last weeks. Why had he come to To-gai? What role might he find there?

Also, in that trance, the Jhesta Tu mystic began honestly to examine his own feelings, toward his heritage, the To-gai-ru, and toward the Behrenese invaders. It wasn't a matter of like or dislike—Pagonel understood well that such sweeping generalizations could not be leveled upon entire races of people—

races comprised, ultimately, of individuals. But there was a matter of justice and implications. The Behrenese had attacked To-gai—unprovoked, by all accounts—and they were not acting the role of beneficent masters!

If the Chezru Chieftain, who continued the long line of his predecessors in declaring the Jhesta Tu heretics, could so simply conquer To-gai, then what of the Mountains of Fire? Everyone knew that the true motivation for the Behrenese invasion of To-gai was the lucrative trade in To-gai ponies, whatever front story concerning To-gai as a lost province of the Behrenese kingdom the Chezru and his cohorts had concocted. Given that willingness to conquer and murder for profit, might the Chezru Chieftain turn his sights to the region surrounding the Walk of Clouds, with all its riches in minerals?

"Is that the reason my vision has led me here?" Pagonel asked quietly, his voice drowned away by the howling wind. "Am I to view the precursor to the attack upon my order?"

He stayed in the sheltered nook throughout the rest of the day and the night, and when the next morning dawned clear, with but a dusting of snow on the tall grasses, the mystic set out again, walking north.

He passed through another town that day and managed to join up with a caravan of To-gai-ru, heading north. All through the journey, Pagonel sat quietly and listened to the tales of frustration, the anger, to tales of horror, where family members had been stolen away by Behrenese soldiers. In all that chatter, the only real measure of hope that the mystic heard came in the name of a rogue leader, Ashwarawu, who was apparently operating in the area.

Pagonel decided then and there that he would seek out this rogue leader.

# CHAPTER 15

## *Expanding His Horizons*

Yatol Grysh welcomed the twenty-square of Jacintha soldiers to Dharyan with mixed feelings. On the one hand, he was glad that Yakim Douan had finally provided him with the strength he needed to restore complete control to the region. But on the other hand, the proud Yatol priest hated having to ask for the assistance. Especially at a time when Chezru Chieftain Douan had hinted that the Transcendence might be nearing, Grysh did not want to appear weak to his fellow priests.

And why had Yakim Douan sent a twenty-square, four hundred soldiers, when Grysh had asked for only an eight-square? Did that signal the Chezru Chieftain's lack of confidence in him?

He stood on his balcony, watching the procession as expected, his visage firm and strong—as much as it could be, considering his lack of any real chin—as the soldiers marched beneath in rows of five. Ten rows, twenty rows, eighty rows!

They passed the temple balcony and assembled in the square to Yatol Grysh's right, lining up in the perfect twenty-by-twenty formation that gave them their name.

Grysh waited patiently for the formation to settle, then gave the many onlookers, including his own city brigade of two hundred soldiers and his war leader, Wan Atenn, time to soak in the spectacle. The Yatol focused on Wan Atenn for a moment, trying to read the proud man's expression. Another Chezhou-Lei warrior had led the twenty-square into Dharyan. Might the war leader of Dharyan be feeling a bit insecure?

If he was, Wan Atenn gave no outward indication, but Grysh knew the stoic Chezhou-Lei well enough to recognize that he could read nothing from that blank look. He would speak with Wan Atenn privately a bit later, he decided, to assure the man that his position was quite secure.

All eyes, soldier and onlooker alike, were up at Yatol Grysh then, expecting him formally to welcome the newcomers.

Before he could begin, though, a horn blew out in the distance, beyond the city gates, a long and plaintive winding: the call for admittance.

Grysh, and Carwan Pestle at his side, and every other person about Dharyan's main square that cold morning, turned to look out. But only Yatol Grysh and his immediate attendants, from their high perch, could see the cause of that horn.

A second contingent of soldiers—a second twenty-square!—stood on the field beyond Dharyan's fortified gate, led by a second Chezhou-Lei warrior in his fine, overlapping armor.

A second twenty-square! Chezru Chieftain Yakim Douan had sent eight hundred warriors to Grysh's call?

It took all the discipline the Yatol could muster to hide his shock. Eight hundred soldiers! That was more than a quarter of Jacintha's standing garrison!

"Yatol," Carwan Pestle breathed. "Are we to conquer Togai all over again?"

Yatol Grysh snapped a cold look over the Shepherd, who lowered his eyes. In truth, though, Grysh couldn't rightly disagree with his companion's assessment, and understood that Pestle had blurted the words without thinking.

Perfectly excusable, Grysh realized, given the enormity of the surprise before them. Two twenty-squares!

As exciting as that prospect might be. For if these soldiers had come in to serve Grysh and not merely as an extension of Chezru Douan's strong arm, then the Yatol of Dharyan had just become the second most powerful man south of the Belt-and-Buckle Mountains. Perhaps this was Chezru Douan's way of showing complete confidence in Grysh, then, in so empowering him before the time of Transcendence.

Too many possibilities, too many questions, assaulted the

surprised Yatol at that time, and so he took a deep breath, consciously forcing himself to relax, reminding himself that he had yet to meet with the Chezhou-Lei leaders of the twenty-squares to determine so many things.

Other questions invariably came to him, though. Suddenly, he had eight hundred new mouths to feed, and eight hundred new bodies to shelter, and with the fierce Dharyan winter already beginning to blow. It was a daunting prospect, to be sure, but Grysh knew that he could handle it.

He signaled to his gate guards to allow the latest arrivals on the field entry to Dharyan, and with the great curving teeyo-del horns blowing, the city gates swung wide. So began the second procession of the morning, as disciplined and perfect in formation as had been the first, marching past the observing Yatol in eighty rows of five, and then assembling on the wide square beside the first group, opposite Wan Atenn and Grysh's relatively minor forces.

While the second group was settling into place, Grysh felt the distant stare of Wan Atenn upon him. He looked down, studying his war leader, and he knew that the Chezhou-Lei warrior was troubled by this unexpected arrival. They had only asked for sixty-four men, after all, and had been sent eight hundred!

Yatol Grysh offered a reassuring nod to Wan Atenn, sincerely given. The Yatol had no idea what Chezru Douan might be thinking, but he was fairly confident that the God-Voice didn't mean to usurp Grysh's power in the region. Given that, Wan Atenn's position as military leader remained secure, because Grysh trusted the Chezhou-Lei warrior implicitly.

The Yatol went through the remainder of the ceremony with an air of disconnection, looking over the procession dispassionately and from a great distance. His thoughts were on the meeting that would soon follow, and already he was formulating some ways in which he might make the best use of the new arrivals.

There was a particularly thorny renegade To-gai-ru that Grysh wanted to be rid of, one who was said to kill without mercy.

\*     \*     \*

"Jilseponie Wyndon," said Chezru Douan, and he was shaking his head as he spoke the name. "Who is this woman, to become a bishop in the Church ruled by men?"

Across from Douan's desk, Merwan Ma held his tongue, for he knew the question to be much deeper than the obvious answer—an answer that both he and Chezru Douan knew well enough.

Jilseponie had been the one to deliver the miracle of Avelyn a decade before, rescuing Honce-the-Bear from the grip of the rosy plague. The companion of the dead Nightbird, Jilseponie was also credited, in part, with destroying the demon dactyl Bestesbulzibar and in helping to win Honce-the-Bear's war against the demon's goblin, giant, and powrie minions. But that was all long ago, and Jilseponie Wyndon was not a name that Yakim Douan and Merwan Ma had heard in several years.

Until this day, when Abbot Olin's messenger had delivered a note, obviously written to convey a sense of distress, that Jilseponie Wyndon had been appointed bishop of the city of Palmaris, and more pointedly, that the woman was being openly courted by King Danube Brock Ursal.

"Abbot Olin fears that she may become queen of the kingdom," Merwan Ma remarked. "Does he believe that this will propel her to the leadership of the Church, as well?"

"It would be unprecedented," Yakim Douan replied gruffly, shaking his head yet again. He had no idea of the significance of any of this, but whatever might happen, the present news was more than a little distressing to the man. Could he risk Transcendence with apparent turmoil brewing in the north, not only with the Church, but with the kingdom itself? And if the worst-case scenario came to pass, with a new Honce-the-Bear that was hostile to Behren, might he be forced to delay Transcendence even more?

The Yatol bowed his head, hiding his frustration from his attendant. He wanted to be done with this body! He wanted to feel again the energy of youth, the excitement and enjoyment of lovemaking, even the thrill of the new relationships he would find with the same group of Yatols and Shepherds who now called him God-Voice.

But now it was obvious to Yakim Douan that all of his efforts, including sending the small army to Yatol Grysh, would
be for naught. He could not and would not attempt Transcendence until the situation in To-gai and in Honce-the-Bear was
resolved, and he could get an honest view of the dangers he
might face in the vulnerable decade before he came to true
power.

"We cannot be overly concerned with the situation in
Honce-the Bear," he announced to Merwan Ma a moment
later. "Recall Ambassador Daween Kusaad, that we might
discuss the situation at length. And ensure that a steady
stream of messengers flows between Jacintha and Abbot Olin
in Entel. A steady stream. I will know week to week what is
transpiring within the kingdom and the Abellican Church."

"Yet there is little that we can do to influence the happenings
in the north, other than continue to provide our friend Olin
with the funds he needs to wage his campaign. Our attention,
therefore, must be focused on settling the issues within To-gai."

"Yatol Grysh has likely received our soldiers by now," said
Merwan Ma.

"Yatol Grysh is a wise man and a powerful leader. He will
use them well, I do not doubt." He ended nodding, instead of
shaking his head some more, as satisfied as he could be that
he was doing all that he could to facilitate the environment he
needed for the desired Transcendence. He took a deep breath
and considered the road before him. He would visit the
hematite regularly from that day on, he decided, to ensure his
health and his comfort.

"Soon enough," he muttered, and when he caught Merwan
Ma's inquisitive look at the curious remark, he just waved the
attendant away.

Three Chezhou-Lei warriors had assembled in his room in
Dharyan. Unprecedented.

But while he was amused by the presence of Wan Atenn's
two peers, Yatol Grysh was not overwhelmed. These great
warriors were his servants, after all, fiercely loyal to the
Chezru Chieftain and to those Yatols serving under Yakim
Douan.

"I am surprised by your appearance, Woh Lien and Dahmed Blie," the Yatol said after Carwan Pestle had served drinks to the three and all had settled into the comfortable chairs in the audience chamber.

"By law, a twenty-square must be led by Chezhou-Lei, Yatol Grysh," Wan Atenn put in.

"Yet I did not expect a twenty-square!" Grysh replied lightheartedly, and he looked right at the two visiting Chezhou-Lei warriors as he continued. "An eight-square would have allowed us to secure Dharyan throughout the winter and spring."

As he finished, he looked to Carwan Pestle, who had been briefed on how Grysh wanted this meeting to proceed.

"Perhaps this is a sign that the God-Voice desires us to do more than secure Dharyan, Yatol," Pestle suggested, and as he finished, he looked to Woh Lien, the older and more experienced of the two warriors.

"We were sent to Dharyan to serve under Yatol Grysh, as Yatol Grysh deemed fit," the Chezhou-Lei warrior said, quite openly and without hesitation. "Whether the strength of the force is a signal to you, Yatol Grysh, is beyond my knowledge."

Grysh nodded, appreciating the openness. A wry smile found its way onto his plump face. "We will see how far your forces will take us, Chezhou-Lei Woh Lien. Has Chezru Douan determined the date of your return to Jacintha?"

"He has not."

*Perfect,* Grysh thought. "Then you are to return when I release you?"

The warrior nodded.

"You understand that, while here, you are both subject to the commands of Wan Atenn?"

The two visiting warriors looked to each other, then to the third Chezhou-Lei, offering deferential nods. "The hierarchies of our order are determined outside the boundaries of the Yatols," Woh Lien explained. "In those hierarchies, noble Wan Atenn is already placed above the two of us. If that hierarchy was different, Wan Atenn would readily and gladly submit to my will."

Grysh started to respond that he was glad of that, but he stopped and sat there smiling instead, realizing that these two had been selected by Douan specifically, and that the Chezru Chieftain had well understood the politics of the Chezhou-Lei. *Well done, God-Voice,* Yatol Grysh silently congratulated.

The Yatol of Dharyan was convinced then that Douan had sent him the forces along with a clear message: secure To-gai once and for all. Put down the pockets of insurgence swiftly and definitively.

"You carry with you supplies enough to get through the winter months?" he asked.

"And more," Woh Lien replied. "We are trained to forage, Yatol, and to hunt. Chezru Douan was concerned that our numbers not strain the resources of Dharyan, and so they shall not."

"That is good," said Grysh. "Then let us put the word out that you have come delivering supplies to me, that we might help the outposters through the difficult season."

"If that is what you deem necessary."

"That is what I deem necessary to tell the people," Grysh explained. "Our task will be much more difficult if the upstart Ru believe that I have eight hundred new warriors under my command. So, as far as the populace is concerned, I do not. Each of you will section thirty-two soldiers to Wan Atenn, that the eight-square I requested will be filled."

"As you order, Yatol," said Woh Lien, and Dahmed Blie echoed the thought.

"Has word of the massacre at Douan Cal been made public?" the Yatol asked Carwan Pestle.

"Limited, perhaps."

"See that it does not spread. Allow the people to know that Douan Cal was attacked, but not that it was eliminated, else it will become common perception that the soldiers are in response to that attack."

"The outpost settlement was eliminated?" Woh Lien asked.

"Our enemy is a Ru called Ashwarawu," explained Wan Atenn.

"A mighty leader?" Woh Lien asked.

"A coward, who strikes at the vulnerable and retreats to the shadows. But of late, he grows bolder, and his attacks come nearer and nearer to Dharyan."

"He will attack us, but only if he believes that we are vulnerable," said Yatol Grysh. "Thus we will make great fanfare of the arrival of a permanent eight-square, and then I will send the eight-square out hunting for him. Though, of course, they will not find him."

"And while they are out, perhaps Ashwarawu will strike for the greater prize of Dharyan," reasoned Wan Atenn.

"Where the jaws of death will be waiting for him," said Grysh. "There are a series of caves to the north, farther into the foothills, where one of your remaining forces can go. As for the other . . ." He looked to Carwan Pestle as he finished.

"Delvin Plateau," the man replied.

"Ah, of course," Grysh agreed, and he turned to Woh Lien. "Delvin Plateau is a small village nestled halfway up the rise that separates the To-gai steppes from the land of Behren. Few know of it, and it is so easily defended, with a cliff on one side, a sheer wall on the other, and only a narrow road allowing access, that Ashwarawu will not go near to it. But from there, if you are alert, you will be able to sweep down to Dharyan in a single night's march."

The Yatol sat back then, nodding, considering the possibilities. Suddenly the idea of going out in pursuit of Ashwarawu seemed a foolish thing to do. Especially if he could somehow manage to lure Ashwarawu in to him.

Of course, other possibilities remained wide open to him. It occurred to him that he could merely send the three mighty Chezhou-Lei warriors out alone in pursuit, and likely have Ashwarawu's head served to him within a month.

But this plan he had just improvised appealed to Grysh more. Better to get Ashwarawu and his foolish rebels in one devastating sweep. Better to crush the resistance at its core.

Yatol Grysh silently congratulated Chezru Douan again, and fully expected that his life on the frontier was soon to become much easier.

# CHAPTER 16

## *Her New Family*

"They pretend that they search for you, but none wish to find you," Barachuk said with a wry grin. He and Tsolona had been coming out of the village every night since Brynn's abrupt departure, knowing she would return. Now, a week after the fight to liberate Runtly, they had been rewarded.

"You killed a Chezhou-Lei warrior," Tsolona added, but her tone, unlike that of her husband, was not mirthful. "And a Yatol. The Order of Chezhou will seek you forever after, and the Yatols will not readily accept the loss of one of their own."

"One of their own," Brynn spat in reply. "Daek was To-gai-ru, yet he turned against our ways, our customs. How deep is the rot that has affected our land?"

"Not as deep as those like Daek would wish," said Barachuk.

"To our people in the village, you are a hero, Brynn Dharielle," Tsolona added. "Our hearts bleed for the horses, trapped in barns and paddocks. To see a To-gai-ru warrior and her horse so defeating the designs of the cursed Wraps brings joy to our hearts, reminds us of who we once were—"

"And who we shall be again," Brynn promised, hardly able to voice the words, for Tsolona's reference to the Behrenese as the "Wraps" had spurred many distant memories within the woman. It was a derogatory term the To-gai-ru had long used against their desert-dwelling enemies, a reference to the Behrenese custom of wrapping their heads in great turbans. Some To-gai-ru wore turbans, as well, but none as elaborate in design as those fancied by the wealthier Behrenese. It wasn't just the word, but the manner in which Tsolona had spoken it that so inspired the memories in Brynn, for at that moment, the old woman had sounded so much to Brynn like her own mother!

"The Wraps are many, and are mighty, and their wealth has brought them the services of To-gai-ru like Daek," Barachuk warned. "Your victory was sweet, but minor, and will be no lasting victory at all if you are hunted down by the Order of Chezhou."

"Let them come," Brynn said grimly. "I will line the steppes with the poled heads of Chezhou-Lei dog warriors."

"You cannot fight a war alone."

Brynn paused and considered Barachuk carefully, recognizing from his tone that he was deflecting her declaration and not trying to halt it altogether. She studied him hard, and he turned from her gaze to look over at his wife, who gave a nod.

"You have heard of Ashwarawu?" Barachuk asked.

Brynn wore a curious expression. She understood the word, but as a word and not as anyone's name, as Barachuk was apparently asking. "He who kills without mercy?"

"Ashwarawu gathers warriors as he roams from village to village," Tsolona explained. "The Behrenese fear him."

"He would welcome a fighter of your skills," said Barachuk. "Already, word of your deeds here are spreading across the windblown steppes."

"You speak as if an invitation has been extended." Brynn's voice reflected her caution. She had come into To-gai hoping that some sort of underground movement was already afoot, but she didn't dare allow herself too much hope at that time. For she knew nothing, really, of this leader, Ashwarawu, and nothing of the force he was assembling.

"Ashwarawu's ears are large, my young friend, and his invitation is open to any To-gai-ru who will raise sword against the hated Wraps!" Tsolona declared, raising her voice so loudly that Barachuk grabbed her and shushed her, fearing that the guards of the village would hear.

"We know where he is," the old man whispered to Brynn. "Or we know, at least, where you can go to be found by Ashwarawu."

Barachuk then rattled off a series of questions to Brynn,

trying to figure out how much she knew of the region and the familiar landmarks. He frowned with every shake of Brynn's head, though, for the young ranger had no points of reference at all south of the mountains. It was just too long ago.

Finally, Barachuk just stepped up to her and physically turned her about, facing her south by southeast. "Three days," he explained. "Two if your horse is swift. You will find an ancient riverbed—we have not yet seen enough snow to cover its unmistakable designs. Follow the riverbed east. You will cross through several ravines, and in one, you will see to the south a mountain face that seems the profile of an old man."

"Barachuk's Mountain," Brynn remarked, drawing a smile from the old man and a cackle from Tsolona.

"A fine name, though I doubt any but you will call it that!" Barachuk replied. "But there, in that valley, Ashwarawu will find you."

"Or I will find him," said Brynn, and she grinned, not expecting the two to take her seriously. They didn't understand her knowledge of tracking, of reading the slightest signs of passage. She had no doubts that if she got anywhere near to Ashwarawu's forces, she would find them with ease.

She took the supplies from the old couple, gave each a warm and sincere hug, then gathered up Runtly and began the long trek to the south.

"How did you find us?" the fierce To-gai-ru warrior demanded, scowling down at the seemingly unremarkable man from horseback.

"Perhaps you are not as well hidden as you believe," the man in the tan tunic and sash of a Jhesta Tu mystic replied, and he gave a little shrug, as if it did not matter.

"I ask you only one more time!"

The mystic shrugged, and the rider growled and seemed as if he was about to run the mystic down, but then came another voice, one that quieted the rider.

"How he found us is not as important as why he found us," said Ashwarawu, walking his strong black-and-white pinto to the forefront. "What do the Jhesta Tu see in our struggles that would so interest you, mystic?"

"I was To-gai-ru before I became Jhesta Tu," Pagonel replied.

"And that means you are loyal to our cause?"

Another shrug, pointedly noncommittal.

"And what of the Jhesta Tu who claim Behren as their heritage?" Ashwarawu asked. "That would include most of your order, would it not? Are they now riding hard from the Mountains of Fire to pledge allegiance to the Chezru Chieftain?"

Pagonel gave a small laugh at that, and took note that Ashwarawu seemed to relax, just a bit. "Hardly that," he said. "Likely they would be killed before they ever neared Jacintha. Our order and the priests of Yatol hold little agreement."

The volatile man at Ashwarawu's side started as if he meant to say something, but the warrior leader held up his hand to silence him. "Allies against a common enemy?"

"The Jhesta Tu do not name the Yatols as enemies," Pagonel replied. "Though neither would we deign to name them as friends. We orbit different realms, to the satisfaction of both."

"Yet you are here."

The simple statement gave Pagonel pause, for in truth the mystic, so fresh from enlightenment, still had not sorted out why he had come to To-gai, and why he had sought out Ashwarawu and his fierce band. All along the path of his travels, once he had hit the midpoint of the steppes, he had heard tales of Ashwarawu and his gang, of vicious retributive strikes against Behrenese outposters. Pagonel had learned why this fierce young man—and he was surprised at how young Ashwarawu really was!—had earned the title of "he who kills without mercy."

The mystic would be lying, to himself as well as to others, if he did not admit that he was intrigued by Ashwarawu and the renegade warrior band. Still, there was more to his journey to find Ashwarawu than mere intrigue, he knew.

"Why did you find me, mystic?" Ashwarawu pressed. "I have no need to ask how—long have I heard stories of the Jhesta Tu witches. Some sorcery brought you to me, I do not doubt. The question I must answer is whether or not that sorcery is being used to the benefit of the Wraps. Are you a spy? Do you seek to lead the Wraps to me, telling them also the strength of my forces?"

"No, to both," Pagonel answered simply and without hesitation. "I have come to To-gai to learn."

Ashwarawu's eyes opened wide at that surprising proclamation. "What is there to learn, mystic? How to fight? How to die?"

"Or perhaps, how to live."

The young Ashwarawu rocked back a bit on his horse at the simple response and spent a long while studying the mystic, head to toe.

"You have come to learn," he said slowly, and he seemed to be measuring Pagonel with each passing syllable. "To learn which side you must choose?"

"I did not know that the Jhesta Tu were involved with the struggle between Behren and To-gai."

"You said that you were To-gai-ru!"

"I once was, and perhaps will yet be again," Pagonel answered. "I do not know. For now, I am Jhesta Tu, and nothing more, and I have come to watch and to learn. And nothing more."

The man sitting beside Ashwarawu spat upon the ground with obvious contempt. "Are we to provide entertainment, then?" he asked his leader.

But it was obvious to Pagonel that his words had intrigued Ashwarawu enough to push them past the point of such simple questions. The fierce leader continued to stare at Pagonel, trying to gain some measure, perhaps, or perhaps trying to weigh the potential good that could come from this unexpected meeting against the potential risks.

Ashwarawu was indeed leaning toward the possible benefits, Pagonel knew. How much stronger might his army become if the Jhesta Tu mystics were to side with him? For though Pagonel was likely the first Jhesta Tu Ashwarawu had ever seen, the legend of the warrior mystics from the Mountains of Fire was surely well-known through both lands, Behren and To-gai. And that legend, Pagonel also understood, had very likely become greatly inflated with each retelling.

"You are another mouth in search of food," Ashwarawu said at length.

"I need no supplies, but will find my own."

"And enough to feed some of my warriors, as well."

"Agreed."

And so on that cold winter day, nearing the end of God's Year 840, the Jhesta Tu master joined the band of a young outlaw, one who was gaining the eyes and ears of Yatol Grysh in Dharyan, and even of Chezru Chieftain Yakim Douan in faraway Jacintha.

Ashwarawu had no idea of what it all meant, but he remained thrilled at the prospects of enlisting the Jhesta Tu in his cause.

Pagonel had no idea of what it all meant, but that quiet voice within him understood that joining up with Ashwarawu's band, even as merely a spectator, would help him more quickly answer the many questions that had nagged at him since his vision after enlightenment had set him on the road to To-gai.

The wind-driven snow rode more horizontal than vertical, stinging Brynn and Runtly, forcing both to squint and often turn their heads. The tough pony trudged along, ears flat, but otherwise uncomplaining.

Brynn wasn't worried. These stinging ice and snowstorms were commonplace on the steppes and rarely amounted to any deep accumulation.

The woman was growing frustrated, though, for she had been in the valley described by Barachuk and Tsolona for several days, with no sign of Ashwarawu and his band, no sign of any recent passage at all. She was anxious to get on with this part of her winding road, for she believed that this turn might lead her to her ultimate goal.

She knew that she wasn't going to track Ashwarawu, or anyone else, at that time, though; and so she was taking Runtly along the northern ridge of the hills, looking for some overhang or shallow cave where they could find shelter.

The wind was howling about her, but Brynn felt very quiet, falling very far within herself. She thought again of those she had left behind, of Belli'mar Juraviel and Cazzira, of Lady Dasslerond and the distant land of Andur'Blough Inninness.

Mostly of Belli'mar Juraviel.

Brynn remembered all the stories the unusual elf had told her about his previous protégé, the famous Nightbird. She shivered, and not from the cold, when she recalled Juraviel's story of his encounter with the demon, Bestesbulzibar, how Lady Dasslerond had come to his rescue, using her magic to take Juraviel and those humans in his charge—and the demon dactyl!—back to Andur'Blough Inninness, where her magic was strongest, so that she could battle the great demon. That fight had left the encroaching rot in the elven valley.

Brynn sighed quietly to herself as she considered the implications of that demon stain. Because of that, Aydrian had been taken in by Lady Dasslerond, who had some mysterious plan to use him to battle the stain. Because of that, Dasslerond's interest in Brynn had become something more than the usual elf-ranger relationship. Thinking that her people might have to desert their fair valley, Dasslerond had determined that Brynn would help to open the road south by liberating the To-gai-ru.

It all tied together in such a strange and unexpected way.

Brynn held no illusions, though. She was not there for the sake of Lady Dasslerond. No, she was there for the good of the To-gai-ru. If Dasslerond and the elves benefitted from her actions taken for the gain of her own people, then all the better.

And she would take those actions, would free To-gai, the young woman believed. She just wished that Belli'mar Juraviel was there to help her along her road, to counsel her and guide her, to tell her when she was acting foolishly and when she was following the right fork in the path.

How she missed him! Both as mentor and friend!

Lost in the memories, Brynn did not notice Runtly's ears coming up suddenly, nor even the little nicker the pony offered, in obvious surprise.

The form came out of the snowy haze in a wild rush, charging right beside the woman, club swinging to knock her from her mount.

Purely on instinct and reflex, Brynn ducked to the side and down and kicked a heel into Runtly's flank, and the strong pony leaped away. The attacker turned to follow, though, and Brynn soon understood that he was not alone.

She brought Runtly into a flat-out gallop, cutting down to the center of the valley, trying to find more maneuvering room away from boxing walls. Riders rose up out of the white-out beside her, all with weapons raised.

Brynn resisted the urge to draw out her sword and instead focused on cutting Runtly into tight turns, kicking him into short bursts of speed, then pulling up fast and changing directions. For these were To-gai-ru warriors attacking her, and not Behrenese, and though their weapons were no less dangerous, Brynn had no desire to kill one of her own.

Of course, the fact that they were To-gai-ru, and on horseback, made them all the harder to shake.

Runtly turned a sharp right, slicing inside the angle of a rider trying to cut Brynn off. The To-gai-ru warrior launched a wild swing at her, his staff coming up far short, but Brynn leaned out and caught the end of it, then quickly turned Runtly back to the left so that she could pull the staff in closer and secure her seat.

The horses passed and Brynn had the stronger seat, and the To-gai-ru warrior tumbled down from his horse. He let go of his club as he fell, and Brynn put it up over her head and gave a great "whoop!"

She brought it around in a circle, then down hard to the side, deflecting the attack of another passing rider, then pulled it in and thrust it back out, catching the man under the arm as he passed and finding enough of a hook there to dislodge him, too, from his seat.

Brynn and Runtly charged straight ahead, directly into the blinding snow. Two large forms appeared before them, blocking the path, but the woman and her pony cut a deft turn.

Right at a tumble of waist-high boulders.

Her strong legs locking on the horse, Brynn went into a half seat and Runtly responded with a great leap, clearing the first boulder, then landing smoothly and launching again after a single stride to clear the second rock. Two strides later, the pony went over the third and largest rock.

Brynn heard pursuit from all around her, but she was smiling, exhilarated, feeling the wondrous interplay of great muscles beneath her.

Rider and horse had become as one, and a series of turns and sudden accelerations had Brynn weaving through the ranks of her pursuers, her staff working furiously to take one, and then another, to the ground.

But then she had to pull up short, for a standing line of dark riders appeared before her, and as she turned her head side to side, she saw that others were filling in about her. At her command, Runtly reared and went right around on his hind legs.

But there, too, behind her, loomed a line of grim-faced riders.

With a growl of defiance, Brynn threw down the staff and pulled forth her sword, and with a thought, set the blade aflame, challenging any and all to approach.

But none did. They sat solemn and stoic, patiently waiting.

And then, after Brynn had turned Runtly about several times, a large man on a black-and-white pinto appeared in the middle of one line, walking slowly and deliberately toward her. He had no weapon drawn, but still seemed to Brynn to be the most imposing and dangerous of the bunch!

He walked his horse right up before Runtly, staring at Brynn unblinkingly.

"Ashwarawu," the woman said, and she was indeed surprised. Not because this was the legendary warrior sitting astride his horse before her, but merely because he was so young! He couldn't even be her age, and she hadn't seen twenty summers as yet!

He was tall and strong-featured, with a wide face and a square jaw and penetrating light gray eyes—made all the more remarkable because of his dark complexion and black hair. His shoulders were wide, as well, a girth exaggerated by the layers of furs that he wore as armor.

His expression didn't change when Brynn spoke his name, and he seemed aloof to the woman, as if he had no doubts that she would know who he was. After a long moment, he held up one huge hand, an unthreatening gesture.

"You are far from any village, woman."

"I am where I meant to be."

The man cocked his eyebrows, smiling at her confident response. "You ride well."

"I am To-gai-ru," Brynn answered. "It is expected of me."

Ashwarawu smiled and nodded his approval.

Brynn knew that the display that she had just put on had impressed all who had witnessed it, particularly the few warriors who had found the misfortune to cross her path. Given that, her matter-of-fact attitude about her riding skill seemed to impress Ashwarawu even more.

Just as she had hoped.

"Who are you, and why have you come?" the leader asked.

"I am Brynn Dharielle," she answered loudly, wanting all about her to hear. "I have no home, and was a wanderer until very recently, when I happened upon a village controlled by a despised Yatol."

"You fled the Yatol?"

"I killed the Yatol, and his Chezhou-Lei lackey beside him," Brynn answered. "And so again, I have no home."

"And others directed you to me," Ashwarawu reasoned, fighting hard, obviously, to keep his expression and voice calm, though those about were murmuring with excitement and disbelief that this young and small warrior had defeated a Chezhou-Lei! To say nothing of the fact that through some magic they did not know, she had just set her sword aflame!

"It seemed a logical road, I suppose," the woman answered.

Ashwarawu spent a long while studying her then, his eyes roaming over her, over her horse, out to her fabulous, still burning weapon. "You are To-gai-ru," he said at last. "We will not turn you out in the winter."

Brynn let her sword's fire burn out and slid the weapon away.

"But neither will you enjoy any treatment of privilege!" Ashwarawu roared suddenly. "You will work for your food and will serve as you are told to serve!"

Brynn nodded, expecting nothing more.

"And I will seek to find out the truth of your words, Brynn Dharielle," the fierce leader promised. "If I find that you have spoken falsely to impress, then know that you have failed. If you have spoken falsely to deceive, to gain advantage for our enemies, then know that a most unpleasant death awaits you."

"And if I have spoken truly?" Brynn asked slyly.

"Then you are welcome as one of my warriors," Ashwarawu answered without hesitation. "Nothing more, nothing less."

Before Brynn could say another word, the leader spun his horse and walked away, passing through the line, which collected into formation behind him.

Brynn waited as the rest of the force walked past her, then took her place at the end of the line, melting into the mountains with the rest of her new family.

# CHAPTER 17

# *The Grim Reality*

Brynn sat astride Runtly near the far end of the long line of To-gai-ru warriors, her position showing her rank within Ashwarawu's band, which was mostly determined by the time when she had joined. Next to her, higher up the ranking, sat a most curious man, dressed in a tan tunic and breeches, finely made, underneath a heavy bearskin wrap, and with a marvelous sash that seemed black most of the time but every so often flashed a myriad of colors in the light, like a tightly woven rainbow.

"Another caravan," Brynn remarked, as the Behrenese train came into view far below in the crisp and clear winter-morning air. "How stupid are our enemies?"

Brynn had been with Ashwarawu's band for three weeks, and this was the third caravan the rebel leader had found out, and now intended to destroy. The first two had proven to be easy victories, with the To-gai-ru warriors sweeping down upon the wagons, slicing apart the drivers and the meager contingent of guards.

"The Yatol of Dharyan hears the desperation of To'in Ru," the monk replied, referring to a large and well-defended outposter settlement in the region, one that Ashwarawu had not yet gone against. "Perhaps the Yatol's compassion for his own people blinds him. Or perhaps he does not understand our resolve."

Brynn always listened carefully to this man, Pagonel, because he had a manner of putting things into a different perspective. It wasn't always one with which she agreed, as now, but often over the last couple of weeks, she had found herself widening her opinions because of Pagonel's softly spoken words—particularly concerning the Behrenese. The others of Ashwarawu's band always referred to them with the derogatory "Wraps," but never did Pagonel. And often, Pagonel dared to assume the likely perspective of the individual Behrenese, though Ashwarawu surely didn't like him putting a human face on their enemies!

A To-gai-ru rider came galloping back then, running the line to the middle, where Ashwarawu sat waiting.

"Twenty soldiers guarding seven wagons," the man reported. "Just like the last one."

"We should take them as prisoners," Brynn remarked under her breath.

"Ashwarawu will not," Pagonel replied quietly.

Brynn turned to regard the mystic. She had not been speaking to him, but could not deny the truth of his response. Ashwarawu had made it perfectly clear to all of them: no Behrenese inside the borders of To-gai would be allowed to live.

Not the women, not the children.

Fortunately for Brynn, she had not been forced into killing noncombatant women and children as of yet. Both of the previous caravans, and this one, too, apparently, had been comprised mostly of soldiers, warriors, instruments of the imperial Yatols. Brynn could fight and kill such men, and a few warrior women, with clear conscience, for these were the invaders, the source of To-gai's ills, the people who would destroy the To-gai-ru culture and heritage.

The woman tried not to think of the inevitable conflict that would arise between her and the fiery, dominating leader when at last the warrior band encountered Behrenese noncombatants.

She turned her attention to the situation at hand, eyeing the caravan as it meandered down below. Brynn understood her part well enough, for in Ashwarawu's sweeping tactics, every role was the same. The raiders would wait until the caravan was directly below them. Then, with war whoops and weapons brandished high, the force would sweep down the sloping ground, slicing through the caravan like a swarm of angry bees, overwhelming the force with sheer numbers and sheer brutality, and with a deep-set confidence, the belief that a To-gai-ru warrior was simply superior to any Behrenese fighter.

The caravan continued along, drivers and guards seeming oblivious to the threat.

And so it began, a whirlwind, a charge, two hundred battle cries rising above the wind.

The drivers and soldiers tried to turn the wagons, tried to get into some sort of defensive position, but the charge was too fast.

On Runtly, Brynn leaped ahead of those closest to her, the strong pony outdistancing the others. Eager for battle, the young ranger veered in toward the center, outpacing even the strong black-and-white horse of Ashwarawu.

She came to the caravan first, her sword alight with fire, slashing across to fell the nearest mounted Behrenese soldier. She veered immediately back to the left as she connected, to meet a second warrior, her pulsating shield deflecting his thrusting spear up high.

Brynn cut even sharper to the left, with Runtly understanding and accepting the angle and smashing hard against the taller horse of the Behrenese soldier. The horse jumped to the side and the man lurched over, and Brynn wasted no time in smashing the soldier across the face with her shield. She pulled Runtly up to a rearing stop and turn, and slashed her sword across.

The soldier's head dropped to the snow.

Runtly burst ahead, leaping the hitch between a pair of horses and the wagon behind them, then Brynn cut him sharply to the left, bringing her down the line along the unde-fended side of the caravan. She stabbed at each wagon driver in line, scoring a couple of hits, one fatal, and forcing three other drivers off the other side.

All semblance of defense was shattered as the frightened horses of those four wagons, some aided by a slap on the rump by Brynn, broke formation.

The ensuing frenzy was just the type of chaos favored by Ashwarawu and his warriors, and each Behrenese, soldier and driver, was quickly isolated from his kin, and quickly slashed, stabbed, or trampled.

It was over in a matter of moments, as fast as a passing avalanche. Only a couple of the Behrenese weren't quite dead, lying bleeding in the snow, crying out in agony, crying out for mercy.

Brynn found Pagonel collecting one of the wayward wagons. She moved to help him, trying hard to ignore the cries of the wounded.

"It is not a pretty business," the mystic remarked, seeing the distress on the young ranger's face.

"I do not enjoy the killing," Brynn admitted. She grabbed up the loose reins of one team then, and started to turn them about, but she stopped, noting that Pagonel was glancing at her and then to the side, silently motioning for her to take notice.

Brynn turned to see the To-gai-ru line reformed beside the bulk of the caravan, with Ashwarawu walking his horse slowly toward her.

"You fought well this day," the leader observed. "As you have in the last encounters. As you did on the morning you were taken into my band."

"I was well-trained," Brynn replied. "And am To-gai-ru." She managed a smile. "And none have ever found a better mount . . ." She stopped, realizing that the proud leader wasn't even listening to her.

"You will move up seven places in the line, closer to me, I think," Ashwarawu said offhandedly.

Brynn knew that she should be thrilled, but something about his tone and demeanor had her quite concerned.

"After you finish the task," he said, and he slowly turned his head to regard one of the Behrenese soldiers lying upon the ground, writhing in pain.

Brynn looked at the man, understanding what was expected of her. But this task hit her hard, assaulting her sensibilities. It was one thing to do battle against an enemy, one she profoundly hated, but how could she view a man lying helpless upon the ground in such a light as that?

She looked back to Ashwarawu, to see him staring hard at her, not blinking, not flinching.

Brynn turned to Pagonel for support, for anything, and found him sitting there staring alternately at her and at the leader, as if weighing both.

The seconds slipped past.

"Finish the task," Ashwarawu said slowly and deliberately.

Brynn found it hard to draw breath. She understood the depth of this trial, understood that if she was not strong, her place among the raiders, among all the To-gai-ru, would be forever diminished. She thought to argue about taking captives again, but knew that Ashwarawu was uncompromising on this point. The raider band did not have the resources to keep prisoners, to feed them or even to watch over them. And since no Behrenese soldiers or caravan drivers would offer any bargaining leverage whatsoever with any of the Yatol leaders, they were worthless to Ashwarawu.

Brynn scanned the leader and the others again, wishing that she had a way out, but understanding that she most certainly did not. She slid down from her pony; she could have done the deed astride, but she didn't want to include Runtly in the dirty business.

Her bloody sword in hand, Brynn walked up to a wounded Behrenese. She chose the most grievously wounded man first, one who could not plead to her, could not even look her in the eye. He gasped for breath, blood pouring from his mouth with each exhalation, and Brynn knew that even if Ashwarawu had agreed to taking prisoners, there was nothing that she and the others could do to help this one.

Juraviel's warnings about the cruelty of war echoed in the woman's mind.

She struck fast and cleanly, stabbing the man through the heart, stilling his body and ending his misery.

The next wounded man looked up at her as she stood over him, his eyes pleading for mercy. He even managed a slight shake of his head, begging her not to strike.

Brynn looked up, then closed her eyes. She remembered keenly the moment when her parents had been murdered, purposely replaying that awful scene in her head again.

She struck, imagining that she was stabbing the man who had killed her parents.

And then she walked away. She held her sword out to the side and called forth its fire, using the flames to burn away the bloodstains.

She heard the cries of encouragement, the cheers, from the To-gai-ru, though she did not feel much like a hero at that moment. She saw the approving look of Ashwarawu.

Or was it an approving look? She had to wonder, for somewhere in the leader's powerful expression, Brynn saw something more, and something far less. He had chosen her to carry out the executions, under the rationalization of glory, that she had performed well and so deserved the task of finishing the battle. But in looking at him then, Brynn understood that Ashwarawu had just tested her, and perhaps, that he had just tried to diminish her, in her own eyes if in no one else's. Had Ashwarawu just taken a bit more control over Brynn?

The woman looked to Pagonel, who sat astride his horse, holding Runtly's reins. She saw a sadness there in his face, and a measure of sympathy that she had not expected.

She took the reins and pulled herself up onto Runtly's strong back, the pony accepting her, as always. She took some comfort in that, for Runtly would not judge her, as she could not help but judge herself.

"They were utterly overrun," Wan Atenn reported to Yatol Grysh in the audience chamber of the great temple in Dhar-yan. "The dead of our people were left on the frozen ground and all but one destroyed wagon was taken." The Chezhou-Lei warrior said it all matter-of-factly, as if the loss of a few soldiers and drivers was no big event.

Yatol Grysh's stern look melted away. "And the foodstuffs were prepared as I ordered?" he asked, grinning.

"They were."

At Grysh's side, Carwan Pestle shifted in his seat and put a curious look over the Yatol.

"The food was poisoned," Grysh happily explained. "That caravan had to ride back and forth several times before the rebels even took notice of it!"

"You sent them out there to be sacrificed?" Pestle asked, in surprise and not in judgment.

"Ashwarawu is a fool, but a dangerous one," Grysh replied. "Of course, he may well be a dead fool now."

The Yatol nodded, trying very hard not to glance in the direction of any of the several slaves—To-gai-ru all—who were working in the temple. He had no doubt that word of the treachery would soon spread to the steppes, and to Ashwarawu's ears, but that was part of the fun of it, was it not? He looked to the stunned Carwan Pestle, and was a bit disappointed that his protégé hadn't caught on to all of this sooner. None of the outposter towns truly needed any supplies, after all, so why had Grysh sent out three separate caravans?

Pestle was too innocent, the Yatol reasoned, to understand the need of such sacrifices. The first two caravans were necessary predecessors to the third batch of poisoned supplies.

Of course, even the third was no more than a ruse. There were no poisons available in any quantities that could kill a large group of men after days and days of sitting in foodstuffs that would not be readily detectable by even casual observation.

No, this too was a ruse, designed to bolster Ashwarawu's confidence—in his own forces, in the incompetence of his enemies, and in the spy network that was so obviously working for him out of Dharyan. No doubt one of the workers in the temple would pass the word of the poisoned food, and another wretched Ru would rush out in the dark of night to find the rebel leader.

Grysh was glad he didn't have to try to hide his sly smile, because he doubted that he could at that time.

He was drawing the rebel fool in, and he had eight hundred trained, professional soldiers at his disposal.

"You are surprised that I take so bold and decisive a step against the fool rebels?" Grysh asked Pestle.

"No, Yatol."

"Yes, you are," Grysh corrected. "Why not wait until the spring, after all, when we could send the might of Jacintha's army against the rabble and be done with them quickly and easily?" Grysh paused, studying the man, mocking him with a wry grin. "Yes, you are surprised, and so our next visitor this day should help you to understand."

With that, he looked to Wan Atenn and nodded, and the Chezhou-Lei relayed the signal to one of his guards by the great double doors. That man turned out to the hall and clapped his hands sharply, twice, and in walked Woh Lien and Dahmed Blie, the Chezhou-Lei leaders of the two visiting twenty-squares.

"Yatol," Woh Lien said, snapping into a formal bow.

"Greetings to you, Chezhou-Lei."

"We have come to inform you that our duties here are done. The supplies have been delivered and distributed. Your requested eight-square has been selected from among the finest of our warriors."

"And so you plan to leave?"

"That is our command, Yatol."

"To return to Jacintha, where you can chase birds from the fountains?" Grysh asked incredulously. "You are warriors, my friend, and here is a war for you to fight. You would turn from that to return to a city basking in peace and security?"

Chezhou-Lei Woh Lien glanced nervously over at his companion, who seemed equally ill-at-ease. "It is not our decision to make, Yatol."

"Yet you are the commanders of your respective forces," Grysh countered. "Surely you hold discretion in emergency situations."

"True, Yatol. But there is no such emergency. Not at this time, at least, and the God-Voice has determined that we are to return, at the first break in the weather."

He continued, but Grysh held up his hand, motioning for him to relent. "Go, then," he said, looking from Carwan Pestle to Wan Atenn, his expression perfectly conveying a sense of worry—an emotion he certainly did not feel. "And let us pray that the wretch Ashwarawu was the first to taste of the last raid's spoils!"

The Yatol, feigning anger and frustration, dismissed them all, then walked with a huff from the grand room, back to his private quarters, an honestly confused and concerned Carwan Pestle close behind.

But Yatol Grysh was not concerned. Not at all. He had a measure of this rebel, Ashwarawu, now. He was beginning to recognize the man's patterns, and he knew that he was adding to the self-confidence that would ultimately bring the man down.

It would be an enjoyable spring in Dharyan.

"You are unnerved," Pagonel remarked to Brynn the day after the caravan raid. Brynn was sitting off to the side of the camp cleaning her sword, alone and apparently calm and composed, but the perceptive mystic had seen through the façade. "It is one thing to kill a man in combat—the rush of fear and the need for self-defense allows for conscious justification. But it is quite another to kill a man lying helpless on the ground. Be relieved, my friend, that there were no uninjured Behrenese after the raid, no men who had just been knocked aside and captured."

"You presume much."

Pagonel gave a disarming smile. "A soldier invading your homeland deserves death, perhaps."

"Any Behrenese entering To-gai uninvited deserves death," Brynn said with as much conviction as she could muster.

"Do they?" The question was spoken, again, with perfect calm and the appearance of sincere reasoning. "If you happened upon a settlement and found a young Behrenese mother with her child, would you kill them? Without guilt?"

Brynn stared hard at him.

"You would put them on the road to their own land, perhaps," the mystic remarked. "And likely with enough supplies so that their road would not be dangerous."

Brynn went back to her work on the sword, her expression intense. "You presume much."

"Presumptions, perhaps, but based upon considerable observation," the mystic explained, taking a seat beside the young ranger. "I watched you at your practice this morning."

The statement froze Brynn in place. She had walked off far from the To-gai-ru encampment early that morning to practice her *bi'nelle dasada*, the elven sword dance, a ritual that she had been neglecting far too often of late. In the elven valley, Brynn had performed the dance nude, but since it was winter here on the steppes, with that constantly chill wind cutting across the iced grasses, she had worn a slight shift that morning. Still, Pagonel's proclamation caught her off guard, and made her feel no less violated than if she had been dancing nude. *Bi'nelle dasada* was an intensely personal exercise, a disciplined series of elaborate motions designed to physically train the muscles in the motions of battle, but even more than that, to extend the consciousness, to heighten the bond between body and mind.

Slowly, the young woman looked up at Pagonel.

"We of Jhesta Tu have similar routines," the mystic explained. "Quite similar, though we rarely fight or practice with weapons. The Chezhou-Lei warriors do, as well. As do certain factions of the Abellican Church to the north. I am curious as to how you came to learn such a dance, for yours, I believe, is quite extraordinary."

"It is not your business," Brynn said, with all the warnings of Dasslerond that *bi'nelle dasada* was a secret not to be shared echoing in her mind. She went back to her work on the sword again, pointedly.

"One day we will speak of it, I hope. But of course, the choice is yours. As for the events of yesterday, I am glad to see that you are troubled by them."

Brynn looked back at him again, her expression skeptical, though Pagonel could not be sure if she was trying to deny the premise of his statement, that she was troubled, or if she was merely confused that he should be glad to witness her guilt.

"You trouble yourself needlessly," he explained. "Those men were dead anyway—by Ashwarawu's hand if not by the wounds they had already received. And you struck with mercy and compassion, which is more than most would have done, and is as much as the doomed soldiers could have expected. Our mighty leader would not allow his reputation to be diminished for the sake of Behrenese soldiers."

"Should he?" Brynn asked, her tone making it fairly clear that she sided with Pagonel on this issue.

"I know not," the mystic admitted. "Ashwarawu's reputation serves him, and To-gai, well, I believe. Can the cost of conscience be weighed against that?"

"If you do not believe that the Behrenese must be forced from To-gai, then why are you here?"

"I do not know," the mystic honestly replied, and he gave a self-deprecating chuckle. "That is a question that I must answer myself. Still, I beg that you consider the question I posed to you, because if we happen upon a village of Behrenese that contains women and children and other noncombatants, you may well find yourself in need of the answer. Will you kill an innocent child at Ashwarawu's insistence? Or are you so convinced that there are no innocent Behrenese?"

"Are you intent upon sowing dissent within our band?"

Pagonel chuckled again. "I speak with none of the others, unless they ask something of me."

"Then why do you take such an interest in Brynn Dharielle?"

"I saw you at your practice this morning," the mystic replied, and he let it go at that.

Brynn started to look back at him, but was interrupted by a figure approaching—a quite intimidating figure, large and chiseled.

"Another glorious victory!" Ashwarawu proclaimed. "Will the trail of Ashwarawu end before it has run right through Jacintha?"

Brynn smiled at him, but his reference to himself in the third person settled uneasily within her. Mostly because Brynn did not believe that Ashwarawu was speaking of "Ashwarawu" as anything greater than himself.

"But the caravans will cease, I fear," the rebel leader went on. "Fat Yatol Grysh will not dare to send many more against the power of Ashwarawu. We may have to destroy a few outposter settlements to garner our supplies through the winter."

Brynn's façade cracked for just a moment as images of herded noncombatants flashed through her mind.

"Or maybe we go right into Behren, eh?" Ashwarawu said with a wicked grin.

Brynn shrugged and held her smile.

"And what of you, mystic?" Ashwarawu asked, turning

abruptly to Pagonel. "Have you decided why you have joined with us?"

"Contemplation follows its own hourglass," Pagonel replied.

Ashwarawu looked at him incredulously for a moment, then exploded into a great burst of laughter. "Well, take your time, then!" he said. "You were helpful in controlling the horses, even if you did not fight. Just continue to be helpful. Continue to earn the food I give to you."

Pagonel decided not to point out the fact that his skilled foraging was bringing in far more food than he was consuming.

"A curious pair, if ever I saw one!" Ashwarawu said, stepping back and surveying Brynn and Pagonel. "Are you certain that you are not father and daughter?"

Brynn winced. Ashwarawu had spoken the words in jest, obviously, but any reference to her father stung. The woman's expression quickly reverted, though.

Ashwarawu cleared his throat, obviously seeing the discomfort he had brought to Brynn. "Well, you fought magnificently yesterday," he said. "I do not relinquish the pleasure of killing the wounded and captured Behrenese easily!"

Brynn merely smiled, hearing Pagonel's warnings in her head.

"Come with me, my warrior," the imposing leader said, and he held his hand out toward a confused Brynn.

She glanced at Pagonel, but his expression offered little advice, and so she took Ashwarawu's hand, stood and sheathed her sword, and followed the large young man away.

He walked her right past the encampment—and Brynn didn't miss several rather lewd snickers she heard from men along the perimeter—to a small tent set up in the distance.

Inside were piles of furs, and Ashwarawu bade Brynn to sit down. She did so, moving to the far side of the small tent, and though she had her back against one side, and Ashwarawu had his against the opposite side, their legs were practically entwined.

The leader began taking off some of his layers of furs, but Brynn thought nothing of it. The tent was warm; no doubt heated stones had been placed under the furs.

"When we chased you about the valley on that first day of

your arrival, you proved your skill," Ashwarawu said. "In the battles against the Wraps, you have proven your worth. Your strength and your will."

Stripped to one shirt and simple breeches, the young man came forward suddenly, going to his knees before the woman. "I feared that I would not find a woman suitable for Ashwarawu," he said, and he moved right in, wrapping Brynn with his powerful arms and pressing his lips against hers.

A rush of confusion washed through Brynn. On the most basic level, Ashwarawu was undeniably handsome, with his strong features and honed muscles, the epitome of To-gai-ru manhood. Add to that the woman's feelings of duty, that her role within Ashwarawu's band at that time was whatever Ashwarawu determined her role to be, and she did not immediately refuse.

Ashwarawu pulled her down to the furs and his hands started roaming about her body, sliding under the furs she wore. He kept kissing her, and started to undress her.

Brynn could not deny some of the tingles his touch excited in her, in ways that the innocent young woman had never known. But neither could she deny her instincts that this was not right. Not for her. Not then and there.

She pushed Ashwarawu away, or tried to, for the powerful young man just grabbed on tighter and pressed his lips against hers more forcefully.

Brynn slipped her hand under his and gave a subtle twist, freeing her enough to pull back.

"No," she said.

If she had picked up a knife and stabbed it into his chest, Ashwarawu's expression would have been no less incredulous.

"You deny Ashwarawu?"

He lessened his grasp as he spoke, and Brynn wriggled free and went back to sitting against the side of the tent.

"I do not even know you," the woman replied. She hated the wounded look on his face, the expression that she had put there. For a moment, she felt very foolish and very ashamed that she was not more of a woman.

"I am Ashwarawu!" he said. "I am the bringer of hope to the To-gai-ru. I am he whom the Behrenese fear!"

"In all those things, you speak truly," Brynn admitted, her voice barely a whisper.

"You should feel proud that I have chosen you to lie with me!"

Brynn looked at him hard, her expression sufficient to keep him at bay, for indeed he had started to advance again. She tried desperately to sort through the myriad feelings and thoughts that were swirling about her mind, but all that she could ask at that moment was, "Is gratitude a reason to make love?"

Ashwarawu sat back, looking very much as if he did not understand.

"I do not know!" Brynn spouted. "I am not sure."

"Pleasure me," the man demanded. "Let me pleasure you, for tomorrow we might die upon the field!"

On one level, his words made perfect sense to Brynn. Did she wish to die a virgin, after all? In truth, to that moment, she had hardly thought about it, for her life had been full of so many other joys and responsibilities.

On another level, though, Brynn could not dismiss her feeling that this was not right for her. Not at that time. So many things about Ashwarawu seemed appealing—his appearance not the least of them. But so many other questions remained in the back of the woman's mind.

"No," she said with conviction. "I do not know you. I serve you with my blade, and with my body in battle."

"You would serve me well tonight," the man complained.

"That is not a role I choose," Brynn said, and though the conflicts remained within her, she was on solid emotional ground, had made up her mind and would not be persuaded otherwise.

"Ashwarawu!" came a voice from outside, some distance away.

The To-gai-ru leader glanced at the tent flap, then back at Brynn, coldly, but then moved and pushed the flap aside.

"Barou is very sick," the distant voice explained. "And others are feeling ill."

Ashwarawu grabbed his furs and crawled for the tent entrance. He glanced back at Brynn once, his expression clearly conveying his demand that the events of that night be kept secret between them. "We will finish this another time," he said.

Brynn didn't know if he was referring to the discussion or the lovemaking, and she even got an uneasy feeling that there was a veiled threat in his statement.

She collected herself then and started to follow, but paused once, considering the irony of it all.

On the field the day before, Ashwarawu had been able to make her put aside the questions of her conscience and take the lives of the two wounded men. In here, he had essentially tried to do the same thing, to use her as an extension of his wishes, whatever her own desires might have been.

So much of what Ashwarawu did offended Brynn at a very instinctive level, and yet, he was proving to be effective. Undeniably.

Was this the definition of a leader?

Brynn did not know.

That night, Barou, a young warrior still in his teens, died, and many others grew sick. It didn't take the To-gai-ru long to realize that the men had been poisoned.

Pagonel stepped in, offering to examine all of the foodstuffs. No one quite understood what the mystic meant to do, but no one questioned him, either.

He approached each bundle of food solemnly, falling deep within himself, and, as an Abellican monk employing hematite might do, he sent his sensibilities right into the food, visualizing any "sickness" within the foodstuff.

He told them which of the supplies were fit to eat, and which were not, and though many sent questioning looks his way, unable to comprehend his methods and therefore doubting his conclusions, Ashwarawu nodded his agreement.

The powerful leader walked up to the first bundle Pagonel had proclaimed as safe, lifted the meat to his mouth, and tore off a huge chunk.

"So, you have found a way to be useful!" Ashwarawu declared, and all of the raiders began to cheer for Pagonel.

Brynn watched it all, scrutinizing Ashwarawu's every move,

studying how he played upon the emotions of the crowd, turning their hope to the benefit of his own stature, but also to the general good feeling and morale. It was obvious to her that Ashwarawu understood that the poison placed in the food could have more emotional impact than the physical toll it had inflicted. The poison could have shaken the confidence of the raiders in themselves, in the weaknesses of their enemy, and in their leader.

That was all behind them now, suddenly, as long as Pagonel's proclamations about the food proved accurate.

Brynn, who understood the deeper levels of magic and perception because of her time with the elves, was beginning to recognize the depth of this Jhesta Tu mystic, and had no doubt that his decisions about the foodstuffs would prove correct.

They did indeed over the course of the next week.

Several uneventful days followed, as the raider band regrouped. As with the period following almost every victory, more soldiers came in to join with mighty Ashwarawu. Brynn watched the leader closely throughout that time period, measuring his words and his actions, trying to determine what he was doing that worked well, and what seemed not so effective. All the while, she couldn't dismiss the obvious fact that Ashwarawu was really a very young man, younger than she was herself.

What he lacked in maturity and tact, though, he made up for in sheer bravery and ferocity.

That was his secret, Brynn decided. His bravery was dominant, so much so that his mere presence lent strength and courage to those around him—as it had when he had lifted the meat Pagonel had said was untainted to his lips and taken a huge bite of it. He had not ordered a lesser to taste the food. And in battle, Ashwarawu did not follow his warriors in.

No, he led, howling and cheering, inviting the enemy to fight him.

Also to the man's credit, Ashwarawu did not pressure Brynn in those days, nor did he try to ignore her. He treated her pretty much as he treated everyone else—except that Brynn often caught him stealing glances at her.

Brynn awoke one morning to find the camp all abuzz. She

found Pagonel not far from her tent flap, the mystic looking on in amusement as many of the other raiders flocked about a middle-aged To-gai-ru woman.

"Ya Ya Deng has arrived," the mystic explained, though the name meant nothing to Brynn.

"An informant from Dharyan," Pagonel went on in response to Brynn's blank stare. "Her cousin works in the great temple of Dharyan and often overhears Yatol Grysh and his leaders."

Brynn nodded and turned back to regard the woman.

"She came in to tell us of the poisoned food," Pagonel went on. "Though she recognized that she would likely arrive too late."

"How convenient for Yatol Grysh," Brynn remarked offhandedly, and though she wasn't really suspicious, the thought did cross her mind that any such informant had to be handled carefully.

"Her information has been reliable on many matters, I am told," Pagonel replied. "Ya Ya Deng is among Ashwarawu's greatest assets."

"She must be loyal to have come all the way from Dharyan, though she knew that her information would not be timely."

"She came in to inform Ashwarawu, as well, that the two twenty-squares of Jacintha soldiers who arrived in Dharyan will not be staying, nor will they be heading west to To-gai," the mystic said. "Apparently, they are to return to Jacintha on the first true break in the weather."

Brynn looked at him curiously. "Twenty-squares?"

"Ashwarawu learned of their arrival in Dharyan. Perhaps that is why we have not been skirting the borderland of late. I believe that our leader feared that his reputation might have grown too strong too far to the east too quickly, catching the attention of enemies he is not ready to face."

Brynn nodded, understanding well why Ashwarawu would welcome the news that eight hundred trained and well-outfitted soldiers were turning back to the east instead of coming his way.

"A fine line, is reputation," Pagonel warned. "While it benefits among allies, inspiring confidence and support, its effects on the enemy are varied. On the one hand, how much stronger are your forces if the enemy is in fear of you because of your reputation. On the other, the game is dangerous when your enemy is powerful enough to destroy you, as the Chezru Chieftain certainly is, concerning all of To-gai."

Brynn nodded but did not reply. This was an important lesson, she knew, and one that she would not forget.

Winter's grasp grew thin on the land early in God's Year 841. Several storms reared above the plateau, only to fizzle as they crossed out of the mountains, turning to a gentle rain or disappearing altogether.

On the last day of the second month, with all of the fanfare they had brought upon their arrival to Dharyan, the two Jacintha twenty-squares marched out of the western Behrenese city. They left behind the sixty-four soldiers Yatol Grysh had requested the previous summer, but seemed no less diminished as they marched, rank upon rank, down the eastern road.

They crossed through Bohgadee, the next Behrenese city in line, two days later, again with horns blaring, and then continued on down the eastern road, into the sandy desert, empty for many miles before the next oasis and city.

And there, in the empty wasteland, the army of Jacintha executed their turn, with Chezhou-Lei Dahmed Blie's group turning south and back to the west, and Chezhou-Lei Woh Lien's group turning north and then back to the west.

Advance groups, posing as simple scouting parties, had already prepared their camps, in the foothills along the mountains northwest of Dharyan, and in the cave complexes along the plateaus southwest of Dharyan.

There they would wait for proud Ashwarawu to err.

# CHAPTER 18

# *Baiting the Hook*

Carwan Pestle settled into his chair at Yatol Grysh's side in the main audience chamber of the temple in Dharyan.

Wan Atenn walked into the room almost immediately, storming up to stand right before the pair.

"You have heard the latest reports of the rebels, I suppose," Yatol Grysh remarked.

Carwan Pestle nodded, for he, too, had heard the reports, which placed Ashwarawu closer to the rim of the To-gai plateau than before.

"Ashwarawu is within striking distance of Dancala Grysh," said the Yatol, referring to a small outposter settlement, just over the To-gai rim, that had only recently been renamed in his honor.

Wan Atenn nodded.

"That settlement must not fall!" Grysh yelled suddenly, rising from his seat, a huge scowl upon his thick-jowled face. "I will not be insulted as Chezru Chieftain Douan was insulted by the fall of Douan Cal!"

"The Jacintha soldiers have departed, Yatol," Wan Atenn reminded. "I have few warriors at my disposal—"

"You have the garrison of Dharyan, bolstered by the men from Jacintha who remained behind. That should be sufficient to crush the fool Ru and his wretched followers."

Wan Atenn stiffened, squaring his shoulders and puffing out his broad and powerful chest. "Even with the additional soldiers, the defense of Dharyan—"

"I did not ask you to defend Dharyan!" Yatol Grysh screamed at him.

"Yatol?" the seemingly stunned Chezhou-Lei warrior asked. "That is my mission, above all. To defend Dharyan and to defend Yatol Grysh."

"And to defend the reputation of Yatol Grysh, you must defend Dancala Grysh," the Yatol explained.

Wan Atenn spent a long while staring at his leader. So did a confused Carwan Pestle. He had rarely seen the calculating Grysh so animated, and could hardly believe that Grysh cared so much about a minor settlement that had borne his name for only a few months.

"Dancala Grysh has only a partial wall, and no defensive emplacements," Wan Atenn explained. "To properly defend it will take nearly as many soldiers as are needed to defend Dharyan itself."

"Then take them."

"Yatol, I cannot," the Chezhou-Lei warrior gasped.

"We have more than three hundred men in garrison," the Yatol said. "More than enough to defeat the one or two hundred known to ride with Ashwarawu, even without defensive emplacements. And even if our losses are heavy in the fight, ridding the land of that dog Ashwarawu will be worth the price. I will call to Jacintha for replacements, if need be, once the battle is won."

"Perhaps you should put out the call now, Yatol," Wan Atenn offered. "Reinforce Dharyan before ordering the garrison out on the hunt."

"Dharyan is secure."

"There are goblins in the mountains to the north."

Carwan Pestle looked at the Chezhou-Lei warrior curiously after that remark. There had been no recent reports of any goblins forming in the mountains—not in any real numbers, anyway.

"You wished to poison the rebels, and so we tried, and so we failed," Yatol Grysh countered. "How many embarrassments must I suffer at the hands of the dog Ashwarawu? No more, I say. He is said to be near Dancala Grysh, and so there you will go with my soldiers. And there he will die, and I will be bothered in hearing his name no more!"

Wan Atenn stiffened again, noticeably. "I will not, Yatol,"

he said calmly. "I am bound to remain by your side whenever I perceive that you are vulnerable. And so you shall be if . . ." He paused and stared at the Yatol, then nodded hesitantly. "When," he corrected, "the garrison marches to Dancala Grysh. They will defeat Ashwarawu without me, I am sure."

Yatol Grysh stared coldly at the Chezhou-Lei warrior for a few moments, then gave a tension-breaking laugh. "Press a hundred men into service to accompany the garrison," he said. "It will take at least that many to make up for the absence of Wan Atenn in the battle for Dancala Grysh. And select another hundred civilians to bolster our walls. The Shepherds can spare a couple of weeks away from their flocks, and this business should be promptly concluded. It saddens me that you will not be there as my personal representative when Ashwarawu is killed, but I will not force you to abandon your vows to protect me."

With a click of his heels and a curt bow, Wan Atenn spun about and strode powerfully out of the room.

"I do not think . . ." Carwan Pestle started to ask, but the Yatol cut him short.

"I am weary and will retire now," he said. "Come with me to my private quarters, that we might speak of these new decisions. Perhaps I will send you as my emissary to Dancala Grysh."

That remark certainly widened Carwan Pestle's eyes, but he held his tongue, obediently following his master from the audience hall, back to the lavish private quarters.

"Speak openly," Grysh said as he fell into a comfortable chair in a small and cozy room.

Carwan Pestle stammered over a couple of words.

"Speak, young Shepherd," the Yatol demanded. "This is a glorious time. Do you not understand?"

"You mean to chase Ashwarawu across the steppes, Yatol?" Pestle asked nervously. "I thought that our policy of bolstering the defenses of the settlements slowly and deliberately, of encouraging walls to be built around every village, and of sending soldiers out to oversee the construction of proper defenses was becoming effective. Over the whole of the winter, Ashwarawu has not struck at a single village. Only caravans."

"Of course it has been effective," Grysh replied. "Ashwarawu cannot risk defeat at a minor settlement when so little gain is to be found and so great is the possible loss. He will attack Dancala Grysh only if he perceives that there is little risk."

"The town is not the best defended of the settlements, at last assessment, but—" Carwan Pestle was stopped short by Grysh's renewed laughter.

"Wan Atenn understands," the Yatol explained. "That is why the glory-hungry Chezhou-Lei refused to leave Dharyan."

Carwan Pestle's face screwed up with confusion, then his eyes gradually widened as he began to catch on. "You believe that Ashwarawu will bypass Dancala Grysh and strike at Dharyan?" he asked incredulously.

"All signs are that his force has grown stronger," the Yatol reasoned. "Ashwarawu's reputation lends courage to all the Ru, and each of his victories sends more warriors flocking to join him. A great and significant victory could mobilize the entire region of To-gai behind him. Ashwarawu is no fool. If he thinks we are weakened here, he will desire that significant victory—one that will carry him to greater glory over the course of the summer. He knows that he cannot continue striking and running, that soon enough we will grow tired of him and send an army powerful enough to hunt him down and utterly destroy him—I am sure that he was a bit worried when two twenty-squares marched into Dharyan at the beginning of the winter, fearing just that consequence. Thus he needs the big strike, the huge victory, to wave as a rallying pennant to the other To-gai-ru. He will come against us, and then he will be mine."

Carwan Pestle sat back and digested it all; and of course, it then made sense to him. All of it. For why would Wan Atenn ever have truly feared for Yatol Grysh and Dharyan with eight hundred soldiers camped within a day's march of the city?

It was all a coordinated plan, all a ruse designed to lure Ashwarawu, to make the rebel leader think that the grandest prize of all was his for the taking. Carwan Pestle stared at Yatol Grysh with sincere admiration then, for the man had been executing this one ruse since the unexpected arrival of the Jacintha soldiers. Each movement he had made, each caravan sacrificed, each accurate message slipped out to the Ru informants, had led to this hoped-for conclusion.

"I know Ashwarawu better than Ashwarawu knows himself," the Yatol said with confidence. "I understand the motivation behind the warrior. That motivation is pride, my young friend, and pride is the easiest human weakness to exploit. Oh yes, he will come. And he will die. And it will be a long time indeed before the Ru find the courage to stand against Behren again. Watch and learn well, my student, for you will likely succeed me and face the next Ashwarawu, and how disappointed I will be in Paradise if I look back upon the earthly realm to witness your failure."

Carwan Pestle nodded, and then, as Grysh exploded into another burst of laughter, let a smile spread across his face. As he considered all that had transpired over the winter—the caravans sent out as bait in very specific order and to very specific locations; the poisoning ruse, done merely to make Ashwarawu even more confident in himself and in his informants; the renaming of the minor settlement—for no better reason, he now understood, than to make his desired defense of it seem more plausible. Carwan Pestle realized that he had very much to learn.

He recalled the last brutal lesson, at the riverbed and the Ru encampment, and couldn't stop a shudder from running along his spine.

Brutal and effective.

Carwan Pestle trusted his teacher, even though he was terrified of the man.

"Our friend from Dharyan challenges us," Ashwarawu was telling his soldiers. "He does not understand how we have grown."

"In numbers and in resolve," Pagonel, who was standing far to the side of the group, whispered so that only Brynn could hear.

The young ranger smiled; they had both heard this speech many times before.

The band was on a high ridge that day, looking down at the distant outposter settlement, and the line of soldiers streaming into it. The estimates of their scouts had put the number of soldiers at near to four hundred, which made it almost twice as large as the force that Ashwarawu possessed, though his forces had more than doubled in the waning days of the winter season.

Still, the confident raiders believed that one To-gai-ru warrior was worth three Behrenese, at least.

"We will answer that challenge," Brynn heard the brave leader declare. "On our terms and in our time."

"Do you think he will lead us against the settlement?" Brynn asked Pagonel.

The mystic shrugged. "I do not think it a wise course, for though I believe that we would win, our losses would be heavy."

Brynn felt exactly the same way, but this was Ashwarawu they were speaking of, and so she had no idea if he would lead the charge or not.

The raider band camped on the ridge that night, sending out scouting arms to encircle the village, while other riders went out farther to the east, looking for a certain informant at every determined rendezvous site.

Ya Ya Deng's information arrived the very next morning, confirming what the scouts had come to believe, that this was the Dharyan garrison, almost the whole of the Dharyan garrison, come out to fortify the settlement.

Once again, Ashwarawu convened his raiders on the ridge overlooking the busy village, and once again, Brynn and Pagonel sat astride their horses to the side of the main body of raiders.

"You seem troubled," Brynn remarked as Ashwarawu began rousing his soldiers.

The mystic shook his head, his eyes never leaving the distant settlement. "Yatol Grysh sends out his garrison so soon after the Jacintha soldiers leave Dharyan?"

"Ya Ya Deng claims that he will not have a village bearing his name fall to Ashwarawu. Perhaps that will inspire our leader to attack at once."

Her sarcasm was not lost on the mystic, but he remained too perplexed and unsure to comment on it. With Pagonel still looking down at the distant settlement, Brynn turned her attention back to Ashwarawu.

"Yatol Grysh brings his forces here, out in the open, as a challenge to us and to all To-gai," Ashwarawu reasoned. "He believes that this paltry force can defeat us!"

"No!" came the cries from many corners of the camp.

"Are we to accept this challenge?" Ashwarawu asked.

"Death to the Wraps!" one man cried, and another and then another echoed his sentiment.

Ashwarawu put on a wicked grin. "Death to Yatol Grysh," he said. "In his arrogance and frustration, he has erred, for his forces cannot match our pace as we ride to the east!"

"I think he just said that we are to attack Dharyan," Brynn remarked to Pagonel dryly.

That got the mystic's attention, and he looked to her, then turned to the distant Ashwarawu.

"Let us take the battle to Yatol Grysh's home, and see how strong his resolve remains," Ashwarawu cried. "Our enemy thinks so little of us that he empties his city in the hunt. He insults us and taunts us. How loud will his taunts resound when Dharyan is in flames?"

That last question elicited thunderous cheers from the gathering, as fierce a war cry as Brynn Dharielle had ever heard, and the woman joined in.

But Pagonel did not. He was looking back at the settlement, then, thinking that this was all a bit too convenient. Certainly the rebels had discussed attacking Dharyan before; they had even made arrangements, through Ya Ya Deng, to build some support within the city if a battle should be joined.

But now, so suddenly, Dharyan seemed ripe for the plucking. Obviously so.

The raider band set out almost immediately, breaking down their camp with stunning efficiency and riding hard to the east. Dharyan was five days away, but Ashwarawu hoped to knock a full day off the journey, so that the city could be struck, perhaps even sacked, before the garrison now settled into the outposter village could hope to get back and help.

The rebel band eagerly accepted Ashwarawu's desired pace, even exceeding it, so that the white walls of Dharyan and the great temple within were visible to them as they set their camp on the third night.

"Tomorrow will bring triumph or disaster," Brynn said to Pagonel.

"A resigned tone is not the voice of a warrior," the mystic observed. "What do you fear?"

Brynn spent a long while sorting through her feelings, then answered quietly, "It seems as if our enemy, Grysh, has erred in failing to understand the strength of our forces. Could he have been so foolish as to strip his walls of trained soldiers?"

"Or?" The mystic's prompting told Brynn that he knew everything she was thinking, that he had likely already sorted these confusing issues out in his own mind.

"Or he wanted us here," Brynn admitted. She gave a great sigh. "But does not every leader faced with such a seemingly wondrous opportunity question it? And are not blunders, exactly like this one that Yatol Grysh has apparently made, often the turning point in a prolonged battle?"

"He does, and they are," the mystic answered.

"Then where does that leave us?"

In response, Pagonel nodded toward Ashwarawu, who was sitting near a small fire, chatting and laughing with some of the newer raiders. Whatever his faults, Brynn could not deny the love the raider band held for this man. She saw them staring, awestricken, at him, looking up to him for guidance.

Looking up to Ashwarawu for hope.

The next dawn came shrouded in a heavy overcast, and the To-gai-ru camp settled in quietly, drawing up their plans, readying their horses and weapons.

Various warriors were selected for various duties: strong riders to carry the torches to the base of the wall; the stealthiest of the group to lead the way in, scaling Dharyan's low wall and quickly and quietly finishing off the sentries.

Ashwarawu wasted no time in approaching Pagonel for

this second task. The Jhesta Tu were noted for the ability to follow the path of shadows, and with no more sound than a shadow might make!

The mystic stared up at the large and imposing man. This was not an easy moment for Pagonel, for if he accepted the duty, he would be thrust into combat. But this was a crucial moment for the raiders and for all of To-gai. If Ashwarawu could win a victory here, in the largest Behrenese city in all the region, then his reputation would explode across the steppes and scores, hundreds, perhaps thousands, of To-gai-ru would flock to join with him.

"I will help to clear the wall," the mystic agreed.

"As will I," Brynn added, and Ashwarawu looked at her curiously, as did his entourage of warriors, for the leader had not asked Brynn.

One of the large men standing beside Ashwarawu broke into laughter, and the others joined in, but Ashwarawu stopped them fast with an upraised hand.

"You have proven your value as a warrior upon your horse," the leader explained to Brynn.

"I am stronger with the sword afoot," Brynn said. "And have been trained well in the art of stealth. The Wraps will never know I am there."

Neither Ashwarawu nor his entourage seemed convinced, but what bothered Brynn at that moment most of all was the incredulous, even disappointed, look that came back at her from Pagonel.

"You will ride in the line, where your fine bow will be of greatest value," the leader said, and he let his look linger long on Brynn, then walked away.

"Do not judge me," Brynn said to the mystic when they were alone again. "Did you not just agree to become an assassin yourself?"

"The word does not flow prettily from your lips," Pagonel replied.

"The word?"

"Wraps," Pagonel explained. "Speaking the word does not become you." He rose and bowed to her, then walked off, leaving her with her thoughts.

*   *   *

Wan Atenn stalked the wall of Dharyan all that day, for he
and his Yatol knew well that Ashwarawu was near. The fierce
Chezhou-Lei relished the coming battle, and only hoped that
he would get the chance to kill many of the hated Ru before
the two twenty-squares closed upon them and utterly obliter-
ated them.

Dare Wan Atenn hope that he might get a chance to kill
Ashwarawu himself?

He had only two hundred men with which to defend the
city, half of whom were mere peasants and certainly not
skilled in the ways of disciplined soldiers. He expected that
Ashwarawu's band would number at least his total, despite
what Yatol Grysh had predicted. And while Wan Atenn knew
that he could easily kill any two of Ashwarawu's warriors, he
did not underestimate the ferocity of the Ru.

The city had to hold firm, with little damage or loss of life,
until the armies arrived.

When night fell and there remained no signs of the approaching raiders, Wan Atenn feared that Ashwarawu had
sniffed out the trap. Perhaps the Ru had noted the approach of
one of the twenty-squares, the soldiers moving into position
barely an hour's march from the city. If that was the case, the
Chezhou-Lei decided then and there that he would take up
the soldiers and pursue the dog, all the way to western To-gai
if necessary!

He was standing by the main gatehouse, instructing a
handful of sentries, when the first unusual sound reached his
ears, one that the other men in the gatehouse didn't even seem
to notice, but one that piqued the interest of the superbly
trained warrior.

"Hold fast your positions," the Chezhou-Lei warrior instructed, and he moved off, silent as death, along the wall.

Pagonel had little difficulty in getting to the base of
Dharyan's wall undetected. Once there, the mystic fell into
his life energy, willing it upward and in doing so, lightening
his body.

The mystic ran his hand along the wall, feeling the grooves

between the large stone blocks. When it had been constructed, a sandy mortar had been used to fill the seals between the stones, but the continual wind off the mountains and the steppes had cleared most of that fill away.

Pagonel was at the base of the highest point in the wall, but it was only a dozen feet, and the mystic went up it as easily as if he was crawling across a floor. At the top, he paused and listened, noting the approaching footsteps of a soldier—he knew that because he could hear the rattle of a weapon against armor.

Still hanging over the side, the mystic brought his legs up as high as he could and set them firmly, then listened, measuring the approach.

The Behrenese soldier spun to his left, facing out over the wall, as the form lifted past. Obviously confused, the soldier never even realized that the springing mystic had gone right above him. He was still staring out at the darkness when Pagonel came down atop him.

Pagonel's foot snap-kicked the man in the back as he descended, blasting away both breath and voice. And by the time the mystic landed lightly behind the dazed soldier, he had already put a twisting chokehold in place.

The soldier never regained enough balance to even offer resistance before he lapsed into unconsciousness.

Pagonel gently and quietly brought him down to the stone, then took his weapon from its sheath and tossed it over the wall.

Then the mystic trotted off, with absolute silence, making his way toward the gatehouse that centered the city's western wall.

He came upon a second soldier soon after, and a few quick moments later, tossed the unconscious man's weapon over the wall.

On he went, with the dark silhouette of the gatehouse in sight. He knew that there would be much more resistance within, likely several soldiers, at least. But he knew, too, that the Behrenese warriors would have more than him on their minds by that time, for out in the darkness to the west, the mystic heard the beginning hoofbeats of Ashwarawu's charge.

\* \* \*

Ten horses, widely spaced, charged the Dharyan wall in a perfect line, each skilled rider holding the same posture, with legs alone guiding their trusted mounts, a pair of oiled torches across their laps, flint and steel ready to strike. They pulled up as one a short distance from the wall and, ignoring the cries of sentries just then realizing that an attack had come, they struck their torches and held them aloft and out to the side.

Now came the main charge, Ashwarawu's warriors, Brynn among them, riding in hard in twenty orderly rows. All had bows, arrows set, and arrow tips treated to burst into flame as soon as they passed the lead riders and touched tip to burning torch.

The archers rode past and let fly their missiles, then turned tight and orderly turns, left and right, to circle for the next shot, setting another arrow as they went.

Brynn came past as the third in her line, and by the time she put her bow up, several fiery arrows had gone over the wall before her, illuminating the top enough for her to pick out the form of a scrambling soldier. With expert skill and a trusted mount, Brynn began her turn before she let fly.

She caught the soldier center mass, the flames catching almost immediately to his tunic. He waved his arms and ran about, frantically and futilely. By the time he fell off the wall, back into the city's courtyard, Brynn was already coming around with her second arrow set.

Crouched on all fours, Pagonel scrambled along the wall. He saw one Behrenese man go up in flames, an arrow in his side, and heard the screams of others as arrows or flames bit at them. He saw a building within Dharyan begin to burn. The mystic didn't enjoy any of it. The whole concept of warfare assaulted his sensibilities, for though the Jhesta Tu were superbly trained warriors, theirs was a pacific philosophy, one that touted battle as the last means of resort for self-defense.

What, then, was he doing there?

Pagonel couldn't stop to ponder the question, obviously, for he was nearing the gatehouse. He winced as he heard the first To-gai-ru scream of pain; he recognized the voice of one of his sneaky companions, not so far away, accompanied by the swishing sound of a sword and the thud of the weapon's impact.

With the small alcove holding the mechanisms to the gate in sight, Pagonel went up straighter and ran on.

He skidded to a stop, though, reversed his momentum, and leaped into a high backspin, as an imposing figure rushed out of that alcove at him, a shining curved sword slashing across at waist height.

Pagonel landed in a defensive stance, ready to advance or retreat as necessary, but his attacker had not come on, but stood there on the parapet, staring at him with obvious surprise. The mystic recognized the overlapping armor plates of the Chezhou-Lei warrior.

"Jhesta Tu?" Wan Atenn asked incredulously, his face a mask of outrage.

Pagonel narrowed his eyes and went lower in the crouch, ready to face the Chezhou-Lei, avowed enemies of his order.

With a roar, Wan Atenn came on hard, his curved sword slashing down, then across, then back across, then up and over to come down diagonally yet again, the Chezhou-Lei taking care to cut through every possible angle of attack.

With only his hands and feet for weapons, Pagonel was forced to back away in response.

Wan Atenn did not take that as any sign of advantage, though. He understood the Jhesta Tu well enough to let caution temper his strikes. He did come forward, stabbing once, twice, and nearly scoring a hit with each.

But like a mongoose dodging a striking snake, Pagonel stayed just ahead of his attacker. His dodges were subtle, a simple twist or bend, for the first Jhesta Tu rule of fighting an opponent of obvious skill was to conserve your energy. Without a staff or sword with which to parry and open an attack path, Pagonel had to count on this one tiring, on the Chezhou-Lei launching an attack slow enough for him to deflect and turn the blade far away, and rush in behind the strike.

The sword came out straight again, then went in, up and over in a flash as the warrior charged the mystic.

Pagonel skittered forward instead of back, diving into a

roll past Wan Atenn on the narrow parapet, as that deadly sword began its downward slice.

Wan Atenn roared and spun about suddenly, recovering so quickly that Pagonel had barely begun his turn and charge before the blade was there, barring the way.

"Why are you here, Jhesta Tu?" the Chezhou-Lei demanded. "Is the fight of the To-gai-ru the fight of the Jhesta Tu?"

Pagonel didn't answer, because Pagonel had no answer.

Fire erupted farther within the city—not the burning caused by the rain of To-gai-ru arrows, but a singular, planned blaze that soared high into the nighttime sky on the tip of a great ballista bolt.

It didn't seem aimed at the opposing To-gai-ru forces, didn't really seem aimed at anything. It just arced slowly, high above the city, rolling out on driving winds to the east.

Pagonel watched it with dismay, for he knew it for what it was, even before Wan Atenn grinned at him and said, "We are not surprised. If the Jhesta Tu have chosen to side with the To-gai-ru, then the Jhesta Tu have chosen wrongly. Watch, mystic, if you live long enough, as the jaws of doom close over Ashwarawu and his murderous companions."

Pagonel didn't understand the details of it all, but they hardly seemed important at that moment. He recognized the signal flare for what it was, and was not surprised when he heard the blast of teeyodel horns, both north and south.

Before he could begin to sort through it all, the fierce Chezhou-Lei came at him again, and the mystic was rolling and leaping, dodging and turning, and ultimately, backing.

He realized that he was running out of room when he heard the cries of a Behrenese soldier behind him, coming on fast.

Her shouts lost in the commotion about her, Brynn galloped Runtly all along Dharyan's western wall, letting fly arrow after arrow, some aflame—on those occasions when she got near to a torchbearer—and others just taking scrambling sentries from the wall top. With each subsequent run, she held closer to the center of activity, the gatehouse, where the wooden doors were burning and Ashwarawu, on his strong black-and-white pony, had backed up close, urging his mount to kick at the weakening wood.

His soldiers about him fired their bows at any atop the wall who tried to draw a bead on their leader, while other To-gai-ru scrambled up the wall, throwing themselves over the top, into the midst of their enemies, with abandon.

The sheer fury of the attack, the sheer bravery and inspiration of Ashwarawu, seemed to Brynn as if it would win the day, as if they would score a huge victory here. While she didn't entertain any illusions that so small a force as this could conquer a city as large as Dharyan, she felt certain that they would inflict a serious wound against Behren here, and return as heroes to the steppes.

Brynn gritted her teeth with determination as she watched a pair of her comrades run to the base of the wall, just to the side of the gatehouse, a huge skin of oil held between them. They rocked it and tossed it up over the wall, and an archer hit it squarely as it went over, the fiery arrow puncturing the skin, creating a huge fireball.

But then Brynn took note of a second flame, a fiery missile arcing over the dark Dharyan sky.

She tried to ignore it, focusing on her aim, and even took another Behrenese soldier from the wall.

She couldn't ignore the continuing distant blare of horns, though, to the north and to the south, and sounding closer with every blast.

Dharyan's gate seemed about to fall, but Brynn's stomach tightened with trepidation.

Though he hated the thought of turning his back on a Chezhou-Lei warrior, Pagonel spun suddenly to slow the charge of two Behrenese warriors. He caught the movement out of the corner of his eye, of something coming over the wall.

Behind him, Wan Atenn charged. Before him, the Behrenese stopped to strike defensive postures, then turned suddenly, surprised, as a twisting form rolled over the wall. Pagonel threw himself backward, falling to his butt and rolling over.

The oilskin exploded, immolating the two Behrenese, startling and blinding Wan Atenn.

Pagonel came around and kicked upward, his feet catching the Chezhou-Lei—who still had his sword up over his head—in the gut, just under the rib cage. The mystic extended full out, double-kicking, but shortening the blow with his right leg, which was closer to the courtyard, and extending fully through with his left, diving the Chezhou-Lei backward and turning him with the kick.

Pagonel came back to his feet on the edge of the parapet, with Wan Atenn falling hard behind him, to the city courtyard. The mystic could have leaped at the Chezhou-Lei then, trying to finish him with a single, clean kick.

But he knew the truth, and he hadn't the time.

He went to the wall then and looked to the south, and saw the torches of the approaching force—a force of hundreds, he realized.

"Fly away!" the mystic cried to the warriors outside the wall, and he climbed atop the crenelation, preparing to leap into the tumult below, waving his arms in an attempt to garner some attention. "A trap! Fly away!"

But his voice was a whisper amidst the thunder of battle.

Expecting his enemy to be leaping down at him, Wan Atenn braced himself and set his sword above him.

When nothing followed him down, and as his breath came back to him, the proud warrior pulled himself from the ground. He wanted nothing more than to scramble back up and pay back the wretched Jhesta Tu, but he could not, he realized—not then. Ignoring the two soldiers burning and thrashing on the ground near to him, the Chezhou-Lei stalked to the gate.

He looked back to see the rest of his command coming forth, as they had been ordered, moving out from the shadows of the nearest buildings toward the gatehouse. He pointed to the commander of the group, then to the burning and falling door, then leaped to a ladder beside the gatehouse and made his way back up.

Confusion had taken the field immediately outside the gate by that point, as the torches of the two twenty-squares drew nearer and nearer and the To-gai-ru came to understand the truth of the trap. Wan Atenn could not spot the hated Jhesta Tu in the scramble, but he did see another figure, one that he knew at once.

Ashwarawu remained at the base of the door, his horse bucking and kicking hard at the wood, the leader howling out for the continuing charge despite the obvious forthcoming turn in the battle.

Ashwarawu!

Suddenly, Wan Atenn forgot all about the Jhesta Tu mystic. He moved to the gatehouse directly above the door, shoving aside those few guards remaining inside the structure and ignoring the fight just to the side, where several To-gai-ru had managed to scale the wall.

His focus was below.

The doors went down and Wan Atenn's main garrison charged out into the thrash of To-gai-ru, streaming past Ashwarawu, whose great sword cut down one man and then another.

Smiling widely, the Chezhou-Lei warrior leaped down from above.

Her bow back in place at the side of her saddle, sword in hand, Brynn brought Runtly in tight maneuvers, chopping away at one Behrenese defender after another. The door was down, the enemy flowing out to meet the attack right there in the bottleneck of the gate.

Not enough enemies to overwhelm the attackers, Brynn knew—not coming from inside the fortified city, at least.

The torches she glimpsed to the north and to the south, though, made it clear to her that the time had come for a full retreat.

Amidst it all, she saw Ashwarawu, slashing away, chopping down enemy after enemy and howling gleefully with each devastating strike. He seemed so much larger than those around him, so above the battlefield, a god among mortal men, that Brynn found herself second-guessing her instinct to retreat.

Could the strength of Ashwarawu take them through the bloody night?

But then a form dropped beside the large warrior, expertly taking him down to the ground.

Brynn forged Runtly in her leader's direction, but she got cut off by a pair of Behrenese entwined with a To-gai-ru rider, and she had to put her sword to fast work to save her compatriot from getting pulled down from his mount.

By the time she looked back toward the gate, Ashwarawu and the man who had dropped upon him were up and facing each other. The raider pulled a huge axe off his back and slashed out wildly.

But he was dazed, it seemed to Brynn, and his overaggressive attack got nowhere near to hitting, while it left him off-balance.

His opponent expertly backed to the side, then came in behind Ashwarawu's strike, stepping forward with the horizontal slash, his fine sword cutting the raider leader's belly. Ashwarawu leaped back and doubled over a bit, and the enemy came forward in a crouch, turning his sword, then straightened fast, lifting the blade and skinning Ashwarawu's face from chin to forehead!

Brynn cringed at the explosion of crimson mist, at the pitiful sight of Ashwarawu, standing there, arms outstretched down and to the side, back bent slightly and his head thrown back from the sheer force of the devastating blow.

Brynn's horror only increased, as well as her fear of this amazing enemy, as the Behrenese warrior spun a complete circle, gaining momentum for his flying blade, and brought it across perfectly to lop Ashwarawu's head from his shoulders.

The woman exploded into motion again, forcing her horse about, screaming for a full retreat, even slapping the rumps of To-gai-ru ponies to spur them on their exit from the battlefield.

Many died right there, more Behrenese than To-gai-ru, but most of the raider band did turn and extract themselves from the mob, riding hard to the west, in a long and unorganized line.

Through it all, Brynn strained to find her one friend among the raiders, a mystic who had become much more to her than mere ally. But she couldn't find him, not on the wall nor in the tumult.

He was likely dead or captured on the other side of the wall, she realized, and with that grim and unsettling thought in mind, and with nothing left for her here in the frenzy, the woman turned Runtly to the west and kicked him hard, sending him leaping away and trampling a pair of Behrenese soldiers in the process.

She went back to her bow almost immediately after she had broken free, lifting her leg over her saddle and turning in one stirrup so that she was facing backward. Arrow after arrow flew back into the Behrenese ranks. She got off nearly ten shots before she was out of practical range, and before she heard the sounds of battle yet again, being joined to the south of her. Thinking only to aid her countrymen, Brynn cut her horse to the south, and saw the truth of their doom.

Ranks of Behrenese, Jacintha soldiers, swarmed over the retreating To-gai-ru, both south and north, closing like the jaws of a killer wolf upon their prey. Tears in her eyes, thinking it all at an end, Brynn plunged right into the wild fight.

She dealt a few blows and took a few in return, and for a while, got the best of those around her—so much so that many started to flee from her rather than engage.

But she was growing weary, was bleeding from several wounds, and standing out so tall among the overwhelmed To-gai-ru certainly invited disaster.

An arrow drove hard into Brynn's side, cracking through her ribs and piercing her lung. All the world swam in blurry grayness then, the woman's orientation fading away.

She slumped forward over Runtly's neck, lost in the swirl of pain—so lost that she did not see the imposing Behrenese rider come up right beside her, his curved sword poised to finish the task that the arrow had surely begun.

For Chezhou-Lei Dahmed Blie, this was a crowning moment of glory, one that would elevate him within the ranks of his mighty order. This To-gai-ru woman had fought valiantly in the brief exchange out here, as many of Dahmed Blie's warriors had witnessed. So he had managed to separate her and have her shot down, and now many would look on as he killed her, claiming the prize as his own.

He lifted his sword above his head and brought his mount up beside the brown-and-white To-gai pinto.

A form, a man, came up over Runtly's other side in a great leap.

Pagonel hooked his foot on the saddle and flank as he crested the pony's back, right behind the slumping Brynn, his shin going down atop the pony's broad back, affording him balance. His lead foot went out ahead, planting against the side of the stunned Chezhou-Lei's mount, but that foot did not break the Jhesta Tu mystic's momentum, for it was not the first contact. That came in the form of Pagonel's thrusting hand, his stiffened fingers perfectly aimed to jab into the surprised Chezhou-Lei's throat, driving through the man's skin and shattering his windpipe.

They held the pose for a long moment, the Chezhou-Lei's sword slipping from his grasp to fall harmlessly into the dirt on the other side of his horse. Slowly, Dahmed Blie's trembling hands reached for Pagonel's extended arm.

The Jhesta Tu mystic snapped free his bloody hand, then pulled back with his hooked foot, bringing him back fully to Brynn's pony. He gathered up the woman in his arms and urged the pony to leap away.

Behind him, Dahmed Blie fell over forward, but was well-secured in his saddle, which turned over with him, leaving the dead warrior dangling in the bloody dirt below his horse.

Away from the battlefield to the south, Pagonel gently lowered the grievously wounded woman to the sand.

He reached inside himself, to the source of his life and his power, and brought forth warmth to his hands, gently massaging the wound, where the arrow still protruded from the side of Brynn's chest. He knew that he had to pull the arrow forth, but first he needed to lend her strength, to channel it from his own body and into hers.

Pagonel heard the vultures overhead, heard the cries on the distant bloody field, of men dying in the dirt, helplessly.

He blocked them out. He focused on Brynn, sent his energy into her.

And then he stopped, his eyes going wide, as he came to know that he was not alone here, or at least, that his energy was not the only healing magic flowing into Brynn's frail body.

Her beret! Pagonel knew then that there was an enchantment upon it.

The mystic nearly chuckled aloud, musing that he had just discovered the truth of why powries were so tough. But even with the aid of the beret, Pagonel could not find any mirth, for he wasn't sure that it would be enough.

He worked with her for nearly an hour. Then, exhausted, and with the bloody arrow lying on the ground, the mystic hoisted Brynn back up, laying her across Runtly's back. He took up the pony's reins and started off again to the south.

Spring slipped into summer before Pagonel and Brynn, who was still comatose from her only slightly improved wounds, entered the region known as the Mountains of Fire. At the base of the five-thousand-step climb to the Walk of Clouds, the mystic stripped the gear from Runtly and gave him a slap, sending him running off in the direction of the low fields, where other horses ran wild.

Then the mystic put the weak Brynn across his shoulders and started his climb, not stopping until he had reached the secluded monastery.

The stares of disbelief that greeted his arrival were not unexpected, for the mystic had surely broken nearly every covenant concerning bringing visitors unannounced to the Walk of Clouds.

Not the least of those surprised looks came to him from Master Cheyes, his mentor.

# PART THREE

# ENLIGHTENMENT

*And so it ended, so quickly, so brutally. When I reflect on how little I knew of this leader, Ashwarawu, I am amazed at the spell he held over me, over so many of us. Where was he born? Among what tribe? Did he witness the death of his parents, as did I? Are his parents even dead?*

*So many questions now occur to me about who this man was and where he came from, about the history that would produce a leader so brave. The strange thing is, when I was with him, when I might have gotten answers to those questions, I never thought to ask them. Like all of the others, I was swept up in the moment, in the hope of freedom, in the glory of our cause.*

*In light of that realization, was it Ashwarawu's greatness that moved us all behind him, I wonder, or our own desperation to believe that we could win back our freedom? Was Ashwarawu a great leader, or simply a strong man thrust into the forefront by a desperate people?*

*Now, these months later, I must consider those questions honestly. For my own heart, at least, I must come to understand and accept the defeat.*

*I was thrilled when I learned that many of my people had not broken to the ways of the Yatols. Not just the old, wishing for times long past, but the young and strong, as well. Most of Ashwarawu's raiders were around my age, and many were significantly younger. We rode with passion and justice behind us.*

*But we lost.*

*When first I arrived at the Walk of Clouds, that seemed impossible to me, a nightmare that could not be. Is there not a god above, a god of justice and honor? If there is, then how could he side with the Yatols against us? Is there justice in their conquest?*

*In their torture? In their reduction of an entire race of people to
the class of slave? No god of justice could side with them!*

*But we lost.*

*And we did not lose because of any godly intervention, or
because of any lack of godly intervention, I have come to
understand through my meditations here. We lost because of
human fault, because of pride, above all. We seemed so unbeatable
out on the steppes, against the caravans, against the settlements.
Even against an army nearing our size, such as the garrison that
moved into the settlement of Dancala Grysh, I had no doubt that
we would win, and decisively. In a battlefield of our choosing,
where we can use our strengths and exploit the Behrenese
weaknesses, the To-gai-ru will cut the Behrenese down. I have no
doubt of this, but in that string of victories, we forgot the key to
those victories: the battlefield of our choosing.*

*The army that came to Dancala Grysh was not there to do
battle against us, but to entice us to turn to the east. When I look
back upon that terrible day with that in mind, how foolish I feel!
How easily did Dharyan play upon the pride of Ashwarawu and
upon us all! We were goaded and baited. We were allowed to
believe in our invincibility. And how ridiculous those illusions
seemed when the jaws of the Jacintha army closed upon us!*

*The agonized cries of that defeat reverberate across the steppes
of To-gai now, I fear. Given the absolute failure of Ashwarawu, a
second insurgence will be much more difficult to organize than
was the first.*

*What now, then? Is the dream of a free To-gai lying dead on the
field outside of Dharyan? Were my plans to battle the Behrenese
and the plans of Lady Dasslerond that I would lead my people to
freedom no more than the folly of impossible hopes?*

*I do not know.*

*That admission pains me. It brings that haunting moment of the
death of my parents crashing around me like the dark wings of
despair. And yet I know that I must honestly answer the question. I
must honestly assess the chances of any uprising, the odds of
every potential battle. If I am to lead To-gai against the Yatols, I
must do so honestly, devoid of the encouragement of hubris. In my
heart I knew, before the battle of Dharyan ever began, that
something was not quite right, that it was too easy and too
convenient and too grievous an error by the Yatol of Dharyan, who
had proven again and again that he was no fool. I sensed the
danger there, and so did Ashwarawu, I suspect. But he—we—were*

*too caught up in the possibility of the decisive win to pay attention to such feelings.*

*Ashwarawu believed in the opportunity that loomed before us because he wanted to believe in it. So desperately!*

*In this most critical test, Ashwarawu failed.*

*I have to carefully examine all that I know of the man now.*

*The first lesson that Pagonel gave to me once I had recovered from my wounds was to force me to admit, to myself, that I was angry at the opportunity lost and angry at the man who had squandered that opportunity. Ashwarawu had beaten me to the war trail and was building that which I most desire, and he failed, and set back my cause—our cause—perhaps irreparably.*

*My first task, then, is to release myself from the bitterness I feel toward Ashwarawu. I have to examine carefully all that I know of the man now. Without blame, I must examine his failures and his triumphs. It is my task to study what he did right and what he did wrong, to learn from it, to better prepare myself.*

*Does this mean that I will take up the reins of battle again, that I still hope to lead To-gai in an uprising against the cursed Yatols?*

*That is my hope, yes, but I cannot know now if ever again I will see the opportunity before me.*

*And while the hope remains, it remains pushed far from the realities of the present. That is not the purpose of my path anymore.*

—Brynn Dharielle

# CHAPTER 19

## *The Play's the Thing*

He looked up the sheer, fifty-foot wall, then glanced over his shoulders at his tiny wings, lamenting that they were nowhere near strong enough to get him out of the hole.

Belli'mar Juraviel could only sigh, reminding himself that even if he could somehow get out of the hole, he would still be a long way from free. He'd have to cross through the lair of Agradeleous, the dragon, and into the adjoining tunnels, and then somehow navigate his way out of the Path of Starless Night. Which way would he go, north or south? With the discovery of the Doc'alfar, and now finding the location of one of the great dragons, it seemed obvious to Juraviel that his road should be to the north, back to Andur'Blough Inninness to speak with Lady Dasslerond.

But now, from Agradeleous' own tales, it seemed as if Brynn had escaped the terrors of the dragon, and in the direction of the To-gai steppes. It was possible that she was already chasing her destiny—one that Belli'mar Juraviel had been charged with overseeing.

And, of course, there remained his promise to King Eltiraaz that he would not return home with news of the Doc'alfar.

And, of course, it was all moot anyway, because Agradeleous was as mighty a jailor as could be found in all the world, and the dread dragon wasn't about to let his prisoners get away.

A noise at the back of the small pit brought Juraviel from his contemplations and turned him toward the one tunnel exit out of the main prison, a long and low corridor leading to a steamy ledge, a waterfall pouring over it and dropping down to sizzle in a wide pit of molten lava. Cazzira, her black hair wet from washing, her creamy skin all red from the steam, entered the chamber, wearing nothing more than her short shirt.

"Has he returned yet?" she asked casually, tossing her wet hair back from her face.

Belli'mar Juraviel just stood and watched her for a moment, letting her question drift away.

Cazzira froze, noting the stare. "What is it?" she asked, smiling, even giggling a bit.

"I was only thinking how much longer this imprisonment would seem if you were not here beside me," Juraviel admitted.

Cazzira's smile only widened and she moved right next to the golden-haired, golden-eyed Touel'alfar, placing her hand gently upon his slender and strong shoulder. Juraviel closed his eyes and inhaled deeply, filling himself with Cazzira's sweet scent. For a moment, he thought of stepping forward and wrapping her in his arms, and kissing her, but that fleeting moment washed away as Cazzira asked him, "Why must you think of it as imprisonment?"

Juraviel stepped back, blinking his eyes open. "Because that is what it is."

Cazzira shrugged. "And your time with my people was imprisonment, as well." The Doc'alfar spun away as she made the remark, moving for her drying clothes spread on a rock at the far end of the wide pit.

"It was," Juraviel called after her. "And less pleasant than this time! Your people kept Brynn and me in a room of mud!"

"Peat," Cazzira corrected. "Where else were we to put you? We chose not to give you to the bog—for that you should be grateful."

A burst of helpless laughter escaped Juraviel. He shook his head and looked back up at the pit's rim.

"And Agradeleous chose not to eat us, or burn the flesh from our bones," Cazzira went on.

"Which I still do not understand."

"He recognized us for who we are."

"And why might that spare us?" Juraviel asked. "When have either the Touel'alfar or the Doc'alfar been allied with the great dragons? I would have thought that any recognition of our heritage by Agradeleous would have prompted the flames all the more quickly."

Cazzira sighed and slumped to the side, tilting her head, her body language reminding Juraviel that they had discussed this issue many times before. "Four races," she said. "Only four. Doc'alfar and Touel'alfar, the children of life, the dactyls and the dragons, the beasts of death."

"That is how it was, not how it is."

"But that is how Agradeleous still views the world," Cazzira explained. "To him, the other races—human, powrie, goblin, giant—are no more than animals, vermin to be exterminated. But we, you and I, represent two of the true races, and to the dragon, we are a novelty, and a chance for companionship."

"Even if our races are avowed enemies?"

"That means little if the races have been reduced to a few creatures. If the Tylwyn Doc and the Tylwyn Tou were at war, and all that remained were the two of us, would we continue the battle?"

A wisp of a smile curled Juraviel's lips. He could not imagine warring with Cazzira under any circumstances, not after spending these weeks beside her, learning so much of her dreams and hopes and philosophy. Not after realizing that he and she were so much alike in so many ways, both enigmas to their respective peoples.

"But the dragons and the dactyl are creatures of darkness," he argued. "When Bestesbulzibar, curse his name, walked Corona a decade ago, there was no parley. There was only war."

"The dragons are not so akin to the demon dactyls, then," said Cazzira.

Juraviel let his line of reasoning end with that, for indeed, there were profound differences between the two dark races. The dragons, always rare, were mortal creatures and were of Corona, while the demon dactyls were creatures of another plane of existence, creatures that found an inviting rift to come and terrorize the world. Elven legend said that this rift was caused by the evil in the hearts of men, and thus, the elves often considered the humans as children of the demon dactyls.

"Will he tire of us?" Juraviel asked. "Will we become vermin in Agradeleous' snake eyes?"

Cazzira held her pose for a long moment, then shook her head. "I think that the dragon has grown fond of us, or fond of companionship, at least."

"Then Agradeleous will never let us go."

Cazzira only shrugged.

Juraviel went back to studying the high walls of his prison, searching for minute ledges, for cracks, for anything that would allow him a handhold, landing and liftoff places where his diminutive wings might propel him out. This prison had been well prepared, however, with the walls fire-blasted to slag that ran down in smooth sheets.

Juraviel walked over to one of the boulders lying about the floor and sat down, dropping his head to his palm.

Cazzira walked up behind him and draped her arms over his shoulders, moving in very close and kissing him gently on the back of the head. "Your friend escaped," she said. "Agradeleous admitted as much."

"Escaped this area," Juraviel replied.

"And likely escaped the mountains altogether, if she is as well-trained as you claim. You must have faith in her, my friend. Perhaps Brynn Dharielle is already leading the Togai-ru against their hated enemies."

Juraviel reached up and grasped Cazzira's elbow, squeezing gently. He tilted his head back so that it rested side by side with Cazzira's, so that he could better smell the freshness of her washed hair.

And then the ground thumped beneath them, a sudden jolt, the footfall of an approaching dragon.

Cazzira backed away and hugged herself tightly, but still, she seemed more at ease than did Juraviel, who just sat there, staring up at the rim.

The reptilian head peered over a moment later, not huge, as it had been when the elves had first encountered the mighty Agradeleous, but about the size of a horse's head. Agradeleous' head, though, even in this diminutive form, was intimidating, covered with rows of reddish gold scales, with pointed, gleaming teeth too long to be contained within his closed maw, and horns jutting out above his eyes—horns as long as great lances when the dragon was in its natural form. Most intimidating of all, though, were Agradeleous' eyes, shining greenish yellow and with black lines running their center, eyes seeming somewhere between those of a reptile and those of a cat. Wisps of smoke wafted out of the dragon's nostrils with each exhalation, framing his face as he moved forward. He came to the lip of the pit, glanced about to locate the elves, then leaped down, his wings, tiny now, almost in the same proportion as Juraviel's, beating the air with little effect.

He landed hard right beside the two elves, who were bounced into the air from the impact.

Juraviel and Cazzira, despite their understanding that Agradeleous would not harm them, could not help but instinctively shrink away, for even in this bipedal form, almost like a large, red-scaled man with a short and thick tail, small wings, and that horse-sized head, he was an intimidating beast, projecting an aura of power that mocked anything that Cazzira had ever seen—and second only to Bestesbulzibar himself in the memory of Belli'mar Juraviel. And while Bestesbulzibar's might was more insidious, was the power to dominate others and use them as pawns, Agradeleous' strength was sheer, brute force, the power of a volcano and an earthquake, of a terrible storm with focused wrath.

His movements were not fluid, but were darting, like the forked tongue that continually flicked out between his long canines. He reached forward, holding a pack, which Juraviel took, knowing it to be more of the nutritious mushrooms that had been sustaining the elves through the months.

"More tales this day," the dragon demanded. Where Agradeleous' voice had been deafening before, in the dragon's true, gigantic form, now it was rasping, but hardly diminished. Each syllable sent a shiver up from the stone of the floor, coursing Juraviel's small frame. "Tell me of this . . . ranger? This man I killed, that you name Emhem Dal."

"I know little of Emhem Dal," the elf replied, and the dragon frowned. "But there is another tale I might tell, one greater still, of a ranger named Nightbird who did battle with Bestesbulzibar, the demon dactyl."

Agradeleous' reptile-and-cat eyes narrowed suddenly, and the dragon exhaled, seething smoke flowing from his nostrils. Though the dragons and the demon dactyls were paired in legend as the races of darkness, though the legends named the dragons as the creations of the demon dactyls, the two races were hardly allied, and it seemed to Juraviel as if Agradeleous would truly enjoy hearing about the defeat of Bestesbulzibar.

The dragon gave a low and long growl, which Juraviel interpreted as Agradeleous' way of saying, "Hmm."

"It is a good tale?" came the rasping question.

"The greatest of our age," Juraviel replied. "And one that, perhaps, is not completely written."

"Then tell it, Belli'mar Juraviel, and let me be the judge of its worthiness," the great wurm decided, and then Agradeleous' voice rose suddenly to stone-shaking volume. "Fear my wrath if I judge that it is not so!"

Juraviel noted Cazzira's look of concern, but he dismissed it with a wry grin. There was no tale that he knew of to exceed the story of Nightbird and his heroic companions. And even if Agradeleous somehow found a way to judge the tale as unworthy, Juraviel understood the dragon's roar to be greater than his bite. Agradeleous would not kill them over a story, not when he craved so many, many more.

And Juraviel began the tale of Elbryan, starting with the sacking of Dundalis those years before, and the rescue of the young man, really just a boy. It occurred to him as he spoke that another survivor of that fateful day, one who would be mentioned often in his recounting, had a story not yet completed, though of course, Juraviel had no idea that the same little girl who had crawled, soot-covered and battered, out of Dundalis was soon to become the queen of Honce-the-Bear!

With great detail, Juraviel spoke of the years Elbryan spent with the Touel'alfar, of his training and of his strength of body and of mind.

"All this from a human?" Agradeleous asked incredulously, more than once, and each time Juraviel nodded, the dragon gave another growling, "hmm," as if the tale was making him reconsider, a bit at least, his previous views of the lesser human race.

Cazzira listened, too, sitting on the very edge of a rocky seat, leaning forward, devouring every word. That pleased Juraviel greatly, more so than he would have expected. He didn't fear that the Doc'alfar was gathering information here—none to use against him and his people, at least—but rather, that she was just enjoying the story. And even more than that, she was enjoying the *storyteller*.

Juraviel went on for a long, long time, and was still not even close to telling of the final ceremony, when Elbryan became Nightbird, when he sat back and took a deep breath, then sat silent for a long while.

"Go on!" Agradeleous and Cazzira said together, and they looked at each other in surprise, then laughed at the shared emotion.

"I am tired, and wish to eat and to rest," Juraviel said.

"But I wish to hear more! I wish to hear it all!" the dragon growled.

"And I fear to tell it all, for what tale shall I tell next that would not pale beside the story of Nightbird?"

"Tell it!" Agradeleous demanded, and stomped his clawed foot, shaking the pit. "And if it is as worthy as you say, then tell it again and again and again, through the years and the ages!"

Juraviel nodded, taking it all in, trying to draw some better measure of the dragon's perceptions and intentions toward him and Cazzira. He wished that he could view this situation as Cazzira obviously saw it, with the contentment that it was a worthy experience, an enriching conversation and meeting, expanding her understanding of this, the rarest of Corona's races—and in many ways the most magnificent. And truly, if Juraviel had not had pressing business at that time, he might have viewed his long time with Agradeleous quite differently. But though months had passed, the elf could not forget the possibility that his charge, his friend, was out there, facing trials that he was supposed to help her overcome, trials that might have a profound and direct impact upon the survival of his own people, should the scar from the demon dactyl continue to grow.

Juraviel needed closure with Brynn, needed to know if she had indeed escaped the tunnels and found her way into Togai, and if she had, how she was faring, before he could begin to accept this chapter of his life beside Agradeleous openly.

So Juraviel went on again, telling of the naming of Elbryan as Nightbird and the passage of the ranger back into the lands of his own people.

"And you did not accompany him?" Cazzira asked. "None of the Tylwyn Tou went with him? I thought that was your way."

"Only with Brynn," Juraviel explained. "Because her journey would take her to lands where we could not readily gather any information."

"And because that information is important to your people?" Agradeleous asked slyly. "Why is that, Belli'mar Juraviel? What are your people planning if not a journey to the south, through the mountains, through my home? And perhaps your army means to take my treasure with it, yes?"

"No! No, no, no, no!" Juraviel shouted, waving his arms, trying hard to slow down the dragon's mounting anger. "How could we have planned such a thing if we did not even know of your existence, great Agradeleous? The only dragons that we know of, if they are even still alive, dwell in the ice pack of the northland of Alpinador, a place where no Touel'alfar goes."

"But if Belli'mar Juraviel could tell his people . . ." the dragon hinted.

"They would stay as far from the Path of Starless Night as possible," the elf countered without the slightest hesitation. "Why would the Touel'alfar wish conflict with Agradeleous? For Agradeleous' treasure? But that treasure is not what we treasure, if you understand. We have the silverel of the dark-fern and a valley of magic and enchantment. Gold holds no great sway over us, as it does with the humans."

The dragon considered the reasoning for a few moments, then nodded and gave what Juraviel took to be a sincere and accepting growl. Juraviel went on, then, in a very animated manner, playing out the many battles he described, even making up a few that fit in with the few props—a single branch and a relatively flat stone that he could hold as a shield—which were available to him in the pit.

He finished, exhausted, at the point where he was accompanying Elbryan, Pony, and Avelyn to the distant Barbacan, before he turned back to the south with the refugees, before his encounter with the demon dactyl. He finished with, "Little did we know that the beast was watching our every move, ready to spring upon us," which he doubted was exactly true, but which he knew would keep the dragon's interest piqued for his continuation the next day.

"You cannot stop there!" Agradeleous roared in complaint, stamping his foot, its report lifting Juraviel right from the ground.

"But I must," the elf replied. "I cannot recount the most exciting of battles when I am too weary to play the role. Allow me my sleep, good Agradeleous."

"Sleep?" the dragon echoed skeptically. "Why, sleep for the centuries and play when you are awake, little one!" And then he laughed, spouting fire that had Juraviel and Cazzira ducking and dodging wildly.

"Very well, then," Agradeleous offered when his mirth had played out. "But I will not let you sleep for more than a year! It is a story I wish to hear!"

Juraviel shook his head emphatically, trying hard to suppress a grin. A year? He had been thinking of only a few hours!

"Not a year," he tried to explain, reminded again of the profound difference between dragons and all the other races. These were the creatures from the dawn of time, who witnessed the early sunrise of Corona. They lived forever, unless they were killed, and saw the passage of time from an entirely different perspective than even the long-living elves. "I need but a few hours to rest and to eat, and then I will call to you, mighty Agradeleous." As he finished, an idea came to Juraviel. He started looking around the floor of the pit, scratching his head.

"What is it?"

"I am trying to discover how I might better embellish the story," Juraviel explained. "No matter—I will think of something."

Agradeleous stared at him, yellow-green eyes blinking, and then the beast shrugged, fell into a crouch and leaped away, easily clearing the fifty feet to the ledge.

"That is power beyond measure," Cazzira remarked, coming over to stand beside Juraviel, who was also looking up to where the dragon had disappeared. She draped her arm comfortably over Juraviel's shoulder, moving her head very close to his.

Juraviel let his still-formulating plans slip away for a few moments then, basking in the sweet scent of this beautiful creature. He turned and considered her porcelain skin and those striking blue eyes.

If it wasn't for the missing Brynn, Belli'mar Juraviel would not have minded the captivity at all.

"You keep stopping!" Agradeleous protested when Juraviel again halted his story and began stalking about the pit.

With a growl, the elf grabbed up one stone and inspected it, then tossed it aside.

"What?" the dragon demanded.

"How can I properly perform with a stage so bland?" Juraviel angrily replied.

"Perform? I asked you to tell a story!"

"But it is a story of battle and courage, of heroes, living and dead!" the elf shot right back. "I would do the memory of Nightbird justice, or I will tell his tale no more!"

"You will tell . . ." the dragon started to argue, and forcefully, but Agradeleous stopped suddenly and glanced all about, at Juraviel, at Cazzira, and at the nearly empty pit. The dragon looked back to Juraviel and nodded. "Come along," he instructed, and he stepped toward Cazzira and grabbed her up tightly with one mighty arm, then similarly scooped Juraviel when he neared.

With a single mighty leap, the dragon exited the pit and set both the elves down on the stone floor of a huge treasure chamber, full of armor and weapons, and mounds of silver and gold coins, sparkling with glittering gems and jewels.

"A grander stage," the dragon explained.

Juraviel nodded and moved about the area, studying the hoard. Were there items here that he might put to better use than as props in a play? he wondered. A mighty sword or gemstone that would bring him freedom?

He dismissed that almost immediately, remembering the foe he would have to defeat, a creature beyond his power even if he held the finest sword in all the world, if he was clad in the finest armor in all the world, and if he possessed the greatest gemstone in all the world.

Besides, Juraviel knew, he really didn't want to do battle with Agradeleous, even if he thought he could win.

That notion stopped him momentarily, struck him with a surprising realization. Had he come to like Agradeleous the dragon?

Juraviel shook the notions away and cleared his throat, then took up his tale, running about the mounds and the various ledges of the room to accentuate the action scenes, taking up a sword at one point to replay the battles that had faced Nightbird and Pony around and within the Barbacan. Again he embellished, adding great detail—and often taking artistic license—because he did not wish to finish quickly.

At one point, telling of the run from the giants at the Barbacan ring, Juraviel ran up the side of a mound of coins and dove over, sliding down the back slope, out of sight of his audience of two. He waited a long while out of their sight.

"Where are you, little one?" Agradeleous boomed, the tone showing suspicion and growing anger.

Belli'mar Juraviel burst out of the coin pile, sword flashing in the air. "So yelled the giants!" he cried dramatically, leaping forward, sword slashing the air about him. "Where are you? And out leaped Nightbird, Tempest's storm flashing about him, driving back the mighty beasts, cutting them and felling them."

The elf danced a ferocious and wild routine as he embellished the story, to the delight of both Cazzira and Agradeleous.

He finished and turned to face the pair, then planted the

sword, tip-down to the floor, and leaned on it heavily. "And so ends my tale for this day," he announced.

To Juraviel's surprise, Cazzira voiced her outrage before Agradeleous had the chance. But Juraviel remained adamant. "In bits and pieces," he explained, tossing the sword to the nearest pile of treasure. "Let your minds linger on that which I have told you this day, that tomorrow's tale might be stronger still."

Agradeleous roared with laughter and jumped up and down, shaking the whole of the chamber and rattling coins.

"Go to your sleep," the dragon bade, and he gathered up Cazzira, and then Juraviel, and carried them back to the pit.

The next day was much the same, as was the next, and in both plays, Juraviel found at least one moment where he could slip away from the others for an extended period of time.

After the third such ploy, Cazzira caught on.

"You are leaving," she said to him much later on, when they heard Agradeleous snoring in the room above them. "That is why you keep running out of sight."

Juraviel put his finger over her lips to silence her. "I am bound by my word and by my duty," he explained.

"And bound not at all by your time with me?"

"More than you can understand," Belli'mar Juraviel replied, and he moved near to her suddenly and unexpectedly, kissing her gently on the lips. Cazzira started to talk again, but Juraviel cut her short with another kiss, and then another, pressing her closer each time, and finding, to his delight, that she was not pushing him back.

They made love that night, in a barren pit in the lair of a dragon, and to Belli'mar Juraviel, it was more beautiful a place than under the stars of the night sky in Andur'Blough Inninness.

Much later on, when Cazzira awoke, she found Juraviel lying beside her, propped on one elbow so that he was looking down at her.

"I am bound to you more than you can know," he said softly, running his hand from her chin, up the side of her face, and along her silken hair. "I am bound by love to exclude you from my desperate plan. I will not lead you to death, Cazzira, though I fear that death will catch up to me in the halls outside of Agradeleous' lair."

"She is only human," Cazzira reminded.

"She is a ranger, and I am bound to aid her, and so I must try."

"And when you are done?"

Juraviel looked away, considering the question honestly, then looked back to her, staring her in the eye, showing her his sincerity. "When I am done, I will return to finish my tale to Agradeleous. If Cazzira is here, then I will remain. If you are not, if you have found your escape, then I will return to Tymwyvenne to be beside you again."

The Doc'alfar smiled and reached up to stroke Juraviel's face. "If you do not, I will lead my people to war against Caer'alfar," she promised. "Battle has been joined for less a reason than this!"

Juraviel bent low and kissed her again, gently, but Cazzira grabbed him tightly and pulled him right over, coming to rest atop him and kissing him with urgency.

A long while later, Belli'mar Juraviel called to Agradeleous to begin what he considered his final performance.

Cazzira watched the dragon leaning forward, every inch of Agradeleous' sinewy, muscular, scaled frame tensed as the dragon awaited Belli'mar Juraviel's reappearance from behind the mound of coins at the back of the large mound. The elf had been reenacting Nightbird and Pony's escape from Mount Aida atop the mighty stallion Symphony. He had buried himself in the coins, thrusting his arm, holding a sword, skyward to represent the mummified arm of Brother Avelyn.

And then he had rushed off to the back of the huge chamber, scrambling over the furthest mound of coins.

The moments continued to slip away.

Cazzira sat back and relaxed, reflecting on the loss. She was surprised at the size of the hole in her heart, the sense of profound loneliness. She knew that Juraviel had acted in what he believed to be her best interest; they didn't expect that Agradeleous would hurt her, after all, though Juraviel had just certainly placed himself in dire jeopardy.

Still, had she realized how painful this separation would be, Cazzira would have found a way to get out with him, to make that desperate run to the south.

She watched as Agradeleous' expression went from intense eagerness to confusion to suspicion, to the mounting anger that only a dragon could exhibit. "Where are you, little one?" the dragon growled.

Agradeleous looked to Cazzira, who shrugged and tried to look as surprised as he. "Soon," she assured the beast.

Agradeleous stood up and narrowed his eyes, peering all about the chamber, issuing a low growl all the while. He took a step forward, turning slowly, and began to sniff loudly. "Little one?" he asked again, the volume of his growl rising.

Cazzira started toward him, but backed away, noted that his iron-corded, scaly arms were trembling with explosive power.

"Little one?"

Several more moments slipped past.

Agradeleous spun suddenly on Cazzira, and with a quickness and power that mocked the Doc'alfar's catlike reflexes, he scooped her up under one arm, took a couple of running steps, and leaped long and far, sailing into the pit. He dropped her unceremoniously to the floor and sprang away, his growl becoming a rock-shaking roar.

"Little one!" the dragon bellowed, plowing through the mounds of coins, sending treasure flying wildly about the chamber. Under one mound, he hit a rock, larger than his present bipedal form, and still his kick sent it skidding away. Not satisfied with that, Agradeleous reached down and lifted the boulder over his head, then hurled it the length of the room, where it smashed in half against the wall.

Behind the farthest mound, where Juraviel had disappeared, there loomed a small tunnel. Agradeleous started down, but stopped and sniffed the air.

The dragon backed away and looked up, to a second hole in the wall, a dozen feet off the floor, a hole that Juraviel, with his wings, could have reached.

Eyes narrowing again, Agradeleous sprang up into the hole, running along on all fours, his small wings curled up on his back, his short and thick tail straight out behind him.

Juraviel ran flat out, but the tunnels outside the chamber were not nearly as well lit from the orange-glowing lava, and despite his keen eyesight, the elf stumbled many times. Even if he had not lost his footing, he realized that he could not simply outdistance Agradeleous. He had to hope that the tunnel forked and branched off, many times.

He heard the rumbling footfalls coming in fast pursuit soon after, and stumbled along in the low light, knowing that he would be caught quickly, unless . . .

The elf breathed a bit easier when he came to the first fork in the trail, one branch winding down and to the right, while the main tunnel continued on straight ahead. Juraviel instinctively went for the branch, but stopped and changed his mind, guessing that Agradeleous would expect him to head down the narrower branch.

He ran on, as fast as he could, hoping that the fork had bought him some time. But then the rumbling behind him stopped, and a moment later, Juraviel heard snuffling sounds. He cringed and ran on—what else could he do?

And then came the dragon's thunderous pursuit.

Several intersections gave the elf a bit of a lead, for at each one, Agradeleous had to stop and locate Juraviel's scent. At one such three-way break, Juraviel ran for many feet down one steeply sloping path, coming to a ledge that dropped off into the darkness. Then he backtracked, and when he turned the corner to enter another of the tunnels, he used his wings to get him up to the top of the large corridor and scrambled along, high up on the wall for a long way.

Again he heard Agradeleous stop and sniff, then nodded with some hope as the dragon's footsteps receded, then ended altogether.

Still, less than an hour later, moving in complete darkness, Juraviel heard the wurm's pursuit again, closing fast.

*Those lamplight eyes,* he thought, and he knew that it

wouldn't take Agradeleous long to catch him, and likely devour him.

Around a bend, the corridor brightened again, and a short while later, Juraviel came to a wide chamber with an arching stone bridge, high above a river of flowing lava. Across the way, the tunnel continued out of the wide chamber. Quickly, he inspected the bridge, hoping that it was weak at some points and would not support the beast, but he understood soon enough that the powries had likely constructed this nonnatural bridge, and that it was quite secure.

Juraviel squinted in the orange glow, looking for some other choice. The air was thick with a sulphurous smell, so much so that he knew Agradeleous could not track him anywhere near here.

The elf had an idea. He looked to the side, to the distant wall, then looked down, gauging the distance against the height of the bridge.

Dragon thunder shook the ground, not so far away.

Juraviel sprinted sidelong across the bridge and leaped high and far, his diminutive wings beating furiously, catching the hot updrafts of the lava across the wide expanse. He hit the sidewall hard, but held on, crawling to an area shadowed by a jag in the warm stone. Then he ducked his head and tried to ball up as tightly as possible.

He heard Agradeleous enter the chamber, and then, hardly hesitating, rush across the bridge. He waited a bit longer, until the dragon's heavy footsteps receded, then gradually came out of his curl, craning his neck to look back at the now-empty stone bridge. If he could only get to it and double back along the corridor . . .

That bridge was a long way from him, though, and above him, and he knew that if he tried to leap from the wall and fly back, he would surely plummet into the lava.

So he crawled along the wall, using his wings to lighten his body and make the climbing easier. Inch by inch, Juraviel worked around toward the wall with the tunnel through which he had entered the large chamber, closer and closer to the arcing bridge. If he could get right beside and beneath the span, he believed that he could leap up and fly enough to scramble atop it.

Inch by inch.

He came to one particularly smooth and difficult expanse of wall and paused, gathering his strength. Then, ready to half fly and half scramble across, the elf set himself and took a deep breath.

"There you are!" came Agradeleous' roar, from not so far away. The dragon's voice seemed enhanced now, even more powerful than Juraviel had heard it a short while before. And the elf saw his own shadow on the wall before his face, as those terrible lamplight eyes cast their glowing beams over him.

He turned his head slowly, but stopped and just closed his eyes, noting the edge of one huge leathery wing, for the dragon was back in its true, monstrous form.

"Treachery!" Agradeleous roared, and the sheer volume shook Juraviel free of his tentative grasp. He scrambled and beat his wings furiously, but he could not find any solid holds. His fingers bloodied as he raked at the stone, and he kicked hard, trying to set his feet.

But he was falling, without the strength to stop or even slow his descent.

He thought of Tuntun, then, an elf maiden who had been his dearest friend of old, and he marveled at the savage irony that his ending would be so eerily similar to hers.

# CHAPTER 20

## *Parallel Journeys*

"You must let go of your anger," Pagonel said to Brynn.

The dark-haired woman looked at the mystic hard. "I saw Ashwarawu die."

"I saw many die," Pagonel replied. "I saw you almost die."

"I saw my parents die," Brynn countered, her lip curling in this dark game of one-upsmanship.

"You must let go of your anger."

"How can I forget . . ."

"I did not ask you to forget," the mystic clarified. "Never that. We each are a composite of our experiences, good and bad, and to release any experience from our thoughts diminishes who we are. Do not forget. Do not dull the images. But do not let those images inspire self-destruction."

Brynn looked at him as if she did not understand.

"Anger dulls the consciousness," Pagonel explained. "Anger sets you on a path that you cannot easily break free of, even if common sense dictates that you take another course. You watched Ashwarawu die, but he died, in part, because he was blinded to the reality of the Behrenese trap, partly because of pride and partly because of anger."

Brynn considered the words for a few moments, and did not disagree. "It will be difficult to raise another band to battle the Wraps."

"That word rings foully off your lips, Brynn Dharielle."

She looked hard at the mystic.

"Wraps," he explained. "A word of belittlement, a word to dehumanize your enemy."

"Belittlement?" Brynn echoed incredulously. "If given the

chance, I would kill every Wrap . . . every Behrenese,"she corrected, seeing the judging scowl.

"Would you? Would you kill a Behrenese child? A poor mother? A man who has never lifted a weapon against To-gai? Are you so hardened by the bitterness of defeat that you have changed fundamentally from that woman who recoiled at the thought of finishing off Behrenese warriors who lay dying in the sand?" Pagonel stopped and smiled, then chuckled aloud at Brynn.

Brynn looked away, but she couldn't resist. The mystic was right—again!—and she felt foolish indeed at her fiery declaration.

"Consider your feelings honestly concerning the Behrenese," Pagonel advised. "Recognize that they are not all of one mind, and not all deserving of retribution. Recognize that they, even those you hate the most, are human beings, are creatures with hopes for themselves and for their children not so different from your own."

"Do you ask that I abandon my cause?"

"No. I ask that you remain truthful to yourself. Nothing more. Your path will not be bloodless, should you walk the road of war again. There will be a heavy price to be paid, for the Behrenese and the To-gai-ru. Is that cost worth the prize that will be freedom?"

"It is!" Brynn said without the slightest hesitation.

"That is all."

Pagonel turned and walked away from her then, leaving her standing on the short stone bridge connecting two wings of the Walk of Clouds monastery, far, far above the floor of a deep and misty gorge.

With just a few words, the mystic had changed her line of thinking, had shifted her perspective—just a bit, but in a direction that Brynn was already thinking might prove to be very productive.

She knew that this would be but one of many, many lessons Pagonel and his brothers and sisters of the Walk of Clouds would teach her in her stay there.

*       *       *

"I am often struck by how similar we all are, though we paint different labels upon our common beliefs, different names upon our common gods, and enact different rituals to reach the same elevated state of consciousness," Pagonel remarked as he exited the darkened room to face the eager Brynn Dharielle.

Brynn looked at him curiously, surprised by his smugness, and more than a little disappointed. She had just taken one of the greatest chances in her life, had just shown to this mystic who had become so dear to her during the last few weeks at the Walk of Clouds one of the greatest secrets of the Touel'alfar. Her teaching of Oracle to Pagonel was a huge expression of trust, for the gifts that Lady Dasslerond's people had shown to Brynn were not to be passed along. She had expected that the mystic would be overwhelmed, would walk out of the room with that same look of disbelief upon his face that Brynn had worn in her first successful Oracle, when she had communicated, she believed, with the ghosts of her dead parents.

He had been in the room for a long time, and Brynn was certain that he had succeeded in reaching a height of intensity, a level of consciousness that transcended the bounds of mortality. And yet here he was, obviously less than impressed.

"There is only one direction, after all," Pagonel started, but he looked at Brynn, whose face showed her disappointment clearly, and paused.

"You know of the Abellican Monks of Honce-the-Bear?" the Jhesta Tu asked a moment later.

Brynn nodded.

"They derive their power through use of gemstones that they consider sacred."

"The ranger who trained beside me was also being trained in the use of the gemstones," Brynn remarked, and Pagonel nodded.

"The Yatols view the stones as sacrilege."

Again Brynn nodded. "And the Jhesta Tu?"

"We have used them."

"And were you impressed enough to incorporate them into

your religion?" Brynn asked, a bit sarcastically, given the mystic's quiet attitude toward Oracle.

"Jhesta Tu attempt to find the same powers as the gemstones offer, the same power that your Oracle offers, within ourselves," the mystic explained. He walked over and tapped Brynn on the forehead. "There is as much magic and power in here," he said, and then he surprised her by running his hand down her face, down her neck, between her breasts and over her belly, all the way to her groin. "A line of strength from there to there," he explained stepping back. "This is the core of your life energy, your Chi, and few are the people who can truly come to appreciate the power of that energy."

"Only the Jhesta Tu?" the somewhat shaken woman asked.

"Only a very few of Jhesta Tu," Pagonel explained. "And only after years and years of study. Internal study." He reached down and untied the black sash from around his waist, holding it up before the woman. "The Belt of All Colors," he explained, "It is the symbol of understanding. Three in the Walk of Clouds now wear it, and of the others, well exceeding one hundred in number, perhaps a handful will one day find the enlightenment to earn this sash."

Brynn reached up reverently to touch the belt, and only then did she see that it was not truly black, but was comprised of fine fibers that ran the length of the color spectrum.

The woman sat back as the mystic stepped away, replacing the sash about his waist. Despite her prior understanding of who this man, Pagonel, truly was, his remark caught her as arrogant at that time, almost belittling her years of training with the Touel'alfar.

"And what is Oracle beside such achievement?" she asked, her voice thick with sarcasm.

Pagonel laughed at her. "It is a very great thing, a precious gift, and a long stride along the road toward enlightenment."

Brynn's expression grew confused. "You seemed less than impressed," she said.

"There is a group giving themselves to the wind this morning," Pagonel said to her. "Come. I will show you our Oracle."

"Giving themselves to the wind?"

"Come," Pagonel said, holding out his hand to her. "As you shared Oracle with me, so I shall share this with you."

Intrigued, Brynn took the mystic's hand. He led her out of the monastery through a door that she had not seen before, exiting the back side of the building. Before them was a single trail, ascending the mountainside. They set off at a brisk pace, with Pagonel leading Brynn at a trot at times. A short while later, still climbing along a bare rock face, the pair spotted a line of a half dozen mystics in their orange-and-red robes, high above them.

"It is getting cold," Brynn observed.

"That is the point."

Brynn stopped abruptly, and Pagonel pulled free of her hand. He, too, stopped, and turned back to regard her.

"What is this?"

"Ever impatient," the mystic observed, and he gave a great sigh and a greater smile. "This is one of the rites of passage through the Jhesta Tu order. Though most of my brothers and sisters who are able to give themselves to the wind are older and more experienced than you, I believe that you should try. Your training has been amazing, I would guess, if you have perfected the meditation you call Oracle."

"And this is the next step ahead of Oracle?" Brynn asked, and still there was a hint of sarcasm in her tone, one that Pagonel caught, if his laugh was any indication.

"This is a step to the side, not ahead," the mystic explained. "This is our Oracle—one manifestation of it, at least."

Brynn held her intended sharp retort. "Then lead on," she decided a moment later, and she took Pagonel's offered hand.

They continued climbing for nearly an hour, their pace slowing as the terrain grew more difficult. Soon, they caught up to the other Jhesta Tu mystics, with Pagonel falling into line behind them, Brynn behind him. The woman feared that she might not be accepted, but none of the mystics seemed to even acknowledge her presence. Besides, she realized, Pagonel was the highest-ranking of their order, along with Master Cheyes and Matron Dasa, and so she supposed that he could pretty much make the rules as he saw appropriate, especially the rules concerning his visitor to the monastery.

By midafternoon, the troupe was high up on the mountainside, with a cold wind blowing fiercely about them, and patches of snow holding fast in the shaded areas. Brynn was about to remark that she was not properly dressed for the elements, but she held the thought private, for the seven Jhesta Tu mystics ahead of her in line were wearing no more than their light robes, and while a couple wore sandals, the others were barefoot.

They came up over a rocky rise, and the path split, veering out to the left, to the facing of the steep mountainside, and continuing to the right, climbing higher. Brynn was surprised when the mystics went left, and even more surprised when she came to the cliff facing, out of the shelter of the rocks and walls. The path dipped lower there, running out to a narrow north-facing ledge.

The wind blew cold, so cold! The mystics went out calmly, the lead brother moving to the end of the ledge and sitting down, cross-legged.

Pagonel stopped and ushered Brynn past him, onto the ledge in place behind the other mystics. She looked to her mentor, then to the others, who were all settling in with that same cross-legged posture.

Pagonel motioned for her to do likewise, and so she settled down.

The others brought their hands up, pressing palms together before their faces. By the time Brynn did the same, the others released their hands down to their hips. In unison, they arched their backs, lifting their hips up and back, then rolled forward slowly but steadily, folding up at the waist so that they wound up bent double over their crossed legs, heads pressing the stone, arms extending up above them.

Brynn looked up at Pagonel, who was still standing, and he nodded for her to assume the same pose.

With a shrug, the woman rolled her hips back, then rotated forward, bending low. She couldn't get quite as far down as the mystics, but she was fairly limber and managed to settle into a somewhat comfortable position.

Then she waited.

And waited.

For a long time, Brynn kept peeking out under her arms to the others, expecting them to shift to another position. But none moved at all. A couple of them moaned softly, but other than that, they were all perfectly still and quiet.

The minutes passed and became inconsequential. After some time, Brynn stopped peeking out, just fell into the moment and allowed her thoughts to drift away, to memories, to fantasies, and then, to nothing at all.

She fell deeper and deeper away from the world.

A cold numbness brought her back to her consciousness sometime later. She blinked open her eyes and was surprised to see that the sun had set.

Brynn felt her muscles contracting; her teeth started chattering. With great effort, she lifted her head into the face of the cold night wind. Shaking, the cold biting at all of her exposed flesh, the woman managed to sit up.

And then Pagonel was there, beside her, wrapping a heavy woolen blanket about her and helping her to her feet, then holding her steady while the feeling returned to her legs.

He started to lead her away.

"What of them?" Brynn asked.

"They will return to the monastery tomorrow."

Brynn stopped, her stare incredulous as she looked from Pagonel to the six meditating mystics. "They will freeze."

"They have consciously slowed their bodies. Their hearts barely beat now, and the cold will not wound them," the Jhesta Tu master explained.

Brynn stared at him in disbelief.

"As you learned your Oracle, so these Jhesta Tu have learned theirs. In time, you will come to understand, if you choose to learn." He started away, and Brynn went along for a short while, before stopping and staring at him hard.

"But you were able to succeed at Oracle on your first try," she said, again with a hint in her voice that something wasn't quite right here, that perhaps Pagonel was mocking her.

"Are you so concerned with how you measure beside me?" the mystic asked bluntly. "Are you so concerned how your training measures against that of the Jhesta Tu?"

Brynn didn't blink.

"All of the mystics now giving themselves to the wind are your seniors," he explained. "And I am likely twice your age. Waste not your time, your emotions, and your talents on such negative feelings, my friend."

"Did you bring me here to fail?" the unrelenting Brynn asked. "To prove to me that I had a lot more to learn?"

"I brought you here not knowing whether you would fail or not," Pagonel answered. "But it hardly matters. I will teach you the technique over the next weeks, and when you return here, you will pass the night in quiet comfort, falling within yourself to shelter from the cold."

Brynn glanced back up the path.

"Even in winter," Pagonel promised. "Even on winter's coldest night."

He led her back down to the monastery then, walking along the dark path with the ease of familiarity.

Brynn began her lessons the next day, with Pagonel teaching her how to focus her thoughts upon one part, one aspect, of her body. He showed her how to consciously relax, strengthening the connection between mind and body, strengthening her control over herself, even to the point of slowing the beat of her heart.

Brynn returned to the shelf three weeks later. The following morning, feeling thoroughly refreshed, Brynn Dharielle walked down the path beside a handful of Jhesta Tu, back to the monastery. None of the mystics said anything to her on that long walk, but whenever she managed to catch their eyes, the looks that she got back were inevitably ones of acceptance.

Brynn went up the mountain to give herself to the wind many times over the next weeks and months, and even though summer had blossomed on the land far below, up there only the discipline she had learned from Pagonel and from the elves allowed her to survive the brutally cold nights. On one occasion, Brynn remained up on that shelf for three days, deep within herself, and within the emptiness of dark peace.

Every time she came back down the mountain, the woman felt refreshed, felt stronger, and felt that the road of her life was a bit more clearly defined.

She left the Walk of Clouds in the other direction often, as well, traveling down the thousands of stone stairs to the valley floor. Finding the grassy fields where the horses ran was not difficult, and a single whistle and call always brought Brynn's best friend galloping to her side.

On one such morning, when the summer of God's Year 841 was giving way to autumn, Brynn and Runtly basked in the sunshine. The woman had brought a bucket and brushes down with her, and she knew all the right places to brush the pony, using just the right texture of bristle so that the pony kept throwing his head with approval.

Brynn had come down before the dawn this morning, so that she had caught up to Runtly just as the sun was rising, intending to spend the whole of the day with the pony, brushing him clean, riding him, just sitting in the grass beside him as he meandered about, seeking out delicious clover.

The young ranger was surprised when she saw a figure approaching, tall and slender, though with a bit of a belly. As he came out of the direct sunlight, she recognized Pagonel.

"Am I needed above?" Brynn asked, concerned, not because of any expression or posture of the mystic, but merely from the fact that he had come all the way down there.

"I thought that I might come and enjoy the day with you," Pagonel replied. "And with him." As he finished, he walked over and stroked Runtly's muscled neck as the pony happily munched at some clover. Runtly's head snapped around and he bit at Pagonel's hand, not seriously, not trying to injure, but merely as a warning gesture.

"He likes you, I am certain," Brynn said with a chuckle.

"Or he likes the way I taste."

"Perhaps he sees our friendship as a threat to my friendship with him."

"Or perhaps he simply likes the way I taste!" Pagonel reiterated, patting the pony hard on the neck.

"I enjoyed several hours of Oracle this morning," the mystic went on.

Brynn knew that he was not lying, nor was he saying that just to make her feel a bit better about her place at the Walk of Clouds.

"A lesson learned in exchange for a lesson given?" she asked.

"A valuable exchange."

"Was it?" Brynn asked in all seriousness. "Do your brethren share your enthusiasm for that which I might contribute to your order?"

"You are anxious."

Brynn considered the statement for a moment, then nodded. "The Walk of Clouds is unaccustomed to casual visitors."

"Is that what you are?"

"Is that what I am?" the woman came right back at him. "I am not a member of your order, yet you share its secrets with me. Does that sit well with your peers, Pagonel?"

"I wear the Belt of All Colors and am thus answerable only to my own judgment," he explained. "There is no questioning, not to me, nor behind your back in whispers It is no Jhesta Tu's place to question your presence here."

"But where do I fit in, in the judgment of Pagonel?" Brynn asked. "Do you think me Jhesta Tu? Do you hope that I will walk that path?"

"I think that you have been walking that path for most of your life," the mystic explained. "Whether you one day choose formally to claim yourself Jhesta Tu is irrelevant."

Brynn started to reply, but Pagonel stopped her with an upraised hand, patted Runtly hard on the neck one last time, then moved over and sat beside the woman. "Many centuries ago, soon after the establishment of the Abellican Church in Honce-the-Bear, one of their missionaries happened upon us, gemstones in hand, to spread the good word of his version of god. He was taken in at the Walk of Clouds, as were you, and shared with us as we shared with him. Both our order and his understanding were strengthened by that commune, I believe, and thus am I strengthened in my understanding by learning the truths as you have learned them. And thus, I pray, will you be strengthened by your experiences here at the Walk of Clouds."

Brynn looked at the older man hard, locking his gaze and not blinking. "Why do you wish me strengthened? Is my cause your cause?"

"I do not know," the mystic admitted.

"Then why?" Brynn asked. "Why did you risk your life to

pull me off the battlefield outside of Dharyan? And why did you then bring me all the way to the south? Would you have done as much if it was another you had saved? Would you have taken another—even Ashwarawu himself—all the way here and opened the secrets of your order to him?"

"No," Pagonel admitted without even considering the words.

"Then why?"

The mystic took a deep breath and leaned back a bit as Brynn leaned in eagerly toward him. After a few moments, he looked away.

"Because I see in you so much of my own heart," he said a short while later, and he turned back to stare into Brynn's puzzled expression, that beautiful face only an inch from his own. "You understand Jhesta Tu—I knew that you would. I knew that both of us would benefit . . ." He stammered a bit, at a loss for words for the first time Brynn had ever seen.

She stopped him, then, putting her finger over his lips. "I know," she said. "I knew it, too, when first we met at Ashwarawu's camp."

She moved her finger away, but Pagonel didn't resume speaking. He just sat there, staring at her, and she at him.

All that Pagonel wanted to do at that moment was kiss her. But he didn't, holding back and reminding himself that he was twice Brynn's age.

All that Brynn wanted to do at that moment was kiss this man, but she wasn't bold enough to initiate that level of intimacy, though in truth, to her, physical intimacy between them could be nothing more than an extension of the emotional intimacy they had been sharing all these months. They were so in harmony, spirit and soul, that Brynn hardly cared about any age difference.

But Pagonel held back, and Brynn, so innocent and unawares in matters of physical intimacy, would not take this first step.

They stayed on the field with Runtly until late that afternoon, then walked together up the long staircase back to the Walk of Clouds, Pagonel's home and Brynn's welcomed sanctuary.

# CHAPTER 21

## *The Relief of Resignation*

Yakim Douan was truly surprised to learn that the Chezhou Kaliit, the master of that warrior order, was in Jacintha to meet with him, for though the Chezhou-Lei were dedicated to the Yatol priests, serving as bodyguards who would throw their own bodies in front of a spear aimed for a Yatol, the Kaliit, an old barrel-chested man named Thog Timig, rarely left his home village, some hundred miles south of Jacintha. His mere presence told Yakim Douan that something extraordinary was afoot.

The door to the private audience chamber cracked open and Merwan Ma entered, leading the old and bent man. The Kaliit was hunched at the shoulders, and while his torso had retained the size and strength of his former warrior years, his arms and legs were spindly things, withered and crooked from an assortment of injuries. But if there was any infirmity in the Kaliit's physical body, it didn't show in his dark and sparkling eyes, strong and intense. He fixed a glare on Douan from the moment he strode through the door, one that showed appropriate respect, but also conveyed the inner power of the man.

"Welcome, Kaliit Timig," Douan greeted warmly. "I have oft feared that I would not have the chance to greet you again before Yatol took one of us or the other to his side."

The Kaliit stiffly, but with great dignity, slid into a chair beside the Chezru Chieftain.

"It will not be long," he replied dryly. "Every storm rages in my body before the sky has clouded."

Douan nodded and smiled, more to himself than to his visitor. He had no idea of the Kaliit's true age, but the man was very, very old, ancient even. Thog Timig had risen to the position of Kaliit early on during Douan's reign as Chezru Chieftain, but while Yakim Douan had been barely more than a boy at that time, those few decades ago, Thog Timig had already been a middle-aged man.

"Which makes your decision to visit me at this time all the more mysterious, I must admit," Douan said a moment later, when the God-Voice noted that the Kaliit seemed to be staring off into nothingness.

The old man turned his head slowly to regard the man beside him. "The Chezhou-Lei will march as one," he explained. "For the first time in three hundred years, the warriors will be recalled from every corner of Behren."

Yakim Douan stared at the man incredulously. What was he talking about? The To-gai-ru had been put down, and definitively, outside the gates of Dharyan, and there had been little stirring over the last months from any would-be rebels. So secure had the situation become that Yatol Grysh had sent the Jacintha twenty-squares marching home again. Even the ever-present pirates along the coast had quieted in recent months, now that the eyes of all of Behren's military power could be turned upon them.

"Recalled to march where?" Douan asked, trying hard to hide his surprise at all of this. "To the west? The north? Do you mean to swim out into the Mirianic and throttle the ragtag pirates?"

"To the south," Kaliit Timig said.

"The south? To the hot jungles and the great Serpent Masur?"

"To the Mountains of Fire and the Jhesta Tu mystics," the Kaliit admitted.

"Jhesta Tu?" Mixed in with Douan's surprise was a fair degree of budding anger. Why would the Chezhou-Lei desire to wake the sleeping tiger that was Jhesta Tu? The old mystics sat up on their mountaintops, removed from all the world—just the way that Yakim Douan wanted it!

"Chezhou-Lei Dahmed Blie did not return with your soldiers from Dharyan," Kaliit Timig remarked.

"No," Douan admitted. "He was among the fallen. The *few* fallen. And I admit my surprise and dismay when I learned that a Chezhou-Lei warrior had been killed at Dharyan. I never would have believed that the pitiful rebels could have struck such a blow!"

"Chezhou-Lei Dahmed Blie was killed, not by a rebel Ru, but by a Jhesta Tu mystic, God-Voice," Kaliit Timig explained. "Our ancient enemies have come down from their mountains and have begun a war."

"You cannot be certain of this."

"The Jhesta Tu was seen in southern To-gai earlier," Kaliit Timig croaked, his voice rising in anger for the first time since he had entered, and for one of the very few times in the dispassionate man's entire life. "The wound was quite telling," he went on, holding forth his crooked fingers as straight as he could get them, thrusting them out, hooking them farther, and pulling back, an imitation of the strike Pagonel had used to kill Dahmed Blie. "It confirmed for us what those who witnessed Dahmed Blie's fall have told. Jhesta Tu killed Chezhou-Lei. There can be no doubt."

"The actions of a rogue mystic, then," a hopeful Douan remarked.

"Even if that were so, God-Voice, the actions of that day were consummated with the killing strike of order against order. It is not a challenge that we can ignore."

Yakim Douan blew out an expression of his complete frustration. Would the web of politics never free him enough that he could leave this old and broken frame in peace?

"A challenge?" Douan asked, skepticism clear in his voice. "A rogue Jhesta Tu joins with the fool Ru and wins a battle against a Chezhou-Lei. You must view that as a challenge? Perhaps this Jhesta Tu is still running about the steppes of northern To-gai. Send Yatol Grysh's warrior, Wan Atenn, and some of his warriors scouring the land."

"We have, God-Voice."

That set Yakim Douan back a bit. The Chezhou-Lei were not an independent order. They reported to him, and to him alone. Or at least, they were supposed to.

"We have inquired all about the region concerning the Jhesta Tu," Kaliit Timig explained.

"And was his presence part of a larger conspiracy from the mystics of the Mountains of Fire?"

The Kaliit shrugged, a stiff and crooked motion. "We have learned little, God-Voice," he admitted. "But it is believed that the slayer of Dahmed Blie has retreated to the south, back to his fortress in the Mountains of Fire."

"And you wish to march the Chezhou-Lei there?"

"We must march, God-Voice," the Kaliit explained. "We must answer this challenge with the sword."

Yakim Douan stood up and walked around to the front of the Kaliit's chair, then bent low very suddenly, his scowling face only a few inches from that of the older man. "You must?" he asked. "Has the God-Voice so directed you?"

"No, God-Voice," the Kaliit admitted.

"Then why do you presume that you must do anything, Kaliit Timig?"

"Our battle with the Jhesta Tu began two thousand years ago, God-Voice," Thog Timig tried to explain. "It is among the most important duties of the Chezhou-Lei, to hold back the infidel Jhesta Tu. We have protected many Chezru Chieftains from the pagans throughout the centuries. Did we not rescue Jacintha from the devilish Jhesta Tu-inspired hordes three centuries ago? Did we not . . ."

Yakim Douan let the Kaliit's words slip past him then, amused by the first reference. He remembered well the day of rioting in Jacintha, when the Chezhou-Lei warriors slaughtered several thousand on the streets outside of the great temple. Yes, there had been rumors that the Jhesta Tu had inspired the insurrection against the Yatol rule, but those were thoroughly overblown, Yakim Douan knew well. The people had rioted out of desperation, because of short food supplies in a time of devastating drought. But the Chezhou-Lei warriors had clung to the belief—the hope, and the heroic legend— that the Jhesta Tu had inspired that mob, and even that several of the mystics had been among the rioters.

When he tuned back into the present, Yakim Douan realized that Kaliit Timig's recounting of the glorious Chezhou-

Lei victories had only gained momentum, and so he stopped the man abruptly with an upraised hand.

"No one doubts the value of the Chezhou-Lei, Kaliit," he admitted. "You are the greatest of Jacintha's warriors, and your loyalty is not, and has never been, in question. But you say that you must travel south, and yet, I have reached no such conclusion, nor have I offered any such edict."

"God-Voice." Kaliit Thog Timig said, rising with great effort to stand as straight and tall as his old and battered frame would allow. "I pray that you will see the truth of my plea. The Chezhou-Lei must answer this act of murder—"

"It was a battlefield, Kaliit," Yakim Douan reminded, and off to the side, Merwan Ma sucked in his breath nervously.

"A battle that did not involve the Jhesta Tu," Kaliit Timig replied steadily. "Their mere presence there should frighten you, God-Voice, for they are a powerful foe."

"One," Yakim reminded, holding up a single finger. "One of them was there. A single warrior."

"It is your decision to make, God-Voice," Kaliit Timig conceded. "I wish only to impress upon you the urgent need for the Chezhou-Lei to respond to this act of murder. We must march south, or all that we are will diminish. I pray that Yatol gives you the guidance you need, that you can see our needs clearly in this matter."

With that, the old man stiffly bowed and shuffled out of the room.

Merwan Ma stood at the door, looking back at Yakim Douan, his expression showing that he was unsure of whether or not he should remain behind.

The Chezru Chieftain waved him away.

Yakim Douan sat for a long time, playing through his options. He truly did not want the Chezhou-Lei marching to some distant land to do battle with the Jhesta Tu. The Chezhou-Lei were Yakim Douan's elite guard, the iron gauntlet upon the closed fist with which he held Behren. He could ill afford to have their ranks decimated in some far-off land, and even if they marched out there and proved victorious, the length of the journey itself would keep them away from Douan's needs for the better part of a year.

And yet, how could he refuse the request of the Kaliit? The Chezhou-Lei were undyingly loyal to the Yatols, to the Chezru Chieftain above all. They asked little in return. And among the Chezhou-Lei, the most important ideals of all were pride and honor. If they felt slighted now by their hated enemies, the Jhesta Tu, then, for the sake of their own sensibilities, they had to go and retaliate. If he said no to them, Yakim Douan knew that they would obey. But what price would they, and he, pay for that decision? What was the cost of denying the Chezhou-Lei their honor?

The weary Chezru Chieftain rubbed his tired eyes.

And what if Kaliit Timig was right in his suppositions about the Jhesta Tu being involved in the battle at Dharyan? What if this ancient order was now siding with the To-gai-ru against the Yatols? Douan knew that he had never been a hero to the heretical Jhesta Tu. The Yatol religion was not one that tolerated their strange views of the world long before he had ascended the position as Chezru Chieftain those generations ago. At one point, in a previous incarnation as Chezru Chieftain, Douan had made some overtures that he might try to mend the division between the Yatols and the Jhesta Tu. That thought had been thrown aside before it had ever manifested itself into any action that would move beyond the temple in Jacintha, for Douan had nearly been overthrown by his own priests for simply suggesting such a thing.

For the Yatols hated the Jhesta Tu as profoundly as did the Chezhou-Lei warriors. This was not a battle that Douan could easily avoid.

And did Yakim Douan really want to hold back his Chezhou-Lei warriors? If the Kaliit was correct, then what might be the implications to him? The Jhesta Tu were the ghosts of the world, mysterious and powerful, and Douan held no doubt at all that they could be the deadliest of assassins if they so chose. If the mysterious mystics had indeed taken up the To-gai-ru cause, then was he, as leader of the conquering Behrenese, truly safe?

This was just one more problem that Yakim Douan did not wish thrust upon him at that time, when he wanted only peace and stability. But like so many of the other problems, it was one that he could not ignore.

He understood then what he must do.


Yakim Douan and Merwan Ma knew from the moment that Master Mackaront of St. Entel walked into their midst that something was terribly wrong in Honce-the-Bear.

"Olin is dead?" the Chezru Chieftain asked, purely on reflex, and Douan bit his lip as he finished the words, angry at himself for the uncharacteristic loss of composure. It was just a thought, an answer to Mackaront's troubled expression, but as God-Voice of Behren, as the unquestioned leader of the Yatol religion, it was not Douan's place to make guesses.

"No, Chezru," Mackaront answered, seeming somewhat confused, as did Merwan Ma, who looked upon his leader questioningly.

It was not a look that Yakim Douan desired to elicit from his flock.

"The College of Abbots has chosen Master Fio Bou-raiy of St.-Mere-Abelle as the successor to Father Abbot Agronguerre," Mackaront explained.

"Abbot Olin is dead," Douan reiterated, this time as a definitive statement and not a question. "His place in the Church is diminished, for he has reached the pinnacle of his power. His road ahead is set, to the end."

Mackaront breathed hard, obviously trying to hold himself steady.

Yakim Douan took a good measure of him, and of Merwan Ma, standing by his side. He had dodged that errant question, he believed, but he knew that he was stretching here. "That is how Abbot Olin feels, at least," he offered. "Else he would not have sent you here."

Mackaront shifted on his feet and straightened somewhat.

"This is unfortunate," Douan remarked, turning away and heading for the chairs. "For Abbot Olin is among the wisest men of your land, among the wisest I have ever known. It is a sad day for Olin, and for the Abellican Church, which would have grown far greater under his leadership. But we cannot change what has happened, and so we must find now our next

best road." Douan understood that he was being a bit condescending, because, obviously, the defeat of Olin didn't weigh
upon him as catastrophically as it did with Mackaront.

"The new Queen Jilseponie of Honce-the-Bear voted against
Abbot Olin, Chezru," Mackaront explained. "Surely that signal from King Danube is of interest to you."

Yakim Douan sat down, motioning for the other two to join
him. He considered Mackaront's words carefully for a few minutes. Was there really a signal here, anything more than the
obvious fact that King Danube of Honce-the-Bear preferred
his kingdom as free of Behrenese influence as possible?

Not really, Douan concluded, and he recognized that Mackaront was just being a bit overly dramatic, and perhaps a bit retributive against Douan's inevitable disinterest.

"Abbot Olin holds my friendship—that has not changed,"
the Chezru Chieftain went on, then he launched into a long
series of stories about some of his past dealings with Abbot
Olin, even admitting that he had once traveled to Entel in dis-
guise to dine with the man at St. Bondabruce.

Master Mackaront listened to it all with growing comfort, and Merwan Ma listened with growing confusion, even
concern.

When he had finished, Yakim Douan stood up suddenly,
with more energy than any had seen from him in a long time.
"Take our friend out to the docks, to his boat, that he might
return to Entel and Abbot Olin," he instructed Merwan Ma.
"Give to him the tapestry that hangs on the left wall of the
entryway—it is a battle that Olin, I am sure, holds dear!" he
finished with a chuckle, one that melted any forthcoming
questions from the obviously stunned Merwan Ma. The tapestry in question, a beautiful and vibrant work, and one of
Douan's favorites, depicted a great sea battle, in which the
Jacintha fleet chased the ships of Honce-the-Bear back to the
port of Entel.

"Abbot Olin will like it!" Douan said to the stunned Merwan Ma. "He and I have discussed that ancient battle in great
detail—he insists that Entel won that battle, sinking the
Jacintha fleet before it could return. We know the truth, of
course, that our proud ships had won a great victory over the

inferior Entel ships, bottling them in their harbor and sinking most. On their glorious return to Entel, though, they happened upon a great storm, and many were lost."

He paused and chuckled again. "Ah yes, we all have our own truths."

When the pair had gone, Yakim Douan stood staring at the door, a grin stamped upon his old face. What a strange and momentous few weeks it had been. First comes news that the Chezhou-Lei wish to march south to do battle with the Jhesta Tu, and now the Abellican Church had just thrown aside the plans of Abbot Olin. Douan knew that this latest news from the northern kingdom should have troubled him, should have once again denied him that which he so desperately wanted, Transcendence. And yet, with these two events, the old Chezru Chieftain felt somehow more alive than he had in so many years.

His had become a cautious existence.

Merwan Ma returned a short while later, his expression showing that he was still perplexed about Douan's reaction to the news from Mackaront and the decision to give away such a prized tapestry.

"Abbot Olin was in need of my consolation," Douan explained.

Merwan Ma seemed to wince a bit at that.

"You wonder why I care?" Douan asked. "He is Abellican, after all. You have never been comfortable with my relationship with the Abbot of St. Bondabruce."

"God-Voice, it is not my place—"

"To question me? No, it is not, and so you do not—openly. But in your heart, my young friend, you have questioned me often."

"No, God-Voice!" the younger man declared.

Yakim Douan held up his hands to show his attendant that it was quite all right, that there was no offense here, and none taken. "Abbot Olin's faith has been shaken yet again by the Abellican Church, and not surprisingly," Douan explained. "Often has he been disappointed by his peers, as we would expect, since they follow a wayward path. Our generosity toward the man has always acted to push him farther from the heretical beliefs of his Church."

"Do you believe that Abbot Olin might be brought to the light of Yatol?" Merwan Ma asked incredulously, and Yakim Douan laughed heartily at that thought.

"I believe that he understands much of the truth of our ways," he explained. "I expect no overt conversion, nor would I desire one, for that would cause the Abellican Church to excommunicate the man, and likely burn him at the stake. No, the transformation of others to the way of Yatol may sometimes be done with abrupt force, as with the pitiful To-gai-ru, but with the more cultured and entrenched societies, such as Honce-the-Bear, our victory will come over the years, the decades, the centuries, as their own failings dishearten them. Abbot Olin was not the first abbot in Entel sympathetic to the way of Yatol, nor will he be the last.

"In the end, we will win, because we are right, my son."

Merwan Ma's smile was genuine, and Yakim Douan knew that he had once again satisfied the man that he was indeed in the presence of a God-Voice, that the machinations of Yakim Douan's actions were far beyond his immediate comprehension.

It was a bluff that Yakim Douan had perfected over many lifetimes.

"What is it?" Yakim Douan asked his attendant, seeing the curious look upon Merwan Ma's face.

Merwan Ma shook his head and seemed embarrassed.

"Tell me, son," Yakim Douan said comfortingly, and he moved over and patted Merwan Ma's shoulder, uncharacteristic behavior that seemed to confuse Merwan Ma even more.

"You seem happier of late, God-Voice," the young man admitted.

Yakim Douan stepped back, surprised by the bluntness, and in truth, surprised a bit by the accuracy of the observation. He was feeling better, and was possessed of more energy of late. It was the gemstone, he knew. Falling into its magical swirl every day was filling him with health and strength.

"I am freed of the bonds of responsibility for now," he replied. "You have gotten your wish, my son, for Transcendence is now an event for the future. Yatol has called upon me to remain here and oversee the momentous events of the day. Our Chezhou-Lei warriors will march south, likely within a couple of months, to do battle with the Jhesta Tu. And now this, Abbot Olin defeated by his brethren. No, Yatol will not let his flock be vulnerable during these times, and so I am called to lead. And lead I shall."

Merwan Ma beamed at the proclamation, but there was something else in his expression that Yakim Douan could not quite decipher, and that unknown reminded the Chezru Chieftain poignantly that he had to remain careful.

Still, Douan could not help but feel refreshed.

Yes, Transcendence had been taken away from him, and yes, the hematite hidden in the chalice was giving him new strength and vitality. But the true change here, the true reason why a smile was often evident on his face, was exactly as he had explained it to Merwan Ma. For months, years even, his focus had been on tidying up so that he could make the transformation to a younger body. Even as the events of the day had continually dictated otherwise, Yakim Douan had stubbornly held on to his hope for Transcendence.

Now he had let go of that dream for the foreseeable future. These two events, with the Kaliit and the abbot, had shut the door and locked it. Now Douan was focused on the events at hand.

Perhaps it was time for him to revel in the present glory.

# CHAPTER 22

# *A Chill Breeze on Leathery Wings*

He felt the searing heat of the lava as he plummeted, and believed that he would simply burst into flame, but then he landed in a great dark and wet cave it seemed. It took Belli'mar Juraviel a few breaths to understand that the dragon had caught him in its mouth, had plucked him out of the air only a few feet above the deadly lava.

The dragon winced and growled, nearly opening its mouth, and Juraviel understood that it had likely nipped the lava on its turn upward. Then came the jolts as the dragon landed back on the stone, a few staggering steps.

Spat out of the beast's mouth, Juraviel hit the ground hard in a bouncing roll.

He came to a sitting position and looked back, then had to look away as Agradeleous began the bone-crunching, flesh-tearing transformation back to a bipedal lizardman form.

The elf glanced down the hallway, thinking that he should use this opportunity to sprint away. To what end, though? He knew that Agradeleous would easily overtake him.

It occurred to him then that he should use this opportunity to attack the dragon, to defeat it, perhaps even to force it back over the ledge into the lava.

Juraviel dismissed that notion with a shrug and a helpless laugh. How might he be able to hurt the great beast, even during this seemingly vulnerable time of transformation? And if he could find a way to win out, if he could find a boulder or something to knock the dragon over the ledge . . .

Juraviel didn't want to. He would not strike at Agradeleous; he had no right to strike at this creature that had shown him unexpected mercy.

He sat down on the floor, closed his eyes, and waited for the dragon to complete its transformation.

A powerful hand grasped him by the back of his collar, lifting him with frightening ease and carrying him along. The elf stayed limp and kept his eyes closed, perfectly resigned to his fate, whatever that fate might be.

Agradeleous ran along the corridors at great speed as the minutes became an hour, and then two, and on and on. Tirelessly, the dragon ran, feet thumping heavily, Juraviel bouncing and dragging, but never complaining. The elf could not believe the beast's stamina, but still, sooner than he imagined possible, Agradeleous stopped and shook him, and when he opened his eyes, he found himself again in the dragon's treasure lair, overlooking the pit, where Cazzira stared back up at him.

Agradeleous growled and threw him down, and only the elf's wings, beating furiously, stopped him from smashing to death on the hard stone. Still, he landed hard, falling into a roll, and then a second, and when he came up, he toppled over backward, too dazed and hurt to hold his footing. Cazzira was there in a moment, cradling his head. "Oh, you fool!" she scolded. "You cannot escape the beast! I should have stopped you from trying."

Juraviel looked up at her and managed to smile, and to lift his arm up to place his hand on her cradling forearm. "You could not have stopped me. I knew the danger, and knew the futility. But still, I was bound to try."

He saw a wounded look upon her face before she sighed and looked away, which somewhat surprised him.

With great effort, Juraviel shifted about and came up to his knees beside the sitting Cazzira, cupping her face with one hand and turning her to face him. "This has nothing to do with how I feel about you," he said.

"It has everything to do with it." Though he held her face toward his own, the elf still turned her eyes away.

"No," Juraviel insisted. "I am bound by duty above all, above even love."

Cazzira looked back at him.

"And I do love you," Juraviel admitted, to himself and to her. "I do. And that, too, tells me that I must get out of here, I must find a way to get us both out of here."

His strength left him as he finished, and he slumped a bit, and Cazzira pulled him in close to her.

And both of them sat there, wondering what would come next, wondering what punishment Agradeleous would rain upon Juraviel.

The jolting landing of the heavy beast jarred Juraviel and Cazzira from their slumber the next morning, both elves leaping up to face the wrathful Agradeleous. The dragon stood there, muscles twitching beneath its scaly hide, clawed hands grasping at the air and squeezing tightly, lizard snout curling back as low growls escaped through jagged, pointed teeth. With a sudden burst of rage, as if the anger simply could not be contained within, Agradeleous exploded into motion. He grabbed up a rock that was nearly as big, and many times as heavy, as either of the elves, and hurled it across the pit to smash thunderously against the opposite wall.

Mouth moving as if the dragon wanted to bite the air itself, the beast took a threatening step forward.

Cazzira rushed in front of Juraviel. "If you are to kill him, then know that I am your mortal enemy!"

The dragon stopped. "Kill?" Agradeleous asked. And then he snorted.

Juraviel pushed Cazzira out of the way and stepped past her to face the dragon directly. He stared at Agradeleous for a few moments, trying to size up the dragon's mood, and he noted a range of emotions, some surprising. Agradeleous was outraged, of course, but there was something behind that anger. It hit Juraviel profoundly then—his action had wounded the dragon, but in the way that a friend might wound another.

"I feed you," Agradeleous started. "You are warm and with companionship. You tell me great tales and I tell you their equal. And you betray me!"

"I did not betray you!" Juraviel shouted back, as emphatically as any dragon's roar. "And it pained me to walk away."

"You deceived me!" Agradeleous countered. "Step by step, you lured me into your grand play, and that play was no more than a ruse to cover your escape!"

"No!" Juraviel retorted, but he bit the word short, and his visage softened as he stared at the dragon. "Yes," he admitted. "I deceived you and I deceived Cazzira."

"Then I should tear your head from your shoulders!" Agradeleous roared, and came forward another threatening step, putting him only one long stride from Juraviel.

The elf only shrugged. "I am helpless to stop you." He looked up, then, noting that Agradeleous had not continued his advance. The dragon stood there, low growls—of frustration, Juraviel realized—escaping its gnashing maw.

"I should not be surprised by the treachery of a Touel'alfar," Agradeleous quietly rasped.

Juraviel realized then that he could not allow the dragon to go down this disastrous road, relating this incident to the less-than-stellar relationship between their races—for Cazzira's sake if not his own. Agradeleous was deeply wounded, and would likely kill him, but if the dragon came to consider Juraviel's treachery as expected from Touel'alfar, and by extension Doc'alfar, then no doubt Cazzira's ending would come swiftly.

"You gave me no choice, Agradeleous," Juraviel remarked.

The dragon's lamplight eyes stared at him hard, seemed to burn holes into him.

"For months you have kept us here, while my protégé walks her dangerous road alone," Juraviel explained. "I am bound to her side, and yet, there I cannot be. While you hold me here to tell you stories, another is being written, one whose writing is supposed to be partly the province of Belli'mar Juraviel. I have enjoyed my time here—I would be lying if I said otherwise. And yet, I must go."

Agradeleous gave a sound that seemed to be a cross somewhere between a mocking laugh and an angry growl.

"How can you claim treachery if you refuse to claim friendship?" Cazzira cut in suddenly.

Juraviel and Agradeleous both snapped their gazes over the Tylwyn Doc. Juraviel's immediate reaction was to shout

out at her to stay out of this, to tell her that it was none of her affair, to protect her from inadvertently entering into the wrath of Agradeleous. But the protests died in his throat as Cazzira calmly, so very calmly, continued.

"If we are prisoners, then you are within your rights to punish Juraviel for his attempt to leave."

"My rights?" the dragon asked with complete sarcasm, as if the whole notion was absurd. This was Agradeleous' lair, where Agradeleous was king, after all, and bound by nothing but the dragon's whims.

"You cannot claim the role of jailor and of friend, Agradeleous," Cazzira went on quietly. "At first, you were the former, obviously. But it seems to me that you have abandoned that mantle, of jailor, as we have abandoned the mantle of prisoners."

"You speak foolishness! He deceived me that he could escape."

"I must go," Juraviel said, and Agradeleous laughed at him.

"He asks you as a friend," Cazzira added, and that stopped the laughter, and in truth, had all three of them wondering what their relationship truly had become.

A few moments of silence slipped past, with all three gazes darting from one to the other.

"And for that, I owe an apology," Juraviel admitted, to himself and to the others. "I should have come to trust in our friendship. I should have come to you directly, and honestly, explaining that I had to leave. It is my duty that I go to find Brynn, and I tell you now, honestly, that if you refuse me this, I will try again to get away from here. Not to get away from you," he added quickly, for it seemed as if the dragon was about to leap atop him, "but to get to her."

"You do not even know if she is still alive," Agradeleous replied, and he seemed much calmer then.

"But I must find out the truth of it."

The dragon pondered the words for a long time, then nodded. "You should have come to me."

"You would not have let me . . ." Juraviel paused and looked at Cazzira. "Would not have let us," he corrected, "go."

"You have tales I wish to hear," the dragon explained. "For hundreds of years, I have slept here quietly. I did not ask you to invade my home, and did not kill you, as is my right against thieves."

"We were not thieves," Cazzira put in. "Not knowingly, at least."

"You cannot argue against my generosity in this!" Agradeleous roared, and he stamped his foot, which shook the chamber and lifted both the elves into short bounces.

"You are correct," Juraviel agreed. "You have been most generous, but that does not change the road I must follow."

"You should have asked!"

"You would not have let me go!"

"Not alone!"

That startled the elves, and indeed, seemed to startle the dragon, as well!

"You would let Cazzira walk beside me out of here?" Juraviel asked.

"I would walk beside the both of you out of here!" Agradeleous answered, and it was obvious that the dragon had just made that decision on the spot. "Yes," he said, nodding, and speaking as if to himself. "It has been too long since I have flown through the wide sky, too long since I have walked the realm of the alfar and the lesser races. We will go to find your Brynn if she is living still, and to make a tale of our own if she is not!"

Juraviel found that he could hardly draw breath, and when he glanced over at Cazzira, he saw that she was equally distressed. What had he just done? What destruction had he just inadvertently unleashed upon the world?

"Yes, it is too long since I have known an adventure, and too many centuries have passed since I have added to my treasures!" Agradeleous declared. "Prepare yourselves. We will leave as soon as you are ready." With that, the dragon, seeming much more lighthearted, leaped away.

Juraviel continued to look to Cazzira, who half walked, half stumbled beside him. "We cannot," she whispered, barely finding the breath to speak.

"We cannot stop him," Juraviel answered. The truth of his

own words struck him profoundly, forcing him to bear responsibility for putting this idea into Agradeleous' head.

"We cannot control him," Cazzira reminded. "How many will die because of this?"

Juraviel tried to keep the edge out of his voice, though the sarcasm remained obvious. "They are just humans, are they not?" He regretted the words even as they left his mouth, for Cazzira turned up at him, her expression wounded.

"Well then, perhaps I fear that Agradeleous will fly over the mountains to attack Tymwyvenne," the Doc'alfar answered. "Because of course I could not learn to care for any humans."

She started to walk away, but Juraviel grabbed her up in his arms and would not let her go, however she thrashed. "I am afraid, Cazzira," he admitted. "I do not mean to wound you, but I am afraid."

From up above, they heard a guttural, rumbling sound, and it took them a moment to realize that the dragon was speaking—no, not speaking, but singing!—in his ancient language. Both Juraviel and Cazzira, whose respective languages bore the same heritage as that of the dragon, understood enough of Agradeleous' song to realize that it was all about pillaging and burning, about the tastiness of man-flesh and the joys of the many artifacts the humans always crafted from glittering stones and metals.

"I think that you should have a long, long talk with our companion," Cazzira said dryly.

"That is what got us into this in the first place," Juraviel reminded her.

The elves stalled for as long as they possibly could, but as the hours turned to days, the dragon's song only became more insistent and frantic. Finally, Agradeleous landed beside them with a reverberating thump, and explained that it was time to leave. Both elves tried to offer protests, but the dragon just scooped them up under powerful arms and leaped away. When they got settled into the main chamber, the elves found that he had set out all of their belongings, along with other general supplies and an assortment of weapons and armor.

"Gather your trinkets and let us go," the dragon insisted,

and when they were finished their outfitting, and just stood there looking at Agradeleous and at each other, the beast asked bluntly, "Do you know the way?"

"We were searching for that when we stumbled upon your lair," said Juraviel.

"Back the other way then!" Agradeleous roared, and Juraviel glanced over at Cazzira, to see her porcelain skin seeming even more pale, and to see her swaying as if she would just fall over.

"No," Juraviel replied. "There are one-way doors, and corridors too twisting to navigate. South is the better course."

"You are certain?" the dragon asked. "I can fly over the mountains with ease. They are no barrier to mighty Agradeleous!"

Again, Juraviel glanced over to see Cazzira growing unsteady on her feet.

"We go south," Juraviel said more firmly. "But before we walk with you into the human lands, Agradeleous, I will have your word of agreement."

The dragon tilted his head, seeming somewhere between amusement and disbelief.

"You will not kill any humans," Juraviel demanded.

The dragon began to growl.

"Except in defense," the elf added.

Still the dragon growled.

"Or in battle," Juraviel went on. "I will determine your course in this, Agradeleous. You may defend yourself, of course, but you will take no actions against the humans, any humans, without my direction and permission. I will have your word on this."

"Or?"

"Or I will not lead you to Brynn and the grand adventure you desire," Juraviel was quick to respond. "If you wish to simply go out from your hole and ravage the land, then do so without me and without Cazzira. If you wish to participate in a war that will change the world, in a tale that will be spoken of for centuries to come, then you will agree to my terms. You will give me your word, and truly, do I ask anything so difficult?"

"Good enough," the dragon agreed after a moment's reflection. "I will trust your judgment on this, Belli'mar Juraviel. To the south we go—let us begin our search down the hole where we lost your companion. If she did not make it out alive, then better that we learn the truth before we step out under the wide sky. Perhaps we will not need to be discerning in whom we kill!"

Now it was Juraviel who truly needed a bit of physical support, but he somehow managed, and so did Cazzira, to follow the magnificent and terrible beast out of the treasure chamber.

It was all guesswork, of course, as the tunnels forked and forked again, and so their progress was painfully slow, and so the days meandered past.

But then Agradeleous stumbled upon a tunnel long and straight and ascending, and with just a hint of current in the air.

It was late autumn of God's Year 841, almost a year since entering the Path of Starless Night, when Juraviel and Cazzira and their newest companion walked out of the tunnel, under a beautiful, crisp, starry sky. The two elves stood there transfixed, hardly remembering the sheer beauty of this sight, and so entranced were they that they didn't notice the crackling of reshaping bones behind them. So they were both taken by complete surprise when Agradeleous issued a dragon's roar—not the rock-shaking roar of his lizardman form, but the rock-splitting thunder of a true dragon!

The two swung about, and for a moment, neither doubted that they were about to be consumed, that the agreement Juraviel had forged with the dragon was a meaningless thing after all.

But Agradeleous calmed his roaring and stretched his great wings out to the sides.

"It is good to feel the breeze upon my wings again!"

# CHAPTER 23

# *What Agradeleous Wants . . .*

Nearly every day, Brynn descended the long staircase of the Walk of Clouds, down to the base of the rocky valley nestled within the Mountains of Fire, and then out the valley trails to the fields where Runtly ran with the other horses. Sensitive to her desires to spend time with her pony, the Jhesta Tu mystics gave her duties that would have taken her to the floor anyway.

As summer gave way to autumn, her job was to collect the black lava stones from the broken landscape and bring them up in buckets so that they could be ground into powder and used to fertilize the many gardens about the monastery. Brynn worked without complaint, taking the burdened climb back up the five thousand stairs in the same stoic manner she had utilized to get her through her years of training with the Touel'alfar. In Andur'Blough Inninness, like all of the other ranger trainees, Brynn had spent many days collecting sponge-like milk-stones from the bog, carrying them back to a distant trough, then squeezing the bog juice out of them. In those mornings, Brynn had learned the power of meditation, of falling within herself to block out unpleasant external events, and so she used that now, slowly walking up the stairs each afternoon, deliberately and carefully placing one foot in front of the other so that she did not twist her leg, with a pole across her shoulders, a full bucket of stones dangling from each end.

It was a good life for the young woman, a necessary respite from the trials of the wider world, a time to reflect and to grow strong again, mentally, emotionally, and physically.

She spent most of her nights with Pagonel and other Jhesta Tu. Unlike her days in Andur'Blough Inninness, her times at the Walk of Clouds were full of openly asked questions and brisk discussions about philosophy and the ways of the various religions. Here Pagonel often led the way, inevitably veering the discussion toward the Behrenese Chezru religion and the concept and ways of Yatol.

Brynn soon enough recognized that he was doing this for her benefit, that in these times, while learning about herself, the young woman was also learning valuable lessons about her enemy. Even more than that, she came to believe that Pagonel was subtly forcing her to view her enemy not as the singular-minded, and thus, singularly hated, Wraps, but as a collection of people following precepts that were not so variant from her own, or from anyone else's.

"You try to distract me from my destiny," she said to the man one night after a particularly heated discussion about how the To-gai-ru, the Abellicans, and the Jhesta Tu were not so different in the artistic renderings of their respective pantheons.

Pagonel looked at her curiously, then merely smiled.

"You do," she accused. "You keep speaking of the Behrenese in very human terms, hoping that I will forget my hatred toward them and, it follows, hoping that I will abandon my course against them."

"Or perhaps I understand that if you do not come to understand the Behrenese, even the Chezru, even the Chezru Chieftain and his Yatols, as people of varying intelligence and desires, then your road will surely end as Ashwarawu's ended, in the bloody dirt."

Now it was Brynn's turn to stand and stare. "Do you believe that I should abandon my road altogether?" she asked after a long pause.

"I believe that you should continue to grow personally," the Jhesta Tu master replied. "And when your heart tells you that it is time for you to go and decide your place in the world, among your own people or among the Behrenese, then you should go. Revelations ultimately come from within, not from without."

"Like your own journey to Ashwarawu's camp," Brynn remarked. "Now that I have seen the Walk of Clouds, now that I have come to know what it is to be Jhesta Tu, your choice puzzles me even more. Why did you go out to the steppes?"

"Perhaps it was simply fate, or a silent command within from a god that I do not understand," the mystic answered. "Or perhaps it was nothing but luck—and only time will tell us if that luck was good or bad." He ended with a chuckle and turned to leave, but Brynn grabbed him by the arm and forcefully turned him back around to face her.

"Do you believe that it was bad luck that you found me?"

Both became acutely aware of how close they were to each other. The tension between them had somewhat cooled since that uncomfortable day on the field below, but now it was there again, palpably.

"No," Pagonel answered. "I could never believe that."

Brynn kissed him before he ever finished the sentence, and then they held each other there in the hallway for a long, long time.

"Another unremarkable village," Cazzira remarked, standing on a ridge and looking down at a small collection of houses, ringed by stables.

"Then let me raze it and eat all the villagers, and its name will be long remembered," Agradeleous offered, and both elves scowled at him, to which the dragon only sighed.

They had spent several weeks moving about the open and empty steppes, with the dragon remaining in his bipedal form—except on occasional nights, when Agradeleous resumed his true and magnificent form and went out hunting, returning with stolen livestock or a wild horse or other things that both Juraviel and Cazzira thought it best not to ask him about.

The trio had encountered two villages previous to this one, and had spent time haunting the areas about them, eavesdropping on the conversations of any who happened by. One such discussion, between a pair of elderly women cleaning their laundry on stones at the side of a small stream, had told of a revolt in a town not so far away, of how a Yatol and a Chezhou-Lei warrior had been slain, though now the town had been reclaimed by the Wraps, and was held more tightly than even before.

And this before them was that village, which Juraviel thought might prove not so unremarkable. Few warriors could slay a Chezhou-Lei warrior, he had come to believe.

But he knew one that could.

"You will remain here this night," he instructed Agradeleous.

"Unless I hear an oxen lowing on the grasses," the dragon replied.

"You feasted last night."

The dragon curled its mouth in a grinning reply.

"I ask you to remain here," Juraviel said firmly. "If you cause any tumult on the grasses nearby, you will rouse the villagers."

Agradeleous' smile faded. "I will stay," he agreed. "Do you mean to go and listen in?"

"It would be wonderful if we could start finding some direction to our path," the elf replied, and at his side, Cazzira certainly did not disagree.

Later on, when the sun went down and the bright stars twinkled above, many people gathered in the village common room, talking animatedly. Just outside, huddled in the shadows beside a slightly opened window, Juraviel and Cazzira sat and listened, as silent as those shadows hiding them.

They heard many discussions about many things, most unrelated to any information they could use. They did hear some Behrenese soldiers boasting about a great battle, though.

"You will all learn your place, you Ru!" one cried out, the man obviously a bit drunk.

"Aye, cleaning the dung from your boots!" one of the To-gai-ru man villagers replied, and all about him laughed.

"Better for you that our boots are covered in dung than in blood, as they were at Dharyan!" the Behrenese soldier shot back, and in the blink of an eye, the room went dead silent.

Both Juraviel and Cazzira peeked up and over the window rim, trying to get a better measure of it all. Another soldier jumped from his seat and grabbed the speaker, holding him steady and bidding him to be quiet.

"They know of Dharyan!" the drunken speaker protested.

"Do you not?" he asked the room, leaning forward and smiling wickedly. "When all of your heroes were trampled into the mud by the power of Yatol Grysh? When brave Ashwarawu's head parted from his shoulders?"

Several To-gai-ru men stood up at that, their chairs skidding out behind them, while others held them back.

"A fairly recent battle," Juraviel observed to Cazzira, for it was obvious that the emotions here were too high for Dharyan to be a memory from the war when Behren had conquered To-gai.

"We remember it," one To-gai-ru from the far corner did respond. "Aye, and well. Almost as well as we remember Yatol Daek Gin Gin Yan and Dee'dahk, and the fine To-gai-ru lass who out them down!"

Juraviel could hardly draw his breath, and felt as if he would simply fall over.

"Speak no more of it!" the soldier holding the drunk ordered the To-gai-ru, and when his drunken friend started to respond, he smacked the man hard across the back of his head.

All the Behrenese soldiers were standing then, and several drew out their weapons.

But it was all bluster and boast, and no real challenge came against them, and soon enough the room settled back into its easy flow of many disjointed conversations.

Over the course of the next couple of hours, Juraviel did note, though, that many of the To-gai-ru veered on the path to the common room's door to a table where a pair of elderly couples sat quietly, and often patted one old man on the shoulders, sometimes looking back as they did to the boastful and drunken Behrenese soldier.

When that old man and his wife left the common room later on, a pair of quiet little figures followed them through the town and to their small and humble cottage, and when they sat down within, at their own table, they did not know that they were not alone.

"I am warmed whenever they speak of her," the old man said, and his companion walked behind him and put her arms about his neck, bending low.

"You think they refer to Brynn?" Cazzira whispered to Juraviel.

The elf nodded, and held his breath as he put his ear back up to the crack in the cottage wall.

"Come, old man, let us find our sleep," he heard the old woman say, and he was sorely disappointed.

"A good one, it will be," the old man agreed, and the elves heard the creak of wood as he stood, and the shuffling of feet as the old couple made their way across the room to their bedding.

"Now what?" Cazzira asked. "Back to Agradeleous or back to the common room?"

Juraviel took a third route, around the house so that he was against the wall closest to the couple's bed. As soon as he got there, purely on instinct, he tapped on the wall.

When no response came back, he tapped again, harder.

"Eh?" he heard the old man say, followed by movement within.

"Tell me of her," Juraviel said to them, though Cazzira was grabbing his arm so tightly that the blood couldn't get to his fingers. "Tell me of the fall of Yatol Daek Gin Gin Yan."

"Who are you?" came a harsh whisper.

"I am a friend."

There came some muffled conversation within, and the elves heard the old woman remark, "A friend of the Behrenese!"

"A friend, I believe, of she who slew the Yatol," Juraviel said, and Cazzira tugged him hard, pulling him away from the wall.

"You cannot do this!" she protested.

"It is the only way!"

They both stopped as they heard the door around the other side of the cottage swing open. Around the corner, armed with a small hammer, came the old man. "Who are you?" he demanded, though neither elf was anywhere in sight. He looked all about, shaking his hammer.

"I traveled with Brynn Dharielle," Juraviel said, using a Touel'alfar trick to throw his voice, so that the old man spun the wrong way in response.

"Then show yourself!"

"That I cannot do," Juraviel replied, throwing his voice to a different place, and the old man spun again. When he had settled, Juraviel started again, his voice coming from a completely different shadow. "She thought me lost in the Path of Starless Night, tunnels beneath the great mountains to the north. But I have found my way to here and, I hope, soon to her side again."

The man's shoulders seemed to slump a bit at that last statement, and a lump wrought of fear welled in Juraviel's throat.

"Bah, but I'll not talk to ghosts!" the old man said firmly. "Nor to Behrenese spies—and how do I know you're not that?"

Juraviel started out and Cazzira grabbed him tightly. "No," she whispered.

"He knows," Juraviel said back at her, and he pulled away.

The old man was heading back around the house by that time, so Juraviel jumped out behind him. "Have you ever seen a Behrenese soldier who looks like this?" he asked, and the man spun about.

And then he stood there, trembling, his hammer falling to the ground at his feet.

"I am no enemy of To-gai," Juraviel declared. "And I am a friend of Brynn Dharielle. Tell me, I beg of you."

*"Tu d'elfin faerie,"* the man stuttered, using the To-gai-ru label for the elven people, a race that was prominent in their fireside tales.

"Belli'mar Juraviel at your service," the elf said with a sweeping bow. "You know of Brynn, so tell me, I beg of you."

"I sent her to her death," the old man remarked, trembling, his hands coming up to hide his face.

"No, Balachuk!" the old woman said, rushing around the house and grabbing at his arms. "We do not know that!"

"She did battle here, against a Yatol priest and one named Dee'dahk?" Juraviel prompted.

"A Chezhou-Lei warrior," the old woman said, nodding. "She killed them both, and others besides, and she freed the horses, though the Wraps have returned to put them back."

The couple exchanged worried looks.

"You'd best come inside," the old woman said. "We saw Brynn once again after she fled, and we know where she went, but it is not a pretty tale."

Juraviel entered the humble cottage behind the couple and took an offered seat at their table, with Balachuk sitting across from him and the woman—Balachuk introduced her as Tsolona—moving to the fire to heat some water for tea.

After a few uncomfortable moments, where Juraviel had to reassure the couple repeatedly that he was no spy, and that, yes, he was of the *tu d'elfin faerie* spoken of in their legends, he managed to coax the story out of them. Balachuk told it, primarily, recounting Brynn's time in the village, and how she had taken down the Yatol priest and the warrior. He spoke of his last meeting with her, when she had left to join Ashwarawu's rebel band.

Balachuk's voice grew solemn as he told Juraviel of the disastrous battle of Dharyan.

"She is dead, then?" the elf asked, barely able to get the words past the lump in his slender throat.

"So I would guess," Balachuk replied, seeming equally troubled.

"We heard rumors that a Jhesta Tu was there, and took her riding off from the battle," Tsolona quickly interjected. "Heard that she, or he, killed another of the Chezhou-Lei."

"Rumors," Balachuk huffed.

"Not all of them died at the gates of Dharyan!" Tsolona insisted.

"Then why did she not return to us?" the old man countered.

"So you just do not know?" Juraviel asked.

"A few To-gai-ru returned from the battlefield and are scattered about the steppes," Balachuk explained. "It is not something they are free to talk about."

"Not in pride or practicality," said Tsolona, echoing a common To-gai-ru saying.

Belli'mar Juraviel paused for a bit to digest it all. "Jhesta Tu?" he asked at length, unfamiliar with the name.

"Group of mystics who live somewhere far to the south," Balachuk explained. "One was said to be riding with Ashwarawu."

"Do you have any idea of where I might turn to find Brynn's trail, if it did lead from Dharyan?" the elf asked, and the old couple looked to each other, but Juraviel knew even before the two blank stares came back at him that they had no idea of how to respond.

Juraviel found Cazzira outside of the house, waiting for him in the shadows.

"A legend comes to life," she said with a grin.

"Let us hope that another one remains alive," Juraviel replied grimly, and they left the village to find Agradeleous, that they might head out to the south and east.

"This is what Yatol has shown to me," Chezru Douan said calmly, bringing his arms in dramatically and crossing them over his chest as he slowly closed his eyes.

Around him, all of the priests in attendance murmured their accord and their prayers, and even one of the other two Chezhou-Lei warriors nodded, his face a mask of acceptance. Kaliit Timig wanted to scream out! He hadn't come for permission to go to the Mountains of Fire, but rather, just to inform the Chezru Chieftain that the Chezhou-Lei warriors had assembled and were ready to begin their march. Months had passed since he had first informed Yakim Douan of the need for the Chezhou-Lei to exact revenge over the hated Jhesta Tu, and not once before this day had Yakim Douan indicated that there would be anything but agreement coming from him.

And now the Chezru Chieftain had walked into the morning audience with the surprising announcement that he would allow Kaliit Timig to take only half of the warriors to the south, and that a force of Jacintha soldiers, not Chezhou-Lei, would accompany them. The Kaliit's frustration was only more profound, since Douan had proclaimed this as a vision of Yatol. The Chezhou-Lei, like all of the Chezru, considered Douan the God-Voice, who communicated directly with Yatol; and thus, it was not their place to question him.

Not publicly, at least.

Kaliit Timig bowed his head. "In what capacity are the soldiers of Jacintha to be used?" he asked.

"In whatever capacity the leader of the Chezhou-Lei contingent desires," Douan answered, his eyes still closed as if he was then in direct contact with Yatol.

Kaliit Timig tilted his head to the side a bit at the surprising words. "The leader" of the Chezhou-Lei? What might Yakim Douan mean by that, since Kaliit Timig was obviously the leader, and had obviously, despite his advanced age, planned to travel to the Mountains of Fire? Had the Chezru Chieftain just subtly stated that Timig would not be going?

"I do not question your words, God-Voice," Timig began, his old voice holding steady, "but—"

"It is good that you do not question Yatol," Douan interrupted, ending that line of probing before it could ever begin. "I am shown that the honor of your order is in need, and thus, whatever my personal fears, Yatol demands that I allow the Chezhou-Lei this journey. But I am shown, as well, that the integrity of Behren rests in no small part upon the valued swords of the Chezhou-Lei, and the kingdom cannot be unguarded for the months of this journey. Appoint your leader—Yatol Grysh's man, Wan Atenn, is battle-seasoned and has earned high regard—and select those warriors who will go to avenge the death of Chezhou-Lei Dahmed Blie. Let them begin their march, and then you and I will determine the best way to redistribute those warriors left to my disposal.

"You do not approve?" Yakim Douan asked a moment later, and Kaliit Timig realized that his expression was betraying his heart. "Do you fear the Jhesta Tu that much? They number fewer than two hundred, closer to a hundred, by every account, and many of those mystics are mere novices, young disciples who have never seen battle. Indeed, it is likely that this mystic who felled Chezhou-Lei Dahmed Blie is the only one of their order who has lifted a weapon, or his fist, against a real enemy. You will send a like number of seasoned, veteran warriors to battle mere children, and I will reinforce your warriors with four times that number. Rest assured, Kaliit Timig, that when the slaughter is completed, the Chezhou-Lei will be given all of the glory for the defeat of the Jhesta Tu."

Kaliit Timig understood that he had been flanked on every front, and since Douan was speaking with the weight of Yatol behind him, the logic walls he had used to surround the Kaliit could not be scaled. The old man snapped a respectful bow, then stood at rigid attention. "Wan Atenn is a fine choice, God-Voice."

"That is the advice of Yakim Douan, not Yatol," the Chezru Chieftain said with a chuckle, and all about him smiled, even snickered, at the sudden break of any tension.

"And it is advice I will take into consideration," Kaliit Timig assured him, and with another bow, the old Chezhou-Lei warrior left the audience chamber and the temple altogether. He had nearly three hundred of the world's finest warriors preparing themselves for the long journey to the Mountains of Fire, choosing their mounts and fitting armor to horse and man. Now he had to go to them and explain that only half would take that ride.

He didn't expect many cheers at that proclamation.

But Yakim Douan was God-Voice and could not be questioned.

And so on a bright morning in the second month of the year, half of the Chezhou-Lei warriors in all the world, a formidable army unto themselves, paraded out of Jacintha to the music of a hundred horns, their armored horses striding easily and proudly down the main boulevard of the city and out the southern gate. Behind them came a marching twenty-square, spear tips gleaming in the morning light.

Chezru Douan and Kaliit Timig watched the procession side by side, on a balcony of the great temple. "Yatol is ever wise," Douan remarked.

"Of course, God-Voice," the Kaliit promptly replied.

"My man in Honce-the-Bear, Daween Kusaad, is not pleased with the new Queen Jilseponie," Douan added, and that caught Timig by surprise, for never had the God-Voice been known to share such political information with his Chezhou-Lei elite guard.

"She is Abellican, you know," Douan went on when Timig looked at him questioningly. "A ranking member of the infidel Church, akin to an abbot in power."

The Kaliit nodded, though he had not heard any such thing, nor did he much understand why it mattered.

"She was instrumental in the defeat of Abbot Olin of Entel in his bid to lead the Abellican Church, an ascension that would have surely strengthened the ties of Behren and our neighbors to the north. I fear that her work toward his defeat may be an indication that King Danube, her husband, will take action against Abbot Olin in Entel, and will weaken the ties between our lands."

Kaliit Timig had no idea of how he was supposed to respond, or even if he was supposed to respond, for Chezru Douan had never spoken to him about such matters, and he wasn't quite sure what the man might be getting at.

But then Douan looked at him directly, his expression stern. "If King Danube moves against Abbot Olin of Entel, then we will support the man—perhaps we will even fight beside him to hold control of his city."

Kaliit Timig's old and drooping eyes widened at that! "You think to sail around the mountain spur and enter Honce-the-Bear?"

"If Yatol so decrees," the calm Chezru Chieftain said, and he looked back to the procession passing along the road below.

Yakim Douan did well to hide his smile at that time. He had no intention, of course, of supporting Olin with anything more than money against King Danube, if Danube was even thinking of moving against Olin overtly, which Douan thought absurd. But on the surface, at least, it all seemed plausible, and by embellishing the events of Honce-the-Bear to the Kaliit, he had given the old man more to think about and less to dwell upon.

He glanced down at Timig and recognized that the man was deep in thought. Up to that moment, Douan had known that Timig was angry that only half of his warriors could march on their road to revenge, but now, with a few well-aimed remarks, Douan had him questioning even sending that many. For the Chezhou-Lei, proud as they were and concerned with their honor, garnered that honor, above all else, by protecting Yatol's Chezru priests and strict order.

Yakim Douan feared no move by Danube, against him or even against Abbot Olin. Queen Jilseponie was no firebrand

seeking conquest, from all the information that Daween
Kusaad had sent back. In fact, she was rarely even in the
Castle in Ursal at that time, for winter was on in full in the
northern kingdom, in their God's Year 842, and kindhearted
Jilseponie was out every day among the poor and the sick.

She and her husband were no threat.

But Kaliit Timig didn't have to know that.

Agradeleous sat on a termite mound, sharpening his claws—
and even in this humanoid form, they were formidable!—
on a large rock he had found, and looking none-too-happy, as
usual.

"Do you think that he will put those weapons to use someday soon?" Cazzira asked Juraviel, the two of them sitting
across the way.

Juraviel shrugged, but in truth, it was a fear that had been
bubbling inside of him for a long, long time. Ever since they
had first come out of the mountains, when Agradeleous had
reverted to his natural behemoth form and stretched his great
wings in the mountain air, Juraviel had worked tirelessly
to keep the dragon calm. For to the beast, all of the creatures about them—the humans included, and perhaps even
particularly—were nothing more than potential meals, or
outlets for his innate aggression. So far, Agradeleous had be-
haved himself well, with not a single human kill, as far as either of the elves knew. But of late, as the weeks had dragged
to months and as the wind across the steppes had become
uncomfortably cold, often with stinging hail or snow, the
dragon's patience had seemed on the wane.

Of late, Agradeleous seemed to be spending more time off
to the side of the encampments, and often flexing his formidable, sinewy muscles, or sharpening those killing claws.

Juraviel understood the dragon's frustration. His own frustration came from the lack of any real information about
Brynn. One time of the many when he had eavesdropped on
the conversations of unsuspecting humans, he had heard ref-
erences to this mysterious Jhesta Tu mystic and the supposed
rescue of the warrior woman from the battlefield outside of
Dharyan, but other than that, he had learned nothing of any

value. For Agradeleous, the frustration was even easier to sort out. The dragon had slept in peace for so many years, and when he had decided to accompany the elves to the surface, he had done so with the intention of finding great adventure. Thus far, at least, that had hardly been the case.

Cazzira's question echoed ominously to Juraviel in context of that realization. On a whim, Agradeleous could level any of the many villages they had seen. It would take a trained army, powerfully outfitted, to bring down the dragon; among the four ancient races of Corona, only the demon dactyls were more individually powerful, and their might came from a combination of magic and physical strength. Even the demons could not match the sheer physical muscle of a dragon. Juraviel had never seen one before he had encountered Agradeleous, and though he had heard the stories of the ancient wurms told over and over again, that one moment when Agradeleous had come out of the tunnel and stretched his great wings had overwhelmed him. He could hardly imagine the devastation this one might cause if he became enraged.

Or bored.

Juraviel glanced across to the dragon, and it seemed to him to hold too much strength and energy within his current form, as if he would just explode back into his greater shape.

The elf was somewhat relieved a short while later, then, when a campfire appeared in the distance. Cazzira noticed it first and quietly motioned to Juraviel, but before the two could come up with any plan that might engage Agradeleous without bringing him dangerously close to the human camp, the dragon, too, spotted the distant light.

"Let us go and see those who would share the land with us," Agradeleous said too eagerly, and the dragon took a loping stride away.

"Better if I go alone, or with Cazzira," Juraviel quickly replied and the dragon stopped and spun about, a slight hiss escaping his mouth.

"At first," the elf quickly explained. "Let us catch them unawares, that they will be more truthful. If they have anything of interest to reveal, we will come back for you."

"If they have anything of interest to reveal, they will tell it to me," Agradeleous answered, and he started away at a fast walk, then a loping trot, and Juraviel and Cazzira had to run flat out to keep up.

Agradeleous stopped outside the light of that fire and was not immediately noticed, for the ten men sitting about the flames were engaged in a boisterous conversation.

"We cannot go back to any town!" one protested. "Don't you think the Wraps will be looking for us? And what a fine prize our heads would make!"

"We cannot stay out here with no food and no wagons to rob," a second argued. "I'd rather die fighting Wraps than freeze and starve out here where only the buzzards will find our rotting corpses!"

"Then you should have died with the rest at Dharyan!" the first man shot back.

"Not that again!" several cried at once, and one continued, "Are we to spend all our days thinking back to that cursed place?"

Out in the darkness, Agradeleous snapped a fiery gaze over Juraviel. "You want answers, and so you shall have them!" he said in his rumbling inhuman voice, and it was loud enough to halt the conversation in the encampment, with several men leaping up and a couple even lifting their weapons.

How they fell all over each other when the huge bipedal lizard walked right into their camp, his wings tucked in tight to his back, his small tail trailing.

One or two froze in terror, one or two screamed out and turned to flee, but these were To-gai-ru warriors here, and before Agradeleous could utter any sort of explanation, several came at him hard, weapons slashing.

Agradeleous didn't retreat an inch, but rather, charged forward suddenly, into the largest concentration of opponents, four men charging shoulder to shoulder. Oblivious to their puny weapons, the dragon slammed in, scattering them, slamming them to the ground. One sword hooked under the dragon's scaled breast, but Agradeleous just snapped his hand in and grabbed it across the blade, tearing it from the man's grasp, then altered the angle of his rush and lowered his shoulder, smashing that man down below him.

And then he kicked the prone man, launching him through the air for a dozen feet.

The dragon spun and squeezed the sword, then threw it to the ground, swinging his hand across to slap aside a spear thrusting for his torso.

From his left, a heavy axe swooped in at his neck.

Agradeleous roared and accepted the hit, which did no damage against his superb armor, and then his powerful legs twitched, launching him right into the axe-wielder, the impact knocking the man back and down.

But not to the ground, for the dragon's hand shot out, engulfing the man's face, and with strength that mocked the warriors, Agradeleous lifted the kicking and thrashing man up into the air.

"Do you wish to speak with me, or should I just kill you all?" the dragon roared, and with his free hand, he caught the swinging arm of another swordsman, and then, with a flick of his wrist, sent the man flying away, head over heels.

"Well?" the dragon demanded, and when he roared, he tensed, and his hand closed a bit on the head of the man he held high, bringing forth a pitiful squeal.

The remaining To-gai-ru held back, circling, weapons drawn, but it was obvious that none wanted to advance.

"No!" came a cry from behind, and the already overwhelmed warriors turned to see two more strange creatures rushing into their firelight. "These are not our enemies!" Belli'mar Juraviel shouted at the dragon. "They are To-gai-ru, kin of Brynn Dharielle!"

"Brynn?" more than one man cried, obviously recognizing the name.

"Were you at Dharyan?" the dragon bellowed, and he gave his prisoner another involuntary shake.

"What do you know—" one of the To-gai-ru started to say, but Agradeleous cut him short.

"Were you at Dharyan?" the dragon boomed, so loudly that the roar echoed off into the darkness, so powerfully that his voice hit the speaking To-gai-ru like a mighty wind, forcing him back a step.

"We were there," he replied. "All of us."

"Shut your mouth!" another of the To-gai-ru warriors cried at him. "You'll condemn us to the Wraps!"

"If we were Behrenese, you would already be dead," Juraviel remarked. "But we are not, and if you rode with Brynn Dharielle, then you are no enemies of ours." As he finished, he looked sternly at Agradeleous.

The dragon put the man down and let go of him, and the poor soul stood there for a moment, staring back at the lizard creature. Then he simply fell over.

"Tell us everything," Agradeleous demanded. "A good tale will make me forget that I am hungry for man-flesh!"

The To-gai-ru to whom the dragon spoke blanched so profoundly that his sudden lack of color was clear to Juraviel and Cazzira even in the dim firelight. Juraviel was quick to his side.

"We are not your enemies," the elf said reassuringly. "And perhaps we are your allies. Pray tell us of that awful day, and of Brynn Dharielle, the warrior, my friend."

It took a long while to settle the camp enough for the man and a few of his bolder companions to relate the story of the disaster at Dharyan, and many of the details were sketchy at best, and often contradictory.

But on one point, there was some agreement. Brynn Dharielle had not been slain—not on the battlefield, at least, though none had any idea if the wounds she had taken there had subsequently proved fatal. She had been taken away on that marvelous pony of hers, by Pagonel, the Jhesta Tu mystic, to where, they did not know.

They did confirm, however, that there was a place far to the south, in a rocky, mountainous land, that the Jhesta Tu called home, a retreat called the Walk of Clouds.

"A tale to calm the hunger of a ravenous beast," Juraviel decided, definitively, before Agradeleous could pass any judgment. "Let us beg your forgiveness for our intrusion and the unfortunate confrontation."

"They started it!" Agradeleous protested, and all the men cowered a bit at the power of the voice.

"I pray that your wounds will heal and that we will all soon view this meeting as fortunate—for us, for Brynn Dharielle, and for all of To-gai," the elf went on, ignoring the interruption, and he rose to leave and motioned for his friends to follow.

"Enough of hiding in shadows and hoping the humans will say what we need to hear," Agradeleous said when they had moved back into the darkness away from the camp, his tone showing that he was quite proud of himself. He ended with a wicked chuckle, one that reminded his two companions of the potential catastrophe that was Agradeleous.

Belli'mar Juraviel boldly walked before the dragon, cutting him off. "Never again!" he warned, wagging a finger at the beast.

Agradeleous regarded him with a somewhat bemused expression.

"These are not our enemies—they are the hope of Brynn's destiny, and woe to us all if your violence turns To-gai from us, and from Brynn!"

"They are just humans," Agradeleous said with a mocking laugh. "To-gai-ru, Behrenese—ha! You speak as if there is a difference."

"In this case, there is."

"Only to you, little elf," said the dragon. "To me, they are an amusement and nothing more—unless we are speaking of a meal to warm my belly!"

Juraviel glanced over to see Cazzira giving him a concerned look, and one that showed she certainly understood the dragon's reasoning.

"I have your word on this, Agradeleous," Juraviel reminded. "And I hold you to it."

"Be silent, elf, else I dismiss our compact altogether," the dragon retorted. "They came at me with weapons drawn. Besides yourselves, they are the first creatures to do that and live to reconsider their course. You should be praising me for my restraint."

It took Juraviel a few moments fully to digest the weight of the dragon's remarks, the threat of breaking the compact, the only real assurance that he had that Agradeleous wouldn't rain terror upon the world, terror as profound as that wrought by Bestesbulzibar. And that last statement, he recognized, was really a demand.

"You did well in not killing any," Juraviel conceded.

"I did well in getting the information, something that you have tried and failed to do for weeks and weeks," Agradeleous added.

Juraviel had to admit that they had indeed made progress, discerning a more definitive possibility and path. But he knew, too, the unique nature of this encounter, with a group of rebels out on the empty steppes. They could ill afford any more outbursts from Agradeleous, and they had much more information to gather.

But he had to give Agradeleous this moment, because the dragon wasn't asking, he was demanding.

And Belli'mar Juraviel was keenly aware of the fact that he had no power to refuse any of Agradeleous' demands.

# CHAPTER 24

# *Ancient Enemies*

They crossed the hot desert sands, spear tips and armor glittering in the unrelenting sun. The mounted Chezhou-Lei led the way, with the Jacintha soldiers marching behind. An army of servants, including many To-gai-ru slaves, came behind them, bearing the armor for the elite warriors' horses, and with wagons and wagons of supplies to get the marching force from city to distant city across the empty sands. At the very head of the column rode Wan Atenn, proud and fierce and dwarfing the man, who was no warrior, riding beside him.

Merwan Ma did not really become comfortable with riding throughout all the days of that journey. He had never even been on a horse until Chezru Douan had unexpectedly ordered him to go along and bear witness to the glorious march, a command that had surely stunned him and all of the others at the great temple of Jacintha. Rarely was the Chezru Chieftain's personal attendant allowed outside the temple. He wasn't to go all the way to the Mountains of Fire, though, for the Chezru Chieftain would not take such a gamble with so important a man. Rather, he was to stop at Yatol Peridan's principal city of Gortha, where Peridan's private ship would sail him back to Jacintha.

Merwan Ma tried to make the best of the tedium, attempting to engage Wan Atenn in conversation throughout the days. At first, he had been met with a polite but cold detachment, but when he had finally turned his chatter from exaltations of the glory of the Chezru Chieftain to honest and curious questions about the Chezhou-Lei and their ancient feud with the Jhesta Tu, the proud warrior actually began to respond.

"Once, before the advent of the truth, we were of the same order," Wan Atenn explained one brutally hot day, the caravan barely inching along. "Those who began the order of Chezhou-Lei were masters of the Jhesta Tu."

"But who were the Jhesta Tu in those ancient days?" Merwan Ma asked, for he had little knowledge of this chapter of Behrenese history.

"Priests. Defenders of the secluded villages from the bandits who roamed the lawless land." Wan Atenn looked over at Merwan Ma and nodded. "Yatol gave order to the land, as the ancestors of the Chezhou-Lei understood, but most of the others of the ancient order of Jhesta Tu would not accept the truth of Yatol."

"And so began the feud," Merwan Ma reasoned.

"And so came the dominance of the Chezru and the Chezhou-Lei, with the Jhesta Tu in retreat to a land even less hospitable than the sands of the desert," Wan Atenn replied, his voice the same even and confident tone that the Chezhou-Lei always seemed to possess. "The truth has won out. Every now and then, we of the Chezhou-Lei must remind our foolish brethren of that."

Merwan Ma settled back in the saddle and let it all sink in. He knew that he was out of his element there, so far out, and dwarfed by the prowess of the warriors all about him, and by those they would soon engage in battle. He was excited, surely, but he was also terrified, and a big part of him wanted nothing more than to be back in the safety of Jacintha's temple, beside his master.

When the procession crossed through each of the cities, the citizens inundated them with new supplies, the farriers rushed to reshoe their horses, to polish armor and repair weapons. And when they left, all the air buzzed with the excited whispers of the populace, watching their greatest going to war.

The route from Jacintha to the Mountains of Fire was not straight. The army followed the coast all the way to the southern edge of the kingdom, Peridan's city of Gortha, where Merwan Ma bade the warriors farewell.

Wan Atenn then turned west, marching a zigzag from city to oasis to city, and thus, by the time the rocky black-and-gray mountains were at last in sight, spring had turned to summer.

The ground beneath their feet changed from sand to rocky ground over the next days, and the shadows stretched over them from the mountains in the west earlier each afternoon. The horses were clad in their plated armor, slowing the pace, and the Chezhou-Lei would only allow a march of a few miles each day. They had to stay fresh and ready for battle, so close to the home of the dreaded Jhesta Tu.

Outside a small village under the shadow of the northern edge of the Mountains of Fire, Belli'mar Juraviel and his two companions first overheard word of the march of the Chezhou-Lei and the Behrenese army. The rumors surrounding that march, that a Chezhou-Lei had been slain outside of Dharyan by a Jhesta Tu warrior, brought even more hope to the elf that he might yet find his dear ranger friend still alive, and only made him more anxious than ever to find the way to this elusive place called the Walk of Clouds.

He noticed, though—as he had since he and his companions had left the rebel band on the steppes far to the north—that one of his companions didn't seem to share his enthusiasm for the journey.

Indeed, Agradeleous had come along more hesitantly each day, a pace that had slowed even more once the small cluster of towering and rocky mountains came into view.

"We must find them before this battle is joined," Juraviel remarked that night as the three settled into a camp in a rocky alcove in the foothills of the mountains. "Perhaps in the dark of night, you can assume your natural form, Agradeleous, that we might fly about the mountainsides for sign of the hidden monastery."

"No," the dragon answered, simply and firmly, and both Juraviel and Cazzira turned curious looks his way.

"Are you too far from home?" Juraviel did ask.

Agradeleous didn't answer, other than to give him a skeptical smirk.

"Then what troubles you?" the elf pressed.

Agradeleous narrowed his reptilian eyes threateningly, and Juraviel knew that he should back off this particular subject.

And then it hit him. The dragon feared, or at least held a healthy respect for, the Jhesta Tu mystics. The revelation surprised the elf, but only at first. Certainly, dragons had been slain in the past, usually by mighty gemstone-wielding Abellicans, and several of the battles against marauding dragons waged by the barbarian Alpinadorans in the frozen north were nothing less than legendary.

Agradeleous did not want to openly expose his true form before the walls of the Jhesta Tu monastery; the dragon apparently held the Jhesta Tu in equal esteem to the mightiest Abellicans. That, too, gave Juraviel some hope that Brynn had somehow managed to escape the tragedy of Dharyan alive.

Brynn brushed Runtly in a small and fairly secluded field around the rocks and through a long and boulder-strewn valley from the monastery stairs. The two had just shared a fast and furious ride from the larger fields where the rest of the wild horses roamed, to the small field near a stream so that she could cool down and brush the pony.

Those were the hours of peace for Brynn, the times of absent reflection, of memories of hopes and of her own feelings concerning this very special interlude in her extraordinary life.

She lost herself there, in the small lea, and so, oblivious to her surroundings, she didn't take note of the movement along the rocky borders of the field and was completely surprised when a voice rang out behind her.

"Stand where you are, or die where you are!" came a rough call, in a dialect that Brynn knew to be Behrenese before she ever turned to regard the speaker.

And when she did turn, she paled indeed, for there stood not just one, but a line of warriors—of Chezhou-Lei warriors!

"You wear no sash," the man remarked.

Brynn didn't even hear him, so caught was she by his presence here. For Brynn recognized him from the battle of

Dharyan, from his leap down from the walls when he had killed Ashwarawu.

"Why do you wear no sash, if you are of the Jhesta Tu?" he asked.

Brynn understood that he did not similarly recognize her, and when she thought about it, she realized that it made sense. She was not outfitted for battle; she hadn't worn her beret or even her sword down from the monastery, and in the fight at Dharyan, while she had seen this one so very clearly, he had likely not even noticed her, just another body in the mass of turmoil.

"I am not of the Jhesta Tu," she answered honestly, keenly aware now that other warriors were moving out of the shadows all about her.

"We watched you come down the steps," the man answered.

"I . . . I am visiting there, but am not of their order," Brynn stammered, having no idea of where she should try to guide this unexpected conversation.

"Take her!" the man growled suddenly. "A prisoner to lure the birds from their aerie!"

A rush came at her from behind, and Brynn responded reflexively, without even thinking, dropping low and skittering underneath the pony.

She came up and around to Runtly's back hard, angling her leading arm to deflect a punch heading for her face, then stepping in closer and snapping her head forward, smashing her forehead against the attacking warrior's nose. As he fell back, Brynn drew his sword from under the sash he wore, rushing past him and shoving him all the way down as she did.

She wasn't used to the curving blade, though, and as she tried to parry the slash of another warrior, she barely connected, and at the wrong angle, and his sword slid up and opened a gash between her thumb and her index finger.

Grimacing through the pain, Brynn turned her blade all the way over, forcing the Chezhou-Lei's sword down to the side. Then, instead of retreating, she reached out her left hand and slapped Runtly on the rump, and the pony responded with a kick. It didn't connect fully, just enough to clip the man and send him stumbling away.

Brynn had him dead, easily so, but several others were closing fast. She started for the vulnerable warrior, and the other Chezhou-Lei moved to intercept.

Brynn threw her sword at them, pivoted about, placing her hands on Runtly's rump and, leaping up, fell into place on the pony's back.

He leaped away immediately, cutting to the side at Brynn's command. She ran a short circle, looking for an opening in the shuffling and shifting line of warriors, and then she darted straight out at the initial speaker.

An arrow just missed her head; another one hit hard in Runtly's flank.

The pony stumbled and almost went down, but Brynn tightened her legs on his flanks and urged him on. He caught his balance in a dead gallop, veering to the side, Brynn bending low over his neck, urging him on.

The Chezhou-Lei warriors blocking the way held their ground until the very last second, then two of the three dove aside. The third moved out a single step, lifting his sword, thinking to unhorse the rider as she passed, but Brynn and Runtly were too in harmony for that. Even as the situation unfolded before her, even as the woman thought that she should veer the pony, Runtly was already doing just that.

The Chezhou-Lei warrior didn't even try to abandon the attack, trading the impact from the charging pony for a slash at Brynn. To his credit, he did score a hit as he went flying aside, but there was no momentum behind it, and while the fine sword did open the woman's leather tunic and put a decent gash across her side, as well, she held her seat and galloped away.

Arrows flew after her, another scoring hard on poor Runtly's flank, and then a third.

Tears welled in Brynn's eyes whenever her beloved pony stumbled, but the gallant pony would not stop his run, would not allow the enemy warriors to catch her.

They went down the rocky ravine, coming out onto the stone-filled clearing at the base of the mountainside staircase. As if understanding the course, Runtly brought Brynn to the base of the stairs and pulled up short.

She leaped from the pony's back, turning to attend to him, but he jumped away before she could begin to tend the arrow wounds, running out the other end of the clearing.

Brynn took a step, as if to follow, but she heard the pursuit, coming hard. Only then did the woman appreciate her own stinging wounds. "Run," she whispered at her fleeing pony, and she turned and scrambled up the stairway. She paused and glanced back at Runtly several times, watching him move away, limping, and she thought of going to him.

But then she heard the shouts as the warriors came on in pursuit. Brynn recognized her responsibility here, to the Jhesta Tu, if not to herself, and so she turned and charged up the stairs, driving on, step after step. Weariness overcame her soon after, along with a deep burn in her side. She reached over and brought her hand back covered in bright blood.

She growled away the pain and shook the weariness from her head and drove on, step after step, pressing onward and upward.

She lost all sense of time, and though she heard no pursuit on the stairs behind her, she wouldn't stop, not even to rest. For she felt that if she sat down to rest, she would not find the strength to get back up and go on again. Growling with every step, the young ranger determinedly and doggedly continued, even going down to all fours and crawling up the steep stairs.

Finally, when she thought that she would have to just lie down and let a cool darkness overcome her, Brynn came over the lip of the ascent, to the landing to the side of the arching stone bridge.

She called out, or tried to, then went down to the stone.

She heard the voices all about her in moments, then felt herself lifted into strong and caring arms.

When the world stopped spinning, Brynn found herself lying on a cot in the main house of the monastery. She opened her eyes to see Pagonel and several other Jhesta Tu looking down at her.

"Chezhou-Lei warriors," she said, gasping. "Many of them. In the valley below."

Pagonel's features crinkled up at that, and he slowly turned to regard the old Jhesta Tu master at his side.

"I have brought the blood of war upon us," he said.

"The Chezhou-Lei should not have come," Master Cheyes replied.

"They march to avenge their dead," Pagonel explained, and Cheyes nodded.

"They will not gain the Walk of Clouds," the old master assured Pagonel. "Not if all of Behren marches behind them. No army can overcome our position."

Pagonel didn't disagree, but his expression remained quite troubled nonetheless. He looked back at Brynn. "Rest easy," he said. "We are in no danger up here."

The two masters motioned to the other Jhesta Tu mystics in the room, then walked out side by side.

"They will issue a challenge," Master Cheyes reasoned. "They count upon your pride to force you down there, that they might avenge their fallen."

Pagonel looked at the old man hard, recognizing the critique hidden within his reasoning. Pagonel had gone out, ill-advised, it would seem, and now that same recklessness could lead him down those stairs and into the jaws of the Chezhou-Lei.

"They will appeal to your—to our—honor," Master Cheyes explained. "But there is no honor in useless battle. There is no honor in dying for no cause other than honor."

"I will not succumb to the temptations of pride," Pagonel assured him. "Let the Chezhou-Lei sit out the season, or all of the year, in the dust below."

Master Cheyes nodded, seemingly satisfied, then walked away.

Leaving Pagonel to ponder again the wisdom of his decision to leave the Walk of Clouds and ride along with Ashwarawu. Indeed there was a part of him which felt as if he had betrayed his order by joining in the distant battle. But when he thought of the wonderful young woman lying in the other room, the mystic found his feelings far more ambiguous. If he had not joined with Ashwarawu, then Brynn would undoubtedly have died on the field outside of Dharyan, and then, Pagonel knew, the world would be a darker place.

He looked up to see Master Cheyes walking easily along a row of red and pink flowers, pausing to pick one, then to

move around the corner to offer it, with a smile, to Mistress
Dasa. It all seemed so ordinary and so normal for the Walk of
Clouds.

Pagonel looked down at the Belt of All Colors that he wore
about his waist, a reminder to him that he was without superiors in his order, that his decisions could not be questioned—
by anyone but him.

And when he looked back to the door of the room
where lay Brynn Dharielle, Pagonel knew that he had chosen
correctly.

Two days later, a lone figure stalked up the five-thousand-
step approach to the Walk of Clouds. He wore the helm of a
Chezhou-Lei warrior, though he had left his other gear far behind, carrying only a waterskin and the white flag of truce.

"I would speak with the Jhesta Tu who fought at Dharyan,
if he is here," the man announced. "And with the master of
this den if he is not."

Master Cheyes and Mistress Dasa stood beside Pagonel on
the bridge, looking down at the lone warrior. "I believe he is
referring to you," Cheyes said, offering a hint of a smile.

Pagonel, his expression grim, stepped forward. "You will
speak with both," he told the man. "For I am just that, a master of the Walk of Clouds and he who rode with Ashwarawu
against Dharyan."

"Was that your place, mystic?" the warrior spat with obvious derision.

"Is this a debate you wish to hold openly, here and now?"

That seemed to catch the man off guard a bit, reminding
him of his position here as an emissary. "No debate," he
stammered after a moment. "Your actions cannot be excused
or explained. You did battle against Chezhou-Lei, unprovoked and without reason. My master, Wan Atenn, demands
retribution, and so it will be gotten."

"Indeed," said Pagonel. "And so you name the protection
of my friend from a murderous Chezhou-Lei as unwarranted?"
He paused and let that sink in, though he understood that the
reasoning would hold no weight with the vicious Chezhou-
Lei. Their journey there had been more based on the excuse

of Pagonel's fight outside Dharyan than in any true retribution for a wrong committed, the mystic understood. Likely, the leaders of the Chezhou-Lei order had been thrilled to find this reason to go into battle against their hated ancient enemies, especially since the situation in To-gai had so calmed.

"Does your master wish to do battle with me, then?" the mystic calmly asked.

"Your attack was Jhesta Tu against Chezhou-Lei," the man replied, confirming to Pagonel his reasoning concerning all of this. "It is order against order and not man against man. Assemble your warriors and come down to the valley floor, that we might engage in honorable battle, and let this be decided!"

"We are not warriors of the heart, young Chezhou-Lei," Pagonel replied. "Go and tell your leader that your journey here has been in vain, for we will not leave the Walk of Clouds and it would be beyond folly for you to try to overtake us. And think not of any siege, though it would be amusing to watch your army sitting day after week after month down in the arid valley, for we are quite self-sufficient."

"You will come down," the Chezhou-Lei warrior retorted immediately, his sudden confidence raising the mystic's suspicions. "Your reticence was not unanticipated. We have gathered all the To-gai-ru people of three nearby villages, and will begin their executions in the morning, one each day until you come down." With that, the man bowed and turned about and started down the steps, leaving a very stunned and very confused Pagonel standing there on the bridge, staring.

Master Cheyes walked up and put a hand on the man's shoulder.

"How badly have I erred?" Pagonel asked.

"You followed your vision, so there can be no error. That is the edict of our understanding. You wear the Belt of All Colors, honestly earned, and so you must follow that which is in your heart, whatever the consequences."

"The consequences to me or to all of our brethren?"

"To both," Cheyes answered. "Your vision and fate has brought this battle to us, but would not the Chezhou-Lei have come anyway, once they came to understand that your heart lies with the To-gai-ru in the struggle against the Yatols? Surely the present incarnation of the Chezru Chieftain has shown a fondness for conquest, and so why would we believe that we are exempt? Perhaps this fight is a better manner of defense for us than if all the Behrenese legions had joined their elite warriors in coming against the Walk of Clouds."

"Then you believe that we are to fight."

"It would seem the proper thing to do," said Master Cheyes.

That afternoon, a Jhesta Tu mystic ran down the steps toward the valley floor, taking a measure of the gathered Chezhou-Lei, then ran back up to report their numbers. The three masters of the Walk of Clouds didn't want to send the whole of the Jhesta Tu down to do battle, though every mystic had expressed a desire to go. But the masters, who had to look ahead beyond the immediate situation, knew that the order had to be preserved, whatever the outcome down below.

As did one other. "This is as much my fight as it is yours," Brynn protested when she learned that she would not be included in the battle. Her wounds had healed already—a testament to the power of the powrie beret and also the fine tending of the Jhesta Tu—and she seemed more than ready to jump back into battle.

"It is not," Pagonel answered curtly.

"You were defending me!"

The mystic chuckled. "The fight outside of Dharyan has nothing to do with this," he explained. "It is an excuse, and nothing more, to begin a battle that has been ongoing for centuries, before Brynn Dharielle ever saw her first sunrise, and one that will continue long after you have viewed your last sunset."

"I can fight as well as most . . ." she started to protest.

"As well as any, excepting myself, Cheyes, and Dasa," the mystic conceded with a smile.

But that smile did not disarm Brynn, not at that time. "Then let me go and fight beside you," she said. "I have studied here through the weeks."

"You are not Jhesta Tu," Pagonel replied. "You could be—perhaps someday you will desire to be. But you are only a visitor here at this time, and so this fight is not your own. And, I fear, any engagement that you have in it will likely hamper your own goals. Have you so forgotten those that you will willingly go down against are the mightiest adversaries that the Chezru Chieftain can offer?"

Brynn stiffened her jaw, wanting so badly to defy that simple logic.

Seventy-five mystics did leave the Walk of Clouds soon after, led by Master Cheyes and Master Pagonel, with Matron Dasa looking on from the bridge, Brynn Dharielle standing beside her.

Brynn Dharielle moved off from Mistress Dasa, allowing her anger and frustration, and particularly her desire to be alone, to show clearly. She understood Pagonel's reasoning for excluding her from the battle, and even agreed with it, based on that reasoning. But that gave her little solace, watching these friends she had recently come to know walking down into severe danger . . .

And so the stubborn young lady, the same little girl who had so often found ways around the strict edicts of the Touel'alfar, took the literal meaning of Pagonel's command to heart. This was not her battle, but that didn't mean that she couldn't watch it! She kept her head down, seeming distressed, until the gathered mystics filtered away, then she took up her bow and her sword and gear, and rushed to the steps, running down from on high.

By the time she neared the rocky valley floor, Brynn saw the two sides squaring off—and it seemed to her as if her friends were at a sore disadvantage indeed! For the Jhesta Tu stood in a long line, evenly spaced and each holding a long spear, while across from them loomed the Chezhou-Lei, armored as the mystics were not, and mounted! How could Pagonel offer so large an advantage to his deadly adversaries as to allow the battle to go forth with the invading warriors on horseback?

Brynn started to mouth a few choice curses, but the words were lost in her throat as the Chezhou-Lei warriors erupted into their thunderous charge, a hundred strong steeds rumbling the valley floor. As one, the Jhesta Tu fell into a defensive crouch, setting their spears appropriately.

Brynn just bit her lip and winced; any skilled rider could take his mount outside the reach of those spears, or take the spear out wide with a feint, veer suddenly, and simply run over the stationary mystic.

In came the Chezhou-Lei, their fabulous swords of wrapped metal spinning up high.

Brynn winced so much that she nearly closed her eyes and missed the spectacle as the Jhesta Tu mystics, again moving as if of a singular mind, exploded into a sudden, whirling motion, bringing their spears up, around, and over, reversing their grips as they firmly set the tips against the stone, even as the horses closed, then leaped up high, the spears bending under their weight, then straightening, lifting the mystics over the front of the charging line!

A few Chezhou-Lei managed to alter their outstretched swords to bring them to bear, mostly ineffectively. A few more reacted quickly enough to veer their mounts out of the line of the flying, kicking mystics. But most caught a Jhesta Tu in the face, literally, and in a few chaotic moments, the valley floor became littered with Jhesta Tu mystics and fallen Chezhou-Lei warriors, with riderless horses milling all about.

Then they were up, both sides, rushing about in sudden and furious battle. Brynn couldn't even keep up with it, with the flash of a hundred swords, the swing of a hundred fists and a hundred kicks, the stab of a hundred spears. She tuned her vision more narrowly, picking Pagonel out of the crowd.

He had taken his rider down cleanly and slid off the passing horse at precisely the correct angle to land with his knee firmly planted into the prostrated man's throat. And then he came up hard, swinging a kick at another Chezhou-Lei as the man tried to rise, laying him low. He sprinted away suddenly, leaving the second fallen warrior to one of his brethren, for off to the side, another of the mystics was in dire need.

Brynn winced, as did Pagonel, as that mystic fell away beneath a crimson spray of his own blood, taken down by the sword of a rider who had not been dismounted.

Brynn knew that rider! She had seen him kill Ashwarawu!

Pagonel charged straight in, leaping high in a full forward somersault, coming around and over with both legs kicking, one to deflect the warrior's attempt to stab him, the other to kick the man hard in the side, nearly dislodging him. The mystic twisted as he followed through, and grabbed on, pulling himself in close to the man, too close for that sword to come to bear.

But the warrior was no novice to battle, and any advantage that Brynn believed her friend had attained was whisked away almost immediately, as a heavy gauntlet smashed into Pagonel's face.

The horse reared under the confusing commands of the struggle, and leaped away, running opposite from Brynn, down the line of continuing battle.

That melee held Brynn's attention then, and her heart leaped, for the Jhesta Tu mystics, with that brilliant initial strike, were fast gaining an advantage.

She looked back to the far end of the line, to see Pagonel and the Chezhou-Lei tumble from the mount, falling hard, out of her view behind a boulder. Despite her agreement to stay out of the fighting, Brynn sprinted away, circumventing the main battle to find her fallen friend.

They stood opposite each other atop a chest-high flat boulder, far to the side of the main fighting.

"I know you," the Chezhou-Lei warrior sneered, his eyes narrowing to threatening slits. "We meet again, mystic."

Pagonel, his arm sorely stung from the fall to the rocks, backed away a step, then brought his hands up together before him, dipping a respectful bow. "I am Master Pagonel," he said. "I would have your name."

"My name before you feel the sting of my sword," his opponent promised. "I am Wan Atenn. Know that my eyes are the last thing you will ever see!" And with that, the fierce warrior came on, his sword spinning up above his head, then chopping suddenly, a shortened blow that Pagonel easily backed away from, and then a quick retraction back up, a short step forward, and a second, more deliberate strike coming in at a downward diagonal for Pagonel's shoulder.

The mystic, moving in perfect balance, could have backed away again, but he decided against that course in the blink of an eye. He found his life energy, that potent, unstoppable line, and focused it into his left arm, then snapped his arm up above him, blocking the blow as surely as if he had used a metal shield.

He came forward inside the blow, firing off a right jab into Wan Atenn's chest, his fist thudding hard against the overlapping armor. But the blow didn't have any Chi behind it, for Pagonel's energy had to hold firm against the powerful sword. While Wan Atenn did stagger back a step, he wasn't really hurt.

The fierce Chezhou-Lei came on again, slashing his sword across, and Pagonel flipped a somersault right over the blade, then skittered out to the side before the warrior could reverse with a deadly backhand.

Or at least, he started to.

Wan Atenn's sword came flashing back, and Pagonel dropped suddenly, right below it, then came up fast, launching a series of punches at his adversary, and taking a left hook on the shoulder and a kick to the knee in response from the skilled Chezhou-Lei.

The two fell back defensively, then came on again, like powerful mountain rams crashing together, head to head. They exchanged hits and kicks, and Wan Atenn drew first real blood, scoring a minor hit across Pagonel's upper arm with his fine sword, but taking a punch to the face in return that nearly dropped him to the stone.

"You fight well," Pagonel congratulated.

"Spare me your worthless insults, dog!" the Chezhou-Lei cried, and in he crashed again.

After another vicious flurry, the two fell back, and Pagonel looked on curiously as a wry grin spread over Wan Atenn's dark face. The Chezhou-Lei started forward, but stopped suddenly.

Pagonel sensed the movement behind him, and knowing

his terrain perfectly, he instinctively leaped up, tucking his legs under him, spinning as he went.

The slash from the second Chezhou-Lei, standing beside the boulder behind Pagonel, missed cleanly, but the mystic knew that it hardly mattered, that the distraction was a fatal turn against the imposing Wan Atenn.

Indeed, as Pagonel came down, Wan Atenn leaped ahead, his sword held in two hands over his head, aimed for a strike that could not miss, that could not be blocked by the mystic, and that could not fail.

The Chezhou-Lei roared in victory, coming in strong.

And then he got hit, and hit hard, across that face, the blow staggering him to the side, dropping him headlong off the boulder. He thought it was a punch, and only realized as he fell away that he had been shot with an arrow.

"Scold me not about honor!" Brynn Dharielle cried, drawing out her sword and leaping atop the boulder beside Pagonel.

"Scold you?" the mystic yelled right back, leaping down onto the newest opponent, driving the Chezhou-Lei back with a series of snap kicks and short punches. "I was going to thank you! I will scold you for coming down here after all is through!"

The Chezhou-Lei warrior turned and ran off, and Pagonel went in fast pursuit, back toward the main fighting.

Brynn started to follow, but heard the movement behind her and realized that Wan Atenn, the man who had killed Ashwarawu, was not yet dead.

So she waited, her back to him, baiting him up onto the rock.

Then, as he leaped up at her, she spun about, Flamedancer slashing hard against his thrusting sword, turning it harmlessly aside. Brynn had to shake away her distraction, though, for her arrow remained in place, stuck through Wan Atenn's cheek, half-buried into his face!

"Do you remember me as well?" Brynn asked, falling into her proper *bi'nelle dasada* stance, her lead, right foot perpendicular to the anchoring left, her right arm extended, slightly bent at the elbow, and her left arm bent out and up behind her. Perfectly balanced.

"Should I?" the Chezhou-Lei replied, his voice slurred and barely decipherable, for he could hardly move his torn jaw. "You are no Jhesta Tu, but merely a cowardly dog who shoots from afar!"

"And stabs from in close!" Brynn corrected, coming forward with a suddenness that surely surprised the warrior. He spun his sword in to intercept, but was too late, and fell back a step at the end of Brynn's vicious blade.

Wan Atenn tried to keep the growl of pain from his throat. He wanted to hurl another insult the diminutive woman's way, but he didn't dare to speak, didn't dare show her how profoundly her stinging thrust had stolen away his breath.

He found his balance, though, and his breath, and came on with sudden ferocity, his sword working marvelous circles side to side, up over his head, even around his back, working from hand to hand, stabbing out and retracting suddenly, only to flash back in at a different angle.

But Brynn, with her forward-and-back balance of the elven sword dance, stayed out of reach, and realized almost immediately that her style was superior, that the Chezhou-Lei, for all his skill, was moving in ways that *bi'nelle dasada* could surely defeat. He was better than Dee'Dahk, but he fought in the exact same style. And that style, with weapons spinning up high and to the side, had little defense against the snap thrusts of *bi'nelle dasada*.

The ranger held her countering thrusts, wanting to find the best opportunity to score a single, fatal hit.

"You would be less impressive without an arrow sticking through your jaw," she did say, if only to spur the already wild warrior on even more viciously.

Let him make one mistake . . .

The scene before him was surely one of misery, of men and women writhing in agony or clashing together like rabid animals, but Pagonel was neither surprised nor deterred.

He kept up the chase of the Chezhou-Lei, and when that man crossed past a comrade, who turned to engage the charging mystic, Pagonel simply leaped over the two of them, spinning as he descended to catch his primary opponent in a headlock, landing and snapping his arms down hard.

The crunch of bone in the man's neck did bring a grimace to Pagonel's face, but hardly distracted him. He stepped back suddenly, ahead of the other's thrusting blade, and that second Chezhou-Lei, knowing he was overmatched against this supreme Jhesta Tu master, backed steadily.

Pagonel did not follow. He turned and sprinted to the side, to join Master Cheyes, to anchor the Jhesta Tu line. A score of mystics were down, some obviously dead, but more than fifty were still fighting, against only around half that number of Chezhou-Lei.

The battle seemed in hand, and the Jhesta Tu masters nodded to each other grimly, with satisfaction.

But then the teeyodel horns began to blow, and the charge of soldiers, hundreds of soldiers, began—the Jacintha garrison moving hard to encircle the mystics, and to cut off the escape route to the stairs.

Pagonel and Cheyes saw it immediately, and called for a retreat to those stairs, with each going to a nearby wounded companion, scooping him up, and starting the retreat.

But Pagonel looked all about and knew the truth: they wouldn't make it.

To an onlooker, their movements would seem nothing more than a furious blur of wild energy, with the Chezhou-Lei's sword spinning like the fans of a favored Behrenese toy, rocking back and forth in front of him, warding away the sudden, and ultimately efficient, thrusts from the elven-trained warrior.

Brynn kept every strike measured, confident that she could defeat the man, that he, with his heavier blade and more exaggerated movements, would have to tire before she did. As soon as that magnificent curving blade of his slowed, she would find her opening, thrusting her fine and slender sword through to a seam in his armor, and into his chest.

But not yet, not until she had him worn down enough that she could be certain he would not, in the last moments of his life when her sword was inside of him, score a wicked hit against her. She thrust in measured strikes and skittered back, always turning, turning, to keep enough of the large and flat boulder behind her for her next retreat.

She scored a stinging hit on Wan Atenn's forearm, then another into the opposite shoulder, but those strikes only seemed to spur the man on even more ferociously.

Yes, it was moving along exactly as Brynn desired.

And Wan Atenn recognized that, as well, and then he surprised the young warrior woman, for as she retracted her blade after one teasing thrust, beginning yet another short retreat, the Chezhou-Lei performed a brilliant spinning charge, his feet stepping and turning in perfect balance, his sword going around in a complete circuit along with his torso.

Brynn saw an open stab at the man's back, and knew she could inflict a serious, perhaps even fatal, wound. But she knew, too, that Wan Atenn accepted that inevitability, and that she was out of room to retreat, so suddenly. As hard as she might stick him, that terrible Chezhou-Lei blade, worn from years of battle—and that wearing only making the remaining wrapped metal even sharper—would come around, and hard!

So Brynn stayed her hand, refusing the opening, and brought her blade in front of her vertically instead.

Around and ahead came the warrior, his rushing, horizontal sword meeting Brynn's weapon at midblade, forcing Brynn's sword backward, forcing Brynn to bend backward. With the new angle, Wan Atenn's blade slid up above Brynn's head, locking both swords.

But Wan Atenn, heavier than Brynn by a hundred pounds, was more than willing to force the contest into a close-in battle of strength. He bulled ahead, holding back her sword with his own, his left hand coming up to launch a devastating punch.

But then Brynn's blade erupted into blazing fire, and the Chezhou-Lei warrior halted, even fell back a bit as he threw the punch.

And Brynn came forward and down, lifting her left hand up and around to grab the hilt beside her right, and to get her pulsing powrie shield up to block the punch.

The woman went forward more, pressing hard against the unyielding Chezhou-Lei blade, and then she dipped, just a bit, and her blade tip slipped free, and all the momentum from the hold shot it forward and down, creasing the helm of Wan Atenn, splitting the man's skull and driving down deeper. She even felt it crack through the shaft of the arrow that was still stuck in the stubborn warrior's face.

Brynn let the sword's fires flicker out, and saw the Chezhou-Lei's hateful eyes staring back at her, from either side of her blade.

The light disappeared from those dark orbs.

Before she could even consider how she might extract her blade from the split skull, Brynn heard movement behind her, and knew she was helpless.

The remaining Chezhou-Lei were more than happy to pull back from the slaughter, stumbling and scrambling to the waiting ranks of the circling Jacintha soldiers.

Pagonel and Master Cheyes worked furiously to organize their remaining fighters in defensive positions about the wounded. There was no way they could hope to get to the stairs, no way they could hope to get out of the tightening ring of spears and swords.

"And so the Chezhou-Lei refuse to do battle fairly," Master Cheyes remarked with obvious disgust. "And so I am not surprised! But history is written by the victors," he lamented, "and so our fall will be spoken of as a grand Chezhou-Lei victory!"

"Brynn will bear witness," Pagonel said grimly. "She must."

Brynn yanked and spun, bringing her sword to bear, but it drooped as her jaw inevitably dropped.

"Juraviel," she gasped. "Cazzira."

And then she nearly fell over altogether as another familiar face, this one of a terrible foe, rose up between the pair. She knew that face, unmistakably, though when last she had looked upon the mighty dragon, that head had been ten times as large.

"Come, and be quick!" Juraviel cried out to her. "The Behrenese soldiers have your companions trapped!" He motioned for Brynn to move between him and Cazzira, while the dragon turned about.

"Right onto his shoulders," the Doc'alfar instructed, and Brynn, after a single incredulous look, lifted one leg and then the other over Agradeleous' strong shoulders, and with pushing from both elves, fell into a seated position atop the humanoid creature.

Almost immediately, Agradeleous began to change, began to grow, and though the dragon fell to all fours, Brynn did not slip lower toward the ground. Cazzira leaped atop the growing beast behind her.

In moments, Brynn Dharielle found herself astride a full-sized dragon, straddling its neck!

"How are we . . ." Brynn stammered. "What . . ."

"There is a time for chatter, and this is not it!" Juraviel explained from the ground, and he held Brynn's bow aloft, then leaped up, his small wings bringing him to Cazzira's side behind the still-stunned ranger. "Many soldiers have come against your friends, and without help they are surely doomed!"

"Die bravely and try to find a Chezhou-Lei to take with you to the afterlife!" Pagonel told his warriors as the ring of enemies, hundreds of skilled soldiers, closed in.

The Jacintha soldiers lifted their spears and swords and cried out to charge, but even as that communal howl began, it was drowned out by a single voice, as mighty a roar as the world of Corona had ever heard.

Agradeleous the dragon swooped past, a line of his fiery breath immolating the Behrenese line that was blocking the mystics from the stairs to their mountain home.

Brynn sat astride the neck, her own fiery sword held high, while Juraviel fired off his own bow behind her, taking down yet another surprised and horrified Jacintha soldier.

Any in the Behrenese line whose legs did not freeze in sheer terror beneath them, broke ranks and fled. Pagonel and Master Cheyes, not taking the moment to question the unexpected turn, gathered their warriors and collected up their wounded and rushed for the stairs. Pagonel and Master Cheyes fell behind the retreat, ready to do battle with any soldiers or Chezhou-Lei coming in pursuit.

But none were. The Behrenese fled before the wrath of the dragon, before the fiery glory that was mighty Agradeleous.

The dragon banked a steep turn and came in hard again, a second fiery blast melting down more soldiers. He caught yet another man in one powerful claw, lifting him from the ground and crushing the life from him, and swept aside several more with his crushing tail.

And so began the day of horrors for the fleeing Behrenese, pursued from on high by the mighty beast and his three riders.

Some soldiers got out of the area, but Agradeleous came in pursuit, and when the startled villagers that had been rounded up by the fierce Chezhou-Lei spotted the confusion and the dragon, they too cried out in terror and began to flee.

"Not the villagers!" Juraviel and Cazzira, and then Brynn cried out repeatedly to the dragon, and it seemed to Brynn as if it took the mighty beast a long while to turn away from the tempting sight of the fleeing mob.

"Fly over them, but bring no harm!" Juraviel instructed, and then he yelled to Brynn, "Tell them who you are! Tell them to take heart, for Brynn Dharielle, the Dragon of To-gai, has come to free them!"

Thus was the legend born.

After shouting her message of freedom to the escaping villagers Brynn directed the mighty dragon to settle near a brown-and-white figure she had seen from on high. She slid down and hurried to her pony, whom she had feared mortally wounded. As she inspected Runtly, though, she breathed a profound sigh of relief, for the stings of the Chezhou-Lei arrows were not serious.

"We are not done with our work," Belli'mar Juraviel called to her, and she turned to see him and Cazzira standing beside an obviously anxious Agradeleous.

Brynn looked back to her pony. "I will come back to you soon and clean those wounds better," she whispered to him. "You just run to the open fields and stay far from danger!"

As if he understood her every word, the pony nickered and galloped away, and it did Brynn's heart good to see him run.

Much later on, after many, many Behrenese soldiers and Chezhou-Lei had been hunted down and killed, Agradeleous, bearing his three riders, pulled up before the bridge at the Walk of Clouds, hanging there for a moment with his great wings beating, as Brynn slipped down to stand before Masters Cheyes and Pagonel, with many others standing in the background, gawking.

Without any hesitation, and without a word from either of the remaining riders, Agradeleous turned and swooped down into the clouds, disappearing from view.

Pagonel started to say something to Brynn, but he just stopped and stood there helplessly, his arms out to the side. And what might be expected of him, after all, since he had just witnessed the arrival of three of the legendary—and, many would argue, imaginary—races of Corona, including the sheer size and power of a dragon!

"I was trained by the Touel'alfar," Brynn stated at once. She held forth her beautiful sword. "And this is elvenmade, forged in the distant valley of Andur'blough Inninness, north of the great mountains. One of my companions is of the Touel'alfar, another is a cousin, a Doc'alfar, and the third . . . well, you have seen the third."

"All in the region have seen the third, dear Brynn," said Master Cheyes, managing a little smile. "Our gratitude is with you this day, for the treachery of the Chezhou-Lei would have brought even more tragedy to the Walk of Clouds had it not been for you and your . . . friends."

"Nearly a score of my brethren are dead," Pagonel added. "And many more are wounded, some badly. But all of us who went down to do honorable battle would have died this day, had it not been for the arrival of the dragon."

"I count the Behrenese losses in the hundreds," the woman replied. "Including nearly all of the Chezhou-Lei who came against you. It is a great victory."

"Victory?" Master Cheyes echoed skeptically. "We do not view war of any kind as a victory, dear Brynn, but as a loss for all of mankind."

Brynn steeled her jaw, not about to agree. "Yet war lies in my path, undoubtedly so," she declared. "And I go with my heart full of hope that my homeland will be free once more. The arrival of the dragon, and of my other two friends, gives me the beginning I will need to drive the Behrenese from the steppes."

"Beware the power of your dragon," Master Cheyes gravely warned.

"More important than the companions are the reputation that they have allowed me this day," Brynn explained, not wavering in the least. "All of the To-gai-ru who witnessed the flight of the Dragon of To-gai will whisper to their fellows, and so the news shall spread throughout the steppes, and so I shall find many, many warriors willing to rush to my side!"

"Many of whom will die," the pacifistic Master Cheyes pointed out.

But again, Brynn was not to be deterred, not in the least. "Then so be it."

Master Cheyes looked to Pagonel then. The other Jhesta Tu did not return the stare, but kept his eyes locked on the remarkable Brynn.

"My time here has come to an end," the woman announced.

"This stay, perhaps," said Pagonel. "The future may hold a day when you, and I, might return to the Walk of Clouds, to study together as we try to make sense of this existence."

His words had Brynn's jaw dropping open, and had Master Cheyes closing his eyes tightly, as if wanting to deny them.

"You will come with me?"

Pagonel nodded. "This is my course, I do not doubt, though neither do I understand. But if you and your friends will have me, then yes, I will stand beside you."

"When I walk into Dharyan," said Brynn.

# PART FOUR

---

# THE DRAGON
# OF TO-GAI

*When first I encountered Agradeleous in his cavern lair, I recognized, or thought I had, the power of the beast. The mere sight of the dragon froze me in my tracks, for a moment at least. I have seen volcanoes and mighty rivers, wild hailstorms on the open steppes, and heard—felt!—the thunder of a buffalo herd charging through the grasses. In all these things I am reminded of the sheer power of the world around us, dwarfing us in our hopes and dreams.*

*So it is with Agradeleous. He is a volcano, a flood, an earthquake, a catastrophe of the highest order, and unbelievably, his power has been given to me! That Juraviel even managed to make such a friend boggles my sensibilities.*

*With Agradeleous has come hope, so say the elves. Upon his back, I can fly the length of the steppes in but a day or two, gathering my armies, inspiring them with the knowledge that they will travel into combat against the hated Behrenese behind the power of a dragon. Is any outposter settlement too great a fortress for us now?*

*Is Dharyan? Is Jacintha itself?*

*But there is another side to the lucky coin that is Agradeleous the dragon. Is his a power truly leashed, truly under my control?*

*I have sought out my answers in Oracle, but have found nothing more than the reminder of my murdered parents. I feel their anger keenly, more at the loss of our old ways than at the particular injustices they suffered. At Oracle, I am convinced more than ever that the ancient traditions of the To-gai-ru must be returned to the steppes, that we cannot tolerate our subjugation to the Chezru Chieftain and his Yatols.*

*Still, I cannot dismiss this power I have been given, this awesome and awful responsibility. Agradeleous will heed to my commands, so said Belli'mar Juraviel. But in those terrible minutes after the ranks of Behrenese had broken, when the dragon went in pursuit with the three of us riding, I understood that Agradeleous truly follows only the commands of Agradeleous. How he blasted through the ranks of the fleeing Behrenese, with his fiery breath and his raking claws, his snapping maw and that crushing tail!*

*I fear what I might see if ever I allow Agradeleous to run loose against a Behrenese city. Will the dragon distinguish between soldier and civilian? Between man and child?*

*And so I have been given a choice, and it is one that surely tugs at my heart. With Agradeleous, I can take great strides toward my long-desired goal. Flying high across the To-gai sky atop the great beast, I can give my people a rallying point, using my own reputation as the "Dragon of To-gai" to give them hope and a focus. Who would not stand behind me?*

*And then I can watch the death and the misery of Agradeleous unleashed. I can turn my head and block my ears, but not my heart, to the screams of the innocents as the dragon fire immolates them. I can watch the outposter settlements burn, perhaps even the great cities of western Behren, burn.*

*Agradeleous is not invulnerable, by the words of Juraviel. An army prepared for the dragon might bring it down.*

*There is within me a small part that might hope for such a thing, after the To-gai-ru have rallied, after enough victories are secured so that the Behrenese will not return to our land. For what might Agradeleous do after the fighting is ended? When and if To-gai is free, what am I then to do with the dragon?*

*For his is a power, I fear, that, once unleashed, cannot be put back in its hole. It is possible that I will lead an army against Agradeleous if I somehow achieve victory over Behren, and that is not a prospect that I enjoy entertaining.*

*Like the Touel'alfar as a whole, Belli'mar Juraviel has brought me hope, but that hope lies along a path made even darker by the prospects of this new and magnificent weapon. Many times during our journey south did Belli'mar Juraviel warn me that to pursue my victory would mean steeling myself to the horrors of war.*

*Agradeleous merely accentuates that point.*

*I pray for strength.*

—Brynn Dharielle

# CHAPTER 25

## *The Walkaway*

Kaliit Timig sat in a darkened room, alone with his thoughts, his guilt, as he had been for most days since the return of the few Chezhou-Lei who had survived the disaster at the Mountains of Fire, and the few dozen Jacintha soldiers who had escaped and who had not subsequently deserted in the wild southland.

All had spoken of a sudden turn in the battle, of the arrival of a dragon, ridden by a warrior woman wielding a flaming sword!

A dragon! Whoever had heard of such a thing? Certainly there were tales of such creatures, the great wurms of legend, but never had any dragon been known actually to take a side in a conflict!

It was all too much for Kaliit Timig to comprehend, or to accept. He was convinced that the beast had been a manifestation of Jhesta Tu magic; the mystics were known for such powers, though never as dramatically as this. The returning Chezhou-Lei had reported that none of the mystic line that had stood against them had shown any indications of any magic use, nor any gemstones, though the hated Jhesta Tu were known to possess a few of those, as well.

Perhaps their greatest wizards had remained high above the conflict, Kaliit Timig reasoned, combining their powers to create the beast, or the illusion of the beast.

Whatever the case, the disaster could not be denied. His vaunted order had been cut in half in one day, with scores of superbly trained warriors, the best in all of Behren, perhaps in all the world, cut down in that barren wasteland. That was his burden, and many times, the old Chezhou-Lei Kaliit had thought it more than he could possibly shoulder. How badly had he erred, how great a failure was his reign as the Kaliit of the elite and ancient order.

He heard the shake of the door chimes outside his chamber, but didn't let it take him from his profound contemplations. He heard the door open, but wouldn't open his eyes and thus, did not see the light filtering into the darkened room.

"Kaliit Timig," came a call, a voice that he could not ignore, no matter how great his desire to be alone. He slowly opened his eyes and turned his head, to see the silhouette of a familiar figure standing in the doorway.

"God-Voice," he welcomed.

"How many more weeks will you spend in here, Kaliit?" Chezru Chieftain Douan asked bluntly. "Hiding away while your order tries to find some way to recover from the catastrophe."

"This disaster is unprecedented," Timig answered softly. "I know not where to turn my attention now. I meditate for guidance."

"You cower in the dark," Douan accused, and behind the Chezru Chieftain there came a gasp, which Kaliit Timig knew to be the surprise of Merwan Ma, Douan's ever-present attendant, who had so conveniently turned away from the army before the disaster.

"I seek to guide my order properly, and nothing more," Timig answered with as much conviction as he could muster.

Chezru Douan laughed at him. "You would have led all of your order to complete destruction if I had not intervened and forced you to hold some of your warriors back. Where would the Chezhou-Lei be now if all of you had gone marching to your destruction in that forsaken land of rock and fire? And for what, Kaliit Timig? To avenge the death of a single Chezhou-Lei, killed in open and honest battle?"

The old Kaliit bowed his head again, having no resolve to fight back against the God-Voice. For indeed, the guilt was there, all about him, like the black wings of despair. There was no escape from it, not out there, trying to rebuild that which was lost, nor in here, hiding in the darkness from the truth.

"You know that many of the remaining Chezhou-Lei seek answers, of course," Chezru Douan remarked offhandedly. "And many others vow revenge and hope that you will send them all off on a journey to the Mountains of Fire."

That last bit brought Timig's head swinging up again to stare at Douan. Perhaps that was the course. To avenge the dead by eliminating the wretched Jhesta Tu altogether! "If you would lend me your army, I could turn defeat into a great victory," he dared to say.

Again came that mocking laughter. "Victory?" Douan asked incredulously. "Victory over whom? The Jhesta Tu? But they are not enemies of mine, nor of Behren, unless they have begun a march of which I am not aware."

"A Jhesta Tu mystic fought at Dharyan, against Yatol Grysh," said Timig. "And that same mystic was back at the Walk of Clouds, engaging in battle, according to those who have returned. Surely that—"

"Means nothing to me," Chezru Douan finished. "The Jhesta Tu are better left in their mountain home, unbothered and unbothering. I'll not awaken the dragon, Kaliit Timig. That, I believe, is more your manner of leading."

Timig squinted against the sting of those words.

"Perhaps I erred in sending my twenty-square behind your warriors," Chezru Douan admitted, but he retracted the words immediately, for it would not do for one who spoke directly to Yatol to make such mistakes. "But then again, had I not sent the soldiers, then none of your Chezhou-Lei would have escaped, and common soldiers are far more easily replaced than are your elite warriors.

"And so it sits fully with you, Kaliit Timig," Douan remarked. "I allowed you your folly, though it was against that which I knew to be true, because of your insistence that honor be upheld, whatever the cost. What is the honorable course for you now, I wonder? You have failed in your capacity, of that there can be no doubt. Do you believe that you should continue to lead the remaining Chezhou-Lei? Or are you too

much a coward to take the only honorable course before
you?"

Again came that gasp from behind him, Merwan Ma apparently as stunned by the heartless words as was the Kaliit.

Chezru Douan merely chuckled again and exited, slowly
closing the door behind him.

Kaliit Timig sat there for a long while, the God-Voice's
words mingling with his own demons of guilt, all of it together taking his gaze inevitably toward the beautifully
crafted curving sword that sat on a decorated stand at the side
of the room.

Hardly even noticing the movement, the battered old man
went to the sword and stared at it hard. Even in the dim light,
its blade seemed to gleam with strength. Timig reached his
hand up to feel the cool metal, wrapped a thousand times over
itself. His was an ancient sword, passed down through the
warrior generations, and so it had seen many, many battles,
wearing away the top layers, making its edge even finer.

Kaliit Timig held the blade up before him horizontally,
studying the intricate runes carved in the metal.

He looked back to the door once, considering the words of
the God-Voice and knowing that they rang with truth.

Kaliit Timig walked back to the center of the room, placed
the butt of his magnificent sword on the floor, then propped
the razor-sharp tip against the hollow of his breast. He had
failed; he could not deny it any longer, nor could he hope to
redeem himself within the Chezhou-Lei order.

With a nod, the man let himself fall forward.

News of Kaliit Timig's death reached Chom Deiru the next
day, and did not surprise the Chezru Chieftain in the least. In
fact, Douan was quite pleased by the turn of events, for this
suicide would allow him to continue to lay the blame in whole
upon Timig's shoulders.

That was all that he truly cared about at that time. Since the
disaster at the Mountains of Fire, several of the Yatols overseeing the surrounding areas had been sending screaming
emissaries to Jacintha, pleading for more soldiers in case the

dragon came after them, and many more had taken up the cry of panic.

But to Douan the defeat was no tremendously important incident. He had a line of couriers spread from the Mountains of Fire all the way to Jacintha, and reports came in every few days. None of those, not one in the months since the disaster, spoke of any ominous activity in the land of the Jhesta Tu. Certainly none had reported any dragons flying about!

The Jhesta Tu had thinned the Chezhou-Lei order considerably, and the loss of leaders to Douan's army was no small thing. But To-gai had been tamed again, it appeared, by Yatol Grysh's cunning feint to defeat the rogue Ashwarawu, and all seemed quiet in the northern kingdom, with no appreciable shifts in policy against Behren after the ascension of the new Father Abbot, Fio Bou-raiy.

Thus, Yakim Douan spent the summer, God's Year 842, in the kingdom of Honce-the-Bear, about the lands of Entel, traveling informally and in relative peace, even beginning to entertain again thoughts that his time of Transcendence was drawing near.

Brynn took a deep breath—several, in fact. There before her lay the first village she had entered on her return to To-gai, a place whose name, Telliqik, she had only recently heard. For the last few months, she and her four unlikely companions had traveled the length and breadth of the steppes, stopping at every village they could find, with Brynn then going in to spread the word about the Dragon of To-gai, about how she would lead the To-gai-ru to freedom, but only if they all joined in with her. Truly it pained the anxious woman to spend these days in relative peace and quiet. After the victory at the Mountains of Fire, with the Chezhou-Lei shattered, it seemed as if Behren was ripe to be plucked.

Belli'mar Juraviel had counseled the woman for patience, though, had reminded her that their enemy remained formidable. And though many villagers had witnessed the great victory and the sheer power of the dragon, communication throughout the land would be slow and inexact, with the story likely changing from one town to another, even from one person to another. The companions would count on that inaccuracy to work in their favor as word spread back to Behren, but they knew that it could well be a liability if it was not parsed correctly on its path through To-gai.

And so they had flown out upon Agradeleous, and the dragon had even taken Runtly along, holding the pony in a harness the Jhesta Tu mystics had fashioned, journeying from town to town to begin the quiet resistance that would signal the start of Brynn's campaign against the Chezru Chieftain.

It was called *Autumnal Nomaduc*, the Autumn Walkaway, and such an action was not unprecedented in To-gai-ru history. Many times before, when one tribe had conquered another, the survivors of the conquered tribe would simply wander away from their conquerors, moving out into the open steppes. Never before had it been tried across all of To-gai, but never before had the conqueror been the Behrenese, and never before had the rebellion leader been an elven-trained ranger, riding atop a dragon!

The ranger stooped over, as if weary and road-worn, and certainly less threatening, and hitched the cowl of her worn cloak up over her head. She murmured to herself in a gruff peasant accent as she approached the gate, and peeked out under the cowl only once, to note the strange looks coming back at her from the guards.

"Oh, but me wagon is lost, and all me poor horses," she said, closing to stand right before the two Behrenese.

"You had a wagon?" one asked.

"A wagon, a husband, and a few friends, I had!" Brynn snapped at him, turning a wild eye his way and moving very close. She didn't really recognize the man, but feared that he might know her, for she had stood tall and distinct when last she was there, that year ago, when she had killed Yatol Daek and Dee'dahk.

"And you lost them?" the man asked with a smirk.

"Killed on the road!" Brynn screeched. "By robbers . . . so many damned robbers! They took me wagon, and killed me friends. Get yer weapons, soldiers! Protectors! Get yer weapons and go out and kill them to death!"

The man was patting the air to try to calm her, and was obviously trying to hold back a smile. Robbers were no major catastrophe in the unruly steppes, Brynn knew, except of course to those victimized. And she knew as well that these guards wouldn't be quick to send out any patrols, certainly not on the word and plea of a lowly To-gai-ru woman.

"Now tell me where this happened," the soldier bade her.

"Fifteen days o' walking," Brynn said, waggling a finger in his face.

"Fifteen days?"

"Fifteen!" Brynn cried. "Now, ye get yer fellows and run south, and ye'll find them. Kill them to death."

Now the man did chuckle, as did his companion. "We will speak with Yatol Tornuk about it."

"I'll be seeing him!"

"No," the man cried back, and then he calmed, and tried again to calm her. "No, good woman. We will speak with him. You just go in and find yourself a place to rest, and get some food."

Brynn stared at him hard, wild-eyed even, but then she slipped past, entering the village.

Her relief was huge when she entered the common room to find the place bristling with To-gai-ru, several familiar faces—including two in particular—among them. Brynn made her way to a corner table and slid into a chair beside Tsolona and Barachuk.

She looked up from under the cowl, smiling widely, then pulled the hood back enough so that they could see her clearly.

"Ah, Brynn!" Tsolona said quietly, and she cupped the young woman's chin in her hands, then bent in and kissed her on the cheek. "So much have we worried for you."

"The Dragon of To-gai, returned for a visit," whispered Barachuk, leaning in across the table.

His reference to her in that manner nearly knocked Brynn right over. How could he know?

"You have come to tell us of the *nomaduc*," the surprising Barachuk reasoned. "Ah, but it is already in place here in

Telliqik. The word outdistances you, and many are eager to follow the way of resistance."

Brynn just sat there, shaking her head.

"Were you really astride a dragon?" Tsolona asked, after looking around to make sure that there were no Behrenese soldiers, or To-gai-ru informants, nearby.

"It is a long story," Brynn replied.

"Then stay with us this evening and tell us your tale," said Barachuk. "And we will tell your tales to our comrades out in the steppes, in whatever manner you wish them related."

Brynn smiled, knowing well that she had fine allies there. She nodded, and stood to leave, and the other two were right behind her as she exited the common room.

The three chatted until late into the night, with Brynn relating the tale of the battle at the Mountains of Fire honestly and openly. She was surprised to learn that the couple had already met one of her elvish companions. She bade the couple not to mention Juraviel or Cazzira, though, fearing that her story might overwhelm any would-be soldiers.

"You can have your old bed back," Tsolona said to her, the hour well past midnight.

Brynn considered the offer, remembering the fine times she had spent with these two, whom she regarded almost as surrogate parents. "I must be out this very night," she answered. "I have but three days to make the final preparations for the *Autumnal Nomaduc*. Everything will move quickly after that."

"You will assemble your army?"

"As many as will join."

"And then strike at the Behrenese within To-gai?" Barachuk pressed. "Like the new dog, Tornuk, who replaced the dog you killed?"

Brynn understood the man's eagerness, for the name alone marked the new Yatol of Telliqik as To-gai-ru. To the proud To-gai-ru people, that betrayal was even worse than the invasion of the Behrenese.

"We will find our ways to gain our freedom, and will pay back those who have brought so much grief to us," Brynn promised. She moved over and kissed Barachuk, then turned to Tsolona, wrapping her in a great hug for a long, long time.

And then she was back out into the dark To-gai night, with Juraviel, Cazzira, Pagonel, and Agradeleous, laying the final plans for the Walkaway.

Three nights later, streaks of fire highlighted the To-gai sky, Brynn astride her dragon flying the length and breadth of the steppes, her fiery sword held high and the fire accentuated every so often by a tremendous gout of the dragon's fiery breath. She flew up very high so the spectacle could be seen from far, far away.

That night, taking the signal, tens of thousands of To-gai-ru slipped out of their respective settlements for the safety of the darkened steppes. There were skirmishes in some towns, where guards caught on to the escape, but in all but a few of the outposter settlements, where the To-gai-ru were outnumbered by the Behrenese many times over, the To-gai-ru got out, moving to appointed meeting places, where new tribes were formed.

Yakim Douan seemed as if he would simply explode. He sat in his chair, his fists clenched so tightly that his knuckles whitened at his sides, and he trembled so violently that his teeth were actually chattering.

Carwan Pestle, who had delivered the terrible news from Dharyan, looked to Merwan Ma with alarm, and the Chezru Chieftain's attendant motioned for the man to step back from the leader's chair.

"Not again," Yakim Douan growled, his jaw clenched so tight that he hardly seemed able to get the words out of his mouth.

"Yatol Grysh begs your pardon, God-Voice," Carwan Pestle offered, bowing repeatedly. "He wished not to trouble you with such unpleasantness as this, but he fears that we cannot ignore the desertion."

"All of them?" Douan asked.

"Yes, God-Voice," Pestle replied. "All who were not captured trying to escape. We have soldiers scouring the steppes; the outposters are banding together for defense."

"And have you recaptured any of the missing To-gai-ru?"

Carwan Pestle seemed to deflate quite a bit. "No, God-Voice," he admitted. "The outposter militia fought one battle, but it was against this . . . this crazy woman, the Dragon of To-gai, and they were overwhelmed."

"Dragon?" asked Douan. "What say your reports? Was there really such a beast as that fighting the outposters?"

"We have heard reports of a dragon flying across the sky on the night of the great desertion, but no, there was no battle against any real dragon. Just against this demon woman and her followers, and their numbers are growing rapidly. Yatol Grysh would not have intruded upon your precious time, God-Voice, but he fears that this foe is more dangerous by far than was Ashwarawu."

Yakim Douan smiled at that remark, for he knew that it had been said for no better reason than to remind him of Grysh's great victory over the fool Ashwarawu at the gates of Dharyan. That was the last good news Douan had heard!

"Indeed he must believe it to be so, to send his closest advisor all the way here," the Chezru Chieftain remarked. "And Yatol Grysh has indeed earned my trust and respect. You ask for two twenty-squares, and so you shall have them, and a third besides! And the mounts to support them, that they will sweep out with great and overpowering speed and strength!"

Carwan Pestle's eyes widened nearly as much as Merwan Ma's! Three twenty-squares, along with enough horses to support them as a cavalry unit? It was unheard of!

"But on the condition that you use them for more than the defense of Dharyan," Douan went on. "I doubt this new leader will be fool enough to charge in to her death, as did Ashwarawu. I will give Yatol Grysh his soldiers—some of the best of the Jacintha garrison!—but he must promise to use them to march across the steppes, destroying all resistance, and punishing the To-gai-ru so terribly that they will never again think to defy us!"

"Yes, God-Voice!"

"Do you understand?" Douan asked, coming out of his chair to stand right before the man. "Do you truly? Tell your Yatol to exact a generational purge of the To-gai-ru. I will not have them as any threat during the time of Transcendence."

Carwan Pestle's face screwed up with confusion, as if he did not understand.

"A generational purge," Yakim Douan repeated. "Eliminate their would-be warriors. All of them! I expect that I will not hear any further requests from Dharyan, but only the news that the To-gai-ru have been properly punished."

Carwan Pestle nodded and bowed, and followed Douan's motion that he should then leave the room.

"What troubles you?" Douan asked Merwan Ma after the emissary from Dharyan had gone, for it was obvious that the young Shepherd was not pleased.

"God-Voice, it is not my place to question—"

"But it is, because I just told you that it was," Douan told him. "You are troubled by my command to Pestle?"

"A generational purge?"

Chezru Douan grinned wickedly. "I grow weary of the stubborn To-gai-ru," he explained. "I'll have no more trouble from them. They have brought this upon themselves—let them suffer the consequences of their insolence and disobedience! Twelve hundred soldiers, my friend, and each square will be led by a Chezhou-Lei . . . no, by two Chezhou-Lei. We will conquer To-gai all over again, and this time to even more devastating effect. And then I can go to my rest, Merwan Ma. My patience is at its end."

Merwan Ma could hardly believe the coldness in Yakim Douan's voice, but he didn't dare to question the man at that time.

He bowed and left the room.

Yakim Douan stood very still for a long while, considering the decision. Three twenty-squares!

But he knew what the stakes were, and after the catastrophe at the Mountains of Fire, they were very high. Douan needed Grysh to put down the rebels and to destroy this newest legend in the making, this Dragon of To-gai.

He took some comfort in the fact that his latest reports put the Jhesta Tu still in their mountain abode, with no signs that they were planning to march in force and join the uprising on the steppes.

# CHAPTER 26

# *Playing to Their Weakness*

"Three twenty-squares," Pagonel reported to Brynn that tenth day of Bafway, the third month of the year.

The warrior woman smiled wickedly.

"Twelve hundred soldiers," Pagonel said somberly.

"Then the blow will prove even greater," the woman replied.

The mystic started to argue, but paused and stared at Brynn's knowing smile. They had spent the winter months rounding up the soldiers willing to ride with Brynn Dharielle, and the number had proven considerable indeed, beyond anything that Brynn dared hope after the disaster at Dharyan with Ashwarawu, for her reputation from that one fight at the Mountains of Fire had swept across the grassy steppes like wildfire. If this woman, this Dragon of To-gai, could destroy such a collection of Chezhou-Lei, and send a Jacintha twenty-square fleeing at the same time, then what did the To-gai-ru have to fear? And so her army had eagerly followed her down from the plateau divide and into the desert sands of Behren, some distance to the south of Dharyan.

"We have near to six thousand warriors," Brynn said to the doubting mystic.

"Only four thousand at our disposal," Pagonel reminded. "A third are out helping the common folk, as you ordered. They will not rejoin us for another month or two, at the least, until the spring is on in full. Even then, by going east, you are ignoring the many secured settlements within To-gai, and now behind our lines."

"You do not agree with me?"

Pagonel gave a helpless chuckle in the face of Brynn's too-innocent tone. "I am playing against your choices," he explained. "As you asked of me."

Brynn laughed aloud and squeezed her dear friend's shoulder. Indeed, she had instructed Pagonel to play the part of her conscience and her better judgment, to question everything she decided with every argument he could find for alternate courses. She just never realized how good the mystic would be at such a task!

"Four thousand will be more than I need," Brynn decided. "Dharyan will fall."

"Burned by the fires of a dragon?" the mystic asked. "I warn you, the city has ballista emplacements—many of them. One shot from such a weapon could bring Agradeleous down to the ground, and once there he would face a concentrated barrage that even his great armor could not withstand."

"Agradeleous will play a small role, if any," Brynn replied, and the mystic's expression became one of surprise. "I do not need him for this."

"But . . ."

Brynn noticed that some of her other commanders had heard that last remark and were now listening more intently than they were letting on.

"I will use Yatol Grysh's confidence against him," Brynn explained. "But we must strike quickly, before the three twenty-squares can be deployed outside of the city."

"You will attack a walled and fortified city, defended by fifteen hundred skilled warriors and a like number of conscripts, with a force of only four thousand?" asked one of her commanders, an older man from Telliqik named Bargis Troudok.

"No," Brynn corrected. "We will attack a fortified city garrisoned by a couple of hundred soldiers with a force that numbers near to four thousand."

That had all of them looking at her curiously, but Brynn only smiled. She had learned so much in her years with the Touel'alfar, and their understanding of battle, small and large, and had learned so much more during her time at the Walk of

Clouds, studying the history of Behren more completely than
the history of To-gai. She understood the Behrenese commanders' expectations and likely reactions, particularly those
of Yatol Grysh.

Yes, Brynn could smile. She knew her enemy at this point,
understood his confidence and his eagerness to repeat the
great victory he had known over Ashwarawu. She knew how
to tease him with just that possibility, and then how to take it
away, oh so brutally.

"He is not happy," Juraviel said to Brynn later that same
day, when the woman had come to see him and Cazzira and
Agradeleous in their separate camp, up on the side of the
cliff-facing that marked the boundaries between the two
countries, and some distance from the main force.

"He hungers for blood," Brynn said with obvious distaste.

"He hungers for adventure," Cazzira explained. "Agradeleous is a patient creature, but you have kept him aside for
months now, serving in no capacity other than mount and
supply caravan. He considers himself your greatest warrior
and has pledged his support for this fight, and yet—"

"I am the greatest warrior!" came the hissing voice, and all
three turned to see Agradeleous entering the area, a dead elk
over his shoulder—and the dragon was carrying it with complete ease, as if it was no more a burden than a shawl. "Or do
you fear that your warriors will see the truth of me, and fall to
their knees, pledging their allegiance to Agradeleous instead
of to Brynn?"

"I fear only to show our enemies the true power before the
optimum time to surprise them," Brynn replied.

The dragon snorted, little bursts of flames spouting from
his horselike snout. "I already showed them the power of
Agradeleous' wrath! In the south—"

"Where few escaped, and those, too horrified and disori-
ented to provide the truth of your power," Brynn argued.
"And need I remind you of the reports that your presence has
been attributed to a trick of the Jhesta Tu? There is much
more to winning a war than battle alone, dear Agradeleous."

The dragon snorted again, as if Brynn's reasoning about

him being no more than some mystic trick was preposterous, though they had indeed heard such a tale from some Behrenese soldiers captured at one settlement.

"I will ride against Dharyan tomorrow afternoon," Brynn announced.

"And I will fly against the city tomorrow afternoon!" Agradeleous announced. "You can choose whether you wish to ride that lunch you call Runtly, or a mount truly fit for one who would be queen!"

Juraviel and Cazzira both turned alarmed looks at Brynn, but the woman only smiled. "You will fly against the city tomorrow night," she corrected. "I hope to fly with you, but if that is not possible, then you, and your other two riders, will know how to proceed."

Brynn's grin told them that there was much more to this, told them all that she had a definite plan, and one that gave her great confidence. And so they all gathered around and held silent, except for the occasional confirming grunt from Agradeleous, as she laid it out to them.

"A daring plan," Cazzira said to Juraviel after the woman had gone. "One designed to exploit every weakness she recognizes within Yatol Grysh."

The elf glanced over his shoulder, to see the dragon quite busy in devouring his elk, and not paying the two elves any heed. "And one designed to win without giving away the truth of the dragon," he added. "Not to the Behrenese, but even more importantly, not to her own warriors."

"You think that Agradeleous recognized the woman's fears?"

"No, but I think that Brynn is too wise to reveal too much to anyone. She knows that even with Agradeleous, To-gai is sorely out-manned by the Chezru Chieftain."

"And still she chooses to go after Dharyan, instead of clearing the steppes of the lesser forces."

"It is because of that very fact that she knows she must strike, and hard," said Juraviel, nodding and staring into the direction where Brynn and Runtly had ridden away, a grin of respect widening on his small and angular face.

*       *       *

"They were spotted traveling north through the valley of the Mazur Shinton, Yatol," Carwan Pestle reported to Grysh. "A considerable force, several times larger than that Ashwarawu led against us."

"And are there any dragons flying about them?" Grysh asked with obvious sarcasm, and a wry crooked smile. He looked away from the map tacked up on the wall to consider his attendant.

"The Dragon of To-gai leads them, we believe," Pestle replied. "A woman, and not a wurm."

Grysh laughed heartily. When the Jacintha soldiers had arrived, he had bidden them to come in quietly, thinking to turn them loose upon the steppes as soon as the weather softened into springtime. How glad he was now that he had delayed! And that he had kept their arrival relatively quiet! For the reports had been coming in daily that the new rebel, this Dragon of To-gai, had come down from the steppes and into Behren at the head of a considerable force.

"They say that she rode with Ashwarawu, you know?" Grysh asked, and Carwan Pestle nodded. "She wants revenge, and so she will come against us, oblivious to the fact that we now have more than twelve hundred new warriors at our disposal."

"Shall we deploy them as we did against Ashwarawu, Yatol?"

"No," Grysh said without hesitation. "This woman remembers well that disaster and she will no doubt look for signs of any armies camped nearby. Our guests are to remain in the city—no one is to leave! Not a Behrenese nor a Ru! Do you hear?"

"Yes, Yatol, it has already been ordered, all about the wall."

"Let the Dragon of To-gai charge right up to our gates. Then we will hit her and her wretched band with a volley of destruction that will overwhelm them where they sit astride their pretty ponies."

"Yes, Yatol."

Grysh looked at the map, at the valley of the Masur Shinton. If the reports were correct, the Dragon of To-gai would arrive at Dharyan's gates early that very evening. And there she would die, as Ashwarawu had died.

That thought did bring a twang of regret to Yatol Grysh, for his friend and trusted commander, Wan Atenn, rotting on the sun-baked stones of a far-distant southern wasteland, would not partake of this glorious victory.

But now he had seven Chezhou-Lei at his disposal, he reminded himself, his new advisor and the six who had come in from Jacintha. That would suffice to destroy utterly this pretentious rebel and her followers. Then Grysh would lead the force personally into To-gai, spending the summer moving across the steppes, bringing harsh justice to the upstart Ru. They would accept the rule of Behren, or they would die.

It was as simple as that.

"Mark the line, left and right," Brynn instructed as her force of nearly a thousand neared Dharyan. She stretched out her front line, spacing the warriors widely, and squared them up to the city, its dark wall back-lighted by the fires burning within.

Beside her, Pagonel sucked in his breath, as did many others.

Brynn looked to him for support. She had pleaded with him not to come out there, but he had refused to be left behind, and in truth, she was glad that he had. Now that the time was upon her, Brynn did not think that she could get through this difficult beginning without him beside her.

But how much worse would it become if he was felled by an arrow?

Brynn growled that dark thought away. "Strike the torches!" the woman ordered, and the call went along the line, and those few brave volunteers who had agreed to wield the torches brought them up in a blaze.

"Cadence slow!" Brynn cried and the drummers began, beating out a slow pace, the whole of the force walking deliberately toward the distant wall. Those drums would be heard within Dharyan, Brynn knew, and in fact, she was counting on it.

More torches went up along that wall, and a voice called out, "Halt where you are and be recognized!"

"Do you not know me, Yatol Grysh?" Brynn cried back. "Have you not heard of the Dragon of To-gai?"

A great cheer went up behind her at that proclamation. "Well said," Pagonel remarked, and it was just the bit of support that Brynn needed at that moment.

"First volley!" she yelled, and a thousand bows bent back and a thousand arrows soared into the dark sky, arcing for Dharyan. They were a long way out, though, and the barrage had little, if any, effect.

Little physical effect, Brynn knew, but this attack was not about that.

Brynn held aloft her sword and set it ablaze. The drums stopped.

"To-gai free!" she cried, and brought her sword sweeping down, and so began the charge, a thousand horses shaking the ground.

A second volley went away, and then a third, with more and more arrows making the wall, even taking down enemies.

Brynn gritted her teeth as they continued their charge, for they were getting close—too close, she feared! When would the response come?

Perched a few miles away, on the cliff-face of the To-gai plateau, Juraviel, Cazzira, and Agradeleous watched the line of torches snaking across the dark plain.

"They will fight without me again!" the dragon complained bitterly.

"No, this is no fight," Juraviel explained. "She waits to turn."

"They grow close," said Cazzira.

"Brynn awaits the revelation," Juraviel remarked. "She needs Yatol Grysh to show his strength to chase her away."

Agradeleous grumbled and shook his head, obviously not catching on to it all.

"She centers the leading line of the charge," Cazzira noted. "Brave, perhaps, but foolish will she seem if she is cut down."

"Then she will lead as a martyr," Juraviel said grimly, but his wince belied his stoic tone.

Arrows came out at them, as well as a few huge ballista bolts, giant spears creasing the air, close enough so that the charging warriors could hear them whistle past. The Dharyan catapults even fired, though their fiery pitch balls were easily spotted and avoided by the skilled To-gai-ru riders.

They were barely fifty yards from the wall by then, close enough to pick out forms scrambling in the torchlight, and so their volleys proved more deadly, and so the cries of agony began, at the wall, and then among the To-gai-ru ranks.

Brynn grimaced, but held fast her plan, knowing that many of these brave warriors would not ride out of this deadly place. They had all known that grim reality, and yet every man and woman in her army—every single one!—had volunteered to ride with her to the base of the wall. Still, this macabre game of nerves was starting to fray hers. "Commit them," she whispered, a quiet plea to Yatol Grysh. "Show us our folly."

Forty yards.

"Sweep left and right!" she ordered her band, though she understood that such a turn might actually leave more of them exposed.

Immediately, the well-drilled To-gai-ru line split down the middle, going left and right. For the skilled horsemen, who hunted the wild steppes while riding, the turn did nothing to deter their attack, and their arrows continued to skim the top of the wall.

But then came a cry from that wall, a familiar voice, speaking in the language of the To-gai-ru.

"A trap! A trap!" Ya Ya Deng, Ashwarawu's informant, cried out, and then her words became a groan, and all who heard it understood that she had been silenced by a sword.

"Hold! Hold and center!" Brynn cried immediately, and how grateful she was for that unexpected assistance, for the excuse to keep her soldiers back a bit farther from the wall.

And not a moment too soon, for even as the split forces began re-forming at the center, and back out to more than fifty yards, the horns began to blow wildly within Dharyan and the top of the wall seemed to grow, as hundreds of soldiers stood up, bows in hand, letting loose a volley that would have surely devastated the force had they been closer. Even as it was, many warriors fell in that devastating volley, stuck with arrows or with their prized horses shot out from under them.

"A trap! A trap!" went the cry along the To-gai-ru line, on cue. "Run away! Run away!"

They milled about in seeming confusion, though in truth, the skilled horsemen knew exactly their course. They scooped up comrades, grabbed horses wandering riderless, and suffered the storm of another arrow volley.

And then they turned and fled, crying out in seeming despair.

All along the Dharyan wall, a cry of victory erupted, with soldiers throwing their arms into the air and yelling out for Yatol Grysh. In the courtyard behind them, the Yatol stood with his seven Chezhou-Lei commanders.

"The Dragon of To-gai!" one spat. "She turns and flees at the first resistance! Coward Ru!"

The others murmured their agreement with the assessment.

"They have ridden all the day," the supremely confident Yatol Grysh told his commanders. "Take your men and their horses, hunt them down, and kill them."

It was an order eagerly received. Within only a few minutes, Dharyan's western gate swung wide and the ground shook under the hoofbeats of nearly fifteen hundred cavalry, the Jacintha warriors and a good portion of the Dharyan garrison beside them.

They came out strong, barely taking the time to form into any coherent groupings, and swung to the south, thundering away in full gallop.

Soon after, the fleeing To-gai-ru force was spotted, still running south, paralleling the plateau. Thinking their prey tiring, the Chezhou-Lei spurred their forces on even harder, gaining ground.

They came into the northern end of one narrow vale, split by a wide and shallow river, and saw the torches of the fleeing

To-gai-ru streaming out the southern end, only a quarter of a mile ahead.

Up went the war cries, the leaders and their soldiers bending low over their mounts, thinking their victory, over a tired and battered foe, at hand.

And then their world changed, so abruptly, so stunningly, as both hills, left and right, came alive with swarms of To-gai-ru warriors, as the Dragon of To-gai's three thousand hidden warriors sprang up, raining death from on high.

At the south end of the valley, Brynn called for a halt and turn, re-forming her line. She didn't turn them loose immediately, but let the rain of death continue, let the Behrenese ranks break apart with terror and confusion, let them thin as soldier after soldier was plucked from his horse.

Then came the charge, left and right, the To-gai-ru forces closing like the jaws of death, angling to seal off any retreat.

And then came Brynn's charge, in a long and thin line, bows humming and then swords clashing.

The Behrenese had nowhere to flee, and no time to regroup into any semblance of a defensive formation. Nor could the Behrenese shoot from horseback with anywhere near the speed and accuracy of the skilled To-gai-ru hunters. Brynn had shaped the battlefield perfectly to fit her forces, and had used the overconfidence of Yatol Grysh to coax his soldiers from behind their defensive walls, out into the open, where they were no match for the fierce To-gai-ru riders

And she eagerly led the way in for close combat when the time was upon them, her fiery sword flashing death to any Behrenese who wandered too close.

In truth, most were merely trying to flee. That only heightened the slaughter.

"My night has just begun," Brynn said to Pagonel when the battle had ended. She found the mystic hard at work tending the wounded, though he had not escaped unharmed, and showed a bright line of blood across his upper arm where an arrow had creased his skin.

The mystic nodded. "You understand the power you now unleash?" he asked.

"I understand that Dharyan will fall in the morning," Brynn grimly replied. "Whatever the cost."

The mystic nodded and Brynn turned Runtly and galloped away to the west, to the base of the plateau divide.

Her friends were waiting for her, Juraviel and Cazzira already sitting astride the great dragon, who was back in his more natural, and more imposing, winged form.

"I feared that we would have to leave without you," Juraviel remarked, obviously greatly relieved to see the woman still alive and unharmed.

"This is not a fight I wish to miss," Brynn replied, climbing up atop the dragon's lowered neck.

"We marked well the ballista emplacements," Cazzira informed her.

Brynn nodded. "A few, perhaps," she agreed. "But the prize I seek is greater."

"Their great spears are the only weapons which can prevent me from razing the city wholly," the dragon argued.

"We will break their heart and their will, and so Dharyan will fall," was all that Brynn would offer at that moment.

Up they went, high into the dark sky, and in moments, the lights of Dharyan were in clear sight.

How much brighter they would soon burn!

Brynn brought the dragon around to the north and then to the east, knowing full well that all of Dharyan's eyes were straining south and west.

Agradeleous climbed high into the dark sky, then he turned and held for just a moment, and then he plummeted, gaining speed. With a tremendous rush, his wind alone blasting surprised guards from the northeastern wall, the dragon crossed over the city. Despite Brynn's instructions, he did veer to cross right above one ballista emplacement, his raking claws and sweeping tail destroying it and its crew as he rushed past. And then he turned for his primary target, and it was not difficult to spot, for the temple of Dharyan was easily the largest structure in the city.

He pulled up before it and loosed his fiery breath, blowing out the eastern windows, lighting the wooden supports.

He shifted up higher and breathed again, and then a third time, his breath igniting fires all about the structure.

Below on the streets, the people cried and rushed for cover, and Agradeleous dropped upon them, strafing a line of fire along one avenue, starting fires along the rows of houses and storefronts.

Behind Brynn, Juraviel and Cazzira worked their bows wildly, sending lines of stinging arrows out at any soldiers they could spot.

"Enough, Agradeleous!" Brynn cried repeatedly, but the dragon wasn't hearing her, or wasn't paying her any heed if he was! He swept along above the streets, his tail thrashing destruction, his claws snapping down at any soldiers he caught in the open, his breath sweeping out to immolate any who were not fast enough or cunning enough to get out of the way.

Soldiers died in that rush, but many more civilians fell to Agradeleous. Women died and children died, and Brynn had to fight back the bile in her throat.

Gradually, the defense began to organize, and arrows whizzed up about the riders, many striking the dragon, bouncing harmlessly off his scales or scoring hits upon his leathery wings.

And Brynn continued to scream at the beast, commanding him to fly away, as they had planned.

And Agradeleous continued to rain death and destruction, all the way to the front gates of the great city, which he leveled with a single blast of his fiery breath.

Finally, the dragon flew off, back into the darkness of night, leaving the screams and the rumble of great fires, behind him. He reached the cliff-facing, but did not land and let his riders down. No, he went up higher, searching among the heights until he found a loose boulder that he could scoop up with his great clawed feet. Then he turned and swept back for Dharyan, flying high above the city, too high for the archers or the ballistae to reach him.

He dropped the boulder, aiming perfectly for the largest fire in the city, and the huge stone smashed through the roof of the Dharyan's temple.

"I can do this all night!" the dragon boasted.

Brynn just wanted to be put back down, and so she ordered the dragon to take her back to where she had left Runtly.

And Agradeleous did so, then he flew off with the two elves, up the cliff-facing to find more boulders and then back over Dharyan to randomly bomb the place.

Brynn came back into the To-gai-ru encampment with a heart heavy from the destruction she had witnessed on the field and especially in the city. One scene in particular, a group of women immolated by dragon fire while they ran along a street, hung thick in her thoughts.

But the warrior woman could not deny that the battle had gone almost exactly as she had planned. More than a thousand Behrenese warriors lay dead in the Masur Shinton valley, and no doubt hundreds more, soldier and civilian, had died in the dragon raid in the city. And the temple of Dharyan was still burning, and would be a complete ruin by morning.

Brynn's own losses had not been substantial. Carving and preparing the battlefield to her choosing had given all the advantage to her warriors and they had used it to near perfection.

Now Dharyan lay ripe for the taking.

But for Brynn, exhaustion had set in, and that only exacerbated the feelings of remorse and of guilt. She said not a word as she walked Runtly into the To-gai-ru encampment, did not even acknowledge the shouts and cheers that erupted around her. She went straight to Pagonel, still at his work in tending the many wounded—only To-gai-ru wounded, for the Behrenese had all been put to swift death on the field—slid down from Runtly and fell into the mystic's waiting arms.

He hugged her close and she buried her face in his strong shoulder, not wanting those around her to see the tears in her eyes.

"What have I done?" she whispered.

"You have struck a blow against your oppressors that will be heard throughout the steppes and throughout Behren," the mystic answered softly. "You have given your people a chance to break free." Pagonel pushed Brynn out to arm's length and looked her right in the eye. "You have given them hope and the courage to fight back."

"Even if they all should die in the war," Brynn said with biting sarcasm, but to her surprise, the mystic only smiled.

"Even if they all should die in the war," he echoed softly, and firmly, and he nodded and smiled, reminding Brynn that some things, perhaps, were worth dying for.

"What is next?" the mystic asked.

"We will deliver our terms for surrender in the morning," Brynn answered.

"Yatol Grysh is a stubborn one," said Pagonel.

"Then he will endure a night of dragon fire the likes of which the world has not seen in centuries," Brynn replied, and there were no more tears at that time, just a determination so cold and so grim that it sent a shiver coursing down Pagonel's hardened spine.

The next morning, Brynn rode at the head of a column of nearly four thousand To-gai-ru warriors, closing to within fifty yards of Dharyan's wall.

"They are all dead, Yatol Grysh," she called out. "Send forth an emissary or your city will be destroyed around you."

She let it go at that, and when no rider came forth from Dharyan's blasted gate, Brynn motioned for her warriors to encircle the place. None would flee Dharyan, and none would enter without her knowing of their approach.

That night, she took Agradeleous over the city again and again, blasting his fire and dropping rocks from on high, above the reach of the Dharyan defenses. Her warriors, too, came forward in short and unexpected bursts, showering fiery arrows into the city.

The next morning, smoke hanging as heavy as the cries of lamentation in the air, Brynn approached the city again, and again called out for an emissary, and this time, she was answered.

A lone rider exited the gate, bearing a white flag of truce. He was not a skilled horseman, obviously, and he nearly fell off several times as he galloped his horse up before the warrior woman.

"I am Carwan Pestle," he introduced himself. "Emissary of Yatol Grysh."

"Come to discuss the terms of surrender," Brynn remarked, and looked over at Pagonel, for she noted that the man looked quite nervous, and uncomfortable, as if he would have to deliver words she did not wish to hear.

"My Yatol instructs me to inform you that he has near to two thousand To-gai-ru slaves within the city," Carwan Pestle began slowly and uncertainly.

"Two thousand reasons for him to evoke my ire no further," Brynn replied.

"He bids you to ride away, back to your own land," Carwan Pestle continued, and he was shaking so hard that it seemed as if he would fall off his horse. "Be gone, Dragon of To-gai, else those slaves will be executed, and most horribly."

Brynn didn't blink, but simply, slowly, nodded and turned to Pagonel. "Tell me, my Jhesta Tu friend, how long would it take for Yatol Grysh to organize such a mass murder as that?"

"Hours, I would guess," Pagonel said with equal calm.

Brynn turned back to Carwan Pestle. "Then I will not give him hours," she said, simply.

Carwan Pestle stared at her curiously, not understanding. "Is that the message you wish for me to return to my Yatol?"

"You?" Brynn asked incredulously. "Oh, no, my good man Carwan Pestle. I intend to deliver my message personally." She looked over one shoulder, to Pagonel, then over the other, to the line of her commanders. "Now," she said. "Sack Dharyan, and extra rations to the man who brings me the dog, Grysh!"

Before Carwan Pestle could even begin to respond, the To-gai-ru line erupted in battle cries, and in the thunder of charging horses.

The response from the Behrenese wall was minimal and fleeting, with the soldiers, mostly civilians pressed into emergency service, throwing down their weapons and fleeing back for their homes. Like a dark flood, the To-gai-ru rolled through the gate and widened out to engulf all the streets, and then above them came mighty Agradeleous and his two riders, swooping in low to blast away any pockets of resistance with a purging gout of flame.

It was over before midday, with all resistance broken, and with most of the two thousand To-gai-ru slaves freed—and many taking up arms against their oppressors.

The killing went on through the day and night, and Brynn heard so many disturbing reports of rape and execution.

On Brynn's orders, no further destruction of property was allowed, and only combatants were to be killed, but it seemed obvious to her that many of her warriors were using any excuse they could find to label Behrenese as combatants, and many of the freed slaves would not walk away without exacting the harshest retribution upon those who had so badly mistreated them.

Late the next morning, a fat, whining man was brought out before Brynn and thrown down in the dirt at her feet. He looked up, his hands entwined in a pleading position.

"Yatol Grysh," explained one of the two To-gai-ru warriors who had brought him out. "We found him hiding in a deep wine cellar, trembling with fear."

"The coward!" the other warrior said, and he spat in Grysh's face.

"Please, I beg of you!" Grysh pleaded. "I am a rich man. I can pay."

"I do not want your money," Brynn said to him. "I want your people out of my city."

It took a moment for the words to register to those around her, but when they did, they brought whoops of delight from the To-gai-ru and a wide-eyed stare of disbelief from Yatol Grysh.

"Bring the emissary to me," Brynn instructed Pagonel, and the mystic rushed off to find Carwan Pestle.

"You cannot think to hold Dharyan," Yatol Grysh dared to say.

"Not Dharyan, no," said Brynn, moving about him and putting her finger to pursed lips as if she was working through some details even then. "No, that is a Behrenese name, and not one I desire. No, we will name it Dharielle. Yes, that is a fitting name."

Triumphant cries erupted all about her, and as the news filtered down the streets, more and more took up the chant of "Dharielle!"

Pagonel and Carwan Pestle arrived soon after.

"Yatol!" the poor Shepherd cried, and he moved for his master but was easily detained by the mystic.

"You were my witness to the conquest and so you shall be my witness before the court of the Chezru Chieftain," Brynn said to the confused man. "Tell him that To-gai is free, and that any Behrenese caught uninvited upon our soil will be killed. Tell him that this city, Dharielle, is now part of To-gai.

"Tell him," she said, moving very close and imposing, staring so hard at the man that he seemed to wilt before her, "that if he ever again sends a single soldier against me, I will burn Jacintha to the ground, and him along with it."

"You fool!" cried Grysh, and somehow, as if he had only then realized that he had absolutely nothing left to lose, he found the strength to stand before her. "Heathen, barbarian dog! He is the God-Voice, the chosen avatar of Yatol! He is—"

Brynn looked to some of her soldiers around her and ended the tirade with two simple words. "Hang him."

The next day, every surviving Behrenese man, woman, and child marched out the eastern gate, down the long and difficult stone-paved roads through the empty desert, exiting the city right beneath the wind-twisting corpse of the man who had ruled over them for decades.

# CHAPTER 27

# *Ghost Town*

Carwan Pestle had entered the same chamber tentatively only a few months before, nervous then because he had been sent by Yatol Grysh to beg for hundreds of soldiers. How much greater that nervousness was now for the poor Shepherd, walking into the chamber of the Chezru Chieftain with the news that Yatol Grysh had failed, that all twelve hundred of the soldiers the Chezru Chieftain had sent to Dharyan were dead, and that Dharyan had fallen!

Merwan Ma shot Pestle a truly sympathetic look as the young man, so much like Merwan Ma in many ways, made his slow way about the room, to stand right before the seated Yakim Douan.

They already knew much of the tale, Carwan Pestle realized, from the sympathy of Merwan Ma to the intense expression on the face of the Chezru Chieftain. The man wasn't even looking up at him, but was staring straight ahead, his thumb and index finger fiddling with his bottom lip.

With his free hand, the Chezru Chieftain motioned for Carwan Pestle to speak.

"I hardly know where to begin, God-Voice," the Shepherd remarked, his voice quivering.

"Is Yatol Grysh dead?"

"He was hanged by the Dragon of To-gai."

Yakim Douan's fierce eyes turned up to bore into the poor man. "The Dragon of To-gai?" he echoed. "Pray you tell me, who, or what, is the Dragon of To-gai."

"A woman," Pestle stammered. "A young and small woman. But fierce, God-Voice."

"Then it is not a true dragon, as if one of the legends of old."

"But she is!" the Shepherd explained, or tried to. "A great beast! She flew over the city at night, her fiery breath setting great fires. On the first night, she destroyed the temple, and killed so many!" He was gasping as he spoke, so overwhelmed that he seemed to be running out of breath with each word.

"And then she flew up high, God-Voice! So high, and dropped great stones upon us! We could do nothing to harm her!"

Yakim Douan patted his hand in the air, trying to calm the man, and eventually, Pestle did pause and take a deep breath.

"And this dragon killed three twenty-squares of my soldiers?" the Chezru Chieftain asked. "Alone?"

"No, God-Voice. The Dragon of To-gai came with a great army—thousands of warriors! I do not know that she even took her dragon form in that battle, and in the end, when she swept over our wall and conquered Dharyan, she was in the guise of a human, a simple woman."

"Not so simple, I would say," Douan said dryly.

"They killed so many," Carwan Pestle lamented. "And their warriors took great liberties with our women, and then murdered many."

"But most of the citizens of Dharyan came down the desert road?"

"Yes, God-Voice. She sent us out into the desert with hardly any food and water. We were lucky to make the Dahdah Oasis with only a few losses. Many are still there, hoping to return to their homes once you destroy this dragon."

"She occupies Dharyan?"

"She has changed the name, calling it Dharielle now."

Yakim Douan nodded. "And tell me, Shepherd Pestle, were any Jhesta Tu mystics involved in this unprovoked and heinous attack?"

"She had one beside her, God-Voice. A man of middle age—some say that he was the same one who had fought at Dharyan with Ashwarawu, though I cannot be certain."

"Likely, he is," Douan replied with a knowing chuckle.

"God-Voice?"

Yakim Douan held his hand up to calm the man. "Rest easy, Shepherd Pestle. You will have your homes back soon enough."

"But the dragon . . ."

"She will fall, quite dead, and her warriors will be sent running back to their forsaken steppes. And there, I will catch them and punish them. Oh, yes, all of To-gai will rue the day that this dragon-woman came into their midst." He finished with a nod and wave of his hand, and a smile so wicked and confident that it surely bolstered Carwan Pestle.

The Shepherd bowed and exited the room.

"Damn her!" Yakim Douan exploded, the moment the young man was gone, surprising Merwan Ma, who, like Pestle, had believed that the God-Voice had all of this under complete control. "Damn this witch and the Jhesta Tu! And damn Yatol Grysh, the failure!"

"God-Voice, it seems as if he was overwhelmed . . ." Merwan Ma dared to interject.

"Overwhelmed?" the Chezru Chieftain echoed incredulously. "Overwhelmed by a ragtag band of To-gai-ru? Yatol Tohen Bardoh captured half of To-gai with fewer warriors than Grysh had at his disposal, and that was on the open plains, not huddled behind a fortified city wall! No, he erred. He erred badly, as Kaliit Timig erred. We are playing to our enemy's strengths, don't you see? We are underestimating them."

"But what of this dragon, God-Voice? Surely neither the Kaliit nor Yatol Grysh could have anticipated —"

"A trick, likely," Douan insisted. "The Jhesta Tu can do such illusions, I am told."

"But you heard Carwan Pestle. He claimed that it was a great beast, a dragon of legend."

"And in the dark night, with fires burning and the city under siege, and likely bombardment from distant catapults, everything that he heard or saw would be multiplied many times over by sheer terror. A dragon? Well, perhaps this fool To-gai-ru woman is such a beast, or has harnessed such a beast. They do exist, or did, and so it is not impossible."

"But then, what are we to do?"

"Kill it," the Chezru Chieftain said calmly. "As we kill all of them. Dragons are not immortal, nor are they invulnerable. Send every scholar to the library to study every legend and detail about such creatures. This Dragon of To-gai has won twice, but both with the element of surprise. The next force we send against her will be ready to deal with any dragon, I assure you. Phalanxes of great bows and poison-tipped arrows will bring the beast down."

Douan paused and chuckled. "If there even is such a beast, and I doubt that there is. But nonetheless, my time of showing any leniency or mercy to To-gai is at its end. They dare to conquer Dharyan? Well, I will respond, do not doubt. As I promised Pestle, I now promise you. Call up all the men of Jacintha. Assemble the garrisons. In a fortnight, we will send fifteen thousand soldiers marching to retake Dharyan, and with them will be the greatest engines of war we can devise. Let the Dragon of To-gai show herself. Perhaps her fiery breath will kill a few, but then she will fall, right before the stunned and horrified eyes of her foolish followers. And then where will they turn?

"Back to the steppes of To-gai? Ah, but we will pursue them, from Dharyan and from the south, where Yatol Tohen Bardoh will march with fifteen thousand more soldiers."

Merwan Ma rocked back on his heels, amazed by how profoundly this disaster had sparked his master to action. Over the last years, skirmishes against To-gai had been just that—minor battles. But now the God-Voice was readying for an all-out war against the people of the steppes, as he had done a decade and more before.

The Shepherd left the audience room quite unsteadily, quite shaken, but also quite reassured that his master was in control.

Yakim Douan paced for a long time, growing more and more agitated. How dare these ungrateful To-gai-ru strike so boldly and mercilessly into Behren? Hadn't he brought the barbarians some semblance of civilization? Hadn't he brought a better way of life to the wilderness of To-gai?

His breath coming in short and harsh rasps, the Chezru Chieftain continued to pace, kicking his heels against the floor with each step.

A sudden burning pain erupted in his left shoulder, spreading like a wave of fire down his arm. Douan stumbled and nearly fell over. His vision blurred briefly, and when it cleared, the man realized that he was sitting in his chair again.

And now the pain was in his chest.

Yakim Douan struggled to regain his footing, then stumbled to the door. He started to call out for Merwan Ma, but changed his mind, realizing where he had to go, and realizing that he had to go there alone.

Step by step, the stubborn old man made his way along the corridors to the chalice room. The pain had lessened considerably by then, but still Yakim Douan grabbed up the chalice eagerly, so much so that he spilled some of the blood on his robes and the floor. Clutching the chalice to his chest, the man fell into the magical gemstone, diving into its swirling gray depths.

He went inside himself, trying desperately to find the harmony of his body, the natural and healthy rhythm. He began to breathe easier almost immediately, and not from his healing powers, but merely from his realization that nothing serious had befallen him, a point accentuated by a series of loud belches.

Yakim Douan laughed at himself and his desperation, a clear reminder of how much he had to lose. He was immortal, but only as long as he remained in control of the situation about him. If a sudden, burning attack felled him, would he be able to spiritually connect himself to the hematite in time to soar out and find a replacement body?

Yakim rubbed the base of the chalice, his fingers separated from the gemstone by a thin sheet of metal. He could feel its presence in there, its tangible power to take him across the generations and the centuries.

A crash from the back of the room startled him, and he turned to see Merwan Ma standing there, a look of both surprise and horror on his face, and a plate of utensils, the sacrificial knife among them, lying on the floor at his feet.

Yakim considered his own appearance, clutching the chalice, blood on him and on the floor, in light of Merwan Ma's expression, and he knew at once that the Shepherd understood that there was something more to this chalice.

"Ah, yes, my young attendant," the Chezru Chieftain said with as much calm as he could muster. "Finishing your duties before going out to the Chezhou-Lei, I see."

Merwan Ma stammered something undecipherable, but otherwise did not respond. He bent low and picked up the utensils.

"What is it?" Yakim Douan asked bluntly, and coldly, and with enough authority to freeze the poor young man where he knelt.

"God-Voice?"

"You are surprised to see me in here."

"Yes, God-Voice. I had thought that you would rest in your audience chamber."

"But it is much more than that, is it not?" Yakim Douan asked slowly and deliberately, moving toward Merwan Ma with each word.

"God-Voice?"

"What do you know of the chalice?"

Merwan Ma began stammering the typical responses concerning the rituals and supposed powers of the sacred chalice, and Yakim Douan let him ramble for some time. Each remark seemed more of an excuse, a front, than anything from the man's heart, though, and so the perceptive Douan began to understand the truth of it, that Merwan Ma knew about the hematite in the chalice.

The Chezru Chieftain sent his spirit into that gemstone, used the portal that was the stone to let him fly free suddenly of his physical body. He didn't slow as he came free, but soared straight for the unsuspecting Merwan Ma, his spirit rushing right into the man, laying bare his soul for Yakim Douan to see.

And he knew then, in that instant, that Merwan Ma did indeed know of the hematite, and that it was the presence of that gemstone, along with Yakim Douan's clutching of the chalice, that had prompted the horrified look upon his face.

Confronted by the spirit of the God-Voice, the poor Shepherd fell back, toppling over to a seated position on the floor, one arm up over his face defensively, as if warding the man away.

Yakim Douan was already in retreat anyway, rushing back to his body, afraid to give too much away here to the curious Shepherd. He went back into his own body and blinked his physical eyes.

"What is it, my son?" he asked innocently.

Merwan Ma gradually relaxed, but only somewhat. He pulled himself to his feet and tried to act as if all was normal. But Yakim Douan saw the truth for what it was. Merwan Ma knew, and was afraid because he knew.

"I must clean these once more," the young man stuttered.

"Go, then," Yakim Douan replied cheerily. "But out to the Chezhou-Lei first. Your duties here can wait."

Merwan Ma paused a moment and stared at his master, but then answered, "Yes, God-Voice," bowed repeatedly, and shrank back out of the room.

Yakim Douan growled in frustration at his own carelessness. He replaced the chalice and wiped the blood from the floor, then moved out of the room back to his own private quarters, cursing with every step.

Merwan Ma knew, and he could not tolerate that. He would miss the young Shepherd greatly.

Chezhou-Lei Shauntil stood at rigid attention before the Chezru Chieftain, the God-Voice, and now—given the disaster at the Mountains of Fire, the failure and honorable suicide of the Kaliit—the only real authority left in the proud warrior's existence.

"You understand the statement of your mission?" Yakim Douan asked.

"To instate Merwan Ma as governor of Dharyan," the warrior recited. "To drive the To-gai-ru from the city and reclaim it for you, then to pursue the rebels onto the steppes, under the leadership of Yatol Tohen Bardoh, destroying them utterly and returning to you the head of this foul woman, the Dragon of To-gai."

"You understand the truth of your mission?"

"As stated," the warrior replied, and he squared his shoulders and puffed out his massive, muscled chest. "Except that it is Carwan Pestle who is to serve as governor until a Yatol can be put in place."

"Because?"

"Merwan Ma will die in a battle."

Yakim Douan nodded and turned away, bitter about issuing such a command against the Shepherd who had become his friend over the last years. He had known for a long time that perhaps he had become too close to Merwan Ma, and now the incident at the chalice had sealed the young man's fate. Yakim Douan simply could not take the chance that Merwan Ma had learned too much, for the mere existence of the hematite would damn him in the eyes of many of the Yatols. Their religion was unbending on this point, that the gemstones were the tools of the demons, were the perverse religious articles favored by the heathen Abellicans in the north.

Merwan Ma knew of the hematite in the chalice, and could easily guess at Douan's connection with it. That revelation, should the Shepherd ever make it, might lead some to guess the truth of Transcendence. And that, of course, the Chezru Chieftain could never suffer to pass.

Still, it bothered him more than a little to so order the death of Merwan Ma. At least he was allowing the man to die honorably. Yes, he would hold a great celebration of the life of Merwan Ma when the tragic news returned to Jacintha.

"Leave as soon as the engines of war, and those designed to defeat the dragon, are prepared," he instructed the Chezhou-Lei. "On the road, your word is rule, as it remains even when Yatol Tohen Bardoh joins you after the recapture of Dharyan, on all matters military. Yatol Tohen Bardoh understands the value of the Chezhou-Lei, I assure you. He knows his place in this ugly business." The last words sent a shiver along Yakim Douan's spine. Indeed, Yatol Tohen Bardoh knew well the means of terrorizing a conquered people. Douan had pulled the man back from To-gai, not because he was ineffective, but because he seemed to be enjoying himself a bit too much. Now, given the sudden turn and the utter stubbornness of the

To-gai-ru, Douan wondered if he hadn't made a mistake in relieving the brutal man.

It didn't matter, he told himself and he waved Chezhou-Lei Shauntil out of his private room. He had other matters to attend—primarily the selection of a new personal attendant, one who would watch over him as he came to maturity in his new body. Only after realizing that he had to get rid of Merwan Ma had the Chezru Chieftain come to understand the depth of his mistake in becoming so close to the man over the years, not only because of his personal grief at having him killed, but because he had not bothered to seed the pool of potential replacements in the event of some unforeseen tragedy.

Again, it didn't matter, he told himself. Transcendence was a couple of years away, at least, and in that time, he would undoubtedly find some overpious fool eager to assume the duties.

Brynn, Pagonel, Juraviel, Cazzira, and Agradeleous watched the marching force with a mixture of awe and amusement. Never had any of them seen such an array of sheer power, with thousands of marching soldiers and hundreds of cavalry, and great war engines, from catapults to gigantic spear-throwing ballistae. This was the power of Behren, the might that had swarmed over To-gai and that kept the often imperialistic Bearmen of Honce-the-Bear, even with their gemstone-wielding Abellican monks, at bay.

"And so I see why you chose not to defend Dharyan," Juraviel said to Brynn. Indeed, Brynn had taken her entire force out of the city soon after sending the refugees down the eastern road toward Jacintha. The To-gai-ru warriors had moved south of the city and were now hiding in the desert, while Brynn and the others had come there, just east of Dharyan, to view the response from Jacintha.

"I did not know it would be so overwhelming," the woman admitted.

Agradeleous snorted, hardly agreeing with that assessment.

"They have prepared for you," Juraviel remarked to the dragon, pointing out the ballistae. "One strike from those would take you down to the ground."

The dragon snorted again, unimpressed.

"We could not have held Dharyan," Pagonel remarked. "Not even for a single day against this force."

"We cannot, can never, fight the Chezru Chieftain, army to army," Brynn explained. "We will frustrate him and his commanders and make them all see that a continuing war is not in their best interests." She turned to the dragon. "This is where you will show your greatest value to our cause, Agradeleous. Pagonel will help us to forage, what little there is to find, but—"

"More than a little," the mystic put in.

Brynn nodded deferentially, not wanting to underestimate the Jhesta Tu in any way. She was quite sure that Pagonel's understanding of the land would prove invaluable. But still, she knew that it would not be enough, not for her warriors and not for their horses. "But," she continued, "it will be Agradeleous with his great speed and strength who will truly supply us. Fly out at night to a river and return to us with buckets of water. Descend upon a herd of deer and bring us more meat than we could possibly consume!"

"There are thousands of you," the dragon remarked, seeming not quite convinced.

"I hold faith in Agradeleous," Brynn answered. "We will construct a great platform and use heavy ropes with which you can bear it." Brynn turned to the others, to see the elves nodding with more than passing curiosity and Pagonel rubbing his chin, considering it all.

"If we can stay mobile, and independent of the few known watering holes, then the Behrenese will have a difficult time in catching us," Brynn explained. "We can maneuver about them and strike wherever they are weakest."

"Then we must always know where they intend to be next," said Pagonel, turning a wry look upon Brynn. The two had already discussed this somewhat, with the mystic explaining that he would serve her well as a spy.

"They have many To-gai-ru slaves among them," Juraviel noted.

Brynn looked from the elf to the mystic. She really didn't want to be apart from him, considering him an advisor who,

in many ways, was even superior to Belli'mar Juraviel. Pagonel understood the Behrenese as well as she did, and knew
even more about the Yatol religion that so dominated the
desert people.

But she couldn't deny that her only advantage here was information, was knowing her enemy better than they knew
her, and so, after many moments of staring hard at her dear
Jhesta Tu friend, she finally nodded her assent.

Pagonel leaned over and kissed her for luck, then slipped
around the back of the sand dune, disappearing into the
desert sands.

That same night, as the Behrenese army camped in sight of
the city now called Dharielle, their contingent of To-gai-ru
servants grew by one. Further to the south, a dragon took to
the air, bearing the warrior woman back to her army of four
thousand. The two elves and Agradeleous did not stay with
Brynn, but took to the air again, scouting the region, then settled back near to where they had parted ways with the Jhesta
Tu mystic, to await his return.

More than two hundred To-gai-ru slaves had accompanied
the Jacintha army on its long march from the east, nameless
and faceless in the eyes of the superior-minded Behrenese,
and so Pagonel slipped into the large encampment with little
difficulty. He wore nondescript clothing, rags like all the
other slaves, and kept his telling and magnificent sash about
his waist, but under his large shirt.

He moved about the encampment for a long while that
night, among the To-gai-ru gatherings, listening far more
than speaking. Their talk of the Chezru Chieftain's outrage
reminded Pagonel just how dangerous this whole game had
become. The might of Behren was sweeping, and dominating, and not even the mighty kingdom of Honce-the-Bear desired to match armies with the Chezru Chieftain. And now
Brynn had turned all that might upon herself, against To-gai,
and the only chance they had was in hitting the Chezru Chieftain where he did not expect it, continually flanking the massive armies and pecking away at vulnerable spots until the
Behrenese decided that they had gone to too much trouble.

Looking at the encampment, a massive, well-prepared, well-drilled, and eager force, the mystic had to wonder if Brynn hadn't stepped a bit too far over the line. He was somewhat bolstered, though, by the whispers of the prisoners whenever the quiet discussions turned to the Dragon of To-gai. Apparently Brynn's fame had already spread—among the To-gai-ru slaves, at least—all the way to the coast. She would find many willing to join her army with each city conquered.

The next morning, the Behrenese army rolled in sight of Dharielle's eastern wall, close enough so that the body of Yatol Grysh could be seen, still hanging before the closed gates. Now Pagonel paid close attention; there were several Chezhou-Lei warriors among the soldiers, he knew from their distinctive armor, and their hierarchy became apparent almost immediately, with one large and powerful warrior taking the lead in delegating commands. With frightening efficiency, the army set up its catapults and ballistae. Riders went out north and south, encircling the quiet city.

Pagonel noted that the Chezhou-Lei leader kept returning to two men, Chezru Shepherds by their dress and the styling of their hair, as if explaining his intent. Pagonel recognized one of them as the attendant of Yatol Grysh.

An hour passed, and then another, and the scouting riders returned with reports that no one had been spotted along the walls of the conquered city.

One of the Chezhou-Lei rode forward under a flag of truce, moving near to the city gates and calling out a greeting in Behrenese and in the To-gai-ru language. But of course there was no response from deserted Dharielle.

That only seemed to infuriate the Chezhou-Lei leader. He stormed over to where the To-gai-ru slaves had been gathered, selected one man randomly from the horde, then stalked away, dragging the man along.

A few minutes later, one of the catapults launched a living, screaming missile over the city wall.

The only responding sounds were the startled cries of the carrion birds within.

Pagonel studied the leader intently, then looked around at his To-gai-ru fellows, reading much from their grim expressions.

The Chezhou-Lei leader began barking a series of commands, and his army fell into its prescribed positions. The catapults let fly more conventional missiles of burning pitch and large rocks, and the ballistae held back, their great spears pointing toward the skies as if expecting the Dragon of To-gai to fly past at any time.

Batteries of archers sent a volley of arrows over the wall, but then they, too, held their shots, scanning the skies above.

And then came the charge, hundreds of horsemen thundering for the gates, foot soldiers falling into ordered defensive arrangements behind them. It was a feint, Pagonel knew, because the Behrenese would never lead with their cavalry, and sure enough, the horsemen got near to the wall, yelling and screaming, and then swung about to the south, running along the wall, looking for some enemy somewhere.

The foot soldiers swarmed for the eastern gate, a large ram leading the way.

They went through without resistance, swarming into the city, and then the cavalry went in right behind.

Pagonel took great amusement in the outraged expression of the Chezhou-Lei leader when he learned that the city, Dharyan once more, was deserted.

With great ceremony, the whole of the army, except for scouts sent to the west, entered Dharyan and began securing the place, putting the slaves to work at patching burned-out roofs and clearing rubble and dead bodies.

Soon after, the unknown Shepherd Pagonel had noted, Merwan Ma, was named by the Chezhou-Lei leader as governor of the city.

Several days went by uneventfully, and it was obvious to Pagonel that the Behrenese army—the bulk of it, anyway—wouldn't remain in Dharyan for long. The mystic waited anxiously for the advance scouts to return, wondering if Brynn's preparations for the deception had paid off. Soon after leaving the city, heading south, Brynn had sent many riders back to To-gai, where they were instructed to find as many of their compatriots as possible and begin a long procession—walking a wide loop—in sight of several outposter settlements, making it appear as if Brynn's army had headed back to the west and melted into the grassy steppes.

She was counting on the Behrenese overconfidence again, with them convinced that the inferior To-gai-ru knew that they could not sustain any kind of a war against Behren.

During those days of waiting, Pagonel positioned himself so that he would be working near the building that had been designated as the command post of Dharyan, where both Governor Merwan Ma and the Chezhou-Lei leader, Shauntil, held audience. He couldn't get into the place, not openly at least, for only selected slave women were allowed inside, but he made certain to befriend many of those women, so that he could continue his spying.

Finally, late one afternoon, a rider returned from the plateau and was taken for an immediate audience with the leaders.

The guards overseeing the work of Pagonel and others hardly seemed to take notice of the To-gai-ru, for they were as anxious for word as was Pagonel. They drifted away from the slaves, never looking back.

Pagonel slipped off to the side gradually, then darted behind a pile of rubble and down an alleyway at the side of the command building. With a glance around to make sure that no sentries were in sight, the mystic fell into his Chi and lifted his spirit, then easily scaled the building, moving beside a window that overlooked the main audience hall, where Merwan Ma, Carwan Pestle, and several Chezhou-Lei, including Shauntil, had gathered to hear the news from the scout.

"Of course they ran," one of the Chezhou-Lei was saying. "That is their cowardly way. They knew that they could not hope to hold Dharyan against the might of Jacintha, and so they fled to their steppes."

"They passed Dancala Grysh only a couple of weeks after taking Dharyan," the scout reported, and Pagonel smiled in admiration of Brynn's cunning deception. "They could be anywhere in the steppes now, or even disbanded."

"They have not disbanded," Shauntil insisted. "They follow this leader, blindly and to their doom. It is their way."

"I was here when Ashwarawu attacked," said another of the Chezhou-Lei. "Shauntil is correct in his assessment. They are like pack dogs, the To-gai-ru."

"We will sweep the steppes," Shauntil declared. "We will catch up with this Dragon of To-gai and give the To-gai-ru the harshest of lessons. When we leave, there will not be enough To-gai-ru men left to mount another attack against Behren."

Some movement below alerted Pagonel that he had to get down, and he started to do so, but then heard Shauntil gruffly dismiss the other Chezhou-Lei, the scout, and Carwan Pestle, pointedly telling Merwan Ma that they needed to speak alone.

Pagonel flattened himself against the wall, not wanting to miss out on this private conversation. But as a Behrenese soldier walked along the alleyway below him, he knew that the chances were great that he would be spotted.

So he leaped out, diving down the fifteen feet atop the unsuspecting soldier. He flew right past the man, hooking him about the head as he did, and he immediately rolled about, his momentum snapping the poor soldier's neck instantly.

The two went down in a heap, with Pagonel rolling away, over and over to absorb the blow. He came back quickly, dragging the soldier behind a pile of rubble in the alleyway, then stripping the body of its uniform and donning it himself.

When he got back to the window, the audience hall was empty. Pagonel moved along the ledge, then climbed again to the top floor of the three-story structure. Then some arguing guided him along, farther to the rear of the building, where he peeked in around a window.

There stood Merwan Ma, against one wall, his hands upraised, a look of sheer terror on his face. A few feet away stood Shauntil, a dead To-gai-ru slave on the floor behind him, a bloody dagger in his hand, pointed toward the new governor.

"You serve the Chezru Chieftain!" Merwan Ma cried.

Shauntil smiled wickedly. "Carwan Pestle will govern Dharyan until a suitable Yatol replacement can be found, while I assume the mantle of Governor General of the region, and all of To-gai."

"Pestle can have it!" Merwan Ma conceded, quite willingly. "I only came out on the command of our common leader, and have no desire . . ." His words trailed away as a knowing, even more wicked, grin widened on the fierce Chezhou-Lei's face.

Outside the window, Pagonel's expression screwed up with curiosity, for it seemed obvious to him that the Chezru Chieftain, for some reason, had sent this poor Shepherd out there to be murdered.

"I have served him for many years," Merwan Ma pleaded as the Chezhou-Lei approached. "I am his choice to oversee Transcendence!"

That last word came out with a gasp as Shauntil plunged the dagger into Merwan Ma's belly.

"But you were murdered, Governor Merwan Ma, by a Togai-ru slave, who was angered because you ordered her brother launched by catapult into the city," the warrior explained, and he pumped his arm, stabbing the poor man again and again.

Shauntil stepped back and Merwan Ma collapsed to the floor.

"Yes, it hurts," the warrior teased. "But I could not kill you efficiently, for, after all, you were killed not by a Chezhou-Lei, but by a poor, frantic slave woman." With that, Shauntil tossed the knife to the floor between them and started for the door.

He paused, though, considering the blood on the robes he had put on, and with hardly a thought, he stripped the outer layer off and tossed it into the hearth, where the dying ember reignited about it.

He looked back to Merwan Ma, then left.

Pagonel dropped back down to the alleyway, his hands working the wall through his descent deftly, so that he landed lightly on his feet. He rushed to retrieve the dead soldier, knowing that time was of the essence, then hoisted the man on his back, moved to the base of the window, and climbed back up once more, this time moving through the open window and into the room.

A soft groan from Merwan Ma told him that the man was still alive, though barely.

Pagonel stripped off the injured Shepherd's bloody clothing and tended the wound as quickly as he could, then put his own clothes on Merwan Ma, and put the Shepherd's clothing on the soldier. He took up the knife and stabbed the dead man in the gut, then placed him as Merwan Ma had been placed.

He rushed to the hearth and pulled out an unburned edge of the robe, then held it to the embers and blew on them until it ignited. He brought his brand to a torn tapestry at the side of the hearth and set it ablaze, the flames spreading rapidly along the dried tapestry and old, dry wood. The mystic tossed the still-burning brand at the chest of the dead soldier, wincing as the fire began to catch. With a deep and steadying breath, Pagonel gathered Merwan Ma across his shoulders.

He heard voices on the stairs, then a shout of, "Fire!"

It was a movement that only a Jhesta Tu, and only a master of that order, could ever have accomplished. Pagonel ran full speed to the open window, reached into himself to buoy his body magically, then leaped out, across the alleyway, flying fifteen feet to the next roof. He sprinted across that roof, hardly slowing, then leaped again, right to the top of the south wall, and then, hardly slowing, hopped over that wall and fell the fifteen feet to the sand below, landing as softly as he could, bending as he hit to cushion the blow for the man draped about his shoulders.

Without delay, hearing shouts from at least one soldier who had spotted him—or had spotted *something*—the mystic laid Merwan Ma out straight at the very base of the wall and fell down beside him, working frantically to cover as much of them as possible with loose sand.

He heard more cries from above, but they weren't directed at him, he realized, but at the fire that was now burning more furiously.

Pagonel lay very still, concentrating on his Chi. He brought his hands to Merwan Ma's wounds and sent his hot life energy into them, transferring his strength, his healing, to the near-dead Shepherd.

The fire burned into the night, and cries of "Murder!" resonated about the streets. Pagonel could only listen with helpless horror as the Behrenese took out their anger over the murder of the new Governor of Dharyan on the other Togai-ru slaves.

Gradually, the screaming died away, replaced by the quiet stillness of midnight.

Pagonel pulled himself from the sand, then lifted Merwan Ma across his shoulders, and in truth, he wasn't even certain if the man was still alive.

And then he ran, out into the darkness, using the stars to guide him. He ran all through the night, and most of the next day, as well, pausing only periodically to use his healing energy on the gravely wounded Shepherd.

That night, he ran on again, tirelessly, stopping only when he heard a command to halt, issued in a telling melodic voice.

Only then did the mystic allow himself to realize his exhaustion, and he slumped into the sand, lowering Merwan Ma beside him.

"A fine gift," Belli'mar Juraviel said to him when he awoke sometime later.

The mystic craned his neck to see Merwan Ma, wrapped in blankets across the small fire, with Cazzira sitting beside him and Agradeleous off in the background.

"It may be," was all that the exhausted mystic could reply at that time, and he lowered his head and went back to sleep, knowing that he would need all of his strength and more if he was to have any chance of keeping Merwan Ma alive the next day.

It was late in the day before he awoke once more, to find Cazzira standing guard over Merwan Ma.

"Juraviel and Agradeleous flew out before the dawn, to keep watch over Dharielle," she explained.

"Dharyan, once more," Pagonel corrected, and he pulled himself up and moved toward the injured man.

"Eat first," Cazzira offered, pointing to the side, to a steaming small pot, and Pagonel veered toward it. "Juraviel believes that the Behrenese will move soon."

"Very soon," the mystic replied. "Into To-gai in pursuit of the Dragon of To-gai and her army."

Cazzira laughed.

"Who is he?" she asked a few moments later, pointing to the injured man.

"His name is Merwan Ma," the mystic explained. "An attendant of the Chezru Chieftain, named governor of Dharyan and then nearly murdered, on orders from the Chezru Chieftain."

Cazzira's look was predictably puzzled.

"A Chezhou-Lei cut him down."

"A rogue act, perhaps?"

Pagonel was shaking his head before she ever finished the question. "They are unquestioningly loyal to the Chezru Chieftain. Never would a Chezhou-Lei take such an action of his own initiative, not when it involved a man so closely tied to Chezru Douan."

"But why?"

"That is what I hope to find out," the mystic replied, and he took another sip of the stew, then wiped his mouth and moved beside Merwan Ma, falling right back into *doyan du cad ray chi*, "the warm healing hands."

Belli'mar Juraviel and Agradeleous returned that night, bringing the welcome news that the bulk of the Behrenese army had marched west and were even then scaling the narrow passes of the plateau divide into To-gai.

"It was all that I could manage in keeping Agradeleous from attacking them," the elf admitted a while later, when the dragon, after transforming back into his humanoid form, stalked off from the camp. "A killing rage grows within him. I know not how long we, and Brynn, will be able to control his fury."

"Because he hates Behrenese?" Cazzira asked.

"Because that is the nature of dragons," Pagonel interjected. "They are creatures of destruction, usually of random destruction. It is remarkable that you and Brynn have placated him enough to keep him in line thus far. Soon enough, I fear, we will see the true fury of Agradeleous."

Belli'mar Juraviel looked out into the darkness, where the beast was out even then seeking some creature to tear and devour. A shudder coursed his spine.

# CHAPTER 28

# *With All the Weapons at Her Disposal*

Runtly plowed through the soft sand, laboring for breath but, like the three hundred To-gai ponies running beside him, not slowing. The feint against the walled city of Pruda had gone perfectly, with very few To-gai-ru lost to the city's defensive volleys.

And predictably, before the fleeing To-gai-ru had gone far, Pruda's gates had swung wide and their garrison of several hundred, along with a seemingly equal number of peasants, all eager to join in the slaughter, had come forth, some riding horses, some on camels, and many others just running behind, brandishing everything from fine swords to farming implements.

Brynn brought her riders along the base of one huge dune, then turned about it and paused, all riders fitting arrows to their bows.

On came the lead Behrenese pursuers, and the To-gai-ru kicked their mounts into another run. Many of the skilled riders of the steppes turned back in the saddle, trusting their mounts to run true, and began letting fly their arrows.

The Behrenese pursuit halted abruptly as the front ranks thinned. Brynn and her riders heard the calls for retreat, for a return to Pruda. When she looked back and confirmed that the Behrenese had broken off pursuit, she halted her force, and gradually turned it about, taking care to send spotters out wide to make sure that their enemies were indeed heading back to the safety of their walls.

Walls they would never reach, Brynn knew, for as she had led her small force and the pursuing Behrenese out into the desert, the bulk of her army had filtered in behind, taking up a position in front of Pruda.

When Brynn and her riders caught up to the retreating Behrenese, they found them stopped in their tracks, desperately trying to form into some semblance of a defensive formation, for they faced a force thrice their size, and one comprised of skilled, veteran To-gai-ru warriors.

Brynn had hoped it would go like this, with the Pruda garrison destroyed right before the city's wall, in clear view of those terrified defenders remaining within Pruda. She noted the leaders of the doomed Behrenese soldiers huddling, likely discussing whether or not they should ask for quarter.

But that was not to be. Not there and not then.

Before their huddle had produced anything at all, Brynn brought Flamedancer up high above her head and cried out for the charge.

Showers of arrows led the way as the To-gai-ru encircled the force.

"They should have tried a charge straight through the line, back to their gates," Brynn remarked to those around her. "Their cowardice has cost them all hope."

Another volley of arrows rained on the Behrenese, and then another, and then came the charge. Even among the Behrenese soldiers, few offered any fight, for they were all too busy trying to scramble away, trying to find some hole in the To-gai-ru line to get back to their city.

Some did manage to get through, but of the force of nearly a thousand who had left Pruda in search of a glorious victory, more than nine hundred soon lay dead or dying on the blood-stained sands.

And a To-gai-ru army of four thousand now stood before the thinly manned gates.

Merwan Ma blinked open his eyes, quickly moving his hand up to shield them from the glare of the hot late-afternoon sun.

He heard the noise almost immediately, but it took him a long while to connect the sounds to the truth of them.

They were screams of terror.

The battered Shepherd forced himself up to his elbows, wincing with pain all the way. He didn't know where he was, but he saw the white walls of a Behrenese city in the distance, swarming forms all about it, and lines of thick black smoke rising from many of the structures within.

The Shepherd's heart sank.

"Pruda," came a voice beside him, and he turned to see the Jhesta Tu mystic, his companion and his savior.

"Pruda?" Merwan Ma echoed, hardly able to get the name out of his mouth. "The greatest center of the arts and learning in all the kingdom. Oh, what are your friends doing?"

"They are fighting to be free."

"Pruda is not a warrior city!"

"Obviously," Pagonel dryly replied.

"They cannot destroy it," Merwan Ma remarked, his words turning into a pained grunt as he tried unsuccessfully to sit up, only to wind up flat on his back, crying softly.

He felt the hot hands of Pagonel on his wounds a moment later, and though they surely brought relief, he tried to slap them away. "Savage!" he said. "Heathen barbarian!"

"But not one who would murder his supposed ally," the mystic remarked, and that notion surely defeated Merwan Ma's attempted resistance.

"Do you think this savagery?" the mystic asked.

"Can you name it any other thing?" came the incredulous reply.

"Do you think it savagery on a scale anywhere close to what the emissaries of your Chezru Chieftain have forced upon the people of the steppes?"

Merwan Ma's generous lips grew very thin.

"You do not believe me."

"My master is a generous and wise man," the obedient Shepherd insisted with as much conviction as he could muster. "He is the God-Voice of Behren, who speaks to and for Yatol."

Pagonel dropped a dagger beside the prone man. "Then do his bidding," he remarked.

Merwan Ma stared from the dagger to the mystic. "A challenge?"

"A challenge to your conscience and your faith, perhaps," said Pagonel. "Your God-Voice wished you dead, so take up the dagger and fulfill his plans for you. I promise that I will not try to heal you once you have plunged the dagger into your heart."

Merwan Ma looked away. "It is a mistake," he said. "A rogue Chezhou-Lei."

"There are no rogue Chezhou-Lei," Pagonel replied. "You know as much. That warrior acted upon the orders of your God-Voice, that you were to be killed and it would be made to look like a murder by a To-gai-ru slave. It is perfectly obvious, to me and to you."

"You know nothing."

"I know that you would be lying dead in Dharyan if I had not carried you away and tended your wounds."

"And you think that I am therefore indebted to you?"

The mystic chuckled and shook his head. "I think that there is a mystery here, one that both of us do not quite understand, but that we both desperately wish to understand. There is a reason that your Chezru Chieftain wanted you dead, and I wish to know of it."

Merwan Ma looked away.

"Consider my words and consider the truth, Merwan Ma," Pagonel said. "There is something very wrong here, from your perspective. Perhaps you believe that you still owe loyalty to the man who would see you dead."

Merwan Ma chewed on his lower lip and did not look back at Pagonel, and the mystic let it go at that, certain that the man was conflicted, at least.

It was a good start.

The mystic shielded his eyes and looked back to Pruda, and knew that the battle was over. Then he looked off to the south, where the two elves and the dragon were waiting, and he knew that Agradeleous would not be pleased that it had ended so quickly and cleanly, and without his aid.

"The Library of Pruda," Brynn heard one of her soldiers mutter in obvious awe. And indeed, the woman felt the same way, for here before her was the great building, the most renowned and revered center of knowledge and learning in all of Behren, perhaps in all the world. Inside were shelves and shelves of parchments and tomes, ancient and new, along with some of the greatest artwork of years gone by. Here were the scriptures of Yatol, and the entire history of the Behrenese religion, along with a multitude of works about the Abellicans and their gemstones, copied from the great library in the monastery of St.-Mere-Abele.

There, before her, was the record of civilization.

"Do not damage this building," she ordered those around her, on impulse, for Brynn was feeling the great weight of responsibility here. "Spread the word that the library is not to be desecrated."

Skeptical expressions came back at her, but no questions, none would question the Dragon of To-gai, who had led them to yet another great victory.

Almost none.

"It is, in part, a Yatol temple," came a familiar voice behind her, and she turned to see Pagonel's approach.

"It is much more than that," Brynn replied.

The mystic moved up beside her and did not disagree. "Why do you distinguish between this place and all of the others that have fallen before you?" he asked.

Brynn looked at him and smirked, well aware that he was testing and teaching her. With his typical distance, he was asking her the question so that she could ask it of herself, so that she could formulate her own answers.

"If I sack this place, then I will have to answer to those historians centuries hence," Brynn answered at length. "They will speak of the To-gai insurrection as a dark time, instead of the glorious time it truly is."

That answer brought a smile to Pagonel's lips. "You are wondering how you will be viewed long from now, when you are dust."

"I wish to ensure that the To-gai-ru are not noted as savage barbarians."

"And once again, you show why you are a great leader, my friend," the mystic replied. "There is more at stake here than the immediate freeing of your people. There comes with your actions a reputation that will follow the To-gai-ru for centuries."

"Then let them know us as fierce enemies," Brynn said grimly. "But let them know us as decent and honest warriors."

"Which side of that description does the hanging of Yatol Grysh fall upon?"

The question stung, but Brynn steeled herself against those black wings of guilt. "We will treat the Behrenese civilians with fairness—as much as is possible," she quickly added, seeing Pagonel's frown, for indeed, the reports of rape and murder had followed the army through Dharyan and into Pruda. Brynn and those about her were working hard to minimize the cost to the civilians, but this was a tricky road to walk. Her warriors were out there, miles and miles from home, in fierce combat and likely to die, and most of them, like Brynn, had watched family members slaughtered by the invading Behrenese.

The conversation was interrupted then, as a small and wiry Behrenese man, dressed in the flowing white robes of a library scholar, came rushing out of the building, waggling a long and crooked finger at the pair. "You leave it alone!" he cried, rushing forward to stand right before Brynn. "Fight your battles as you will, but the Library of Pruda does not belong to you, or to any man . . . er, woman! This is a place of the ages, and for the ages, and—"

"Enough," Brynn interrupted. "Your library will stand."

"Well, good enough then!" the fiery little scholar yelled back at her. "Then just be on your way." He ended by waving them off with his hands, but neither Brynn nor Pagonel budged.

The mystic turned to Brynn, as did the scholar, looking to her to lead the way.

She stood there for a long while, chewing her lip, considering her options and weighing them carefully, then began to nod slowly. "In conquering Pruda, I became the keeper of this library," she explained to Pagonel.

The little scholar scoffed. "Chezru Chieftain Douan will have it back soon enough!" he declared.

Brynn called to some of her men nearby, motioning for

them to join her. "Empty the library," she instructed when they arrived. "Clear it to its stone, and take everything from the city."

"What?" the scholar cried, hopping up and down frantically. "You cannot! I will not have it!"

He finished abruptly, as Brynn's sword flashed out and thrust ahead, coming to a stop with its tip firmly against the man's throat.

"Be well aware that the hand you force holds a sword to your throat," she warned. "Take care as to which direction you force it."

The scholar blanched and fell back a step, but Brynn paced him, keeping the sword tight against his throat. "You will go and tell your fellows that they are to stay out of our way, and beware, any who hoard even a single parchment will suffer my wrath!"

"Barbarian!" the man squealed.

"Never forget that!" Brynn shouted back at him, her eyes going wide and wild, and with a yelp, the little scholar ran off.

Brynn sheathed her sword and turned back to Pagonel.

"I do believe that you would have killed him," the mystic remarked.

Brynn only smiled and shrugged.

"I must enter the library before your warriors commence their work in full. Our friend over there"—he nodded toward Merwan Ma, who was off to the side, sitting and with a pair of soldiers closely guarding him—"has hinted that there is something unusual going on in Jacintha, though I have not yet discerned what it might be."

"You think that you will find some answers to the present state of Behren in there?"

"I think that I will understand better that which is unusual if I have a better grasp of what is usual," Pagonel answered.

Brynn nodded, not about to argue, and quite certain that her mystic friend was doing her a great service with his information gathering. Knowing one's enemies was vital—her understanding of Yatol Grysh and the Behrenese mindset had allowed her to turn their weaknesses back against them at both Dharyan and Pruda, and now had a great Behrenese army of nearly fifteen thousand warriors wandering the steppes to the west in search of her.

She knew that Pagonel would not disappoint her.

He started up the long flight of steps, but paused and turned back. "There is one other problem you must attend. I stopped by to look in on Juraviel, Cazzira, and Agradeleous before entering Pruda this day. They are right where you left them, and ordered them to remain—but Agradeleous is not pleased. The beast does not wish to be left out of the fighting."

Brynn took a long and steadying breath. She was thrilled, of course, that she had taken Pruda without the dragon's aid, and without much loss of To-gai-ru life at all. In fact, the number of To-gai-ru slaves within the city of the elite scholars was so large that Brynn's army had actually grown by several hundred after the battle. And she was glad that she had not been forced to loose the terrible dragon upon the people of the city, as she had done in Dharyan. She could still hear the screams of the civilians scrambling futilely along the lanes as Agradeleous had approached, and it was not a sound that she wished to replicate.

But she understood the mystic's grave tone, and wholeheartedly agreed with it. Agradeleous was a creature of action— destructive action. Such a beast as the dragon would not be ignored throughout the war.

"How many days were we to linger out here while you led your pitiful humans to battle?" the dragon's angry voice greeted Brynn as she trotted Runtly to the camp of Juraviel and Cazzira.

"Do you think it wise that we reveal our strongest and greatest weapons when they are not needed?" Brynn asked, both innocently and incredulously.

"Do not play me for the fool!" Agradeleous roared back at her.

Brynn looked to the elves, and neither wore a reassuring expression.

"Our friend has not enjoyed watching from afar," Juraviel remarked.

"That is not why I left the comfort of my home!" Agradeleous added.

"You agreed that you would serve me in this matter," Brynn bluntly replied. "That means that you will defer to my judgment."

"My patience is not without end."

Brynn slid down from Runtly and walked to stand right before the dragon. "I will use you as I need you, and nothing more than that," she said. "Our enemies suspect the truth of Agradeleous, and that is a dangerous thing. You saw the great engines of war they dragged along with them down the road from Jacintha."

The dragon snorted. "The toys of children!"

"Dangerous toys," Brynn argued. "Toys that could bring Agradeleous from the sky." The dragon started to argue, but Brynn wouldn't allow the interruption, shouting over him until he quieted and listened.

"You are not a spectator here, but a valuable tool—perhaps my most valuable tool," she explained. "I'll not risk you when there is no need. A lucky shot from the Behrenese could spell disaster for me, while you are needed for far more than sacking a barely defended city like Pruda!"

That last statement seemed to pique the dragon's curiosity, for he tilted his head to the side and—more importantly— stopped arguing.

"There is a great force canvassing the steppes of Behren unchecked," Brynn explained.

"You would send me against them?" the dragon asked, obviously hopefully.

"I will use your speed as I used it in the *Autumnal Nomaduc*," Brynn answered. "I must keep a watch over that army, and use your speed to ensure that my forces within To-gai are apprised of their movements."

"I am a scout?" the horrified dragon asked. "I could sack a city without you! I could—"

"And so you shall!" Brynn promised. "When there is need. For now, this night, I need your speed. Fly me to To-gai, great Agradeleous. Let us find Shauntil's army."

Agradeleous stood quiet for a moment, staring at her. Then

he nodded, seeming somewhat appeased, for the time being at least.

Soon after dark, Brynn felt the wind on her face as she and the dragon soared high and fast over the plateau divide and into To-gai, across a distance and terrain that would have taken her army a week or two to traverse.

The dragon went up high in the sky, and the fires of many villages could be seen dotting the landscape.

And the fires of a great encampment, a huge glow, showed far in the north.

Brynn urged the dragon that way, and Agradeleous soared off at tremendous speed, the ground rolling along below them. The glow grew and grew as they neared, and only then, from that high vantage point, did Brynn truly appreciate the might that had been assembled against To-gai. And from the way the dragon slowed suddenly, and then went up even higher, she knew that Agradeleous, too, had come to understand.

The dragon's head snaked around, his face moving close to Brynn. "You wish to attack?" he asked, and she sensed, for the first time, a bit of a tremor in Agradeleous' great voice.

Brynn shook her head, not even trying to shout loudly enough for the dragon to hear her in that deafening wind.

She spotted a second glow, then, farther to the north, and she prodded Agradeleous, and when he looked back, she pointed it out.

Brynn knew what the second encampment was before the dragon even flew past it. It was a band of To-gai-ru, likely a sizable chunk of the army she had left in the country. It all sorted out for Brynn at that moment. The Behrenese were in pursuit of the To-gai-ru, were hot on a trail they would not forsake.

Brynn scanned all the dark steppes, looking for some answers.

She got an idea from a third set of lights that she marked, not the fires of an encampment, but the smaller glows typical of a settlement. She banked Agradeleous down to that area, a few miles south and west of the Behrenese army, and did a low fly-over.

An outposter settlement, she recognized. Perhaps her army

had been heading for it before the arrival of the Behrenese warriors.

On Brynn's urging, the dragon set down some distance away, and the woman slipped from his back and stood staring at the lights of the outposter settlement. She understood well the choices here before her, and didn't have to glance back at the mighty dragon to understand the horrors of those choices.

But she could not let her army be caught and destroyed, not if there was anything that she could possibly do to prevent it.

"You were angered that you were not involved in the last battle," she remarked.

Agradeleous' long neck snaked his head around, to come up right beside her, his eyes narrowing dangerously.

"The village," Brynn explained. "Destroy it. Let the flames fly high so that the Behrenese army can see them." The woman found her breath coming in short gasps as she finished, for she could hardly believe the command—no, not the command, but the permission—she had just given to this most terrible of weapons.

The dragon's great head swiveled about to regard the settlement, and he issued a low, horrible growl.

"You will ride?"

"I will stay here," the woman replied, and she felt as if she was acting the part of a coward. But what good would come of her accompanying Agradeleous on his rampage? Would she be able to save a single outposter? Would she wish to?

Any contemplation at that time was moot, anyway, for the dragon hadn't waited a second. He leaped up and his great wings beat the air, launching him away.

Within a couple of minutes, Brynn watched Agradeleous' first pass over the sleepy outposter settlement, a low strafing run, his fiery breath running a line of destruction the length of the settlement.

He did a series of stoops and fire-breathing runs, and the cries of the terrified, doomed outposters filled the night air. And then the dragon fell upon the village, dropping down, all claws and teeth, beating wings and smashing tail.

Brynn looked away and lowered her gaze, second-guessing herself with every heartbeat.

It went on and on, and then the sounds began to quiet, as more and more voices were forever stilled, and then Brynn noted another sound, that of running horses.

She turned around to see Agradeleous gliding down beside her. Past the dragon, the woman saw the high fires, burning bright—brightly enough so that the Behrenese army would have to take notice. Those horses were likely the typical trailing scout cavalry of the main army, a small and mobile force.

Brynn motioned for the dragon to lower his head so that she could climb atop him. "I believe that some of the soldiers have come to investigate," she explained as she scrambled on. "I do not wish them to report that the town is destroyed."

Agradeleous loosed another of those low and angry growls, and leaped away once more, and in no time, Brynn was above the burning, ravaged city. To the north, in the glow of those flames, the flyers saw the forms of the Behrenese cavalry.

Brynn lifted her sword and sent forth its fiery blaze, and Agradeleous swooped down from on high. Some of the stunned Behrenese soldiers shrieked in horror, others even managed to wheel their mounts about and start away.

But it didn't matter. There were only twoscore of them, and not a one had a bow in his hand.

Agradeleous destroyed them.

Back up in the night sky, Brynn and the dragon saw much commotion about the distant Behrenese camp and knew that the invaders were already trying to break down their bivouac and prepare for battle.

"Fly past them, high and to the side," she instructed the dragon.

"Let us fall upon them!"

"No!" Brynn screamed. "No! They are ready for us, for you. Past them, I say, and put me down to the side of the To-gai-ru force."

The dragon growled, and Brynn could feel him stiffening with frustration as they flew past the Behrenese army. But Agradeleous, somewhat sated by the destruction he had wrought that dark evening, obeyed her command.

Less than twenty minutes later, Brynn, flanked by the sentries she had met at the perimeter of the To-gai-ru encampment, walked in to speak with their commanders. How pleased she was to find old Barachuk among them!

"We have heard that another great city has fallen!" the old man said, trembling with excitement, tears streaming down his face, after he and Brynn had shared a great hug.

"Pruda," Brynn told him, told all of the many who were then gathering about her. "The city is ours, though we will leave it behind us, as we left Dharyan."

"Is the Chezru Chieftain to suffer no permanent losses?" asked one of the other men, a scowling giant of a man, with dark eyes and many battle scars.

"He has suffered many already," Brynn replied. "And many more will follow. The Chezhou-Lei are in disarray, those who did not die at the Mountains of Fire and in the two conquered cities. He has lost many, many warriors, and suffers the weight of thousands of refugees, streaming down the roads from the west. He has an invading army running loose about his kingdom, while his army, a great force, chases ghosts on the To-gai plain." She looked back to the south, where the fires of the distant, destroyed outposter settlement were still sending a glow into the night sky. "And one outposter settlement," Brynn finished. "My attack there has turned the Behrenese army."

"They have pursued us doggedly for several days," Barachuk explained.

"Then I have given you some time to widen your lead on them."

"What force did you bring with you?" the scowling giant man asked. "Enough so that we can do battle with the Behrenese army here and now, and finish this?"

"If I had brought the whole of my force with me, I would not do battle with the Behrenese army," Brynn replied. "Let them continue to run over the empty ground, to meander futilely in To-gai, while I rain destruction inside Behren. Stay ahead of them, I beg, and lead them ever farther westward and northward, into the foothills of the mountains."

"And when are we to fight?"

Brynn shrugged and shook her head. "Every day that you take them further from Behren gives me two days to convince the Chezru Chieftain and his people that this war is folly. Pruda has fallen, and we have many more cities in line." She stared hard at the man as she spoke, and it was obvious to her that he was not enjoying her answer. She understood well enough; he was a warrior and wanted nothing more than to do battle with the Behrenese, whatever the odds. In looking around him, Brynn saw that many others seemed to share his sentiments.

"You will get your fight, my friend," Brynn promised. "On the ground of our choosing, at the time of our choosing."

"Not soon enough," the warrior replied. "I will see every dog Wrap out of my homeland, or dead on the grasses!"

"Hold faith in us, in me, I beg of you all," Brynn said. "Each conquered city will grow my army, as both Dharyan and Pruda already have. Wear this force thin. Make them long for home. Send out smaller bands around them if you can, and destroy any supply caravans. Attrition greatly favors those defending their homeland. The Behrenese soldiers hate this land because they do not understand it, and if you are cunning and quick, you will make them hate it all the more. Watch their numbers thin as hungry soldiers give up and run away."

"Not one will get out of To-gai alive," the scowling man declared.

Brynn walked up to him. "What is your name?"

"I am Tanalk Grenk of Kayleen Kek," he declared, and Brynn stepped back, her eyes widening, at the mention of her old tribe. And at a name that seemed familiar to her.

"I was of Kayleen Kek," she said, and the man was nodding, and looking past her. She turned and noted a nodding Barachuk.

"I remember you," Tanalk said, "though you were but a child. It pleases me to see you again."

Brynn turned back and put her hand up on the large man's strong shoulder. "Take the fastest and strongest twoscore," she said to him. "Lead them against the caravans. Strike wherever you can, and as hard as you can. Live off the bounty of the land, as you—as we all—were taught, while the Behrenese stumble and starve."

A wicked smile widened on the large man's face and he nodded slowly.

A tremendous roar rumbled through the night, from somewhere out in the distance.

"I must be away," said Brynn. "Back to Behren, back to our kinfolk army, now in the conquered city of Pruda. I will return as I can, if I can. But whether any of you ever see me again, I beg of you to hold fast the old ways of the To-gai-ru, and to deny to your last breath the will of the Behrenese conquerors."

A great cheer went up about her, with many weapons brandished high in the air.

She let that cheer echo in her thoughts behind the veil of wind as she sped back to the east that night, past the Behrenese army that had broken camp and begun their march to the burning settlement. She and Agradeleous went past that settlement, and a dozen more beyond, down over the plateau rim and across the wavy, blowing sands.

She knew the danger of the situation, knew that these early victories would likely be the easiest, and knew all too well that one day soon, those cheers of hope might well turn to cries of despair.

But so be it.

Brynn had not started this war—that had been done by the Chezru Chieftain more than a decade before. But she meant to fight it until her dying breath, if need be. That grim determination was her only defense against the awful images and sounds of that dying outposter settlement.

But so be it.

# CHAPTER 29

## *Exacting a Promise*

Pagonel found Brynn at her morning ritual of *bi'nelle dasada*, something he thought quite curious, for he had not seen the woman performing that exercise in many weeks. She seemed very earnest about it, though, falling into the steps and movements with an intensity beyond anything he had previously witnessed from her.

He knew then that she was using the dance as a shield of some sort, burying emotions behind a wall of discipline.

He found her robe nearby and took it with him, then approached her as she danced.

She looked at him curiously when she saw him, for he knew better than to disturb this ritual!

Pagonel continued his earnest approach, and tossed the robe to the nude woman.

Brynn caught it and stood there for a long while holding it and staring at Pagonel. Then, suddenly feeling very naked indeed, the woman wrapped the robe about herself and continued to stare. "What do you know that so troubles you?" she asked.

"What I know does not trouble me," the mystic calmly replied. "The looting of Pruda is complete, with supplies packed, treasures hidden, and one cache sent to the south with the contingent, as you ordered, to go and hire whatever mercenaries they might find, including fierce pirates. What I know tells me that the war progresses better than we could ever have hoped. It is what I do not know that troubles me."

"About Merwan Ma?"

"About Brynn Dharielle."

Brynn studied him intensely, and he moved right up to her, then began walking about her, staring hard. "You cannot hide, you know."

"Am I trying to hide?"

Pagonel smiled at her sarcasm, but his look went serious almost immediately. "Tell me of your return to To-gai last night," the mystic bade her.

"I found the Behrenese army chasing our own, with the cunning To-gai-ru leading them far to the west," Brynn replied, with too much calm by Pagonel's estimate.

"And so you hide from me, and I have no lights to reveal your shadows," the mystic said. "But does your dance truly allow you to hide from yourself?"

Brynn snorted and waved him away. "You speak like a fool," she said, and snorted again.

But that last chide was cut short by a sudden gulp of air, a sudden pang of overwhelming guilt. Brynn turned away quickly, trying to hide her horrified expression from the mystic, but Pagonel was there, right beside her, lifting her chin in his strong hand so that he could look deeply into her moistening eyes.

"What did you see?" he asked softly. Brynn tried to turn away, but he held her firmly. "What did you do?"

"They would have caught up to our fleeing force," the woman blurted suddenly. "Their great army! They would have overrun Barachuk and the others in a short time. I had to widen the lead until the terrain favored our forces."

"You set Agradeleous upon the Behrenese," the mystic reasoned.

"Not the army," Brynn admitted. "They were too strong, even for the dragon. But there was a village nearby, an outposter settlement." As she finished, she fell into Pagonel's arms, burying her face against his strong chest.

"You set the wurm upon the village?" he asked, and he felt Brynn's nod against his chest. The mystic pushed the woman back to arm's length.

"Agradeleous burned it to the ground. None escaped, I am certain."

Pagonel nodded, both knowingly and sympathetically. "I once asked you if the price was worth the end," he reminded. "Are the horrors of war—of any war—worth the end result of freedom for To-gai? You believed that they were."

Brynn paused a moment to reflect upon that conversation, and upon the resolve that she had shown for so long, weighing against the black doubts that fluttered all about her. "That was before I was handed the power that is Agradeleous."

There was a logic in that statement that was hard for the mystic to deny.

"Yet it was your army, and not the beast, that destroyed the Pruda garrison utterly and overran the city," he did remark. "Surely the destruction here was great, as was the stench of death in the air. It is not so different."

"That was honest battle, man against man," Brynn countered. "With the village, it was . . . it was just slaughter."

"And how do you plan to prevent that in the future?" came a melodic voice to the side, and the two turned to see Juraviel and Cazzira approaching.

"Why do you not tell me?" Brynn snapped back at him, quite harshly. "You brought this beast upon me, this scourge."

"You presume that I could have stopped Agradeleous if I had wanted," the elf calmly replied. "When the dragon determined that it would leave its dark hole, I had no power to convince it otherwise. But I did bring it to the cause of freedom—that is something, at least."

"Is it?" Brynn asked, pulling away from Pagonel to stand before Juraviel. "In using the beast, am I—are we—any better than the Behrenese who conquered To-gai? Or are we worse, since we have loosed upon them a power that we cannot truly control?"

"A question for each of us to ask," Juraviel replied with a shrug. "But know this as you seek an answer: The beast is out, and not I, and not you, can put it back in its dark hole. Will you now wage war against Agradeleous? How many will you lose, and how lost will be your cause?"

Brynn looked back to Pagonel, but the mystic had no answers for her.

"I could not prevent the rising of the dragon," Juraviel went on. "But was it not better that I flew him to the south and distinguished his enemies as the Chezhou-Lei and not the Jhesta Tu? Is it not better that Agradeleous' destruction is aimed at the oppressor instead of the oppressed?"

Brynn sighed and looked at the elves and the mystic helplessly. "I feel the weight of a responsibility too great."

"Yet because you bear that weight with compassion, the artifacts of the Library of Pruda remain intact," Pagonel pointed out. "You have not indiscriminately loosed the power of Agradeleous upon the Behrenese."

"Tell that to the outposters of that village," said Brynn.

"And how many other villages did you pass on your flight west, and then back to the east?" asked the mystic. "Were they all set ablaze?"

That did make Brynn feel a bit better, obviously, and she just nodded in reply, and said, "I hate this war."

"I hate any war," said Pagonel. "And so I ask you again, and you must ask yourself, every day if need be, if the price is acceptable for the outcome. Is the concept of To-gai free worth the horrors that will take her there?"

Brynn glanced over at Juraviel and gave a helpless shrug. "I wish the wurm had stayed in its hole."

"You should wish more that the Yatols had not invaded your homeland," the elf replied.

"I could not tell you the routes if I wished to, for I am as unfamiliar with this land as are you," Merwan Ma said defiantly when Pagonel came to him in the back of a covered wagon, bounding along a dry riverbed later that day. The whole of the Pruda citizenry those who had survived the assault, had been set on the road to the east, and then Brynn had turned her own army south, leaving the emptied city to the hot winds and the carrion birds.

"The Dragon of To-gai asks nothing of you," the mystic replied, settling in beside the still-wounded man. Pagonel reached down and pulled back Merwan Ma's shirt, then nodded hopefully at the continuing progress of his healing upon the dagger wounds.

Merwan Ma looked away, at first defiant, but then his eyes gradually lowered and a great sadness swept over him, and he began to sob.

"Why were you sent away?" Pagonel asked him. "Why did the God-Voice of Behren think Merwan Ma such a threat? I have read much of the Chezru hierarchy in the tomes I found in Pruda, including one unfinished reference of Chezru Chieftain Yakim Douan. That tome mentioned Merwan Ma. Your loyalty to the God-Voice seems obvious enough."

"You would say that, yet you expect me to betray him to you?" the Shepherd asked.

"I am voicing the questions that you are afraid to ask of yourself," Pagonel explained. "There is confusion within Merwan Ma, great and devastating. You are horrified to think that Chezru Douan would have you killed, and yet it is obvious that he tried to do exactly that. But you remain afraid to ask the questions, and so I have asked them for you."

"You would heal my heart as you mend my wounds?" came the sarcastic response.

"Perhaps," the mystic replied with all sincerity, and he looked at the scars crossing Merwan Ma's belly one more time, then crawled out the back of the wagon, leaving Merwan Ma alone with the unsettling thoughts.

The Shepherd tried to put his head back against the side of the bouncing coach, but his wounds would not allow such a stretch, so he scrunched over instead, folded his arms onto his bent knees, and buried his face there. He tried to deny Pagonel's words, over and over again, tried to reason that Shauntil had acted the part of a rogue, had grasped for power on his own by trying to murder the Chezru Chieftain's choice for governor of Dharyan. Yes, and if only he could get back to Chom Deiru and inform the God-Voice, Shauntil would be punished for his heinous act.

Merwan Ma told himself that over and over again. And yet he understood, somewhere deep in his mind, that if he returned to Chom Deiru, he would likely be summarily executed.

But why?

He scoured his memories for any offense he might have offered against the God-Voice, however unintended. He could see nothing glaring.

But one image, that of a bloody Yakim Douan cravenly clutching a chalice, kept coming to mind.

That had been the turning point, obviously, but what crime, what sin, had he committed concerning the chalice? He knew of its unexpected content, that gemstone, but had told not a soul. Nor could he even be certain that there was anything amiss concerning that gemstone. Perhaps it was nothing more than a decorative filler block, that the great and ornate cup could be filled without draining too much blood from those offering the sacrifice.

There was nothing amiss about that, after all. Yatol did not forbid gemstones—only the use of magical gemstones, such as those of the Abellican heretics.

At least one of those heretics was a close personal friend of the God-Voice.

Finally, Merwan Ma tilted his head back, ignoring the stretching pull across his scarred tissue, too consumed by the awful possibilities that loomed all about him even to notice the discomfort.

It all made no sense, all seemed a preposterous trick of this Jhesta Tu mystic, attempting to bend the awful actions of one rogue Chezhou-Lei to some personal gain. And yet, though he denied it consciously and vocally, it seemed undeniable to Merwan Ma's heart.

Chezru Chieftain Yakim Douan, his beloved God-Voice, the man to whom he had given the service of his entire adult life, had ordered him murdered.

Brynn surveyed the landscape, the flowing brown dunes sweeping like great breakers toward the one spot of varying colors, where date trees swayed in the hot wind and grasses grew thick about their trunks, bordering a long and narrow lake. Rows of small houses lined that lake, leading up to a single brown castle, squat and thick, with weathered brown walls pierced with arrow slits and a roof that sloped in varying angles.

It had taken her three weeks to bring her army there, mostly across empty sand, for they wished to follow no course that their enemies could predict. A welcome sight indeed was this place, as any settlement would have been to the weary and battle-hungry To-gai-ru.

"Garou Oasis," Pagonel said to her, sitting astride a horse beside her and Runtly.

"A city with no walls," Brynn remarked.

"Typical for an oasis stop," the mystic explained. "This is the waypoint for caravans, who pay a large tithe to water their animals and themselves."

"As we shall do, though we'll pay no tithe."

"The settlers of the houses will flee before us, no doubt, into their castle," said Pagonel. "From there, they will shower us with arrows."

"Then we will flatten their castle before we drink," Brynn said matter-of-factly, a coldness that was not lost on the mystic.

"Take care with this place," Pagonel warned. "The castles of the Behren oases are the strongest fortresses in all the country. They need not house many—I would guess that fewer than five hundred live here—and yet they normally hold great storerooms of wealth, for the tithe of using an oasis is never cheap. They are built to withstand an army, and you'll not lure them out, as you did at both Dharyan and Pruda."

"We shall see," Brynn said, and she turned Runtly and walked him away.

They came in as a swarm of destruction, churning the soft and hot sands all about the oasis. Unlike her previous victories, Brynn held nothing back against Garou Oasis, charging her entire force, which now numbered closer to five thousand than four, in a tightening ring. Those Behrenese in the outlying houses didn't even try to offer resistance against the To-gai-ru horde, fleeing straightaway for the defensive castle.

Most got in ahead of the To-gai-ru surge, though some were trampled down. Barely moments after the attack began, the oasis was quiet once more, with Brynn's army surrounding the last bastion of Behrenese defense.

One group of Behrenese was not inside, though. A visiting caravan milled about the castle door, denied entrance, with nowhere to run or hide.

Brynn wouldn't bring her soldiers in close to the well-armed fortress, though, nor did she allow the To-gai-ru to cut down the trapped merchants with their great bows.

She walked Runtly around to that side of the castle, close enough to make eye contact with some of the frantic Behrenese—and many began pounding on the door once more at the sight of the woman given such deference by the other To-gai-ru as to mark her obviously as the fierce leader of this army.

Brynn lifted a hand to the Behrenese and motioned for them to approach.

They held back, some still pounding on the unyielding iron door.

"You have nowhere to turn," Brynn called out to them. "Your surrender will be accepted, if offered. Else you will die where you stand."

Those simple words seemed to break the will of many of the merchants, and they exchanged despairing looks and threw up their hands, walking out toward Brynn and bowing repeatedly.

The first volley came forth from the castle then, a hail of arrows aimed primarily at Brynn. Most fell short, though, some even cutting into the poor merchants as they made their way out from the castle.

They all scrambled, as did Brynn, leaping Runtly aside, but not before one arrow struck the pony's foreleg, digging a deep gash and making him rear, nearly dislodging the woman.

The Behrenese merchants were in a full run, then, fleeing in terror from their own countrymen. Brynn's soldiers pulled them in roughly, herding them to a central point, while Brynn, with Runtly back under control, marched defiantly back to her previous position.

"Despite your insolence, I offer you a similar chance to surrender," she yelled out to the castle.

"Go away!" came a curt reply. "You cannot defeat our thick walls, fool, and we'll not run out to do battle with you. Water your horses if you choose, for we cannot stop you, but your victory here has reached its end! Go away!"

Brynn held her sword aloft and sent a burst of fire running the length of its blade. "I am the Dragon of To-gai!" she cried. "Dharyan has fallen. Pruda has fallen. There is no escape for you. I will knock the walls of your fortress down around you!"

The answer came in the form of another volley of arrows, but Brynn was already moving her precious mount out of harm's way.

"Water the horses and resupply on the far side of the lake," she instructed her commanders as she crossed by them. "But keep a perimeter of scouts up and ready. If they try to flee the castle, chase them into the open desert."

"What of them?" one tall and stern To-gai-ru warrior asked, pointing out the twenty merchant prisoners and their slaves, which included some To-gai-ru.

"Our countrymen will join with us—find them mounts from among the captured," Brynn instructed. "Allow the Behrenese servants to go. Give them mounts and supplies enough to get them to the next town in line. And the merchants . . ."

Brynn paused, considering what value might be gleaned from the unexpected prisoners. "Send them south with the next group bearing wealth in the hopes of employing mercenaries. Tell our leaders in that action to use them for ransom."

The warrior, and many others, looked at her skeptically, an expression that Brynn returned with one of inquisition.

"We agreed long ago that we would take no prisoners," the man explained.

Brynn looked to the groveling merchants, men and women grown soft from living most of their lives in almost decadent luxury, from having others do all of their menial tasks for them.

"They will hardly hinder us," she decided. "As we take this war more fully into Behren, employing greedy pirates and mercenaries, we will need even greater wealth, and I suspect that this group will offer anything to save their soft skins, whatever the cost to Behren."

"Yes, my Dragon," the warrior agreed with a brisk bow.

The title hit Brynn like a slap. She knew that many had taken to referring to her in that manner, but given what she knew of Agradeleous' true, destructive nature, she wasn't sure that the title was quite the compliment intended.

The warrior woman, ranger and trained in Jhesta Tu, steeled herself against those twangs of guilt. She had told the impudent Behrenese that she would topple their walls around them, and she meant to do just that. The fortress at Garou had been built to withstand the fastest spears thrown by ballistae, the heaviest shot of catapults, and the thunder of magical gemstones, the greatest engines of war ever devised by man.

But Brynn had a greater weapon than that at her disposal.

Juraviel and Cazzira turned their heads in unison to see the approach of Brynn, the woman walking and not astride Runtly. The elves, along with Agradeleous, had put up behind the shelter of a high dune, a half mile from the besieged oasis, and as with the victory at Pruda, and despite the night of devastation he had rained upon the outposters in To-gai, insatiable Agradeleous did not seemed pleased to be left out of the fighting.

The dragon's lip curled up over his fangs and he gave a low grumble and moved away as Brynn neared the elves.

"You did not try to lure them out," Cazzira remarked. "I was surprised to see the whole of your force charging to battle."

"Not the whole of her force," came Agradeleous' sarcastic remark.

"Different tactics for a different battleground," Brynn explained. "I wanted them forced within the castle, and so they are, and now I mean to tear it down."

All three heads turned on that cue, to regard the suddenly interested dragon, and Agradeleous' lip curled again, this time with apparent delight.

Brynn walked between the elves, approaching the dragon

directly. "This will be your most difficult challenge yet," she said.

The dragon scoffed, a curious sound, hissing and rumbling all at once.

"I will take you against the fortress, destroying the shell around our enemies that my army can swarm over them," Brynn explained.

"You should have begun the battle like that," Agradeleous growled back at her.

"I offer you this opportunity, as I did in To-gai that night three weeks ago," Brynn said, and again the dragon scoffed.

"Do you believe that you could stop me if I decided to take this opportunity?"

Brynn walked to stand directly before the wurm, who was in his lizardlike humanoid form, and she eyed him hard, unblinking. Behind her, Juraviel and Cazzira exchanged concerned looks, and both rushed up to stand beside the brave, and apparently foolish, woman.

"I will allow you to continue to follow my army, Agradeleous," Brynn said firmly. "But I offer this opportunity to you only with your promise that when I require it, you will return to your lair and haunt neither To-gai nor Behren any longer."

Agradeleous' wide-eyed scoffing response seemed the prelude to a sudden and deadly attack, so much so that Juraviel pulled Brynn back a step and Cazzira leaped before the dragon, waving her arms to distract him and give him a moment, at least, to reconsider the strike.

But Brynn didn't blink.

"I could destroy you here and now, human!" the dragon roared. "I could burn you where you stand, to ashes! Or grab you up in my hands and tear you in half, with hardly an effort."

"With no effort at all, likely," Brynn agreed. "But to what gain? And to what long-term detriment?"

The dragon narrowed its reptilian eyes, seeming hardly convinced.

"You will agree, or your time here is at its end," Brynn said.

Agradeleous issued a long and low rumble.

"And you will be handsomely paid for your service!" Belli'mar Juraviel said suddenly, moving before Brynn. "For when To-gai is free, we will deliver a line of treasure to your lair, wealth fairly earned for your services!"

Agradeleous tried to hold his angry glower, but one eye did widen, tellingly, at the appeal of that offer.

Brynn, though, was much less thrilled that Juraviel had offered anything, or that he had intervened at all in this necessary showdown between her and Agradeleous. For in reflecting upon that horrible night in To-gai, Brynn Dharielle had decided that she would either assure herself control of the beast, or she would dismiss the beast. There could be no compromise.

"A treasure delivered by five hundred human slaves!" Agradeleous demanded suddenly, eyeing Brynn with every word.

"No!" the warrior woman shot back, and there was no compromise in her tone. "Delivered by men of free will."

"Who will entertain me with stories—and if I find those great tales of adventure acceptable, then perhaps I will not devour them!" Agradeleous pressed.

"No!"

The dragon roared.

"Name me as your enemy here and now, then!" Brynn demanded, pushing past the elves to stand right before Agradeleous. "Strike me dead with your fiery breath and know that all the peoples south of the mountains will rise against Agradeleous. And they will take you down, united, for the war between Behren and To-gai will seem inconsequential beside the true horror of a wild dragon. What place will you find, mighty Agradeleous, where you might sleep well again? For I know the way to your lair, and have spread out many informants, who will deliver those directions to mighty enemies if I am betrayed and killed by you."

The dragon's eyes narrowed to threatening slits.

"I desire to ride upon your back this night, that you and I, as allies, will topple the fortress of Garou. But I will not do that, Agradeleous, until I have your word that when I am done with you, you will return to your lair and bother the race of man no more."

"And what will I have from you, Brynn Dharielle, the Dragon of To-gai?" the wurm hissed.

"Treasure," Brynn answered, nodding deferentially toward Juraviel. "Finely worked pieces, and delivered by To-gai-ru bards, who will sing to you and tell you great tales—proper reward for your service to our cause.

"But it must be to *our* cause, Agradeleous, and not to your own!" the woman added fiercely. "That is the leash I demand about your neck."

"You demand?"

"I demand!" Brynn countered with striking intensity, her eyes widening and sparkling with inner fires that seemed to more than match the dragon's own.

Agradeleous fell back a step, and for one horrible moment, both Brynn and the elves expected the beast to pounce upon her and devour her. Then came the dragon's laughter, grating and mighty bellows.

And then it stopped, suddenly, and Agradeleous stared back at Brynn. He moved with awesome speed toward her.

But not to throttle her or devour her. Rather, Agradeleous fell to one knee before her in the sand.

"Climb on my shoulders, Dragon of To-gai!" he said. "Let us show our enemies how feeble their fortress walls are against the power of Agrad . . . against the power of To-gai!"

"I have your word?"

"Tell me when I may go and rest. I am growing weary of this adventure already."

Brynn looked over to Juraviel, who wore a perplexed, but ultimately pleased, expression.

The air was still that night, crisp and clear and with a thousand stars twinkling above, but no moon shone over the desert sands. And so it was dark, and so none noticed that some of the stars seemed to wink out momentarily, briefly blocked by a moving line of blackness.

Alone astride Agradeleous, Brynn did not light her sword. Riding her engine of destruction, the woman glided down quietly toward the mighty fortress, repeatedly checking the

leather straps she had secured about the dragon as a make-
shift saddle.

"Straight and strong," she whispered to the great wurm,
though she doubted that he could hear her words against the
rush of air.

The dragon folded back his wings and dropped like a gigantic spear toward the dark mound of the fortress. Just before impact, Agradeleous swooped back up, opening wide his
great leathery wings and landing hard against the side of the
fortress, his huge clawed feet digging deep footholds in the
soft sandstone, shaking the castle so forcefully that waves
rippled across the oasis pond fifty feet away.

Cries began immediately from within the place, and when
Brynn lifted her sword and set it ablaze, her soldiers ringing
the fortress took up great cheers and war shouts.

Brynn held on tight as the dragon went into a frenzy, his
great tail smashing at the walls, his forelegs and great maw
tearing at the stone. An arrow came out at him from one
nearby slit, bouncing harmlessly off his scaly hide, and the
dragon responded by putting his mouth against the slit and
breathing a burst of great fire within.

How the howls inside increased!

But the resistance from within erupted suddenly, as well,
with many arrows coming out, buzzing in the air about
Agradeleous and Brynn, clipping off the dragon's thick
scales to poke and stick against his leathery wings. That only
increased the dragon's fury, and he leaped up from the side
and dropped back down, again and again, shaking the whole
of the place, weakening the integrity of the thick walls. His
tail continued to smash hard, as well, and wherever he saw an
opening, the dragon breathed his fire.

"The gate! The gate!" Brynn bade, for she had purposely
brought Agradeleous in against the front side of the place,
with a definite plan for opening it wide.

The dragon hopped a few more times, smashing and tearing, then finally seemed to hear the shouting woman. He
snapped his snakelike neck, sending his maw hard into the
soft stone just above the iron gate, and there he focused much
of his wrath, burrowing through the soft stone, biting and

gnashing until at last his teeth clamped on something more substantial.

With a great heave, Agradeleous retracted his head, pulling the slab of iron right through the soft stone, then snapping his head high and to the side, launching the great gate of Garou Castle far into the night, to splash into the oasis pond.

Agradeleous' head snapped down even lower and he filled the castle entryway with his killing fire.

And then he thrashed some more, and a great slap of his tail at last toppled a portion of the wall, dropping great chunks of stone on the helpless defenders inside.

But the stubborn Behrenese kept up their rain of missiles, which now included great spears hurled from ballistae.

"Fly free!" Brynn ordered the dragon.

Agradeleous continued to thrash, snapping his head into the opening left by the toppled wall, grabbing one man up in his toothy maw.

Brynn winced, hearing the bones crunch under the weight of that terrible bite, and then the man was gone, just like that.

"Fly free!" she yelled again, and the dragon spun out and slammed his tail against the weakened wall once more, knocking a larger chunk free to topple inside. And then, to Brynn's great relief, Agradeleous leaped away, his great wings beating the air to lift them far away in short order.

Brynn closed her eyes and allowed herself to breathe. The dragon had obeyed.

Then the woman opened her eyes and looked back to the battered castle, to see the opened gate area and the even larger gouge in the wall to the side. Smoke was rising from both openings, and from the roof as well, from fires no doubt begun by Agradeleous' breath. Now, seeing Brynn's sword held high as she and the dragon flew away, her army began its charge.

By the time Agradeleous set Brynn down beside the elves and Runtly, and she was able to ride her pony back to the oasis, the fighting was done, the fortress taken, and the few defenders left alive had been herded together in a small circle.

Brynn rode to that circle and dismounted. Then she walked about the terrified, overwhelmed Behrenese. "Supply them and send them on their way," she told her warriors, and then to the prisoners, she instructed, "Go and tell your countrymen of the fate of Garou Oasis. Tell them of the Dragon of To-gai, of the fate that will befall them, all of them, unless the Chezru Chieftain declares To-gai free. There are no castle walls strong enough to defy me."

And then she walked away.

# CHAPTER 30

## *One Angry Cat, One Clever Mouse*

"From Alzuth?" the Chezru Chieftain asked, referring to the next city in line south of Pruda, and, to his thinking, the next city in line for the Dragon of To-gai. Only a couple of weeks before, Yakim Douan had heard of the fall of Pruda, and now, hearing that frantic men had arrived bearing news of another disaster, he expected that Alzuth had fallen.

His new attendant, a skinny and tall Shepherd named Took, shook his head slowly. "Garou Oasis, God-Voice," he said quietly.

The others in the room, Yatols who had come in with reports of increasing pirate activity and other unsettling events, began to whisper nervously. The Chezru Chieftain motioned for them to remain calm, but his own expression showed that he, too, was a bit unsettled by the unexpected news. For Garou Oasis was not along the plateau line directly south of Pruda, as he had expected the Dragon of To-gai to run, but was farther inland, farther east, and along the southwestern road out of Jacintha.

Yakim Douan slumped back in his chair, his face tight with concentration.

"God-Voice, what does it mean?" Yatol De Hamman asked desperately. "Does the Dragon of To-gai intend to charge at Jacintha?"

Again, the Chezru Chieftain patted his hand reassuringly in the air. "Show the emissaries in," he instructed Took, and the man bowed repeatedly, skittering for the door, and returned in a moment with three dirty men, one of whom, Doyugga Doy, Yakim Douan recognized as an ambassador from Garou.

"God-Voice," Doyugga said, prostrating himself on the floor before the Chezru Chieftain. "I beseech you! She is mighty beyond words! Her horse can change into a great dragon, wielding fire as she wields fire! And the barbarians follow her without regard to their own lives! They are mad, God-Voice! Mad, I say!"

"The oasis was overrun?" Yakim Douan asked calmly.

"Crushed!" the man replied. "They swept in like a sandstorm. I think that they were sand, yes, magically transformed sand, sweeping in on fast winds. My master, Yatol embrace him, brought in all of the villagers, as many as our fortress could hold, but the Ru leader turned her horse into a dragon and smashed down our walls! And then her warriors flew in on the wind, as many as grains of sand!"

The other Yatols began talking amongst themselves nervously, exclaiming "dragon!" or "sandstorm!" repeatedly, but Yakim Douan was less impressed. He had been hearing these stories over and over again, about every war that had been fought in the last few centuries. Without fail, those fleeing exaggerated the strength of the enemy, if only to put aside any blame they might otherwise have to shoulder for running away in the first place.

Still, Yakim Douan understood that he had to take this threat seriously, though he doubted that the To-gai-ru, even if all of their tribes had combined into a singular force, could have any chance of doing much harm at all to mighty Jacintha.

But there remained the issue of this dragon . . .

"You saw the wurm yourself?" he asked Doyugga, and the man's head began to bob.

"God-Voice, it was as large as a great house! Its breath was fire, its tail thunder! Its claws dug the stone as easily as if it was mud! It pulled my friend Yuzeth, Yatol embrace him, right from out beside me, crushed him in its great jaws and swallowed him! I saw, God-Voice, I saw!"

He was bobbing up and down and sobbing uncontrollably as he recounted the story, and so Yakim Douan motioned for a pair of guards to come and gather him up and drag him out of there.

"Where is Yatol Tohen Bardoh?" the Chezru Chieftain asked his attendant.

"He marches north along the plateau ridge, and should make Dharyan in a few days, God-Voice."

"Will you send him, too, into To-gai?" came a question from Yatol De Hamman, and only when Yakim Douan fixed him with a threatening stare did he seem to realize that he was way over the line of good judgment. The fact that Shauntil and fifteen thousand Jacintha warriors were running about the seemingly empty steppes of To-gai, while this Dragon and her army were cutting a swath of destruction across Behren did not sit well with Yakim Douan—and Yatols offering sarcasm on the matter might well find themselves hanging by their necks outside the Chezru temple.

Yakim Douan's stare reminded the upstart and angry De Hamman of just that.

"Send word to Governor Pestle to turn Yatol Bardoh and his forces straight east for Jacintha," the Chezru Chieftain commanded. That brought murmurs of discontent among the gathered Yatols, most of whom commanded cities in the western provinces of the country, and who would depend upon that great combined force now led by the fearsome Bardoh for protection from the Dragon of To-gai.

"They wish to lead us on a fruitless chase about the desert, but Yatol will show me the way to them, and this unpleasant business can be finished once and for all," Yakim Douan said to quiet them. He glared at Yatol De Hamman before the man could utter a word.

"You were going to note that Yatol led me errantly in sending Shauntil into To-gai?" he asked.

The man blanched. "No, God-Voice. Never would I—"

"Spare me your lies, Yatol," Douan replied. "I understand your fears."

"If you were in our tentative position, you would feel the same," Yatol De Hamman said defensively. "The pirates that Yatol Peridan has coddled have been bought by the Dragon of To-gai's ill-gotten gains, and now attack my coastline mercilessly."

"No," the Chezru Chieftain insisted. "If I were in your position, I would trust in Yatol, and hold all confidence that this Dragon of To-gai would soon enough run out of tricks and out of luck. I will find her, and I will destroy her and all of her followers. And if there is truly a dragon, a great beast of mythology, flying beside her, then I will destroy it as well, and what a fine trophy its horned head will make upon my wall!"

That brought some murmurs of excitement, even a bit of laughter, from the gathered Yatols. But Douan ended it abruptly by fixing Yatol De Hamman with an imposing stare. "And when I am done with her and her followers, I will indeed send Yatol Tohen Dardoh into To-gai, to join with Chezhou-Lei Shauntil to punish the upstart To-gai-ru for the trouble they have caused to me."

The next day, a report came in from southern Behren that a band of outlaws had attacked a small settlement before being hunted down by the local Yatol's forces. One of the captured raiders had invoked the name of the Dragon of To-gai, and had carried a pouch bulging with coins bearing the Pruda stamp.

A few days later, an emissary from Avrou Eesa, Yatol Bardoh's own city, arrived with news that demands of ransom had been sent to prominent merchant families, payment for the return of a band of merchants captured at Garou when they had been denied entrance to the fortress.

"Find Doyugga Doy and learn if this is true, that a band of merchants visiting Garou Oasis had been denied entrance to the fortress at the time of attack," Douan instructed Took.

"I will return with the response, God-Voice," Took said obediently, offering yet another series of his ridiculous bows. Watching him, Yakim Douan could only think of a drunken stork, and how he missed Merwan Ma at that time!

"That is not necessary," he said to the attendant. "Ask the question and hear Doyugga Doy's answer."

"And if it is true?"

"Have him hung in the square, publicly, and speak his

crime as cowardice," Yakim Douan declared. "This is not the time for cowards, my friend. I'll not suffer them to live."

"Yes, God-Voice," the obviously shaken Shepherd said repeatedly, backing out of the room and continuing his endless series of ridiculous bows.

Douan, glad to be alone, slumped back and blew a frustrated sigh. This one was getting the better of him. She, if it truly was a woman, was hitting helter-skelter, and finding perfect tactics to overwhelm each target. Douan had spent the morning with some of his Chezhou-Lei, going over the reported descriptions of the battles, and they had all agreed that this Dragon of To-gai was a cunning adversary.

Two weeks earlier, Garou Oasis had fallen, which meant that even now, the Dragon of To-gai might be looking across the sands at Jacintha.

So Yakim Douan had sent his Chezhou-Lei out to gather every garrison within the area and form a defensive perimeter about Jacintha, even before the arrival of Yatol Tohen Bardoh and fifteen thousand soldiers. He expected that many of the outlying Yatols would soon be crying for an audience—and De Hamman would scream loudest of all—fearful that he was protecting himself at their expense, but so be it. He certainly could not let Jacintha fall!

But while Yakim Douan could feel secure in his own safety and in that of Jacintha, he understood well that he could not allow the Dragon of To-gai to continue her rampage through the outer provinces. So far, his scouts had been unable to find her.

Reports of the fall of another city, Teramen, located between Garou and Dahdah Oasis, came in the next day.

Yakim Douan huddled about a large map with the newly arrived Yatol Tohen Bardoh and a few of his Chezhou-Lei commanders. All of them were surprised indeed at this latest choice of target.

"But it does make sense, God-Voice," one did admit. "From Teramen, the Dragon of To-gai can resupply, and can then hit back to the northeast, at Dahdah Oasis, or can even turn back to the northwest and strike at Dharyan once more, within a week."

Yakim Douan let his head loll forward at that prospect. Had he not just brought in Yatol Bardoh and fifteen thousand soldiers from Dharyan?

"I will force march back for Dharyan, God-Voice," offered Yatol Bardoh, a man of nearly sixty years, but in fine physical condition and with angry fires burning bright in his dark eyes.

"To Dahdah Oasis," Yakim Douan corrected. "Then split your force, with one contingent marching fast for Dharyan, and the other turning southwest to cut off any escape by the Dragon of To-gai to the south. If she hits at Dahdah, you will have her. If at Dharyan, then force her north into the mountains, or back to the To-gai steppes, where your forces and Shauntil's can close about her and destroy her."

"Yes, God-Voice," the man replied, and he stormed out of the room, his hard soles echoing loudly against the white-and-pink marble.

"She will beat us to either location, and so she may get one more victory, perhaps even two," Yakim Douan told his warlords. "But then she will be mine."

They all seemed quite pleased with themselves.

Of course, when Yatol Bardoh and his force arrived at Dahdah Oasis, they found the place perfectly quiet and secure. Those who force-marched ahead down the western road were greeted at Dharyan by the blowing horns of intact Governor Carwan Pestle. And those who hastened along a southwesterly route traveled all the way to the foot of the plateau divide without any sign of the invading To-gai-ru army.

A few weeks later, with the summer of God's Year 843 fast turning to autumn, Abellican reckoning, a fleet of many ships—mostly Behrenese pirates—sailed out of Entel for the open Mirianic. The fleet bore Aydrian Wyndon, Brynn Dharielle's friend of old—and all of old Abbot Olin's hopes—to a distant island that was rumored to be covered with millions of valuable gemstones. That same day, in Jacintha, Yakim Douan heard the first reports of lines of beleaguered refugees streaming down the road from the conquered *southern* city of Alzuth.

\*     \*     \*

"They fought well," Pagonel remarked to Brynn, when he caught up to the woman outside the conquered city of Alzuth. The place had been fully looted and gutted, with all Behrenese survivors sent on the road to the northeast.

Alzuth had proven to be the toughest battle yet. Brynn had used her bait-and-ambush tactic, and indeed, a force had come charging out the gate behind her fleeing force.

But a second force, great in number, had followed the first, coming on the battle even as Brynn's main army had descended upon the pursuing Alzuth force. While the fierce To-gai-ru had won the day anyway, several hundred had fallen out in the desert, prompting Brynn to use Agradeleous once more in the attack upon the city.

So Alzuth had fallen, yet another great victory for the Dragon of To-gai, and greater still because her followers understood that her ploy of unpredictability had worked yet again, luring thousands of Behrenese soldiers out along the road much farther north, far from the actual fighting. With Agradeleous continuing to supply the To-gai-ru, their mobility could not be matched and their route could not be predicted.

Still, they were only five thousand strong, and so a city like Alzuth, braced for battle, proved a formidable foe.

"The Behrenese defended their homes well," Brynn admitted, and the mystic nodded.

"The Chezru Chieftain will begin a sweep south, likely," Pagonel said. "And one west and south from Jacintha. Soon enough, I expect, he will recognize that he cannot hope to outguess you."

"My warriors are weary and battered," said Brynn. "Many carry wounds that require rest, though they'll not rest if I show them a city to conquer."

Pagonel nodded again. It was true enough—nearly every To-gai-ru warrior had been wounded at one point or another, and many of the horses carried scars.

"We should turn south and take respite," Brynn decided. "In the fields about the Mountains of Fire, perhaps. We rest and heal, and then Behren will be an open slate upon which we can strike our next mark."

"As long as you keep the wealth flowing to the mercenaries and the pirates, the Behrenese will know no rest," said Pagonel. "Though your delay may allow the Chezru Chieftain finally to pull his wayward force out of To-gai."

"Unless we make him believe that we have returned to the steppes," Brynn said with a wry grin. "I will take Agradeleous out there and level several outposter settlements. Perhaps we can lure even more of the Chezru Chieftain's soldiers out onto the open steppes, where the winter winds will find them and bite at them."

The mystic nodded, then he motioned to a pair of diminutive forms walking toward them.

Brynn's smile was genuine, and only then did she realize that she had not spoken with Juraviel and Cazzira in many days.

"A fine morning," the elf greeted. "Though Agradeleous warned us of a dust storm growing in the west."

"And where is Agradeleous?" Brynn asked, glancing all about.

"Out fetching water," Cazzira replied.

"We have all the water we can carry from Alzuth," said Brynn, a bit of suspicion creeping into her voice. As she hadn't seen the elves of late, she hadn't seen the dragon since the fall of Alzuth.

"Perhaps he has found nomads to destroy," Juraviel remarked, and when Brynn looked at him with obvious alarm, he merely shrugged. "It is his nature."

"He will go back to his hole when I instruct him to do so," said Brynn. "I have his word."

"And the word of a dragon is to be trusted," Juraviel assured her. "But did Agradeleous give to you his word that he would not fly out and take any offered opportunities to attack our enemies?"

Brynn shook her head. "I will have that word next."

"Take care how tight you hold the leash about Agradeleous," Cazzira warned. "The dragon's curiosity and loneliness has brought some conciliation from him, but that is not the nature of such beasts. And Agradeleous is well aware that you need him as much as he needs you—more so, perhaps, both in tilting the course of difficult fights and in keeping your army supplied well enough to move freely about the desert. The dragon understands his value, even if he does not enjoy his role as supplier and not warrior. If you push too far, Agradeleous will use that value against you, do not doubt."

It was good advice, Brynn knew.

"I have heard whispers that we will break now from the battle," said Juraviel.

Brynn nodded. "We are weary and wounded. It is time for some rest, both for our health and to put our enemies further off-balance. Let them march hard against the windstorms, and the snows of the steppes, while we prepare for renewed battle in the spring."

Juraviel and Cazzira exchanged looks which struck Brynn as somewhat out of place.

"What?" she prompted.

"Perhaps the break in the fighting would be the proper time for me and Cazzira to take our leave of Behren," Juraviel replied. "We have become no more than observers in this fight, for now your hold over Agradeleous is even greater than our own. Cazzira longs for Tymwyvenne, as do I, for another adventure awaits us in the north, one more pressing to both our peoples."

Brynn winced at the unexpected words, and for a moment, true panic set in. How could she continue to wage the war without the counsel of Belli'mar Juraviel? Even though she spoke with him less and less, she had always taken great comfort that he would be there for her when she most needed him. She looked to her human companion, at first desperately, as if silently asking him to intervene and argue against that course. But then, in just seeing Pagonel, Brynn came to understand that he, and not Juraviel, had become her true advisor.

Still, when she looked back at the elves, at Juraviel, who had been her companion for years, she feared that she would miss them terribly.

But she understood, as well, their desire to be gone, for a great adventure indeed awaited them in the lands north of the mountains. Brynn had no doubt that these two, so spiritually joined, so alike of mind and temperament, would find a way to unite their peoples. Then how much stronger Lady

Dasslerond's position would become, should the demon dactyl's stain push the Touel'alfar out of Andur'Blough Inninness, if she had Tymwyvenne's strength and friendship behind her.

It occurred to Brynn then, for the very first time, that the discovery of the Doc'alfar had greatly lessened the importance of her journey to free To-gai, from the perspective of the Touel'alfar. She looked at Belli'mar Juraviel curiously, and then appreciatively, recognizing that he could have left her long ago, that he could have left the dragon's lair heading north and not south.

"What will you tell Lady Dasslerond about my efforts?" she asked.

"I will tell her that you have performed amazingly well," the elf answered without hesitation. "I will tell her that if To-gai is not free by the hand of Brynn Dharielle, then Behren is simply too great a foe for To-gai to break. There is nothing more that you, or anyone, could possibly do to facilitate a successful revolution. Every course you have taken is the correct one, from dodging the Behrenese armies to outguessing the leaders of each walled city, to enlisting mercenaries and pirates in the south and east. Even your actions in controlling and utilizing Agradeleous have been beyond anything I could have expected."

Brynn took all the compliments with the severe caveat that they were being given as justification for Juraviel, perhaps her greatest friend in all the world, to leave her.

"It is a story not yet fully told," she countered. "Though one that will likely be completed, for good or for ill, within the next year. Are you not bound to see it through to the end?"

Juraviel paused and stared ahead blankly for a bit, digesting it all. "Would you have me stay?" he asked, simply and sincerely, and Brynn understood that if she said that she would, then he would not leave.

But the honesty of that question evoked a sense of true responsibility in the woman. She understood the emotions driving Juraviel, for a return to Tymwyvenne, and then with the Doc'alfar to Andur'Blough Inninness, could be as important to the elves as these battles in Behren were to the To-gai-ru.

Given that, was she acting responsibly as a friend by imploring Juraviel to stay here with her?

"When the war is complete, if we are victorious, I will send couriers to the land about Tymwyvenne to give a full recounting of the events," she offered, and then she smiled widely, "But only if I have Cazzira's promise that my couriers will not join the army of the Tylwyn Doc!"

Both elves laughed at that, as did Brynn, but Pagonel just looked from one to the other curiously.

"I will explain it another day," Brynn offered to the Jhesta Tu.

"A day when I am far, far away, no doubt," said Cazzira, and the three shared another laugh.

They chatted easily for some time then, about the adventures that had taken them to To-gai, and with many promises that one day they would meet again. Then Juraviel walked up to Brynn and took her hands in his own.

"There are those among my people who doubt the wisdom of training the rangers," he explained. "When they do, we speak to them of Mather; of Andacanavar, who still roams the wilds of Alpinador; and of Elbryan the Nightbird, who saved the world from the demon dactyl. And now, when the doubters speak up, they will be reminded of Brynn Dharielle, the Dragon of To-gai, who freed her people from the oppression of Behren."

"The To-gai-ru are not yet free," Brynn reminded.

"But they shall be, and soon enough," said Juraviel.

Brynn bent down a bit then and kissed her dear friend on the cheek, and they hugged tightly and for a long while, and more than one tear made its way down her brown cheek.

"Let us set the army on the road south," she said after a bit. "Then I will fly you to the base of the mountains, a quick start on your road to Tymwyvenne."

They heard a distant call for Brynn at that same time; one of her commanders needed her assistance. She backed away from Juraviel and wiped away her tears, then squeezed his hand once more and headed away with Pagonel.

"It is more difficult to leave her than you expected," Cazzira remarked to Juraviel when they were alone.

"I knew it would be hard. I found Brynn after I had lost a

dear friend, Nightbird, and feared that I would never mend the hole in my heart. I miss him still, I always will, but Brynn Dharielle taught me to smile once more. She reminds me yet again of why we train the rangers, of the good that they can do in the world."

Cazzira stepped in close beside him and took up his hand in her own, squeezing it gently. Juraviel turned a grateful look toward her, but one that fast shifted to a more serious and fearful expression.

"Do you think that she will win?" the Touel'alfar asked in all seriousness.

"I do not truly appreciate the power of her enemies," Cazzira replied. "But Pagonel does, and I believe that he thinks she will win out."

"You are surprised by these humans," Juraviel remarked.

"It makes me regret our practice of giving them to the bog," Cazzira admitted. "Never have my people viewed them as anything more than the goblins. I did not understand that they could be so self-sacrificing for principle, or so loyal."

"Tymwyvenne will change in the years ahead."

"Tymwyvenne already has," Cazzira replied. "The fact that you, and especially Brynn, still draw breath is proof of that!"

Juraviel, still watching the woman and Pagonel walk away, merely nodded.

"Have you yet solved the riddle of why your Chezru Chieftain desired you murdered?" Pagonel asked, sitting beside Merwan Ma that same night, in a sheltered place off to the side of the main To-gai-ru encampment.

Merwan Ma looked at him and snickered. Always the same question, every day. "You are a patient one," he said.

"I am willing to allow you to come to accept the truth of it in your own time," the mystic replied. "I believe that you will tell me, one day soon, because you will realize that the cause I support is just."

"Just?" the Shepherd scoffed. "You call the destruction of cities just? You believe that the blood of the thousands spilled upon the desert sands is just?"

"Regrettable, but unavoidable," the mystic answered, breaking out his pack and handing some food to his prisoner. "Do you believe that there is any other way for To-gai to break free of the iron grip of your former master? Or is it that you believe that grip to be just?"

"Chezru Chieftain Yakim Douan is the God-Voice," Merwan Ma insisted, and he pushed the food away. "His decisions are inspired, divinely so. He conquered To-gai to show the To-gai-ru a better way of life, and though there was immediate pain—"

"He conquered To-gai to fatten the purses of his greedy Yatols," Pagonel interrupted. "And to increase his own power, though now, with Brynn's campaign, he may be regretting that decision!"

"You know nothing."

"I know what I see, and what I have seen from your God-Voice is imperialistic and opportunistic, and nothing more."

"Because you do not understand that he speaks with Yatol!"

Pagonel drew out his knife again, and flipped it over in his hand so that the handle was out toward Merwan Ma. "You know what Yatol commanded concerning you," he said dryly.

"I know no such thing," the defiant Merwan Ma replied. "I know what a rogue Chezhou-Lei tried to do, and I am grateful that you saved my life. Beyond that, I have only your reasoning that the act was somehow connected to my master."

"My reasoning and your own memory," said Pagonel. "For you understand more than you will reveal. You know something, about the Chezru Chieftain likely, that he finds dangerous. Deny it as you will—to me, for you cannot deny it to yourself. When you view the act of the Chezhou-Lei and my reasoning in light of your own memories, you know that I am correct."

"I will not betray Yatol, however you choose to twist my words!"

Pagonel smiled and rose in response, leaving the food beside the troubled young man. "We are moving this very night, so you should eat, and eat well."

"To another city, to justly murder everyone within?" the Shepherd asked sarcastically.

"To the Mountains of Fire, to heal our wounds and rest out the winter sandstorms," the mystic replied, and a horrified expression crossed Merwan Ma's gentle face.

"The home of the Jhesta Tu!" he said.

"Near to it, though few, if any, will view the Walk of Clouds."

"But I am doomed to that fate, I suppose," said Merwan Ma, eliciting a puzzled expression from Pagonel. "That you might use your ancient torture techniques upon me to gather the information you desire," the Shepherd reasoned.

"Ancient torture techniques?"

"I know all about your order, about how you can take the skin from a man without killing him, that his whole body burns with horrible fires! I know about your rituals, drinking the blood of babies and enemies. You believe that because you hide in the mountains far to the south that the world would have forgotten about the atrocities of the Jhesta Tu, but we have not, I assure you!"

His bluster was somewhat tempered by the sincere laughter of Pagonel. "You know the stories the Chezhou-Lei tell, and the Yatols tell, because they fear that if their subjects learned the truth of the Jhesta Tu, we would not be so hated. And they need to hate us, don't you understand? Because, without an enemy to hate, without a threat from somewhere, keeping a nation in obedience is a much more difficult process."

Merwan Ma hardly seemed convinced.

"Yes, you will visit the Walk of Clouds, Merwan Ma," Pagonel remarked. "If only because I wish you to see the truth of the Jhesta Tu with your own eyes."

"Why would that be important to you?"

"Because I suspect that you are intelligent enough to see the truth, of my order and of so much more," Pagonel replied, and he bent low and patted the man on the shoulder. "I will leave you to your thoughts, and to your memories, my friend," he said, and walked away.

A perfectly miserable Merwan Ma lowered his head into his hands, wanting simply to clear his mind of concerns and memories, and of future problems. But that last word Pagonel had uttered, "friend," stayed with the poor Shepherd for a long, long time.

Once he had thought Yakim Douan to be his friend.


"You rode three horses into the sand to rush here to tell me that Yatol Bardoh will not be following you back to Jacintha, as I have ordered?" Yakim Douan said to the poor, trembling courier.

"Yatol Bardoh instructed me to deliver his response to you as quickly as possible, God-Voice," the man stuttered.

"His response?" Douan asked incredulously. "What makes you, or him, think that he has the option of any response? He is to do as I instructed, do you hear?"

"Yes, God-Voice!"

Yakim Douan eyed the man threateningly for a short while, watching him squirm under that withering glare. Then he put on a disgusted look and waved the man away. "Ride five more horses into the sand, if that is what it takes," he instructed. "Find your Yatol and tell him that the God-Voice is watching his every move closely, and is not amused."

"Yes, God-Voice," the trembling man said repeatedly, and he bowed with every retreating step.

Yakim Douan waved everyone else out of the room, as well, and collapsed in his chair, thoroughly frustrated. With the Dragon of To-gai nowhere to be found, he had ordered Yatol Bardoh and his fifteen thousand soldiers back to the Jacintha perimeter, to set defensive positions against this most frustrating of enemies. But Bardoh's courier had come in to inform Douan that the man was turning for Avrou Eesa, his home city, and was taking the soldiers with him, ostensibly to help guard the farther reaches of Behren, the outer rim of the country, which was obviously more vulnerable to the Dragon of To-gai.

But Yakim Douan had lived through centuries, and he understood the southern turn to be much more a militarily tactical movement. Yatol Bardoh was using this time of crisis to further his own position, obviously. With Grysh dead, Bardoh was probably the second most powerful man in all of

Behren, especially when he had fifteen thousand of Yakim Douan's soldiers at his disposal!

Both Douan and Bardoh knew that the outer cities were not very pleased with the tight defensive stance about Jacintha and her neighboring cities, and were feeling abandoned and afraid. So now Yatol Bardoh could act the part of savior to them, and if Douan went overtly against him, even under the pretense of commands from Yatol, he would risk losing the loyalty of all those people in the outer regions. Yes, they were Chezru by religion, but the pragmatism of simple survival often trumped the tenets of religion.

So now Yatol Bardoh apparently saw his chance to further his own position among all the towns of the south and west. Given the fact that Yakim Douan had been speaking fairly openly about a time of Transcendence for a couple of years, who could guess how powerful the man hoped to become?

Yakim Douan took a deep, deep breath, trying to steady himself. He had to look beyond the immediate situation, beyond the Dragon of To-gai. She would be put down soon enough, obviously, but because of Yatol Bardoh's impudence, Douan had to look ahead to the time of Transcendence. He had to find a way to placate the man, to satisfy his ego and his craving for power and glory, then he had to make sure that the man would follow the precepts of Transcendence.

Else all could be lost.

"Damn you, Dragon of To-gai!" Yakim Douan said suddenly, and he pounded his fist forcefully on the arm of his chair.

He heard a scuffle to the side then, and turned fast to see Shepherd Took staring at him wide-eyed.

"What is it?" he demanded.

"I wanted to tell you that Yatol Bardoh's courier is already away, God-Voice," the man stuttered. "Riding hard down the western road to Dahdah Oasis, and then to Dharyan."

"Get out," Douan ordered, and he waved his hand.

With many bows, Shepherd Took retreated.

Yakim Douan made a mental note that he would have to execute his latest attendant in the morning for spying upon him.

With a frustrated growl, the Chezru Chieftain ran a hand through his thinning hair, for that thought only illustrated how absurd and out of control this whole situation had become. How he missed Merwan Ma!

He reconsidered then his order to kill the man, and was sorry for a moment to think of the faithful and competent attendant lying dead under the sands of Dharyan. How extraordinary Merwan Ma truly had been, he had to believe then, for the string of prospective attendants that had followed the man had been anything but.

And Yakim Douan understood well that he could not risk Transcendence without a thoroughly competent and undyingly loyal attendant at his side.

# CHAPTER 31

# *Her Winter of Discontent*

"I am certain that I will come to dread this day and chastise myself for agreeing to let you leave," Brynn said to Juraviel and Cazzira. The three were back in To-gai, far to the north, at the southern entrance to the Path of Starless Night in the foothills of the Belt-and-Buckle. Behind them, Agradeleous stretched his great leathery wings and roared repeatedly into the winter wind.

"It was not your decision to make," Juraviel replied. "Nor one that you could have changed, if you sought to."

"If I begged Belli'mar Juraviel to help me, he would not?" Brynn asked, batting her eyes and putting on a purely wounded tone, almost sounding like the lost little girl who had first arrived at Andur'Blough Inninness.

All three shared a laugh at that.

"He would indeed," said Cazzira. "Belli'mar Juraviel has a reputation among his own people, he tells me, that he is more fond of *n'Touel'alfar* than of Touel'alfar, and it is a reputation that he has truly earned!"

"Only if you consider Doc'alfar as *n'Touel'alfar*!" Juraviel shot back, adding in a wink at his lover and friend, and the three laughed all the louder.

But that mirth couldn't hold, for the reality was that these three were saying good-bye. Juraviel and Cazzira were abandoning Brynn and her quest for their own, which seemed much more pressing to their respective peoples now that Brynn's campaign was in full swing. The reality was that it seemed quite plausible that Brynn Dharielle would never see Belli'mar Juraviel again.

They both knew it, but neither spoke that possibility aloud. Instead, they shared a good meal and told many, many tales, mostly Juraviel and Brynn recounting to Cazzira some of their adventures together back in Andur'Blough Inninness, like the time Brynn had lured a deer with a sweet plant, that she could pass the challenge of touching the animal—turning what should have been a test of her stealth and understanding of her surroundings into a test of her charm. How many tales Juraviel had to recount of Brynn frustrating him and the other Touel'alfar, circumventing their plans while reaching every goal they had set out for her!

Late that afternoon, with daylight beginning to wane, they shared some hugs and some tears, some hopeful words about a reunion, and some assurances to each other that they would all succeed. And then the two elves walked into the deeper darkness of the Path of Starless Night, and suddenly Brynn Dharielle felt very much alone.

She hugged herself against the cold winter wind and reminded herself that Pagonel was back to the south, at the Mountains of Fire and the Walk of Clouds, waiting for her. Still, she stared into the black hole of the tunnel, feeling lonely and empty and fearful.

Behind her, Agradeleous roared.

"Are we to fly all the way back to the south this night?" the dragon asked some time later, with Brynn still standing there, staring into the tunnel.

She was no longer thinking of the two elves, though. Rather, she was formulating her continuing plans. The previous night, the last leg of the journey that had brought them up there, they had spotted several large encampments of the Behrenese army, still floundering about the To-gai steppes. Brynn was glad that the winter had caught the Behrenese still in To-gai, confident that the vicious weather would erode their morale, possibly even their numbers. She was thinking that she should find some way to keep the soldiers there, in misery, and perhaps even lure more in.

She glanced back at Agradeleous. "No," she answered. "My army is at rest and needs us not at all. Perhaps you and I should find some fun in To-gai."

The dragon looked at her curiously. "Fun?"

"You have wanted your fights, Agradeleous—more than I have allowed you, certainly. Perhaps it is time for you to have those fights."

The dragon's lips curled eagerly and a low growl escaped his lips, along with a trickling line of smoke.

"Let us go down this night, and however many it takes, for us to learn as much as we can about the situation in To-gai, that we might find ways to strike hard at our enemies."

The dragon's wicked grin receded more than a little. "Months of gathering information?" he asked, seeming none too pleased.

"Days," Brynn assured him. "Only days. I desire battle as much as you. There is an enemy army within my country, likely making life miserable for my kinfolk."

"We will chase them away!" Agradeleous roared.

"No," Brynn corrected. "We will make them miserable and strike at their flanks, but above all else, we will keep them here."

Again came that curious look, but Brynn gave a sincere smile in response, for the plan was already taking definite shape in her mind.

Brynn kept the dragon aloft for as long as she could stand the cold wind that first night and the next, mapping out the deployment of the Behrenese forces. They had several encampments, and it was obvious that the army was using a number of the settlements in the region for their bivouac, as well. Also, they weren't as far west as they had been when Brynn had previously encountered them, and she was guessing that her To-gai forces had taken them on a chase out to the north and west, but that they had, for some reason, turned back.

Nor were the encampments static, for that second night, she noted that the westernmost groups had moved to the east, leap-frogging their fellow Behrenese. Brynn didn't even need to see the movement before the third night to know that the pattern would be repeated, an organized, well-defended retreat back to the plateau rim, perhaps even back into Behren, to Dharyan.

She wasn't surprised.

On the third night aloft, Brynn and Agradeleous found another encampment, a large one, further to the south and west. Recognizing it for what it was, Brynn had the dragon set her down far to the side, and then she walked in, greeting the To-gai-ru perimeter sentries.

They seemed to recognize her almost immediately, but when she drew out her sword and lit its magical fires, their smiles grew wide indeed, and they hustled her into the encampment.

Brynn's initial thrill at finding the To-gai-ru was dampened quite a bit as she made her way through that huge encampment, for this was not the same group of eager warriors she had encountered on her last visit. Or at least, it was much more than that same group. Where that previous band had numbered two thousand, this one had to be ten times that number! Most of the people here were not warriors, however, but were the very young and the very old, were mothers with their children. And it was obvious to Brynn that they were not faring well. Only then did it hit the woman how profoundly her kinfolk back home were suffering because of the war. They had left the settlements—the *Autumnal Nomaduc* had seen to that—but forced together in a conglomeration of all the old tribes, they could not yet retain their old ways

In a tent with the leaders, including old Barachuk, the woman quickly got her answers.

"The Behrenese hoard all of the food, slaughter all of the elk and deer. They leave those which they cannot take to rot on the steppes," said a man whom Brynn surely recognized: Tanalk Grenk of her old tribe, Kayleen Kek. "They stockpile the foodstuffs in their outposter settlements and guard them fiercely."

"They continue to seek us," added another leader, a fierce-looking woman who could not have been much older than Brynn. "If we reveal ourselves by striking at a settlement, they close a wide noose about us."

"We have lost several battles and many warriors," said Tanalk. "We have five thousand ready to fight, but we cannot hope to defeat the thousands of the Behrenese. And as the numbers of our warriors have grown, so, too, have our responsibilities."

"We are in no condition to do battle against them!" a third interjected angrily. "We cannot repair our weapons. We cannot refill our quivers! Our horses starve, and we starve!"

Brynn took it all in stoically. Until this moment, she had viewed the distraction of the Chezru Chieftain's great army as a blessing, allowing her to run wild through western Behren. But now she understood the brutal truth. Now she questioned her decision to initiate the *Autumnal Nomaduc*. Would her people left in To-gai have been better off to remain conquered, to remain under the control of the Behrenese, even if that meant that Brynn's army would be having a much harder time of it in Behren?

"The winter will not be kind to us," another voice piped in, and many concurring murmurs followed.

"We have won great victories in Behren," she said, if only to judge the reaction. And that reaction was more positive than she had hoped, with Barachuk leading a cheer for Brynn Dharielle, for the Dragon of To-gai. Tanalk, who had obviously gained great respect among the folk, readily joined in. That these beleaguered people still stood behind her despite the terrible conditions her revolution had exacted upon them, struck Brynn profoundly and made her vow then and there, silently to herself, that she would not forsake them through this difficult season.

"I will return to you tomorrow night," she promised. "We will find a way to bolster your supplies and your readiness We will find a way to strike hard at the Behrenese, to chase the remnants of their once great army out of To-gai!"

She was surprised again at the response, for it seemed much more somber.

"They are strong," Tanalk Grenk remarked quietly.

"Where will we hide this time?" Agradeleous asked her sarcastically when she returned to him out from the encampment.

Brynn didn't immediately answer, going instead to the pile of netting and large skins on the ground beside the dragon. She had intended to make a supply run during her return to the Mountains of Fire, using Agradeleous in his customary role. That was fortunate, she now knew.

"Hide?" she replied skeptically. "We have several hours remaining until the dawn. Why would we hide?"

The dragon looked at her curiously.

"Let us find a settlement to destroy," Brynn said grimly, and the dragon's lips curled back.

They swooped down like a great bird of prey, right into the middle of a small outposter settlement. For those Behrenese still awake and near to the area, the first warning came too late, a sudden rush of air, the flap of a leathery wing, just in time for them to look up and see their doom as the dragon breathed its killing fire over them.

Agradeleous banked back up, hovering for just a split second, long enough for Brynn to leap down into the village and scramble into the shadows. She would be no spectator this time.

Alarms went up, as did a pair of bows from the sentries near the gate. But Agradeleous was upon them in a rush, jaw snapping, wings and tail smashing, and the sentries were dead and the gate crushed. Then the dragon flew off into the night, turning up high and out of sight, lining up his next angle of attack.

Brynn darted from shadow to shadow, listening to the sounds of the wakening town, measuring the screams. She put her back up against the wall of one cottage, right beside the door, and when it swung open and a man rushed out, the ranger turned and struck hard, a slash across his chest that sent him back inside, sprawling to the floor.

Another man loomed right behind him, a son or a brother, perhaps. He gave a shout and awkwardly tried to put up his axe in defense.

But Brynn leaped over the prone, dying man, to stab the second through the heart.

The ranger turned and rushed out into the village, avoiding the central area, where great flames leaped high into the night sky and the dark forms of terrified outposters rushed all about.

She turned down an alley between two long buildings, realizing at once that they were storehouses. Brynn put her sword up high and lit its blade, but only briefly, the pre-arranged signal with Agradeleous to mark where he should not loose his devastating fires.

Around the back corner of the building, Brynn turned to see three men running her way. Confident that they had not noticed her, she slipped back around the corner, sword in hand, and concentrated on their footsteps and chatter.

Brynn stepped out right in front of them, skewering the man on the left and tripping the one on the right. She stepped and turned past the stuck man, tearing free her sword and coming around all the way in perfect balance to bring her fine weapon in hard against the side of the third, trailing man. Brynn winced, and the outposter collapsed screaming, as his arm fell free to the ground.

Brynn heard the charge from behind, and purely on instinct brought her sword up horizontally over her head, intercepting a downward chop from the man she had tripped up. She spun and slashed, opening his belly, then stabbed ahead once, slipping Flamedancer deftly past his feeble parry and into his chest. Then she retracted it quickly and stuck him again, this time in the throat. He fell away, and Brynn retreated back into the shadows of the alleyway.

Agradeleous came across then with his second devastating pass, and a line of buildings on the opposite side of the village went up in flames.

By the time Brynn came out the other side of the alleyway, no semblance of organization remained within the doomed village. Outposters raced all about, screaming and crying. Many headed out over the wall, or through the smashed gates, fleeing desperately into the cold dark night.

Brynn caught another duo running her way, but looking back over their shoulders at the dragon, who had set down near the rear wall and was even then slaughtering outposters by the dozen. By the time the second man even looked ahead again, his companion lay beside him, mortally wounded, and Brynn's sword was rushing for his chest.

He fell beside his friend.

It was over quickly, with the village deserted and most of it in flames. Brynn and the dragon did not give pursuit; the woman wanted those who had fled to bear witness to the sudden and devastating strike. The dragon, so excited from the destruction, had to be reminded of this tactic, but to Brynn's surprise, he agreed. He went out from the village then, not to hunt down the fleeing Behrenese, but to retrieve the netting and skins, then joined Brynn at the warehouses.

As the pair rose again into the night sky, they noted the torches of the nearest section of the great Behrenese army, rushing for the dying outposter settlement.

It took Brynn a long time to convince Agradeleous to hold his course steady, to the south and the west.

Just before dawn, Brynn walked into the encampment of To-gai-ru once more, bidding the perimeter guards to follow her out into the darkness, to a mound of foodstuffs and other supplies.

"There will be more," she promised grimly. "Every night. But keep your eyes out far, for the Behrenese army will be marching swiftly, trying to find you, and to find me. Stay ahead of them—I will find you and feed you."

With that, she was gone, and the legend of the Dragon of To-gai had grown a bit more.

Over the next few weeks, Brynn and Agradeleous hit settlement after settlement, scattering their attacks far and wide to avoid any organized attempt by the Behrenese army to trap them. As the woman had promised, she returned often to the To-gai-ru encampment, delivering stolen supplies. And so the To-gai-ru grew stronger while the Behrenese chased ghosts and died by the score. And the word went out, throughout To-gai and into Behren, that the Dragon of To-gai and her army had returned to the steppes of their homeland.

In western Behren, the news was received with mixed feelings, more relief than trepidation. Though Brynn was running unchecked throughout the steppes, and many Behrenese were being slaughtered, at least she was out of Behren, they believed, where the army had been unable to find and destroy her, and every city seemed vulnerable.

In Avrou Eesa, Yatol Bardoh took the news as an invitation to brag that he and his soldiers had chased the Dragon of To-gai away, often punctuating his long-winded speeches with promises that he would march out in the spring and finish the Dragon of To-gai once and for all.

Many To-gai-ru slaves in Avrou Eesa heard those boasts, and relayed them out of the city. Thus Pagonel and the To-gai-ru army, wintering safely and quietly in the fields scattered within the Mountains of Fire, heard them, too.

# CHAPTER 32

## *Hit and Run?*

"He has a great army at his disposal," Pagonel reminded Brynn. Farther north, the winter snows were beginning to relinquish their grip upon the land, and there near the Mountains of Fire, the day was almost uncomfortably warm. "Yatol Bardoh boasts because he believes himself to be safe."

Brynn looked around at her army, now more than six thousand strong. They were eager, she knew, hungry to be back on the roads that would lead them to the next Behrenese city that would fall before them. And though Brynn had seen much fighting over the winter, she too longed for a great battle, man against man, army against army.

"Do you believe that the dog Bardoh will come out after us, as he has declared?" she asked.

Pagonel shrugged noncommitally.

"Do you believe that we might lure him from his city?"

Pagonel shrugged again, and looked at Brynn hard. "Even if you do, going against that army would be folly, for it is as great a force as is now in To-gai. And Yatol Bardoh . . ."

He paused as Brynn spat upon the ground.

"He is reputed to be a fine military leader," the mystic finished.

"He is a murdering dog, and nothing more," said Brynn. "And before this is ended, I will have his head."

Pagonel's expression became even more puzzled. "You would risk all to go against him?"

Brynn's hard look didn't answer the question in the least, and for a moment, the mystic honestly feared that Brynn would do just that.

"I will get him out of Avrou Eesa and into Behren," Brynn declared. "Not too far over the plateau rim. I want him to see the smoke from the fires when I destroy his city."

Pagonel had never seen her so grim and so determined.

Brynn said no more, but walked from the encampment and through a long and rocky pass, to where Agradeleous waited. She and the dragon had made several journeys back there during the winter months, but this one would be the shortest stay, for that very night, after only a few hours among her forces, the Dragon of To-gai was back in the air, flying fast for the north.

They stayed along the plateau rim for a long way, with Brynn taking careful note of the terrain, a plan already beginning to form.

Yes, she would lure Yatol Tohen Bardoh from his home, and let him sit up on the plateau helplessly while his home burned.

She found Tanalk Grenk and her To-gai forces right where she had left them, and surprised them indeed when she ordered a split among them, with a portion of the strongest warriors riding south and east, and the rest, accompanying those who could not fight, fleeing straightaway to the southland.

"Now, with the weather at last breaking, you will get your fight," Brynn told the force that would travel with her, and that brought as many concerned murmurs as eager grins. The To-gai-ru understood the power of the Behrenese forces assembled against them, after all.

"We will strike, and we will run," Brynn explained. "Leading our enemies back toward Behren, to the edge of the plateau rim."

"And into Behren?" one man asked.

"We will take them to a point where there seems no route into Behren," Brynn answered. "Where they will believe us trapped by the plateau rim and where they will likely find allies to strike against us."

More murmurs filtered throughout the gathering, but Brynn, growing more and more confident, merely smiled.

And so it began, with the newest To-gai-ru army, two thousand strong, overrunning an outposter settlement teasingly close to the frustrated Behrenese army. A week later, a second settlement fell, far to the south and east of the previous. While flying about on Agradeleous that night after the second battle, Brynn noted that the Behrenese army had turned more to the south, and she also noted a line of couriers riding out straight to the east. Yes, her enemies knew where they were, and knew well the terrain.

She was counting on that most of all.

Through it all, the ranger kept Agradeleous in check, tightly reined. She was not willing to reveal him further to her enemies, for all of this, in the end, would come down to his ability to serve her army well. She did fly out to the south, to the Mountains of Fire, to instruct Pagonel to begin the march toward Avrou Eesa.

Two days later, a Behrenese supply caravan was flattened, and the chase continued, and the word continued to spread into Behren that the Dragon of To-gai had indeed returned to the steppes, but was fighting her way back toward Behrenese soil.

Right in the region immediately west of Yatol Bardoh and Avrou Eesa.

The march from Bardoh's city began the very next day, heading for a pass that would bring the glory-hungry Yatol and his fifteen thousand onto the To-gai plateau to the north of Brynn's position, with the second army, led by Chezhou-Lei Shauntil, circling fast to the south. At that particular juncture of the two kingdoms, there weren't many easy routes up or down the plateau, and it seemed obvious to the Behrenese that the Dragon of To-gai had erred, for Yatol Bardoh would beat her to the north pass, arriving within a week, and Shauntil had the west and the south already cut off.

Brynn's To-gai based army continued its flight to the east, seemingly walking into the jaws between the mighty Behrenese forces.

And then, a few days later, they were out of room, with the cliffs of the plateau divide blocking their way to the east, and with south, west, and north blocked by the two pursuing armies.

"Burn your fires bright this night," Brynn instructed her warriors.

"For tomorrow, we will fight and die!" one man called out, and neither he, nor any of the others, seemed bothered by that grim possibility.

"For tomorrow, we will begin our ride across the sands of Behren," Brynn corrected, and she pointed out over the cliff. "Down there." She finished with a whistle, and the great dragon Agradeleous rose up over the edge of the cliff, higher and higher, and bearing under him a huge platform, secured to his talons by thick ropes.

They rode like the sandstorm whirlwinds across the open desert, the great storm that was the Dragon of To-gai and her followers. Before Yatol Bardoh and Chezhou-Lei Shauntil had even charged their way out of the steppes and back onto Behren's light brown sands, Brynn and her two thousand had the city of Avrou Eesa in sight.

The woman looked to the south, knowing from the previous night's dragon flight that Pagonel and her main force was still several days away. If she waited for them, the assault on Avrou Eesa would have to happen right before Yatol Bardoh returned, and then they would have to flee wildly, with the Behrenese in hot pursuit.

But Avrou Eesa was a prize that Brynn would not let get away, for she keenly remembered the grim fate of her parents at the hands of Yatol Bardoh.

That night, she went in with Agradeleous, swooping about the city, setting buildings ablaze and toppling defensive positions and great catapults, blasting down the many remaining soldiers who came out against them.

And then, from on high, Brynn yelled down to them, told them to flee Avrou Eesa or be destroyed. "Run down the eastern road!" she cried. "I claim this place for To-gai. Be gone!"

The response came in the form of a volley of arrows that had Brynn ducking tight to Agradeleous' back and had the dragon roaring in protest at the pestering stings.

"Destroy that group," Brynn ordered, and the outraged Agradeleous was more than happy to comply, tucking his great wings and falling into a stoop that shot him right past the archer battery as he leveled out.

By the time Agradeleous flew out past the Behrenese line, many had died before his breath, others from his wing, and he clutched two screaming men, one in each talon. Now he and Brynn went up high over the city, back to their original position, where Brynn repeated her warning that any who did not flee the city would die in it the next day.

To accentuate her warnings, Agradeleous then dropped the two men, one after the other.

At dawn the next day, Brynn and her two thousand charged Avrou Eesa's western gate, with the dragon coming in to support them from the north.

There was little resistance, and when Brynn walked into the conquered city soon after, moving to the high tower that anchored the eastern wall, she noted the lines of Behrenese who had fled at the onset of the attack, running wildly to the east.

Late that same day, Brynn's scouts came in, reporting that Yatol Bardoh and his forces were coming down from the plateau in the north, and Chezhou-Lei Shauntil and his were coming down along the route to the south.

"We will have the city pillaged before the dawn, then we can flee out to the open sands," one of her commanders remarked.

Brynn shook her head. "Pillage the city and hide the supplies and the valuables out in the desert," she did agree. "But we will not run. Not this time."

That brought many surprised looks from those leaders standing about her, all keenly aware that somewhere around thirty thousand Behrenese warriors would soon converge on Avrou Eesa.

"Pagonel is not far," the woman explained.

"We would still be sorely outnumbered," one man observed.

"Only if we fight them as a singular, or even as half, of their force," Brynn replied, a grin widening on her face as she thought of yet another way she might stick a pin into the eye of the Chezru Chieftain and his marauding people, and particularly into the eye of Yatol Tohen Bardoh.

"What do you know?" one To-gai-ru woman asked her.

"We can outride them. We can outrun them," Brynn answered. She turned her gaze to the west, to the line of distant heights that marked the To-gai plateau. If the armies were filtering down the narrow passes out of the steppes, north and south, then she and Agradeleous could catch them in a vulnerable position indeed.

She nodded as she considered that her fighting that day was not done. She had to go out with the dragon, anyway, she knew, to go and inform Pagonel of his role in the upcoming daring battle.

"A large group of the fleeing Behrenese have camped just to the west of us," another scout reported soon after, and beside the woman, Tanalk Grenk issued a low growl as threatening as any Agradeleous himself had ever grumbled.

"Leave them there," Brynn replied, issuing that order to all of her fierce leaders. "Let them tell Yatol Bardoh of our approximate strength."

"That he might overrun Avrou Eesa with complete confidence?" another man asked.

"That he will encircle Avrou Eesa to prevent any escape."

"Your great dragon cannot fly us all out of here quickly enough, as it did to bring us down from the plateau," came one concerned reply.

But Brynn only smiled all the wider, thinking that it was indeed time to take a gamble, and time to engage some Behrenese soldiers openly.

As dusk fell over the steppes, the desert already dark behind them, Brynn and Agradeleous saw the long line of torches, winding down from the To-gai plateau along a narrow and rocky descent to the Behrenese floor.

"He force-marches through the night, hoping to catch up to us," Brynn yelled to the dragon. "The dog Bardoh is angry, and his anger will be his downfall!"

Agradeleous beat his wings more powerfully, speeding them along the plateau line, sweeping down from the north.

Brynn urged the dragon straight across that long and narrow line. The beast banked and swept past, breathing forth his

fire, immolating those poor Behrenese who could not flee or
find any cover behind the rocks. The dragon's tail thrashed as
he passed, splintering stone and sending men flying to their
deaths.

Caught by complete surprise, it took the Behrenese a long
time to organize their archers up high on the plateau ledge
and for those caught along the narrow trail to find cover, or to
scramble down among the massing defensive formations already on the desert floor.

Brynn and Agradeleous struck hard and struck repeatedly
during that time of confusion and tumult. And then, as the organization grew stronger, as volleys of arrows filled the sky
and great ballistae prepared their deadly shots, Brynn
brought the dragon out from the plateau, and shouted down,
"Avrou Eesa is mine!"

And then she and Agradeleous rushed off to the south, flying fast along the plateau line and repeating the destruction
on the second Behrenese force, that of Shauntil. This army,
under the crack command of the cunning Chezhou-Lei, organized more quickly and sent Brynn and Agradeleous fleeing
fast for safety with little damage done and only a few Behrenese lost.

The ranger and her dragon flew to the south and then to the
east, and eventually, they saw the distant fires of Pagonel's
force.

There, the dragon set Brynn down outside the encampment, and she went to her allies.

"It seems a desperate plan," Pagonel warned her privately,
after the gathering of commanders had dispersed so that
the warrior woman and her friend could share some private
moments.

"Every movement grows more desperate, with the pursuit
growing more organized," Brynn replied. "The Chezru Chieftain will send even more out against us. A third force will
march from Jacintha, and then a fourth, I am certain, and they
will catch us, and any one of the forces could likely destroy
us, or at least weaken us enough to render us ineffective."

Pagonel nodded grimly. "You knew from the outset that

even if you organized all of To-gai behind you, you could not defeat the Behrenese in force."

Then it was Brynn's turn to nod, and grimly. "Avrou Eesa has fallen, and Yatol Bardoh will force-march all the way to the broken gates. Let us sting him again—I pray to Joek that I will find the chance to wet my blade with cursed Bardoh's own blood."

"Even if that opportunity costs you the greater war you have waged?"

The question made Brynn back off a bit, quieted her eagerness, and made her consider carefully her current course.

"These plans will work," she said.

"Is it a necessary chance?"

"It is one that seems plausible, and that will afford us a great gain."

"Great?"

"Great enough," Brynn insisted. "Every victory will become more difficult as we draw the Chezru Chieftain's power out of Jacintha. Let us take every victory as we find it. On my way here, Agradeleous and I struck at both Behrenese forces filtering down from To-gai. We did not kill many—a hundred, perhaps—but likely many more than that now desire to flee the army, for in return for their dead, they got nothing. No kills. No blood for blood. That is the most frustrating thing of all for a warrior."

The mystic nodded his agreement. "If Chezhou-Lei Shauntil is as focused on his march toward Avrou Eesa as you presume, then he will not see us."

"And then my plan . . . ?"

"May indeed sting the Behrenese once again," Pagonel admitted. "But we will be sorely pressed, and running fast with an angry army in close pursuit."

"With Agradeleous, we can supply; they cannot," Brynn insisted. "And To-gai-ru can outride Behrenese. How long will they chase us? How soon will we forge enough of a lead to flatten yet another city?"

"How soon will Chezru Douan send another thirty thousand out against you?"

The question was sobering, because Brynn understood that Douan could do just that.

But Brynn only nodded and accepted the possibilities. "You understand your role, and the timing?"

"We will be there," Pagonel assured her.

Brynn smiled, and kissed him on the cheek.

Soon after, she and Agradeleous were gone, flying back to the north. Brynn didn't strike at Shauntil's force on the return trip, recognizing with a couple of high fly-bys that the Chezhou-Lei warrior had his army ready to strike back hard immediately. But they did indeed hit at the less-prepared army of Yatol Bardoh, swooping down from on high and scattering the final lines of soldiers making their way down from the plateau, for Bardoh had not even kept his earlier forces assembled below to provide cover, instead riding them straight out toward Avrou Eesa.

Agradeleous feasted on the weakened end of that Behrenese line, more than doubling his kills for the night. Brynn took great satisfaction in seeing many other Behrenese warriors turning from their assigned course, fleeing north and south, apparently deserting Bardoh's army.

That was her strength, the ranger realized, the strength of To-gai, for she and her leaders would never have left so many behind in pursuit of a goal. Yatol Bardoh cared nothing for his warriors, beyond the goals he desired; Brynn knew that her own warriors recognized that she did not subscribe to that losing philosophy.

# CHAPTER 33

## *The Dragon Ruse*

Brynn stood on the western wall of Avrou Eesa, staring out over the desert to a distant cloud of stirred sands. She questioned herself repeatedly, her decision to remain there, to try to sting again before disappearing into the open desert. Was it her hatred of Yatol Bardoh that was driving her? Was she hoping for a chance to avenge her parents' murder? And if so, was she risking too much to find that chance?

She took heart that Pagonel and her larger army would arrive on time, as arranged. Given that, the plan didn't seem so desperate, as long as her guess concerning Yatol Bardoh's reaction to the loss of Avrou Eesa proved correct.

She was standing there, mulling it all over, when an unexpected companion walked up beside her. Brynn turned, startled, for she had not seen Agradeleous in his lizardman form in some time. She noted, too, that the dragon was limping a little bit.

"Their arrows sting you," she remarked.

"It will take more than arrows to bring down Agradeleous," the dragon assured her.

Brynn nodded and looked back to the sandstorm. "Our enemies," she said.

"Our?"

The woman turned and studied the dragon, surprised by the comment, though when she thought about it, it made perfect sense. Agradeleous, it seemed, didn't really care who or what he was destroying.

"I must soon ask you to go out through a hail of arrows

again," she said. "I will need you to convince Yatol Bardoh that we are attempting to flee to the east."

The dragon nodded, seeming unconcerned.

"I plan to draw his line about the city," Brynn started to explain, but her voice trailed off as she realized that the dragon wasn't paying her any heed. "None of this matters to you, does it?"

Agradeleous' eyes narrowed as he regarded her more closely.

"There is no difference between us—me and my people, and the Behrenese—is there?"

The dragon blinked, but did not otherwise respond.

"And if a Behrenese ally had found you in your lair and brought you out, you would be fighting for them, as you are now fighting for me. Correct?"

Another blink.

"Or is it that you are not fighting for me?" Brynn reasoned it through. "You are fighting for Agradeleous, and nothing more. I offered you a deal that you thought acceptable, and so your fires char the Behrenese soldiers." She paused and stared at the dragon hard, waiting until she had his full attention. "Do you not understand why I wage this war?"

"I do not understand the wars of humans, nor do I wish to," the dragon finally replied. "You fight for your freedom." He shrugged, his great muscled shoulders rising up almost over his head. "It all makes so little sense to me, that humans would enslave humans in the first place. You are a curious race, and a lesser race, from all that I see."

Then it was Brynn's turn to narrow her eyes.

"You think me a creature of wanton destruction, and to an extent, you are correct," the dragon went on. "When I care not at all about the creatures in the line of my flames, I find it exciting to breathe forth the fire. And I care not at all about humans."

Brynn noted that there was something less than convincing in that statement, some subtle hint from the dragon's tone.

"Behrenese, To-gai-ru . . . you are all the same. No dragon would think to enslave another dragon."

"So if a Behrenese agent had found you, you might well be

flying against me now," Brynn reasoned, and again the dragon shrugged, as if it did not matter.

"Then thank your good fortune," he said. "Or call it the ultimate justice of fate, the gods themselves shining upon your cause for freedom, if that brings you comfort."

Brynn turned away sharply. "There is a difference," she stated through gritted teeth. "A difference between what they have done to us, and what we now try to accomplish."

"Indeed."

"The To-gai-ru have never tried to conquer Behren," Brynn remarked against that sarcasm.

"Because they have never been able to," Agradeleous was quick to point out. "When you have the power, only then can you measure the relative morality of your peoples."

Brynn wanted to argue, wanted to find some words to deny the logic of the dragon's observations. But in truth, she could not. Would her people have acted any differently, had they been the conquerors? Had they acted any differently in their first large victory, when Dharyan had been overrun? Until she had intervened, the Behrenese had been subjected to many of the same injustices they had shown to the To-gai-ru.

But she had intervened. Brynn had to remind herself at that uncertain moment, with Agradeleous, of all people, laying bare her conscience, and with Yatol Bardoh and thirty thousand Behrenese warriors coming to destroy her relatively insignificant army.

"You are quite observant for one who does not know humans," Brynn remarked.

Agradeleous gave a rumbling laugh. "Detachment allows for that."

Brynn turned to face him once more, locking him with a serious stare. "Will you fly out against the archers?"

The dragon put on a perfectly awful grin. "With pleasure."

The storm swept in across the blowing sands, thirty thousand strong, led by riders waving the huge curved swords favored by many Behrenese warriors. They charged at Avrou Eesa's western gate, and for a brief moment, Brynn's heart sank in the fears that Yatol Bardoh would abandon all caution and just overrun his conquered city.

But then the lead riders broke, left and right, their horses thundering about Avrou Eesa to encircle the wide city. With the discipline of a superbly trained army, the Behrenese soldiers filtered to their appropriate positions. By late afternoon, Brynn and her army were fully encircled, the enemy line secured like a hangman's noose, and with the devastating war engines already assembled out to the west of the city.

The bombardment began soon after dusk, with balls of pitch soaring in to smash walls, splattering all about.

Brynn's warriors let many of the ensuing fires burn, for they had no desire to save any more of Yatol Bardoh's city than those sections they needed for defense.

The first charge came soon after, with infantry marching in from all sides, shield to shield.

Brynn knew that Bardoh was trying to draw her out, to see how much firepower she and her warriors could throw back at him. And so she did not disappoint, lining the walls, particularly the eastern one, with archers and meeting the charge with volley after volley of arrows.

And then she went out, upon Agradeleous, sweeping first to the south, scattering the terrified Behrenese before her, then turning to the east, where that line broke almost immediately and rushed back to the cover of their own archers.

Brynn banked Agradeleous sharply, putting the dragon in fast flight right over the city and beyond, sweeping to the west, flying right over the surprised Behrenese infantry and right over the reserve cavalry, all fighting to hold their terrified horses steady, and right through the hail of arrows the Behrenese archers launched their way.

Agradeleous bore down on the war engines with a vengeance, setting a catapult ablaze, then banking up to hover beside another, his great tail smashing hard against the supporting beams.

"Fly away!" Brynn cried out frantically. "Agradeleous, fly away!"

Too excited and enraged, the dragon didn't even hear her,

and so his surprise was complete when a ballista bolt smashed hard against his side, knocking him from the sky.

The Behrenese warriors cheered and charged, long lances flashing in the firelight.

"Up!" Brynn commanded. "Up and back to the city!"

The dragon spun about and charged into the coming line of soldiers, taking hit after brutal hit, but giving out killing blows with great claws and chomping maw, beating others aside with his great wings and launching still more far away with his deadly tail.

Brynn kept urging him up, as more and more Behrenese soldiers charged in fearlessly.

The woman's respect for her foes increased dramatically in those few minutes.

Finally, to Brynn's great relief, the dragon leaped up into the air, his great wings beating immediately to send him flying back toward Avrou Eesa's western gate. The pair set down in the courtyard just beyond the gate, Brynn leaping down from the dragon's back to inspect his greatest wound, where the ballista spear had hit home.

The warrior woman winced, more at her own thoughts than at the wound—for she had allowed herself, for a brief moment, to hope that the wound would prove fatal. In the end of all this, whether To-gai was free or not, Brynn Dharielle would have to deal with the fact that she had been instrumental in letting a dragon loose upon the world, and though she had exacted the necessary promise from Agradeleous, she was not sure that it would hold.

"How bad?" she asked the dragon, moving around to face him directly.

Agradeleous growled and reached for the ballista spear with his foreleg, then tore it out. He reared on his hind legs, roared defiantly, and hurled the bloody spear across the sands, into the midst of the still-scrambling Behrenese far beyond the gate.

Then came the bone-crunching sounds as Agradeleous began his transformation to his bipedal form. All about him, To-gai-ru warriors blanched and retreated, as fast and as far as they could run.

But Brynn stood right there, before the dragon, grateful to him for his sacrifice that night. A necessary sacrifice, and one that had turned the Behrenese charge into a fast retreat.

Lookouts on the walls were even then calling down that their enemies had broken off, all about the city, had returned to the encircling perimeter and were striking camp.

"I will need you again in the morning," Brynn whispered to the dragon. "When Pagonel arrives."

The dragon growled, and nodded.

Brynn took a deep breath and headed away, cursing herself silently for her moment of selfishness, when she had hoped the dragon would die.

No, it wouldn't be that easy. For the sake of To-gai and all her dreams, it couldn't be.

The timing could not have been better for Brynn and her companions. Dawn broke over the city of Avrou Eesa, bright and clear, and the Behrenese began their charge, their perimeter collapsing inward. And at that same moment, Brynn saw the flashing signal out in the distance beyond the westernmost Behrenese cluster that told her of Pagonel's arrival.

"Eastern wall!" she cried, and more than half of her warriors ran that way, launching arrows out at the charging Behrenese, though they were still too far away for any effective barrage. As the warriors bent down behind the wall, they propped helmets in place, decoys to make it look as if they intended to hold the wall.

And then they abandoned their posts, running to their waiting mounts, who were assembled in the western courtyard before the gates.

Brynn, meanwhile, went to Agradeleous. She sent the dragon flying away to the east, dropping down to attack the Behrenese advance. As the lines broke apart, the eastern gates of Avrou Eesa were thrown wide and many horses charged out.

Riderless horses. Captured Behrenese horses.

From her post on the western wall, Brynn took hope as she saw the Behrenese lines beginning to veer toward the west. Yatol Bardoh had anticipated a breakout, and following logic and the dragon's strike, he expected the breakout to be to the east.

But Yatol Bardoh did not know that a second To-gai-ru force, thrice the size of the one he had contained within Avrou Eesa, was just to the west of him.

The city's western gates flew wide and out came the charge of Brynn and her two thousand warriors, bearing down on the main Behrenese force west of the city.

And then came the battle cries and thunder of the second To-gai-ru force, charging east, bearing down on the same enemy positions.

Caught between the vise, the Behrenese forces scrambled to find some defensive posture.

Brynn drove her charges in hard, her sword all ablaze, Runtly answering her every command and improvising when necessary. The To-gai-ru came through like a swarm of locusts caught on a fast wind, slashing the Behrenese ranks, forcing soldiers to dive aside or be trampled.

They did not stop to engage, though, but continued their charge until they had linked up with the larger force, moving west to east with similar brutal efficiency.

And then they turned, as one, to the north and the open sands, riding hard and outdistancing the surprised and confused Behrenese.

By the time the main numbers of Yatol Bardoh's warriors had come around to the western line, Brynn and her warriors were a dust cloud on the northern horizon.

They left behind a field of carnage, of many fallen Behrenese and more than a few fallen To-gai-ru, as well. But the breakout had worked—another devastating blow to the Behrenese morale, and a lightning fast battle that claimed the lives of ten times more Behrenese than To-gai-ru.

And then came Agradeleous, just to accentuate Yatol Bardoh's embarrassment, sweeping past the Behrenese field, accepting the volley of hundreds of arrows and returning a strafing line of killing fire, and even managing to catch up a Behrenese warrior in his tearing claws.

And then the dragon, too, was gone, flying fast to the north.

\* \* \*

Coming from his position east of Avrou Eesa, where they had expected the breakout, Chezhou-Lei Shauntil did not arrive on the true battlefield until long after Brynn and her minions, including Agradeleous, had long departed. The warrior found his commander, Yatol Bardoh, leaning on the wreckage of what had been a catapult, staring vacantly to the dust cloud rising in the north, and suddenly looking all of his sixty years of age.

"Yatol," the warrior greeted, snapping a curt bow.

Yatol Bardoh's head slowly turned, that he could regard the man, but then swiveled back to the north, his face a mask of blank horror.

"Hunt her down and kill her," he said.

"She is a gnat, Yatol," Shauntil replied. "She flies about us while we swipe futilely at her, but her stings are not lethal. We have missed thus far, but one hit—"

"Hunt her down and kill her."

"Yes, Yatol. She is a cunning foe, and she has not erred of yet. But while her perfection of tactics has kept her alive, it has not truly wounded us. When she makes her first error, it will be her last."

"Hunt her down and kill her."

"It will be done, Yatol," Shauntil assured him. "We learn more of her with each movement. It is her dragon that allows her army to run about the open desert, supplying her forces, perhaps even flying them at times, as surely it must to have escaped our vise at the plateau divide. But we are seeing the limitations of the beast—it was almost brought down this very day, and every city will become more prepared to deal with it, should it arrive. Once it is gone, this woman and her armies will be no more."

Yatol Bardoh's head swiveled about again and he fixed Chezhou-Lei Shauntil with the coldest and most determined stare the warrior had ever seen from the man—from the man who had murdered hundreds in his years of terror in To-gai, the man who had lined the plateau divide overlooking this very region with the crucified bodies of a hundred To-gai-ru women.

Yatol Bardoh said slowly, without emotion, "Hunt her down and kill her."

# CHAPTER 34

## *Sacrilege Revealed*

"They are hot and thirsty," Chezhou-Lei Shauntil reported to Yatol Bardoh, as the two of them, along with many others, looked over the destroyed remains of a supply caravan. For a month since the recapture of Avrou Eesa, they had been chasing Brynn across the desert. They knew that they could not outpace her, and so they had continued to try to outguess her.

She had doubled back behind them, somehow, and had flattened the closest supply caravan.

For the second time this week.

"She must have a smaller force operating in the area," Yatol Bardoh announced, nodding with every word. "She uses her main force to keep us moving in one direction, and has splinters hidden among the dunes to interrupt the supply line."

"The caravans are well-armed and guarded," Shauntil dared to reply, drawing a scowl from his frustrated master.

"Against the likes of a dragon?" Yatol Bardoh snapped back, and the Chezhou-Lei bowed apologetically for his obviously errant thinking.

"We must stretch our line longer as we pursue," Bardoh remarked, and it seemed to Shauntil that he was more thinking out loud than addressing the warrior. "Yes, we will spearhead long points whenever we think we are near her, and sweep our forces in behind, a left or right flank. Or split to flank both ways, encircling her as we did in Avrou Eesa, but with no walls between us!" As he finished, he looked to Shauntil for confirmation, but the Chezhou-Lei was shaking his head, not nodding.

The warrior stopped, though, and stood at attention, not about to question unless the Yatol called for his opinion.

"A bold maneuver," Bardoh insisted, but Shauntil, despite his discipline, wore an expression of disagreement.

"Speak your mind!" the Yatol scolded.

"I fear any bold movements against one who has been as cunning and as lucky as the Dragon of To-gai," the warrior admitted. "We must be dogged and patient in our pursuit. We must arm and train any city we pass by. If we lose a thousand men to attrition and by moving them into city positions, then it is not so devastating to our great army, and surely we can replace them many times over if necessary. But every loss must weigh heavily on the Dragon of To-gai, for in this land that is not her home, she will find replacements difficult to come by."

"Her army has swelled with freed slaves," Yatol Bardoh reminded him. "How clearly we saw that as they burst free from my city."

"Yes, but that was in the beginning, and in Dharyan and Pruda, the two cities, other than Jacintha, with the most slaves. And even those former slaves must be second-guessing their decision to join the woman, as they spend the days wandering through the desert heat. Surely their existence under Behrenese control was more comfortable than that which they now endure, even with this dragon apparently delivering supplies."

"Do you ask that the whole of Behren cower behind city walls, that this barbarian witch can run free all about our lands?" the Yatol asked with obvious skepticism and anger.

Shauntil straightened his shoulders as if he had been slapped. "No, Yatol!" he answered with obedient enthusiasm. "Never that. I wish only to ensure that we do not err and allow the Dragon of To-gai to win any more impressive victories. Time is on our side, I believe. We have erred in underestimating her, and she has made not a single error to date. But she will."

"And one error will be her last," Yatol Bardoh added immediately. "But only if we are close by and prepared to seize upon her moment of vulnerability. I will see Behren free of her, Shauntil, and I intend to be the one who personally executes her in front of a grateful populace. And you are the one who will deliver her to me, whatever it takes. Do we have an understanding?"

"Yes, Yatol."

Bardoh nodded and looked one last time at the destroyed caravan, then waved his hand in disgust and walked away.

Shauntil relaxed immediately and blew a frustrated sigh. Bardoh was playing right into the Dragon of To-gai's hands, he knew.

But he was Chezhou-Lei, and sworn to follow the orders of the Yatols.

The Yatol and the warrior repeated the scene and the discussion while looking over the remains of yet another destroyed caravan three weeks later in the desert region east of Pruda.

Yakim Douan dropped his head into his hands and clutched tightly at his thinning hair. It took all of the discipline he could muster to not scream aloud!

Avrou Eesa. The Dragon of To-gai had taken Avrou Eesa, and had then escaped right through Yatol Bardoh's encircling line!

And now Bardoh and Shauntil were wandering the open desert with more than twenty-five thousand soldiers, trying to catch this woman, who remained as elusive as a ghost. The Behrenese legions were taxing the stores of every city and every oasis they neared, hauling out supplies by the wagon-load.

Douan understood the dangers of this game. For the To-gai-ru, every day spent ahead of the pursuit pleased them and made them bolder, while each passing day in the brutal heat no doubt wore at the resolve of his great army.

"I will send them all back into To-gai, to scorch the land as they pass," he said aloud, addressing his newest attendant, the eleventh since the departure of Merwan Ma. The thin young man didn't nod and didn't say anything, as he had been instructed. He was there to listen and nothing more! "Yes, that

will force the Dragon of To-gai back onto the steppes in a
desperate attempt to salvage some homeland to free!"

Even as he finished, the Chezru Chieftain shook his head
and growled. He had already tried that with Shauntil, and the
man had found very little to burn, and very few To-gai-ru to
punish.

"Yatol damn it!" he swore, standing up fast, and his attendant, eyes wide, backpedaled. Douan looked at him with obvious disgust and said, "Get out, you idiot," and waved him
away, and the young man nearly fell over himself with his repeated bows as he exited.

He returned shortly afterward, though, with a group of
emissaries from various Behrenese districts, mostly the south
and the west. One from Yatol De Hamman complained of increasing pirate activities, and pointedly blamed Yatol Peridan
for tolerating the criminals. One from Peridan spoke of mercenaries raiding his smaller outlying towns—mercenaries
hired by the Dragon of To-gai, and possibly supported, his
message hinted, by Yatol De Hamman.

Yakim Douan understood the significance of having all of
these emissaries come in together; this was akin to a unified
protest, one on the border of revolt and one struggling against
itself, from the outlying and vulnerable provinces.

"All of you return to your Yatols, and at once," he bade
them after hearing them out in full. "Bid your Yatols to travel
with all speed to Jacintha, that I might tell them of my plans
to be rid of the Dragon of To-gai. Assure them that I have
heard their words and fears completely, and that when we
turn the tide against the To-gai-ru—an imminent event, I assure you—they will get their revenge on all who wronged
them. And you two," he warned the emissaries of De Hamman
and Peridan, "advise your masters that their words do not
please me, and do not please Yatol. If we are to fight among
ourselves, then the Dragon of To-gai becomes a greater foe
by far!"

As all of the emissaries filed out, talking excitedly among
themselves, it occurred to Yakim Douan that he had better
come up with the promised plan to be rid of the Dragon of
To-gai rather quickly.

\* \* \*

With reverence and fear, trembling fingers and dry lips, Yakim Douan lifted the sacred chalice in the ceremonial room in Chom Deiru. He looked around many times, remembering the unfortunate discovery that had cost him his valuable servant and friend, Merwan Ma.

After the emissaries of the various Yatols had departed the city, Douan had spent many days sitting in the dark, meditating upon the great problem that was the Dragon of To-gai. He held little fear that she would overrun Behren, or even Jacintha. Yatol Bardoh's reports put her army at around ten thousand, at the most; in a crisis, Jacintha alone could muster five times that number. But this rebel had indeed become a great concern to the Chezru Chieftain. Her antics were fraying the always fragile alliances between Douan's Yatols, and in conquering three Behrenese cities, the woman had put tens of thousands of refugees on the road.

And she had cost him Merwan Ma, and Yatol Grysh, and the Kaliit of the Chezhou-Lei, and many of his warriors.

It was bad enough that Yakim Douan could not even begin to consider Transcendence any longer, but now he was beginning to see real reason to fear a general revolt among his own subjects!

He looked at the chalice as he considered that awful thought, for he knew that he was taking a great chance here. For months he had been using the hematite to help keep his aged body strong, and even those minor trances brought him fear of discovery. This scheme absolutely terrified him.

But Master Mackaront had arrived from Entel that day, and had confirmed what Yakim Douan had suspected: that Abellican monks had sometimes used hematite, the soul stone, to fly free of their bodies and traverse great distances with their disembodied spirits. Father Abbot Markwart had been especially deft at such tactics, Mackaront had said.

Of course Douan knew of spirit-walking. He had used it against his enemies within Jacintha and to spy upon visiting Yatols on occasion. He had used it to trick Yatol Thei'a'hu into betraying Yatol Bohl. But this was something beyond that.

That night, he intended to fly far, far from Jacintha, out

into the open desert where he might locate the Dragon of To-gai and her elusive army. He had already ordered his newest attendant—he could never remember the man's name!—to set up a line of signalers to Yatol Bardoh and Shauntil, explaining that he would seek divine guidance to help them with their quest.

Now all he had to do was find the Dragon of To-gai.

In his private room, the door securely bolted, Yakim Douan took his first tentative steps into the swirling depths of the hematite gemstone, using the magic within to separate his spirit from his body. His incorporeal spirit went out across the city easily, moving to the western gates.

And there he paused. Never before had he gone out from Jacintha in this form.

Before he could second-guess himself, the Chezru Chieftain sailed out across the open desert, his spirit flying free and fast. He sped to the west, past Dahdah Oasis, then turned south, for the latest reports from Yatol Bardoh had the Dragon of To-gai somewhere to the east of Pruda.

He could not believe the amount of ground he covered that night, running a line from Dallabad to Pruda, and then back to the northeast, back to Jacintha. But he saw no sign of the woman and her army. His relief was profound when he returned to his own body to discover that nothing was amiss, that none in Chom Deiru apparently had any idea that anything unsavory had occurred that night.

And so he went out again the next night, this time moving more to the south and less to the west.

He knew at first, distant sight, that the encampment he spotted was that of the To-gai-ru and not of Yatol Bardoh.

"Pruda has been garrisoned once more, and no doubt with many spear-throwing ballistae in case our dragon should make an appearance," a scout reported to Brynn that same night.

The woman nodded, hardly surprised. The pursuing Behrenese were having little luck in catching her, but Yatol Bardoh was doing well to outfit every nearby city against possible attacks.

"No doubt they have been told of our typical tactics, as well," Pagonel said to her when the scout left them alone. "What new tricks will we find to shape the upcoming battle-fields to our liking?"

Brynn shrugged, having few answers. "Agradeleous grows impatient once again," she noted, for she had been speaking with the dragon nearly every night. "How many weeks has it been since he has seen any large battles?"

"You give him free rein to destroy the caravans."

"But that is hardly the adventure he so craves."

Pagonel looked at her intently. "Hold the course," he advised. "As miserable and hot as we are, our pursuers are even more so. Let us run Yatol Bardoh all across the hot sands of Behren, finding opportunity to sting where we may."

It was true enough, Brynn realized. There was no way they could turn about and do battle with the pursuing Behrenese army, even with a dragon at their disposal. Agradeleous had been fairly injured at the escape from Bardoh, and to Brynn's surprise, she had learned that dragon wounds were cumulative, that they really didn't heal very quickly. As much as the dragon desired battle, Brynn knew that she had to take great care, using him only when he was most needed.

"Your guidance keeps me strong," she said to Pagonel, stroking the side of his head and neck gently. "We will hold our course and run Yatol Bardoh into the hot sands. And when winter comes, we will return to the steppes, quietly, and next spring wage war against every outposter settlement."

"And when the Behrenese army charges into To-gai to stop us?"

"We will turn again upon Behren," said Brynn. "We will sting them over and over again—it is all we can do—and hope that the Chezru Chieftain will come to see his expansion onto the steppes as a fool's—"

She stopped suddenly, her face locked in a strange and confused manner, and she blinked her eyes repeatedly.

"Brynn?" Pagonel asked, moving toward her.

She lashed out suddenly, her fist speeding for his chest, but the supremely trained Jhesta Tu snapped his hand up to deflect the blow gently.

She punched out again, and again, and then began to thrash about, and it became apparent to Pagonel that she wasn't attacking him, but was struggling against some unseen enemy, some demon within herself!

"Brynn!" he cried repeatedly and he finally found an opening to grab the woman and bring her down to the ground. "Brynn! What is it? Tell me!"

Undecipherable, almost feral, sounds escaped the woman's lips and she shuddered violently, nearly tossing the Jhesta Tu off her.

And then she lay very still, staring at Pagonel, her face a mask of confusion.

"What was it?" he asked, recognizing that the danger had passed.

Brynn shook her head. "It was . . . someone else . . ." She stammered and shook her head, unable to fathom what had just occurred. She finally started to better explain it when the pair heard a scream from the neighboring tent, where Pagonel had secured the captive Merwan Ma.

"Someone else?" Pagonel asked as he started to rise, pulling Brynn up beside him.

"Looking, into me . . . looking through my eyes!"

By the time the two got into Merwan Ma's tent, the poor Shepherd was curled up in a corner, trembling with obvious terror, and whispering "God-Voice," over and over again.

"God-Voice?" Brynn asked Pagonel.

"The Chezru Chieftain," the mystic replied, and he turned to Merwan Ma. "You have seen him?"

The Shepherd just continued to tremble, and shook his head repeatedly.

Brynn and Pagonel looked to each other, then back to the man.

"He has seen him," Brynn remarked. "The Chezru Chieftain was here—in spirit, at least." She looked back to Pagonel. "But how is that possible?"

"With a gemstone," the mystic replied. "A hematite." He watched Merwan Ma as he spoke, and noted that the man's eyes widened a bit more, a subtle but telling sign.

"What do you know?" the mystic asked the captive.

Merwan Ma looked away.

"The use of gemstone magic is strictly forbidden by the Chezru religion," the mystic explained to Brynn, who was nodding, already well aware of that fact. "And yet, there is no other way that Chezru Chieftain Yakim Douan could have come to us. The Jhesta Tu know how to walk out of body, but that is a secret we guard carefully, and only our greatest mystics can achieve the state.

"But Yakim Douan did come out here, did he not, Merwan Ma?" Pagonel went on. "He came to Brynn and then to you, and you recognized him clearly."

"You know nothing!" the Shepherd yelled, and he turned about, burying his face in the tent side. "Nothing!"

Brynn and Pagonel looked to each other.

"Leave us, I beg," the mystic whispered. "I believe that this entire picture is beginning to focus. Our friend here knows something—that is why the Chezru Chieftain wanted him killed—and that something is perhaps linked to the surprise we have seen this night."

"The Chezru Chieftain uses a gemstone?" Brynn whispered, but she was too excited to keep her voice low enough so that Merwan Ma could not hear, and he shifted and let out a small whimper.

Pagonel shook his head, then shrugged. "If he does, he would not want anyone to know."

"Enough of a threat for him to order this man killed?"

"Perhaps," the mystic reasoned.

Brynn left then, and Pagonel knelt beside Merwan Ma. He grabbed the man by the shoulder and began to turn him about, but Merwan Ma tugged free and turned back.

Pagonel took him more roughly by the shoulder and pulled him around. "I have been more patient with you than you deserve," he said bluntly. "You—we—were visited this night by a spirit, and one that you recognized as your God-Voice."

"No!"

"Yes! And now you will tell me the truth of why Chezru Yakim Douan wished you dead. Is it because you knew his secret? That he possessed a soul stone?"

The man blanched but did not answer, and Pagonel took
that as an answer in itself, a clear indication that he had hit on
something, something very important. Still, the depth of this
escaped him. Yakim Douan had been in power for decades,
without threat, for indeed, none of the Yatols would threaten
him. The hierarchy of their religion left no room for any such
dissension. Given that, why would Yakim Douan even need a
soul stone? Or perhaps, in desperation, he had enlisted the
Abellicans to help him in his search for the To-gai-ru army.
That made some sense to Pagonel, but offered only a partial
explanation. For if it was indeed the God-Voice who had
come out to them in spirit, then the man's flirtation with such
a gemstone could not have been anything new to him. It took
years of training, even with the aid of a hematite, to attempt
even a small spirit-walk, let alone the near possession he had
witnessed with Brynn. No, it made no sense.

"We will sit here all through the night, and tomorrow as
well, if that is needed," Pagonel said to Merwan Ma. "I will
know the truth of it. And why you so protect this man who
would see you dead, I do not understand."

"It was the Chezhou-Lei, and not the God-Voice!" Merwan Ma screamed, but his voice lost all power and all conviction at the end of the declaration, and he melted into sobs.

Pagonel sat back and let him alone for a bit, trying again to
sort through all of this startling news.

With mixed feelings did Yakim Douan re-enter his corporeal body back in Jacintha. He had found her! Had found this
woman—Brynn, he had heard her called—and her band of
marauding rebels! Now he could direct Yatol Bardoh and destroy the Dragon of To-gai once and for all.

But he had found Merwan Ma, as well, alive and sitting in a
tent right beside the woman and her Jhesta Tu companion.
Merwan Ma! Douan had thought him dead and gone, murdered, burned, and buried in Dharyan! What implications did
this hold? What dangers might Merwan Ma bring to him personally, whatever the outcome of his hunt for the Dragon of
To-gai?

Few or none, he decided. He would send word out among

his troops that the man was a traitor and was guiding their enemies across the desert. He would offer a huge reward for Merwan Ma—no, not for Merwan Ma, but for Merwan Ma's severed head!

Yes, that was it.

Douan hustled through Chom Deiru, back to the circular room, where he replaced the chalice. Then he ran to find his attendant—how he wished he could remember the young dolt's name!—to proclaim that he had heard the word of Yatol, and that Yatol would deliver their enemies unto them.

"Your God-Voice has enlisted the aid of the Abellicans in finding us," Pagonel reasoned to Merwan Ma the next day, after spending more than half the night grilling the man.

The Shepherd shook his head.

"It is no secret that he is friends with the abbot from Entel, Abbot . . ."

"Abbot Olin," Merwan Ma said, the first words he had spoken in hours. "Yes, Jhesta Tu, the God-Voice knows Abbot Olin of Entel well, but never has he shown any interest in procuring gemstones from the Abellicans. The gemstones are what separate us—"

"But he has a stone in his possession, a powerful one, if he can use it to spirit-walk this far from his city."

"You believe that you know so much."

"Knowledge is the way of Jhesta Tu, Merwan Ma," said Pagonel. "We know of the To-gai-ru and the Behrenese. We understand the word of Yatol and of St. Abelle. We know of the gemstones, including their properties. I, myself, have used a hematite to walk out of body."

"They are sacrilege," the Shepherd grumbled.

Pagonel laughed at him. "To the Jhesta Tu, they are tools, my young friend. As fire is a tool. Some consider them the gift of God, others use them as proof that their religion is better since they forsake them."

Merwan Ma looked away.

"And yet, your God-Voice has one, does he not?" Pagonel pressed, and he moved around, putting his face very near the shaken young man. "Admit it. That is why he wanted to kill you—and it was Yakim Douan who ordered you dead, not some rogue Chezhou-Lei trying to grab for power in Dharyan. Why would a Chezhou-Lei warrior even wish for some power? They are warriors, not governors! They are—"

"He has a stone!" Merwan Ma shouted back, and fell back in horror at his own words and sat there, gasping.

"A hematite?"

The Shepherd nodded.

"You have seen it, and Yakim Douan knows that you know of it?"

Another nod.

"And that is why he wanted you dead," the mystic reasoned. "Your knowledge of his . . . indiscretion, frightened him. Profoundly so, it would seem."

"It is in the chalice," Merwan Ma admitted somberly. "A sacrilegious Abellican soul stone embedded in the Chezru Goblet, in the Room of Forever."

"The chalice filled with the blood of those chosen for sacrifice?" Pagonel asked.

"It is among the most important relics in Chom Deiru," Merwan Ma replied, and he held up his hands and pulled up his sleeves, showing the mystic the line of scars along his wrist.

"And you found the hematite within that chalice?"

The Shepherd nodded. "And then I saw the God-Voice with the chalice," he admitted, shaking his head, his expression full of horror as he remembered that awful moment.

"And he knew that you saw him?"

"Yes."

"And soon after, you were sent to Dharyan to serve as governor," said the mystic, and it was all beginning to come together then, even a definite feeling within Pagonel that this was something deeper than just the God-Voice using a soul stone.

# CHAPTER 35

# *Head-On*

Word left Jacintha in the form of a series of flashes on a shiny metal plate. And so it went, down a long, long line, from signaler to signaler. By afternoon that day, the signal had crossed through Dahdah Oasis, and continued on, to the south now more than to the west.

Two days later, the words of Chezru Chieftain Douan reached Yatol Bardoh and Shauntil. They stood over a large map of the region and used Douan's instructions to pinpoint the location of the Dragon of To-gai and her forces—or at least, the position of that encampment two nights previous.

"We will receive word every second or third day," Shauntil explained to his leader. "Soon we will have the woman's pattern, and can anticipate her movement. Already, if we begin to move our forces here and here"—he pointed to locations on the map, moving his finger to show a swing farther to the south and then east around the point indicated by the message—"we will begin to limit her options."

"Forcing her north or back to the west," the Yatol observed.

"North to the road where more Jacintha soldiers might join us in encircling the To-gai-ru," the Chezhou-Lei explained. "And west back to the steppes. It would be better if we pushed her out of Behren altogether, I believe."

"She will be harder to find and destroy in the steppes."

"But Behren will be secure, and the people will be calmed, and that, I believe is a primary goal of Chezru Chieftain Douan."

"Do not presume to know the will of the God-Voice!" Yatol Bardoh snapped back, and then he recoiled, fearing that his suddenly excited tone would reveal much of his thinking. For Yatol Bardoh did not wish any help from Jacintha in ridding Behren of this To-gai-ru witch, nor was he concerned about calming the populace. Bardoh understood well that turmoil was his opportunity to strengthen his own position, and that the more credit he could take for killing the Dragon of To-gai, the more power and influence he would attain throughout the kingdom. He especially needed that great victory now, given his disgrace in losing Avrou Eesa to the woman. Even though the city was firmly back in Behrenese hands, the scars of the Dragon of To-gai's attack would be enduring indeed.

And so the man was somewhat ambivalent about this new assistance, where his master, the Chezru Chieftain, claimed to be communicating directly to Yatol. Yes, Bardoh was thrilled to have the intelligence he needed to finally catch up with his adversary. But on the other hand, it galled him that the assistance was coming from Jacintha, and thus stealing his glory.

"If we do not catch this Dragon of To-gai, and soon, then the people may come to look upon us as failures, Yatol Bardoh," Chezhou-Lei Shauntil dared to remark, quietly, so that only the Yatol and not the other commanders in the map room could hear.

Bardoh straightened and stared hard at the perceptive warrior, but he calmed quickly and even nodded his appreciation. It was an important reminder.

"Let us begin to herd the witch," he said.

"They knew that we were moving south," Brynn said to Pagonel. From a high dune, the pair could see the distant lights of a long Behrenese encampment, stretched out across the desert.

"Their line is thin," the woman went on. "We could break through it."

"And lose more warriors in the fight."

"We would kill many more than we would lose."

"And they can afford to lose many, many more," the mystic reminded. "Our pursuers try to force fights, even skirmishes.

They dog us and look to attrition to thin our ranks. We are not on the steppes, and while you know that we are fighting for your homeland, our mere presence here forces the whole of the Behrenese population to feel the same way. If we break through and kill a thousand, and lose only a hundred in the process, then the day will still belong to Yatol Bardoh and not to Brynn."

"We must continue to ride hard, then," said a determined Brynn. "Our opportunities may prove fewer in number, and so we must be vigilant to find and exploit each and every one."

Pagonel nodded, but he could not wipe the grim expression from his face. He understood what was going on, and with the Chezru Chieftain using a soul stone to locate the To-gai-ru and relay their position to the pursuing army, Brynn's greatest advantage, unpredictability, was no more.

He and Brynn had even discussed the possibility of breaking up the single army into many swifter independent forces. It had been a fleeting thought, though, for how would they supply so many divisions? No small force would be able to take on a city, and Behren was a kingdom of great cities, not small enclaves.

Pagonel didn't voice his fear then, but he knew that Brynn already understood that she and her forces might soon be running across the To-gai steppes once more.

Even there, they would be effectively hunted.

Agradeleous' expression told Brynn that he hardly wanted to hear her words of encouragement. She had come to him to explain the need for their continuing run, to beg him to fly off more often and gather the supplies to keep the riders and their mounts fresh and ready to flee.

"Attack them!" the dragon demanded. "Let us vanquish our enemies here and now and be done with this folly!"

"You stand straight no longer," Brynn observed, and the dragon, whose wounds from the breakout at Avrou Eesa had indeed bent him a bit to the side, growled.

"It is not time," Brynn said.

"The opportunity will get no better," Agradeleous countered. "They follow us as if you yourself are directing their movements!"

Brynn couldn't deny the truth of the observation, so she didn't try. She wasn't about to tell the dragon about the spirit of Yakim Douan. Pagonel had assured her that there was no way the Chezru Chieftain could use the stone in any detrimental way against a beast as great as Agradeleous. Even attempting to possess a mighty dragon would likely destroy the man. But Pagonel and Brynn had agreed that they would have to watch Agradeleous carefully, now that the tide was turning against them, and now that they needed the dragon to increase his more mundane duties.

"Our enemies will continue to err, and we will continue to exploit those mistakes," Brynn said, rather unconvincingly.

Another low growl escaped Agradeleous.

"I need you. To-gai needs you, now more than ever," Brynn said. "On every night that you fly out for supplies, pause and gather a great stone or two and drop them upon our enemies from on high, above the reach of their great spear-throwers."

She had to give him that bit of fun, at least, she knew, though she understood that they would likely gain little from such excursions. Dropping a rock upon a burning city was one thing, but hitting a target the size of a stretched encampment to any effect was more a matter of luck than skill. And if the dragon, in its bombing, got excited and tried to attack, then the Behrenese would fight against it viciously.

Brynn understood all too well that if she lost Agradeleous, her only reliable source of supplying her army, she would have but two choices: initiate the great battle against the overwhelming odds, or flee back to the To-gai steppes and disband into small marauding bands, many of which, she knew, would soon give up the fight altogether.

Brynn retired late that night full of trepidation and exhausted, so exhausted that she did manage to find some sleep, though it was a light and restless one.

That would prove fortunate.

\*     \*     \*

This was nothing that Pagonel often attempted, for it was trying and disturbing, and left him quite vulnerable. Still, the mystic thought it important to try to gain even footing with their adversaries, to spy on the movements of the Behrenese as the Chezru Chieftain was now spying on the movements of the To-gai-ru.

The mystic fell into himself, sending his consciousness to his line of Chi, his energy of life. And then he filtered that energy out beyond his physical body, out into the open air. He glanced back at himself, sitting alone in his small tent, legs crossed tightly before him, hands on his knees, palms upward, a look of complete serenity on his face.

Pagonel moved out slowly from his relaxed form, to the edges of his tent, and then he floated up through the tent, slowly rising, looking back, then looking all about at the quiet encampment.

He noted one form, moving out of a tent to the side of his own, and thought nothing of it for a moment, until he realized that it was moving with purpose, and not toward Pagonel's tent as the mystic had anticipated, but toward the tent of Brynn Dharielle.

That too would prove fortunate.

The shadowy form slipped silently through the tent flap, leaving it open just a bit so that he could navigate the darkness within.

There lay Brynn, curled under a blanket against the cold desert night air, and there to the side lay her fabulous sword, Flamedancer.

The form moved in closer, his hand reaching for the weapon.

Caught in fitful dreams, Brynn didn't hear any of it. But then, through her dreams, came a face she knew and trusted, the image of Pagonel, speaking to her directly.

*Get up!* the ghost implored her, and his tone was one of dire warning, a silent but insistent cry that warned her of imminent danger.

The woman was moving before her eyes even popped

open, rolling to her belly and flipping a forward somersault, rolling to her feet.

She saw the glint of metal, flashing off the low firelight outside, and moved instinctively, snapping her arm down and across while turning her hips out of harm's way.

She did get nicked on the forearm, but it was no serious wound, and nothing that slowed her as she worked out from the side of the small tent, trying to find some maneuverability even as the attacker retracted and realigned the blade.

The sword thrust came in fast and low, but awkwardly, the man's retraction before the strike giving the skilled Brynn more than enough time to compensate and set not only her defense, but her return attack. She leaped forward, turning over above the blade in a tight somersault, bringing her legs around to slam down atop the man's shoulders. He brought the sword up in response, but there was no strength behind the movement.

Brynn was quite glad that this one didn't understand how to ignite Flamedancer at that moment!

Her legs clamped about the man's neck as she came over and down, and a quick twist sent the man spiraling off to the side, tumbling headlong against the tent as Brynn let him loose.

She was up before him, and as he tried to turn about and bring his sword to bear, the ranger bore in, too close to be warded by the blade. She shouldered the man back against the tent flap, knocking him completely off-balance. Then she went for the sword arm, driving stiffened fingers into his forearm muscle, stealing his strength, while grabbing at the sword hilt with her other hand.

Falling and stung, he couldn't hold the sword away from the strong woman. She pulled it free and stepped up against him, moving just off to the side as she reversed her grip, turning the sword point down and behind her.

Even as she began the killing strike, her tent flap flung wide and Pagonel cried out to her, "Do not kill him!"

Brynn held the blow, and as the man sorted himself behind her, she launched an elbow into his face, laying him low. Then she came out and swung about, reorienting the sword so that its deadly tip turned in toward the helpless man.

Pagonel came in, bearing a torch, and the woman recognized her attacker as Merwan Ma.

She looked to Pagonel, confused, for he and the man had seemed to come to an understanding—so much so that Brynn had relaxed all guard over their captive.

"It was not Merwan Ma!" Pagonel said against her doubting and angry look.

The mystic rushed to kneel before the sobbing man. "It was not you, was it?" he asked.

Merwan Ma waved him away.

"Tell me!" the mystic insisted, grabbing him by the shoulders and squaring him up. "It was the Chezru Chieftain, was it not? Come out with his soul stone to possess your body? Tell me! Your God-Voice possessed your body. He threw out your free will and substituted his own."

The Shepherd broke down completely then, falling to the floor and covering his head with his hands.

"What does it mean?" Brynn asked.

"It means that Merwan Ma has seen the lie that is his life," Pagonel answered. "The Chezru religion cannot tolerate such a thing as has happened this night, and yet, it was the Chezru Chieftain himself who perpetrated this horror upon Merwan Ma." He looked down to the sobbing man. "And he knows it."

"Shackle him and put him under guard," Brynn demanded.

The mystic nodded. "The danger is mostly past now."

"But tomorrow?"

Pagonel was shaking his head before she ever asked, obviously anticipating the question. "The theft of a body is no easy task, even for those Abellicans most skilled with the soul stone. Merwan Ma left an opening for his God-Voice, one wrought of confusion. But now he knows the truth and will be more vigilant, and I will teach him to resist such intrusions."

With Brynn's accepting nod, the mystic helped Merwan Ma to his feet and ushered the man out of the tent and back to his own. He offered a few instructions, a few mental games the man might use to help him battle the attacking spirit, should it return, and then he set a pair of guards outside the Shepherd's tent and returned to his own to contemplate these newest, troubling developments.

There in the dark, in his meditation, Pagonel considered the startling events and the good fortune alone that had allowed disaster to be averted. He thought of his own reasoning as to why Merwan Ma had been possessed, of why the man had not been up to the task of ejecting the attacking spirit. For surely Pagonel would have had no trouble at all in repelling Yakim Douan, and Brynn had done so in mere seconds.

All it took was a little mental discipline, a bit of understanding that such an act was wrong in the extreme.

Pagonel popped open his eyes, staring straight ahead, seeing something then so simple and basic that the biggest surprise of the revelation was that he had not recognized it before, and that Merwan Ma apparently had not. He unfolded himself and rushed from his tent, past the guards, and into the tent of Merwan Ma, where he found the man sitting and staring blankly, hopelessly.

"Tell me of Transcendence," the mystic implored him.

Brynn used every trick that she or her leaders could think of. They intercepted flashing signals and sent some of their own along the line, and managed to turn the dogged pursuit off course several times.

On one such occasion, apparently running free up along the north road that connected Dharyan with Dahdah Oasis, the ranger made the decision to continue north, into the foothills of the Belt-and-Buckle, reasoning that her warriors would find more rest there, more supplies for them and their horses. Also, the thinking went, if the Chezru Chieftain came out to find them, he'd have a harder time spotting their encampment along the craggy rocks and canyons of the steep foothills.

And so they shook off the pursuit of Shauntil and Yatol Bardoh for several weeks, as the summer of God's Year 844, Abellican Reckoning, turned to autumn, marking the second anniversary of Brynn's rise as the leader of the To-gai-ru rebels.

"It has been a good two years," Brynn said to Pagonel and some others one night about the campfire. "We have struck hard into Behren, harder than any of us might have hoped."

"It was a good first year and a half," one of the leaders, the ever-grumbling Tanalk Grenk, replied. "Now we hide, while the Wraps tighten the noose about our necks."

There was little Brynn could say in the way of argument. They had won a couple of minor skirmishes that summer, mostly over supply caravans, but the victories had been few and far between, and always with the knowledge that Yatol Bardoh and Shauntil and their legions were not far behind.

"We must strike again, and hard!" the man went on, rising and brushing off his worn breeches. He paced about the fire, staring into the hard eyes of his seasoned warrior companions. "Let us find again the glory of battle! Let Behren tremble beneath the thunder of our charge!"

"Where?" Brynn asked, stealing a bit of his bluster, and quieting the murmurs of excited agreement that had begun. She too rose and paced about. "To take a city would delay us longer than our pursuers allow. And to turn and fight the pursuing force would be folly."

"Then let us turn for To-gai," another man offered. "Let the Behrenese chase us about the land we know, and that they do not!"

The murmurs began anew, and Brynn closed her eyes, for this was exactly what she had been fearing as the war had ground to a halt. She and Pagonel had been over this time and time again, and in considering the return to Behren, they had always come to the same grim conclusion: that such a turn would mark the end of the campaign. For in To-gai, their warriors would find other pressing duties, and with the pressure off the Chezru Chieftain to come to resolution, attrition would weigh against them, and not for them. With the army running about To-gai and not Behren, the Behrenese would have no reason to seek peace.

Little was settled that night at the campfire, and a frustrated and troubled Brynn went back to her tent. She had only begun her typically fitful sleep when a call awakened her. She rushed out to join several others, Pagonel among them, as they stood on a nearby ridge, staring to the south, where the fires of a huge encampment could be seen.

"And so the chase begins anew," one man muttered, and walked away.

"Douan has found us," Pagonel remarked.

"Is there any way to hide from his spirit eyes?" Brynn asked.

The mystic turned to her and shook his head. "We can prevent possession, likely, but out of body, he is swift, and he can fly high to gain proper vantage points. Even if we lit no fires at all, not even those concealed in deep fire pits or in the shadows of overhangs and caves, he would find us."

"Send the scouts out far and wide," Brynn instructed. "Let us turn now to the west, and use our speed to outdistance our pursuit."

"Back to To-gai?"

"So it would seem."

"And you believe that her efforts will falter once back in her homeland?" Merwan Ma asked Pagonel soon after, the two sitting alone near one low-burning fire, for the winter chill was blowing up there already.

"The odds were never in her favor," the mystic replied. "In truth, I never believed that she had any chance at all of breaking free of Behren's immoral stranglehold, unless the Chezru Chieftain and his Yatols came to understand that To-gai was worth less than the effort required to hold it."

"And she must have known as much, as well," said the Shepherd, and the mystic nodded.

"She, we, all expected to die. And so we likely will."

"Then why did you try?"

Pagonel looked at him as if the question itself was preposterous, and that expression conveyed all the reasons Merwan Ma needed to know.

"Brynn's world has crumbled," said Pagonel, and he paused and looked at Merwan Ma, waiting for the man to return his stare. "And so has your own."

Merwan Ma sat back and folded his arms over his thin chest, letting that realization sink in deeply. He knew that

Pagonel spoke the truth, knew that his entire life had been tossed aside, simply because he had seen the Chezru Chieftain in the illicit, even sacrilegious, act of using the hematite gemstone. And Merwan Ma, the keeper of that sacred chalice, the appointed attendant to the God-Voice and mentor to the new God-Voice, once one was found, had come to recognize, as had the mystic, the deeper implications to all of this. Merwan Ma had felt the intrusion of Yakim Douan keenly, and understood that the God-Voice had almost forced his spirit from his body entirely, taking the corporeal form as his own. If he could do that to a grown and intelligent man, what might he do to an unsuspecting infant in the womb?

"I am not going west with Brynn," Pagonel said to him, drawing him from his contemplations.

"South to the Mountains of Fire?"

"East to Jacintha."

Merwan Ma's eyes opened wide. "They will kill you. They will not hear you!"

"This is a bigger issue than my life."

"You say it as simply as that?"

"I do."

Again, Merwan Ma sat back, staring hard at this unusual man. "And what of me?"

"I will ask of Brynn that you be set free," Pagonel replied. "And she will not argue the course. If you choose to go south, to the Mountains of Fire, I will tell you proper phrases, passwords, that will ensure your acceptance in the Walk of Clouds. Your road will be your own to determine."

Merwan Ma continued to stare at him, trying to read the thoughts behind the words. "My road will be mine to choose, but you are hoping that I will choose to go with you, to Jacintha."

Pagonel smiled.

"They will kill me, too," Merwan Ma said, and the mystic did not disagree.

Merwan Ma shrugged, and gave what might have been his first honest smile since entering the city of Dharyan so long ago.

The next day, the pair stood before Brynn, their gear heavy on their backs.

"You have my love and my respect," Pagonel said to her. "I know that you will choose correctly in every course you take." He gave her a hug and kissed her on the cheek. "May good fortune keep you alive, Brynn Dharielle. Your home is the Walk of Clouds if you cannot find it again in To-gai."

"I only hope that I will be buried in the soil of To-gai," the woman said grimly, her tone telling the mystic that she understood well that her war was fast ending. If her force could not outguess the Behrenese, they had no chance of victory.

"There will be others who come behind you," Pagonel replied. "Who use the name of Brynn Dharielle, the Dragon of To-gai, to inspire those who would follow them. The quest to see To-gai free does not end with you, even should you fail."

"And you will plant the seeds of dissent among the Chezru, that Yakim Douan will find his power wavering," Brynn replied.

"And perhaps, in the time of Transcendence, which is not so far away, another will take up the cause of Brynn Dharielle, and use the tactics of Brynn Dharielle, and how will Behren fight back then?" said Merwan Ma, and the other two looked at him with perfectly stunned expressions, then broke out in laughter.

"Jhesta Tu mind tricks, to bend him to my will," Pagonel quipped, and Merwan Ma, after a quick, panicked look to make sure that the mystic was joking, joined in the laughter.

And so they parted ways, with Brynn leading her riders out to the west, and Pagonel and Merwan Ma beginning their long walk down the eastern road, some two weeks from Jacintha.

# CHAPTER 36

## *Defensive Position*

"She has turned west," Shauntil informed Yatol Bardoh when the news arrived from Jacintha in the morning.

"The mountains were her last refuge," the Yatol reasoned. "Now that we have found her once more, she is out of room. She runs for home."

The Yatol turned to face the warrior and chuckled wickedly. "Swing the line to block all passes into To-gai."

The Chezhou-Lei warrior put on a confused expression. "We cannot hope to pace the To-gai-ru, with their fine steeds."

"We will trail," the Yatol explained. "Send those we already have in the west to block the passes. Have them set their great ballistae in defensible positions in case the dragon makes an appearance."

Shauntil's expression did not change. "The only forces we have close enough to the plateau divide are those you sent north to Dharyan, Yatol."

The man nodded.

"If they swing east, it will leave the city undefended."

"And so the Dragon of To-gai may get her last victory," Yatol Bardoh said. "And then we will have her, and all of her forces, bottled up and waiting to be destroyed. Do not consider me in such a manner!" he scolded when Shauntil's expression grew even more doubting. "We must look upon that which will achieve the greater good. If Dharyan is sacked once more, it will be rebuilt, but once we destroy the Dragon of To-gai, there will be no one to replace her."

The Chezhou-Lei warrior snapped to attention. "Yes, Yatol," he said, and he found that he was beginning to see the wisdom of Bardoh's thinking. Indeed, if they could finally be rid of the Dragon of To-gai, then the price of Dharyan would not seem so great a thing.

"If they catch me with a Ru servant, they will tear the flesh from my body," Merwan Ma said excitedly, addressing a group of soldiers at Dahdah Oasis. The place was crawling with the Jacintha garrison, another several thousand marching down the western road to link up with Yatol Bardoh and Shauntil for the final defeat of the Dragon of To-gai.

Behind the Shepherd, Pagonel kept his head bowed and his hands, bound much more loosely than they appeared, in close to his torso.

"You should give your servant over to us, here and now," one of the guards remarked, and he turned to his friends, laughing, then continued, "that we might launch him by catapult into the midst of our enemies!"

They all broke out in laughter then, including Merwan Ma, though the Shepherd certainly wasn't pleased at the grim reminder of that horrible sight.

A couple of the soldiers moved toward Pagonel.

"No!" Merwan Ma shouted at them, and they did stop, and turned to stare at him hard.

"He is needed for the service of the Chezru Chieftain," the soldier standing before the Shepherd declared angrily. "You would deny us?"

"I am a Chezru Shepherd!" Merwan Ma replied. "Once attendant to Chezru Yakim Douan."

"So you say!"

"Would you dare to guess that I am wrong?" Merwan Ma shot back, not backing down a bit. "I can name for you every member of Chezru within Chom Deiru! I am only now returned from the retaking of Dharyan, with word from Governor Carwan Pestle, my peer and my friend. So would you challenge my word, soldier? Would you risk the wrath of Chezru Douan and his Chezhou-Lei?"

The man blanched and fell back a step, and Merwan Ma, scowling with every stride, led Pagonel by the group and across the oasis, heading out again down the eastern road toward Jacintha.

All that day, they passed columns of soldiers, marching to partake of the end of the Dragon of To-gai.

"You took a great chance for me this day," Pagonel remarked to Merwan Ma when they were alone that night.

"I took no chance for you," the Shepherd declared.

"You could have turned me in to them and been done with me then and there," the mystic reasoned. "And you might even have redeemed yourself in the eyes of the Chezru Chieftain if you had."

"Redeemed myself?" the man echoed with a snort. "I am not even sure where such redemption should come from anymore. We decided upon the plan to walk through Dahdah, and I gave to you my word."

"To many men, their salvation is worth the price of that word, particularly to an enemy who holds them captive."

"Is that what you are?"

The mystic shrugged.

"If I chose to walk away from you now, would you stop me?" Merwan Ma asked.

"No."

Point made, the Shepherd rested back.

"But you will not walk away, Merwan Ma," Pagonel went on. "You have come to see the truth of this, and this journey to Jacintha is as much your quest as it is mine."

"More," the Shepherd said, his voice as grim and determined as Pagonel had ever heard, indeed, as grim and determined as it had ever been. "You speak of salvation, and that was the promise of Yatol. But what is that promise if all else is a lie?"

"You do not know that all else is a lie."

"I know that Transcendence is the miracle that binds the Chezru religion," the Shepherd explained. "Those who witness the miracle of the fully conscious and knowing child are forever affected. They go to their graves happy, because they know that Yatol is all-powerful and looking over them."

Pagonel noted a bit of a tremor growing in the man's voice as he continued.

"But if the Chezru Chieftain himself, the God-Voice of Yatol, cannot trust in that, then how can we? And without that miracle, then where is the binding force of Yatol?"

Pagonel had no answers, no words at all to comfort the man. For if their guess was correct, if the Chezru Chieftain now was merely the same spirit, taking the corporeal forms of unborn children down through the centuries, then what argument was to be made?

"When we are done with this, come to the Walk of Clouds, my friend," he did offer. "There you will learn the truth of who you are. There you will come to understand the fleeting nature of the body and the eternal energy of the soul."

Merwan Ma did smile, but he snorted again, as well. "We will not be done with this, my friend," he said, and it was the first time he had addressed Pagonel in that manner. "We will walk into the fortress that is Chom Deiru. We will not walk back out."

Again, the mystic found that he could offer little argument against that logical statement.

"Then we will break through their pitiful lines!" declared Tanalk Grenk with his typically imposing tones.

"To be slowed, stung, and pursued," another remarked, and so it went, all about the campfire where Brynn and her commanders had gathered. The reports from the scouts had come in for the last three days, making it apparent that the Behrenese knew exactly where Brynn's force was, and where they were heading. Now the Behrenese seemed to be forcing a fight, breaking their great army into three groups, the smallest to the east—though reports told of another great force marching down the road from Jacintha—the largest to the south and moving swiftly, trying to keep pace with Brynn, and one to the west, setting defensive positions along the base of the plateau divide and blocking all known passes.

"We can run straight west and use the dragon to get onto the steppes," one of the woman leaders remarked.

"But many would be caught before the dragon could lift them," argued Grenk, who was obviously itching for a major fight. "The enemy is too close and too determined."

"Most would get away," the woman commander countered. "The others, myself among them, would turn and fight the Behrenese to the last!"

Many nods accompanied those strong and determined words, but Brynn's was not among them. She had spent another night arguing with Agradeleous, with the wurm growing more agitated by the day, as eager as was Tanalk Grenk to do battle, but for very different reasons, obviously. Agradeleous had long ago grown tired of this retreating action, and Brynn doubted that he would cooperate in a maneuver designed solely to run away. More likely, they would run to the base of the plateau divide and Agradeleous would force them to turn and fight the pursuing Behrenese, then and there, whatever the outcome.

"To the steppes, and then where?" the ranger asked them all. "Even if we dodge them this time, to what gain?"

"Then fight them!" Tanalk Grenk growled. "Here and now!"

"Or from a defensible position, where we at least will have a chance to inflict tremendous damage upon them," Brynn reasoned.

"I will send scouts at once to find such an area!" the excited man replied.

"I already know of one," said the ranger, and all eyes turned her way and all held quiet, waiting for her to explain.

She looked to the southwest, her expression grim. "We could fight them from behind the wall of Dharielle."

"You mean Dharyan."

"No," said Brynn, her gaze locked, her face tight, her voice perfectly even and steady. "I mean Dharielle."

The very next day, the city was in sight and the To-gai-ru formed their ranks on the high ground just to the east and north of the place.

"The Dragon has returned," said Pauche, the new garrison commander of Dharyan, as he and Governor Carwan Pestle stood on the wall, looking up to the northeast, where the line of enemy soldiers could be seen.

"Where is Yatol Bardoh?" Pestle replied. "Where is Chezhou-Lei Shauntil?"

"Several days away," Pauche answered. "We will hold until they arrive!"

"We will be overrun in a single day," Carwan Pestle remarked with all certainty. "The Dragon of To-gai will visit us this very night, do not doubt, raining fire and death, and in the morning, we will have little resistance against the charge of the horde." Carwan Pestle closed his eyes and recalled the first defeat of Dharyan, remembering how easily the Dragon of To-gai had overrun the place once the Jacintha twenty squares had been lured out to their deaths. With soldiers pulled to block the western passes into To-gai, Pestle's garrison now was not even as strong as it had been then! And all reports indicated that the Dragon of To-gai's army was twice the size of the one that had overrun Dharyan.

"Prepare a horse for me," Pestle ordered.

Pauche did not move, just stood staring curiously at the man.

"Now," Pestle prompted. "A swift horse and a flag of truce."

"You will go and bargain with her?"

"I will go and try to save us all."

Still the man did not move, and his stare shifted from curiosity to a simmering anger.

"Now!" Pestle ordered. "I am the governor of Dharyan. The decision of how to conduct this is mine alone. Now, fetch me a horse and a flag of truce, or I will have you relieved!"

"Governor Shepherd Pestle," Pauche said, dipping a tight bow. "We can fight them. We can hold the walls until Yatol Bardoh arrives with his legions."

"You do not understand the power of the Dragon. The beast will set Dharyan ablaze in a single night, and destroy our defenses. And then we will die. All of us." As he finished, he couldn't help but remember the image of Yatol Grysh, hanging below the eastern gate, and he imagined himself in the man's place, as surely he would be.

He rode through that gate soon after, galloping his horse hard to the distant line of enemies.

"I would speak with the Dragon of To-gai," Carwan Pestle addressed them with as much courage and strength as he could muster.

A small woman stepped her muscled brown-and-white pinto

pony out from the line, walking it to stand before Pestle's taller horse. "We meet again," said Brynn. "You were the attendant of Yatol Grysh, were you not?"

Carwan Pestle sucked in his breath. "I am Shepherd Carwan Pestle, now governor of Dharyan."

"Dharielle," Brynn corrected. "And I have appointed no governor."

Pestle felt the sweat beading on his forehead. He knew he was trembling, and knew that it would show in his voice. He took a deep breath and tried to hold his response as steady as possible. "Chezru Chieftain Douan has reclaimed the city. It was he who appointed me as governor."

"After the unfortunate death of Merwan Ma, no doubt," said the woman, and Pestle's eyes widened.

How could she have known that?

"So, you claim the city for your Chezru Chieftain," Brynn went on a moment later. "And will you deny me entrance in his name?"

"I have come to negotiate a compromise."

"A surrender, you mean?"

Carwan Pestle shifted uncomfortably on his horse. "I request some conditions."

"Concerning your neck?"

Pestle paused and took another deep and steadying breath, and then another. "I—we—do not wish to battle you again," he said.

"Then surrender," came Brynn's uncompromising response.

"I will have guarantees for the safety of my people," said Carwan Pestle, and he felt stronger suddenly, recognizing that he really had nothing to lose there, that he had, in effect, lost everything already.

Behind Brynn, the To-gai-ru warriors began many conversations, with many voices raised in anger. The woman held up her hand and soon enough all chatter stopped.

"And if I allow you and your warriors to walk free, then you will no doubt turn around and wage battle back against me, once your friends have arrived," Brynn reasoned. "Is that not so?"

"We will not."

That proclamation brought a renewal of the doubting and cynical discussions, but Brynn cut them short once again, lifting her hand.

"I cannot trust in that," she said. "All of your old and young may leave, and if we are allowed to occupy Dharielle unopposed, then you and your warriors will be considered as prisoners, and treated humanely. My city has a jail, does it not?"

"A large one," said Pestle. "Enough to hold the two hundred garrison of the city."

"Then ride back and throw wide your gates," said Brynn. "And be warned, Pestle, if this is a trick, I will slaughter every man, woman, and child in Dharielle, and will let your body dangle as did the body of Yatol Grysh!"

The man bowed his head, then turned his mount and rode back to the city. Soon after, a line of refugees began to wind their way out of the city.

Brynn led her force into the place, declaring it as Dharielle once more. The eight thousand warriors she brought in went to work immediately, separating potential combatants from obvious civilians among the remaining captives, imprisoning the former and escorting the latter through the eastern gate. Then they began defensive preparations: repairing catapults and ballistae; bringing oil to the wall, to be heated and dropped on attackers; and setting up caches of many, many arrows.

Brynn and Agradeleous watched it all with grim determination.

"Fight as long as you desire, then fly to your mountain home," the woman told the dragon.

"You promised me bards with many tales, and a line of treasure," the dragon reminded.

"And I shall fulfill that promise, if I am able."

Agradeleous snorted, little puffs of flame escaping his nostrils.

"You can leave now, if you prefer," said Brynn.

"I could have left whenever I chose. But I chose to stay, and so I choose to stay now. This promises to be the grandest fight of all, the one of which the bards will long sing. Better that I am a part of it, to make the songs more enjoyable to those who will hear them centuries hence!"

The dragon's sudden enthusiasm brought a smile to Brynn's face. "I will not command you in the battle," she said. "I trust that you will find the best spots in the enemy line to attack."

Agradeleous growled and grinned, seeming quite pleased.

Four days later, all the horizon about Dharielle darkened with the march of the legions of Yatol Bardoh and Shauntil.

"They outnumber us nearly four to one," one commander observed, as the To-gai-ru leaders assembled at the main gate tower to survey the oncoming storm.

Brynn's answer was direct and to the point. "Then kill five."

The bombardment of Dharielle began that very night, with lines of catapults launching balls of burning pitch through the night sky, to splatter within the city, lighting ablaze everything nearby. The To-gai-ru responded with their own shots, but the steppe nomads were not trained with such weapons and their target was much less substantial, and so they did little damage in return.

Agradeleous did fly out and attack, but then he returned, stuck with a thousand arrows, it seemed.

Brynn watched it all with deep trepidation. The Behrenese were ready for her this time. She could not shape the battlefield.

Her dream would end there, and it would take To-gai many years to recover from the loss of so many.

But so be it, she decided, remembering the words of Pagonel. The legend of this fight would live on, to feed the seeds of resistance sometime in the future. For now, Brynn meant to make this battle a costly one for the Behrenese.

She worked right alongside her warriors, battling the fires and trying to keep them all prepared for the charge that would likely come soon after the next dawn.

# CHAPTER 37

# *To the Bitter End*

The western side of Dharyan was still in predawn darkness when the charge began, the great ring of Behrenese closing as one on the city. The To-gai-ru responded with typical ferocity and bravery, manning the walls, great bows in hand, showering their attackers with a killing rain. But the Behrenese came on, too many to be denied, rank upon rank throwing themselves wildly against the deadly volleys in the name of Yatol and their beloved Chezru Chieftain.

Rushing through the courtyard to bolster the southern wall, Brynn found Agradeleous, standing in his lizardman form, growling angrily as he looked all about. "Is this the end?" the dragon asked.

"I know not," Brynn admitted.

"You will die here?"

"If that is my fate. But I will do so with my blade stained with Behrenese blood!" She started away, but the dragon grabbed her by the shoulder and stopped her dead in her tracks.

"And is that enough for you, human? To die here is acceptable because you know that you are right?"

"I'd rather live," Brynn replied with a grin. "And I pray that we win out, or hold out."

"But if you do not?"

Brynn had no answer, but neither did the possibility shrink her proud shoulders at all.

"I hope you live," Agradeleous said to her, and he let her go, and Brynn stood there for a long while, staring at him, until the cries from the wall told her that a breach was imminent.

She ran off to a ladder, scrambling up to the parapet, to find as many Behrenese in that area as To-gai-ru, and with more enemies scrambling over the wall with each passing moment. Brynn's sword came to fiery life. "To-gai!" she cried, and pushed past her fellow defenders, driving hard into the forming Behrenese line. Those invaders gave way a bit before that blazing sword, and that single waver was enough for Brynn to gain a breach in the line.

Spearheading a wedge, she pushed through, shouldering one man off the parapet, stabbing a second man in the belly. She retracted the blade and fell forward to her knees, spinning about, an errant Behrenese sword swishing harmlessly over her head.

Flamedancer took that man out at the knees, and then Brynn was at the ladders, and a thrust to a face had another enemy tumbling back out. That falling man clipped the one behind him on the ladder as he tumbled, and as that second man struggled to hold his balance, the drifting ladder moved out from the wall.

Brynn leaped atop that wall and kicked hard, dislodging the ladder altogether.

A line of arrows came at her from below, but she turned quickly and got her pulsating powrie shield up to deflect most of them. One did clip her across the calf, a burning wound.

She shrugged it off and leaped away, driving back another disintegrating line of enemies.

The breach was closed.

Agradeleous watched it all with sincere admiration, understanding more clearly Belli'mar Juraviel's words to him concerning the value of humans.

"I hope you live," he whispered to Brynn, though she certainly could not hear, and then the dragon fell within himself, bringing forth the transformation into his more natural, huge and terrible form.

Over the eastern gate he flew, above the line of ducking and scrambling Behrenese. Only a few got their bows up to offer meager shots.

Gaining speed with every passing foot, the dragon rammed hard into a catapult, scattering the crew and destroying the

war engine. His head swung about and his fiery breath immolated a handful of fleeing soldiers.

Then the arrows began, but Agradeleous ignored them and
attacked the next catapult, and then the next. He saw one man
rushing to organize the defense—a man wearing the armor of
a Chezhou-Lei. Off the dragon swooped, crashing amidst the
leader and those about him, accepting the heavy blow from
the man's sword and returning it tenfold with a savage claw
rake that nearly took the man in half.

Several others fell and Agradeleous leaped back up into
the air, his great wings bringing him higher. His attack had
stopped the entire charge at that eastern wall, had allowed the
defenders within the city to peel away and reinforce other
vulnerable areas, for the Behrenese were turning back upon
the wurm, with cries naming the dragon as their primary target. Now the volleys of arrows showering Agradeleous increased, but the dragon roared through it and charged on,
destroying another catapult.

A ballista bolt shot past him, then a second, but the dragon
pressed on, breathing forth his fire to light both catapult
and crew.

His wings brought him up high and he dove immediately,
passing low over one group of Behrenese cavalry, unhorsing
most as he sped past on his way to another catapult battery.
Now the dragon swooped back around and up, hovering for a
split second to line up his fiery breath.

Just as one ballista crew had anticipated.

The dragon fire came forth, then stopped abruptly as the
huge spear smashed against his side, crushing bone at the
base of his wing. With a shriek that deafened those nearby,
Agradeleous rolled over in the air, then tumbled down into
the sand.

Immediately, the Behrenese soldiers swarmed over him,
bows twanging, swords slashing, but the dragon went into a
thrashing frenzy, his tail swiping out men by the dozen, claws
digging and raking, his maw snapping to and fro, biting men
in half.

But the dragon was in trouble, and he knew the truth of it.
Soon his scrambling had purpose, turning him about, then

running him flat out for the wall of Dharyan. He neared and leaped, crashing over the wall and tumbling hard into the courtyard.

Brynn was on that wall, urging him on, and as soon as the dragon passed over her, she and her batteries of archers drove back the Behrenese pursuit.

"The west gate!" came a frantic cry, and Brynn spun about to hear the screams of anguish and anger, and she knew that the city would be lost, that if the Behrenese got through that western gate, their flood would sweep her and her army from the city.

And she couldn't get there in time.

But down below, her greatest warrior was moving again, clawing and fighting his way along the streets, his blood drawing a red slick behind him.

Agradeleous arrived in the western courtyard just as the gate began to crumble, and the To-gai-ru, seeing his approach, cleared the way.

The gate fell in, and in charged the Behrenese.

Or at least they started to, and then they were dead, melted in dragon fire. There Agradeleous stayed for the remainder of the attack, a living barricade.

Behind him, on the walls, Brynn rushed from spot to spot, bolstering the defenses with her cries of victory and with her deadly sword and bow.

Soon after, the Behrenese line retreated. Dharyan had held through the first day.

There was little revelry within the city, though, for many To-gai-ru lay dead about the walls. Several thousand Behrenese had fallen to less than one thousand To-gai-ru, but in looking at her depleted resources, and in looking at the gravely injured dragon, Brynn could not claim victory that day. They had held, and that was something.

But that was all.

Thanks to the heroics of Agradeleous, the barrage from catapults would be less that night. But several huge fires did erupt, forcing the weary men and women to battle them—all with the knowledge that their enemies would come on again in the morning.

\* \* \*

Pagonel and Merwan Ma had little trouble getting into Jacintha, for the city was in seeming turmoil, with people rushing all about, selling and buying all sorts of staple goods. Soldiers marched about all the avenues, schooling hard the lessons they knew they would soon put into real combat.

"It would seem that Brynn's efforts have been felt far, and to the heart of Behren," Pagonel remarked to Merwan Ma, the mystic still playing the part of the Shepherd's slave.

"Many of the brigades are from visiting districts," Merwan Ma explained. "I have seen the pennant of Yatol De Hamman and Yatol Peridan, Yatol Shie-guvra and—"

"Does that mean that the Yatols have assembled here?"

Merwan Ma nodded. "That would be the usual reason for their garrisons to be about Jacintha," he explained. "But who can say in these strange times?"

"Can you find out?"

The Shepherd nodded and moved across the crowded square, to a merchant selling baskets of dates. He bent in and whispered to the man, then nodded, reached into his pouch, and produced a few coins—which Pagonel had given to him out of the loot from one of the conquered cities.

The smiling merchant took the bribe and bent in, whispering to Merwan Ma for a long, long time.

"The Yatols are in Jacintha," the Shepherd reported to Pagonel a few minutes later. "And they are not pleased by the continuing war. Brynn's efforts in hiring the mercenaries and pirates have played into the ancient rivalries between some of the Yatols, particularly those trading rivals along the coast-line. Now the Yatols are angry that so many soldiers have been pulled from the disputed zones in the east and sent along to the west to join in Yatol Bardoh's pursuit of Brynn."

Pagonel nodded, considering the words. He wished he had known of this internal strife before, long before, when there might have been some opportunity to exploit it further.

"There is word from the west," Merwan Ma went on, his voice going suddenly grim. "Brynn has conquered Dharyan once more."

Pagonel nodded, knowing what was coming next.

"Yatol Bardoh is even now moving to encircle her and destroy her there," the Shepherd went on. "Likely the fighting has already begun."

Pagonel took a long moment to digest the information, then took a deep and steadying breath and stared hard at his companion. "It is irrelevant to our present course." As he finished, the mystic looked across the way, to a large structure, the largest in the city, set upon a hill lined with beautiful gardens and fountains.

"Chom Deiru," Merwan Ma explained, following that stare. "It will be heavily guarded—it is always heavily guarded, and even more so now, I would guess, with the tension so high."

"But you can get me in," the mystic reasoned.

"To what end?"

"To reveal the truth."

"It is a truth that will get us both killed." Merwan Ma stopped short, seeing the unblinking stare coming back at him, a reminder to him of all that he had learned of late.

"I will get you in," he said to Pagonel, his voice steady. "Or I will try."

The mystic nodded, and Merwan Ma led the way across the city, to the base of the hill of Chom Deiru and the first guard house they would have to pass.

They did so, quite easily, for Merwan Ma knew all the passwords through these preliminary checkpoints. Soon enough the pair were up the hill and moving up the steps of the temple proper, through the great arching doors of Chom Deiru.

A pair of guards inside crossed their spears before the entryway, commanding them to halt.

"I have come from the west," Merwan Ma said to them, then spoke the usual passwords, "The setting sun cannot elude the Chezru's eyes."

It was the proper phrase for any returning scout to use, but Merwan Ma noted that one of the guards betrayed his stoic expression for just an instance, as if in a flicker of recognition.

"What is your name?" the man asked.

"I am . . ." the Shepherd paused, feeling suddenly that

something was very wrong. He didn't really recognize the guard, but he had the feeling that this one had known him from his time as Douan's assistant.

"My pardon, Governor Pestle," Pagonel said behind him, and he began bowing repeatedly. "I should have been more prompt in arranging for your formal announcement."

The two guards looked to each other, and then one retreated behind the door.

A long moment passed, the silence growing more and more uncomfortable. Finally, the door cracked open and the guard poked his head out, whispering to his companion.

"Welcome to Chom Deiru, Governor Carwan Pestle," the other guard said as his companion disappeared behind the door once more. "You will be announced to the Chezru Chieftain at your convenience." As he finished, he stepped aside and pulled open the door, motioning for the two men to enter.

Merwan Ma should have been dead the moment he stepped through, and would have been, had not Pagonel's finely honed reflexes launched the mystic at the back of Merwan Ma's legs, laying him low, and making the stab of the other guard's long spear miss the mark.

Pagonel was up in an instant, spinning to face the spearman. He dropped his shoulder and leaped ahead, spinning diagonally down low. Then, as he came around and set his feet, he leaped up high, over the poor attempt to reorient the unwieldy weapon. He snapped his foot into the guard's face.

The man fell away with a grunt.

Pagonel landed lightly, turning sharply about to see the guard from outside charging in at Merwan Ma's back, and with the stunned Shepherd only then even pulling himself from the floor, facing away from the thrusting spear.

Out went the spear tip, but in the flash of the mystic's well-aimed, stiffened hand, the weapon was no more, chopped in half.

Pagonel grabbed the broken shaft of the weapon in his left hand, stepped in against it, and swung around backward, his right elbow lifting high to smash the man in the face. The guard dropped like a stone, but stubbornly tried to rise.

Pagonel's stiffened fingers smashed his throat, and he went down and stayed down.

The mystic was moving even as the man hit the ground, running past Merwan Ma and sweeping him up in his wake. Noise echoed from both side corridors, likely other guards rushing to see what the commotion was all about.

"Where do we run?" the mystic asked.

Merwan Ma's horrified expression told him much. "I must get to the Room of Forever," the Shepherd explained. "But the way is long and the shouts of the pursuit will bring many guards out before us!"

The mystic stopped and looked all around at the great corridors and huge pillars. "Which way to the Room of Forever?"

Merwan Ma looked across the anteroom and through the large hall behind it, motioning toward some distant stairs. "Up there, and along many hallways."

Pagonel retrieved the remaining spear from the fallen guard, and smashed the man again as he began to stir once more. "Go. I will keep the guards occupied."

Merwan Ma spent a long moment studying the mystic, then put his hand on Pagonel's shoulder. "There is much I wish to say to you," he began tentatively.

Pagonel stopped him with an upraised hand. "We will find the time to talk," he said with a smile, though neither he nor Merwan Ma expected that they would ever speak again.

The mystic ran off then, into the larger hall and to the right, and when a guard yelled out upon sighting him, he launched the spear, far and true, into the man's chest.

Merwan Ma faded back against the wall behind a pillar as the commotion grew, as more and more guards and servants rushed all about. The whole commotion moved down to his right and the shepherd started off to the left, hugging the wall of the larger room until he made the stairs. Then he fell back into the shadows again, as a group of guards, including a Chezhou-Lei warrior, rushed down the stairs and right past him, giving chase to the now distant shouts of an intruder.

Up went the Shepherd, and he breathed a sigh of relief when he crossed out of the stairway and into the hallways of the palace's second floor. He ran along, then down corridors so familiar and yet strangely out of place, past rooms that had once been his home, but now seemed foreign and uncomfortable.

Pagonel ran on, one step ahead of his pursuit—and well aware that the pursuit was growing with each passing corridor. He turned down one arched corridor, rushing right past a pair of surprised guards.

They yelled and took up the chase, but Pagonel surprised them again by stopping short and spinning about, leaping their leading spears and double-kicking, left and right, laying them both low.

Another guard came in right behind, swinging a huge curved sword. The mystic caught his wrist and pulled it aside, stepped in close, and hit him with three short but devastating chops to the chest. The man gasped repeatedly and started to fall, but Pagonel grabbed him by the tunic and pulled him back up, then threw him hard to the ground, right before a pair of charging soldiers. They didn't trip, but the tumbling man held them up and stole their attention.

Long enough for the mystic to come in high and hard, above their swords, kicking and punching.

As they fell away, Pagonel didn't move in, but turned and ran along the grand-arched corridor. A large group was close to him, he realized, and when he turned back to note them, he picked out a Chezhou-Lei warrior among their ranks. The mystic put his head down and ran on, knowing that he couldn't turn and confront this group. A Chezhou-Lei was enough of a problem all by himself, but with several guards on his side, the fight would not fall the mystic's way!

The hallway bent in a wide arc, and the mystic came to guess that he was circling a large room. The pursuit remained dogged, and close, and now others were coming out from side corridors off to Pagonel's left as he continued to circle around to the right. He was running out of room, and he knew it. The only corridors down which he could turn were to the left, and those seemed full of enemies.

Pagonel stopped and turned to face the wall, putting his

fingers against it, feeling the grains within the stone. Then he fell within himself, ignoring the shouts closing in behind, and more shouts coming from the left. The mystic found his Chi and lifted it high, and then ran along with it, spider-crawling up the wall. As he neared the top, with some oblivious guards running past beneath him, the mystic heard much arguing and talking from within the huge circular room.

Before he could even consider that, though, a cry from below told him that he had been spotted. He moved along more quickly, now thirty feet from the floor.

An arrow skipped past him.

"More bows!" came the shout from the Chezhou-Lei. "Shoot the pest from the wall."

Pagonel glanced down, and considered dropping upon them, perhaps killing the Chezhou-Lei, at least, before they slaughtered him. But to what end? he realized. Was he going to kill for spite, or out of anger?

That was not the way of the Jhesta Tu. Truly there was nothing for Pagonel to gain by dropping on the Behrenese at that point, not for him and not for Merwan Ma, and not for the cause of Brynn Dharielle and To-gai.

"Your Chezru Chieftain is a fraud," he yelled down. "He possesses an Abellican soul stone, and uses it!"

His answer came in the form of an arrow, driving deep into his calf and nearly dislodging him.

With a grunt, the mystic climbed higher, nearing the ceiling, and only then did he realize that the wall upon which he was perched was not solid, floor to ceiling, but had an alcove at the top. And in the rear of that ledge area, the mystic found a grate, overlooking a wide circular chamber, full of rows of seats, and full of arguing Yatols!

His respite there wouldn't last long, he knew, for the alcove wasn't deep, and all the archers had to do was step back across the hall to spot him.

Dismissing the unsettling thought out of hand, Pagonel gripped the bars of the grate and focused his life energy into his hands. His palms grew hot—hotter than they had when he had used his healing techniques on Brynn and Merwan Ma.

He dove deeper into the energy, forcing it to his fingers,

heating them even more. He didn't contain the energy there, though—to do so would have melted his hands!—but rather, let it flow out of his digits and into the metal of the bars, heating them and softening them.

Ignoring the uncomfortable heat, Pagonel began to pull with all his strength.

An arrow soared into the alcove, deflecting off the ceiling to bounce hard against the mystic. But it didn't disrupt Pagonel's concentration. With the metal practically glowing under his mystical touch, the man pulled the two bars of the grate apart, bit by bit, until they were wide enough for him to slip through.

He squirmed onto the ledge in the huge audience hall, then moved to the lip, marking the gathering below him, figuring out at once that it was Yakim Douan himself who was addressing the Yatols from a dais across the way, in front of a long and sweeping, ascending stairway. The chairs were all before him, set in a semicircular pattern: a thousand chairs, though only those at the very front were occupied.

Pagonel studied the room for a moment, but knew he didn't have much time, for below, the Chezhou-Lei was yelling for the guards to enter the audience hall and protect the Chezru Chieftain.

Pagonel rolled to the lip and leaped off, dropping the thirty feet to the floor and landing easily in a shock-absorbing roll. All heads turned his way, and a group of guards, standing behind the dais that held Yakim Douan, rushed to the front of their beloved Chezru Chieftain, forming a line before him.

"Jhesta Tu!" one of the nearby Yatols yelled, and all of the others began to shrink away from Pagonel, whispering excitedly.

"What is the meaning of this intrusion?" Yakim Douan yelled. "Who are you to violate this sacred place?"

"I am Pagonel of the Walk of Clouds, Chezru Chieftain Douan," the mystic answered with a bow. "I am he who knows the truth of Yakim Douan! I am he who knows the truth of Transcendence!"

No one in the place missed the wide-eyed look of surprise and horror that came over Yakim Douan at that moment, but

before anyone could begin to question it, the great doors of the
audience chamber burst open and a group of soldiers charged
into the chamber, bearing down immediately on Pagonel.

"I have seen you at use with your soul stone, Yakim Douan!"
the mystic cried.

"He is a fool and a liar!" yelled the Chezru Chieftain. "Kill
him at once!"

Pagonel dodged a thrown spear, then another, then fell into
a roll to move to the side of a trio of warriors charging in at
him. He came up and kicked back the other way, tripping one
up, but had to fall back farther and couldn't finish the move as
the other two bore in. The mystic ran behind the chairs and
leaped atop the back of one, then ran along, chair back to
chair back, so balanced that none even began to tip.

He ducked instinctively; an arrow cut the air above him. He
ducked again, and then again, altering his run as the guards
began to herd him, always seeming to be between him and the
Chezru Chieftain. He knew that it couldn't last for long, and
knew that he couldn't get anywhere near the man, so he stopped
suddenly, still standing atop one chair-back, and yelled out,
"You have spirit-walked, Yakim Douan. That is how you found
the Dragon of To-gai! Each night you go out and seek her—
and you cannot go out without a gem—"

He stopped suddenly as an arrow bored into his side. Then
he got hit again, in the hip. He tried to leap away, tried to hold
his focus, but he got hit again, the missile creasing his shoulder, and then he was falling, smashing through a bunch of
chairs.

"Finish him!" he heard Yakim Douan yell, and it seemed to
him suddenly as if the Chezru Chieftain was far, far away.

Blood ran from a dozen wounds and one of her eyes was
closed from where a mace had slipped off her powrie shield
and clipped her, but Brynn showed no signs of slowing as she
ran along the wall, rousing her allies with cries for a free To-
gai, and with her magnificent swordplay, with enemy after
enemy falling to her flaming blade. So great was her reputation growing as she moved along the wall that the Behrenese
shrank back from her wherever she appeared, with some even

going back over the wall, outside of the city. That only made her furious charge even more effective, of course.

Down along the avenues, Agradeleous moved from gate to gate and wall to wall, bolstering the defenses with blasts of killing flame. At one point, the eastern wall was breached, with hundreds of Behrenese warriors swarming in, many heading to throw wide the gates so that their cavalry could overrun the courtyard.

Agradeleous alone stopped that attack, wading through lines of soldiers, taking and accepting punishing hits with the single-minded purpose of destroying those who meant to open the gates.

The gate held, and those Behrenese who had come over the wall were soon cut off, as Brynn solidified the defenses on the parapets and the dragon turned upon them along the streets.

All that day, the Behrenese came on and were pushed back, and when it ended, thousands more lay dead. But so did scores of To-gai-ru, and as the ring about Dharyan settled once more, Brynn was again hard-pressed to consider the event any kind of a victory.

Even worse, that same night, another garrison arrived from Jacintha, five thousand more warriors to replace the fallen.

Brynn could not look to the west for similar help, she knew.


The mystic lay on the floor, knowing that each passing second brought his enemies in closer. He reached into his life force, finding that line of power between his forehead and crotch, the center of his energy, his Chi. Then he blanked away the many pains, put them outside of his consciousness.

He heard the soldiers, two at least, standing over him, bending to finish him.

With a sudden burst of sheer power, the mystic swung over and sprang up, soaring into the air between his attackers, seeing three and not two.

He kicked out ahead, then left and right, landed lightly and sprang up again, lifting into the air before the one man who still stood there and the second, who was staggering but not down.

A kick left and right again had them both down, and Pagonel landed in perfect balance on the back of the nearest up-right chair and began his run anew.

Another arrow clipped him, but he held his course stubbornly, working his way around the now-sheltered crowd of amazed Yatols.

"You must hear my words!" Pagonel shouted. "For your own sake and not my own! The Chezru Chieftain possesses a soul stone, an Abellican hematite! He lies of his course and of Transcendence, which is no more than—"

He stopped suddenly as a Chezhou-Lei warrior popped up before him and smashed him hard in the gut with the end of a thick staff.

"Transcendence is possession of an infant," the mystic cried, falling away as he got smashed again, and then again as he lay helpless on the ground.

He felt hands grabbing him by the arms a few moments later, but could offer no more resistance as they stood him upright. He tried to talk again, and his efforts got him slugged hard in the stomach, and then across the face.

"Behold!" he heard the Chezru Chieftain yell. "We have before us the killer of Chezhou-Lei Dahmed Blie!"

"What of his words, God-Voice?" came a cry that sounded somewhat accusatory.

"The heathens have no other answer to the visions of Yatol!" Douan shouted immediately. "They seek to destroy us from the inside, since their feeble attempts to destroy us otherwise have miserably failed! And now this one is dead, and they have lost their ties to the Jhesta Tu. Yet another blow to the army of the pitiful Dragon of To-gai!"

Pagonel had no strength to argue as the cheers went up about Yakim Douan, so he fell within himself, trying again to gather his life energy, trying merely to keep some bit of consciousness.

He did hear the Chezhou-Lei warrior ask Yakim Douan if the prisoner should be hung publicly, or burned, and was not surprised when the Chezru Chieftain told his warrior to finish Pagonel then and there.

And the mystic couldn't begin to stop the blow. He tried to

open his eyes, wanting to look into the eyes of the man who would end his life.

"Wait!" came a cry from somewhere in the back. "Hold your weapons and your judgment!"

Pagonel did open his eyes then, to see Merwan Ma rushing down the long stairway behind Yakim Douan, a magnificently decorated chalice in his hand.

Yakim Douan worked very hard to keep his expression stoic as he watched the traitorous Shepherd rush down the stairs, bearing the damning chalice. It took him a moment to steady himself, to try to play through this potential disaster— and in that moment, Merwan Ma was not silent.

"He hides the stone—he has hidden the stone for centuries!" He reached into the bloody chalice and pulled forth the gemstone, then tossed the ceremonial cup aside. "In here!"

Gasps arose all around him, but Yakim Douan held his calm and motioned to the side, to a bank of archers.

"It is all a lie!" Merwan Ma cried. "Transcendence is a trick and no miracle." He ended with the air blasted from his lungs, as arrow after arrow bored into him.

He was sitting then, though he knew not how, and knew not why, whispering, "A lie," over and over again.

And then Yakim Douan was there before him, reaching down.

"God-Voice," the confused and dying man gasped.

Douan pulled the hematite from him and walked away.

"How clever!" the Chezru Chieftain shouted. "Look at the conspiracy that our enemies have created about us! Give them credit, my friends."

"Was that not Merwan Ma, your former attendant?" asked one of the visiting Yatols.

"It was," answered Mado Wadon, who had served beside Merwan Ma for so many years.

"Obviously fallen traitor to us for the cause of our enemies," said Douan.

"But he was murdered, in Dharyan!" cried another.

Yakim Douan held his smile and held his calm. This one wasn't going to be easy to wriggle out of, he realized, but he knew that delay was on his side. Soon enough, reports of the fall of the Dragon of To-gai would flood in, and his people would be more receptive to whatever explanation he offered.

"It is a puzzling riddle," he said. "But one that we will unravel, I assure you."

"And what of the stone?" asked Mado Wadon.

Yakim Douan fixed the man, the Yatol who would obviously succeed him if not for Transcendence, with a hateful glower. "It is a gemstone, a hematite, I believe."

"What the Abellicans call a soul stone," another offered, suspicion evident in his voice.

"Why, of course," said Douan. "Else their little ploy would have been for naught. I will summon Master Mackaront of Entel in the morning and present it to him."

It pained Pagonel greatly to see Merwan Ma slump down on the stairs, so perfectly still that the mystic knew that his friend had died.

The warriors holding him had relaxed their grip as they, along with the Chezhou-Lei who was supposed to deliver the killing blow, stood and stared dumbfounded at the surprising events about them.

Pagonel weighed the reaction as much as he could. He heard the buzzing of the Yatols, recognized the doubt in their words and whispers, but he heard too the continuing assurances of Yakim Douan in a debate that was now one-sided.

He and Merwan Ma had done exactly as they had intended, though, and for that, he was grateful. They had planted the seeds of doubt, and perhaps those would take root and grow, ending the reign of the tyrant Douan.

Pagonel had only one more thing to do.

He fell into himself again, gathering his energy, bringing every ounce of life force he could muster together in one collected ball, preparing for one burst.

He reached out tentatively, hoping that the Chezhou-Lei would continue to delay, would give him the moment he needed.

Then he felt the connection to the hematite held by Yakim Douan.

"I do give credit to our enemies for their clever ruse," Douan was saying, laughing.

Pagonel grabbed his life energy together. He opened his eyes and with a sudden burst of movement, ran his arms in circles, then out, dislodging the two men holding him and shoving them aside.

The Chezhou-Lei warrior moved immediately, but so did the mystic, gathering his energy, then throwing his arms forward and sending that ball of power out across the way, reaching for the hematite, diving into its depths, flooding it with the pure power of Chi. Long Ago, the Jhesta Tu had learned the secrets of the gemstones, had come to know that the energy contained within the stones and was the same basic energy as within their own Chi, the same energy that permeated all of the universe. The strength of any gemstone depended upon the amount of energy contained within, and the amount that any gemstone could hold was a finite thing.

Spent, Pagonel was already falling as the Chezhou-Lei's staff whipped around, smashing him to the ground.

Across the way, the hematite blew apart, shards spraying back into surprised Yakim Douan, hurling him to the floor.

Cries erupted for the death of the mystic, but before the Chezhou-Lei could follow that course, Mado Wadon yelled at him to hold his strike and to drag the prisoner away to the dungeons.

Other guards were ordered to bear the wounded Douan away, as well, to a comfortable bed. The Chezru Chieftain, semiconscious, resisted them at first, scrambling desperately to find some piece of his precious soul stone, some chunk of the enchanted gem that would allow him access.

"God-Voice?" came a simple question, and he looked up to see Mado Wadon and several others, including Yatol De Hamman, staring down at him incredulously.

"It may explode again," he said unconvincingly.

"Yes, God-Voice," said Mado Wadon. "Go with the soldiers now. You are wounded, and we must ensure that Chom Deiru is now secure."

Yakim Douan nodded repeatedly, trying to sort through it all, trying to find some line of deception that he might follow to minimize the risk. And, of course, he had to discern a way he could gather another soul stone. Olin would help him. Yes, and he could keep it secret through the next couple of years until things settled, until he had reestablished himself enough to chance Transcendence once more.

Of course, none of this would make any difference at all in forty or fifty years, when all the witnesses would be dead and buried, and Merwan Ma's name would be long forgotten!

That fool Merwan Ma!

Soon after, the God-Voice of Behren was resting comfortably in a bed in Chom Deiru, guards securing his door. His wounds were not nearly as serious as feared, only minor cuts and bruises, and the first Yatols who had come in to see him had expressed great regret that such evil conspirators as Merwan Ma and the Jhesta Tu had ever gotten into the palace.

"Where is the Jhesta Tu?" Douan asked Mado Wadon.

"He is dead, God-Voice," the Yatol replied. "As you commanded, though it would have given us all great pleasure to see him burned publicly before the palace."

"Too dangerous," Douan said.

"Of course, God-Voice," Mado Wadon replied with a bow. "Rest now. The first reports of the battle at Dharyan are coming in."

"The Dragon has fallen?" Douan asked, coming forward excitedly.

"Not yet, God-Voice," the Yatol replied. "But soon. She has nowhere left to run."

Yakim Douan rested back, comfortable in those thoughts.

For the third time, they attacked, and for the third time, they were repelled.

"You cannot continue to throw our warriors against the walls," an angry Chezhou-Lei Shauntil dared to say to fuming Yatol Bardoh after that third retreat.

"Dharyan should have fallen long ago!" the Yatol declared.

"Agreed, but the city is fortified by the fires of a great dragon," Shauntil reminded. "And we must never underestimate the strength of this woman. She is possessed of demons,

my warriors say, and every breach is met with her fiery
sword."

Yatol Bardoh clenched his fist and slammed it down on the
small table before him, knocking it to the floor. "I will have
the city!" He looked up at Shauntil. "You deliver Dharyan to
me, and soon!"

"If we continue to attack, and continue to be chased away,
leaving hundreds dead behind us, you will find your ranks
thinning by more than the dead, Yatol," the Chezhou-Lei honestly reported.

"Are we to abandon Dharyan?" came the incredulous
response.

"We can resupply. With her dragon downed—and it is
downed, by all reports—she cannot."

Yatol Bardoh's expression went from anger to curiosity.
"What are you saying?"

"Besiege her," said Shauntil. "She cannot hope to break
out. Without the walls and fortifications, her army would be
crushed in short order. Besiege her. Let the Ru eat their
horses!"

Yatol Bardoh gave a perfectly awful chuckle. "They would
not like that."

"Besiege her, that is my advice," Shauntil said again. "Demand her unconditional surrender, then hang the witch and
her commanders, destroy the dragon, and send the rest back
to the steppes."

Yatol Bardoh looked at the man doubtfully. "Or we say that
is the condition of the acceptance of surrender," the scheming
man remarked. "And then, when she is dead and the dragon is
destroyed, we put the remaining Ru on the road to the west.
And there we kill them, every one."

Shauntil, an honorable warrior, didn't particularly like that
plan, but neither did he question it. "I will see that the defenses are set to ward against any breakout," he assured his
master. "I will have the catapults rebuilt, that our bombardment may begin anew."

"Every bit of their misery pleases me greatly," was the Yatol's response.

A lone rider approached Dharyan's eastern gate soon after,

declaring the city besieged, and calling for the unconditional surrender of the Dragon of To-gai.

Every To-gai-ru near to Brynn when she heard that call spat profanities back at the man, patting their brave leader on the shoulder and assuring her that they would die to the man and woman before they would ever allow her to surrender.

Brynn appreciated the support, truly, but she understood the reality of their grim situation. She looked around, wondering how long that support would hold, wondering how strong would be the determination when bellies began to growl with hunger.

Yatol Peridan, wearing a suspicious expression, met Yatol Mado Wadon coming out of the dungeon stairwell.

"You told the Chezru Chieftain that the Jhesta Tu was dead," said Peridan.

"And so he is."

"You just came from him. What deception . . ."

"You did not find his claims intriguing?"

Peridan stopped as if slapped, and nodded his concession. "The Chezru Chieftain explains it as a ruse, a clever one at that."

"My uncle was a Yatol, here in Jacintha, many years ago," said Mado Wadon. "Often did he tell me of the miracle of Transcendence, of the amazing blessed child who could recite so clearly the verses of Yatol's teachings, who seemed to know, so instinctively, the present state of the kingdom." He fixed Peridan with a telling stare. "As if with the wisdom of the ages."

Peridan sank back.

"More Yatols have come in?" Mado Wadon asked.

"As you requested," said Peridan.

The Yatol of Chom Deiru nodded.

Later the next day, Mado Wadon met with the visiting Yatols, laying bare his suspicions and reminding them that none of this made any sense along any other lines of reasoning, especially with the cries of Merwan Ma. The man had been appointed governor of Dharyan, after all, and had been subsequently reported murdered by a To-gai-ru slave. With so much glory and honor lauded upon him, how or why would he ever go over to an obviously losing side?

Mado Wadon had spoken with Pagonel that morning, had heard the story, one that made much more logical sense, in depth.

After the brief meeting, Mado Wadon led all of those visiting Yatols, twenty-three in number, into the bedchamber where Yakim Douan was fast recovering.

"The Dragon?" Douan asked immediately.

"Yatol Bardoh continues his battle," Yatol De Hamman replied from the side.

"I have brought the chalice, God-Voice," Mado Wadon explained. "The interruption of ceremony is unprecedented, but we believe that all can be put in order."

"That is good," said Douan. "Thoroughly cleanse the chalice, that the stains of the Abellican gemstone placed within by the treacherous Merwan Ma be washed away."

"Of course, God-Voice. It has already been done."

"Consult the scholars, then, and determine the proper rituals for renewing the once-tainted chalice."

"Yes, God-Voice," said Mado Wadon, perfectly calm and in control. "But that is why we have come to you."

Yakim Douan looked at him curiously.

"Were you not the one who initiated the ceremony of the chalice in the Room of Forever?"

Yakim Douan returned a puzzled look, but one that fast turned grave. "What foolishness is this?" he asked, catching on. "The ceremony was determined centuries ago . . ." He stopped then, his eyes going wide as Mado Wadon produced the other part of the ritual gear, a sharp, ceremonial knife.

"What foolishness is this?" the God-Voice asked again, though he knew from the Yatol's face what treachery was coming.

"Wait! Wait!" he pleaded. "This is insanity! I have found the true way of Yatol! I can show you eternal life!"

"Through a gemstone?" Mado Wadon asked, pausing.

"Yes!"

Mado Wadon stepped forward and plunged the knife into Yakim Douan's chest, then stepped back and calmly handed it to the next Yatol in line. And so it went, around the gathering, until all twenty-three had taken their stab at the old wretch.

Yakim Douan lay there for a long time, stubbornly clinging to life.

"There is no gemstone, God-Voice. Nothing through which your spirit can flee this fate," Mado Wadon said to him, leaning in so that his face might be the last thing Yakim Douan ever saw.

"Sacrilege," Douan whispered.

"Perhaps it is," Mado Wadon answered. "We will await the coming of the blessed child to tell us of our folly."

Yakim Douan tried to answer, but he could not. Consciousness left him soon after, as his blood continued to pool about him.

The Yatols filed out solemnly later on, with Mado Wadon ordering the guards to go and ring the bells of Chom Deiru, the Cadence of Grief.

# *Epilogue*

"I have assumed control of Jacintha, as is commanded by the tenets of Yatol," Mado Wadon told several of the more important Yatols later on that fateful day.

"But you are not Chezru Chieftain!" Yatol Peridan insisted. Peridan had been viewing all of this with mixed feelings. He had agreed with Mado Wadon's argument that Douan had to die, in light of the revelations, but the practical implications of that action did not shine favorably on him. Mado Wadon was a friend of De Hamman.

"I am not, nor do I pretend to be," Mado Wadon calmly replied. "We are each brothers in the greater cause of Yatol, with our own areas of responsibility. Mine is now Jacintha."

He didn't say it, but it was well understood that the control of Jacintha meant control of the legions, greater power than any three other Yatols combined could muster.

But that was indeed the tenet of Yatol.

The meeting broke up sometime later, after many speeches of solidarity and common cause to rebuild. Underneath all the words, though, loomed an unmistakable aura of suspicion and trepidation. Under the Chezru Chieftain, the Yatols united the kingdom of Behren, but that religious grasp over the peoples of the many tribes had always been a tenuous thing.

Yatol De Hamman caught up to Mado Wadon alone a short while later.

"Peridan will move swiftly against me," the man insisted. "With the Jacintha garrison tied up at Dharyan, he will know that the moment is now, or is never."

"I have already warned Yatol Peridan that the time has come for caution."

"He will not heed your words," Yatol De Hamman insisted. "Chezru Douan pulled many of my soldiers from me to send off along the road to the west. Peridan knows that I am under-manned, and he will seize this moment!"

Mado Wadon sighed deeply, finding it hard to disagree. He knew that the weeks ahead were going to be quite difficult for Behren, and he honestly expected that the next Chezru Chief-tain, when one could be found and brought to maturity, would likely have to rebuild many parts of the disjointed kingdom.

That was even if another Chezru Chieftain would be found, for any child now selected, given the believed deception of Yakim Douan, would face a brutal inquiry period. And if that child uttered nothing miraculous—truly miraculous!—he would be rejected and the kingdom would be thrown into even more disarray. On one level, Mado Wadon regretted the decision to kill Douan. Perhaps they should have allowed him to go on with his practice of stealing the bodies of unborn children to use as his own.

Would Behren survive?

Would the Chezru religion survive?

And should it? Mado Wadon had to ponder.

"Yatol Peridan is the least of your troubles," an increas-ingly frustrated De Hamman stated suddenly, drawing Mado Wadon from his disturbing thoughts. "Your eyes should focus upon Yatol Bardoh and the legions he commands."

"The Jacintha legions are mine," Mado Wadon said.

"Bardoh commands them. It is no secret that he has used Chezru Douan's inability to capture the Dragon of To-gai to foster his own ends. How much more powerful will he be-come once Dharyan is recaptured and the rebels are all dead."

Mado Wadon winced at the thought.

He went back to the lower levels of Chom Deiru almost immediately, down the cold and wet steps to the dungeons and to the filthy, barred hole in the wall where Pagonel of the Jhesta Tu had been placed.

"We must speak," he said to the man.

Pagonel, dirty and unshaven, his wounds thick with infection, looked at the man curiously, blinking his eyes repeatedly against the sudden intrusion of light.

"Tell me of the Dragon of To-gai," Mado Wadon bade him. "What does she desire?"

Pagonel continued to stare at him.

"Time is short," Mado Wadon said. "Save yourself."

"I will not betray my friend."

"Betray?" the Yatol echoed incredulously. "I offer you the chance to save her." Mado Wadon leaned in closer, his face barely inches from Pagonel's. "I offer you the chance to realize her dreams."

"You will pardon my skepticism."

Mado Wadon nodded, expecting as much.

He did notice that Pagonel's mood had brightened considerably the next day when they sat together on the wagon in the midst of a great caravan rolling down the western road out of Jacintha.

"They will not eat the horses," Tanalk Grenk said to Brynn. "Nor will they stay in here to starve."

"They want us to try to break out," she replied, looking down at the besieging army, as she had for more than a week.

"We have a few days more of food, even if we starve the prisoners."

"Which we shall not do!"

Tanalk Grenk's expression grew intense for a moment, but he relaxed and nodded. "I would rather die with a sword in my hand," he said. "And not with that hand limp from starvation."

Brynn looked hard at him, and at those others standing along the wall, listening in to the conversation. Gradually, she began to nod. "As would I," she said. "As shall I!"

A cheer went up about her.

"Let us consider our options more carefully," she said to Grenk. "Perhaps we can make a ruse of a breakout, luring our enemies in to us one more time."

The man's expression was doubting, and when she thought

about it, Brynn could not disagree. "Or if not, then let us ride out in full force and kill as many as we may before our end."

"I will begin formulating the plans," the fierce To-gai-ru warrior offered, and Brynn nodded.

It wasn't the end she had hoped for, but it would have to do.

The next morning, the To-gai-ru leaders met and argued over the plans, with some thinking it would be best to charge east, instead of the expected burst to the west. "If we are not going to break through anyway, then better to gain even more surprise," one argued.

The banter settled much, and Tanalk Grenk and Brynn broke away to draw up the final plans. They were nearly finished, when a call from the wall roused them.

"A lone emissary!" came the cry.

"No doubt to reiterate their call for surrender," Tanalk Grenk reasoned as the pair made their way to the parapets. "We should send his head back without his body."

His words were lost in his throat as he gained the wall and looked out. No response was forthcoming from Brynn, either, for both recognized the lone figure walking toward them, his gait the practiced and balanced walk of a Jhesta Tu mystic.

Brynn fell into Pagonel's arms as he came through the gate, burying her face in his strong chest.

"Yakim Douan is dead," Pagonel said to her, to all of the warriors gathering about. "The new leading Yatols wish to discuss the terms of peace."

"We have already dismissed their calls for surrender!" Tanalk Grenk said angrily. "We will die as warriors before surrendering the freedom of To-gai!"

That brought a cheer, of course, but Pagonel held calm. "I said peace, not surrender," the mystic replied.

The expressions were doubtful, even Brynn's.

"Their kingdom is in disarray," the mystic explained. "They cannot hope to continue a unified struggle to hold To-gai."

"But this is the hour of their victory," reasoned Brynn.

"A victory that many of them fear more than defeat," Pagonel replied. "Come with me, Brynn, and you, Tanalk Grenk, to the tents of our enemies."

Brynn wore a puzzled expression, but Tanalk Grenk's was one of open suspicion.

"This is no ruse," said Pagonel. "For they need none to finish this battle. We have caught ourselves in the middle of their political games, and they would all prefer that we leave."

"Those are my terms," Brynn said coldly, after three days of arguing with Mado Wadon and the others at the Behrenese encampment encircling Dharyan

"Preposterous!" said Yatol Bardoh, Brynn's greatest enemy at these discussions, and the Yatol who least desired peace. Pagonel had explained it all to her, and so she understood that Bardoh wanted this fight to strengthen his own position in the aftermath.

Brynn moved out from the table, to the back of the tent, and motioned for Yatol Bardoh to join her.

"I know you," she whispered.

The man looked at her curiously.

"I watched you murder my parents, a decade and more ago."

Bardoh glared at her wickedly.

"Know that if this battle ensues, the Behrenese will likely win," Brynn assured him. "But my dragon has healed, and with his help, I will find my own victory among the ruins, for I will avenge my parents. Of that, do not doubt."

The man blanched, and Brynn patted him on the shoulder and returned to her seat at the table.

It amazed her how much more responsive Yatol Bardoh became after that little private conversation.

But still, when Brynn and Pagonel returned to Dharyan that night, nothing had been settled, and now the food was beginning to run thin.

"We will meet one more time," the woman said to Pagonel. "And then we will fight."

"You could relent," the mystic replied. "They have offered you a chance to run back into To-gai and be free of Behrenese rule. Is that not all that you wanted?"

Brynn took a deep breath, understanding that she was playing a very dangerous game. But she held firm to her resolve against the doubts. Her demands were the insurance against another invasion, one that she knew would come soon enough after Behren solidified itself once more, if Yatol Bardoh had his way.

The next day, Mado Wadon came alone to Dharyan, under the flag of truce, as Brynn insisted. In a quiet room, the Yatol, the Dragon of To-gai, and the Jhesta Tu mystic sat and talked.

"Dharyan-Dharielle, then," Brynn improvised, as the Yatol again argued the one sticking point in the negotiations. "We will call the city Dharyan-Dharielle, and leave it as an open city, to Behrenese and To-gai-ru alike."

"And what would possibly prompt the Behrenese to come here, other than to scorn the invading To-gai-ru?"

"Invading?" Brynn echoed. "It is a word you should take care when speaking. Your people will come for the trade, open trade, between To-gai-ru and Behrenese. And your scholars will come for the library."

"Library? Do the To-gai-ru even write?"

"The library formerly of Pruda," Brynn said with a crooked smile, and Yatol Mado Wadon's eyes widened indeed!

"Yes, I have it, buried and hidden in the desert, never to be found unless I so deem it," Brynn explained. "I will retrieve the items, and build a new and grander library here, open to all the scholars of our respective kingdoms."

Mado Wadon waved his hands and shook his head. "You speak foolishness! Why should I hear these words? Why should I allow for any concessions from the Behrenese? You are beaten, if we choose to attack! Never forget that!"

"But at a great cost."

"Greater costs have already been paid!"

Brynn nodded, conceding the point. "But greater gains are hard to find," she said. "Yatol Mado Wadon, I asked you to come out here alone this last day of our discussions because you above all others should understand the true prize I offer to you now."

"And that is?"

"Alliance," said Brynn.

"Between To-gai and Behren?"

"Between Dharyan-Dharielle and Jacintha," Brynn corrected. "Between the Dragon of To-gai and Yatol Mado Wadon. If you force me from this city, then who will replace me? One loyal to Jacintha, or to Avrou Eesa?"

The man did not reply.

"And if you send your hordes against me, or I charge mine out against you, then who will be blamed for the thousands of Behrenese dead on the sands, and the hundreds I will execute in my dungeons? Yatol Bardoh or Yatol Mado Wadon?"

Brynn leaned forward and grabbed the man's hands suddenly, moving very close to his face, locking his gaze with her own. "And I offer to you a vision of a better way between our peoples, one of strength and not of animosity. Can you not see the wisdom of that course?"

"Do you believe that you can eliminate centuries of mistrust and hatred in one action?" the Yatol asked sincerely.

"I believe that we two can take one large stride, that is all," Brynn replied. "And will Jacintha not benefit from the alliance with Dharielle?"

"Dharyan-Dharielle," Mado Wadon corrected a moment later, and Brynn smiled wide and looked to the side, to a nodding Pagonel.

The great army encircling Dharyan-Dharielle stood down that same afternoon, even sending supplies in to the beleaguered To-gai-ru.

"It was not done without arguments among the Yatols," Pagonel assured Brynn.

"Let them fight, then," the woman replied.

"You risked much."

"Every step of my journey," said Brynn.


The city under Brynn's control actually had more Behrenese citizens than To-gai-ru, once the situation had sorted itself out after that long winter of God's Year 844–845. Many To-gai-ru did come down from the steppes though, including some old friends, Barachuk and Tsolona.

"You will be prized advisors," Brynn said to them, after many hugs and kisses. "Our way is not yet clear."

"Indeed," said the old man who had just come down from

the steppes, where the tumultuous ripples of Brynn's surprising victory were only then reverberating. "Indeed!"

As she had promised, Brynn Dharielle left the gates open to men and women of either land, and many Behrenese merchants flocked in to reap the rewards of open trade with the To-gai-ru for their prized horses.

Late that spring, the first column bearing items from the Library of Pruda arrived, while craftsmen worked to construct a new and more fabulous library. Though the scholars of Pruda offered a letter of defiance and complaint, they did begin showing up in the city to peruse the ancient tomes.

Brynn heard reports of many battles being fought in the east, mostly south of Jacintha along the coast, and she knew that Pagonel's estimate of the crisis now befalling Behren had not been exaggerated. She determined to be a good neighbor, though, and take no gains from the Behrenese distress. In truth, she had enough trouble in keeping her own kingdom, To-gai, united—and for the first time! Things were not going smoothly on the steppes, for there remained many outposters and much bitterness.

But they would get through it, Brynn believed. After what she and her friends had accomplished, no obstacle seemed too great.

That spring brought a pair of partings, as well, one expected and somewhat welcomed, and the other one that caught Brynn completely by surprise.

"Agradeleous has agreed to fly me to my home before he returns to his own," Pagonel announced to her, the dragon standing behind him.

"My wounds have healed enough for me to fly again," Agradeleous added. "How good it will be to feel the wind upon my face!"

"You will return to the Walk of Clouds?"

"I must," Pagonel replied, and he took her in his arms. "For how long, I do not know. But it is my place to go to Master Cheyes and Mistress Dasa, that we three might determine where the Jhesta Tu can fit into this new order of Behren and To-gai. With the death of the Chezru Chieftain and the Kaliit

of the Chezhou-Lei, there may be some gains to be made between our orders. It must be explored."

Brynn wanted to argue against it all, wanted to beg Pagonel to stay beside her as she continued to work through this
confusing and dangerous time. But as she had let Belli'mar
Juraviel and Cazzira go, so, too, must she grant Pagonel this
priority.

"I will return there one day," she promised.

"And I will be there to greet you, with arms open wide," the
mystic replied. "Unless, of course, I have already returned to
you, in which event, I will escort you up the five thousand
steps, to a place of greater enlightenment."

Brynn fought back the tears and so did Pagonel. It was a
bitter parting, but was made with the sincere understanding
and belief between these two that they would indeed meet
again.

"And of you, good Agradeleous," the woman said suddenly, turning away from the mystic. "You will return now to
your mountain home?"

"I will mark a cave for the bearers of treasures and the
bearers of tales," the dragon replied, reminding Brynn of
their bargain.

"Promise me that you'll not eat them."

"You ask much."

"Agradeleous—"

"Promise me that their tales will be good!" the dragon
roared.

They shared a laugh.

"If I need you again, will you come out?" Brynn asked.

Agradeleous put on that typically awful grin, and despite
the joyous mood, both she and Pagonel shivered as the dragon
replied, "With pleasure."

Each day brought new challenges, new victories, and new
frustrations, and though she worked tirelessly, Brynn felt as if
she simply could not keep up with it all. For To-gai, she demanded solidarity, a unison of purpose, though she did not
argue when the leaders of her people insisted that they return
to their ancient tribes.

Of the Behrenese, Brynn asked for little and was asked for less, as their kingdom continued to dissolve into chaos, with open wars declared. Through it all, the woman hoped that she would one day find the opportunity to exact her revenge upon Yatol Bardoh.

But it was a fleeting fantasy, lost in the swirl of the everyday realities of governing both a city and a kingdom behind it. She had to establish profitable trade, to keep her people happy and prosperous, to allow them to work through the centuries of tribal feuding that had made them vulnerable to the Behrenese in the first place.

It struck her as curious how the situations in the two kingdoms had suddenly reversed, with To-gai uniting and Behren breaking apart. There was a difference, though, in that Brynn and her people would never try to take advantage of that situation, as Yakim Douan had done.

There had to be a difference, else all of it, the killing and the dying, the loosing of Agradeleous upon Behrenese cities, and the last desperate fight to hold Dharyan-Dharielle, would truly prove meaningless.

Brynn knew that, in her heart, and so she was glad when the turn of autumn brought the first open market in Dharyan-Dharielle, one that attracted Behrenese caravans from all across the desert kingdom.

But then, soon after, she was confused, as well, for word came to her that fall of God's Year 845 that the kingdom north of the Belt-and-Buckle, too, had been shaken to its core, that a new king had ascended the throne. It was a name Brynn knew all too well.

King Aydrian, the son of Elbryan Wyndon.

And she who had been schooled in the elvish tongue recognized the surname the young man had chosen, as well—*Boudabras*—and understood its true meaning.

Maelstrom.

As armies clash and darkness spreads across the lands of Corona, Pony, mistress of the gemstone magic, is the only one who can stop her son from his cataclysmic quest to destroy the world. But even she might not be able to free him from the grip of evil . . .

Read on for a sneak preview into the thrilling climax to the seven-book DemonWars Saga:

# IMMORTALIS

## *Warnings on the Winds*

The feel of the breeze on their faces came as welcome relief to the two elves who had spent weeks wandering the dark ways of the Path of Starless Night. This journey had taken much longer than their original trek under the mountains, when they had been heading to the south, for Belli'mar Juraviel and Cazzira of Tymwyvenne were determined to properly mark those paths leading through the Belt-and-Buckle, from Tymwyvenne to To-gai, the land they hoped now to be securely the province of Brynn Dharielle. For while Juraviel had left the ranger in the southland, he had not done so with a light heart, and he was determined to keep track of her progress in freeing the To-gai-ru from the conquering Behrenese.

Despite that burning curiosity and his deep feelings for Brynn, Belli'mar Juraviel hadn't regretted his decision to turn back to the north. His responsibility was, first and foremost, to his people, the Touel'alfar, and to his home, Andur'Blough

Inninness. Lady Dasslerond had sent Brynn to the south to free To-gai because she had thought the To-gai-ru more sympathetic to her people than the Behrenese and because she feared that the stain of the demon dactyl, the rot that had begun to infect precious Andur'Blough Inninness, might force the Touel'alfar on that southern road in the near future.

That need seemed much lessened to Belli'mar Juraviel now that he had come to know Cazzira so intimately, however. Not because the stain of the demon dactyl was any less dangerous to his precious homeland, but because he had found the race of the Doc'alfar, the lost cousins of the Touel'alfar. And as his relationship with Cazzira had grown, Juraviel had come to understand and believe that the elves of Corona would indeed reunite into one community.

The two races were different, physically. Though both about four feet in height and lithe of build, the Touel'alfar were possessed of translucent wings. And while the Doc'alfar had dark hair and very light skin, the result of living in their dark and foggy homeland bogs, the Touel'alfar had colors more reflective of the daylight: bright hair and light eyes and skin glowing with the warmth of the golden sun.

But now, over the months, Belli'mar Juraviel had come to look deeper into Cazzira, beyond their physical differences, and had come to see a soul that was very much akin to any of the Touel'alfar. They were one people, of one heart, and with mostly superficial physical differences that would fade over time as their communities rejoined.

That was Belli'mar Juraviel's hope, at least, and his plan. And so he had come back through the mountains, to the northern slopes near the Doc'alfar land of Tymwyvenne, with Cazzira by his side, and with a third elf, not yet born, growing within Cazzira's womb.

"This is not the same tunnel that we entered with Brynn those years ago," Juraviel remarked, squinting as he surveyed the region, his eyes unaccustomed to the light—even though it was late afternoon and the sun was already beginning to set.

"But we are near," Cazzira assured him, and she pointed to the northwest, to a distinctive mountain peak that looked somewhat like the wrinkled face of an old man. "Close enough, perhaps, so that the scouts of Tymwyvenne are looking upon us, their deadly weapons readied to strike at you should you make any untoward movement against me," she added, flashing Juraviel that mischievous grin of hers.

"Let them attack, then!" Juraviel cried dramatically, and he flung himself against Cazzira, crushing her in his loving hug, the both of them laughing. He pushed his lover back to arms' length, his golden eyes locking with hers, which were no less distinctive and startling, the lightest shade of blue that contrasted so starkly with her raven locks. How deeply did Belli'mar Juraviel love this Doc'alfar! And in looking at her, every time he looked at her, he knew that Lady Dasslerond would come to see the beauty of it all, and the benefit of rejoining their long-lost cousins.

Sometime later, with the moon Sheila shining brightly overhead, the two elves moved along the lower slopes of the foothills, Cazzira leading in a generally westerly direction. They would not make Tymwyvenne that night, she had explained to Juraviel, but she was fairly certain that they would see the magnificent woodwork of the elven city's great gates early on their second day of travel.

They set camp on a clearing up above the bogland and skeletal trees that marked the region of Tymwyvenne, taking little care to conceal their campfire. For they were in the realm of the Doc'alfar now, secure from any intruders save those of Cazzira's own people.

The night was quiet about them, with only a gentle breeze blowing. A bit of a chill carried in on that breeze, but it was nothing their generous fire couldn't defeat.

"You will press King Eltiraaz to send us off immediately to your people?" Cazzira asked as the two lay side by side, staring up at the moon and the stars.

"Better that you and I make the first journey to Caer'alfar," Juraviel explained. "Lady Dasslerond will be no more trusting of your people than your King Eltiraaz was of me when first I ventured onto your lands. It is my Lady's duty to move with caution concerning the welfare of her people, and I would expect no less of her." He rolled to his side so that he was facing Cazzira directly, looking into her light blue eyes that had so captured his heart. "But you will melt her caution," he said quietly. "Together you and I will forge the bond anew between our peoples, to the gain of Touel'alfar and Doc'alfar alike."

"To the gain of Tylwyn Doc and Tylwyn Tou alike, you mean," Cazzira teased, using the Doc'alfar names of the respective races, and pointedly and playfully putting her own people first. She moved her hand onto Juraviel's shoulder as she spoke, and he suddenly grabbed her wrist and pulled her arm back, pinning it.

"Touel'alfar and Doc'alfar!" he demanded.

"And if I refuse?" Cazzira countered.

"Then I shall have my way with you!" Juraviel replied. "Unless, of course, the wondrous sentries of the Doc'alfar are about, ready to spring to your defense!"

Cazzira laughed. "The same wondrous sentries who managed to capture Belli'mar Juraviel on his first pass through their land, and with ease!"

"Aha!" Juraviel said dramatically, pointing one finger into the air. "But how do you know that was not my plan all along? To get captured so that I could steal from your people."

"Steal?"

"Your heart, at least."

"My heart?" Cazzira echoed incredulously. "Could you be so foolish as to believe that I have any romantic feelings toward you, Belli'mar Juraviel?"

With great dramatic flourish, Juraviel rolled away from Cazzira, clutching his heart as he went. "Ah, but you have shot an arrow into *my* heart!" he cried. "Mortally wounding—"

"I had thought to do the same," came a third voice, startling both from their play. Juraviel increased his roll and twisted about, coming swiftly to his feet, while Cazzira propped herself up on her elbows.

Both relaxed when they saw a familiar figure enter the firelight, that of Lozan Duk, who had accompanied Cazzira on the initial capture of Juraviel and Brynn Dharielle. He looked much like Cazzira, except that he was a bit broader in the shoulders and his eyes were dark, not light. The Doc'alfar scout spent a long moment studying the pair, his expression curious and obviously amused.

"Your journey to the southland was successful, I presume," he said. "Has the ranger Brynn unified the To-gai-ru tribes as securely as Juraviel and Cazzira have unified themselves, I wonder?"

Cazzira scrambled to her feet and rushed across the clearing to wrap her dear old friend in a great hug. Juraviel followed her over, taking Lozan Duk's offered hand in warm embrace.

"You have been gone too long," Lozan Duk said to Cazzira. "Our land has seemed empty without you. We have found so much less fun in hunting intruders." As he finished, he turned his smile and his gaze over Juraviel.

"Too long, indeed," Cazzira agreed. "I cannot wait to look upon Tymwyvenne again!"

"But you mean to stay only a short while," Lozan Duk prompted, glancing from Cazzira to Juraviel and back again.

"And how long were you spying upon us?" Cazzira asked.

Lozan Duk laughed aloud. "When first I came upon you, and recognized that Cazzira and Juraviel had returned, I wanted to rush right in and welcome you, both of you," he explained. "But then it seemed as if I was intruding on a personal time, and so I started away, prepared to return in the morning."

"And then you heard my mention of returning home, with Cazzira," reasoned Juraviel.

Lozan Duk looked at him earnestly and nodded. "You speak of momentous things, Belli'mar Juraviel of the Tylwyn Tou."

"I hope for momentous gain, for my people and for yours," Juraviel replied.

Lozan Duk really didn't have a response for that, so he just paused for a bit to consider his dearest of friends, returned to his side. For many years, he and Cazzira had been hunting partners, and partners in just about everything else. There had never been anything romantic between them, so there was no jealousy in his eyes as he considered her now, just gratitude that she had returned.

That expression of gratitude fast shifted to a look of curiosity, though. "There is something. . ." the elf started to say.

Cazzira's smile gradually widened, until the whole of her delicate and beautiful face was beaming in the moonlight.

Lozan Duk's jaw dropped open and his eyes followed Cazzira's gaze down to her slightly swollen belly. "You are . . . ?"

"I am," Cazzira replied. "It will be the first child born in Tymwyvenne in a quarter of a century, unless other births occurred during my absence."

"No others."

"And it will be the first child born of Tylwyn Doc and Tylwyn Tou parentage in . . ." She paused and looked over at Juraviel.

"In more than the longest memory of the eldest elves," he answered.

"But what does it mean?" Lozan Duk asked, a simple question that held so many layers of intrigue for all of them. Was this child to signify a union of the peoples, a reunification of sorts? Or was it to become a bastard child of both races, accepted by neither?

"It will mean what we make it to mean," Cazzira said determinedly. "The child is a product of love, true and honest love between Tylwyn Doc and Tylwyn Tou. Let there be no doubt of that."

Lozan Duk shook his head slowly as he considered his surprising friend, and gradually his gaze shifted over to Belli'mar Juraviel, this surprising visitor to his land.

"What says Lozan Duk concerning the child?" Juraviel asked bluntly, not sure how to read that expression.

The other elf took a long moment to consider the question, to digest all of this startling news. "If you make Cazzira happy, then you make Lozan Duk happy, Belli'mar Juraviel," he said at length. "She is my friend—as true a friend as I have ever known—and I stand beside her in all of her choices. She has chosen Belli'mar Juraviel as her companion in love, and has chosen Belli'mar Juraviel as the father of her child. That is all that I need to know about the truth of Belli'mar Juraviel's heart." He looked down at Cazzira's belly and smiled warmly. "Any child of Cazzira will be a beautiful creature."

"As will any child of Belli'mar Juraviel," Cazzira added.

"Then the child is doubly blessed," said Lozan Duk, and he held out his arms, and Cazzira fell into a welcome hug.

From the side, Belli'mar Juraviel nodded hopefully.

Lozan Duk led the pair away soon after, moving quickly along the trails leading toward Tymwyvenne. They met other Doc'alfar along the way, and all greeted Cazzira and Juraviel with open arms.

As did King Eltiraaz when at last the companions came before his gleaming wooden throne in the great hall of Tymwyvenne. He rushed down from his royal seat to embrace Cazzira and welcomed Juraviel back with a warm handshake.

"So much we have to share," he said, returning to his throne. "I wish to hear every step of your journey to the south and hope that all went well, and is well, with Brynn Dharielle, this extraordinary human that has made the Tylwyn Doc reconsider our actions against human intruders within our borders. You will be pleased to learn, Belli'mar Juraviel, that not another human has been given to the bog since you and your companion passed through."

Juraviel was indeed thrilled to hear that news. When first he and Brynn had encountered the Doc'alfar, it was behind an army of zombies they had created from human intruders, giving the people to the bog in a ritual that put them into an undead state.

"The humans are not without merit," Juraviel replied.

King Eltiraaz nodded, his thorny crown bobbing. "But they are a volatile race," he said. "They lack the stability of the Tylwyn folk. Even now, my scouts are out to the east, where momentous changes have come over the kingdom of the humans." He gave a great sigh. "I do not pretend to understand them and their frenzy, but perhaps we will learn.

"But enough of that," King Eltiraaz went on. "Your tale will be a long one, I trust, since you've walked a road for years. Begin at the beginning, if you will!"

Cazzira was smiling, and even started to speak, but when she turned to regard Juraviel, and when King Eltiraaz likewise looked at the Touel'alfar, they saw he wore a troubled expression.

"What is it?" the Doc'alfar king prompted.

"What changes in the east?" Juraviel asked.

King Eltiraaz and all the Doc'alfar looked at him curiously, as if they did not understand why that could possibly matter. "The human kingdom shifts often," Eltiraaz said. "I doubt—"

"Please, tell me what you have learned," Juraviel pressed, for a nagging feeling of dread filled him, and a sudden great fear for his friend Jilseponie. "Is not Danube Brock Ursal the King of Honce-the-Bear?"

"He is dead, from what we have learned, though you must understand that even my scouts most knowledgeable of the ways of the humans do not understand the subtleties of their language."

Juraviel held the elf king's stare and fought hard to keep his breathing steady. Something within was telling him that those friends he had left behind were somehow involved, and probably not for the good.

"King Danube is dead," Eltiraaz went on, "and his wife, Queen Jilseponie—"

"Jilseponie? Queen?" Juraviel blurted. It made sense to him, of course, for before he had left Andur'Blough Inninness with Brynn, the Touel'alfar had heard rumors that Danube had been courting Jilseponie every summer.

"Yes, her name was Jilseponie," King Eltiraaz explained.

"Was? Is she not still the Queen?" The panic was evident in Juraviel's tone.

"Upon Danube's death, she left the great human city," King Eltiraaz told him. "From what we have learned, she is not in the favor of the new king."

"Who is this king?"

"Aydrian," Eltiraaz replied, and Juraviel sucked in his breath.

"Yes, and apparently he is a new addition to the royal line," King Eltiraaz explained. "He is not of the blood of Ursal, but of that of Wyndon."

Belli'mar Juraviel felt as if the whole world was sliding away from him at that awful moment, felt as if he was receding into some surreal dimension. Aydrian was king? He knew in his heart that Dasslerond had never planned such a thing, and that if this really was the Aydrian he had known in Andur'Blough Inninness, the child of Elbryan and Jilseponie, then something had gone terribly wrong.

"You know of him?" Cazzira stated as much as asked.

Juraviel hardly heard her. "I beg of you, King Eltiraaz, learn more of these events, for they hold great consequence, I fear, for my people."

"How so?"

"If this Aydrian is who I believe, then my people are either more intimately tied to the humans than ever before, or they are in more danger from the humans than ever before," Juraviel honestly replied. "I must learn more of this new human king, and quickly."

Cazzira put her hand on his arm, and when he glanced at her, he realized that the desperation must have sounded clearly in his voice. He looked at her helplessly for a moment, then turned back to the Doc'alfar king. "And I fear that my time here is short," he went on. "I must be away, as soon as is possible, to my people." He looked back at Cazzira, who nodded. "I pray you allow Cazzira to accompany me, and perhaps others of your court."

King Eltiraaz wore a curious expression. "I thought that we had long ago agreed on a decidedly more gentle approach to heal the ancient breach between our peoples. Such a meeting cannot be forced, we agreed."

"If Aydrian is king of the humans, then I fear for my people," Juraviel admitted.

# Visit www.delreydigital.com— the portal to all the information and resources available from Del Rey Online.

- Read sample chapters of every new book, special features on selected authors and books, news and announcements, readers' reviews, browse Del Rey's complete online catalog, and more.

- Sign up for the Del Rey Internet Newsletter (DRIN), a free monthly publication e-mailed to subscribers, featuring descriptions of new and upcoming books, essays and interviews with authors and editors, announcements and news, special promotional offers, signing/convention calendar for our authors and editors, and much more.

To subscribe to the DRIN: send a blank e-mail to join-ibd-dist@list.randomhouse.com or sign up at www.delreydigital.com

The DRIN is also available at no charge for your PDA devices—go to www.randomhouse.com/partners/avantgo for more information, or visit www.avantgo.com and search for the Books@Random channel.

Questions? E-mail us at delrey@randomhouse.com

 www.delreydigital.com